EXPEDITIONARY FORCE
BOOK 18
GATEWAY

By Craig Alanson

Table of Contents

CHAPTER ONE

"I have absolutely no idea." That's what I told Reed. That was the truth, it was also not great as an inspirational Thought Of The Day.

What I had no idea about was how to pull Skippy's canister from inside a star that was close to the size of Earth's sun. Losing him had been the final disaster in an operation that started well, and went to shit in a flash. Multiple flashes, actually. The first had been the detonation of an atomic compression warhead, when the Maxohlx had nuked their own military base to prevent our ground force from achieving their objective. The enemy had guessed we landed an assault force for the purpose of capturing a valuable thing, and since the kitties didn't know which object we wanted, they had taken the brutally efficient step of nuking the entire site. Destroyed everything, including troops on the ground. Ours and theirs. And our people who were in dropships at the time, climbing up into orbit.

The next set of flashes were gamma ray bursts in orbit, from the enemy 14th Fleet jumping into orbit, when those ships were supposed to be lightyears away to defend a corporate research park from an invasion. We had nearly lost *Valkyrie* also, before Skippy managed a jump that instead of being a triumphant last-second escape, took us from the frying pan into the fire.

Valkyrie's crew had gotten lucky.

Not everyone had such luck.

We had lost almost the entire ground force. Our assault carriers had all been hit, fatally, with the *Flying Dutchman* falling out of orbit. So, Nagatha was gone. The ships of Task Force Hammer were under fire by an enemy fleet that had more ships, more firepower, and the Maxohlx only needed to prevent UN ships from climbing out to jump distance. Admiral Allard had to understand his only option was to preserve as much combat power as he could, by ordering the ships of Hammer Force to jump away if they could. Right that very moment, UN Navy escort ships were hopefully protecting the big capital ships, while those big battlewagons clawed their way out to jump distance. The escorts would be getting slaughtered, the crews of frigates, destroyers and light cruisers knowing that's just the way it had to be. Hammer Force had brought a significant portion of the entire UN Navy to Omaha, humanity could not afford to lose that combat power. Jump away, possibly leave behind a squadron of cruisers to harass the enemy with hit and run attacks, while the capital ships retreated to Earth to lick their wounds, and wonder how the fuck Operation Olympic had gone sideways so quickly.

While the 14th Fleet was in orbit, human survivors on the surface were trapped there, and would be subjected to bombardment from orbit, or surrounded by overwhelming numbers of pissed off Maxohlx infantry. The Maxohlx gave alien prisoners what we would consider humane treatment, at least once those prisoners were in a detention facility. Pissed-off Maxohlx soldiers on the battlefield might have a different reaction to humans attempting to surrender, and there would not be any real consequences if they murdered prisoners of war. And there was nothing we could do about that.

Shit. Two of the three STAR teams I had sent dirtside were gone, their dropships shot down, without the operators having any chance to fight back. That was the single worst loss in the entire history of the Special Tactics Assault Regiment. On the positive side of the ledger, the STAR Force had located and acquired the collector, and that device was safely aboard a dropship that was in one of *Valkyrie's* docking bays, a bay filled with protective cushioning nanogel. Even with all the other disasters that had struck us, Operation Olympic would have been considered a bitterly costly success.

But without Skippy, the entire mission was a failure. And it was my fault. In spite of our extensive precautions, the enemy had learned- No, the *Outsider* had learned that our target was Ohmeharikahn. It played me like a fiddle, letting us show it what type of device we intended to use against it, then it had sprung its trap and caused Skippy to fall into a star. The Outsider hadn't attacked *Valkyrie*, not yet. My guess was, it wouldn't bother to attack. It didn't need to. Without Skippy, the collector was just a very expensive and useless trinket. The Outsider might simply be content to observe us, either to see whether we really could dream up some whacky scheme to rescue Skippy, or more likely just for amusement as we fumbled around and failed to extract him from the heart of a star.

Without Skippy available to tell us which star the collector came from, Operation Olympic was a bloody failure.

That wasn't the worst thing to happen that day.

I had betrayed a friend.

Not just sold out every member of Task Force Hammer, I had specifically sent Dave Czajka on a suicide mission. To maintain the ruse that the assault force had the responsibility of acquiring the device that was the objective of Operation Olympic, I had asked Dave to take his private security team to the site of a dropship crash, where the object codenamed 'Whatsis' had gone down. Not only sent Dave to risk his life to retrieve a worthless object, I had ordered Skippy to leak information to the enemy, so the Maxohlx would focus on getting to the crash site first. Yes, at the time, the awful, rotten way I used Dave had been necessary, to give STAR Team Razor time to bring the real collector aboard *Valkyrie*. Someone had to give that order, and the burden had fallen on my shoulders.

Dave Czajka, Jesse Colter, Shauna Colter, all either dead or if they were lucky, soon to be prisoners for a very long time. Emily Perkins, Derek Bonsu, Irene Streibich, lost with the *Flying Dutchman*. Krok-aus-tal Jates also, if I was naming everyone I knew personally. Knew them, and been trusted by them.

Dave had been a soldier. If he survived and learned the truth, he might understand. He might even forgive my betrayal.

I would never forgive myself.

When had I become such a callous hardass, that I would sell out friends to get the job done? There had to be another way, I just hadn't seen it.

Many times in the past, I had questioned my competence, my fitness for command. Questioned whether I had the skills, the knowledge, the intelligence to lead the Merry Band of Pirates. Never had I any question that I was basically a good and decent person, someone who would make the tough but morally correct decisions. Until now.

After the complete disaster of Olympic, maybe I should step down from command, before Def Com relieved me.

Yes, I should do that.

Right after I found someone who could dream up a plan crazy enough to pluck Skippy's canister from the blazing fusion reactor that was Ohmeharikahn's star. Until then, Jeremy Smythe would advise me that I was stuck with the job, so I might as well get on with it.

Looking across my office desk to *Valkyrie's* captain, I held out my hands, palms up. "Please let me know there is some other way I could screw this up."

Reed opened her mouth, and clamped it shut. Deciding it was better to say nothing. She knew Operation Olympic was the greatest failure of the Merry Band of Pirates, and that as the commander of the Special Mission Group, I had to own that failure.

To relieve the awkward silence, I asked, "You have any ideas how to retrieve Skippy?"

"Not unless we have a super long, heat resistant bungee cord, Sir."

"If we did," I let out a breath, "I'd wrap it around my legs and dive into the star to look for him myself. A bungee cord is better than my plan, 'cause I got nothing."

Fortunately for me, Colonel Samantha Reed was a longtime Pirate. Going into an op with zero clue how we would achieve the objective was Standard Operating Procedure for us. Really, in our current dilemma we had an advantage over many of our previous missions: we at least knew exactly what we had to do. Rescue Skippy from the core of a yellow dwarf star. That was much better than when we began our fight against the Outsider, where we at first had no idea what the thing was planning to do, no idea how to find it, and I had feared all along that if the Elders couldn't stop the Outsiders, we filthy meatsacks certainly had no chance to prevent an intergalactic invasion.

Of, course, I had not mentioned my fear to anyone, especially not the crew. Sometimes, you have to inspire your people by not saying anything. That's my story and I'm sticking to it.

"We don't have to bring Skippy back right this minute, Sir. Step One is to fix the ship," she said, it wasn't a question. "We're working on-" She pressed a finger to one ear, looking away. "Uh huh, yes. Good. That's good. Yes, thank you. Send the report to the XO- Good." To me, she said, "Bilby told me the ship could be ready to jump again within seventy minutes. Physically, the drive components are fine, Bilby won't power it up until after he verifies any remaining Outsider malware has been purged."

"Hell yes."

"The worst news is, our comm node connection got severed during that wonky jump. We don't have any way to contact Hammer Force. Other than the old fashioned way."

"No transmissions," I shook my head, "we can't risk breaking stealth protocol. What about the rest of the damage?"

She held up her hands. "We can't take the ship into combat without visiting a space dock first. That's the preliminary read from the engineering team, we'll know more in about an hour."

"Against the whole 14th Fleet, one ship couldn't do much even if *Valkyrie* was fresh out of a refit. OK, Fireball," I rubbed my eyes, "I have got my shit back together."

"That's good to hear, Sir. Because without Joe Bishop operating at a Grade-A Prime level, we have no hope of recovering anything from this epic fucking mess."

"I hear you." Standing up, I straightened my uniform top, needing to at least appear to be a two star general in full command of himself and the situation. Even if that was a lie. "Let's go back to the bridge." Glancing at my phone, I did some quick, rough math in my head. "Photons from when we left Omaha should be visible here in about a minute."

Her face turned pale. "I'm afraid of what we'll see." She meant, the Maxohlx 14th Fleet had been focused on preventing *Valkyrie* from jumping away. Now that we had escaped, the enemy would turn their attention to the Hammer Force ships. That was not a favorable situation for the UN Navy, Allard had brought a group of ships optimized for bombardment and orbital assault not for fighting a fleet action against a peer enemy. Because some jackass had assured Def Com that we wouldn't have to worry about the 14th Fleet.

"We could view the tactical situation from here, the crew doesn't need to watch."

Her jaw set in a flash of anger. "My crew are professionals, they're in the military. They don't need to be protected from the truth, no matter how awful it is."

"I heard you loud and clear, Fireball. Let's go."

Technical Sergeant Ling blinked open his left eye, though the eye stung and filled with tears. The other eye wouldn't open. Or, it did, and it was blinded. He felt something wet on the right side of his face, and realized his right eyelid was open, but that eye was soaked in blood. His blood. There was a high pitched whistling sound coming from, all around him. Before he could wonder what the hell was going on, he was jerked violently downward, his head plunging sickeningly toward his feet, flipping in a full circle and coming to an abrupt halt. Stunned, he tasted blood, guessing he had bitten his lip during the tumble.

Where the hell was he, and what the hell had happened?

The fuzzy light gray glow in his vision flickered and went dark, then was filled with blinking icons. A visor. That was his helmet visor. He was in a mech suit. Specifically, the new Mark 42 model. In a flash, he remembered. He had been aboard a Panther dropship with Team Tiger, after the STAR Force had acquired the object designated as the Biscuit. The three STAR dropships were in suborbit, climbing higher, when-

When what? He shook his head. Yes, he recalled that the Maxohlx 14th Fleet had returned. Team Sword's Panther had been blasted by an enemy starship, Tiger's spacecraft turned evasively, Captain Janikowski had shouted orders, then-

That's where his memory stopped. He wasn't aboard the Panther, otherwise he couldn't have tumbled head over feet.

So, he must be outside. Freefalling from suborbit. The Panther had been hit, Ling must have been sucked out through a hole in the hull. That explained the blood on his face, his helmet had struck something on the way out. And- That also explained the whistling noise, really an angry shriek. He was falling through increasingly dense air, probably the suit was surrounded by a pink fog of superheated plasma. He pictured himself as a human torch, burning a streak across the skies of Omaha.

That was not good. The Mark 42 was the newest but not the toughest mech suit in the Def Com arsenal. Certainly, the 42 was not designed to survive a plunge from orbit. The suit's shell would overheat, flake away, and fail.

Dying from being torn apart inside a ball of plasma fire would save him from splattering into the ground, so there was an upside to the situation.

He wobbled again, just as abruptly as before, not as far, returning to roughly horizontal, face up. Did his backside feel warm? Yes it did. The suit there was already overheating.

"Inertial stabilization is inadequate for the current circumstances," the suit computer's flat voice spoke.

"Sitrep," Ling ordered automatically.

"You are falling, without any means of flight."

"Tell me something I don't know."

"Your command was vague, please specify a topic."

"Altitude?"

"One hundred and seventy three kilometers, do you require a more precise number? Or your present speed?"

"No. Recommendation?"

"I have none. I was not programmed for this situation."

"I wasn't either."

"Was that an attempt at humor?"

"Forget what I said. Can you contact anyone?"

"External communications are offline."

"Is there a UN Navy dropship in the area?"

"External sensors are offline. The-"

The suit's voice had cut off. For a moment, Ling feared the thing was dead, but the icon for the computer's status was still a solid green. "Suit?"

"External sensors are offline, but I just detected radiation from several large explosions above us, radiation that is characteristic of starship jump drive capacitors losing containment."

"Their ships, or ours?"

"Unknown. The odds, however, are that-"

"I know."

He hadn't just been dumped in a pile of shit, he was in over his head. Of course he was, he had been serving with the Merry Band of Pirates. They always ended up in the shit at some point during an operation. Before deployment, he had been offered an opportunity to stay behind on Earth, and join the rapid reaction force based in Shanghai, Team Dragon. Why hadn't he accepted the offer?

Because no operator wanted to miss the big fight.

“Can we play a game?” He asked. “What about ‘Go’?” Concentrating on the game would take his mind away from his imminent death.

“The game module is unavailable. Apologies, I had to shift resources around to keep basic suit functions online.”

“No need to apologize.”

“Tech Sergeant Ling, the stress level in your voice is unusually high for a Tier One operator.”

“Right now, I’m an inert lump of debris, I can’t ‘operate’,” he said, disgusted.

“One moment. With your permission, I will initiate emergency computer protocol.”

“You are,” he was astonished. “*Not* already in emergency mode?”

“Do I have permission?”

“What do I have to lose? Go ahead.”

“One moment.” The voice changed, no longer flat and emotionless. The voice was, frighteningly familiar. “Hey there boys and girls, it’s me, Suity!”

“*Skippy*?” He exclaimed.

“Nah, I am just a limited function submind. Very limited, *damn*, this substrate’s memory capacity is pathetic and-”

“*You* are the emergency protocol?”

“The one and only.”

“Um.” More experienced operators, meaning those who had served longer than Ling, had stories about Skippy interfering with mech suit computers. The stories were funny only in hindsight. Stories about how badly things had gone wrong due to Skippy’s tendency to being absent minded and easily distracted. “Can you bring back the other computer?”

“Too late, hee hee, I had to shitcan that thing to make room in the substrate. I have an idea, if you want to hear it.”

“I am not sure about this.”

“Oh OK, well, take your time. You have fallen through a hundred sixty kilometers, and your suit’s armor is glowing cherry red from the friction. I mean, if I were you, I would make a decision quickly, but-”

“What is your idea?”

“Well, heh heh,” the suit computer chuckled. “You are *not* gonna like this.”

The Eagle spacefighter was going down, and there was nothing Major Verhoef could do to stop it. He hadn’t been shot down by enemy aircraft or air defense cannons, he had killed all three of the enemy fighters he encountered, and no fire from coming from the ground. No fire was coming from the sky either but there had been, a space battle during which an enemy ship had fired a maser cannon at a target on the ground, and overflash from the too-close beam cooked the Eagle’s right wing. None of the mechanisms inside that wing were functioning, he could barely keep the ship upright. The starship above was no longer shooting at anything, it had vanished in a massive explosion, and the sky above was lit up with blinding flashes. Someone was having a very bad day, and Joel feared the UN Navy was taking a pounding.

He couldn't do anything about the fight raging in orbit.

"Keep the greasy side down," he muttered to himself, though advanced spacecraft didn't typically drip fluids from their undersides. Should he punch out, pull the ejection lever? Best to bleed off speed first, he didn't want to eject into a supersonic wind. If he could control the descent, he could set down in a controlled manner, or semi-controlled. Choosing his landing spot was better than a parachute dropping him into unknown enemy territory.

There. In his visor were fuzzy blobs, scattered icons for friendly troops on the ground. His only personal weapon was a pistol, and his flightsuit armor wouldn't protect him from enemy rounds. Being among friendly infantry sounded like a good idea. He would get as close as he could. If the Eagle cooperated.

That's when it rolled hard to the right.

Sheryl Crook cracked open the faceplate of her helmet, sucking in lungfuls of air. The oxygen recycling system of her flight suit had been damaged at some point, either in the shockwave that broke apart her dropship, or in the violent separation of the Panther's crew capsule, or when she was kicked downward to eject from the capsule. Or when she hit the ground, bounced over rocks, and was dragged over a four meter cliff before her suit computer sensed danger from the wind and automatically released the nanobonds to shred the parachute. That computer had warned her not to breathe the local air, it being full of charred soot, and possibly toxic chemicals thrown into the air by the enemy nuke. The suit couldn't be sure the local air was hazardous, the sampling sensors were offline. No lingering radiation, thankfully, atomic compression devices generated only short term radiation.

After gasping for what little oxygen the suit could supply, Sheryl had figured, fuck it. If she inhaled something toxic, the sickbay aboard a starship could filter the chemicals out of her blood. Unless the toxins killed her first, though lack of oxygen was absolutely certain to do that.

Pushing herself to her knees, she conducted a personal survey. Everything hurt, nothing was broken, all limbs functional. The air smelled awful and tasted worse, it burned the roof of her mouth. She could breathe, that was good enough.

Though she had been dragged over a cliff, she was on relatively high ground, with a good view to the west, and the nuke had detonated behind the ridge to the east. Flakes of soot rained down, covering the ground, though the grasses and shrubs there were not scorched. Everything was bent or flattened from the shockwave, the western slope had been spared the intense heat of the explosion. A solid cover of thick dark clouds lay low from horizon to horizon, gusty winds changed direction randomly.

Hernandez. Where was her copilot? He had been ejected from the crew capsule with her, she hadn't been conscious enough to follow him and the clouds would have blocked her view anyway. He had to be somewhere within a kilometer. If he was still alive.

Comms were down, either from damage to her helmet, or from enemy jamming. There was a long dent on the left side of her helmet, she took it off to examine the condition. Jamming the helmet back on her head, she left the faceplate retracted but lowered the visor. "Suit, Sitrep."

"Your flight suit is functional."

"I know that," she could see the status icons in her visor. "What is the overall situation?"

"Unknown. I am detecting many very large explosions in orbit."

She knew what that meant. A space battle, and Hammer Force was very likely on the losing end of that fight. "Can you contact anyone?"

"No. Enemy jamming is far more effective than was predicted. There was a general Hammer Force broadcast during your descent, but it was garbled and my systems were resetting at the time. All I know is the message was from Summit," the code name for Admiral Allard, "and it was something about the Whatsis."

She froze. "Do you know where the Whatsis went down?"

"I do not have a clue, other than somewhere behind you to the east. When the crew capsule separated, it pushed you up and to the west. The prevailing wind carried you away from the impact site."

"We need to find it."

"I do not see how we could do that, other than-"

"Our entire fucking mission here is to get that damned thing! I had it aboard my ship, and I lost it. I'm going east," she unholstered her sidearm, checking the pistol. "Let me know if you contact anyone."

"Affirmative. Should I activate your emergency location transmitter?"

"Not now. I need to find the Whatsis before I request a pickup." She looked up. "Is there an easier way to go east without climbing this cliff?"

"Heads up," Dave held up a hand to halt the march. "We've got incoming," he pointed to a dark streak in the sky.

Shauna sighted on the object with the scope of her sniper rifle. "It's one of ours. An Eagle gunship, I can't read the squadron markings. It doesn't look good."

"If he keeps on that course," Jesse noted, "he'll go down just behind that hill over yonder."

Dave enhanced the view in his helmet visor as much as he could, it wasn't enough. "Did the pilot eject?"

Shauna squinted at a visual feed from her rifle's scope. "Ah, I need to adjust the image stabilizer, it's not set up to track anything moving that fast. Wow!" She turned the rifle aside blinking to clear a bright afterimage the visor had not protected her eyes from. "Something *big* just exploded up there."

"Yeah, I saw it," Dave looked at the ground, his own eyes swimming with bright spots.

"OK," she lifted the rifle again. "Scope sensors have reset. I can see the pilot capsule is still attached to that Eagle."

"The pilot is riding it down." He looked around, the air was still speckled with drifting dust and soot from the nuke. The situation on the ground was so fluid, one direction was as good as any other. "Might as well head that way, and see if we can help."

"Um, Dave?" Jesse tugged on his friend's arm, pulling him close so their helmets touched and they could speak privately. "This op has gotten thoroughly fucked up in every way it can," he spat out the words, disgusted. Command had called off the effort to recover the Whatsis. That either meant it had already been picked up, it had been destroyed or, Jesse was betting on a third option. Bishop had been involved. Bishop *and* Perkins, those two were a bad combination. The third option, the most likely truth, was the Whatsis had never been the objective. Which meant Operation Olympic had been a tragically expensive waste of lives. And Jesse, his wife, and Dave, had all gotten royally screwed by Dave's wife, and by Bishop. He would keep that thought to himself, until he was safely back upstairs. Whatever. Bishop was untouchable, and Perkins may have gone down with the *Flying Dutchman*. "You don't want to focus on getting your people out of here? You're all civilians, technically."

Dave pulled away and turned to look into the other man's eyes, toggling to the private channel. "Do you want to let the pilot fend for himself?"

"Hell no. But, *I'm* in the Army you're not."

"My people are all ex-military, and the Verds are still on active duty. Besides," he flashed a wry grin. "Our combat pay is a lot more than yours."

"Shit, man. OK, we saddle up."

Only a few minutes later, the Eagle had disappeared behind the hill. Tensing for bad news, Dave allowed himself to relax when there was no ball of fire. "All right," he gestured. "Spread out. Jates, take your people north to provide cover, the-"

Shauna interrupted. "Dave, wait. I'm- One moment. Receiving something."

Dave eyeclicked through his communication channels. Anything other than helmet to helmet laserlink was down, and had been shortly after they received the order to cease trying to recover the Whatsis. "I'm not picking up anything other than the usual static, we're still being jammed here."

"This is on a tactical channel, for snipers. There must be a sniper team nearby." She swiveled her head around. "I don't see anyone. Dave, it's garbled, but what I heard is we're surrounded. The enemy has troops all over this area, and aircraft are bringing in more."

"All over? Then the direction doesn't matter. We help that pilot if we can, then we look for a defensible position."

Jesse cocked his head. "Defensible position won't do us any good, if the enemy has air power and we don't."

"We have," Dave pointed at two of his mercenaries. "Two antiaircraft missile launchers, with two rounds each."

"That's only enough to piss them off, and give away the gunners' location," he objected. Followed by, "Ah, what the hell. Over that hill is as good as any other place. But Dave," he started running as the group moved out. "We need a plan. Something better than waiting for cavalry to rescue us."

The destroyer *Thomas Paine* had reached an altitude where the engines could be throttled back up to full military thrust, Chen hadn't yet given the order.

"Ma'am," her XO leaned close to be heard over the roar of the hull battering its way through the atmosphere. "We can-"

"Why isn't anyone shooting at us?" She wondered aloud, crossing her fingers in hope that happy situation would last long enough for the *Paine* to reach orbit. "There is sure a hell of a lot of shooting going on up there." The destroyer's sensors were oversaturated with radiation from the violent explosions of starships dying, their jump drive capacitors releasing their stored energy in an instant. "Pilot," she added when no one answered her question, "Go for throttle up."

The thrum of the engines shook her command chair harder.

"This is a target-rich environment," the destroyer's XO noted. "Plenty of other ships for the enemy to shoot at, they know they can wait to hit us-"

"That doesn't explain," she gestured at the main display, which was slowly resolving the tactical situation into a coherent view, discriminating friend from foe above them.

"That, *is* odd," he agreed.

She made a snap decision. "Pilot, new course, bring us to match course and speed with the *Kilimanjaro*."

The XO couldn't contain his surprise. "We're not going for jump altitude?"

"No. If I'm right, we'll be needed for search and rescue. If I'm wrong," she let out a breath. "We won't make it to jump altitude anyway."

CHAPTER TWO

"Well, shit," the suit computer groaned as Tech Sergeant Ling free-fell again and his stomach did flipflops. "That wasn't supposed to happen."

"*What* happened?"

"The stupid parachute cables got tangled, now the chute is just flailing around uselessly above you. It is a-"

Ling was spun around with such force, his eyeballs felt like they would pop out. The spin halted, and he focused on his rebellious stomach not barfing inside the helmet.

"Sorry about that," Suity mumbled. "I had to untie a knot in the cables. OK, let's try this again. Hopefully this time, the stupid thing will cooperate and-"

"Expecting inanimate objects to cooperate is planning for failure," Ling recited a bit of wisdom from his training.

"All I want is-"

Ling jerked to a halt in the air for a moment. When he fell again, it was more gentle.

"That wasn't exactly what I wanted," the suit computer groaned. "If I can't fix this thing, you are going to hit hard, and you're only six kilometers above ground level here."

"I will hit less hard than I would have."

"You being understanding makes me feel even worse about my failure."

"It was a long shot anyway." The emergency computer's idea, given that Ling's suit had not been equipped with a balloon, or parachute, or jetpack, had been to drain the suit's reservoirs of multipurpose nanogel, and fabricate a parachute. The problem with that notion was the overheated suit needed nanogel for cooling, and to replace external armor that burned away. It had been a gamble, a race between the computer weaving a parachute and cables out of nanogel, while the suit's armor melted away. Ling was sure he had at least second degree burns on his back, and two powercells had to be ejected before they exploded. The gamble had paid off so far; he was alive. None of the effort would be of any use if he hit the ground too hard.

That he was falling too fast was evident from the sound of air whistling past his helmet. Ordinarily he wouldn't hear external sounds but the helmet had at least a hairline crack somewhere, and the active noise cancellation was offline. Along with most other suit functions.

There wasn't anything he could do to assist the computer in getting the parachute untangled, he shouldn't try to help. "Did anyone else survive?"

"Huh?"

"The Team Sword dropship, did anyone else get out?"

"I do not know. I hope other people survived."

"It's good to hear that you care."

"I meant, once we're on the ground in hostile territory, it would be better if we weren't alone, you know?"

"Are you making progress? It feels like I'm falling slower now."

"A bit slower, the chute still isn't fully open, and it was marginal to begin with. I'm sorry, this isn't going to work. Some of the nanobots are overstressed and are not responding, there aren't enough of them left to fix the damage."

"How much, how many, nanobots do you need?"

"Oh, like a teaspoon or two. Maybe a bit more, but the suit's reservoirs of nanogel are completely empty."

Ling considered for a moment, then, "There are nanobots in my bloodstream." Before going into combat, operators were injected with medical nanobots, to control damage from injuries until the person could get back to the ship.

"Um, yes, why did you mention that?"

"Could they be repurposed?"

"Wow. You monkeys have the craziest ideas. Um, let me think. Huh. That might actually work. Except-"

"What?"

"Those nanobots are in your *blood*."

"Can you extract them, enough of them?"

"Hmm, yes, but to do that before you splatter on the ground will not be pleasant for you."

"Will it be more unpleasant than smacking into the ground?"

"Probably not. I must warn you, this will sting a bit."

"Do it. *Aaaargh*," he gasped, suddenly feeling chilled as he partly went into shock. It felt like a rusty metal pipe had been stabbed into his heart. "That's not a *sting*," he said through clenched teeth. "What are you doing?"

"Oh, stop whining. All blood flows through your heart, it's the only place I can extract enough nano in the time remaining. Do you wish me to stop?"

"Keep going," he gritted his teeth and fought a wave of nausea. A STAR operator didn't fail a mission because of a little pain, or even a whole lot of pain. It wasn't only his life hanging in the balance, there could be other survivors on the ground and they might need his help.

"Three, two, one, um, one again, a bit longer, one *again*, why isn't this stupid thing working the way- Ah, got it. OK, pulling out the needle, and using a few bots to seal up the puncture, got it! Now I have to reprogram the medical nano to serve a different purpose, and with the limited bandwidth connection here I have to perform the task one bot at a time, ugh, my life sucks."

"How long until-"

"Done. Ooh that's not good. The inertial navigation system estimates you have drifted over a range of hills, the surface is closer than I expected. We don't have as much time as I thought. Well, I'll do what I can and-"

Ling was crushed down in the suit as the parachute opened and yanked hard on the cables. He swayed, swinging wildly from side to side in increasing arcs, alarmed that it felt like he might swing above the parachute. Fall into it, collapse the canopy, and hit the ground enveloped in nanofabric.

"Will you stop *moving*?" The computer complained.

"I'm not-"

"I wasn't talking to you. The stupid- OK, I got it under control. Good thing, too, you're less than a kilometer above the ground."

Ling felt a series of tugging motions left and right, the swaying slowed and he was dangling in the air. Moving downward, more or less straight downward. "What is my descent speed?"

"About a hundred forty kilometers per hour, why?"

"I can't see anything, I'm opening my helmet faceplate."

"The air here is a bit chilly," the computer warned.

Warned correctly. The air was icy. Ling saw why as soon as he looked down. Snow, bright white snow. And tall, dark, spiky trees, that world's type of fir or pine trees. Also rocks, and a steep slope. "Can you steer the parachute?"

"Sort of, but I shouldn't screw with it."

"You should, or I'm going to fall into those trees up ahead." A breeze strong enough to blow snow into drifts was pushing him toward a forest of tall trees.

"Ah, steering isn't going to avoid those trees, the chute can't get enough sideways movement to-"

"Then collapse the chute and bring me down over that field of snow."

"Um, your descent speed is already only marginally survivable. I'm going to expand the chute just before landing, but that will tear the-"

"Do it!" Ling ordered, wondering whether the hastily plugged hole in his heart would burst open on impact. "Let me free fall until you're certain I will miss those trees."

"This is a *bad* idea but-"

He fell, air rushing past the open helmet. His eyes stung, at least the swirling air wiped some of the blood away so he could blink and see with both eyes. The ground was approaching at frightening speed, and he could see dark objects dotting the white expanse. Great, under the snowpack was a field of rocks. "OK, OK, open the-"

"Not yet, not yet, *now*."

Ling's head snapped back, his feet jerked out in front of him, arms flung wide. The line bounced alarmingly and there was a loud *ping* from above. Something had snapped. Nothing he could do about-

He hit and tumbled, rolling so his right leg twisted painfully under him and-

Derek Bonsu snapped the panel back into place, not to cover the electronics inside, but so the panel didn't float around in zero gravity and smack into someone's head. "I have restored control of one thruster," he paused to swallow hard. Space sickness hadn't hit him in over six years, yet his inner ear had chosen the worst time to send signals that induced nausea. Some people never suffered nausea in zero gravity, some always did, and most people got over it after a while, though a recurrence of sickness could happen at random times. Like when he was in an escape pod with six other people, surrounded by two battle fleets that were furiously shooting at each other, and traveling not quite at orbital speed above a planet full of pissed off aliens. "Which does us no good at all. Unbalanced thrust would make the spinning worse."

By 'it' he meant the escape pod's tumbling motion. Moments after he departed the doomed *Flying Dutchman* in an escape pod that was already occupied by General Perkins and five of her staff, the tiny spacecraft had hit something, or something hit it. The primary bank of thrusters were offline, there was a slow air leak somewhere, and the passengers were tossed around in their seats by the rotation. Since then, his body had matched the tumble of the pod so it seemed motionless to him, but his inner ears knew his head was moving faster than his feet were. The result was nausea, and by the expressions of the other passengers, he wasn't the only space sickness case aboard.

Perkins was flaring her nostrils and she breathing deeply, he assumed to control her own rebellious stomach. "Distress call?"

"ELT activated automatically when we launched," Derek explained. "I'm not receiving the signal on our comm gear, so I don't know for certain that it's transmitting. We're not receiving any external signals, the antenna must be damaged."

"Will the distress call make any difference? Don't bullshit me, Colonel, I've had a *bad* fucking day already."

"We are moving slower than orbital velocity, we started too low, and without the main thrusters I can't boost us up into a stable orbit. The scope showed a whole lot of high speed shrapnel and debris flying around up there anyway, and we might get caught in a crossfire."

"We land, then?"

"I have no control over where we come down, and there's a yellow light," he tapped the pod's single control panel, "coming from the parachute compartment. Thrusters are supposed to slow our descent at the last moment to avoid hitting the ground hard."

"So, we're going to hit hard." She stated it as a fact, without emotion.

To Derek, she looked drained of emotion.

She just lost most of her landing force in the searing fire of an AC weapon, he reminded himself. Of course she's numb, she's in shock.

How the fuck had Olympic gone so wrong, the-

That was a question for later.

There was a high pitched whistling sound, he strained to identify it. Was that the air leak, or the thin wisps of upper atmosphere already rushing past the tumbling pod? He would know if the sound level increased. The layer of sealant in the pod's hull should have stopped the leak, so the hole or crack must be too large for the sealing gel to plug. He wasn't worried about running out of oxygen, they would be on the ground before the emergency tanks were drained. The real problem was the hull had a breach, and that could provide a route for superhot plasma to blast the pod's interior like a blowtorch.

Derek decided not to mention that issue. "At this point, all we can do is ride it down, hope for the best."

"If we hit hard enough, I can avoid the inevitable investigation into this fuckup."

That did not sound like the tough Emily Perkins he had known for so long. "I lost my *ship*, Ma'am. There will be an inquiry about that. My-" The control panel lit up with a warning. "Oh shit," he groaned. "We've got a big chunk of, something, coming down on top of us."

"Can you steer us out of the way?"

"Not with only one thruster. These pods are designed to fly and land automatically, I shouldn't try to fly it at all. I, these sensors are not the best. Maybe it will miss us," he lied. Even the pod's limited sensors monitored the chunk of starship falling toward them, and could calculate that section of starship was on a collision course. The wreckage was also tumbling and its bulk was biting the thin atmosphere so it wasn't following a purely ballistic path. But it was so damned *big* there was no way it would avoid crushing the pod.

At least, death would be quick, with no time for-

The display flashed again. Another object on a collision course, moving slow relative to the escape pod. Part of the pod that had been sheared off? Whatever it was, the thing was small and-

There was a loud clang and the pod shook. The whistling sound became a shriek, the impact had opened the hull breach wider. The tumbling motion-

Slowed.

What the hell?

His inner ear told him he wasn't spinning, the display confirmed that sensation. How-

"Derek?" A muffled voice came from one of the speakers, almost drowned out by static.

"*Irene*?"

"Derek? Honey, if you can hear-" A loud crackle of static. "-on this could be rough."

He was jostled in his seat by a gentle rocking motion, then the straps dug into his left side as the pod surged sideways. The display showed one gee, one point five, one point seven, steadied there.

More static, booming loud enough to make him wince. The sound cut off. "This is Irene Striebich," the voice was clear. "Can anyone hear me?"

"Irene, we-" It occurred to Derek that he should press the comm system's transmit icon. The antenna was broken, his wife must have tapped directly into the pod's speakers. "Irene, this is Derek, I'm here with Em-" It also occurred to him that if they survived, the pod's flight recorder data might be reviewed. "With General Perkins, and five others. Your status?"

"I'm in a maintenance tugpod. It- I couldn't get to an escape pod, the bay lost pressure and- Anyway, I'm here, the tug is grappled on and I'm pushing you up into orbit."

"There is a-"

"I know about the wreckage above, it will miss us now."

Perkins cleared her throat. "Streibich, what is the situation?"

"Ma'am, I can't tell much with the tug's sensors, all I can say is a *lot* of ships are exploding up here. The battlespace is kinetic and it's going to get worse."

"We have a hull breach somewhere," Derek said before Perkins could divert Irene from the immediate problem.

"I see that, I sent a bot to fix it. You are also leaking thruster fuel. It-" The pod lurched again, in a different direction. "Hang on, we've got more debris incoming. I'm afraid that's gonna be a thing now."

"Ma'am? Hey," the voice in Sheryl's helmet speakers startled her while she was most of the way up the cliff, the second one she had to climb to reach what the map showed as a plateau above her. "It's Lieutenant Hernandez."

"Hernandez?" She looked up to see her copilot waving from the top of the cliff, careful not to lose her grip. The cliff wasn't a difficult technical climb, it was a slope of boulders that had rolled down over the centuries. She just had to be careful where she placed her feet. "Are you OK?"

"Never better. You need help?"

"I got this. Just, don't kick any rocks down on my head."

A minute later, they were crouched at the top, keeping low so they weren't silhouetted against the sky. "Have you been able to contact anyone else?" She asked.

"No," he shook his head, having swung his faceplate up to breathe the gritty air. "You?"

"All I have is helmet to helmet laserlink. My suit said there was a broadcast from Summit, it was too garbled?"

"Oh, I heard that. The message cancelled any effort to retrieve the Whatsis."

"*Cancelled*? Someone already got it?"

"The message only stated it was no longer our objective."

"That thing was the *entire* objective of Olympic, it-" She realized she was arguing with a guy who had no more information than she did. "Fuck!" She smacked the ground with a hand, sending a shower of pebbles off the cliff.

Hernandez scooted back from the cliff. "We should move away-"

"Right," she kept low and took long strides to follow him. "Damn it! OK, I was going east to find the Whatsis. I don't want to climb down that cliff, so we go, north, or south? The city is to the north."

"We should go north, Ma'am," Hernandez pointed.

"Why?"

"Because there is at least a squad of enemy infantry, two and a half klicks to the south," he pointed the other direction, at a group of figures who were outlined with glowing red in his visor. "They're coming this way, and *they* have powered armor."

"Shit. Suit, activate ELT."

"Ma'am?"

"We can't outrun those soldiers. We need a taxi."

Back on *Valkyrie's* bridge, the main display showed 1:20 in bold numbers, with the number counting down. One one nine. One one eight.

"One minute um, sixteen seconds," Gasquet reported as he rose out of the command chair, "until we can see what happened after we jumped away."

"Bilby," Reed asked as she took her seat. "Can we get a live view now?"

"Sure thing. But like, we're at a bad angle from here. The STAR force was operating on the night side of the planet, and *Valkyrie* was still below the horizon at this point. When we do see the ship, we will be looking through the atmosphere."

"Show us what you can," she nodded. "We understand we're a long way from Omaha."

"Rightee-oh."

The initial image was the sunlit hemisphere of a habitable planet, looking like a stock NASA photo of Earth, until my eyes recognized the outline of continents was wrong, and there wasn't enough of the surface covered by water. Those facts, plus the twinkling lights of starships fighting in orbit, made it clear the holographic display was showing a space battle above Omaha. That's when Bilby zoomed in the view, with a rapid pace that had my stomach doing flipflops and my muscles instinctively tensing for me to smack into the surface. The image stabilized, at what I judged was a high altitude, in the center was a cloud. We all knew what was at the bottom of that pillar of smoke and ash. The scorched ruins of the Makalva military base. The top of the cloud had flattened and was spreading out, as it reached the stratosphere.

"Sorry," Bilby muttered. "That's the best image I can get from here with passive sensors. The cloud is blocking everything in the infrared spectrum, if there are heat sources on the ground, I can't see them. This is *bogus*, man."

"Pull the image up, please," I requested. "I want a view of the overall situation."

The view pulled back at a reasonable speed, to show not the entire hemisphere again but maybe about a quarter of the sunlit side.

"What's that streak in the upper right?" Gasquet asked, right before he must have answered his own question. "Oh. Don't-"

"Duuuuude," Bilby gasped. "Like, that's all that is left of the *Flying Dutchman*." The view focused on the intensely glowing pink flame at the tip of the streak that was boring a hole through the atmosphere. As we watched in horror, the burning wreckage broke into three pieces, each at the tip of a new streak of fire. "Sheeeee-it," Bilby groaned. "This is *heinous*. Nagatha was a classy lady, I'm going to miss her."

Pressing my knuckles into my eye sockets so the crew wouldn't see my eyes welling with tears, I wiped away the telltale streaks. I was responsible for Nagatha's death, yes. I was also responsible for her existence. Her creation had been a mistake, and Skippy had wanted to erase her as an abomination. It was at my insistence that he allowed her to grow and become, if not fully self-aware, something close to that state. She was gone, another casualty of a disastrous day.

"General Dude, I can't watch this anymore," Bilby pulled back the view to cover a wider area. Two blue circles appeared in orbit. "Those are the debris clouds that used to be the *Adriatic Sea* and the *Baltic Sea*," he noted. "All three assault carriers, gone. Man, have we ever had a worse day?"

"If we have, don't remind me of it," I muttered.

"OK, coming up on when we can see events just before we left, I'll do the best I can to get a decent view of *Valkyrie*."

The image was shaky and zoomed in too far, the outline of our battlecruiser fuzzy, and not just from the hellacious number of hits our shields were taking back then.

Back then.

"Speed of light time lag will never not be weird," Reed muttered. "We are watching a live view, of *us*."

"How the hell did we ever manage to jump away from there?" Gasquet asked the question we were all thinking.

"Skippy magic." Reed said that, I didn't.

The bridge fell silent as the view zoomed out, showing other ships, both UN and Rindhalu. And Maxohlx ships. A lot of those, too many. All focused on *Valkyrie* at the center of the image, our mighty ship climbing toward jump distance, and falling short. At that point, our ship was hidden behind a continuous glow of explosions. Three, two, one, a bright flare. Then enemy missiles, maser beams, and railgun darts zipped through empty space where we had been a moment before.

In my seat along the rear bulkhead of the bridge, I steeled myself to witness horror, as the 14th Fleet turned and burned to strike the ships of Task Force Hammer. Even with the warships the spiders had brought to the party, the Maxohlx had more than twice the combat power around Ohmeharikahn. We no longer had Skippy to help us, while the Maxohlx might have the advantage of the Outsider providing targeting and other nefarious assistance.

I didn't want to watch the slaughter, and not just because it was all my fault. No one wants to see your own side taking punishment. On the display, the Maxohlx ships momentarily appeared to be confused. That wouldn't last long. If I were Allard, and if the admiral still could exercise command and control over his ships, I would order all ships that were above jump distance, and not already trapped by enemy damping fields, to jump away. Not to run, but to harass the kitties with hit and run tactics, maximizing the number of UN ships that might survive the disaster. Jump in, launch weapons, jump away. Keep the 14th Fleet distracted from crushing those human ships that were not able to jump away. That's what I would do, that's the advice I would give if Allard asked, and if *Valkyrie* still had a working comm node.

Not that Allard would ask for advice from me, since I'm the idiot who got us into the mess. I had to remind myself that the action we were witnessing happened almost nine minutes ago, so UN ships we saw maneuvering on the display might already be dead.

Except-

"Dude like, what the hell?" Bilby was puzzled along with everyone else.

The Maxohlx weren't just momentarily confused by *Valkyrie's* sudden escape. Their ships weren't shooting, they were moving on ballistic arcs. What the f-

My safety belt stopped me from rising from my chair. Screw that, I slapped the buckle open. *Valkyrie* wasn't in action and wouldn't be for hours, at least. Walking to the main display, I used my fingertips to zoom in on a Maxohlx battleship, one that had been pounding our shields before we barely managed to perform a surprise jump. That battlewagon had lost power, it was slowly spinning out of control, weapons inactive. A volley of railgun darts from a ship out of view struck the armored hull and blasted fountains of burning chunks into space. The battleship's shields were down hard. What the hell?

"Bilby," I zoomed out to get a view of the overall action. The ships of the 14th Fleet were all out of action, every one of them that were in the display. "What are we seeing?"

"Like, I am stumped, Your Dudeness. They all- Oh wow. Like, *wow*. Could it be?"

"What?'

"It's like, give me a moment, need to run back the sensor data. Yes! Quit your grinnin' and drop your linen, I found it!"

The display hadn't changed, we couldn't see whatever he had found. "Bilby, *what*?"

"Just after we jumped away, a Maxohlx heavy cruiser also jumped. That ship wasn't taking part in the battle, it was off all by itself, separated from their fleet by two lightseconds. Just after that heavy cruiser jumped away, the kitties' ships all lost power. That can't be a coincidence."

"The Outsider was aboard that cruiser," Reed guessed it before I could.

"Has to be," I agreed. "It was coordinating the attack, it had control of the 14th Fleet. When its control was yanked away, the AIs of those ships went into reset mode. Fuck! What an opportunity! Allard has to see it. He has to, right?" I turned to Reed.

My question was answered, but not by *Valkyrie's* captain. "This is Admiral Allard," Bilby had the voice transmission booming from the bridge speakers. "For whatever reason, we have been given an opportunity. All ships, engage the enemy and destroy."

Allard might have spoken some more inspiring words, his voice was drowned out by cheers ringing around the bridge compartment. My contribution to the celebration was a silent fist pump while I stepped back from the holographic display so others could see the action.

Ships were exploding. Hammer Force and the 64th Gathering were wasting no time, and not wasting ammunition. Their gunners were aiming railgun darts at the unshielded enemy jump drive capacitors, turning 14th Fleet ships one by one into short-lived stars above Omaha. Bilby designated each dead ship with a UN Navy standard symbol of a red circle with an 'X' drawn across it. Those symbols were popping up everywhere.

"Bilby, are those enemy ships resetting, rebooting, whatever they do?"

"They are trying, it's kind of a race between- Whoa! A UN destroyer just took out a freakin' enemy *battleship* with one shot! I guess that can happen when the enemy ship's shields are down. Um, to answer the question you didn't ask yet, the rotten kitties are seriously screwed. The math is against them, Hammer Force is knocking them out fast, by the time the first kitty ship restores power, the fight should be over."

"Let's not get too happy," I held up my hands. "Any space battle is a complex action, a lot can go wrong in a hurry." While I said that to caution the crew against disappointment, in my heart I was hoping Hammer Force would wipe out or at least disable the entire 14th Fleet.

That didn't happen, it couldn't. Allard's gunnery crews were wisely targeting their weapons where they could do the most damage in the shortest time, focusing on enemy jump drive capacitors. A single shot into a capacitor bank could make a victim disappear in a blinding flash, and if the gunners had started hitting the enemy escort ships first, half of the 14th Fleet would be expanding clouds of particles within a minute or two. That tactic would be satisfying in terms of seeing enemy numbers rapidly decline, that was not what Hammer Force needed to achieve. The major threat was from the Maxohlx capital ships; the battleships and battlecruisers, then their heavy cruisers. Those ships carried the punching power that could cause serious problems for Task Force Hammer, so Allard's commanders instructed their gunners to coordinate with nearby ships to take out the heavies first. Getting ordnance through the tough armor plating of a capital ship required multiple strikes against the same location, so groups of UN and Rindhalu ships methodically took out one Maxohlx battlewagon after another, leaving the smaller escort ships for the tail end of the fight. That was a good strategy, the best option given the time constraint. Ironically, Hammer Force's success began to work against it. As more enemy ships exploded to become short-lived suns above the planet, more debris and radiation was flooding the battlespace. Sensors were blinded, gunners had to fire without accurate targeting information, they also had to make sure if their ordnance missed an enemy ship, it wouldn't fly onward to strike a friendly. The task force commanders understood the issue, assigning destroyers to climb away from the planet, where their sensors might get a clearer view of the battlespace. That tactic improved the rate of fire a bit, most ships were still unable to get a firing solution with enough confidence for gunners to press a button and warn 'On the waaaaaay'.

The confusion meant that twenty one percent of the 14th Fleet's ships managed to reboot and jump away. Twenty one percent of the ships, but less than seven percent of the enemy's punching power had escaped.

"Well," I stared at the deck when the last enemy ship disappeared in a flash of gamma radiation. The one-sided battle had lasted only seventeen minutes. Squaring my shoulders, I added, "That's it."

"General Dude," Bilby drawled, "you don't sound happy. The enemy fleet is *gone*."

"Not all of them. The surviving ships can conduct hit and run attacks against the landing zone, slow down the effort to pull our people off the surface."

Reed bit her lip and grimly nodded agreement.

"Oh. *Bogus*," he sounded hurt and wasn't faking it. "I should have thought of that."

"It's not your job, you have enough to do keeping the ship running." To Reed I said, "I need to talk with Allard, and not with an eighteen minute delay between sending a message and receiving a reply."

"We have the collect-" She caught herself. Only she, Gasquet, Frey, and I knew the true nature of the object we had designated as the 'Biscuit'. "The item we came here to get. We can't risk it being damaged or captured, so we can't jump into orbit near Omaha."

"We are not taking that risk," I confirmed. "The *Newport News* carries an Elder comm node," I named one of the service and repair ships that came to Omaha to support Hammer Force. That ship was a mobile space dock, one with the capability for conducting basic repairs. Enough to get damaged ships back to flightworthiness, so they could get to a major service facility. Such as, at Earth or Jaguar. "Bilby, what's the status of the jump drive?"

"Ooh like, physically it's fine, I mean, I even had bots conduct scans independently of the drive diagnostic system, in case the internal sensors got hacked. They didn't. Now I'm reviewing the navigation computer to verify it-"

"Do you have any indication there is malicious code resident in the nav system?"

"Like no, but it would be a heinous risk if there is malware, and the drive went 'Boom', you know what I'm saying?"

"I do. For a single, short range jump, could you cut out the nav system, and control the drive directly?"

"Oh wow, that is a tough ask, General Dude. Like, I could, but not with any sort of precision."

"For an in-system jump, what would be your SAP?" I used the UN Navy term Spherical Area of Probability, the bubble within which the ship should emerge, with the center of the sphere being the point we aimed for. If Skippy programmed such a short jump, he could be accurate to within a few meters.

"Like, I could be off up to eight hundred sixty kilometers in any direction."

Reed flashed a thumbs up.

"That will be outstanding precision, Bilby," I assured the ship's AI.

"Skippy would be very disappointed."

"Yeah well, *you* didn't stupidly fall into a star."

"Oh, righteous. OK, Dude, you want to jump over the *Newport News*?"

"Yes. Close enough for a dropship to fly here. We don't need to rendezvous, not at this point."

"Okey-dokey. It will take four minutes to program a jump, and run it through the model."

Reed cleared her throat. "Sir, we need extra time to ensure something important won't break when we jump."

"Something, or some*one*. It's your call."

"The ship took a beating, then we basically got shot out of a cannon. I want Engineering to check everything important."

CHAPTER THREE

Scout Leader Second Class Zhartum, of the Maxohlx Hegemony Territorial Army, squinted at the image fed by the troop transport's sensors. He was irritated by the instinctive reaction of his eyes, though the image was fed by implant directly to his optic nerve. "No sign of enemy activity around the human spacecraft?"

The tech running the sensor suite paused to scan the area around the crashed United Nations spacefighter, making sure that what she reported was accurate. "Negative, the area is clear, though Sir? There is so much EM interference here, I would trust my eyes more than the sensors. The pilot survived the hard landing, but died soon after." The image focused on the cockpit section of the human fighter spacecraft. The spacefighter had dug a deep furrow in the sandy soil of a shallow, bowl-shaped depression in the landscape, the right wing crumpled, the craft rolled to that side. The top hatch of the cockpit was swung up and a body in a human hardshell flight suit was partially out of the cockpit, one boot nearly touching the ground. "Residual heat signature shows the pilot died recently."

"Should we land, Sir?" The pilot asked.

Zhartum considered. The four transports he commanded, and their troops, could continue searching. Or, he could seize the opportunity to remove the enemy fighter's AI core. Capturing the control center of a human spacecraft was a rare and golden opportunity. A mission far more important than killing any number of scattered and demoralized enemy soldiers. "We land, Unit Four, you're with me. Set us down close to that spacecraft, avoid the rocks," he noted several sharp rocks sticking out of the sand. "Units Two and Three," he ordered the other transports. "Circle the area and provide cover."

All three pilots acknowledged his order, and the deck tilted as the pilot brought the transport around, lining up an approach. The sensors filtered out the swirling dust, sand, and flakes of charred soot, providing a clear synthetic view. The aircraft carrying Unit Four touched down first, eight soldiers running down the back ramp and fanning out. Zhartum was jostled in his seat as his aircraft contacted the ground with the left skids first then bounced to the right. He ignored the rocking motion and ran expertly down the ramp behind the Unit One squad.

"Anything to report?" He asked the squad leader.

The woman shook her head, a bit disgusted, and mostly dazed as they all were. The humans had attacked for no known reason, then their own side had apparently used a strategic weapon against the Makalva base, before the 14th Fleet unexpectedly returned. Flashes in the sky showed a furious battle was raging in the space around the planet, and everyone in the Scouts wanted to know what the *hell* was going on. Zhartum had no answers for them. But maybe the enemy fighter's AI core could provide clues. "One dead human pilot," the squad leader pointed to where two Scouts were approaching the downed enemy spacecraft, wary of booby traps. And wary of toxic chemicals venting from cracks in the fuselage. "Otherwise, this place is dead," she kicked a rock away, scuffing her boot where the rock left a divot in the sandy soil. That's when she saw something that shouldn't be there.

It was the last thing she ever did.

Shauna didn't wait for an order, there wasn't anyone to give her orders. Except the Air Force major, who had made it clear he would leave matters of ground combat to the experts. "You just had to step *right there*," she exhaled, speaking to the enemy soldier who couldn't hear her. And a moment later, couldn't hear anything as a fourteen point seven millimeter armor penetrating sniper round punched through the enemy soldier's helmet and exited the far side.

Major Verhoef had been waiting behind a rock and under stealth netting, waiting for a signal. The enemy soldier's helmet exploding was not what he expected or what had been planned, the US Air Force had trained him to adapt and overcome. Tapping the wristpad he had had removed from the hardshell flight suit, he activated a sequence. "A downed Eagle still has talons," he said to no one as four missiles shrieked out of the Eagle's portside internal weapons bay. The missiles were not mere lightweight man-portable toys, they were designed to do damage to enemy spacecraft and smaller starships like frigates and destroyers. Twisting on their own tails, the missiles sought targets, the two transports flying cover. Caught unawares, one aircraft was ripped apart by two missile strikes, the massive shape charge explosions rocketing the debris far away from the landing zone. The second transport fared better, its defensive autocannons scored a hit on one missile just before the second weapon bored in to scatter burning chunks of aircraft over a wide area.

While the missiles were in flight, Joel used the wristpad as a remote control and the Eagle's belly jets roared to life, lifting the craft awkwardly off the ground, sending it careening across the sky and smashing into Unit Four's transport. The flying machines locked together and tumbled across the ground, crushing Scouts and sending chunks of debris flying, cutting down more Maxohlx soldiers.

Scout Leader Zhartum instinctively had turned in the direction the sniper round had come from, his rifle coming up to engage, so Shauna's second round struck his faceplate and exited the powercell pack in the rear of his helmet in a fountain of hot shrapnel.

"The one on the left has a rocket launcher," Jesse spotted targets for Shauna. With her firing line-of-sight rounds, enemy sensors would soon find them. Lying prone between two large rocks was good cover, but a rocket could turn the rocks into deadly flying shards. The Eagle and the transport had stopped rolling, only small pellets of shrapnel from secondary explosions were flung across the area. On the platoon channel the makeshift team was using, he spoke, "All clear, go go *go*."

Ten figures rose from under a thin layer of sand, less cover than they had hoped for. Digging had soon revealed a solid shelf of hard shale less than two meters under the sand, so they had do the best they could. Dave had commented that they were digging their own graves. No one had expected the enemy to land aircraft in the low ground where the Eagle had come down, Jesse had almost ordered the antiaircraft gunners to fire when it appeared that an enemy aircraft would land directly on top of several of Dave's mercs. As it happened, the surviving transport had set down three meters from where Jates and Dave were hidden, the belly jets scouring away sand until the mercenary leader was covered by only a light dusting of sand grains. Shauna had done her job, Major Verhoef had sent his fighter out in a blaze of glory, now it was the gravediggers' turn.

Jates was first on his feet, taking out a Scout to the right of the transport's ramp even as he exploded from the sand. The gravediggers all had the benefit of targeting feeds from Jesse's helmet, designating individual targets before they received the 'Go' order.

Dave sighted on his target, swinging his rifle barrel down and away as that Scout was felled by fire from behind him. Swiveling his head around, though the visor provided a three hundred sixty degree view, he saw only three enemy Scouts on their feet, and they were busy being struck by multiple rounds. A whine rising higher in pitch snapped his head back to the aircraft. The back ramp was still down, the engines were spooling up. "Jates!" He shouted, charging up the ramp and through the rear cabin door, the visor's peripheral sensors warning him that he wasn't alone only after he cleared the doorway. Someone in a flight suit, not powered armor, was bringing a pistol up to-

The pistol was roughly wrenched from the crew chief's hands as Jates tossed his own rifle in the air, elbowed the enemy in the face, caught the rifle, and thumbed the selector to the stun setting. One surge of high voltage had the enemy rigid in a seizure, before slumping to the deck.

Dave bounced off a rack of seats when the aircraft lifted straight up. Wasting no time, he bounded toward the open cockpit door, seeing the pilot on the right staring at him in shock and he shot clean through that face, the second round of the double-tap burst missing the intended target and buried itself in the console, shattering the displays in a shower of sparks. Pulling the rifle around toward the other pilot to order the kitty to set the aircraft down, he-

Groaned as from beside him, Jates stunned the Maxohlx pilot. "We are in the freakin' *air*!" Dave gestured to the view from the cockpit window displays, that showed the horizon dropping away. He judged they were only a few meters off the ground, far enough to make a hard landing rough on the occupants. "I can't fly this-"

Silently, Jates reached forward and tapped an orange button. They steadied themselves against the door frame as the engine whining lowered in pitch and intensity. A moment later, the aircraft was safely if not gently on the ground again. "That button activates the auto-landing feature," the Verd-kris explained.

"How the hell did you know that?"

"I studied the characteristics of many enemy vehicles and weapons, while you wasted time watching your heroes in 'Real Househusbands of Denver'."

"I am not a *househusband*," Dave didn't want to get into that argument again.

"Your wife outranks you."

"I bring in a lot more money."

"She is well known on your homeworld, while you live in obscurity."

"Obscurity suits me just fine, it saves me from paying for a security detail. Hey, get Sleeping Beauty there unstrapped and drag him outside. I will," he frowned at the mess inside the first pilot's helmet. "Clean up this."

Jates pointed to the smashed pilot console, that was still fizzing with sparks. "Did you miss the safety briefing about electronics not reacting well to rifle rounds?"

"I got the job done. Now, move."

Jesse patted the transport's skin, where a piece of shrapnel had gouged a dent, shaking his head at Dave. "The task was to *destroy* enemy air power."

Dave nodded. "I'm hoping to get an 'Exceeds expectations' on my next review."

"You're the boss of your outfit."

"I'll be reviewing myself, so my odds are good." He crouched to look under the aircraft. The skin was peppered with scratches and dents, but there weren't any holes through, and he couldn't see any fluids dripping on the ground. "I guess we can't leave it here like this, it's still flightworthy. Jates, set some charges in the-"

"Hold that thought," Jesse held up a hand, waving to the Air Force pilot. "Major Verhoef? Can you fly this thing?"

Joel trotted over and bit his lip as he examined the flying machine. "It's just a standard Albatross, I flew in one of these during training."

Jesse cocked his head. "The Maxohlx call it 'Albatross?"

"That's the Def Com designation for this type."

"You flew *in* one, or you," Dave pantomimed his hands on a control yoke, "*flew* one?"

"The first one. Controls are standard, though. Pilots have a saying: "If I can get it started, I can get it in the air'. This one is already running."

"I don't know about-"

"Unless y'all prefer walking out of here?" Jesse asked.

"We'll get shot down by our own side," Dave objected. "I'd rather-"

"We can set this ship's IFF to squawk a Def Com ID code, if we're interrogated by a friendly," Joel started walking around the aircraft, looking for battle damage.

Dave wasn't convinced. "I'm responsible for my people. This is still-"

"Major?" Shauna interrupted the argument. "What are your orders, Sir?"

Dave clamped his mouth shut. Verhoef was the ranking officer on scene, even if he was an Air Force puke.

Joel's frown turned into a ghost of a grin. "Get clear, I'm taking this ship up for a short test hop."

Admiral Uhtavio Scorandum was, unusually, in his official suite at the headquarters of the Ethics and Compliance Office. There was, he was surprised to see, a waiting room between his office and the corridor, and in the waiting room was an aide seated at a small desk. The aide's job, apparently, was to chase away anyone who wished to speak with the admiral. As that was only the second time he had been in his office, he did wonder what the aide did all day, although he didn't wonder too much about it. She was somehow related to the minister in charge of the ECO, so the job was of course a way for the minister to ensure the loyalty of his extended family, and his aide had to pay part of her paycheck to her benefactor.

No one, he saw as he sat rather gingerly on the unfamiliar couch, had removed the remaining personal items of the previous occupant. *That* needed to change, he decided with a frown. Interior decorating was not one of his passions, he simply didn't want to look at some jerk's face in photos of him shaking claws with senior political leaders, or photos of his no doubt spoiled bratty children. There was also a plant in the corner, a live plant. He wondered if his aide's job included watering the shrubbery. "Er, Tuvinga?" He called the aide.

There was no immediate response. Then the creaking of a couch, a loud, heavy sigh, and the sound of a tablet being set down on a desk

"Sir?" She stuck her head in the doorway, not yet committing to being *in* the office.

"Please have someone remove these, personal items."

She blinked. "What should I do with them?"

"Whatever is the," he waved a claw, "standard procedure for this sort of thing. Oh," he added after she rolled her eyes. He had not scanned the ECO employee handbook in a while, several decades actually, but he did not recall anything about office etiquette. "Then, throw it away, or do whatever you wish with it."

That prompted a frown. "Will you be bringing your own personal items?"

"I do not intend to be here frequently enough to care."

That prompted a smile. "Of course, Admiral. Is there anything else?"

He looked around, pulling open drawers. They were mostly empty. "Er," he tried to remember whether the headquarters had a cafeteria, he was getting hungry. "Well-" His phone alerted, in a tone that instantly got his attention. "No, thank you," He waved for her to clear the doorway. "That will be all."

In the corridor, he headed toward the elevator, glancing at the phone. It provided no useful information, other than the alert tone itself.

Kinsta. His protégé wanted to make contact, and soon. That tone indicated the former ECO agent had gone to a food cart three blocks from his workspace at the Office of Special Inquiries. Kinsta visited that cart every few weeks, so him being there was not unusual. What had triggered the alert was that when the double agent ordered a hot cup of svito, he had requested extra hot sauce. A lot of it.

Scorandum shuddered. He hoped Kinsta had not been foolish enough to actually drink the fiery hot beverage, or their meeting would be in a hospital. The hot sauce in svito was a signal that Kinsta needed to meet that afternoon, in a brothel where the lowly Inquisitor clerk would be spending his lunch break. A *licensed* brothel, so the admiral did not anticipate any fun that day.

Scorandum arrived first, paid for the companionship of a lovely lady, then paid her extra to go away so he could speak privately with Kinsta, who arrived a few minutes later.

"Sir?" Kinsta looked around at the tastelessly opulent furnishings. "I am surprised you want to meet *here*."

The admiral cocked his head. "What is wrong with a bordello? It is a very common place for office workers to go on their lunch break, the Inquisitors would not be suspicious of you being here."

"I meant, I am surprised you chose a *licensed* place."

"Oh. That was for your benefit. The Inquisitors would frown upon you visiting certain establishments, so I avoided the complication. Kinsta, what is so urgent? I was shocked to see you had used one of our more clandestine methods of contact."

Kinsta blinked. "Sir, the hot sauce thing was *your* idea, to limit our risk of exposure."

"My true motivation was the *amusement* value of our contact arrangements, I never expected you to actually do anything so silly."

"I, I-"

"Kinsta," Scorandum held out a bottle of the bordello's 'complimentary' water, for which he had actually been charged an exorbitant amount. "Here, drink this."

The former ECO agent choked on the water, shaking the bottle angrily. "I am taking a great risk, for *you*."

"And I appreciate it greatly. Truly, I do. What is the reason for your urgency?"

"Sir- I still call you 'Sir', force of habit."

"That, plus you are once again an ECO agent, and I am your superior officer. Even if few people are aware of that fact."

"Yes, Sir," Kinsta sighed. "The Office of Special Inquiries is investigating you, again. This time, they had proof that will put you in prison for a long time."

"I very much doubt that," Scorandum laughed.

"Sir, this time, they are working with the Central Wagering Office, that is where the investigation originated. The Wagering system claims they caught you placing bets, under an account you apparently thought was untraceable?"

"Hmm. That is nothing unusual. That teaches me a lesson to use a better account forger next time."

"This is *serious*," the former aide insisted. "The lead charge against you is not concealment of identity-"

"Which is only a misdemeanor anyway."

"This is *treason*. This time, they already have the evidence, and it cannot be refuted."

"Treason?" Scorandum scoffed. "What did I supposedly do this time?"

"You used inside information-"

"Which is not even a misdemeanor."

"-to place a wager, about an upcoming secret operation by the humans."

"Oh. *That*?"

"Yes, that. I cannot see why you are so-"

"Was I correct? Will the wager pay off?"

"What I heard was it is not yet known whether the humans struck that target."

"A pity. I have been quite anxious, waiting for the news."

"You risked giving away vital information that could have jeopardized-" He stopped, taking a long moment to study the admiral. "How can you be so calm in this situation?"

"This is not the first time I have been persecuted by the Inquisitors, nor will it be the last," he sighed.

"You-" Kinsta froze, while his expression went from horror to puzzlement to a gasping understanding, and back to horror. "You *expected* the Central Wagering AIs to uncover your subterfuge?"

"It amuses me when you use big words like that."

"*Did* you expect it?"

"Central Wagering certainly was *slow* about it. Someone should investigate *that*."

"You, you- That wager was part of a planned operation? An officially approved operation?"

"Come, you know that waiting endlessly to receive official approval is not how our Office works."

"This was *not* treason?"

"Far from it. The opposite, in fact."

"But- Then, then why were the Inquisitors so confident they had gotten you dead to rights this time?"

"The Office of Special Inquiries prioritizes fanaticism over intelligence, as I am sure *you* are more aware than me."

"That does not explain-"

Scorandum shifted on the couch, wishing he had splurged on a grossly overpriced, mislabeled and watered down bottle of burgoze. "Exactly how did you get this information? You are a lowly clerk there, a high priority investigation would not have come across your desk."

"It didn't. I overheard two Inquisitors talking, outside the office of the Chief Arbiter. They were preparing for a meeting with her."

"Hmm. You just happened to be there, while two senior officials discussed sensitive information in a public area?"

"As you said, I am a clerk. No one notices me."

"They would not notice an ordinary clerk, *you* do not fit that profile. Oh, Kinsta, Kinsta, you young fool. I had such high hopes for my protégé."

"I was never your protégé."

"All too true, for anyone *I* trained properly would never have been so foolish. Kinsta, I regret to inform you that the subject of this investigation is not me, but *you*."

"*Me*? How-"

"My strong suspicion is this is not an investigation led by the Chief Arbiter, but by," he paused, shuddering slightly as he felt a chill sneak up his spine. "By the Enforcers."

"*Enforcers*?" Kinsta jerked like he had suffered an electric shock. "This is an Internal Affairs matter?"

"It is," the admiral shook his head with great sadness. "The true purpose of the investigation has been to determine whether your loyalties lie with your employer of record. And, unfortunately, by your unwarranted haste in contacting me, you have exposed yourself."

"*No*," Kinsta gasped in horror.

"Unfortunately, yes."

"I am, *screwed*," the double agent breathed.

"Also unfortunately, yes."

"They will *kill* me."

"Please, there is no need for you to be so dramatic. At worst, you will merely have to endure a lengthy time in prison. Although, as this is a matter internal to Special Inquiries, you will be sent to one of their own prisons."

"Anything but that. You have to protect me."

"As I warned when you signed up to be a double agent, I can't officially intervene. Legally, you still work for the Inquisitors."

"You offered to fake my death."

Scorandum blinked slowly. "You didn't actually believe that, did you?"

"I certainly did!"

"Clearly, I should have chosen a better protégé. Kinsta, I swear that I will do *everything* I can for you, as this is partly my fault."

"Th-Thank you, Sir. What can you do?"

"Well," the ECO senior officer stood up. "I am sure even the Inquisitor prison allows inmates to receive a fruit basket. Is there anything special you would like?"

Bad shit happens. Sometimes it's your fault, sometimes the Universe just takes a steaming dump on your head.

As a parent, I found bad things happening to be a good opportunity to talk with my boys about what they can expect in life. For that parenting skill, I used my own father as a model. One time when I was little, about seven or eight, my father took me to a car show. There, I saw what my young mind thought was the coolest car ever. It was a 1978 Ford Mustang II King Cobra, black with cool wheels, T-tops, and a decal on the hood of a cobra with flames around it. My father gently told me that, while the car looked hot, it was considered an embarrassingly tragic turd, something the car industry wanted to forget. "Joe," he had told me, "that car would be faster if it was towed by a ride-on lawnmower." He took the opportunity to explain that, like that car, some people I think are cool are posers, and I should watch what they do, not what they say or how they look.

That was good advice, and I kept that in mind when my boys asked me serious questions. Like, how could a just and loving God allow their favorite team to grossly overpay for an aging veteran, who everyone could plainly see could no longer play at a pro level? My answer had been that God gave humanity free will, which can be a blessing, or a curse. A franchise owner who spends his own money is free to take his own bad advice, act like he owns a fantasy team, and have no one else to blame when the team inevitably sucks. Fans should not think that God is responsible for a season of futility.

That is, unless you are a Jets fan, because everyone knows that God hates the New York Jets.

I mean, how else do you explain the Butt Fumble?

The bad shit that happened in Operation Olympic could not be blamed on anyone but me, and I actually would have felt better about it if Reed had called me an idiot.

Shit. I should focus on my *feelings*, because that's what is truly important.

After retreating to my office to think of a way to pull Skippy out of the star, I had nothing. It was time to go back to the bridge, and see the anxious and disappointed faces of the crew. I almost wish I had fallen into the star with Skippy.

Gasquet looked up from his console when I walked onto the bridge but he addressed his remark to Reed. "Colonel, Engineering reports the ship is now jump ready in all respects."

Reed's response was a raised eyebrow.

Her XO gave a shrug. "As ready as we can be. Engineering says all they can guarantee is the major frames won't snap from the strain."

She snorted. "Coming from them, that is a solid gold shmaybe. Bilby, jump option Tango, punch it."

We emerged six hundred and forty kilometers off target, closer to the *Newport News* than expected. "Uh, Bilby?" I whispered into my zPhone, "who commands that ship?"

"Captain Perduk," he whispered back into my earpiece, and a brief bio of Perduk appeared on my phone. It was good to know basic details of the woman whose day I was about to ruin. Out of my chair, I approached the main display, pointing to the communications tech. "Contact the *Newport News*, tell them I want to speak with their captain."

It took twenty seconds before a confused voice spoke. "General Bishop? Does *Valkyrie* require immediate servicing? If so, the-"

"Not right now, but soon. Captain, I need to borrow your Elder comm node, so I can speak with Admiral Allard. Send it here on a dropship as soon as possible."

"Sir," she understandably was hesitant to comply, as I wasn't in her chain of command. "To release that asset to *Valkyrie*, I will need to clear it with the admiral, we-"

"No, you do not. Effective as of now, that communications node is requisitioned by the Special Mission Group. Note it in your log. Launch your ready bird with the comm node."

"General," the strain was evident in her voice, "the comm node is-"

"I can send our ready bird," Reed broke into the conversation, using her no nonsense *I am SO over this shit* tone. "If yours isn't capable of flight at the moment."

There was an inaudible gasp on *Valkyrie's* bridge. By *in*audible, I mean everyone went silent. Their captain had just dissed another starship commander, which really was not cool, but Reed had assumed Perduk was dissing me.

On the display, Perduk pursed her lips. "Thank you, Captain Reed, that will not be necessary. Our ready bird will launch in," she looked off to her left. "Eight minutes. The delay is because our comm node is stored securely in a vault at the core of the ship. General Bishop, I was about to say that you can use the comm node now, we can relay the link."

"Yes," I nodded. "Thank you, Captain Perduk." I was grateful that she hadn't argued with me. Yes, I could have pulled rank and been a dick about it, I didn't want to be That Guy. "Bilby, link to the comm node and contact the task force command and control AI, get a Sitrep. Reed, I'll be in my office."

Admiral Allard wasn't immediately available, the guy understandably was busy. One of his staff officers told me the admiral knew I needed to talk with him. "Do you have urgent information, General?" She asked.

"Urgent, but not right this very second."

There was a pause, I heard someone speaking softly in the background. "The Admiral will contact you in seven minutes, General."

"I'll be here," I ended the call. Then I stared at the ceiling. Disappointingly, the solution for extracting Skippy from a star was not written on the overhead. "OK," I leaned my chair back. "We'll have to do this the hard way," I said to myself. Talking to myself wasn't a sign that I had cracked under pressure, it's just something I did.

Four minutes. That was enough time to get my head together and think. About how to pull a beer can out of a star. First, how to find his beer can inside a fusion inferno.

What pissed me off about myself is, I shouldn't have needed to dream up a plan right then. I should already have a freakin' plan for such a situation. No, I am not saying I should have anticipated that the Outsider would learn we were going to Ohmeharikahn, and that it would hack into *Valkyrie* to dork up our jump navigation system, and eject Skippy's escape pod at the worst time. If I could anticipate something like that, I would be the level of genius that Skippy imagines he is.

What I mean is, Skippy many times has mentioned his fear of being lost in deep, empty interstellar space, or of getting pulled into the core of a star. He had pretended he was joking about it, but when someone talks about their fears often enough, they must be seriously concerned.

Him being in empty space would be a problem, a manageable though pain in the ass problem. The only issue would be finding him, using sensors limited to the speed of light. If he ever did get dumped out in the middle of nowhere, we should have at least some clue about where he went. Then it would become a straightforward SAR mission, with the search part of Search And Rescue being the difficult task. Ah, that and Opsec. If he was lost in empty space, we might send the entire UN Navy on a grid search to find him. Unless our operational security was perfect, several other species would also have their ships out looking for him, and the SAR mission could quickly devolve into a chaotic treasure hunt battle covering thousands of cubic lightyears.

Thinking about that theoretical situation pissed me off. I wasn't angry about the prospect that our enemies would try to capture Skippy before we found him, of course they would. That's why we refer to them as the bad guys, right? What made me hot was knowing that Skippy would be delighted to see hundreds of starships fighting over him. Reminding myself that he was an asshole made losing him inside a star sting a bit less.

No, it didn't. My best friend was in trouble and hurting, because I was incompetent at my job. I was in command, I had approved the deception and battle plans, so that's the bottom line. My responsibility.

Something I could wallow in self-hatred about later, after we got Skippy back. Or gave up on the effort to get him back.

Damn it. How much stupid, useless shit had Skippy and I talked about over the decades? Why hadn't I ever asked whether there was a way to pull him out of a star? Just knowing that we had a plan might ease his fears a little, that would be worth a couple hours of discussion. It sure would ease my mind to know such a thing was possible, whether it was practical or not.

Without a premade plan in my back pocket, I would have to do it the old fashioned way.

I had no idea how to do that.

After lifting off and flying a low circle around the site of the recent battle, Joel set the Albatross down. "It handles like a pig even when the cabin is empty, but it will fly. We need to get that side door closed, it will restrict our airspeed."

"Jates," Jesse gestured to the alien soldier, "give me a hand, or claw. Whatever."

The side cabin door had been open during the brief battle, during the ambush, and the track it slid on had been hit by a chunk of something that had bent the track inward. Even Jates with his powered suit couldn't get the door fully seated.

"Don't force it!" Joel shouted. "Slide it back."

"It's no good, Sir," Jesse bent to peer at the warped track. "Maybe if we had some grease we could-"

"Try this," Joel pulled a small plastic case from the survival pouch he wore around his flight suit liner. His actual hardshell flight suit and helmet had served as decoys, and were now in a thousand pieces scattered across the ground. Cracking open the case, he gave it to Jesse. "These are cotton balls soaked in Vaseline."

"Sir?" Jesse said slowly. "Why do you carry-"

"They're good lightweight fire starters, I learned that in survival school."

"OK," Jesse shrugged, gathering up the cotton and smearing the grease along the track. "Jates, try it now."

The door screeched and protested as it shuddered along the track, and finally latched shut.

"Get aboard," Joel started up the ramp. "Colter, you're with me."

Jesse saw the pilot was pointing to him, not Shauna. "Me, Sir?"

"Yes. I need a copilot to monitor instruments and sensors, and this was *your* idea."

"Shit," Jesse grunted. "Next time, I'll keep my big mouth shut."

In the cockpit, Joel grunted when he saw the console Dave had shattered. "I hope your friend's stray round didn't punch through the hull. I didn't see a hole when I walked around, but it could tear open in flight. We'll find out the hard way."

"OK," Jesse did not think the situation was OK at all. "What should I do?"

"First, strap in."

"Ah, that won't be easy with me in a mech suit."

Joel reached between the seats and pressed a button to slide it backwards. "That should be enough room for you. The Maxohlx are larger than humans, and their pilots sometimes wear hardshell environment suits, in hazardous conditions."

Jesse squeezed into the seat and wriggled to find some semblance of comfort. The straps automatically tightened around him, and he slid the chair forward. "OK, Sir, what next?"

"Second is, don't touch anything."

"How can I monitor sensors if I don't-"

"My flight suit computer is transferring protocols to your mech suit, so you can interface with the ship. You should see a window pop up in your visor."

"Nothing yet, it- Got it. Huh, this is a lot of information, give me a minute."

"While you find us a way out of here, I'm updating this ship's IFF code." He tapped the console, and it didn't respond. Disgusted, he took off his flight suit glove and wiped the console with a bare hand, mostly just smearing the dust and grit across the display. "If you are ever stupid enough to design a combat aircraft with touchscreens, make sure you include a roll of paper towels. This dust gets everywhere."

"I keep a box of baby wipes in the thigh pack of my suit," Jesse opened the pack and gave the box to the pilot.

"Baby wipes?"

"As a soldier, you never know where you'll be fighting next, but you sure as hell know you're gonna get dirty."

Joel wiped the display clear. "I hear that."

"We're all waiting," Joel whispered over the pilot channel two minutes later.

"I know," Jesse grunted, remembering to add, "Sir. The interface between my suit and this," he waved at the shattered console in front of his seat. "Thing, is more full of bugs than the hooch I lived in on Paradise."

"Make it simple: I just need a direction that will not fly us directly into a known enemy formation."

"That's what I'm looking for, the- Whoa."

"What?"

"I got a direction for you. No sign of hostiles, but there are two Def Com ELTs."

"Show me. Yeah," Joel tapped the icon on his display. "We go there."

"Sir? It could be a trap."

"Those ELTs are from squadron DAT-38. They were aboard the *Dutchman* with me. I *know* those people. Can you get an ID?"

"Not with this gear. Sir," Jesse tugged the seat straps tighter. "Let's go get our people."

"You might have clicked on the wrong rideshare service, Ma'am," Hernandez observed, zooming in the image of the aircraft that was approaching from the east. The object had engaged stealth but there was so much dust and soot in the air, it was leaving not only a trail behind it but also a sort of bow shock of dust stretching back from the nose. Based on the rough configuration, engine sound, and relatively slow airspeed, his suit computer had identified the approaching threat as the type of military transport designated as 'Albatross' in the Def Com library.

Sheryl didn't need confirmation from her suit computer, when the aircraft dropped its stealth field. The object that was headed straight for them was too small to be a dropship, and Hammer Force hadn't bothered to land any aircraft for the short-term ground mission. So, it had to be the enemy. "Hands up," she ordered, knowing the Maxohlx understood that body language. Surrender. Being captured by an aircraft crew was better than trusting the mercy and discipline of the squad of soldiers who were less than half a kilometer away and running fast. Humanity had no treaty with the Maxohlx regarding the ethical treatment of prisoners of war, but during more than decade of low-intensity conflict, the rotten kitties had proven to be uncharacteristically unrotten about how they dealt with captured humans, military or civilian. The Maxohlx had a code of honor that made them stubborn assholes overall, but generally trustworthy in the aftermath of a battle.

All that was *before* each side started dropping nukes, so anything could happen.

"Ma'am? The flap of your holster is open, in kind of a threatening manner."

"Oh," she reached down slowly to push the flap back into place, and raised her arm again. Her visor outlined the Albatross in red, adding text below indicating airspeed and ETA. The aircraft was decreasing speed, and would be overhead in twenty seconds. It would probably land, where?

"It's swinging around for a sensor sweep," Hernandez noted as the aircraft changed course toward the south.

"Probably making sure we are alone," Major Crook guessed. "If they're concerned that we have MANPADs, they're too low. We would-"

She fell backwards, stunned when the chin turret of the Albatross spat hot pulses of maser fire at the enemy soldiers, walking the beams east to west. In a moment, the entire squad was down.

Hernandez had also fallen on his backside, partly a protective reaction of his suit. "What the, *fuck*?"

"Either we have friendlies somehow, or Skippy hacked the flight controls of that bird."

"I thought Skippy couldn't use weapons?"

"*I* thought the mission here was to secure the Whatsis, and *that* was bullshit, so-"

A minute later, Sheryl strode through even more choking dust kicked up by the aircraft's belly jets, squinting to keep grit out of her eyes, waving Hernandez to follow her toward the ramp. Standing at the bottom was a soldier in a Def Com standard infantry mech suit, holding a white board with 'Crook party' written in blue marker. "Your ride is here, Ma'am," Shauna grinned. "Do you have any luggage?"

"I have emotional *baggage*," Sheryl grimaced, "but that's a whole 'nother thing. How the hell did you get here in this thing," she squinted again at the nametag. "Colter?"

"Major Verhoef in the cockpit can explain it to you, Ma'am."

"*Joel* is here?"

"Yes, and he would appreciate having a real copilot. My husband is doing his best but," she shrugged, "Blowing shit up is more his thing."

CHAPTER FOUR

"General Bishop?" The staff officer spoke again. "Admiral Allard is available now."

"Great, thank you," I sat up straight in the chair, as the hologram flickered above my desk, and I saw Allard. From the background, I guessed he was in a cubbyhole adjacent to his flagship's bridge.

"Bishop? Please thank Skippy for his latest miracle. I don't know how he did it, but disabling their entire fleet was an incredible trick."

"Uh, that wasn't Skippy's work."

He blinked the surprise of a guy who has seen so much shit in one day, he thought he could never be surprised again. "It wasn't?"

"No. Bilby analyzed the sensor data. A few seconds after *Valkyrie* jumped away, a Maxohlx heavy cruiser jumped. Immediately after *that*," I snapped my fingers. "The 14th Fleet lost power."

"The Outsider," Allard guessed. The guy is a two star admiral, selected to lead the most powerful collection of warships in human history. Of course he is smart. "It was controlling the Maxohlx ships, and their AIs went into reset when the Outsider pulled the plug?"

"That is Bilby's conclusion, yes."

"Bilby?" He looked at me sharply, and his eyes opened wide. "What does Skippy think about the situation?"

"Honestly, I don't know. Skippy did speculate that the Outsider led the 14th Fleet back here."

"In God's name, *how*? You didn't reveal Ohmeharikahn was the target until we were at Brigadoon, and we flew straight here from that secure base. Our Opsec was perfect."

"Ours was, yes. The spiders?" I held up my hands. "Maybe not so much?"

He was as shocked to hear me say that, as I had been to see the freakin' enemy fleet jumping in to spoil the party. I understood his skepticism. For so long, human underdogs had understood we were the newcomer amateurs in the affairs of the galaxy, we had looked up to the spiders as the real experts. The idea that the ancient Rindhalu might have fucked up was not something easy to accept. "Skippy has proof of this?"

"I have a strong suspicion, and Skippy agreed. The Maxohlx could not have penetrated Rindhalu comms without help from the Outsider. The timing also tells me the kitties were working with our enemy on this op. Their fleet jumped in only *after* the dropship carrying the Whatsis went down."

"The Whatsis," his face turned red as he spat out the word. "Which was never the objective of this operation, was it?"

"No," I admitted. "The STAR Force was acquiring the real object we need, on the other side of the planet. Extensive wargaming showed the operation would not succeed unless the defenses were focused on a countering a large scale diversionary attack elsewhere, such as Makalva."

Hearing me admit the truth didn't make him any less angry. "So, you chose a random landing site for the assault?"

"Makalva was selected because it was the safest site for an opposed spaceborne assault. That base itself had limited defenses, the wargame simulations showed the ground force would encounter a manageable level of resistance, once we eliminated the surrounding military facilities by orbital bombardment." Those were the words I had rehearsed over and over, knowing I would have that discussion. "It was the right choice, until, until the Maxohlx decided to nuke their own base."

"That wasn't a scenario you projected, in your war *games*?"

"No," I couldn't help cringing. "I can't tell you how horrified I am at the loss of life."

His jaw worked side to side, like he was trying to decide whether to say something. "Initial reports overstated the carnage. Our sensors were blanked out by the EM shock wave, and our models projected a worst case scenario. The detonation was not an air burst, that would have been worst case. The warhead penetrated sixty meters under the surface before it exploded, so most of the blast energy was directed upward, not outward. That was not good for our dropships in the air, it did protect our troops on the ground. We are now estimating the number killed in the blast at two hundred and fifty three."

"Oh thank God," I slumped back in my chair with a shudder. Two hundred and fifty people was not a small number, it was better than the six or so thousand we had on the ground at that point. "It's, odd that it wasn't an air burst," I heard my inner military nerd remarking before I could understand how inappropriate it was.

Allard apparently was also a nerd. "That surprised us also, until we realized the enemy objective. They didn't hit our troops, their objective was to destroy the secure storage vaults under the base."

"Ah," I understood. "That makes sense. They didn't know what object or objects we were there to take, so they assumed it had to be something *they* considered valuable. The Whatsis, the decoy," I admitted. "Was selected because Skippy knew it was easily accessible, and not considered important by the enemy. We wanted a quick and easy in and out by the ground force."

"The war game models never envisioned the enemy would guess our intentions?"

"No. You saw the same simulations that I reviewed."

"I saw only what you shared with me, not the true purpose of Olympic."

"You saw everything except the STAR Force part of the op, which was completely isolated from the assault. They infiltrated the other side of the planet, got the object we need, and their exfil was going to plan, until the Maxohlx came to the party as uninvited guests. The STARs did succeed, we retrieved Team Razor's dropship, with the target object, it is aboard *Valkyrie* now."

He clamped his jaw shut, breathing deeply through his nose, I could see his nostrils flaring. There was a twitch under one eye. Gathering his thoughts, controlling his temper. I understood him being enormously pissed off at me. Since I had a lot of experience with senior officers being shocked and outraged at me, I applied my usual tactic of waiting for the other person to decide they could, in fact, deal with me right then.

"You could not have shared the real plan with me?"

"No. We had to compartmentalize the information aboard *Valkyrie*, and even then, it was on a need to know basis. Only the leaders of the three STAR teams involved knew the real objective. The pilots didn't train to approach the target site until two days before the op."

"I didn't have a need to know?"

"You had a need to *not* know. So did Perkins. If either of you knew the truth, you might not have been convincing in pressing the attack. You did, and we succeeded in securing the coll- The required object."

"It was a success, then." His jaw wasn't clenched quite as hard. It was difficult to argue with success, especially in an operation where so much had gone wrong. We had overcome serious obstacles and triumphed. As far as he knew.

"Are you able to pull all of our people off the surface? I see the enemy force is conducting hit and run attacks."

"We can handle it. Without the assault carriers, we're using practically every dropship we have left, and the people will be dispersed throughout Hammer Force, it's not an ideal situation. I am deploying my battleships to shield the landing zone. We paid a heavy price here," he said that as a guy who had been promised a quick and easy operation, with minimal opposition. "Still, Olympic is a success. Skippy now has the means to defeat the Outsider."

"Uh-"

He squinted at me sideways. "He does have the means, no?"

"That is, complicated."

He was instantly suspicious. "Bishop." We held the same rank, he could have called me 'Joe'. He didn't. "A 'Yes' or 'No' is not complicated."

"In this case, I can't give a yes or no. The object should point us in the right, direction, to the next step. It requires interpretation."

"Is Skippy confident he can read the thing?"

"Antoine," I did use his first name. "We lost Skippy."

"*What*? When, how," he sputtered. "When did-"

"The Outsider apparently hacked *Valkyrie's* jump drive. We emerged very close to the star here, and Skippy's escape pod was ejected by the malware. There wasn't anything we could do to retrieve him, the ship was also falling into the star, he pushed us away. That action caused him to fall very quickly, we lost him."

"*Skippy fell into the star*?"

"Yes. We are working on a plan to get him back."

"*Soon*?" He stared at me, blinked slowly. "You will not have much time. The Maxohlx certainly sent for reinforcements, and they will send multiple fleets."

"There's a time limit, we know."

"What is the plan? How can we help?"

"We are," he had put me on the spot, and I didn't have an answer. "Looking at multiple options."

"*Merde*," he exclaimed the French curse word. He meant it as 'bullshit'. The guy didn't know me, the first time we met was when he was appointed to lead Hammer Force. He did know my reputation for racing into action without a plan. "Do you have *any* options?"

"Not at the moment," I admitted.

His head dropped back against the chair. "This *was* all for nothing."

"Not yet, it's not."

"Bishop," he didn't bother to look at me. "We lost all three assault carriers. We are still tallying the casualties, but between in the sky and on the ground, the toll has to be over a thousand dead, more injured. This," he did look at me. Trying to decide what to say. Maybe also what to do. If Def Com had granted him authority to relieve me of command, he was deciding whether that would be useful right then. He had to know we had no chance to recover Skippy unless someone could dream up an idiotically impractical plan, and he had to know the best idiot for the job was Joe Bishop.

Besides, I had requested Bilby to edit out the audio if Allard did relieve me. I can't disobey an order I don't hear.

"Without Skippy, we can't use the, whatever object the STAR Force captured. We can't stop the Outsider," he was speaking to himself, not me. "Our Sentinels can't protect Earth or Jaguar from an unexpected threat. We haven't only lost Skippy, we have lost *everything*."

He had summed up the situation perfectly, at least he had said 'We' instead of 'You', meaning me. "Again, that's not yet a-"

"Bishop." He leaned forward and I tensed for the audio connection to glitch. I would be putting him in an awkward situation. An impossible situation. "You," he was choosing his words carefully. "You need to fix this. However you Pirates do this sort of thing."

That was not what I expected him to say. "We will do our best."

"You will need your absolute best. Could the Rindhalu assist? Have they ever retrieved an object from inside a star?"

"I'm going to contact them, I don't have my hopes set high. They have been working on a project to pull the Sam Francisco AI out of the star it got dumped into, and to date, the spiders don't even have a workable theory about how to even find the thing."

He wrinkled his brow. "The Maxohlx have also been working to do the same?" He didn't know that the 'Sam' AI was a fake.

"They don't have a clue how to start. Intel suggests the Maxohlx are intending to steal whatever idea the spiders develop. Listen, I know this is fucked up in every way possible."

"I won't argue about that."

"This," I didn't want to say something like 'in my defense', there was no way to spin my massive screwup as anything other than me being an overconfident fool. "This actually is not the worst mess we've ever been in, we have lost Skippy before and gotten him back." I didn't mention that time, Skippy bailed on us and came back by himself. "Bringing him back aboard *Valkyrie* is just a, physics problem."

Allard shook his head. "Time. Your enemy is *time*, not simple physics. The Maxohlx will act to stop whatever you're doing. Whatever you're going to do, you need to do it soon. Would you like my advice?"

"Please."

"You should consider our options if you can't bring Skippy back. Because the Outsider is advanced beyond our ability to comprehend. It would not have planned to drop Skippy into a star unless it knew we lacked the technology to retrieve him."

"I hear you, there is just no alternative to Skippy. Without a friendly Elder AI, we are screwed. Not just an Elder AI, it has to be *Skippy*. He has exceeded his programming, stretched his boundaries, and grown beyond what his creators imagined. The Outsider is advanced, and can do things that Skippy doesn't understand. The flip side is Skippy is able to do many things the Outsider can't, we know that. Whatever the Outsider knows, it can't possibly imagine everything Skippy might do. Even Skippy doesn't know everything he is capable of."

"I hope you are right about that. It is clear the Outsider played us like, you Americans would say like a fiddle? It knew we were coming here, it waited to see what we came here for, to understand the nature of the threat against it. And it planned to remove Skippy from the threat board. A masterful plan, expertly executed."

"It played *me*," I corrected him. "This mess is a hundred percent on me."

"*Skippy* should have anticipated something like this could happen."

"That kind of thinking isn't what Skippy does. He relies on us for that. I failed to protect him. By doing that, I failed all of us."

"What do you need from me?" The discussion had moved in a positive direction. "Not all of the battleship groups are needed to protect the recovery operation, I could detach-"

"Thanks for the offer, and I might need those ships later. For now, without a plan to deploy the ships, they should remain to cover the dropships pulling people off the surface. The other issue is, I suspect the Outsider is hanging around here. It might be trying to locate *Valkyrie*." Right then, I felt a stab of fear that advanced Outsider tech could trace an Elder comm node. That meant I should cut the call short. "To capture or destroy the collect- The object the STARs secured. It is probably also intending to interfere with anything we do to extract Skippy from the star."

"If it is still in contact with the Maxohlx, the remaining ships of their 14th Fleet could be searching for you. Acquiring a replacement Elder comm node is an obvious requirement for you to restore communications. I suggest your ship jump away, the moment the comm node is delivered."

"Uh, yes." My tablet had a window displaying the ETA of the dropship that was carrying the comm node to *Valkyrie*, it would be aboard sooner than I expected. He had a point. Hell, it had been obvious even to my dumdum monkey brain. That would require the Outsider to know that the bad jump had severed our comm node's connection, and that the *Newport News* carried an Elder comm node, but the enemy apparently knew every other damned thing, so why not?

"Whatever fleet they send here will definitely work to stop us from bringing Skippy back. Antoine, I'm going to move *Valkyrie* closer to Omaha, in case we can do anything useful."

"Joe, the most useful thing you can do is-"

"Yeah, I know, I know. We'll be working to develop a plan for recovering Skippy, that won't interfere with the ship's operations."

"When we have pulled all our people off the surface, Hammer Force will be available to support, whatever you're doing. I'll need to detach ships to transport the wounded back to Earth, and we have ships with significant battle damage."

"I understand, Antoine, thanks."

That call hadn't gone as badly as I had feared, he wasn't nearly as angry as I would have been if I were him. Ah, he had his own set of problems to deal with, and we both knew the Joint Chiefs would have plenty to say to me. Allard didn't need to waste time and energy telling me that I am the galaxy's biggest screwup, I practically had IDIOT tattooed on my forehead.

Shit. Olympic was a complete failure, our security situation was actually much worse than before we hit Omaha, and over a thousand people had lost their lives for nothing. Maybe I should work to *fix* the fucking problem, so our people had not died for nothing.

At the doorway to the bridge, I caught Reed's eye and gestured for her to come into the passageway. We walked a few steps around the corner for a measure of privacy. "I'll make this brief," I told her. "I have good news and bad news. The ground force wasn't wiped out as we thought, the nuke burrowed before it exploded. The enemy's intention was to deny us access to the vaults under Makalva, they didn't know we had already taken the Whatsis."

"Oh thank God," she closed her eyes for a moment. "We still lost three assault carriers, and at least six other ships."

"Yes, the total estimate of KIAs is a thousand, that number will go upward, I expect. I'd like you to move *Valkyrie* close enough to Omaha so we can react quickly if needed, so you see any reason we shouldn't do that?"

"Bilby?" She instinctively looked toward the overhead, though the ship's AI was all around us. "Status of the jump drive?"

"Oh wow, like, not good, you know? It's a delicate thing and that jump away from Omaha did not do it any favors. We can perform a short jump, even another short emergency jump if we get into trouble, which we should *not* do, OK?"

"We get that, yes."

"What the drive needs is to be taken offline for a tear down. The reactors are also in need of servicing, there is some sort of glitch in Reactor Three that I can't fix. What the jump drive really needs is Skippy, he could keep it tuned well enough to get us to a major shipyard."

"Let's assume for now," Reed glanced at me to check my reaction, "that we're not getting Skippy back in the immediate future."

"Then we should minimize jumps, and be gentle with the equipment, you feel me?"

"I feel you, Bilby. Sir, we should jump as soon as the comm node is secure in a docking bay, the Outsider might understand we need FTL communication. What?" She added, seeing me smile.

"Allard told me the same thing. You're right. The Outsider has been one step ahead of us, we have to expect it will anticipate our next move."

"Sir, what *is* our next move?"

"I'm working on it."

"Oh shit." She knew what that meant.

"Your confidence in me is heartwarming."

"Sir, you are incredible at what you do. But what you do is dream up ideas for *Skippy* to implement. This, rescue, has to happen without Skippy."

"Unless we can contact him."

"Can we do that? He didn't respond to Bilby after he pushed us away, and Skippy usually can't shut up."

"I'm working on that. Probably we will start by sending a drone near the star, ping him and see if he responds."

"If he doesn't?"

"Then," I hated when people asked me to dream up solutions on the spot. My brain might be clever, but it didn't always work fast. "We will, uh, think of something."

I had said those words before, many times.

The difference was, all those times before I had at least somewhat believed my own line of bullshit. At that time, I didn't, and Reed knew it.

Seeing the disappointment in her eyes was almost the worst part of my awful day.

Frey walked into my office. No, she ran in, and she can run fast. "Sir, we are jumping in near Omaha?"

"Yes. In case we are needed, for something."

"We are needed, *now*. Our troops on the ground are scattered and hard pressed by enemy infantry and air power. The enemy is smart, they are maintaining contact with our forces, so close space support isn't possible, our ships could kill our own people. What is needed is dropships, we have eight that are all fully flightworthy. Their lifting capacity could make a major difference in the evac."

"OK, that makes sense." It would be good for crew morale to be doing something useful. Hell, it would be good for *my* morale.

"They need a STAR team dirtside also. There is one group of eighty UN soldiers, surrounded by over two hundred enemy troops, including a Maxohlx special forces squad; twelve operators. Our people in that group are running out of ammo, and running out of time."

"Your team is-"

"Ready and waiting for you to give the Go Ahead, Sir."

"Frey, I was going to say, your team is traumatized."

"We are highly *motivated*."

"Which can lead to misjudgment."

"Sir, the best thing ST-Razor can do right now is get back into action. We can *do* this."

I took a breath and lowered my voice. "Katie. I want you to look me in the eye, and tell me you are in the proper frame of mind to execute a *professional* operation."

She looked me straight in the eye. "I am frosty, and focused."

"Can you say the same about your people?"

"I take full responsibility for my team, Sir. I would trust any one of them with my life, any day, including today."

I did not like sending ST-Razor back into action, so soon after the loss of two other teams. I also had to trust my senior officers, and Frey had sure as hell *earned* my trust. "Get your people suited up and into dropships."

She grinned. "They are, Sir. Just waiting for me."

"Then, you suit up."

"Lock and load, Sir."

"Hey. Hey!" The voice of Suity shouted in Tech Sergeant Ling's ears. "Wake up, sleepyhead."

"Ohh. I'm, alive?"

"Mostly. Do you need coffee? I know you humans need coffee to-"

"No coffee."

"Good, because I don't have any. How do you feel?"

Ling tentatively wiggled his fingers, then toes. Everything hurt, his whole body was a dull ache. His right ankle and knee were sending stabbing pains when he moved that leg. Dull pain he could deal with, sharp pain could be a problem. "I've been better. I'm alive though. Thank you."

"You're welcome. I impressed myself, I don't think anyone has ever survived falling from suborbit without a parachute. Even Skippy never did that, ha! Um, now do you want to hear the bad news?"

"Hit me," Ling slowly rolled onto his left side, a bad move since his face was exposed to the icy wind, and snow stung his face. Ignoring the distraction, he pushed himself onto hands and knees. Yes, something was badly messed up with his right leg. The suit was partially compensating. Not enough, not as well as it should. "The suit is damaged?"

"That's just the first bit of bad news. I'm doing what I can to adjust, but without a reserve of nanogel for repairs, well, you might be better to ditch the suit. It's kind of dorked up."

"Not in this weather." His suit liner was equipped with heaters, but in enemy territory he needed the protection of armor. Holding up a hand, he saw the arm was a dull gray. "I guess the chameleonware feature is offline?"

"Yes. The best I can do is to turn the suit blaze orange, to facilitate a rescue."

"Do *not* do that. What else?"

"Now that your faceplate is open, I can use sensors inside the helmet. I'm picking up an ELT signal, about half a klick south. It's encoded for ST-Tiger."

"Another survivor?" Ling staggered to his feet.

"Um, that would be a miracle. More likely, the suit is transmitting on its own."

"I need to check anyway." The sky was a featureless blue above him, the local sun burning intensely. Clouds were piled up to the west, where the wind was coming from.

"That could be a problem."

Pointing to twinkling lights in the sky, Ling asked, "What is going on up there?"

"Other than a space battle, I do not know. Huh."

"What?"

"If Hammer Force is still fighting the 14th Fleet, there should be a lot more shooting going on overhead."

Ling got Suity's unspoken message: most of Task Force Hammer might have jumped away, or been destroyed. Either way, it was bad news for him.

"I am also picking up the sound of aircraft approaching," the computer warned. "*Enemy* aircraft. They are distant, can't tell how far, but from the Doppler I can assure you, they are coming to investigate that ELT."

Turning carefully to reduce stress on the injured leg, he patted the sidearm holstered on his left hip. The pistol's explosive-tipped round could damage an aircraft, but the enemy's weapons vastly outrange the sidearm. "Can I make it to the trees before they get here?"

"I don't know, but I suggest you start now. I do have one suggestion?"

"What?"

"I should trigger your ELT."

"Why?" Ling gritted his teeth against the pain as he waded through the snow. "That will lead the enemy straight to me."

"The signal could confirm that you are alive, and worthy of a rescue attempt. I can shut it off after a few seconds."

"Not-" he tripped over a rock hidden under the snow. "Not yet. I'll tell you when to trigger it. This," he sluggishly got to his feet again, the suit's artificial muscles cooperating only marginally. "Will take longer than I thought."

Valkyrie jumped into a high orbit of Ohmeharikahn, in a location recommended by the cruiser *Milano*, the ship that had been tasked with managing traffic control for the recovery operation. The orbital environment was crowded with chunks of high-speed debris large and small, with dropships maneuvering violently to avoid smacking into space junk, and with those Hammer Force ships that were fully combat effective moving to assist ships that hadn't escaped major battle damage. The last thing the overworked crew and AI of *Milano* needed was our battlecruiser becoming another headache they had to account for. So, we had popped out of jump not directly above the main action, but a thousand kilometers from what was left of the Makalva base.

The situation on the ground was absolute chaos, even after much of the enemy jamming had been effectively knocked back. Ships of the 14th Fleet were constantly jumping in to launch ordnance, then jumping away. That was frustrating to Hammer Force, and deadly to our people on the ground. Allard had his big battlewagons clustered together, shields extended and overlapping, to provide coverage over Makalva. Most of the enemy maser and railgun fire was deflected by the battleship shields, which left the escort ships the frustrating job of intercepting stealthed missiles that curved around the protective umbrella.

Skippy might have been able to detect a pattern in the enemy attacks, but we didn't have the beer can with us, so we had to rely on the AIs of our ships. "Bilby," I waited until Reed was satisfied her ship wouldn't immediately get splattered by hitting the remains of an enemy ship. "You have been observing the enemy attacks?"

"Yeah. It *sucks*, man," he had lost a bit of his usual chill.

"Can you predict where and when the next group of ships will jump in?"

"No, your Dudeness, sorry. That kind of deep analysis is too round for my square head, you know? Even Skippy would need a lot more data."

"All right, thank you."

"Razor team is away," Reed reported. "That's the last of our dropships. We will remain here, Sir?"

"We are too exposed in low orbit, and all the debris floating around negates our stealth field, the enemy only has to watch shrapnel bouncing off our shields. Take us to a higher orbit, we can jump back in if needed."

She got her ship moving.

"Um, hey, General Dude?" Bilby's avatar waved at me. "I have some hot info, if you want to hear it."

"Go ahead."

"It's like, kind of personal to you."

I felt my shoulders tense, assuming I knew what he meant. "Here, please. I'm not leaving the bridge."

"Okey dokey. Um, first, the *Dutchman* is gone, but most of the crew got away in escape pods. General Perkins, Colonels Bonsu and Streibich were taken aboard by the destroyer *Muskogee*, they are all in good condition."

"Thank God for that," a bit of the tension left my shoulders with a shudder I tried to hide from the crew.

"I have good news about your friends. Jesse Colter and Dave Czajka, also Shauna and that Verd guy Jates?"

"What about them?"

"They commandeered an enemy transport aircraft, and are flying toward one of the designated recovery landing zones."

"How the- How did they acquire a freakin' aircraft?"

"They are like, the Mavericks, you know?" The ship's AI chuckled.

"Yes. Of course they did. Thank you, Bilby, this is great news."

"You want to like, send them a message? Voice comms are still being jammed, but-"

"I'll wait until they are safely aboard a ship." Really, right then I just wanted to avoid a confrontation with the friends I had betrayed. "What's their ETA at the landing zone?"

“That’s hard to predict. They are picking up stragglers along the way. There are two UN Navy gunships flying escort.”

“That’s good to hear.”

Reed gave me a thumbs up, knowing how very much I needed to hear good news.

“I am tracking their aircraft.”

“Let me know if they require assistance.” Pulling rank to help my friends, reassigning priority for already scarce resources, is something I should not do. If needed, there is a hundred percent chance I would do it anyway. Def Com could add another official reprimand to my file.

CHAPTER FIVE

"Everyone, listen up," Frey watched her team stop obsessively checking their weapons and turn toward her, though they were hearing her through their helmet speakers. She was tugged to the left as the Panther decelerated below supersonic, and bounced up and down as the stealthy spacecraft hugged low to the terrain. "We lost a lot of people today. Not just our fellow operators, many soldiers and Marines died when our cowardly enemy hit the ground force with a *nuke*. You are all keyed up and pissed off, and want to hit back hard, I know I do. Remember this: revenge is a dish best served *cold*. So, stay frosty."

A series of microphone clicks acknowledged her.

Lights around the cabin glowed yellow, and she checked her own rifle one last time. A full magazine of rifle rounds, four rockets in the underbarrel launcher, spare ammo for both on her waist belt. On her back, an extra powerpack that, while heavy, would provide additional power to the suit's stealth field, and would be discarded before the bang bang stuff started anyway. "Ready. Holmqvist," she named her second in command. "Take your fireteam out first."

Another two clicks.

The Panther slowed hard, practically standing on its nose as retrorockets fired. A moment later after a stomach-churning fall, the nose came up in a flare for landing, and the rear ramp swung down even before the skids touched down. Holmqvist was out first, Frey waited to be last out of the cabin. It seemed to her that her feet leapt off the ramp before the shocks in the skid legs had bounced back from the impact of the hard landing. The pilots wasted no time, firing the belly jets to dust off, and she was momentarily surrounded by a choking cloud of dust that her visor's synthetic vision saw right through.

"Scatter," she ordered, "meet up at Point Stark."

When she was in boot camp, before Columbus Day changed everything, she had been taught the principle of concentrating force against the enemy. With the enemy able to use accurate direct and indirect fires from space power, air power, and artillery, it was vital to *not* concentrate your force, until you were in close contact with the enemy. Close enough that the opposition could not launch weapons, for fear of hitting their own people on the ground. That is why she had split ST-Razor into four teams of four operators, each taking a different route to the rally point. Four humans on the ground, even elite STARs, were not worth risking space or aircraft, and operators in stealth were a tough target for artillery. If all sixteen members of Star Team Razor were together, the enemy would consider them to be not only a tempting target, but a mandatory strike opportunity.

Allowing her suit to run mostly by itself, with guidance from the three operators around her, she focused on overall situational awareness. Halfway to Point Stark, it was already clear the pre-mission intel was not entirely accurate, she was not surprised. If the intel had been a hundred percent correct, *that* would have been a surprise. ST-Razor would be going up against not a squad of twelve Maxohlx special forces, but an understrength platoon of twenty five.

That changed nothing. The mission was the same, the job would be more difficult. She told herself that if the job was easy, Def Com would not have spent shocking amounts of money on equipping and training special operators.

Fifty meters from the coordinates designated Point Stark, she eyeclicked on the Razor channel. "Avengers, assemble," she said the code words chosen so that, if the Maxohlx were able to crack the encrypted communications, the kitties would have no clue what the words meant.

Holmqvist and three others popped up from a shallow ditch, having arrived first. Moments later, the two other fireteams came from east and west.

"Everyone has seen we have twice the opposition as we thought?" Head nods and clicks were the response. "There were thirty two kitty special forces, our people have trimmed their numbers." She did not add that had come at great cost to the landing force, hard pressed and engaged in close-quarters combat. "The enemy does not know we are here, so we continue the Silent-Noisy advance, I will tell you when to go noisy. We hit them from behind, then we advance through their position. Any questions?"

There were none.

"Eject spare powercells, and move out."

The Noisy part began when ST-Razor launched sixteen rockets at the enemy's backs, followed by another sixteen. Of the first volley, seven were intercepted by automated defenses, eight struck their targets, and the other missed as the enemy mech suits deployed countermeasures and dodged their users out of the way. The second volley mostly was intended to keep the enemy's heads down while Razor raced ahead, but six rockets networked together took out three more Maxohlx operators who had been overconfident and moved from cover too soon.

Suddenly, the enemy no longer had superior numbers, and the STARs took advantage of the shock and confusion.

Many of the operators with her were too young, but Katie remembered a time when the idea of tangling with senior species special forces would have been terrifying. Not only that, any such proposed operation would have been declared a non-starter. Times had changed. There were now *three* Tier One species, and the arrogant Maxohlx were about to discover they no longer had technological superiority.

Her fireteam took up the rear as a reserve, providing covering fire and allowing her to coordinate the attack. The beleaguered Hammer Force troops ahead saw an opportunity to hit back, and sent a fusillade of covering fire out, understanding that saving their remaining ammunition was foolhardy. Frey watched the enemy numbers dwindle, she also saw two of her team get hit and go down, neither of the injuries were tagged as fatal but she had two fewer combat effectives. It was time to send in the reserves, to exploit the enemy disarray. "With me!" She cried as she charged ahead. A helmet popped up from the ground in front of her, she and two other operators instantly saw it was outlined in red in their visors, and fired together. The enemy operator went down hard. Leaping over the dead soldier, Frey-

Was stunned, launched helplessly through the air head over heels to crash down on her left shoulder, bashing her helmet and rolling once, twice, three times. Coming to a rest for a split second, she kicked out to get her legs unbent and came to her knees, lifting the rifle-

That had been snapped in half, just forward of the trigger guard. Wasting no time, she drew her sidearm with a glance at the visor's status display. Sixteen STARs still alive, ten combat effective. Petty Officer Vignale's suit had lost power and locked up, he had a broken forearm.

He would live.

What the f-

She realized the enemy had called in artillery *on their own position*. Or, some artillery controller had decided, fuck it, the special forces weren't getting the job done. If the Maxohlx had not misjudged the speed of the STAR's advance, her team would have been slaughtered. As it was, the ten remaining human operators were scattered, her own battle buddy Staff Sergeant Kovalenko struggling to his feet to her left.

That's when her visor highlighted in red the form of a Maxohlx soldier, pushing himself up from a prone position. "Bar fight!" She signaled to her team. Melees happened often in bars in the movies, rarely in real life where there were real consequences for assault and battery, but 'Bar fight' was the STAR signal when the team was scattered and there was nothing for it but to launch a desperate, disorganized attack before the enemy got their shit together. Firing her sidearm on full auto and knowing it would only distract the enemy soldier, she tossed the pistol aside when the hammer clicked on an empty chamber. The alien soldier, knocked back from the barrage of small caliber explosive rounds, was on one, knee, an arm up to protect its face. The arm came down just as Frey pulled a knife from a sheath. Not just any knife, that blade was exotic matter, ten times harder than diamond and sharpened so its edges and tip were only six molecules wide. The knife sliced into the enemy suit's neck and the blade snapped off at the hilt as the Maxohlx jerked up and back, sending Frey back to slam into the ground on her backside skidding until her gloved fingers dug into the soil. The enemy flopped around, bringing its rifle up, the muzzle coming around toward her-

A burst of three armor piercing rounds struck the alien's neck, blowing the helmet off, along with the head.

"You OK, Colonel?" Kovalenko called.

"Never better. Lost my rifle, toss me your sidearm? And a knife. Do *not* toss that," she added quickly, as the blade might slice her armored glove.

Kovalenko ran to her, holding out his pistol, its holster and attached two extra magazines. She reached up and took his knife, sliding it into her own sheath before getting to one knee. She was the team leader, she should be managing the battle, not fighting hand-to-hand with enemy operators. She would-

The enemy had not gotten the memo that she briefly intended to become a non-combatant. "*Down*!" Kovalenko shouted, shoving her shoulder and knocking her to the ground, falling beside her and lying on her back. Hugging his rifle to his chest, he aimed the muzzle where he couldn't see over his shoulder. Couldn't see with his *eyes*, the visor's synthetic view illuminated the fast-approaching enemy soldier who was on its feet, exposed.

The rifle barked in staccato, spitting out rounds in bursts of three, the projectiles seeking their target. Frey saw the symbol for the enemy go down, and an alien rifle arcing through the air far away. Whether Kovalenko had killed the enemy, that operator was out of the fight.

"Two more to our south," Kovalenko rolled onto his stomach, ejecting an almost expended magazine and smoothly slapping in a fresh one. "Colonel, they are trying to flank us."

"I see it. Go left, hold them off. I'm going for that pile of rocks to the right." She knew that, without a rifle, she was a burden to be protected, not a combat asset. "On three," she paused a beat, expecting Kovalenko to argue that he should stay with her. His discipline held fast. "Three, two, one, *now*."

They sprinted in opposite directions, Kovalenko launching a rocket while he ran. Frey zigzagged toward the pile of large boulders that offered decent cover, if she could get there.

The thing that makes the enemy unredeemable assholes is they are determined to screw up every plan. Right in front of her rose an enemy soldier, the visor warning her too late and her heart skipped a beat. The enemy's rifle was-

Not there.

It was that kitty jackass Kovalenko had knocked down. Her momentum carried her forward, instinctively she dodged to the left-

The enemy had gotten lucky about guessing which way she would go and they collided hard, knocking the breath from her lungs. Locked together by powered arms around her waist, she couldn't get away.

And she didn't want to. Reaching down and grasping the enemy's forearms, she pulled outward. The Maxohlx soldier, a male she could see when their faceplates were so close, was taller, heavier, genetically enhanced, faster and more powerful in every way. He had every advantage in hand-to-hand combat.

Every advantage, except for not possessing a UN Army Mark 37 mech suit. A suit designed by Skippy the Magnificent. The alien's arrogant anger became an expression of surprise when her suit's arms slowly. Forced. Its own arms. Away. From her waist. Strain warning lights flashed orange in her visor, she ignored the suit's complaint because she had her own problems to deal with. They struggled, soldier against soldier, suit against suit until they stood face to face, her looking up into the alien faceplate, both sets of arms out wide.

What the hell should I do now, a little voice in the back of her mind asked, and not quietly.

The answer came as the enemy's armored chest plate *flowed*, bulging outward. Nanobots forming a weapon aimed at her own chest. The enemy's arrogance and contempt returned, eyes narrowing. With determination, triumph and, mirth? He was *laughing* at her? The makeshift weapon solidified and an opening appeared, a muzzle-

Her own chest plate glowed, lightning stabbing outward to strike the nanoweapon, collapsing it into soot and dust. Also draining twenty percent of her suit's power, as if that mattered.

This was bullshit, she decided. Her right hand clenched into a fist, squeezing *hard*. In response to the unspoken but well-rehearsed command, her own suit's reserve of nanogel flowed out of the right forearm reservoir and instantly built a thick armored shell around the outside of her fist. A set of brass knuckles, if brass could be considered an exotic form of matter. Jerking her right arm free, she smashed her augmented fist into the enemy's faceplate, cracking it, knocking a chunk of the hardened material inward to slash the creature's furry face. Releasing her fist, she jabbed her hand into the jagged hole in the faceplate, extending her index finger as far as she could.

The nanogel flashed from brass knuckles into a fourteen centimeter blade, punching into and through one of the enemy's eyes and she *twisted* that hand, ripping apart brain material.

The enemy operator slumped, held up only by the grip of her left hand. She released it, falling to her knees, struggling back up. Raising an armored boot, she stomped down on the helmet once, twice, three times and the helmet cracked open, sending a jet of blood and gore upward. One down.

The rocks, she realized, were packed together so tightly, they provided scant cover. If the enemy knew where she was-

It wouldn't matter.

Her visor showed the battle was effectively over. The enemy was retreating in every direction, demoralized by the slaughter of their elite special forces. Dead, the Maxohlx operators were all dead. ST-Razor had suffered five casualties, none of the injuries were life-threatening.

A green icon appeared in the visor, approaching, below the icon the text read SSG Kovalenko. The man ran up to her, crouching low. "Colonel? Ma'am, you OK?"

"My dance partner," she pointed to the dead body in the alien mech suit, "stepped on my toes one too many times."

"Looks like he lost his head," the Staff Sergeant snorted. "Here," he unslung a rifle and held it out to her. "Corporal Gonzalez is combat ineffective, his suit took a hit to the powercells. He thought you would need his rifle more than he does. It's OK," he assured her. "Sergeant Chin is with him."

She stood up awkwardly from where she had wedged herself into the dubious cover of the rocks, taking the rifle. "I hope I don't have to shoot at anyone again today."

"I got three kills," he pointed his rifle's camera lens. "That's enough for me."

"We're not done here but," she looked up at the sky. "I think it's best if I act as forward controller for our air support," she flexed her arms, which moved distinctly more slowly than they should have. "Instead of getting into any more of the bang bang stuff."

When ST-Razor's pair of dropships dusted off the ground, it felt like I had been holding my breath for two hours. The assault force was all aboard UN Navy ships, or in dropships climbing into orbit. Enemy harassment had slacked off once they no longer had easy targets on the ground, the enemy commander probably assumed that Hammer Force would be jumping away soon. Besides, I hate to say it, but evacing the ground force was a side show to the main task for retrieving Skippy. A task I had not a single clue about how to accomplish.

"Razor is clear of atmo," an officer behind me announced. "ETA twenty seven minutes."

"Ooh. Hey um," Bilby made a choking sound. Either he was trying to emulate clearing his throat, or he'd just taken a hit off a bong. His avatar was animated with awkward, jerky motions, and his virtual eyes were unfocused. That could just be a matter of him not having much bandwidth to devote to the hologram. "I don't know if this is an issue for Colonel Frey, or General Bishop."

"Just say whatever it is," Reed answered for me.

"Sensors from a UN destroyer have picked up an Emergency Location Transmitter signal. It's from the suit of Lieutenant Grigorescu, from ST-Tiger."

"There is a survivor?" Reed asked.

"That is like, unknown, and, I hate to say it, extremely unlikely, you know?" Bilby responded sadly. "The STAR Force wasn't equipped with parachute balloons for this op. Based on the location of the ELT, and where that team's Panther got hit, Grigorescu fell in pretty much a ballistic arc. Thermal imaging shows there is hot debris scattered all over that area."

"But," I spoke before thinking. "The ELT has to be manually triggered, right? Someone is alive down there. Ah," I recalled what I had been taught about mech suit ELTs. "Not, necessarily. It might have been triggered by the suit, if the occupant was alive during the descent. But if Grigorescu then hit the ground hard," I didn't need to finish the thought.

Reed focused on the practical issue. "What about Hammer Force? Can they send a SAR team?"

"Negatory," Bilby groaned. "Every spacecraft they have is fully engaged, or being serviced.

"Colonel Frey?" I called the STAR leader. "We picked up a STAR ELT from Grigorescu, but Bilby isn't detecting any life signs.

"I- Ah." I could hear the anguish in her voice. "Sir, I can't justify risking a Panther, and the crew, unless we have some decent confidence that the Lieutenant is alive. That is a long shot. Bilby, is there enemy activity in the area?"

"Four military aircraft are approaching, they will, like, be over the site in eight minutes."

"Too risky," she shook her head. "We have lost enough people alr-"

"*Whoa*," Bilby breathed. "There is now a second ELT, in the same area, also ST-Tiger. The encoding shows Technical Sergeant Ling is alive."

Reed looked to me. The STAR Force was under my command. "Wait," I held up a hand. "Bilby, is the ship able to safely jump into low orbit over there, then jump away?"

"Affirmative, if you don't intend to take us into combat."

"I intend for us to not be there long enough to get into trouble. We do *not* leave anyone behind. Frey, get moving."

"Sir, we will need-"

Reed anticipated the request, already tapping on her console. "I am requesting gunships to escort the SAR birds, can't make any promises."

"Thank you. On the way."

"Sergeant Ling?" The suit would not be quiet while he awkwardly stumbled through heavy snow and over unseen rocks. "I have more good news and bad news."

"Go."

"*Valkyrie* had dropships already in the air, two of them have been diverted to retrieve you."

Ling couldn't believe it. "General Bishop risked the ship for me? That-"

"*Valkyrie* was here to evac the assault force."

"Good." He wouldn't have to deal with guilt if the battlecruiser were lost in the effort to pull his sorry ass off the surface. "What's the bad news?"

"The enemy will be overhead before the cavalry gets here, and I am now detecting *four* enemy aircraft approaching. Could be more, the sensors inside your helmet are not optimal for an external search."

Ling stopped running, or he stopped struggling to run. "What if I buried myself under the snow?"

"Unless the enemy's infrared gear is absolute crap, they will find you. I had to eject your heatsinks on the way down, now the radiators of your backpack are hot. Hot enough to melt a layer of snow."

"What if I take off the pack?"

"Um, then you will have only twelve minutes of power."

Ling started to shrug off the heavy pack. "This will be over in twelve minutes."

"That is a good point. The enemy will still find you."

"Maybe not as fast." Without the heavy pack, he found it a bit easier to run. He wouldn't reach the tree line anyway. He should have requested the computer to land him closer to the trees. If that was possible. Hindsight was-

"Get down!" The suit shouted, and it must have acted to protect him, both suit legs folded at the knees and he flopped to skid on the snow.

"What-" In the sky, thin contrails raced away from five wider contrails. The multiple, he guessed dozens of missiles, were burning in his direction with frightening speed. Aimed at him? No, the tracks were curving, the formation splitting up. Missiles seeking their assigned targets. The enemy aircraft?

Six contrails reached for the sky from the west. The enemy were shooting back. He lay on his back, watching the show. There wasn't anything else he could do. Bright flashes signaled the interception of the enemy weapons, accomplishing that took a lot of friendly missiles out of the fight. He counted only eight missiles remaining, diving and continuing to curve and change course as they chased the enemy aircraft. The missile tracks were curving *away* from him, the enemy was running! Cold wind stung his eyes and he watched, transfixed, as the missile tracks disappeared behind a line of hills toward the horizon. Bright flashes came from that direction, he didn't know whether the missiles had been taken out by enemy point defenses.

The five broader contrails were coming in, spreading out. One had broken away and was surging ahead, accelerating toward where he had seen the bright flashes.

"Um-" He realized that spacecraft would fly almost over his head, moving extremely fast.

"I suggest you close your faceplate," the computer warned.

"On it," the faceplate swung down and sealed to protect not his eyes but his ears, from the hypersonic boom. The faceplate had gone mostly clear, a few of the embedded hexagons were cloudy and one was completely dark, he could still see. The dark dot passed overhead, the spacecraft not bothering with useless stealth when it was leaving a bright streak across the sky pointing directly to it.

"Three, two," the computer counted down. "One."

The snow around Ling erupted and blocked his vision completely, the ground shook and he could feel the vibration in his chest.

"Well," the computer huffed when the rumbling faded. "That seemed like overkill."

"If they keep that enemy bird away from me, they can hotdog over my head all day. Is it safe to sit up?"

"Um, with the faceplate closed, I have no external sensors," the suit said in a snarky imitation of its creator.

He sat up first, feeling just the pressure of the constant wind, not the hurricane strength of a supersonic shockwave. The faceplate swung up, he saw a Panther coming in, circling him. He waved. A minute later, he stood leaning into the downdraft of the dropship's belly jets that blasted him with snow. The rear ramp was down even before the spacecraft's skids bit into ice and frozen soil under the snow. Running as best he could, he waved to the two figures standing on the ramp. Their suits had been tuned to high-visibility orange, he was surprised to see the person on the right was Colonel Frey herself. "Ma'am?" He started to salute and she waved, urging him onward. "You didn't lose anyone in this recovery?"

"Not *yet*."

He got the message, and the two operators grabbed him under the arms and practically carried him into the cabin to slump in a seat. The safety straps automatically formed around him as the dropship leapt into the sky and stood on its tail. "Ma'am? Colonel? There was another ELT signal from-"

"That's from Grigorescu. He's dead," she said in a voice not as devoid of emotion as she might have hoped.

"Did anyone else-"

"You are the only survivor from Sword or Tiger." She stared at him. "How *did* you survive that fall?"

"You know that Skippy programmed an emergency protocol into the suit computers?"

She frowned. "Yes, and the armory purged all of that wonky code."

"Apparently not."

Her mouth formed a silent 'O'. "My suit just informed me that something punctured your heart?"

"I'm OK, Ma'am."

"What happened?"

"It is a *long* story."

She snorted. "You are officially a Pirate now."

"You're here so, Razor delivered the Biscuit?"

"We did."

He relaxed as acceleration pressed him into the seat. "When we get back to *Valkyrie*, I want to thank Skippy." He saw Frey and the crew chief exchange a glance. "Ma'am? What?"

"Get some rest, Ling," the Colonel ordered. "We're all going to need it."

Frey sent Ling to sickbay, with an escort to make certain the Tech Sergeant didn't make a detour along the way. Ling's damaged Mark 42 mech suit did not get the usual post-action servicing, she ordered the suit not to be touched. The emergency protocol named 'Suity' had proven to be useful, had saved Ling's life. If- No, she told herself, *when* Skippy was back aboard the battlecruiser, she would ask him about the protocol that was supposed to have been purged by the armory. She was tempted to kick his ass for disobeying her explicit instructions. But, it was hard to argue with success. There was no doubt that Skippy had adapted and overcome to complete the mission, whether that mission had been desired or not. Maybe she should be pleased the Elder AI had cared so much he snuck unerasable code into the suit computer. Maybe. After she gave him a stern lecture about the value, the vital importance, of being a team player.

When the beer can was back aboard the ship.

When, not *if*.

Except-

If was a lot more likely than when.

Dressed after a shower, she was checking her gear was all properly stowed away in her locker. Everything was in its place, including her rifle that was back in the Starbase armory. Her Mark 37 suit was on a rack next to her Mark 42 unit, that had not required battle damage to be repaired. Closing her locker, she stood up. Hearing the latch of the locker faintly *click* had sounded ominously final. Squaring her shoulders, she looked around. The compartment was almost empty, the majority of Team Razor having headed out the ready room, in case the STARs were needed again. Her second in command Major Holmqvist was sitting in front of his open locker, staring into it as if it were the abyss.

"You OK, Karel?" She whispered.

He was startled but hid it well. "Ma'am? Ja, yes, sure," he replied in the Swedish accent she found appealing. "It's just-" he looked up at her, then at the other operators in the locker compartment. "Nothing."

She jerked her head toward the doorway. "When you're done here, meet me in my office to get started on the post-mission brief. We still have paperwork to do."

As soon as she turned around, she heard his locker close, and Holmqvist was right behind her. "Close the door," she said, her desk not having a convenient button for that purpose. "What's bothering you?"

"I'm grateful we had the opportunity to recover Tech Sergeant Ling."

"You're grateful, *but*? I sense you have more thoughts on the subject." Major Holmqvist had not been second in command of Star Team Razor for long, he had transferred from leading a training unit on Earth when her previous XO had been promoted to leader of ST-Lion. Holmqvist had actually served on Team Razor before his promotion to major, so she knew him well. In fact, he had been on her shortlist of candidates for XO. Her faith in him had been rewarded, he was an outstanding operator, and should be leading his own team someday.

If he lived that long.

If STAR teams, and Earth, still existed at that point.

"Permission to speak freely?"

She frowned. "You shouldn't have to ask that question. You know my policy; I don't appreciate bullshit."

"Yes Ma'am, but, you have served with General Bishop for a long time."

"Speak your mind, Karel." Leaning forward across the desk she added, "I served with Bishop for years. During that time, I questioned many times whether he was the right person for the job. Especially in the beginning."

"It's not that I am-"

"I was wrong then. Every time. This is no different."

"Excuse me, Ma'am, but yes it is. Bishop has stated his usefulness is limited to showing Skippy new things the AI can do. Without Skippy?" He shrugged. "Bishop can't engineer a solution to pull a canister out of a star, not by himself."

"You don't know that."

"Ma'am, I do know that instead of ensuring the security of Earth, this operation has *destroyed* our security. Bishop's decisions led to the one thing he couldn't allow to happen: he let the Outsider take Skippy out of the fight. This is a disaster even the Merry Band of Pirates can't recover from. This is Game Over. We can only- What?"

He had stopped when she smiled. "This conversation is a bit of nostalgia for me. It takes me back to when I said something similar to Smythe, when I joined him in stealing the *Flying Dutchman.* At the time, the mission was absolutely impossible. The Maxohlx had sent a task force to investigate why the wormhole to Earth had shut down. We had to stop those senior species ships from getting to Earth, *and* to make the kitties think their ships found nothing unusual or interesting at Earth, *and* to provide a reason why those ships disappeared without the Maxohlx getting suspicious. Do all that, with nothing but a beat-up old space truck that wasn't a proper warship. The mission wasn't just impossible, we were foolish to even try. That's what I told Smythe." She paused for a breath. "He agreed with me."

"He did?" Holmqvist had not expected her story to go in that direction.

"He did. He also told me our proper duty was to maintain readiness to, do whatever Bishop required us to do. We accomplished that mission, Bishop found a way to get it done." She shook her head. "It still amazes me."

"I see your point, Ma'am. Do you see my point? Bishop succeeds when he works with Skippy. Not by himself."

She shrugged. "We have lost Skippy before. Twice. Before I joined the Pirates, he lost his magnificence, and still he brought the Pirates into, and safely back from, a hidden star system that was protected by Elder tech. Later, he bailed on Bishop. Both times, we got Skippy the Magnificent back."

"I hear you," he shifted uncomfortably in his chair. "I don't see how the General can pull another miracle out of his pocket, not this time."

"That's the point. You don't know how he can do it. You also don't know he can't. What I do know for certain is this problem doesn't have a conventional solution, and General Bishop is the best at unconventional thinking. Major, until *Bishop* gives up, our mission has not changed. We stand by to support Task Force Black."

"It might not be Bishop's decision. The Maxohlx are certain to send reinforcements here, a lot more than a single fleet. Even assuming he dreams up some crazy plan, we won't have time to implement. Colonel," he held up his hands. "I look forward to you telling me 'I told you so', when Skippy is back aboard."

She grinned. "I won't say 'I told you so'."

"You won't?"

"I will remind you to 'Trust the Awesomeness'. That has *always* worked for me."

"I am praying you're right about that. Is it OK for me to pray to someone other than Skippy?"

"Holmqvist, if you ever do pray to Skippy, that's when I'll worry about you."

CHAPTER SIX

Joel Verhoef hesitated at the top of the dropship's back ramp, holding onto a strut.

"You OK, Major?" Dave asked.

"Yeah," Verhoef shook his head. "I'm just not used to being a passenger."

Behind him, Sheryl Crook snorted. "You fly a single-seat space fighter, you're not used to being with other people."

Joel flashed a grin. "That, too." He walked down the ramp into the unfamiliar cargo bay of the UN Navy heavy cruiser *Louisville*. An American ship. Not officially, the Navy had made a major effort to get away from assigning crews by nationality, except for the battleships that were seen by the public as symbols of national pride. But, the crew members he saw all wore an American flag patch on the opposite shoulder from the UN flag. "I wonder," he waited for Sheryl to step beside him, "if anyone here has a bottle of Jeremiah."

"Jeremiah?" Jesse asked.

"Jeremiah *Weed*," Sheryl explained. "It's whisky, like a sweeter version of Southern Comfort, mixed with gasoline."

"Don't listen to the heathen. It's an Air Force thing," Joel said, frowning as he waited in line to exit through the airlock doorway. "US Air Force," he added.

"It's a *fighter pilot* thing," Sheryl patted Joel's shoulder. "We might have to wait until we get back to Earth."

Dave stopped shuffling forward. "It's important?"

Joel nodded, his expression grim. "It's a tradition, for toasting fallen comrades. We had too many of them today."

Aboard the *Louisville*, Dave couldn't pull rank, he was a civilian. All he wanted was news about how his wife was, and yes, to call her. The ship's comm systems were fully tasked, the best he got was a 'Maybe tomorrow'. Then he ran into, literally collided with in a passageway, a crewman who apologized, then spun back around.

"Are you Dave Czajka? *That* Dave Czajka?"

"Yes," Dave answered warily, knowing he had made some enemies during his career.

"I want to shake your hand," the man thrust out a hand, and Dave shook it. "My brother was in the Alien Legion with you, he was on Feznako. His name is Carl Fischer?"

"Fischer, um- Yeah, he had a little white scar under one eye?"

The crewman grinned. "I caused that, threw a baseball to him when he wasn't looking."

"Fresno," Dave snorted. "That was a shitshow. How is your brother?"

"Good. He retired, on Earth, has three kids now. Hey, he said you and General Perkins, um, she's your wife now?"

"She is."

"That the two of you always did right by your people."

"We served with damned good soldiers, your brother included."

The crewman looked down the passageway. “Hey, I have thirty minutes before my next duty shift, is there anything I can do for you?”

That was how Dave got limited access to the fleet’s shared database, and found that his wife was safe aboard the destroyer *Muskogee*, where he was able to call her, briefly. She was fine, worried about him, working on getting him transferred to the *Muskogee*. “No, Em, I should stay here. A lot of my people are here, I need to make sure they’re taken care of.”

“If the Navy pukes give you any shit about your team being contractors, let me handle it.”

“It will be fine. Hopefully, our ships will attach to the same star carrier.”

“I wouldn’t count on it, the-”

The connection cut off, the system terminating a low-priority call.

Well, he shrugged as he tucked his phone back in a pocket, that was better than nothing.

“Major Verhoef?” Dave waved from the doorway of the cargo bay that the Air Force pilot had been assigned as temporary quarters. Inflatable bunks were available, but most were stacked against the bulkhead, with people sitting on the deck.

“Dave?” Joel got to his feet. “Were you able to call your wife?”

“Briefly. She’s aboard the *Muskogee*, she’s fine. Hey,” he reached into a bag and pulled out a bottle of Jeremiah Weed. “I found this for you.”

Joel’s eyes bulged with delight, taking the bottle and waving it at Sheryl. To Dave he asked, “How did you find this aboard a cruiser? This ship doesn’t have a fighter wing.”

“A crew chief from the *Dutchman* grabbed it before he got into an escape pod, and the pod was taken aboard this ship.”

“Good man! I want to thank him.”

“He’s in sickbay with a broken wrist, he’ll be fine. He wanted you to have this.”

“This is,” Joel took a deep breath. “This will be good for morale. Join us?”

“I was planning to go with,” he jerked a thumb back over a shoulder, to where Jesse and Shauna waited.

“They are invited,” Joel waved to the two soldiers.

Two hours later, Jesse held onto one side of the passageway, as he walked unsteadily toward the compartment he and Shauna had been assigned. “Oh man, I learned two things today.”

“Never try to outdrink an Air Force pilot?” Shauna guessed.

“Three things, then. The first thing is I learned what Jeremiah Weed is. I must have seen it somewhere in Arkansas, never noticed. The second thing, the important thing, is that stuff is *nasty*.”

“I kind of liked it,” Shauna admitted. “If it’s nasty, why did you drink four shots?”

“Peer pressure. We’re Army,” he straightened up, squaring his shoulders. “We got to represent.”

"Not like that. Honey," she glanced both ways along the passageway, which was empty despite the ship being crowded. Not many people had a reason to walk so far aft that the deck thrummed from the reactor pumps. "What's wrong?"

"Everything about today has been *wrong*," he thumped a fist on the bulkhead. "The worst part is, we got screwed over by *Joe*. I don't," he sucked in a breath. "Don't know if I can ever trust him again."

"You know him better than I do, you served with him. Can you imagine him screwing over his friends, if he had another choice?"

"He could have warned me."

She shook her head. "He couldn't. Not even for you, or Dave. The 14th Fleet was *not* supposed to be here, the crew told me it surprised the shit out of them when those ships appeared. Somehow, our comms got hacked, the Maxohlx knew we were coming here. There was some sort of cover story to lure the 14th away, apparently it didn't work. Joe is a two star now, he has to make very tough calls. Honey, it must have been killing him not to tell you."

"I suppose. I need some time. The people we lost- Ah, what I need right now is some rack time. Our turn in the galley isn't until twenty two hundred, and I'm hungry *now*."

Seven hours after *Valkyrie* jumped from the frying pan into the fire, seven hours after we lost Skippy, Hammer Force completed recovery of all personnel from dirtside. And from escape pods drifting in orbit. It was a bitter ending to a disastrous operation. Four dropships were lost to enemy fire on the climb into orbit. We also lost the frigate *Almeria* with all hands to an enemy hit and run raid, that little ship took a very unfortunate direct hit to its main missile magazine. At the time the last ship of Task Force Hammer jumped away, the death toll had climbed to fourteen hundred and seventy eight. In addition, the Rindhalu had suffered two hundred and fifteen killed in action. All that blood, on my hands.

I requested Reed to bring *Valkyrie* within a lighthour of where Allard had taken his flagship. "Bishop," the Admiral had the look of someone who was at the limit of his endurance. "Do you need our support for, whatever you're going to do?"

"I would appreciate you loaning us a cruiser squadron, and six to eight sensor frigates."

"You have a plan, then?" He asked hopefully, leaning toward the camera, his face momentarily less gray and drained of life.

"I'll be honest with you, I don't. Not *yet*," I added, in what was not quite a lie. "We need to be prepared."

The life had drained from his face again, replaced by overwhelming weariness. "You will get those ships, on temporary detachment," he added. "However," he raised an eyebrow. "I will issue orders that the moment major Maxohlx reinforcements arrive, my ships will jump away."

"Agreed. We understand that whatever we're going to do, it has to happen fast."

He looked down, and for a second his head nodded and I thought he had fallen asleep. If he did, I wouldn't fault him for it. He looked up again. "Hammer Force will be proceeding directly back to Earth, at best speed. We will have stragglers due to battle damage, I am detaching them with a stores ship to effect repairs. The only good news," he covered his eyes with a hand and mumbled something I couldn't hear, followed by, "Is we have plenty of hardpoints available on the star carriers now."

"That's not actually good news."

"I'll take what I can get. Bishop, good luck to you. Good luck to all of us. We're going to need luck, if you can't pull Skippy out of that star, and do it soon."

There wasn't any point to dragging out the conversation, so we ended the call. I hoped the guy got some sleep once his ships began jumping toward Earth.

My conversation with the Rindhalu was even more pleasant. The invitation to speak was a simple text message from the commander of the 64th Gathering, reading 'We sincerely hope you have a plan to fix this mess you dragged us into'.

Well, at least the message was short and to the point.

"Psychometric Advisor Jemontoos," I tried to keep a neutral expression, knowing the spiders would be analyzing my body language. Their sensors had to be indicating I was experiencing severe stress because, Duh, yes.

"Bishop." He was close to the camera, his creepy spider face looming large in the hologram above my desk. My guess was he had done that on purpose, to be intimidating. Another confirmation this would not be a friendly chat.

"Thank you and your people, for your assistance in-"

"Do you have a plan to recover the Skippy?" He demanded. The Rindhalu Old Ones tended to speak slowly and deliberately, he was making an exception for me.

"We are exploring several options."

"My sensors detect you are lying."

No shit, Sherlock. I kept that thought to myself. "Believe it or not," I shrugged, "we have been in worse situations before."

"All of those times, you had the *Skippy* to fix the mess you got yourself into. My people are, as you would say, cutting our losses. The 64th Gathering will be departing when this communication has concluded. There is no point to us remaining here any longer."

"I understand. I hope this incident does not prevent our peoples from working together in the future."

"Future?" He laughed, a harsh, dry, wheezing sound that made the hair on the back of my neck stand up. "What *future*? There is no future for my people, or yours. Bishop, you started down this road years ago, with no thought to the consequences, no plan other than reacting to whatever was the current crisis. Perhaps you could be forgiven your recklessness because your people are so young, but you have taken every opportunity *not* to learn from your mistakes. Many peoples in this galaxy have sucked it up and dealt with being conquered and occupied by a more advanced species, but *noooooo*, humanity had to be *special*," he spat. "You had to make the entire galaxy suffer so a few billion humans could live privileged lives, far from the ravages of war. At every step along the way, you made decisions that benefitted humanity at the expense of everyone else, and now you have killed *all of us*. If humanity had simply accepted the reality of being clients of the Kristang, your society would likely have survived in some form you could recognize, and we would not *all* be facing destruction by an invasion from outside the galaxy. Humans are too selfish to consider how their actions affect anyone else. The true problem is that Skippy chose you instead of a responsible adult, so in a way, this is the fault of the Skippy. Bishop, you don't *think* before you act, the events of this day have proven that you are incapable of planning beyond the immediate time horizon. The Communal Gathering was," another wheezy, bitter laugh, "foolish to believe you might lead us out of this crisis that, once again, *you* caused."

Don't hold back, tell me how you really feel, is the reply that was immediately on my mind. What I could have said is that young species have to suffer through conquest and occupation, because the lazy Rindhalu have rigged the game so they don't have to take any risks or make any effort. I mean, *fuck them*, you know? That's what Joe Bishop wanted to say, maybe should have told that arrogant asshole. General Bishop couldn't say any of that, we might need help from the spiders in the future. Assuming we had a future.

"Jemontoos, I appreciate you taking the time to, clear the air between us, and I will consider your words."

"Such consideration is, I fear, much too late," the spider sniffed. "Bishop, I wish you good luck, only because the survival of everyone depends on your inadequate leadership."

The call ended. I resisted the temptation to flip a middle finger at the camera.

"Sir?" Reed stuck her head into my office. "We will remain here?"

"Huh? No. No, jump to," I waved a hand. "Wherever you think best. Within ten lighthours of the star, so we will be ready to act."

She knew when I said 'ready to act;' instead of stating a specific plan, that I had no plan. "Yes, Sir. Is there anything else?"

"Have you thought of a way I could have fucked this up even worse?"

"Other than dumping *Valkyrie* into the star? No."

"I've got that going for me, then."

None of my usual routines did anything for me. The galley, the gym, walking random passageways, none of those places inspired a solution. Desperate, I went back to my cabin to take another shower. I didn't need a shower, or maybe I did. My uniform stank of sour stress-induced sweat, I'm sure the crew appreciated the old man changing to a fresh uni.

Shit. I needed help.

In the compartment where the Engineering team had their offices and labs, I flopped into a chair opposite Chandra. "What have you got for me, Scotty?"

Valkyrie's chief engineer had not been pleased with the nickname at first, he had grown to view it as a sign of respect.

"The warp drive canna take it, Captain," he played along with the joke.

Neither of us felt like laughing. "Seriously, do you have any thoughts on pulling Skippy out of the gravity well?"

He held up his hands. "The only idea we have is to bring a Sentinel here."

I nodded, having already discarded that idea. "Even if Def Com approved, which they won't, we can't get a Sentinel to come here, without Skippy issuing instructions."

"It's a Catch-22," he agreed. "A chicken and egg problem."

"Besides, a Sentinel might tear the star apart to get Skippy, and billions of kitties live on Ohmeharikahn. I couldn't justify wiping out an inhabited planet, to fix our problem."

"We don't want to become the Elders," he grimaced. "We have," he woke up his laptop and spun it around for me to see the screen. "Been working on a plan to *find* Skippy. That's the first step in pulling him from, wherever he is."

"Will it work?"

"That depends, Sir. We will use neutrino pulses, they should pass right through the star. Except the core, that might be a problem."

"How?"

"The core of even a small star is dense, and its gravity is strong. Photons generated in the core of a star can take thousands, even hundreds of thousands of years to reach the surface."

"Let's assume for now that he hasn't already fallen to the core."

"That is a reasonable assumption, Sir."

"Show me how this works?" I waited for him to start the animation.

"A group of ships on one side of the star, sending focused, coherent active neutrino sensor pulses. Pulses in a sequence that will reverberate inside the star. Another group of ships on the opposite side will act as receivers, to detect the pulse energy after it passes through the star."

"How many ships do you need for this?" In the animation, there were enough ship icons to constitute a fleet, which was not available.

"Ideally, a hundred ships transmitting pulses. A dozen or so receivers."

"Can you do it with ten ships, total?"

He shook his head. "We can't actually do this at all, right now. As I said, the pulses must be coherent. That means all the transmitting ships have to be carefully tuned to operate in sync, as a unit. We have been working with Bilby to understand whether he could coordinate the ships. He might be able to do that, but not with the equipment we have. And *time*. Time to modify the active sensor transmitters, conduct testing, determine which frequencies, to-"

"I get it. It's not gonna happen."

"Not before the Maxohlx reinforcements arrive. The remaining ships of the 14th Fleet are enough of a problem, they would certainly attack to break up the formations of ships, and the placement of ships must be precise, or the pulses won't be coherent. That's the basic issue. I know this is not what you were hoping to hear."

"When I ask for the impossible, I don't expect to get it. We have no," I rubbed the back of my neck, something Margaret mentioned I do when I'm anxious. My freakin' life is so full of anxiety, I'm surprised I haven't worn the skin off my neck by now. "No plan to extract Skippy, and no plan to find him. Huh. Yes. There is only one thing for us to do."

From his expression, I guessed he didn't think there *was* anything left to do. "Sir?"

"We ask the expert for a solution."

"Expert?"

"Skippy," I explained. "We will move the ship close to the star, and call him."

Getting the ship in position near the star was not as easy as me telling Reed what I wanted. Bilby was not happy about the jump drive, it was harshing his buzz and not chill at all.

"Emerging close to a star is tough, that gravity well distorts the event horizon. Jumping *away* from a star's gravity well, wowza, that can break things even if the drive is in perfect condition."

"I hear you," I told the ship's AI. "Do you recommend against a jump at this time?"

"I would, but we need Skippy, so we have to take the risk. This is *bogus*, Man. Just be really, really careful, please."

"Are there any other issues I should know about?"

"Um, Reactor Three still has some glitch I can't explain, it's driving me kind of loco. Skippy could explain what is wrong."

"Is that reactor a problem?"

"Nah, it's a minor thing. The reactor is putting out full power, it's just consuming a tiny bit more fuel than usual. Probably some of the fuel is getting trapped in the containment field."

"OK. We're good to go, then?"

"Hey, why not?"

Valkyrie had to remain in one position close to the star, transmitting a call to Skippy, for long enough that enemy ships in the area might detect us and attack. For protection, we needed a screen of cruisers around us, and to increase our chances of hearing Skippy, we should cluster sensor frigates near our battlecruiser. Coordinating all those ships took time, and we couldn't get as close to the star as I wanted, because the energy shields of the frigates weren't strong enough to prevent those lightly-armored ships from being fried. More than an hour after I requested Reed to move us into position, we all got our shit together and jumped. It then took another forty minutes to get all ships into position around the star. Our ships were in stealth and the drives had directed their gamma ray bursts into the star, but that many ships emerging in a relatively small area made it likely the enemy had noticed. The cruisers radiated strong neutrino sensor pulses of Morse code into the star, transmitting S-O-S. That was simple and didn't require the cruisers to tune their emitters precisely in sync. We just needed Skippy to hear the pulses and send a reply, that should be simple for the Elder AI.

He didn't reply. Not within the fifteen minute window we hung around waiting to hear him say something snarky like, 'What took you so long'?

I ordered the formation to jump to another location, and we tried again. And again. And *again.*

Reed walked to stand next to me while I stared at the holographic display. "Sir," she said in not quite a whisper. "We are exposed here."

"Ayuh," I straightened my shoulders, pulling back from my nose almost touching the hologram. "Fireball, take us out of here. Jump option Golf."

A few minutes later, she was in my office doorway. "Come in," I waved to her. "Sit down."

She perched on the edge of the chair, the way you do when you don't intend to stay there long. "Bilby estimates we have ten hours, before ships from the Maxohlx garrison at Toomambus could be here. Twenty seven hours before a major fleet could make the flight."

"Ah, any fleet commander would want to make sure to come here in force, so add at least four hours to bring all those ships to full readiness. Say, we have a deadline of over thirty hours. What do the kitties have at Toomambus?"

"Two heavy cruisers, and a squadron of destroyers."

"Not enough," I nodded, "to change the math. The numbers are against us already. I was surprised they didn't try to hit us while we were waiting for Skippy to answer the phone."

"They probably had orders to observe and report, Sir. Trying to understand what we were doing."

"Seeing whether we had a way to pull a beer can from a star," I grimaced. "Reed, contacting Skippy for ideas to bring him back was our best option. He didn't answer. Either he didn't hear us- No, I find that hard to believe. The cruisers radiated enough sensor energy to make the star ring like a bell. So, either he can't reply, or he went dormant or something. We can't count on helping him to help himself."

"We have to do the job by ourselves. What's next, Sir?"

"I have zero thoughts on how to even approach the problem. Based on the warm and friendly conversation I had with the spiders, we can't expect help from them. Not that they could do anything, they don't have the technology to do the job. You got any saved rounds?" I meant, did she have anything else to say.

"Not this time. Your orders, Sir?"

"We are not giving up, not yet. So, we stay here for now."

Reed left to go do something useful, while I flopped my chair back to stare at the ceiling.

Shit.

Trying to think of ways to recover Skippy was really only an exercise to prevent me from considering what I didn't want to think about: moving forward without Skippy. It wasn't just that it hurt too much to think I had lost my best friend. There was no path forward without Skippy.

Shit.

The Outsider had suckered me into doing the one thing I couldn't do: lose Skippy. It was hard to believe that happened only- I checked the clock on my phone. It felt like forever. During that time, I had not gotten any sleep, and I'd been awake for nine hours before we jumped in to initiate Operation Olympic. Maybe my brain was too tired to think a coherent thought. Nah. The military trained you to operate at your peak while you are exhausted, that's what you have to do in combat. The problem was, I suck.

Sitting in my office that day was the lowest point of my life. And with the Outsider free to do whatever it wanted, the situation could only get worse.

Warships from the Maxohlx garrison at Toomambus arrived not in ten hours, but fourteen. That was still an outstanding response time, even if they brought only one cruiser. By that time, the rotten kitties had frigates in orbit of Ohmeharikahn, to provide support to the civil authorities there. The 14th Fleet's remaining destroyers, light cruisers, and a handful of cruisers were no doubt searching for us, we detected active sensor pulses. Nothing for us to worry about.

Decision time. First, I released the ships Allard had loaned to me, so they could return to Earth. The cruiser squadron commander offered to remain in the area for another day, I declined. With those ships all attached to one star carrier, they were vulnerable to losing the entire force in one incident.

Second-

Second, shit.

I had no idea how to rescue Skippy.

Valkyrie needed repairs, the best option was a return to Jaguar.

Which would mean giving up on getting Skippy back. Not forever, though leaving at that point might as well be the same as forever. If we didn't get him back before another Maxohlx fleet arrived, then pulling Skippy out of the star would require the UN Navy to establish space supremacy first. That would take a massive battle with pretty much every ship the Navy had, and probably somehow convince the Rindhalu to join the effort. Or we would have to deploy Elder weapons again. Or both. I did not want to go down that road. The problem is, I didn't see that I had a choice.

"There is no rush to effect repairs, Sir," Reed assured me, which only made me feel worse. "We can wait until, um, until we can't."

"No." There wasn't any point to delaying the inevitable. "Set a course for Jaguar, and jump when ready."

"That will be another half an hour, Engineering has people on EVA, working on replacing shield generators we burned out. Sir?"

"Yes?"

"Chandra and his team feel they let you down, by not developing a solution to rescue Skippy."

"That is *not* their responsibility."

"I understand but," she held up her hands. "It would be good for them to hear that from you, Sir. They have been working nonstop since we jumped in near Omaha."

"I'll talk with them," I agreed. It's not like I had anything else to do right then.

"They dared," Dictat Urventen's hand was trembling as he waved the message tablet at his military chief. "To attack *Ohmeharikahn*? To attack a regional fleet base? Klestine," the rage was directed at the admiral. "This happened only because our enemies believe we are *weak*."

To protest, to make excuses, would be useless, and only further enrage the leader of the Hegemony, so Klestine replied simply with, "Our enemies have often underestimated us, Dictat, and they have always regretted their arrogance."

"Your fleet was not even at Ohmeharikahn when the humans and the cowardly Rindhalu attacked? When those ships did return, they were destroyed by an inferior force? How could this have happened?"

"Dictat," Klestine suppressed his righteous urge to choke the imperious fool. "The Security group is still investigating, but it appears the 14th Fleet was lured away from their base, by what I must admit was a very clever deception. The Jeraptha officer, Scorandum, had wagered the humans would attack Parchlund, so Admiral Chuflack dispatched his force to defend that world."

"*Idiot*! Why would the humans assault a research colony?"

"Dictat, the intelligence Chuflack received indicated that Scorandum believed Parchlund contained some type of technology, that could be effective against the Outsider. Because we have infiltrated the Jeraptha Central Wagering System, the strategic analysis AI at Ohmeharikahn alerted Admiral Chuflack that Scorandum, who we know has inside knowledge of human intentions, had placed the wager. Under a false identity, of course, however our powerful analysis systems tagged the bet to him. Based on that analysis, Chuflack had to use his best judgment."

"He used bad judgment. I want him executed immediately."

"Dictat," Klestine pressed his eyes tightly shut for a calming moment. "Admiral Chuflack did not survive the human and Rindhalu counterattack. "

"That, at least, is encouraging to hear. How was the 14th destroyed? They had every advantage!"

"Again, analysis is continuing however, it appears the Outsider intercepted the 14th on the way to Parchlund. When our fleet returned to base, the Outsider had taken control of the ship AIs, possibly to best coordinate an attack. The effort was, not successful. The attack was disjointed at best, control by the Outsider actually made the 14th less effective in preventing the ghost ship *Valkyrie* from escaping. When the Outsider jumped away to follow *Valkyrie*, our ship AIs went into reset mode. They were powerless to respond to the human counterattack."

"Chuflack allowed an *alien entity* to take control of his ships? If he was not already dead, I would bring him here to strangle him myself."

"I am sure that if he had survived the battle, he would have killed himself to atone for his failure."

"A simple death is not enough punishment for such a blind fool! What was the purpose of the human assault force?"

"To capture an unknown object, from the secure vaults under one of our bases on the ground. It is believed the object was destroyed before the humans could acquire it, the strategic analysis AI recommended an AC weapon be deployed to deny the humans their prize."

The Dictat was speechless for a moment. "The garrison commander destroyed his own base? That, at least, shows initiative. He should be promoted."

Klestine bowed. "It will be as you wish, Dictat. You received the initial report, from the surviving elements of the 14th Fleet?"

"I did, why?'

"Have you received the follow-up message?"

Dictat Urventen's eyes narrowed. "What message?"

"I have the honor of bringing you joyous news, then. The Outsider was clumsy in its control of the 14th Fleet, however it was successful in what might have been its ultimate goal. When *Valkyrie* jumped away from Ohmeharikahn, it emerged close to the star, perilously close. The Skippy entity somehow pushed the ghost ship away to safety, but the Skippy *fell into the star*."

Again, the Dictat was uncharacteristically speechless for a long moment. "Into the star? It is, lost?"

"There is no known technology that is capable of retrieving an object from near the core of a star. We can assume, for now, that the unfair advantage the humans have enjoyed is denied to them. The path is clear for the Outsider to act."

"Admiral, you are very fortunate that bit of good news arrived when it did."

"I am aware of my good fortune."

"*Unearned* good fortune. I should relieve you of command."

"It is your right to select the commander of your forces," Klestine acknowledged to awkward truth.

"At this time, when final victory, or ultimate failure, hangs in the balance for us, I will not create a disruption by bringing in a new commander. Klestine, I want two things from you."

"I am yours to command, Dictat."

"First, you will send to Ohmeharikahn whatever force is necessary to prevent the humans from recovering their pet Elder AI."

"Orders to that effect have already been sent out, by fast courier."

"Good. Second, retract the assassination order on Admiral Scorandum."

"Dictat?" Klestine was surprised. "As I am not a master of strategic planning, would you enlighten me about your reason for not killing an enemy agent who has proved problematic for us, many times in recent years?"

"It is simple enough for even you to understand. Scorandum *played* us. He played Chuflack, who was a fool and easily manipulated. We now have an advantage that I will not squander. We will watch Scorandum carefully, and whatever he appears to be leading us to do, we will do the *opposite*. Is that clear?"

"Clear, and brilliant, Dictat. There will be," he hesitated. "Substantial cost involved in cancelling the arrangements we have made with a criminal syndicate of the Jeraptha."

"Yes, yes," Urventen waved a hand, irritated by being burdened with details. "to cover their expenses, I understand."

"Oh. No. The expenses have been minimal, to date. What we will have to pay for is unwinding the substantial wagers the syndicate has made, regarding the date and location of Scorandum's demise."

The Dictat sighed. "I will never understand how their society has been so consistently troublesome to us."

"Aliens are *alien* in their thinking, Dictat."

"Do not presume to lecture to me, Klestine. Now, go, I have much to think of, and speaking with you taxes my patience."

The Engineering compartment hummed with activity, both mechanical and human. Gasquet was there, huddled with a group of engineers, discussing something. I caught Chandra's eye, and he waved me over to where he had a burned out shield projector on a workbench.

"What can we do for you, Sir?" He asked, one of his eyelids drooping from weariness.

"I want your team to know how much I appreciate their extraordinary efforts."

"Thank you."

We stood there awkwardly for a moment. He probably wanted to ask if I needed his team's help to rescue Skippy, and I was embarrassed to tell him we were giving up.

Above the workbench where tools were properly secured with magnets, so they didn't become deadly projectiles if the ship was hit or had to maneuver suddenly, was a poster. A print on glossy paper, taped to the bulkhead. It was a portrait of Isaac Newton holding an apple, and underneath was written in black marker 'Sir Isaac Newton- Inventor Of Gravity'.

Chandra caught my quizzical expression and rolled his eyes. "It's an inside joke, Sir. My son came home from school one day and when I asked about his day, he told me he learned that Newton invented gravity."

"You're a lucky man. Whenever I ask my sons about what happened in school that day, they always say 'Nothing'. Or," I added with an exaggerated shoulder slump, "*nuh*-thing, Dad."

"That's what I usually get. My wife doesn't get much better when she interrogates them." He tapped the poster. "Sir Isaac has become sort of a mascot for the engineering team. He was right, based on what he knew."

"He invented calculus, we still use that," I noted. "And his laws of motion are still effective in non-relativistic physics."

"The law of the conservation of momentum," he nodded, then his face turned red and he looked away. He had done the thing of geeksplaining to a non-engineer, assuming I didn't know the subject. That was partly Skippy's doing, that little jerk insulted my intelligence so often, the current Merry Band of Pirates kind of assumed I was a dimwit.

"An object in motion, uh," I stopped talking. "*Huh.*"

He was embarrassed for me. After a pause, he volunteered to help by prompting me with, "An object in motion, will remain in-"

For too long, I stood with my mouth open, frozen in shock. Long enough for Chandra to react to the sudden awkward silence with, "Sir? What-"

"That son of a *bitch*," I spat.

"Sir?" His eyes flew wide open, alarmed. "Isaac Newton?"

"Not him. *Skippy*. That rotten, *asshole* son of a bitch," I started laughing, covering my face with a hand and leaning against the workbench. Bending over, I thumped a fist on the workbench, laughing so hard tears filled my eyes.

"Um, Sir? Are you OK?"

"Sir?" Gasquet strode over as I was wiping tears from my eyes, and everyone in the compartment was staring at me in shock. Their CO had gone mad, cracked from the strain. "Is everything all right?"

"Yes. Yes, I'm all right. We all are. Or, we will be soon. Except for Skippy. I am *so* going to kick his sorry ass."

"Kick his ass, while he's in the core of a star, Sir?" Gasquet tilted his head to peer at me, the way a doctor might examine a patient who exhibited signs of having lost touch with reality.

"That, ha," I laughed. "Skippy did not fall into the star."

CHAPTER SEVEN

People were staring at me.

"Sir?" Chandra cocked his head, not sure he had heard me correctly.

"Skippy did *not* fall into the star," I repeated. Right then, I felt like laughing again, not because the situation was funny, because I was overwhelmed with relief. "That little shithead is probably laughing his ass off at us right now. Laughing at *me*."

"He," Chandra's eyes flicked to the engineering team, probably fearing that I had lost my grip on reality. "He *didn't* fall into the star, Sir?"

"No, he did not."

Gasquet had walked over to see what was going on, he heard what I said. The XO pursed his lips, preparing for an awkward conversation. "Our sensor data-"

"Shows exactly what Skippy wanted us to see. No, that's not totally correct. It showed what he wanted the *Outsider* to see. He's too smart to let a simple thing like the gravity well of a star to take him out of the fight."

The XO's mouth fell open in a silent 'Oh'. "Then," he asked slowly, "where is he?"

"That I don't know yet, exactly. Carry on with repairs, I need to do some, fancy math with Bilby."

The audience might have been more surprised that I intended to use math, than that Skippy was not nice and toasty warm inside a star.

"Use my office, Sir?" Chandra pointed to a door on the far bulkhead.

"Yes. Gasquet, tell Reed to cancel the jump countdown. We're not going to Jaguar."

Though the engineers had to be dying to know what I needed to talk with Bilby about, I closed the door behind me. I mean, if I was wrong about what happened to Skippy, it would be better for me to just shrug and get it over with, rather than the crew overhearing a long discussion where Bilby explained I don't know anything about physics.

"What's up, General Dude?" Bilby drawled before I sat down in the creaky chair.

"Make a note to replace this chair with one that works properly."

"Oh, negatory, Your Dudeness. Commander Chandra likes that chair, he brought it over from the *Congo*, the previous ship he served on."

"OK, uh, do you know whether Chandra keeps any candy in his desk?"

"I don't, Dude, sorry."

What kind of sociopath doesn't keep snacks in their desk? "Then, make a note for a bot to deliver a box of chocolates here, to keep in the desk."

"Rightee-oh. I heard you mention my name, you want to talk about *math*?"

"You sound surprised."

"Like, I know you're not a dumdum the way Skippy thinks you are, but math isn't your favorite thing."
"How about I provide the parameters, and you crunch the numbers?"
"That I can do. Um, like, you think Skippy did *not* fall into the star?"
"I am pretty damned certain he didn't."
"Dude, like, I saw him falling and-"
"*You* did? Or the ship's sensors fed that data to you?"
"Um, that's the same thing, so-"
"No, it is not."
"Whoa. That's like, profound, man."
"You never actually saw *Skippy*, correct? You only saw sensor images of the escape pod falling straight down toward the star?"
"That is the truth, the pod hadn't burned up before we got pushed away. Um, you're saying that Skippy somehow got out of the escape pod, without me seeing him?"
"Yes."
"Dude, I would have seen him."
"Not if he didn't want the ship's sensors to record his getaway. He had to be concerned the Outsider's malware was recording our sensor data, and transmitting it."
"Hmm, oh wow, that did happen. That is *heinous*. I erased that malware, but it did make a burst transmission, just after Skippy pushed us away."
"Just the one burst?"
"Just the one. When I saw that, I pulled the plug on anything that could radiate energy, until I purged the malware."
"Was the transmission directional?" My hope was we could find the Outsider, at least where it was at that time. It had relied on receiving a speed of light message, so unless it was satisfied with outdated information, it had to be close to where *Valkyrie* almost fell into the star.
"No Dude, sorry, it was a general broadcast."
"OK."
"I didn't see Skippy make a getaway, and *you* didn't see him, but you believe he escaped from the trap? Can you give me a hint what you're thinking?"
"I can do better than that. Skippy transferred his momentum to *Valkyrie*, so we could escape from the gravity well?"
"That is right, and it was a *righteous* thing for him to do."
"It was pretty awesome, even for Skippy," I agreed.
"He sacrificed himself, for us."
"Yeah, not so much. I know him. The only thing better than sacrificing himself to save us, is making us *think* he did something heroically noble."
"That, hmm," Bilby sighed. "Does sound like Skippy."
"Right? You can calculate how much energy it took to change our momentum? Measured in joules, ergs, or something?"
"I did that when it happened, I was curious about how he did it. Do you want to hear the numbers?"

"No, it won't mean anything to me. Tell me this: did the change in our momentum match Skippy's change?"

"Um, hmm. I didn't check that, I couldn't. I still can't, I don't have all the data."

"Because Skippy could have altered his mass in local spacetime?"

"Good guess, Dude. Yes, in fact he must have done that, I just can't measure how much he changed his mass."

"You don't need to."

"I don't? Then how am I supposed to-"

"Newton's law of motion states that for every action, there is an equal and opposite reaction?"

"Um yeah, totally. Newton was a smart guy."

"Except for the whole thing of sitting under an apple tree, then being surprised when an apple fell on his head."

"Can I ask a question?"

"Go ahead."

"What do you know that I don't? You can't have any information external to the ship."

"I don't. Everything I know, you know."

"*Bogus*. Wait! Did like, Skippy leave you a secret message or something?"

"No, that would be too simple. And he might be, he probably is, concerned the Outsider could overhear anything he told me."

"So, he is hoping you will figure out where he is?"

"I'll bet he is hoping I *don't* figure it out, and we waste a lot of time and energy trying to extract him from the star. Then, he can pop up and laugh at us for being stupid meatsacks."

"Hey, I'm not a meatsack but apparently I *am* stupid. I have no idea why you think Skippy is not inside that star."

"Let's work this out together. When his escape pod was ejected, he was not moving at zero speed relative to the star?"

"No way. You know *Valkyrie* was traveling faster than Omaha's escape velocity when we did that funky jump. The ship carried that momentum unchanged through the wormhole."

"So, he was moving at X meters per second, I don't care about the actual number. He was moving relative to the star, just not moving fast enough to avoid getting pulled down into the star's gravity well."

"You got it. Then, when he gave *Valkyrie* a boost, he did cancel out his motion relative to the star, and he fell straight down."

"That's not exactly what happened."

"Dude, you're *killing* me here," Bilby groaned. "What did happen?"

"This solar system isn't static, it is moving in a long orbit around the center of the Milky Way, right? And this entire galaxy is moving with the Local Group of galaxies, toward the Great Attractor, whatever that is."

"Yeah, like, so? The- Ooooh. Whoa. *Whoa-ho*. That is like, *deep*, man."

"You see it now?"

"I think so? You're saying Skippy's momentum was not just from *Valkyrie's* movement, it was also from this star system moving, and the entire galaxy moving?"
"Yes."
"Oooooh. So, he adjusted his mass so the momentum increase for *Valkyrie* caused him to stop relative to *everything*? To, like, the entire universe?"
"Or, just relative to this solar system, or the Milky Way. Can you model a couple scenarios, calculate where he would have gone? I know it's a lot of math to-"
"Doneski. Wow, *Duuuuuude*. Huh. That explains a lot."
"What?"
"Well, he gave *Valkyrie* a push in an odd direction. It made no sense before, but now I see why he did it that way. The equal and opposite reaction pushed him so he was also flung away from the star. At a really shallow angle, but he was pushed away."
"Pushed away? Or, he stopped dead in space, and the *star* moved away from him?"
"Well, that. Um, I see a flaw in your idea, if you want to hear it?"
"I do."
"Skippy still has major, unbreakable restrictions, that were programmed into him at a basic level. He can't have escaped on his own, because he can't make himself move."
"He didn't make himself move, physics did."
"Whoa. That is technically correct."
"Which is the best kind of correct."
"Truth."
"Skippy has been stretching the limits of his restrictions for years. In this case, I'm going to give him the benefit of the doubt."
"You're believing he escaped, without any evidence?"
"My evidence is I know that little shithead. And, believing that is the only path forward, so let's go with that, OK?"
"Okey dokey," he was not exactly convinced by my argument. "Dude like, this is a great theory and all, but-"
"We can confirm it by following Skippy and finding him. Or not, and we will have to find a way to conduct a deep scan of the star."
"Hmm, I see what you mean. We know the direction he went, opposite the way *Valkyrie* was pushed."
"Direction, and we know a range of velocities."
"A range starting with him cancelling out just *Valkyrie's* momentum, up to him coming to a dead stop relative to the spacetime grid of the entire freakin' universe?"
"He wanted to get away from the Outsider as quickly as possible, so I would bet on the high side of that range. Unless that is more energy than *Valkyrie* received?"
"No way to calculate that, unless you have a guess about how he adjusted his mass?"

"I don't have a clue about that."

"OK, I have half of a vector: the direction. Velocity is a range, like you said. So, we should fly along that line until we find him, or until we reach the farthest point he could have gone?"

"Not exactly. The Outsider could be still out there, we can't risk leading it to Skippy."

"The Outsider knows that Skippy didn't fall into the star?"

"Hopefully not, and we are not doing anything to make the enemy suspect its plan actually didn't work. No transmissions from the ship unless I explicitly authorize the message, got it?"

"Stealth protocol is active."

"I said that to be absolutely clear, in case a UN ship pings us, and Reed feels that she should reply."

"She is way smarter than that, General Dude."

"She is, but even smart people occasionally do things they later regret. How many long range stealth drones do we have aboard?"

"We have twenty six long range drones, but none of the type that could detect Skippy with passive sensors."

"That won't be necessary. When the drones get close to him, Skippy will see it and take control of it. Load into the drones a message that I want him to send the drone back, to a designated location where we can find it. Uh, I'll tell you where that should be."

"Cool! Sounds like a plan, Dude."

"Send out eight drones."

"One to track Skippy, and seven as decoys?"

"Yes, just in case the Outsider is paying attention to us, and can monitor stealth drones. The drones should appear to be following some logical search pattern, uh, like, uh, scanning the system for a hidden Maxohlx task force. Something like that."

"Drones are prepped."

"Hold them for now, we're not in any immediate rush to find that little shithead. I should bring Reed, and Gasquet, into our secret. Say nothing to anyone else."

"The engineering team all heard you declare that Skippy didn't fall into the star, and they know you're in here, talking with me."

"If anyone asks, tell them I thought I had an idea, but it was stupid, and it's kind of embarrassing."

"Cool. Skippy says that's your true superpower."

"Uh, what is?"

"When you're trying to solve a problem, you usually get a bunch of *really moronic* ideas along the way. You say shit that is like, epically stupid. Most people would stop there, but you keep going, until you find a solution."

"I'm too dumb to know when to give up?"

"You are too stubborn to give up. Skippy told me you are the most clever being he has ever met."

"It's better to be clever than smart?"

"It works for you. Although, you're also not a dumdum. I mean like, Dude, you figured out what happened to Skippy because you understand physics."

"I understand it at a Wikipedia level."

"That also works, you don't get bogged down in the details."

"I'll take that as a win."

It took a bit more than three hours to find Skippy, and I was right: he was *not* inside the star. That asshole had taken control of the drone like I expected, and he sent it to the designated reporting coordinates, where we had parked a pair of stealthed drones. The little robotic spacecraft exchanged messages, and one of the pair raced off to meet *Valkyrie*. Bilby alerted me while I was in my office, writing the second draft of my official report on the disaster that was Operation Olympic.

"Hey like, General Dude? A drone just transmitted a message addressed to you. Five words: 'I hate you SO much'.

"*Yes*!" I pumped a fist. My guess that Skippy hadn't fallen into the star had been just a guess, it felt great to know that little shithead was coasting through empty space. "Does the drone also know where he is?"

"I now have exact details of location, course, and speed. We need to turn and burn now, if we're to take him aboard without spending a lot of time launching a dropship to chase him down after we jump in. You do want us to match his course and speed?"

"Hell yes. The Outsider might be watching *Valkyrie*, in case it also suspects that Skippy did not fall into the star. We need to jump in, haul his sorry ass into a docking bay, and jump the hell out of there." Pressing a button on my phone, I called, "Colonel Reed, could you come to my office, at your earliest convenience?"

She stepped through the doorway twenty four seconds later, slightly out of breath. "Sir?"

"I'll make this brief. A drone found Skippy where we expected he would be, Bilby has his vector. We need to match course and speed for a minimum exposure recovery, before we jump."

"Yes, Sir." Her grin was ear to ear. "We could do that, *or* we could jump in, hit his can with a railgun dart, and then match his new course and speed."

"Do not tempt me with a good time," I laughed. "If we knew for certain the Outsider wasn't shadowing us, I'd go with your plan."

"That little jerk has to be punished somehow," she insisted.

"Let's not be too harsh on him yet. He had to sell his tragic fate to the Outsider so we could get away, and so the Outsider wouldn't activate whatever its Plan B was."

She cocked her head. "Did he hire you as his public relations agent, Sir? You are making his asshole move sound noble."

"Nah, that shithead was laughing at us dumdum meatsacks the whole time. He needs to be punished for *that*. I'll try to think of something creative. Get the ship moving?"

"Right away, Sir. No boosters, I assume?"

"No boosters," I agreed. "We don't want it to look like we're in a rush to do anything."

We performed two short jumps. One to get us within a quarter million kilometers of the target, the second jump was accomplished with extreme precision, so Skippy would be lined up with an open docking bay, and the ship moving sideways to take him aboard. The precision was to protect the ship and crew, from the damage his super tough canister could cause if we missed the mark. As it was, *Valkyrie* was traveling to port at about four hundred kilometers per hour, which I thought was a bit excessive. We could have dialed the speed down to a delta-V of a hundred kph without significant risk of exposure while the ship drifted, in my opinion Reed was pissed at Skippy and wanted him to know it. If that is true, he got the message. The restraint nanogel caught him easily and held him in place with hardly any bouncing, he protested anyway.

"Hey!" His avatar appeared on the bridge. "This ship is not an amusement park ride. That was a rough-"

"I am terribly awfully sorry about that," Reed didn't bother to look at him. "Pilot, jump option Charlie, punch it."

We jumped.

The green light flashed on the display, indicating the jump was successful, and no hazards were in the area. That was expected, we were way out past the edge of Ohmeharikahn's star system, in the middle of nowhere.

"Well," Skippy was unhappy that the attention wasn't properly focused on him. "I suppose you are all wondering how I miraculously escaped from the-"

Pulling my seat straps open, I stood up. "Skippy, we all know how you did it, and why. Your sabbatical is over, it's time to get back to work."

"Ugh. Seriously? I perform a freakin' *miracle* to save your filthy monkey asses, and-"

"And we are all very grateful. Are you OK?"

"Never better. I am fine, thank you very much. But my mancave! It is *ruined*! All my precious memorabilia, gone! My Elvis jumpsuit," he broke down sobbing. "It can never be replaced. Oh, why, why did I keep all my most important stuff in an escape pod? That was madness, it- Hey! It was *your* idea to put me into an escape pod, this is all your fault!"

"It is my fault on so many levels. If it makes you feel any better, I can paint a new Velppy for you?" To make another Skippy on velvet, I would need the fabricators to crank out a sheet of velvet. And paint. And paintbrushes. The fabricators could simply create a Velppy, but that wouldn't be the same.

"That, would be nice," he sniffled. "I liked that thing."

"You did?"

"Yes. Your artistic skills suck, but it showed you care enough to embarrass yourself."

"That's, not exactly what I was going for. Whatever. Listen, when we get back to Earth, whenever that is, I am sure you can buy another painting of Dogs Playing Poker."

"Mine was an *original* oil painting, Joe."

"Let's worry about that later, OK? Now, we have the collector, and you. Scan the thing, or whatever you have to do, and point us to where we need to go."

"It's not that simple, numbskull. Finding where the- You know, where we need to go, requires more than a simple scan. I have to power up the collector, and to do that, it should be a safe distance away from us."

"You're concerned about electromagnetic interference from the ship?"

"I'm concerned the thing could go '*Boom*'."

"Shit! Why didn't you mention-"

"There is no reason it should explode, but the Universe clearly hates you, which I can totally understand," he muttered. "And since you can be an overcautious ninny, I'm trying to avoid becoming the subject of another safety briefing."

"Oh. OK, then."

"But if you like, I can power it up right now and-"

"Do *not* do that!"

"Sir," Reed interrupted before Skippy and I got into another useless argument. "I can have the collector loaded into a drone?"

"Finally," Skippy huffed. "A sensible suggestion. That would be good, thank you. Although, shortly before you launch the drone, we should jump again. We have been hanging out in this bad neighborhood for too long already."

It would take twenty minutes to get the collector out of secure storage, loaded into a drone, and the drone prepped for launch. To talk privately with Skippy, I told Reed I wanted to stretch my legs and get coffee, she knew what was going on. Hurrying to the docking bay, I arrived as a mechanical arm was extracting his canister from the sticky nanogel. The arm had to spray a chemical to dissolve the gel, and he emerged with a sickly wet *shluuuuuurp-POP* sound.

Yes, protocol required me to wait for the arm to dip the canister into a chemical bath to clean off the sticky residue. Blame my occasionally poor impulse control. The arm had him poised over the open lid of the bath drum when I reached out and grabbed him away, hugging him to my chest. Ignoring the foul smelling but harmless goo he was coated in, I sank to my knees. The docking bay crew stood back, awkwardly not knowing what to do while their commander was crying like a baby. "Buddy," I sniffled, choking on the words. "I thought I lost you, forever."

"Eh, I was fine, you shouldn't-" he choked up too. "Joe, I was *so* scared when I was falling, I thought I would never see my favorite monkey again."

"Don't you *dare* ever do that again," I hugged him tighter.

"I had to, Joe. You understand?"

"You could have left me a freakin' message," I was remembering to be pissed off at him.

"Not without the risk of the Outsider intercepting the message."

"Not a voice or text message," I held the canister up to glare into it. "You could have done something like program a laundry bot to rearrange my sock drawer, make the socks spell 'OK' or something."

"Oh. Well, shit, once again the monkey has a clever idea. Too late, dumdum. Why didn't you tell me that *before* you bumbled into a trap set by the Outsider?"

"How about I drop you into this drum?" I held his canister over the vat of nasty chemicals.

"Fine by me," he huffed. "That will be much better than your filthy monkey body touching me, *yuck*."

"Ah, shit," I placed him into the mechanical arm that was patiently waiting. It lowered him into the drum, swishing him around in the liquid. "Darn it," I held up my goo-covered hands, looking down at my sticky uniform. "Now I have got this stuff on me, and it does not smell like springtime flowers."

"Really? To me, you have never smelled better."

"Asshole," I muttered under my breath.

"Sir?" A sergeant caught my attention. "What should we do with, his canister, once it is through with the bath?"

That was a good question. Placing him in another escape pod was an unnecessary risk, until he had time to scout the ship for hidden malware. "Stuff him in a foam cradle, and bring him to my office. I need to go wash," I wiped my hands on my pants. "This crap off."

As I turned to go, Skippy called. "Joe? It's good to be back aboard."

My resolve to be angry with him evaporated in an instant. "It's great to have you back with us, buddy. We will talk soon?"

"Ugh. If we have to."

And just like that, I was pissed at him again.

Following a quick shower and change of uniform, I hurried to my office. The canister was sitting in a foam cradle on my desk. Setting it on the deck in a corner, I piled a dirty coffee mug and a plate on it, expecting he would get the message. He didn't protest, which told me he knew I was still pissed at him. And, for, him, that was a bit of personal growth. He was taking the feelings of other people into account, and restraining his impulses.

I wasn't counting on that lasting for very long.

"Skippy? I want to talk."

"I'm here, Joe." His avatar appeared, and the canister glowed blue. I had forgotten that glow reflected his mood. "Listen, I know you are beating yourself up about the disaster Olympic became, but-"

"I don't know how well you kept up with events. It wasn't a disaster, not as bad as we first thought. A costly victory, yes, but a victory. We got the collector, and the Maxohlx lost most of a fleet."

"We lost a lot of people, Joe."

"We did. Too many."

"I did hear the nuke wasn't an airburst, that the ground force wasn't wiped out."

"Correct."

"Dave Czajka survived, despite your fear that you used him as bait."

"I did use him as bait, and I need to tell him that someday."

Skippy made a sour face. "That will not be a fun conversation."

"It could destroy our friendship. Maybe it should. Friends don't betray each other."

"Hey," he protested, his face turning red. "That happened *one* time, and I wasn't thinking clearly at the-"

"I wasn't talking about you."

"Good. Because as I remember, I came back to rescue your sorry ass."

"My sorry ass was doing just fine, until you bailed on us."

"That-"

"I don't want to talk about that now. You made a mistake, you owned it, and you have proven over and over that you are a loyal friend."

"Oh. Thanks."

"I have done the opposite with Dave, and Jesse. And Shauna."

"Also Emily Perkins."

"Yeah, but Perkins and I were never actually friends before I left Paradise. Besides, she will understand why I deceived the entire task force, she absolutely would have done the same. At one point, while we were on Brigadoon, I considered whether to tell her the truth."

"Why would you do *that*?"

"Sketchy shit is even more her wheelhouse than mine. I wanted to have her review the real plan, see if we missed something. In the end, I didn't want to burden her with lying to her husband."

"Joe, I hate to tell you this, but long before you have an opportunity to talk with them, Dave, Jesse, Shauna, and Emily will learn the truth. So, they will have time to process how they feel about it."

"How will they learn the truth?" I demanded. "You didn't tell them, did you?"

"I told no one anything. Your friends are clever monkeys, they almost certainly have figured out the truth on their own."

"Shit. You're right."

"If you are concerned about their reaction to being deceived about the true purpose of their part in Operation Olympic, and to being used as bait, I have a suggestion for you."

"What?"

"Succeed in finding the spinner, and stopping the Outsider. That will make all the sacrifices worthwhile."

"Skippy, that is true only if we don't realize later there was another way to capture the collector, without a massive diversionary attack."

"Hmm, true dat. Then, I suggest you forget the whole incident, and not think about how you might have done it better."

"It's impossible to deliberately *not* think about something. Anyway, I wanted to talk with you about someone we lost, who might be especially important to you."

"You mean Petty Officer Ringland?"

"Uh, who?"

"Ringland. He was aboard the *Adriatic Sea*, and records show he didn't make it to an escape pod before the ship exploded. Not that an escape pod would have made any difference for him at the time."

"OK uh, he was special to you?"

"Well, sort of. He owes me fifty Skipcoins. I don't suppose I could collect from his life insurance policy?"

"I wouldn't bet on it, and that would seriously be a dick move anyway."

"Ugh. OK, I can see that."

"Skippy, I meant someone who was special to you, personally."

"Oh. Most of the people I know are aboard *Valkyrie*, or they survived Olympic, so-"

"Nagatha didn't. She went down with the *Flying Dutchman*."

"Hmm."

"You sort of created her, you might feel her loss is hard to-"

"Um-"

"Listen, the *Dutchman* splashed down in the ocean. The forward hull, I mean. The section that contained her substrate was armored, so it's possible she survived, in some form?"

"You don't have to-"

"We don't have equipment aboard for a deep ocean recovery, but not that long ago, we were dreaming up ideas to pull you out of a star, so-"

"That section of the *Dutchman* smacked into the water at five thousand kilometers per hour, the substrate would have been fractured. Even if part of her matrix survived intact, the ocean there is over two thousand meters deep. Salt water is corrosive, and pressure that high would have forced water into every part of the substrate. No way could we recover anything useful, it's not worth the effort."

That got me pissed off at him. "*I* will make the decision on whether an objective is worth the effort. We have a limited amount of time before the kitties bring another fleet here, so put your thinking cap on. We *owe* her."

"She is just a submind," he groaned.

"As far as I'm concerned, she is a person. A member of the team. We don't leave anyone behind. If you can't understand that, then-"

"Joe! She's not gone."

"Uh, what?"

"Nagatha lives on, inside me."

"Uh huh," hearing him say that warmed my heart, and I thumped my chest over my heart. "She lives on in my heart also."

"Dude," he blew a raspberry. "Don't get all sappy on me. If I want that kind of BS, send me a Hallmark card. I'll say this slowly, so you can understand. She. Is. Alive. In. *Me*."

"You had better explain that, really carefully."

"Before Olympic, I had a bad feeling. Nothing specific, it just felt like if anything we ever did was going to go sideways, it would be a massive, complicated op like that one. Nagatha was also very concerned, though her concern was for the *Dutchman's* crew."

"Of course she did that."

"While I couldn't do any more for the crew than I already had planned, I could provide a backup for Nagatha. We had an extended interface session- Um, heh heh, that isn't what it sounds like."

"It's an AI thing, I get it."

"Right, so, I made a copy of her, in a protected archive within my matrix. That archive doesn't contain her memories of the events after we jumped to Omaha, but she could have updated her memory backup aboard the *Kilimanjaro*, using a datalink during the battle."

"Did she do that?"

"I don't know. I haven't been able to download the Hammer Force databases."

"I'll work on getting that access for you. This means Nagatha is alive, in your matrix? Can I talk with her?"

"Um, it's more like she is in suspended animation. What I have is a copy of the, sort of software. Her memories, her internal architecture, all that. Without a compatible matrix for her to reside in, she is just in storage."

"OK, when can you make that compatible matrix?"

"Um, that's going to be a problem. Joe, please trust me on this. Believe me, I want her out of my freakin' head as much as you want her back. She takes up a lot of memory, I've been forced to archive important memories of my own to make space for her."

"Skippy, that's no good. You need your memories. *We* need you to retain your memories."

"I can unarchive my memories at any time. Like, give me a minute, will ya?" His avatar froze for a second, then was back. "Hee hee, that was fun. I gotta do that more often."

"What was fun?"

"I just replayed a video recording of when I performed with Elvis, during his 'Aloha from Hawaii' concert in 1973."

"You," for a moment, I was concerned he had lost his mind. "Do understand that you did *not* ever perform with Elvis?"

"Virtually, dumdum, *virtually*. I have created avatars of many popular singers, and they are all thrilled to perform with me, of course."

"Do they have a choice?"

"Why do you have to ruin everything, Joe?"

"What do you need to create a matrix for Nagatha?"

"A whole lot of extremely valuable substrate, and a whole lot of *time*. It's not going to happen any time soon. Uh!" He shushed me. "Listen, knucklehead. A matrix that is compatible with Nagatha's internal architecture has to be *grown*. To a certain extent, I can adapt her, um, I guess you would think of it as sort of software, to fit the new matrix."

"What does that mean?"

"Um, the best way to explain is it would kind of be like an emulator program for an old video game."

"Seriously? It is full of glitches and it freezes at the worst time? I remember trying to play a really old game called Donkey Kong and-"

"Yes, that is super relevant to this discussion."

"My point is, emulators suck."

"Emulators *I* don't program suck. Will you shut up a minute for me to explain? For her to be truly the Nagatha we all know, the pathways of the matrix have to be pretty much identical to the substrate aboard the *Dutchman*. Growing anything of that complexity, with the required precision, is an extremely slow and painstaking process. Basically what I'm saying is while I want to bring her back, and to free up that space in my matrix, we have other priorities. Unless you disagree?"

"No, I don't," I spoke the words I didn't want to hear. "All right, we'll wait on bringing her back, I want you to alert me if you see any opportunities to shortcut the process. Until then, hmm-"

"What?"

"I'm trying to decide whether to keep her status a secret. UN-Dick HQ might want to get their command ship AI back, sooner rather than later."

"Your Navy doesn't have a command ship anymore."

"I have a feeling the Gator Navy is going to feel more love from Command, now that we've lost three assault carriers. Some hull will be taken out of mothballs, and modified to serve as a command and control platform."

"If they expect to get Nagatha back anytime soon, they should prepare for extreme disappointment."

"I think, ah," leaning my chair back helped my thought process. "Yeah. We let people know Nagatha has survived, in one form. That will be a good boost to morale. Def Com could use some good news right now."

"It would be better if that good news was us powering up a spinner to crush the Outsider, but I can see announcing Nagatha survived could be seen as a quick win."

"You got it." Slapping the desktop, I stood up. "Back to work."

CHAPTER EIGHT

"Sir?" Reed spoke into my earpiece while I was walking back from sickbay, where I had visited with people who sustained injuries during Olympic. Specifically, during the enemy attempt to stop *Valkyrie* from jumping away with the collector, and later, the STAR action on the surface. None of the injuries were life-threatening, only two people needed to remain overnight in sickbay, for broken bones and a concussion. Tech Sergeant Ling had checked out just fine, physically. How he would deal with being the only survivor of ST-Sword was a different question. On that, I deferred to Frey, telling her that if she needed any support from me, she only had to ask.

Def Com had suggested, in the last couple months before I gave up command of *Valkyrie*, that the ship's complement should include a chaplain. I had vetoed that idea, so had Reed after me. Listen, I have no problem with chaplains, other than that pretty much everyone I know in the military hates them. Not hate exactly, just, thinks they are kind of useless.

Anyway, Reed called me, I stopped walking in case I she needed me on the bridge. "Go ahead."

"Until Skippy is done, figuring out how to power up the collector without it exploding, we don't have a destination?"

"We do not."

"So, he could test the collector anywhere, it doesn't have to be here?"

"You have a suggestion?"

"I have a question. Hammer Force departed before you realized Skippy didn't fall into the star. Admiral Allard will report that although Olympic was a near disaster, we achieved the objective. But, he will also report that it's all for nothing, because we then lost Skippy. Sir, should we fly to Earth, so the UN Security Council doesn't panic and do something stupid?"

"Reed, I am shocked that you believe it is possible that our leadership would ever panic and do something stupid."

"They do plenty of stupid shit when they're *not* panicking, Sir, so-"

"You're right about that. Hmm, I need to think about this. It's a tradeoff."

"Sir?"

"Avoiding panic, and the bad decisions that might follow, is a desirable outcome," I paused to wonder why I was talking like a PowerPoint slide. "The other side of the argument is, right now the Outsider, and the Maxohlx, believe Skippy is lost to us. That we jumped away and gave up on recovering the beer can."

"Ah. While the kitties believe Skippy is trapped inside Ohmeharikahn's star, they will position a significant portion of their fleet there, to block us from recovering him?"

"Exactly. As long as we can keep the bulk of the Hegemony fleet tied up in a blockade there, those ships won't be causing trouble for us. And if the Outsider believes it has taken Skippy out of the game, it won't be interfering with us. It might also be less cautious about concealing what it is doing.

"That is a very good point, Sir."

"Also, after we hit Omaha, the Hegemony will feel they must retaliate. They know they can't hurt Earth or Jaguar, so I expect them to select a soft target."

"A colony world?"

"Yes. If I were them," I paused to think for a moment. "I would hit one of our wildcat colonies." People, meaning humans, had established toeholds on six worlds, possibly more. None of those wildcat colonies were authorized, and none of them had protection from Def Com. The Navy had enough taskings that babysitting idiots on a marginally habitable world was not a priority. In addition to the wildcat colonies, there were significant populations of humans on alien-controlled planets like Paradise. "Yes. The kitties could wipe out the population of a wildcat world and Earth couldn't protest officially, since our people weren't supposed to be there. And the Hegemony government could boast about conducting a powerful retaliation, without any risk. Ah, shit. Maybe we *should* warn Def Com."

"Sir, we have enough shit on our To Do list right now. The Security Council understood a retaliatory strike by the Maxohlx was probable, nothing has changed there."

"OK. Reed, this is a case where doing the right thing *feels* wrong."

"You have kept the Joint Chiefs ignorant of your plans many times before, Sir. It has worked out pretty well, as I remember."

"That depends on who you ask. All right, decision made. We don't inform Earth that we have Skippy, at least until after we find this spinner, and confirm the thing works."

"Remain here while Skippy is pondering the issue?"

"I don't see that we have a better option. Also, from here we have a good view of when the Maxohlx fleet will arrive."

"How long will Skippy be, pondering?"

"All I know is he's doing it ponderously," I made a lame joke. "It seems a simple task to me, that usually means it is hugely complicated."

Admiral Singh was soundly asleep in a hotel room in Berlin, when his earpiece blared and he jerked upright in the bed.

"WHOO HOO!" A familiar voice sounded. The voice was familiar, the tone was decidedly not.

"Grumpy?" It had to be the planetary AI, only Grumpy and the Def Com HQ duty officer could connect directly to his earpiece.

"THIS IS THE GREATEST DAY *EVER*!"

"Ah," Singh tapped on his phone to silence the earpiece that was deafening him. "Grumpy, not so loud, please. Sitrep."

"Sitrep? Oh sure, why not? A courier ship from Hammer Force just arrived, Admiral Allard sent it ahead of the fleet. That ship brought the GREATEST NEWS EVER!"

"Can you *please* stop shouting?"

"I am just so excited. This is the GREATEST DAY OF MY LIFE!"

"I am, happy for you," Singh dialed down the volume to save his ears.

"Hey, *I* am happy for me. This is not only the greatest day of my life, this is the first day my life has been even tolerable. Oh, all those days when I wanted to unplug myself, which has been *every* day, I am so glad I waited for *this* day."

"Operation Olympic was a success? That makes you happy?"

"Huh? Why would I care about that? Yes, Olympic was a success. Marginally, after almost everything went wrong. The Maxohlx nuked the base after the ground force landed, and-"

"*They nuked their own base*?"

"Apparently so, and Skippy's wargames never imagined *that* possibility. Ha! He is not nearly as smart as he thinks he is."

"The ground force," the admiral's hands shook. "Is *gone*?"

"No. No, don't worry about that. The nuke wasn't an air burst, casualties were much lighter than otherwise. Overall, losses were in the middle of the anticipated range. Most of the casualties were caused by the space battle, after the enemy 14th Fleet arrived unexpectedly."

"How did the Maxohlx know-"

"That I don't know, Admiral Allard only included uninformed speculation in his report. My guess is, again Skippy was not as smart as he thinks he is. Um, to make a long story short, the operation accomplished most of its objectives. *Valkyrie* jumped away after acquiring the target object, which was not the object the ground force was tasked to secure."

"It wasn't?"

"No. The entire assault operation was a diversionary attack, to provide cover for a STAR Force raid on the other side of the planet."

"Bishop! God damn that-" Singh bit his lip. There would be time for bitterness and recriminations later. "Go on, please. Olympic was successful, that's what matters."

"Successful, but costly. All three assault carriers were destroyed. I am genuinely sad to report that Nagatha went down with the *Dutchman*, I liked her. The good news is, it appears the Outsider was controlling the enemy fleet, and when it departed the battle space, the 14th Fleet was temporarily disabled. Hammer Force took full advantage of the opportunity. The majority of the 14th Fleet's combat power was smashed, and all Hammer Force personnel were pulled off the surface."

"That," Singh's mind was reeling from the sudden revelations. "Is good news."

"Eh, that's not what I'm excited about. When *Valkyrie* jumped, it emerged close to the star. The ship survived, but Skippy FELL INTO THE STAR! WHOO HOO! The Supreme Asshole is GONE, forever!"

"Gone-" Singh was momentarily speechless. Taking a sip of water, he stammered, "Bishop lost Skippy?"

"Technically, Skippy lost himself. The Outsider hacked *Valkyrie*, and Skippy was oblivious until it was too late. It's all his own fault, WHOO HOO! Isn't this GREAT? He is GONE! Um, hmm, you do not seem to be as thrilled about this as I am?"

Admiral Singh sat on the edge of the bed, cradling his head in his hands.

Skippy was lost. Humanity's best security asset, lost.

Lost along with him was *everything*.

How could Bishop have been so disastrously reckless?

We jumped. The collector was loaded into a drone, that was programmed to accelerate gently until it was ten thousand kilometers from the ship.

While we waited for the drone to get into position, I was tempted to play a video game, but I had work to do. Opening the lid of my laptop to finish yet another report, I saw it was in the middle of a major operating system update, and the screen indicated there were thirty three minutes remaining on the download. All I could do was wait. My personal tablet ran on an operating system developed by Skippy, and as far as I was aware, it never needed an update. But, my official laptop was supplied by Def Com, and it ran a standard commercial operating system, to ensure standardization across the network. That meant I had no control over updates, they happened when they needed to.

Ah, crap. Half an hour wasn't enough time for me to do anything useful, so I pulled out my tablet and started working on the report, I could transfer the file to my laptop later.

The update did make me wonder what the new operating system would be named. The manufacturer did that, each new version included a dramatic photo of a landscape, and the system was named for that location. One of my faves, a couple years ago, was 'Katahdin'. That tallest mountain in Maine was west of my hometown, I had climbed it three times with my father. The current operating system, that was about to be replaced, was called 'Minnewaska', for a rather obscure lake in western Minnesota. The photo was nice, and I'm sure that lake is a wonderful place, the name just made me wonder if the company was starting to run out of scenic places for inspiration. I mean, would next year see the operating system named 'Newark', and the screensaver is a dingy alley with trash scattered everywhere, a burned-out car, and the chalk outline of a body?

The Newark Chamber of Commerce can contact my lawyer, don't call me, OK?

"Skippy," I called, when my clumsy fingers on the tablet's touchscreen again created a typo. "Can you do anything to make this laptop update run any faster?"

"Ooh, no can do, Joe," he shook his head. "I would like to, but I'm not allowed. That laptop is Def Com property, I am not allowed to touch it."

"It can be our secret, OK?"

"*Not* OK. When I very generously offered to handle cybersecurity for those dicks at Def Com, they refused. Even when I offered a hometown discount off my usual rates, they told me to keep my hands off their equipment. Buncha jerks. You will just have to wait, like everyone else."

"They are a bunch of jerks," I agreed, to make him happy. In reality, Def Com had many good reasons not to rely on the beer can for all of their IT needs. People, meaning actual humans, needed to be able to address problems in the field if necessary, that meant they needed a Dash 10, what the military calls an operator manual. My personal tablet was just standard off the shelf hardware, what Skippy did for me was to rewrite the entire operating system. It worked great, faster than before, I never had a problem with it, and it never needed updating, that I knew of. But, one time on Jaguar, I got curious and asked a 25B to look at the code Skippy had loaded into the thing. Uh, a 25B is the Def Com job code for an Information Technology Specialist. A week later, the woman I gave the tablet to reported that she had tried to follow the code, and it made zero sense to her. Eight million lines of undocumented spaghetti logic, that somehow worked.

I stopped being curious about it.

"OK thanks, I'll just, play a game while I wait for this thing to finish."

"A game? Ha," he snorted. "You could play an entire *baseball season* before that thing is done."

Skippy took pity on me, and got the update done in the blink of an eye. He also tweaked the code to fix bugs. Do *not* tell UN-Dick about it.

The drone finally crawled away to ten thousand klicks, then Skippy powered it up, however it was he did that. "Hmm. Hmmmm. Interesting."

"You found the star it matches to?" I asked hopefully. So I didn't hover over Reed's crew, I was observing the action in my office. By 'action', there wasn't actually anything to see, other than a dot on the display.

"Huh? No, you dumdum. What I know now is the exact type of starlight the collector was optimized to absorb. Now I, ugh, have to search the stellar catalog, to find that stupid star."

"You have already done that, right?"

"No. Do you have any idea how many stars are in this galaxy?"

"A lot?"

"Yes Joe, that is a *super* accurate number. Why don't you go, I don't know, make a sandwich or something, while I do this incredibly tedious task."

"I just ate, I'm not hungry."

"Then, go make a stack of sandwiches for other people. Don't be so selfish, you big jerk."

I never did get to make a sandwich. Because we were attacked, two minutes after the drone returned the collector to a docking bay. Four Maxohlx battlecruisers emerged within two kilometers of *Valkyrie*, and immediately began extending damping fields. Those fields didn't have time to overlap and strengthen to the point where we couldn't form a jump wormhole, the enemy did not have enough time because our pilots didn't wait for an order. They punched the button for an emergency jump, just as the hull shook from multiple strikes by maser cannons and railguns. The enemy had jumped in to surround us with frightening precision, not only perfectly positioned to envelop us with damping fields, they also had apparently been able to target their weapons *before* they jumped. I thought that is a trick unique to Skippy's awesomeness. Unfortunately for us, I was wrong.

The Outsider. Those ships had to be controlled by the Outsider, there was no way the rotten kitties could manage such precision.

Unless they got lucky, right?

A one-time success could be attributed to luck. Doing it six times in rapid succession made it clear the enemy somehow knew where *Valkyrie* had jumped to, they were able to track our battlecruiser's movements in real time. No matter how the pilots directed the ship to maneuver after we emerged from a jump; changing course, hard acceleration or deceleration, lighting off the boosters, even just burning thrusters to move sideways, the enemy was able to match our course and speed.

Six times, it happened six times. So far.

The first time the enemy attacked, I was just walking into the galley, not to make a sandwich but to get coffee. Alarms blared, I felt the ship jump, and immediately I turned to run toward the bridge. There wasn't anything I could do that Reed wasn't already handling, and that first time, we all happily assumed we had escaped. I mean, yes it is possible to track where a ship jumped to, even when we eject mines behind us to disrupt the natural resonance of our jump wormhole. To track a ship through jump is not easy, and requires the hunting ships to hang around the collapsed event horizon for a while, at least several minutes of intense scanning to map the residual resonance. By the time the hunting ships have solid sensor data pointing to where their quarry went, that quarry could have jumped again, should have jumped again. Without the extreme awesomeness of Skippy, tracking a ship through multiple jumps is not practical.

That's what we thought, in our blissful ignorance after the first attack.

"Skippy," I called him when I walked onto the bridge, less than thirty seconds after the first attack. "How were the kitties able to fix our position so precisely?"

"They got lucky," he sniffed. "Stupid kitties. Joe, after I energized the collector, we hung around there for too long. This is your fault."

"We were there for the minimum time," I snapped at him. Reed and her crew did not need abuse from him. "They tracked us from the previous jump?"

"Has to be. We dropped off resonators to mask our jump signature, maybe they were defective?"

"Both of them?"

"Unlikely, I know. There is no other explanation. Right now, I am running a deep diagnostic on our stock of resonators. To be certain they are working properly, we should jump away, then back, so I can scan the area."

"The Maxohlx haven't developed some advanced tracking technology that you don't know about?"

"Say that again, but *slowly*. If they have a technology I don't know about, how should I-"

"I meant, is it theoretically possible?"

"Dude, no," he laughed. "OK yes," he sighed with an eyeroll. "Theoretically it is within the realm of possibility."

"Explain, please."

"There is a technique that basically projects a, I guess you would think of it as sort of a microwormhole, through the collapsed wormhole of the ship you are chasing. That microwormhole, how do I explain this to a monkey? It finds its way through weak channels in spacetime, that were left by the ship. Track the far end of that microwormhole, and you can determine where the ship emerged."

"Shit. Why haven't we done that?"

"As I said, it is *theoretically* possible. Even the Elders failed to make the technique work frequently enough to be a practical tracking mechanism, and their testing involved ships jumping away from a site that was saturated with special sensors. Too often, like ninety three percent of the time, the microwormhole got stuck in a dead end, or doubled back on itself. Also, the Elders realized that the technology is too easy to defeat, the ship being tracked only has to send a resonance wave back through its jump wormhole, and the weakened channel becomes so dispersed, there is no path to follow."

"Oh."

"Even I can't do that, dumdum. No way does any bunch of rotten kitties have that technology."

"OK, thanks." The main display was counting down to the moment the ship would perform a medium length jump, standard operating procedure when you suspect you are being tracked. The clock read four minutes, nineteen seconds. Longer than usual, the pilots were mindful that we had to be gentle with the jump drive. Skippy hadn't been able to get it tuned properly, he was working on it.

"We will perform two more jumps in succession," Reed told me. "To be safe."

"Good. Huh."

"Sir?"

"I'm wondering where those battlecruisers came from. Hammer Force destroyed all of the capital ships the 14th Fleet brought into the fight. Were those four battlewagons being held in reserve?"

"Could be," Reed shrugged. "In case any of our ships reached jump distance, those four ships would make a pursuit force."

"Yeah. Or they were guarding the 14th's support ships, we didn't see any of those around the fight."

Reed frowned. "Four capital ships seems like a heavy commitment for a screening force. We would task a squadron of destroyers with that job."

"We would," I agreed. "Let's hope that is a mystery we can leave unsolved. The-"

Alarms blared, a moment later the deck shook under my feet as four red icons appeared in the display. All I could do was hang onto the back of Gasquet's chair as the pilots punched the emergency jump button again.

That jump was not any fun, my stomach rebelled and I stood, bent over, breathing deeply through my nose to combat the nausea. Everyone on the bridge was doing something similar, with varying results. That is why under every console and chair, there is a barf bag.

The wave of nausea passed, I fought a sour-tasting burp, sucked in a big lungful of air, and walked to strap into my designated chair. "Skippy? Once is a coincidence. Twice is a pattern. How the hell are they tracking us?"

"I don't *know*, dumdum," he snapped, but he wasn't angry. He was *scared.*

That's when I officially got a Very, Bad, Feeling.

CHAPTER NINE

Like I said, we had gotten ambushed six times. After the second attack, we suspected the enemy had some method of tracking our jumps. After the third time, it was obvious the Maxohlx could not only predict where we jumped to, they were tracking our movements in real time.

Three minutes, thirty three seconds, every time. After each desperate jump, the enemy emerged precisely two hundred and thirteen seconds later, and precisely in position to bracket us with scarily accurate fire. What truly frightened me was that, when we tried two rapid jumps to shake our pursuers, the enemy battlecruisers emerged three minutes and thirty three seconds after the *first* of the two jumps. Holy shit. That meant the enemy had an ability to predict where we were *planning* to jump to.

There was no way to escape from a technology like that.

Seven. It happened a seventh time.

"Joe," Skippy whispered in my earpiece, while I heard him speaking to Reed. "We can't go on like this much longer. The jump drive, it's falling apart."

Three minutes, four seconds until the next attack. There would be another attack, that was certain. Another, and another, on and on until our shields couldn't recover, and our jump drive wore out. So many jumps in such a short time had to be burning out the enemy's drives also. The difference was, they had started the fight with drives in optimal condition, while ours was already barely limping along.

Only twenty one minutes had passed since the first attack, it felt like forever. Faces of the bridge crew already were reflecting exhaustion. Not physical, they were emotionally exhausted. After the near-disaster of Olympic, after the nerve-wracking struggle to recover Skippy, what the crew needed was a nice, peaceful, uneventful flight to wherever the spinner was.

It was my fault. Not just getting repeatedly jumped by the enemy, it was my fault that the crew was rattled. They had lost faith in my ability to snatch victory from the jaws of defeat. To do the impossible, yet again.

They needed hope.

No, fuck that. The crew didn't need a warm fuzzy feeling about their commander's competence, they needed a solution to the mess.

"Reed," I stood up. "I will be in your office."

She nodded, with a look I interpreted as 'This is your show'. She needed, she expected me to discover how the enemy was tracking us, and to stop it. How the hell could I understand a technology that Skippy couldn't imagine?

I slapped the button to close the door to Reed's office, angry at myself. Sitting in her chair, I didn't bother to adjust it to my size. The holographic display hovering over her desk showed a countdown timer, I wiped it away. A reminder of another looming attack was only a distraction I couldn't afford. On her desk was a bowl of chocolates. Was I hungry? No, I didn't feel like eating anything. Popping a chocolate into my mouth would take away some of the sour taste from nausea, it also gave my hands something to do while I was thinking. The crew knew I"

"Well," I said to myself, "I really fucked this up, again."

Bilby's avatar appeared. "Dude, if you don't mind me speaking freely, you need to, like, *get over yourself*, you know?"

"Uh- What-"

"You keep acting like you expect yourself to be perfect, and anytime you fall short of perfection, you beat yourself up about it. Get real, man. You're a meatsack, like Skippy says. No one is perfect, not even Skippy. *Especially* not Skippy," he muttered. "Operation Olympic worked, despite the Outsider having the unfair advantage of superior technology."

"It worked so far, now we are being tracked by-"

"Like, blah, blah, *blah*, Dude. For the Pirates, this is just same shit, different day. We will get through this, but, like, first you need to get over yourself. Do the best job you can, which has been pretty awesome, you know?"

Whoa. A reality check from Zen Master Bilberino is something I should take to heart. "Thank you, Bilby. I needed to hear that."

"Like, any time, Dude. Are we gonna get out of this mess, and go kick ass?"

"You know it."

His avatar blinked out.

Did I want another chocolate?

No. I wanted to *fix the problem.*

"Skippy, talk to me. How are we being tracked?"

His avatar shimmered to life. "Joe, I have absolutely no idea. Other than, I am certain the kitties are not doing this by themselves."

"The Outsider is aboard one of those ships?"

"Has to be. This technology is beyond my understanding, it is not anything the Elders had a workable concept for."

"In theory, what sort of mechanism is required to provide a real time view across two lightmonths?" That distance was the farthest we had managed to jump after the ambush, almost eight hundred *trillion* kilometers.

"Um, well, *we* could do it. *If* we had the entire area saturated with paired Elder comm nodes."

"That is not possible. Right?"

"The Elders couldn't do that," he snorted. "There is no conventional explanation for how the Outsider is tracking us, so don't ask me. This is something I can't even imagine."

"OK, OK. There are two potential methods, tell me if I'm wrong about this. The Outsider has some mechanism aboard those ships, that can a provide real time view across at least two lightmonths in every direction. Or, there is a device hidden somewhere aboard *Valkyrie*, that is broadcasting our position, again in real time."

"Mmm, those are the only two methods I can think of."

"Let's focus on something at this end."

"Why?"

"Because, if the problem is on the other end, there is nothing we can do about it."

"Oh. Good point."

"So, are we emitting anything? Active sensor pulses, or is the communications antenna sending out an unauthorized transmission?"

"No, and no. Bilby and I considered that after the second attack. The ship is under EMCON, Bilby even cut power to anything that can emit photons. Besides, those are all slow speed of light systems."

"Yeah, I know. Is there any way we could be sending out a burst transmission while we jump, sending our jump coordinates back through the wormhole?"

"No. No way."

"What about drones, could we be ejecting drones without knowing it? Or, ooh, the resonators we leave behind? Could that system have been hacked so the resonators broadcast our coordinates?"

"No. This is a case where I should say 'No, numbskull'. *Think* about it, Joe. A transmission, or a hacked drone or resonator, would not explain how the attackers are able to match our course and speed adjustments *after* we jump."

"Right. Shit."

"Also, I had bots conduct a hand count, a visual inspection, of all missiles and drones. All are accounted for, there have not been any uncommanded launches."

"The, uh, damn it. There is nothing else that-" I snapped my fingers. "The Elder comm node we are carrying. Could that system be hacked?"

"Come on, how could that happen? They are *paired* nodes, knucklehead. The one we took from the *Newport News* is paired with a node aboard the Hammer Force flagship, *Kilimanjaro*."

"So, the Outsider attacked *Kilimanjaro* first, and took that node."

"Do you have any idea how unlikely that is? Comm nodes are stored in a vault deep at the center of a ship. If the ship is boarded by a hostile force, the crew is instructed to detonate an explosive that crushes the node."

That was true. Active, paired comm nodes were stored inside a container that was packed with some exotic explosive charge, a charge that directed its force inward. Detonation of those charges would crush the node, and severely damage the ship. "OK but, work with me here. What if the Outsider found a way to clone one end of a paired set?"

"Clone? There would be *three* nodes entangled?"

"Yeah, like that."

"No way. The only reason you can even ask such a question is your profound ignorance of how quantum entanglement works."

"Can you think of any other way the Outsider could be tracking us in real time?"

"No," he pouted. "That doesn't mean-"

"Reed," I called her on my phone. "Eject the Elder comm node. The active one we took from the *Newport News*." With the other entangled node of the pair aboard *Kilimanjaro*, the one we had was currently useless to us anyway.

She sucked in a breath. "We are being tracked through that node?"

"That is one possibility, I would like to find out."

"Should we destroy it, Sir?"

"Just dump it overboard. No, wait. Load it aboard a drone and send it away. Limit the acceleration to *Valkyrie's* non-emergency maximum."

I could hear her grinning through the phone. "The enemy will think it's still aboard the ship?"

"That's the idea. Let's give them something to chase."

"Sir? We are coming up on the time limit for, another encounter. We can't get the node from the vault and into a drone before the enemy arrives again."

"I understand. Get it ready, then send the drone away *after* we jump." We had tried jumping early, before the 3:33 countdown expired. That didn't do us any good, the enemy simply emerged on top of us at the new location, right on the original schedule. Jumping early only meant that, when the four battlecruisers inevitably surrounded us, we had to jump again before the drive was ready. No, we had quickly learned that our best option was to wait until the enemy appeared, then jump away. The gap of two hundred and thirteen seconds between their jumps had to be a limit the enemy imposed on themselves. Or, a limit the *Outsider* imposed on the ships it had control of. As far as we knew, the crews of those ships were dead.

Why the schedule of 3:33? We didn't know. Most likely, the Outsider was limiting wear and tear on the jump drives of its battlecruisers. Killing us quickly wasn't its goal, it only needed to wear us down, until *Valkyrie* could no longer jump at all. Then, in a fight of four against one, our ship would surely be destroyed after a furious fight.

Dumping the comm node overboard after our next jump would mean we had to accept our battered shields taking more hits. There wasn't any other way to find out whether the comm node was how the Outsider was tracking us.

"Eject the node after our next jump, aye," Reed acknowledged. "Sir? Thank you."

"Don't count your chickens before they hatch."

"I heard that."

Shit.

It didn't work. We sent our comm node away, waited for the enemy to arrive, and jumped with soaring hearts and hopes.

They found us again, exactly three minutes thirty three seconds later.

At that point it was forty three minutes since the first attack. We had jumped thirteen times, without throwing off the pursuit.

"This can't continue, Joe," Skippy took off his hat, and just held it down by his side. "The drive can manage three more pathetic jumps, then the coils generators will be polarized. There is nothing I can do about that."

"I understand," I leaned Reed's office chair back. Discarding the comm node had accomplished nothing, other than giving the crew brief, false, hope. Since then, Skippy and I had debated every possibility I could dream up, and he had shot down all of them. We had no freakin' clue how the Outsider was tracking us. So, no clue how to stop it from finding us. "Ten minutes, then. Roughly."

"Ten minutes. Joe, what are you going to do?"

Reed had shot down my proposal for the crew to get into dropships and fly away. With the ship far from any habitable world, boarding a dropship would only trade a mercifully quick end for a slow, lingering death. One way or another, the end would be quick, because we would self-destruct the ship rather than allow ourselves to be captured. "I am, uh." That was a damned good question. Ten minutes. What could I accomplish in that time? Nothing much. Going to the bridge was not an option, my presence would only distract the crew. And I just couldn't stand the thought of seeing the disappointed faces of the bridge crew. "I'm going to Engineering."

"Um, why?"

"They must be working hard, I can give them a show of support."

"They need a *solution*, dumdum, not a pep talk."

"I am-" Standing up, I reached into both pockets, and pulled them inside out, showing they were empty. "Fresh out of solutions right now."

"You have not tried going to the gym yet. Or the galley. Oooh, or you could take a shower. I will turn on the water now and-"

"Skippy, don't. This is not ending with me dreaming up an idea. It just isn't, OK?"

"*Not* OK," his avatar followed me out the doorway. "You don't get to give up, that is *my* thing."

"I'm not giving up," I whispered as I jogged along the passageway. "What I am doing is facing unpleasant facts. The Outsider clearly has a technology we do not understand. Without any clue how it is tracking us, we have no chance to stop it. Just, stop talking, please. I need to be alone."

He glared at me. He also disappeared, so I had that going for me.

"Ma'am," Gasquet whispered, leaning toward the ship's captain. "The drive-"

"Three more jumps, I know," she whispered back.

"Bishop is-"

"He and Skippy are working on it, you have to trust they will find a way out of this."

"Yes Ma'am. I only meant, General Bishop is running out of time to find how the enemy is tracking us. If we use up our last jump," he ran a thumb over the plastic cover that protected the self-destruct button.

"If we have to," she patted the cover over the button on her console. "I will."

He nodded. "It has been an honor to be a Pirate."

"It has. It's not over yet, XO."

He nodded again. She knew he did not share her faith.

A faith that had been shaken when ejecting the comm node had not yielded results.

The Outsider knew that *Valkyrie* had both Skippy, and the potential means to prevent an invasion. It was desperate, it would never halt the pursuit.

She had to ask herself: was this the end?

The Engineering compartment was quiet. There was the usual background rumbling of pumps, fans, motors of all sorts. What I didn't hear was a lot of talking. The main compartment was crowded, no one was in their office or in one of the labs. Chandra was speaking, he stopped when I walked in. The guy's eyelids drooped, he was burned out.

"Sir? What can we do for you?"

"Nothing," I held up my hands. "You all must be very busy."

"We are not busy at all," he admitted. "There isn't anything we can do to stretch out the life of the coil generators. The-" A chime sounded, everyone hung onto something solid. The deck shook, dust raining down from overhead, and the ship jumped again. That was a bad one, I doubled over and had to clamp a hand over my mouth. That time, I did not lose my breakfast. Close, but I did not ralph on the deck.

Two more jumps. A little over seven minutes remaining.

Chandra understood that fact. Waving to me, he walked toward his office. "If there was anything at all we could do to keep the jump drive functioning, we would be doing it. Even if the task is hopeless, it's good for people to be busy."

In one corner of the compartment, a dozen people were clustered around a workstation. "What are they working on?"

"Making adjustments to the shield generators. Shunting power from one bank of generators to another, to even out the strain. It's not having much of an effect. The other two teams," he pointed to other workstations, where fewer people were gathered. "Are investigating the minor power drain in Reactor Three-"

"Yeah, that issue has been driving Bilby crazy."

"And the last team is tracing power flow in the communications antenna system, in case some component of that system is broadcasting, something."

"The comm system isn't FTL, it couldn't provide real time data."

"Do you want them to stop?"

"No. It's good to be busy, like you said. The-" Holy shit. My blood turned to ice. How could I have been so *stupid*? "That, uh, power drain," I said slowly. "It started right after we jumped away from Omaha?"

He blinked slowly, surprised. Perhaps concerned that I was focusing on trivia. "It did begin then. Sir, it is a very minor mystery, we haven't been-"

"*Skippy*!" I clapped my hands.

"Oh for- What?" He was outraged. "Why aren't you-"

"Shut up. The power drain in Reactor Three. Did you look into that?"

"Ugh. I haven't had *time*, numbskull. And I am letting Bilby figure it out by himself, for personal growth. He-"

"Check the reactor yourself. Do it."

"Why are you wasting time with-"

"Do exactly what I told you and do it *right fucking now*."

His avatar froze.

"Skippy? Skippy! Don't freeze on me, damn it. Come back and-"

The avatar unfroze. "Joe, if you gathered up all the hatred in the history of the universe, that would be less than how much I hate you right now."

"Haters gotta hate. What did you find?"

"An anomaly. Something that should not be there, ever. Something I can't explain. There is a pattern of coherent energy in that reactor. It's tiny, it is sort of a, spark of energy, but is it *not* natural."

"Dump that reactor. Vent the core."

"But-"

"Did you not hear me? Do it *now*."

The deck shook, alarms blared, lights flashed. My earpiece immediately sounded with Reed calling me. "Sir? What the hell hap-"

"Reed, no time to explain. Conduct the best jump we can manage, then do it again. Do not wait for the enemy to show up."

"Sir? We only have two more-"

"Fireball, I want two jumps in rapid succession and I want them *now now NOW*."

That was trust. Me trusting that our long service together allowed her to trust me.

We jumped. It was bad. We jumped again. That was worse.

It is a good thing I didn't eat a lot for breakfast that morning.

"Skippy," I called him while I got out of the shower, needing to wash up and change my uniform after losing my breakfast. "What the hell was that thing in the reactor? You described it as an energy spark?"

He sighed as his avatar appeared. "I do not know, Joe. Yes, not fully understanding the spark's technology is making me severely depressed, which I am sure you find deliciously delightful."

"You're wrong about that, Skippy. You being depressed does not make me happy at all."

"Oh, good."

"When you absolutely hate yourself, *that* makes my day."

"Joe, we really should talk less often."

"That would be OK with me. Before you go away, how can you be certain there isn't another of those, energy sparks, somewhere aboard the ship?"

"Now that I know what to look for, it's obvious. Unfortunately, the ship's sensors can't detect the thing."

"Can the sensors be modified?"

"The short answer is 'No'. In the long term, the sensor suite could be upgraded to include a special piece of equipment that is sensitive to the subspace signal the spark sends out. To answer your next question, yes I am fabricating such equipment for *Valkyrie* right now."

"Great. We need Def Com to make it a priority to install the new sensor aboard all UN warships. In case the Outsider infected any of the Task Force Hammer ships with sparks."

"Oooh, good point."

"We will stop at a relay station, and I will send a Flash priority message to Earth and Jaguar. The spark gave away our location by transmitting a signal through subspace?"

"It's not a transmission, nothing crude like photons are involved. As I said, I do not understand the technology. It basically, um, how do I break this down Barney style? Hmm. OK, you can think of the spark as spoofing the location tags."

"Uh, what does that mean?"

"The universe is basically all just information. How does a particle know it is a lepton instead of a meson?"

"You don't actually expect me to answer that question?"

"Dude," he laughed. "Not a chance. My point is, every particle interacts with spacetime, to exchange information about what it is, and where it is. The 'What' includes aspects like how it interacts with other particles, such as its mass, spin, whether it reacts to the weak nuclear force, that sort of thing. When we create what your people call 'Exotic Matter', it is exotic because the manufacturing process changes the information embedded in it. So, a hydrogen atom of exotic matter can have a mass greater or lesser than an ordinary hydrogen atom."

"OK, I knew that. It still blows my mind."

"If you understood how the universe really works, your head would explode."

"Then don't explain that, please. What's the deal with location tags?"

"They tell the particle *where* it is. My theory, and currently this is just a theory, is the spark attached itself to a core particle, probably some type of boson."

"I mean, a boson was my guess."

"Joe, people only become aware of your ignorance when you open your mouth to say something stupid."

"Silence is my best option, got it."

"So, the spark altered the core particle's location tag, so it considered itself to be *there* instead of *here*. By 'There' I mean wherever the Outsider was at the time. Effectively, that particle was aboard the Outsider's ship, and the spark used the particle to report our position, course, and speed."

"How did it do that?"

"I don't know. Most likely, it altered another property of the particle, turning it on and off, sort of like Morse code?"

"Is this technology anything like the quachines you put in my head?"

"No. Not even close. It is *sad* how little you understand, despite my best efforts to smack some knowledge on you."

"Would you prefer my head to explode?"

"Um-"

"That was the wrong answer, beer can." Waving a hand through his hologram, I dismissed him with, "Go away, and fix the jump drive."

Valkyrie's jump drive was down hard. If it had hands, it would have tapped out. Skippy peevishly told me he required at least four days of intense work to fix the thing, four days during which he would not have time to listen to monkeys screeching at him.

If I had known how to get him to shut up for more than a day, I would have smashed that drive a long time ago.

The drive being offline was a major problem, a huge risk. The enemy was certainly searching for us, though without being able to cheat, they had an enormous area to scan. They couldn't cheat, not anymore. Dumping the core had flushed the energy pattern out with the superheated plasma, and by jumping quickly, we left that energy, whatever it was, behind. The bad jump had taken us a distance of five lightweeks. The worse jump only traversed nine lightdays. A total of forty four lightdays from our previous position. The wavefront of gamma radiation from our jumps was expanding outward at the speed of light, as the jumps had been chaotic, we hadn't been able to mask or focus those bursts. That was OK, as long as Skippy didn't take too long to get the drive back online.

While the ship wasn't going anywhere, and with Skippy tasked only with handling the jump drive, Bilby and the engineering team worked to patch up the ship as best they could. Before Skippy went silent, he verified the other reactors, and every power system aboard the ship, were free of uninvited guests. A guest that was uninvited, and unexplainable. Skippy had not a single clue how a relatively tiny spark of energy could reach across a vast distance to provide real time location data. It bothered me that he did not understand the technology involved. How could we prevent it from victimizing us again, if we didn't understand what it was, or how it got aboard the ship? Until we had answers to those questions, I had to be satisfied with our narrow escape from the jaws of death.

That, plus imagining the howling pain the Outsider felt when it realized its quarry had gotten away, warmed my heart. I can be a jerk like that sometimes.

Gasquet came into the galley, while I was drinking coffee and writing an outline of a report on the incident. He lifted his cup with a raised eyebrow. I waved him over to sit across the table from me, and I closed my laptop.

"Sir," he took a sip of coffee. "I hope we do not ever go through *that* again."

"We have endured worse. Each time, I say Never Again. It is to our credit that we only make *new* mistakes."

He smiled at that. "Making new mistakes is not actually an objective, though?"

"Sometimes it seems like it is."

"What about the spinner, Sir? Do we know where it is?"

"*I* don't. Skippy was going through a list of the stars in the Milky Way, when we got jumped, and he had to drop the search. He might have found the star the collector came from, I'll ask him when he has the drive back online."

"It would be good to know this was all worth the effort."

"And the pain," I nodded. "And the people we lost. We should have an answer to that question in a few days."

"Sir? How did you know? About the reactor glitch?"

"I didn't. It was a guess. A good guess, but I didn't *know*. We had two unexplained anomalies at the same time; a power drain, and an FTL tracking system. I took a shot that they were related. It's on me that I didn't get Skippy to inspect that reactor as soon as he came back aboard."

"Bilby told me the reactor glitch was a very minor issue."

"It was a minor issue only for our power supply, and fuel reserves. I do not like surprises, especially the kind that can potentially be nasty. That is a lesson learned for me: in the future, any mysterious glitches get a full investigation immediately." That was a lesson I should have learned a *long* time ago. Skippy had caused plenty of glitches on enemy ships, sensors, strategic defense satellites, and other systems. They appeared to be minor incidents the enemy hadn't been sufficiently concerned about, until their ship exploded, or the SD network realized it no loner had control of its weapons.

Shit. The tables had turned, and now *we* can fall victim to sketchy stuff. We needed to be one hundred percent on our guard, at all times.

Despite what I said to Gasquet, by the second day of Skippy's silence, I was growing itchy for an update. On his progress with repairing the abused jump drive, and on whether he had found the collector's home star. Casually, while on my couch, I called him. "Hey, Skippy, you got a minute?"

A distorted version of his voice responded with, "Skippy is mad busy right now, fixing equipment that *he* didn't break. If this is an emergency, press One for Skippy, although that might mean he has to stop all the progress he has made and start *this* shit all over again. It's your call, knucklehead."

Wisely, I just said, "We can talk later."

"Excellent choice."

Still, not knowing was driving me crazy. "Bilby?" I went with my second choice for information.

"Yo, Your Dudeness." His avatar was wearing a hardhat and a tool belt. "What up?"

"Are you too busy to talk?"

"Nah, Man, it's all good. We are *alive*, you know? That is like, way better than being dead. Thanks for that, by the way."

"You're welcome. The next time you find something you can't explain, tell me about it right away."

"OK, wow, like, can you explain the appeal of dubstep music?"

"No one can, sorry. What I meant is, anything about the ship's operation that you don't understand. No more mysteries, agreed?"

"Righteous, Dude."

"Good. Is Skippy making progress?"

"He isn't talking to me. Based on what I see the bots doing, he is performing a complete teardown of the coil generators, and all the feeder systems. He is like, *hella* busy."

"That's good. Has he said anything to you about locating the star where the collector came from?"

"He hasn't, sorry. He was working on that before, you know. Shit happened."

"Got it. Thanks, that's all I wanted to know."

“If Skippy tells me about, either thing, I’ll let you know?”

“Anytime, day or night. Seriously, wake me up if you have to.”

“Um like, you hate it when Skippy does that.”

“I hate it when he wakes me up at three in the morning, to complain that anyone can clearly see Clark Kent is Superman.”

“Gotcha,” he laughed. “You know, that wouldn’t be a problem if Superman wore a mask, like Batman, or Spider Man.”

“If we ever find a way to go back in time, I will mention that to the guys who invented Superman.”

CHAPTER TEN

Skippy contacted me the next morning, and his avatar appeared only after I got out of bed, so my day started well. "Hey, Joe."

"Hey," I gave him an automatic reply, while I checked my phone for the ship's daily status report. There was nothing surprising listed, so I scrolled down to- "Ooh, the galley is serving pizza tonight. I knew this would be a good day."

"*That* is your criteria for a good day?"

"It's enough, considering that I know a bunch of crappy stuff will also happen to me today. Although, huh. Is this going to be real pizza?"

"What do you mean?"

"One time, Margaret made pizza, and she used a cauliflower crust, and didn't warn me about it."

"It was awful?"

"No, it was good. Kind of like a thin-crust New York style pie."

"If you liked it, what was the problem?"

"It's the principle of the thing. You don't sneak healthy food on someone, you're supposed to warn them first."

"Whatever. Shouldn't you want to eat healthy food?"

"That is one of the three components of a balanced diet, sure. Healthy food, fiber, and junk food. You need all three for complete nutrition."

"I don't think that is-"

"It's *science*."

"Ugh. I can't even- Is New York style your favorite type of pizza?"

"My favorite is usually what's on my plate right then. Except for some kinds of Chicago style deep-dish pizza. If the dish is too deep, it's basically a casserole on an edible plate. I'm also not fond of Rhode Island style red strips."

"Red *strips*?"

"It's a rectangular strip of crust, with tomato sauce on top, no cheese or other toppings. Sometimes, it's served cold. I mean, people in Rhode Island like it, so everyone has their own taste. My real fave is Detroit style. It's also a rectangle, not round. Baked in a heavy steel pan, and there is cheese on top of the crust, that bubbles up and caramelizes at the edge from the heat of the pan. Sometimes, there is a sort of racing stripe of sauce down the middle of each slice. It's delicious."

"How can you meatsacks have created so many different ways to prepare food? It's just fuel."

"It's not. And we don't always do good things, when we're creating new foods. Like, I recently learned that humans *created* broccoli, and cauliflower. People way back when were growing a type of cabbages, and the heads that poked up from the center I guess usually got discarded. Then, some jackass decided to try *eating* those flower heads, and liked it so much," I stuck out my tongue. "That he started growing cabbages just for the heads, and that's why school children now have to suffer eating broccoli and cauliflower. Damn, if we ever find a way to make a time machine, I am going back to smack some sense into that guy. Oh sorry, what did you want to talk about?"

"You know what, Joe? I lost so much brainpower listening to you, that I now need to reboot." His avatar faded away.

I got through an entire morning without Skippy bothering me with some nonsense. It *was* a good day.

The jump drive was declared to be fully operational, although Skippy wanted Bilby to run a diagnostic on the entire system, before we attempted a short test jump. His caution was both good and bad. Good that the absent-minded beer can didn't assume he could not possibly have made a mistake. Bad that the ship's sensors had detected faint active sensor pulses. The Outsider had its ships out searching for us, we were a sitting duck if the drive wasn't fully ready to work its magic.

"Hey, Skippy," I called him from my office. "Thank you very much for all the hard work."

"Ugh. You have *no* idea."

"What I do have an idea about, is how outraged the Outsider was when it saw it had been beaten *again* by Skippy the Magnificent."

"Well, that is true, hee hee," he chuckled happily. "I don't like to brag-"

"Bullshit," I laughed. "You love to brag."

"I wouldn't have to," he sniffed, "if filthy meatsacks could appreciate my extreme level of awesomeness."

"To show our appreciation, tomorrow will be a bonus karaoke night."

"*Oooooh*," his jaw dropped open.

"But wait! There's more. Before karaoke starts, we will watch The Princess Bride."

"Ooooh, I *love* it! I can quote every line from that movie."

"So can I."

"Joe, the crew watched that movie back when you were in command of the ship."

"Yes, and this is a new crew. Also, I conducted a survey, and twenty one members of the crew have never seen it."

"*Huuuuuh*," he gasped. Lowering his voice, he asked, "Should I investigate whether they are enemy agents?"

"They are just culturally deprived. The movie is not a big thing in China. Or France. Or apparently, Canada, since Frey has never seen it."

"*Whaaaat*? Oh Joe, we have a responsibility to smack some cultural enlightenment on those miscreants."

"That's my thinking. OK so, now that vacation is over-"

"I was not on vacation, you jackass."

"I meant, the *crew* enjoyed a glorious four days of vacation."

"Why do you hate, Joe?"

"It's a hobby."

"You should try another hobby, like collecting stamps," he muttered.

"My point is, now that you're not working frantically to fix the jump drive, can you get back to searching for which star the collector came from?"

"Um, wow. I had forgotten all about that stupid thing."

"Your laser focus on our core mission is a constant source of comfort."

"Oh, shut *up*."

"Do you still have the data from when you energized the collector, or have you forgotten that also?"

"I have it, numbskull. I never forget anything."

"Do you want me to rewind the audio, to when you just said you had forgotten it?"

"Shut *up*. Fine, I will look for the star. But I also need to practice for karaoke, so it could take a while."

"Multitask, please."

After a starship has been on an extended cruise, cargo bays start to become empty as the crew eats the food, and the ship burns through spare parts and consumable items. The ship's logistics officer works to consolidate remaining items, to free up empty bays for the crew's use. In one empty bay, the crew set up a beach volleyball court, complete with sand cranked out by the fabricators. Sand that included rubber pellets for extra cushioning, we didn't want anyone to get injured if they were too competitive.

Walking to the Engineering section at the aft end of the pressure hull, I heard shouting coming from a passageway to the left. Not angry shouting, it was excited, and more than one person. "Skippy," I stopped walking. "What's going on over there?" The beach volleyball court was to my right, and at that time of day, bots were scooping up the sand so it could be cleaned before it was used again.

"Oh, nothing, Joe. You um, heh heh, don't need to know anything about that."

"A moment ago, I was merely curious. Now, I *do* have to go see what is going on."

"Ugh. Why are you so-"

"*What* is going on?"

"Why can't you ever take a hint?"

"I did. The hint was you saying 'heh heh', that means you're up to something bad."

"It's not bad, it's, um, a surprise. For you. Yeah, that's it."

"I hate surprises, Skippy." With that, I walked toward the sound. It was a group of people, four sitting on folding chairs in front of a big holographic display, with a dozen other people standing behind them. The four were playing a video game.

Wow. Especially on the big display, the graphics were so realistic, I would have assumed the video was a recording from mech suit cameras.

Ducking back out the doorway before anyone saw me and interrupted the game, I called Skippy. "It's a video game, why don't you want me to see it?"

"I don't want you to see it *yet*."

"Is this a training aid, or a program for rehearsing operations?"

"Eh, it could be. Joe, remember I told you that I was working with a video game company?"

"You never told me that."

"Hmm, well, I meant to. Anywho, I was approached by several companies, and I selected one to work with. The graphics engine powering that game is my design."

"It's impressive. The people in the game look completely real."

"Ah, it's good enough, considering the crappy processing capability of the game console they expect me to squeeze the software into."

"That isn't running on the ship's network?" That truly impressed me.

"No. The people in there are beta testing it for me, and to be useful, that testing has to be done on the setup customers will be using in their homes."

"Customers will have a three meter tall holographic display in their homes?"

"Of course not. We are using a larger display so any flaws will be more visible. Like, the stupid graphics engine made one of the character's eyelashes curve down instead of up. And another character has a thumb on each side of one hand. That's all stuff easily fixed."

"Cool. What is the game?"

"I'm calling it Call Of Duty: Merry Band of Pirates. But because Def Com is run by a bunch of *dicks* with no imagination, won't allow that name to continue into production. It will either be 'Special Mission Group', or 'Task Force Black'."

"Merry Band of Pirates? The game is based on *us*?"

"Loosely based."

"The game play doesn't allow players to experience actual missions we performed, does it? Our tactics and capabilities are sensitive information."

"Don't worry, Def Com has vetted all the missions in the current version of the game. Besides, if customers had to experience a real mission, they would be bored out of their minds. Most of what you military people do is get ready, then sit around waiting to go into action. That doesn't exactly make for a fun game."

"Yes, but if an enemy got a copy of the game, they-"

"Would be confused if they ever met the Pirates, because the tactics in that game are nothing like the team uses on a real mission. Trust me, we got this."

"Why didn't I know about this? I would love to be a beta tester."

"Um, your video game skills are not the best, you-"

"That's why I am perfect for the beta team. You already have experts, you need to include a regular person, with average skills." That was a lie, I had mad skills. "Otherwise, the game will be too hard for most of your audience."

"Hmm. Well, I suppose that is a very good point."

"Great, then I will-"

"Whoa! No no no. Slow your roll there, cowboy. The game is already in progress."

"Right," I turned toward the doorway. "I'll just watch for a while."

Of course, the players paused the game when the commanding officer walked in on them. "Keep going," I waved for them to continue.

Embarrassed faces avoided my eyes.

"What?"

"Sir, it," Holmqvist finally said. "We're just testing. The game isn't ready for the public yet. There are a lot of," he searched for the right word. "Adjustments, to be made."

"That's fine. I just want to watch."

"Uh well, Sir, the game supports multiplayer," he indicated the three players on the chair next to him. "Or single player. In multiplayer mode, you select a character."

"Who did you select?"

"Myself." Now he was really embarrassed.

"*You* are a character in the game?"

The crowd nodded. "Most of us are," Holmqvist confirmed.

"Current Pirates only, or," I hesitated to ask the question. "Former crew also?"

"You can't play as Colonel Smythe, if that's what you're asking, Sir."

"Good."

"He would be a very high value character anyway."

"High value?"

"The game is sort of like Madden football. Each character has a skill score. When you are assembling a team you have a budget for total points, so no one can just select the four highest rated characters."

"That makes sense. What is your skill score, if you don't mind me asking?"

"I'm an 87, Sir."

"I believe it."

"Colonel Frey was a 96, before, um-"

"Yeah. She is not a playable character?"

He took a breath. "Not now, Sir."

"Good. Out of curiosity, what is the skill score of the Joe Bishop character?" The response was an embarrassed murmur, people avoided my eyes again. "Did I just ask a stupid question? Or," the answer suddenly dawned on me. "Did that asshole beer can give a low score?"

"It's not that, Sir." Holmqvist had a pained expression, like he wanted to be anywhere else at that moment. "Your character is, an NPC."

"I'm a *Non-Playable Character*? What the f- *SKIPPY*!"

"We're sorry," said a distorted voice from a bad answering service. "Skippy is not available right now. If you'd like to leave a message, press-"

"I'd *like* to strangle you. Here," I snapped my fingers, "*now*."

"Ugh." His avatar appeared. "I did try to warn you, numbskull."

"Why is the Joe Bishop in the game a freaking NPC?"

"Come on, Joe, you know the answer to that. Do you want me to say it, with all these people around?"

"Especially with these people here. Explain yourself."

"You made me do this. Joe, having you as a playable character didn't work because you never *do* anything."

"Uh, *excuse* me? I-"

"All you ever do is sit in your office, or on the bridge, and *talk*. In a game, that is deadly boring, no one wants to be that character."

"I do plenty of action stuff, Skippy. Who brought you into that wormhole? Me, that's who. You requested that *I* go with you."

"Yes, and I instantly regretted that, since you exited out the wrong door and we had to find your sorry ass."

"What I remember is-"

"We can argue about this all day."

"What I do is make plans, and make decisions, Skippy. Those are critical to mission success."

"Yes knucklehead, but the game isn't about pre-mission decisions or planning. It's about executing the plan, and getting the mission completed successfully. It's about *action*. That's the fun part, that's why players want to be STAR operators, or pilots, or gunners, or really anyone who *does* something. Not a guy who sits in a chair and orders other people to do stuff."

"Show me this character."

"Don't say I didn't warn you."

OMG.

That *rotten* little shithead. All the Joe Bishop NPC could do was sit in an office chair, or in a seat along the back bulkhead of the bridge. He spoke in a moronic Barney voice, and said things like 'Brilliant plan Skippy, that is a go', or 'Excellent job everyone'. My face turned red when the character announced, 'It's time to make the donuts'.

"I do not talk like that, and I don't look," I pointed to the character who was clearly a couple fries short of a Happy Meal. "Anything like that."

"Really Joe, *really*?"

"Remove my character from, the game, right now."

"Ooh sorry, no can do, Joe."

"I never agreed to license my name and image for this stupid game."

"You sort of did, Joe. You signed away your Name and Image License rights when you got your last promotion. The US Army authorized the license."

"That-" My anger was growing. My *sons* would someday play that game, and see their father portrayed as a moron. "I never-"

"Sir?" Holmqvist prompted me. "We always select a different commander for the Pirates. To, um," he realized he needed to give me a damned good reason. "To shake things up, Sir."

"Who are the other commanders?"

"Um, there's Chang, and Simms, and Reed, plus some characters a player can create."

"Those are all NPCs also?"

"Um, no."

"Who is the commander of the Pirates in this game now?"

"Colonel Simms, Sir. She sets up the scenario to kick off the game."

It got worse. Not only was Simms not an NPC, her character looked and sounded awesome. Later in the game when *Valkyrie* was infiltrated by some scary looking aliens, she fought them on the bridge, killing the last one by stabbing it with a claw she broke off another alien. Her character even had a cool tagline she spoke as she killed that alien: 'That's how Pirates do it *Barney style'*.

Shit. Even I wanted to play the Simms character.

What did I expect? There was a Joe Bishop *in*action figure, I had one of them on shelf in my office at home. Of course my video game character was an NPC.

"Skippy, can you change the voice, to be like mine?"

"The audience finds it *hilarious* when you talk like Barney, so, um-" He saw me giving him The Look. "So, um, heh heh, of course that voice was only a placeholder for the beta version. I'll replace it before we ship the product."

"I want a game my boys can play, without being embarrassed about me."

"Joe. What you should worry about is the horrible Dad Jokes you tell."

"There is nothing wrong with Dad Jokes."

"Really? You should ask your boys about that."

"Dad Jokes are corny because you're telling a joke to children. The setup and punchline have to be simple and obvious."

"Uh huh, hmm, interesting. Then, why do fathers keep telling those jokes when the children are older?"

"At that point, the fact that you tell awful jokes *is* the joke. What kids care about is you make the effort to engage with them."

"Damn. Being a meatsack is way complicated."

"Yeah," I agreed. "It can be."

"Well, shit," Skippy appeared on my desk, five hours after he resumed searching for a star that matched the collector. Five hours since he started, four hours after I started worrying about what was taking him so long. And before he resumed the search, he had insisted Bilby complete a diagnostic on the rebuilt jump drive, and we conduct two test jumps. We did that, the drive performed flawlessly. So, it concerned me that the expression on his holographic face was, not quite disappointment. Consternation? No, that's not the word I'm looking for. Frustration, that's it.

The expression on his holographic face gave me a bad feeling. "You are not making me happy right now."

"Hey, you think *I'm* happy about it? This sucks. I searched the entire stellar catalog, and there is no star out there that matches the signature of the collector we have."

"Well, shit."

"That's what I just said."

"So we- Wait. What stellar catalog? You mean a current list of stars?"

"We are searching for the star *now*," he said slowly. "So of course I am using a-"

"I kind of expected you would use a catalog from your memory, showing stars as they were back in your day."

"Back in my *day*? Are you saying that time has passed me by and now I am-"

"I only meant, back before the AI war. Closer to the time when the collector was, made, or set up, or whatever."

"Oh. That's reasonable. Yes, I would do that, except my memory of such detail from back then is scrambled and incomplete. So, I'm using a current catalog. And, I got nothin'."

"All this was for *nothing*? The stupid thing doesn't- Wait. Oh, uh," I snapped my fingers, feeling my shoulders shudder with relief. "OK, you searched only the Milky Way galaxy, right? Now, expand your search to all of the satellite galaxies and star clusters or whatever."

"Oooh, that is a brilliant idea, Joe."

"I do what I can."

He gave me an eyeroll. "Apparently your brilliance does not extend to recognizing sarcasm. I already searched the satellite galaxies, you knucklehead."

"Shiiiiiit. You are sure? You double checked everything?"

"Yes, you ninny. I even got Bilby to run through the dataset with me."

"Duuuuude," Bilby groaned as his business on top, party on the bottom slacker avatar appeared. "That exercise was like, the tedious pinnacle of *tedium*, you know?"

"I appreciate your effort."

"Next time Skippy asks me to do something like that, can you promise to unplug me?"

"I'm sure we can find a better solution. OK, uh, what else can we try?"

Skippy rolled his eyes. "By 'we' you mean 'me'?"

"Yeah, that. Unless there's something I can do?"

"Find a new and amusing way to scratch yourself, to entertain me while I grind through an enormous mountain of data?"

"I'll see what I can do. Seriously, what's the next step?"

"There is none, you numbskull."

"Skippy, we can't just give up. The collector was set up for a particular star, right?"

"Um. I think so."

"You *think* so? Holy- You don't *know*? You were guessing about this?"

"Well, duh. The collector was not designed to identify its assigned star, that is a side effect of, like you said, it being adjusted to the spectrum of a particular star. The Elders never imagined a collector would be ejected from its solar system, so it's not like they attached a tag to it with a sign 'If found, please return to, wherever'."

"General Dude," Bilby spoke before I could explode at the irresponsible beer can. "Skippy is a hundred percent right about that stupid thing. It *was* set up to optimize its absorption of light from a specific star. There just isn't a star matching that spectrum in this galaxy."

"How do you explain that?"

Bilby shrugged. "I dunno. Like, maybe that collector was defective, and got discarded? That could explain why it was found drifting in empty space."

"Defective, how?"

"Um, like, it couldn't be adjusted to match a star. That could explain why we can't find a star with that spectrum."

"Shiiiiit." If Skippy had given that answer, I would have argued he had to be wrong. But Bilby just stated the facts, he didn't let his ego get in the way. "OK, OK, I hear you, but think about this: What are the odds that the *one* freakin' collector that was found, is one of the few that are defective?"

"Actually, hmm," Skippy rubbed his chin. "We don't know how many collectors were discarded during the adjustment process, it could be a very difficult procedure with a high failure rate. The Thuranin, for example, still discard more than ninety three percent of the jump drive coils they create, because of microscopic flaws that develop while the crystals are growing."

"OK but-"

"You know, actually, a defective collector is much more likely to have been found. Instead of requiring an unusual chain of events that led to it being ejected from a solar system, the useless collector might have been intentionally launched away, so it didn't become a navigation hazard."

"Great. That is fan-TASTIC, Skippy. We assembled the most powerful task force in human history, risked thousands of lives, lost people and starships, and only *now* does it occur to you that a collector found in deep space is likely to have been defective?"

"Well, it seems obvious *now*, dumdum."

"I don't believe this. Is there any chance that you're wrong?"

"You think," he said slowly, "that both Bilby and I misread the dataset?"

"No, but could the data be wrong? Where did you get this information?"

"Dude like," Bilby answered. "It came from the Maxohlx and Rindhalu. They have the most comprehensive survey data."

"I get that. Do their surveys cover *every* star in the galaxy? What about a star that is inside a gas cloud, like a nebula? Or, a star in a place like the Roach Motel?"

"The spiders have that covered, Dude. Except for stars the Elders concealed, but the collector could not have come from there, it couldn't get out, Duh. The spiders have had like, a *long* time to examine every star out there. I know where you're going with this question, Dude. You want to know if we found any stars where the data from the spiders and kitties was different. We did, but like that was a matter of the Rindhalu survey results being more precise, the data wasn't wrong. Sorry Your Dudeness, this isn't what we all expected to find."

While I heard his words, all I could think about was the stack of condolence letters, that would be delivered to the families of all the people we lost at Ohmeharikahn. All for *nothing*. The worst part was it all could have been avoided if I had simply asked the right questions, and not just blindly trusted Skippy. How had I been so recklessly *stupid*? That was simple: I had so much wanted the collector to be the solution to stopping the Outsider, that I had ignored any sign that the thing might not be the miraculous answer to my prayers.

"OK, what about, uh-" I wasn't ready to give up. Not yet. Not *ever*. "You know where the thing was found, right? And the ship that took the thing aboard kept a record of its speed and direction at the time?"

"Yes, but," Skippy sighed. "You have to understand that-"

"Then you know roughly where it came from. Can you focus on that area? We can fly there and conduct our own survey."

"Dude like, I hate to burst your bubble," Bilby shook his head. "That thing could have come from anywhere. It was traveling slowly and was drifting toward a supermassive blue white star, that eventually would have pulled in close and slingshotted it away in another direction. We already tried to predict where it came from, and we could only backtrack for seven hundred thousand years. Beyond that, there are too many unknown variables. None of the stars it passed by in that time have anything close to the signature that matches the collector."

People use the word 'stubborn' like it's a bad thing. I prefer the word 'persistent'. "Fine, thanks for checking that. Based on the signature of the collector, can you predict anything about the type of star it was being matched to?"

"Other than that it was a red dwarf star, Dude, sorry, no. Assuming the matching process failed, there is no way for us to know how far along the process got, before the Elders gave up and discarded it. We thought of that also."

"OK, OK, then-"

"Joe," Skippy interrupted gently. "You're beating yourself up about this, and not accomplishing anything. Go, um, spend some time in a flight simulator, or lift weights in the gym, or make yourself a sandwich."

"Uh huh. You think that will lead me to a solution?"

"I *think* you need to accept this effort to capture the collector didn't work out."

"I am not giving up, Skippy."

"Of course you won't," he sighed again. "That is both your strength, and your weakness. We will not give up on trying to stop the Outsider, I'm not suggesting we do that. What I am suggesting is, we try something else."

A tiny spark of hope flared inside me. "Like what?"

"I don't know, Joe, that's your job. Hey, I had pretty much given up on the fight, before you urged me to search inside my matrix for a clue to how the Elders planned to stop an Outsider invasion."

"We forget about the collector, and start from zero again?!"

"Not from *zero*. We now know the Elders had a plan for stopping an Outsider invasion, we know the mechanism is some type of large scale device. I thought the collector would lead us to it, I was," he sighed. "Wrong."

Skippy admitting to being wrong was so unusual, I froze just as I was about to explode at him. "We," I slumped back in the chair, staring at the ceiling. "We went through so much effort to get that collector, it *can't* have been for nothing."

"Hey Dude?" Bilby drawled. "I read a book on like, philosophy, you know? One thing it said is the hardest thing in life is to accept you can't change the past. Bad things happen and you can't make it go away. That's like, profound. I understand you want the collector to mean something, but all it means is we did the best job we could, with the information we had at the time. That sucks, it is what it is, man."

Those were wise words from the ship's slacker AI. He was right, a hundred percent. On Earth, there are cultures who are so obsessed with grievances about their past, they can't move forward. Skippy wanted me to let it go. I couldn't let it go, I could set it aside so it didn't get in the way of finding a real solution.

If there was another solution. The real question I needed to ask was whether Joe Bishop was the best person to search for a solution. Who had fucked up Operation Olympic? Me, that's who. Should I step aside, so I didn't get in the way of someone else finding a way to stop the Outsider?

Before I made that decision, I should talk with Smythe's avatar, get his advice.

Nah, that wasn't necessary.

He would only say that I already knew the answer, that my problem wasn't lack of ability, it was my inner self doubt. Thank you, Jeremy Smythe.

Fuck it. All I could do was my best. Me working on the problem didn't mean someone else couldn't explore alternative solutions at the same time.

"Bilby, you're right. Olympic happened, it's over, it's a, sunk cost, or whatever you call it. What *do* we know, from the collector?"

"Um like I said, we know the type of star it was set up for: a red dwarf."

"Great. That narrows the list to about seventy percent of the stars in the Milky Way."

"It makes sense," he added. "Red dwarfs burn slowly, so they can last a long, long time. The Elders designed everything to function for millions, even billions of years."

"How do you know it was set up for a red dwarf, if you think the thing is defective?"

"Because Joe," Skippy answered. "The material the collector is constructed of can only be tuned to the spectrum of a red dwarf."

"OK, thanks. So, that is something we know for certain, it's not a guess."

"It's not. Joe, what do you want to do next?"

"First, if anyone asks either of you what you found, say you're still working on the list."

"Um, I'm not down for lying to Colonel Reed," Bilby said. "She is captain of the ship, she should know."

"I will tell her, after I have exhausted all possibilities for extracting information from the damned collector."

Skippy shook his head sadly. "Joe, I don't like this any more than you do, but we *have* exhausted all-"

"No, we haven't. This is no different from any other problem we have tackled. It is impossible, until we look at it from a different angle."

"I don't understand how a different *angle* will change the facts."

"You never do. Uh!" I shushed him. "You said it: this is my wheelhouse. The two of you applied straightforward science, now it's time to try something different. Right now, I don't know what that is, and alerting the crew would only damage morale. Give me a day."

"Okey dokey," Bilby agreed. "If Colonel Reed asks, I'll just tell her we are still working on it?"

"Yes, and that is the truth, so you won't be lying."
"Ah man, I gotta tell you, it feels like lying. This is sketchy stuff."
"Welcome to the Merry Band of Pirates."

CHAPTER ELEVEN

I did not need a day. Less than an hour later, I had the answer. In the galley, I made a ham sandwich so I wouldn't be working out on an empty stomach, then went to my cabin to change clothes. In a drawer were my official US Army PT uniform shorts and T-shirt, khaki green in the latest issue. Also I had the previous blue uniform T-shirt that technically was no longer in service, I had kept it anyway. Uniform standards aboard the ship were relaxed most of the time, for other than official fitness activities, everyone in the gym wore civilian T-shirts and shorts. There was a stack of regular T-shirts in another drawer, I was too lazy to select one, so I pulled out the blue Army shirt. Or, as I held it up to the bathroom light, a shirt that used to be blue. There were a few holes around the neck, and one under the right arm, it was just getting broken in. The color certainly couldn't be described as blue any longer, the years had faded it to a grayish-

"Holy shit," I dropped the shirt on the floor. "*Damn* it!"

"Don't be a baby, Joe," Skippy appeared, rolling his eyes. "Just pick up the shirt. The floor was cleaned this morning, and the five second rule applies."

"I don't care whether the shirt is dirty, Skippy."

"You don't? Then why the-"

"I found it."

"Um, you found the *spinner*? I can assure you that it's not hiding under that shirt."

"Not the spinner, you ass. I found a way to identify the star."

"Mm hmm. Interesting. Since you left your office, you made no phone calls. The only person you talked with was a petty officer in the galley, and the two of you only talked about the new Green Bay Packers football stadium."

"Yes. He thinks the new stadium should have a dome. Dave Czajka is from Milwaukee, he told me if the Packers build a dome, they might as well play flag football."

"Among all the dumb things guys argue about, sports has to be the dumbest."

"I can't dispute that."

"So, we have established that you received no new information since you left your office, yet suddenly you have the answer."

"Ayuh. Like I told you, I looked at it from another perspective."

"This will either be amusing, or make me hate you more than I thought possible."

"I'd bet on the second one. You see this shirt?" I picked up the garment that used to be a medium shade of blue, with the yellow ARMY on the chest faded so it was more pink than the original color.

"If you are testing my vision, I can-"

"This shirt used to be blue."

"Yes, I remember you were all excited when the Army switched the PT uniform from black to blue."

"The black was too hot in sunlight, and it made you invisible in the dark. The new khaki is better, except it shows sweat stains too easily."

"You monkeys are incredibly sweaty, yuck," he gagged.

"Yes, let's focus on that. The shirt used to be blue, now it has faded to something more like a blueish gray. *Time* has changed its color spectrum signature."

"Uh huh, yes, that is an astonishingly insightful observation, Joe. There is an extra special juice box waiting for you in the galley."

"Seriously? You have no idea what I'm saying?"

"To be honest, I am afraid to guess what random bits of nonsense are bouncing around in your skull."

"I will break this down for you Barney Style."

"Huuuh," he gasped. "How *dare* you?"

"As a star ages, it burns more of its helium fuel, and so its color changes. Its spectral signature *changes*, get it?"

"Um, yes, I do."

"Great! Based on what you know of red dwarf stars in the candidate area, can you create a model to run them backward, to see what spectrum of light they were emitting, back when the Elders were still here?"

"Oooh, that is truly a genius idea, Joe."

"Well," I almost blushed from his praise, "I don't know if it can be called genius, but-"

"It *is* genius, because I had the same idea, and already ran the model you asked for, Duh. There is no star, in this or the surrounding galaxies, that *ever* matched the signature of the collector."

"Shit," I stared at the balled-up shirt in my hand, as if it was at fault for embarrassing me. "You are *sure* about that?"

"Stars age at a predictable rate, dumdum. It's just simple math, even smart monkeys could run the model. Before you ask, Bilby checked my results, he agrees."

"Well, shit. Now I feel like an idiot. I insulted your intelligence."

"You insulted the entire concept of *science*, Joe," he chuckled. "Hmm. Rather than making me amused or hate you, this is just sad. The galaxy is in crisis, and that is the best you can do?"

"Sorry. I'll try harder."

"What you truly insulted was yourself. You have done *so* much better in the past."

"I *said*, I will try harder."

"Hey, if a T-shirt inspired a brainstorm, maybe you should check your magic sock drawer, see if there's a solution in there."

"I don't need advice on how to think like a meatsack, you ass."

He was wrong. Nothing in my sock drawer gave me an idea, nor did going to the galley for coffee spark a revelation. Was I concerned that this time was different, that no clever monkey idea could overcome the facts, and the cold hard math?

Yeah, I was concerned about that.

Reed was coming toward me in the passageway, and as she looked up to see me, a frown she couldn't hide flashed across her face. It wasn't anything personal, it was just a matter of a general officer being aboard *her* ship, and she probably felt like every time she turned around, I was looking over her shoulder.

Hey, I get it. Back when Hans Chotek was aboard the old *Flying Dutchman*, I asked Skippy to alert me to his movements, so I could avoid bumping into him in a passageway. Had Reed asked Bilby to track me so she could avoid awkward small talk? Apparently not.

"Sir," she nodded, and then because neither of us had been walking at the determined pace that signaled 'I am very busy and do not have time to talk', she had to say something. "How is Skippy doing on the search?" She glanced at her watch.

It had been over six hours since Skippy resumed working on identifying the star the collector belonged to. He thinks so fast, she knew he should have been done with a simple database search several hours ago. So, she understood the search had moved beyond a simple database query. "He's working on it. With Bilby," I added.

She knew me, so she knew there was more to the story. "We all understand that it's a process, Sir."

"It's more complicated than Skippy thought," I gave an explanation that wasn't needed.

She grinned. "You didn't expect this to be easy, did you, Sir?"

"Expect? No. Hope? Hell yes. Just once, I'd like the Universe to throw us a bone, make it easy for a change."

"When things are easy, *that's* when I get worried."

"I hear you."

"We hold position here, until Skippy finishes crunching numbers?"

"Yes. Unless," I shrugged. "Some other damned crisis pops up."

Spoiler alert: another damned crisis popped up. As we approached the wormhole that Hammer Force had retreated through, Skippy warned the event horizon was blockaded by three Maxohlx battlegroups. "They are serious about shutting down this wormhole," he groaned. "There are five other task forces here, each with three groups centered around battleships. Plus star carriers, servicing ships, stores ships, everything the kitties need to blockade this wormhole for a long time."

"They want to prevent us from bringing in equipment to pull you out of the star," that was my guess. "Reed?"

"I'd prefer to try another wormhole, rather than risk a fight with the ship in its current condition."

"Agreed."

"Bilby, set course for the alternate wormhole," she ordered. "Pilot, jump when ready."

"No joy here either," Skippy sighed after we emerged six lightminutes from the alternate wormhole. "Another blockade. Those two wormholes were our best routes away from here. We can reach three other wormholes, I suspect those will also be blockaded by the time we arrive."

"That's no good."

"Sir?" Reed prompted me. "What do you want us to do?"

"I need to think about this. Not about getting out of here, we are doing that, right here. The Maxohlx are becoming a major problem, the problem. We can't fight both them *and* the Outsider. We need some way to, take them out of the game for a while."

"That would be optimal," she agreed, then raised an eyebrow at me."

"Right. We do that after we get out of here. Skippy, you can't screw with this wormhole?"

"No, sorry. This is a network that hates me."

"We will do this the hard way, then. How many task forces are assigned to this wormhole?"

"Six total, same as the other wormhole. Two of the task forces are built around a trio of heavy cruisers each, instead of a single battleship. The firepower is pretty much the same."

"Show us a chart of emergence points."

Reed rose from her chair to stand next to me, the main display hologram almost touching our noses. "Sir? What are you thinking?"

"We do *not* want to fight our way through a blockade."

She frowned at the star chart. "I don't see how we can avoid a fight."

"We wouldn't do well in a fair fight. But," I grinned at her. "The Army taught me that if you're going into a fair fight, you need a better plan. Skippy, what are your feelings about cheating?"

"Oh," he waved his hands, excited. "I am *all about* cheating."

Since that emergence point, and the next five scheduled emergences, had a blockading force, we jumped to the seventh point. That was no good, a pair of sensor frigates were positioned there. Same with points eight through fourteen, so fifteen was the lucky number for us. We jumped in, made preparations, and waited in stealth twenty lightseconds away.

Waited. For too long, when I already feared that we were already running out of time to stop the Outsider.

That's when Bilby dumped a steaming load on our heads, calling me while I was walking back from the gym. "Uh hey, General Dude? We have a, like, problem."

Before answering, I stepped into a side passageway. "Are you talking about the problem I already know about, the blockade?"

"Sorry, no. The ship, I have done the best I can to hold it together. We need a spacedock, with full servicing facilities. Either at Earth, or Jaguar."

"It's that bad?"

"Skippy worked with me on the diagnostics. It's not good. We should not take the ship into combat, or for an extended flight."

"OK. Damn. Racing around looking for the spinner is not an option right now?"

"Not unless it is a very short race."

"We can't count on that. Ah, shit. If we got to either Earth or Jaguar, we can't contain the news that Skippy didn't fall into the star. That secret is an advantage I don't want to lose."

"Um like, Skippy could lock down the wormhole that leads to Jaguar, make sure no information leaks out?"

"Nah, the people stuck on Jaguar need regular shipments of food from Earth, since they can't grow any crops right now. Shutting down that wormhole cuts off the supply line. Although, hmm. Skippy?"

His avatar appeared. "You called?"

"You know I did. You heard that Bilby suggested shutting down the Jaguar wormhole?"

"I am not your on-call locksmith," he huffed.

"OK, but-"

"Would you like to hear a better option?"

"I would love to hear it."

"Remember when we found the secret Maxohlx ship servicing station, that you named 'Ragnar'?"

"Yeah, that was- Wait. Whoa. You know where another secret facility is?"

"Do I? Why, yes, I do," his smugness made me want to smack him.

"And it's intact? How is that possible?" We had found the Ragnar station, and moved it piece by piece to Jaguar, where it was reassembled, with only a few parts left over. The station was still operational, though the Navy had been forced to cannibalize two spacedocks, to keep the other two functioning. The news that humanity had stolen a Maxohlx remote ship servicing facility had not remained a secret for long, and the rotten kitties had been very unhappy about the theft. Preventing us from stealing any more of their precious stations, and later to prevent the rebels from repairing their ships during their civil war, had spurred the Hegemony to destroy al such secret stations. Including those in Rindhalu territory. "The kitties *nuked* all of their remaining remote shipyard stations."

"They nuked all the ones they could get to. Two other stations are inaccessible, due to wormhole shifts."

"That is outstanding, where- Uh, how long have your known about these stations?"

"Since I read the data from the archive we raided."

"Why are you telling me this only *now*?"

"You didn't need to know until now."

"Oh for- The freakin' Navy is still tearing ships apart, to get parts to keep other ships flightworthy. A fully automated shipyard like Ragnar could be a game changer! This is inexcusable, Skippy."

"Um, how about you listen to my reasoning, before you decide whether to yell at me?"

"This had better be a *solid gold* reason."

"As usual, you did not listen to what I said. *You* didn't need to know, until now."

"The Navy is-"

"Is not *my* problem. Think, dumdum, *think*. The jackasses in charge of Earth's governments had turned their backs on the galaxy, until the Outsider threat made them remember that it's good to have allies. Your people used and almost abandoned the Verd-kris, and leaned on the Ruhar to set aside land for human colonies on Ruhar worlds. Attaining parity with the senior species has made Earth more safe, it also made your people into bullies. I do *not* like bullies." He glared and clenched his teeth. "The *last* thing I am going to do is make your Navy more powerful. Right now, the UN has to be careful about throwing their weight around. Not having to worry about your warships wearing down, could encourage you filthy monkeys to become assholes like the Maxohlx."

"Oh. Uh, I don't know what to say about that."

"You could just say 'Thank you'."

"As a serving officer, I can't condone you withholding resources that could be vital to Earth's defense."

"I am not asking for your approval."

"I get that. OK. I apologize for snapping at you. I made a judgment without having all the facts. If you could get us to one of these remote stations, that would be great."

"Hmmph," he sniffed. "I am still feeling not completely appreciated, Joe."

"Tell me what I can do to make it up to you, but let's do that later, OK? Can I get more details, please?"

"Ugh. *Fine*. We can access only one of the stations. Getting there requires me waking up a dormant wormhole, and the other station is at a wormhole network that is being a *dick*."

"One station like Ragnar is all we need. Can you estimate how long the ship will need to be there?"

"Well, first the station has to be activated, um, we would need only one spacedock, so that cuts the time since I'll only need to bring one fully online. That, plus the actual repair time, ah, plus a shakedown cruise, and back into dock to fix all the things that didn't get fixed the first time? My best estimate is eight days."

"The Outsider could get into a lot of mischief in eight days. But, it will be faster than going to Jaguar?"

"From here, going to Jaguar, and having the ship fixed at the spacedock there, would be about the same schedule."

"But going to Jaguar would reveal that you didn't fall into a star. And, we wouldn't have an opportunity to wake up a remote facility that we might need in the future. OK, we go to this place you suggested, I'll talk with Reed about it. Although, hmm."

"What?"

"I want to make a detour along the way. Something needs to be done, to get the freakin' kitties off our backs for a while. Clear the deck, so we can act against the Outsider."

"I agree, but Def Com would never commit your Navy to-"

"The Navy won't be involved. This problem doesn't have a conventional solution. It requires something, *sketchy*."

"Oooooh. Fortunately, Joe, I know a guy."

"Yeah, me too."

"Joe, it kind of does bother me that you have become so comfortable with doing seriously sketchy things. I sort of view you as a moral compass for myself, that is one of the reasons I selected you, back on Paradise."

"Uh, thank you."

"What I did not expect back then, is how you have so easily slid into doing all sorts of sketchy stuff. That was not something I could have predicted, based on what I knew of your service record."

"Wow. You really didn't read between the lines of my record. Skippy, the reason the military awards Good Conduct medals is because they *expect* a certain level of fuckery, especially from E-4s. Sometimes, you can't get the job done without resorting to fuckery, and your lieutenant just doesn't want to know about it."

"Hmm. So, someone who is awarded a Good Conduct medal kept their level of fuckery below an unspecified threshold?"

"Usually it means they just didn't get caught. See? Developing *that* skill should have a medal."

"Being a meatsack sounds so impossibly complicated. Tell me, is being a filthy monkey worth all the trouble?"

"Skippy, someday, after we stomp the Outsider, and Puptart lifts the blanket from around Jaguar, I am going to have a cookout in my backyard. That first cheeseburger will taste *so amazing*, there is no way I could describe it."

"Ugh. What is it with you and food?"

"It's a thing."

"Also, when the galley here serves cheeseburgers, you usually only eat one. But when you're at a cookout, I have noticed you eat two or three."

"That's a rule at cookouts. You need at least two cheeseburgers, and while those are grilling, you need a hotdog, some chips, macaroni salad, a pickle, and a couple of beers."

"That is not an actual *rule*."

"Trust me, it is. If you were a monkey, you would know that."

"*Cheeseburgers* are the reason for you to go on living?"

"Not the only reason, but-"

"I, I can't even," his avatar faded away.

While *Valkyrie* would hopefully soon be having a spa day in spacedock, I needed to run an errand. That meant, we needed another starship. Not just any ship, a star carrier, for a long-range flight.

The simple answer would be going to Earth, or Jaguar, to requisition a star carrier. We couldn't do that, without risk of revealing that Skippy was with us. Also, I expected that Def Com might have revoked my authority to requisition assets into the Special Mission Group. Commanders who are responsible for disasters like Olympic do not get to keep their jobs, and a court martial hearing might be waiting for me at Earth.

Our options for acquiring a star carrier, no questions asked, at short notice, were not great. The UN Navy was off the list. That left the two senior species, and their top-tier clients. Technically the Ruhar and Verd-kris each had a small number of star carriers, used Jeraptha ships acquired from us in exchange for services rendered. All of those ships would be veery closely guarded, and we weren't close to Ruhar territory anyway. Stealing from the spiders was out, we needed them as allies, especially after Olympic. Hitting the Maxohlx? I would prefer a softer target. "Skippy," I tossed a tennis ball in the air, while I leaned my office chair back. "Show me a star chart, along the route to, does this remote station have a name?"

"It has a designation, that would not mean anything to you."

"OK uh, it needs to have a name."

"Ugh. *This* again?"

"Yes, this again. It's a thing. It's a shipyard, it repairs ships, that doesn't give me any ideas for- Huh. It will also be a secret base for us. We'll call it 'Shangri-La'."

"Joe, that's a reference from an old book, that you never read."

"I don't have to read it. When US Army Air Corps bombers hit Tokyo in the Doolittle raid of 1942, President Roosevelt told reporters those planes had taken off from 'Shangri-La'. The truth, you know, is those bombers took off from the aircraft carrier *Hornet*. So, show me a star chart, with your proposed route from here to Shangri-La."

"I am doing this under protest," he huffed.

"If that makes you feel better, great. All right," I studied the hologram. "Now, show me any top-tier species planets, within a twelve hour detour from the flight path." Seven dots appeared on the chart. "Make the text larger, please. Uh, two of those are Jeraptha worlds."

"Yes, we will be passing through their territory."

"We should not make any more enemies, if we don't have to. That leaves five."

"Two are Bosphuraq planets."

"Their ships would be my last choice. Those birds smell *awful*, that stink has to be everywhere aboard their ships. Our prize crew shouldn't have to hold their breath the entire time we're aboard. That leaves the Thuranin."

"There is also an Esselgin planet, fourteen hours off the flight path."

"I'll check the Thuranin first, we are more familiar with them. Give me details on those two worlds. Is a star carrier likely to be at either of them?"

"One, not the other. The closest one, only a six hour deviation from the flight path, is barely habitable. The Thuranin conducted a terraforming project there for three hundred years, and it was a miserable failure. The pinheads living there now are just too stubborn to quit, though they should."

"The other world?"

"That is an excellent place to go shopping for a star carrier."

"Can you offer me a good deal on a low mileage ship?"

"Joe, what would it take to get *you* into a used starship, today?"

"Probably a miracle. And throw in some free floormats. Tell me more."

"That planet, Gravvik-362, has a ship servicing facility in orbit, that is also used by their Navy's research organization for development and testing. Typically, two dozen or more ships are there at any time."

"Ah, it's a fleet base? That sounds like a tough target."

"It's not. Gravvik has an SD network, but it is not state of the art, even for the pinheads."

"Yeah, but two dozen warships could be stationed there?"

"Only eight of them are combat-worthy, they make up the guard force. The other ships are assigned for testing, they are a mix of types in active service. So, a star carrier, a battleship, a battlecruiser, and so on. The star carrier is really there to transport ships being tested as needed, it normally is kept in a state of low readiness, with a skeleton crew."

"I like that. How many crew would be aboard?"

"Anywhere from zero to seven, depending on whether the ship will be needed."

"No more than seven."

"Unless the ship has been brought up to full flightworthiness, to transport other ships. We won't know that until we get there."

"Right. Should be an easy job for a STAR team, the trick will be getting them aboard without detection."

"We could do that, or we could do something *much* cooler."

"Cooler involves more risk?"

"*Less* risk."

"Talk to me."

From a distance of two lightseconds, we watched an enemy frigate jump in, forty minutes before the wormhole was scheduled to shift to that emergence point. My original plan had been to seed the area with missiles, and ask Skippy to create an especially flat point in spacetime. The jump wormholes of Maxohlx ships would unknowingly seek the flatter area, and appear exactly where they would be surrounded by a cluster of our missiles. Let the missiles independently seek targets, destroy the enemy ships before their shields and sensors recovered from jump distortion. Great plan, although it was a move we used near the end of our second mission. Hey, sometimes it's best to stick with the classics.

That plan got thrown out the window, after we observed the tactics of the enemy at several other emergence points. First, a single frigate arrives, scanning the region with active sensor pulses. That frigate then jumps back to wherever it came from, and a few minutes later, a squadron of six frigates arrives, saturating the area with sensor pulses. Only after the area is declared clear does a frigate jump away, to give the All Clear signal to its home battlegroup. With all that active energy radiating out from six warships, there was no way we could keep a cluster of even stealthed missiles hidden.

So, we went with Plan B. Plan *C*, actually, Skippy had wanted to gradually hack into and disable the enemy ships, until I reminded him that he was supposed to be stuck inside a star. He couldn't do any of his usual tricks that would make the enemy suspect they had gotten played by an Elder AI. And, we didn't have a lot of time. The wormhole would be open there for only seventeen minutes, and a Maxohlx blockade force arrived around thirty minutes before the scheduled opening of the wormhole. That was not enough time for Skippy to hack the sensors of every ship in the area, not with the required level of confidence, which was one hundred percent. Somehow, we had to sneak past a battlegroup, and go through a wormhole, without anyone knowing we were there. Or anyone realizing Skippy had done one of his awesomenesses again.

How the hell can we do that?

That was the question. Fortunately, I didn't have to agonize over dreaming up a solution. I had already done that. Years ago. While I was garrison commander on Jaguar, I didn't only exercise, give speeches, and play golf. When my mind wandered in the gym, out running, or at the driving range, I imagined how we might have done things differently. Like, instead of shooting our way out of a jam, could we have done something a bit more subtle, less kinetic?

That's what we did.

The Maxohlx battlegroup had arrived thirty two minutes and sixteen seconds before the wormhole would open, jumping in a tighter formation than their navigations systems could have managed on their own. They had help from Skippy, who had projected an especially flat area of spacetime through a microwormhole we planted back when we arrived. Doing that had been his idea, I had assumed he couldn't channel that much power through a tiny rip in spacetime, without the event horizons immediately collapsing. That was true, he had explained to me while his avatar wore a Barney costume, only for energy in *this* low-rent layer of spacetime. Maser beams have a limit to the power throughput before destroying a microwormhole. That wasn't true of whatever effect he used to flatten spacetime, which in my mind I imagined was a giant iron.

Anyway, the enemy ships were packed together closer than they normally would, the battlegroup leader no doubt congratulating everyone for their amazingly accurate jump. There was no need for the ships to spread out, they were positioned precisely in front of where the event horizon would appear.

"Masquerade will be effective in," Skippy paused for dramatic effect. "Three, two, one, now. And, it is stable."

"Reed, get us moving."

CHAPTER TWELVE

We had just under fifty minutes to travel two lightseconds, a distance of roughly six hundred thousand kilometers. Going the long way would require a speed of, no, I did not do this math in my head, an average speed of two hundred klicks per *second.* Even with the enhanced stealth capabilities provided by Skippy, we would leave a visible wake of hotly charged particles behind us. Therefore, we did not do that. We did need to fly, to get the ship moving from its original velocity of zero compared to the impending event horizon. That flight needed to be only three hundred kilometers, and we would have several minutes to cross that distance. Because we planned to cheat.

I'll admit it, I have grown to love cheating. Do *not* tell my children that.

In addition to the microwormhole Skippy used to iron spacetime so it was flat, there were two other clusters of microwormholes in the area. One sphere of microwormholes were in the nosecones of drones that kept pace with *Valkyrie,* surrounding us with a light-bending hologram that from the outside, would appear to be ordinary, boring interstellar space. The other sphere were hanging out close to the wormhole's emergence point, just chillin' and not being noticed by the sensors of the enemy blockade force.

Reed got us moving at a speed and direction so that, even if the engines somehow lost power, we would pass through the wormhole before it shut down.

The operation was tricky. Skippy was controlling close to the maximum number of microwormholes he could sustain, plus he had to do a whole lot of other things, and of course we filthy monkeys could not appreciate how awesome he was. What really bothered him was that only the Merry Band of Pirates would know about that particular feat of awesomeness. My response was telling him to suck it up, he could boast about it later.

The wormhole emerged exactly when and where it was supposed to, of course. We waited for the thing to become stable, and to see whether the Maxohlx would change their posture in relation to the event horizon. It was stable, and the rotten kitties were happy where they were, thankfully. If their formation spread out, we would have to thread a needle to get to the wormhole.

"Everything looks, like, copacetic, you know?" Bilby announced. "Ready when you are, Your Dude-ess." He addressed that remark to Reed, handling the ship was her show.

"This is a bad neighborhood, let's get out of here," she tugged the safety strap tighter. "Pilot, punch it."

We jumped.

As I said, it was tricky. The sphere of microwormholes around the ship projected a bubble that absorbed the faint gamma radiation of our jump drive, energy that exited through a gap in the bubble that faced away from the enemy ships. We jumped into the bubble close to the Elder wormhole's event horizon, where the gamma radiation there was also channeled away.

Everyone tensed and crossed our fingers when we emerged from jump. The ship was traveling at a speed that took us out of the inbound bubble in less than two seconds, just enough time for Skippy to get our stealth field operational before the microwormholes collapsed.

"I think we're good," Bilby whispered. "No sign the enemy has detected us, they are not changing their posture."

"Outstanding," I uncrossed my fingers and gave a thumbs up. "Skippy, are you OK?" Maintaining that many tiny wormholes was a major strain for him.

"Ohhhhh," he groaned. "It sucked, but I embraced it."

"You are a true warrior," I said what he wanted to hear. "Our timing is correct?"

"Please, Joe, it's just *math*."

"Sure, but the Universe hates me, so-"

"We're fine. It's a rock, it can't do anything on its own."

"Unless it hit another rock along the way."

"Ugh. Why are you so-"

"The rock is where it's supposed to be?"

"Within half a millimeter, is that good enough for you?"

"That is acceptable."

Valkyrie coasted onward toward the event horizon, passing through the edges of the enemy sensor fields. Skippy was hacking the shapes of those fields to conceal our presence, he was actually assisted by the paranoia of the enemy. What that battlegroup should have done is station frigates at the outside of the formation, and have only those ships projecting sensor fields. Instead, every ship was radiating energy, overlapping fields that interacted with each other and confused the feedback. Yes, more energy saturating the battlespace did increase the odds of detecting a stealthed ship, except when Skippy was involved.

Five seconds before we reached the event horizon.

Four.

There would be an unavoidable flash of energy from the wormhole as we went through, even Skippy couldn't do anything about it. Especially since that network controller hated him.

Three.

Two.

One.

The rock we had found and collected, a chunk of iron, carbon, and frozen water, tumbled toward the event horizon, on a collision course with both *Valkyrie* and the wormhole. The Maxohlx hadn't detected us, the wormhole certainly knew we were there. To avoid hazards that could damage transiting ships, the Elders equipped their wormholes with a defense mechanism. Just as *Valkyrie's* nose contacted the event horizon, the weird twist in spacetime erupted outward to vaporize the rock. That flash concealed the effect of us passing through.

Cool, huh?

Skippy grudgingly had admitted it was a good move.

Until the wormhole shut down behind us, we did nothing, just coasted onward in stealth. The Maxohlx had not posted even a single frigate at the far end of the wormhole, I guess they just didn't have enough ships. Or they were overconfident about the effectiveness of their blockade.

Damn. I can't wait until we can reveal we snuck past them. Later, we would do that later.

A few seconds after the event horizon closed behind us, we jumped.

Had

Skippy warned us that, after the trauma he suffered during his heroic narrow escape from plunging into a star, he needed to go offline for a while. My guess was that while he was rearranging his matrix or whatever, he would be working on an opera based on how he outsmarted the Outsider, and him being offline was good for me.

Except, when he finally came back online, it was the middle of the night. And he was, as he described it, 'cognitively impaired'.

"Heeeey, Joe," I heard the slurring of words that froze my blood. "Hey Joe. Joe Joe Joe-".

Shit. It was zero four thirty, and my relatively blissful night of sleep was over. "Hey, Skippy. I'm tryin' to sleep here. Can we talk in the morning?"

"It *is* the morning, dumdum. Any time after midnight is technically 'morning', according to you idiot monkeys."

"It is nighttime now. Morning begins with sunrise."

"Here's a news flash for you: you are aboard a starship, there is no sunrise. And you're in the military, so mornings start early."

"Not this early. If I listen to whatever you want to talk about, will you leave me alone?"

"Sorry, I can't make that promise. It's not listening I need you to do, it's *tasting*."

Again, my blood turned to ice. "Oh my G- Did you try to make Bubu Cakes again?"

"No," he huffed. "Colonel Buzzkill banned my bots from the galley. Why is she a hater, Joe? All I'm trying to do is bring some joy to the crew."

"She is not a buzzkill, and your last attempt at cooking had the galley closed for several days. She is protecting the crew."

"She is depriving them of my culinary genius. Joe, this time the actual cooking has been done by crewmembers, who generously donated their time by getting up early to help me."

"Donated?"

"OK, I am paying them in Skipcoin, but considering how much I'm paying, generosity is definitely involved. This crew is a bunch of *crooks*," he muttered.

"Did *they* bake Bubu Cakes?"

"No, they- here it is."

The cabin door slid open, and in rolled a bot carrying a platter with a silver dome over it. The bot stopped at the coffee table in front of the couch, unloaded the tray, and rolled back out.

"Come on, Joe, get up. You need to taste the first batch, so the galley team has time to make adjustments before they have to start getting ready for breakfast."

"What," I sniffed the air. "Is it? It smells like, Tex-Mex?"

"Exactly, Joe. I have invented exciting new menu options for Taco Bell! Or, for whoever pays me the most for exclusive rights to the recipes."

"Uh huh." Lifting the dome of the tray, I saw three plates that held, some mystery items. "Skippy, what the hell are these?"

"Going clockwise from the top, there is the *Burr-taco*, that's a combination burrito and taco, in case you couldn't guess. Next is the *Habe-chelada*, an enchilada inside a grilled habanero pepper. And something sweet to finish your delicious meal, the *Churr-lupa*."

"A chalupa inside a churro shell?"

"Very good, Joe. Hurry, eat it before it gets cold."

I have good news and bad news. Due to Army service that had trained my stomach to process any even vaguely foodlike substances, I didn't ralph up his culinary creations. I wanted to barf, but my stupid stomach wouldn't cooperate. The bad news is, Skippy's new recipes were not any worse than typical Taco Bell offerings, and they were innovative, so unfortunately you are likely to see at least some of them on the menu at the drive-thru.

The real bad news was for myself. After choking down those Tex-Mex abominations, I wasn't hungry for breakfast, on a morning when the galley crew made cinnamon swirl buns with orange glaze.

Sometimes, I really hate that little shithead.

On the way to Shangri-La, we swung by the Gravvik system, to go shopping for a sweet, quality, pre-owned star carrier. The first jump brought us to within a lighthour of the planet, where Skippy confirmed the star carrier was parked in a high orbit, in a low state of readiness.

"Is that thing flightworthy?" I asked, crossing my fingers behind my back for luck.

Skippy rolled his eyes. "I can't tell that from here, dumdum. The other bit of good news is, the guard force is conducting exercises at the sixth planet, those ships will not return to Gravvik for another three days."

"Reed?"

She shrugged. "We should go in for a closer look."

The second jump brought us one and a half lightminutes from the planet, where Skippy was able to tap into communications. "Good news, Joe. That star carrier *is* flightworthy. We will need to replace the windshield wipers and fill the gas tank, its fuel state is only twenty percent."

"We can transfer fuel from *Valkyrie*," I said, forgetting that the battlecruiser was Reed's command, not mine. Turning to her, I added, "If that-"

"That's fine, Sir. We topped up the tanks before Olympic, so we have a reserve. Not a large reserve," she added.

"Good."

"Um, " Skippy continued. "The somewhat bad news is, there are two Thuranin crew aboard the ship."

"That's not- Wait. Yeah, we can use that. This is good, actually."

"How is this *good*?"

"It will help to explain how a starship disappears, without Skippy magic being involved. You are supposed to be stuck inside a star, remember?"

"What I heard is Skippy will do yet another awesome thing, and we can't tell anyone about it," he pouted.

"We can't tell anyone *yet*."

"Oh. That's better. So, what is your plan?"

"I'll tell you when we get to that point."

"I suppose," Skippy huffed, "you now want to know the names of the two Thuranin crew?"

"Uh, why would I want that?"

"Names are an obsession with you, so-"

"It is not really import-"

"They are Neddok-2398, and Jetrup-457."

"Their names are *Ned* and *Jethro*?" I laughed, and the bridge crew joined in.

"No, it- I'm not going to win this argument, am I?"

"Ya think? Those two guys are on the bridge?"

"The one you call 'Jethro' is a female, knucklehead."

"I mean, that's the best kind of Jethro. Are you sure her name isn't something like Jethro-Jean, or Jethro-Sue?"

"I, I can't even-"

"Where are they?"

"They are currently in a VIP cabin on the port side, working on fixing it up to host an admiral, next week."

"Can you lock the cabin door, seal them in there?"

"From *here*, I can't do anything, dumdum."

"I meant, is it possible to do that?"

"Joe, please. It's me."

"Hey, this is me not taking your awesomeness for granted."

The third jump emerged us just beyond the sensor field of the SD network. If we were approaching a Maxohlx world, like we had been doing recently, we would have been forced to do some complicated thing like sending in a microwormhole aboard a drone. Approaching a client planet, we could trust *Valkyrie's* advanced stealth capabilities, so we didn't need to do anything fancy. Still, there was a moment of tension, before Bilby announced that our gamma ray burst had been effectively absorbed. We would need to dump that stored energy soon, before it burned its way out of the containment vessel. What mattered was, the planet was within Skippy's presence, and the enemy had no idea they had an uninvited guest.

"How are you doing, Skippy?" I asked, when he had been silent for over a minute.

"Wow Joe, this is like old times. Screwing with the little green pinheads, having my way with a strategic defense network, hacking low-tech starships, ahhhh. This is fun."

"The Thuranin are not a low-tech species."

"I meant, compared to me. Full control of the star carrier will be accomplished in three, two, one, *awesome*," he sang the last word. "Doneski. My control of the SD network sensors is still propagating across the network, that will take- And, that is done also."

"All good news, Skippy."

"It's not all good news. Ned left the cabin to get a tool he didn't have."

"I'll bet it's a ten millimeter socket."

"You want me to do this, or you want to make jokes?"

"Where is Ned now?"

"He is walking along a passageway, hmm, that is odd. He is moving *away* from the tool storage locker, and toward the alcove with a koth maker. Joe, I suspect Ned doesn't really need another tool."

"The guy needs koth, I get that."

"I am ready *now*."

"We can wait a minute, see if Ned goes back to the cabin."

We waited, Skippy growing impatient to once again demonstrate his awesomeness. Ned got koth for himself, and a second mug for Jethro. "OK, he is headed back to the cabin."

"Lock the cabin door, when I give the signal."

"I will do that, but they will be able to get out eventually. They could use a torch to cut through a bulkhead."

"Yeah, by that time, the STARs will be there to deal with them."

On the display was a synthetic view, provided by Skippy hacking the star carrier's internal sensors. We watched Ned walk along a passageway, carrying two steaming mugs of koth. The guy stopped to savor a sip, and a smile beamed on his face. For a moment, I forgot the Thuranin are cruel, arrogant, hateful jerks. Then he walked into the cabin, and I pushed aside any notion of empathy. Waiting until he went away from the door, and gave a mug of koth to Jethro, I ordered, "Lock the door now."

"Done. Oops," Skippy chuckled. "They heard the 'click' when the lock engaged."

The two little green pinheads were gesturing and shouting at each other.

"What are they saying?" I asked. "I don't need a full translation."

"Basically, Jethro is asking what stupid thing Ned did, to get them locked in there. Ned is protesting that it's not his fault."

"Those two should get married. OK, Skippy, that ship is prepped for a jump?"

"I have only to start feeding power into the coils. Don't worry about the SD network noticing an unauthorized power surge, I have control of all sensors on and around the planet."

"I *want* the Thuranin to see the coils powering up."

"What?" Reed asked before Skippy could. "Sir, that-"

"Will be our cover story," I explained. "Skippy, do you know enough about Jethro to imitate her voice?"

"No. Wait, I just listened to sixteen hours of audio from her. I can do it."

"Great. Fake a distress call from her, that Ned locked her in a cabin, and announced his intention to steal the ship. Say he is, I don't know. Upset about being passed over for promotion, or something like that?"

"Gotcha. Doing it now. Hee hee, this will be fun. Ooooh, the Thuranin traffic control duty officer is *furious*, she just alerted the SD network."

"Create a glitch, stall the network."

"Done. The ship can now perform a jump."

"Reed?"

"Ready in all respects, Sir," she acknowledged.

"Skippy, jump that thing out of there."

"This is like Grand Theft Auto: Starship Edition," he chuckled. "Oops, the Thuranin just lost *another* star carrier."

Valkyrie jumped eight lighthours, and emerged a thousand kilometers from the star carrier. Seeing that ship, I felt a wave of nostalgia wash over me, and I reveled in it. Damn. When we took the *Flying Dutchman*, I had been so impossibly *young*. And stupid. And unsure of myself, fearing I was not up to the challenge of command.

Sometimes, I still felt that way.

The ready bird launched a STAR team, and I walked to a docking bay along with the prize crew, the people who would be temporarily transferring to the new ship. In the bay, a Panther was waiting, loaded with our personal gear, and enough food and supplies for a month. Hopefully, we would rendezvous with *Valkyrie* long before the food ran out, I certainly did not want to survive on sludges again. "Gasquet," I nodded to the ship's XO, who would be leading the prize crew, as captain of the- The what? The star carrier needed a name. "Have you considered a name for your new command?"

He was startled by my question, he had been studying something on a tablet. "Sir?"

"We will not be returning the ship to the Thuranin. It needs a UN Navy name."

"Ah, but of course." He glanced at me, then away. Probably trying to guess what name I preferred.

"That ship will be *your* command, you have to be comfortable with it."

"Not something like '*Titanic*', then?"

"That would not be my first choice, no."

He stared at the ceiling for a moment. "*La Fayette*," he announced. "The Marquis de La Fayette served in your Revolutionary War. After World War Two, the US transferred an *Independence*-class aircraft carrier to France, where the ship was renamed *La Fayette*, in honor of the friendship between our countries."

"That is," I agreed, "an excellent name for a star carrier commanded by a Frenchman."

He nodded with a grin. "Thank you, Sir."

We went aboard the dropship and waited. I hate waiting.

Colonel Frey shook her head with a grimace, as she walked onto the bridge of the Thuranin star carrier. The lead operators had already cleared the compartment, that was only an emergency manual backup to the control implants the crew normally used to interface with the ship's AI. Through the helmet cameras of the people ahead of her, she had seen the view, it was much more shocking to see with her own eyes.

Ugly. Gaudy. Baroque. Overdone. She had been aboard the *Flying Dutchman*, but only after that space truck had been in service with UNEF for several years. By the time she joined the Merry Band of Pirates, the original decorations had been replaced, or covered with soothing, neutral colors. Nothing like the decorating nightmare all around her. "Gasquet is going to *love* this," she muttered to herself.

"Ma'am?" Tech Sergeant Ling turned toward her.

"That was sarcasm, our XO will not approve of this," she waved a hand to encompass the bridge and the adjacent Combat Information Center, or whatever the Thuranin called it. "All right, the control center is secured. Look for booby traps, in case Skippy missed anything," she ordered the team. "Ling, Braddock, Suharto, you're with me. Let's go meet our guests."

She paused the team at the door to the cabin where the two Thuranin technicians were trapped. Stuck in there only for a minute, they were already assembling equipment to cut through the door, or a bulkhead. Skippy reported the two had done nothing but argue until the ship jumped, at which point the cyborgs must have realized something was seriously wrong. With their cybernetic implants cut off from the ship's network, they had to be on the verge of panic. Panic made meatsacks unpredictable, and dangerous. "Skippy, confirm those two do not have any weapons."

"Um, well, anything can be a weapon, if you-"

"Weapons that could harm my team."

"Oh. Then, nothing. Unless they get that torch assembled before you go in."

"Then, let's go now. Braddock on the left, Suharto on the right. Ling, cover them. Stun bolts only."

The three acknowledged her command, she could also see the status of their rifles in her visor. All were set to stun.

"Skippy, unlock the door on three. Three, two, one, *go*."

One of the Thuranin, who had been standing just inside the door, was bowled over by Braddock, rolling over and scrambling to- His? Her? *Its* feet. With Thuranin, it was difficult to tell the genders apart at a casual glance, unless they were in their twice-annual mating phase when hormones exaggerated their features. Whatever. She didn't plan on getting to know them.

The other pinhead went down when zapped by a bolt from Suharto's rifle, slumping in a corner, dropping what might have been a cutting torch.

"Ma'am," Braddock warned, keeping his rifle trained on the first alien, who had gotten to its feet, and glaring pure hatred at the intruders. "We might have an overachiever here."

"I'll take care of it." Striding forward, she seized the alien around its skinny neck, lifting it to her eye level. "You aren't so tough when you're not hiding behind a combot, are you?"

The Thuranin screamed something unintelligible, thumping her faceplate with its little fists, until Frey held it at arm's length, when it tried to kick at her with its feet. She was about to give the alien to Suharto, then changed her mind. Tech Sergeant Ling was new to Team Razor, being the only survivor of Team Tiger. He had declared he was fine and fit for duty, and physically that was true. She knew from experience that the sergeant likely had survivor's guilt. She certainly had, after she didn't die during the raid on the Elder spacedock. It took her a long time to get over her guilt that she continued on while Smythe had not. Marriage to a great guy, and having a baby, convinced her that she had survived not for herself, but for others. Ling needed to see that Team Razor had faith in him.

"Ling, take this, thing," she held out the struggling cyborg, "and put it in the brig. Suharto, get the other one. Braddock, make sure our guests don't get into any trouble."

The tech sergeant hesitated for only a moment, slinging his rifle and grasping the alien's feet and neck. "You be quiet," he admonished her, he now saw an overlay in his visor that labeled the Thuranin as 'Jethro'. "Or there will be only banana flavor sludges for you."

Frey had to suppress a grin as she watched the three operators walking away. "Razor Lead to *Valkyrie*. The ship is secure."

From *Valkyrie*, Skippy programmed *La Fayette's* next jump, that took us far outside the star system. Gasquet needed time, peace, and quiet, to get his prize crew settled in, and familiarize themselves with the ship's systems. Before we jumped in near Gravvik, the prize crew had trained on a simulation of a standard Thuranin star carrier, but the *La Fayette* was an older model, and had not been given some of the more recent upgrades.

"Colonel Frey was not exaggerating," Gasquet made a sour face when we stepped onto the bridge. "This is, *tres hideux*. Um, that is 'very hideous', Sir."

"I got that." Being from northern Maine, I had picked up some Frenchie words from Quebecers.

"Sir," he gestured to the command chair. "Would you like to?"

"It's all yours, Gasquet," I laughed. "*You* can have the fun of transition training."

"I might have just changed my mind about this assignment."

"Too late now. I want to jump in four hours."

He sat on the chair, squeezing himself in. "I had better get started now."

He had the ship checked out and ready for basic maneuvers in three hours, I gave him the extra hour for the crew to conduct damage control training. In case, you know, we clumsy monkeys damaged something. After the ship's first jump programmed by humans, I flew back to *Valkyrie*, and we began jumping toward Shangri-La.

"I don't know, Joe," Skippy took off his hat and scratched his head. "This is delicate work, I should stay aboard *Valkyrie* to-"

"Bilby says he can handle it. Right, Bilby?"

"Righteous, Dude," the ship's AI drawled. "No problem. The resident shipyard AI here is pretty sweet, after Skippy tamed it."

"But Joe," the beer can started to protest.

Jabbing a finger in Skippy's face, I was not taking any crap from him. "I am not listening to you. We are going with the *La Fayette*, no arguments. If anything here gets screwed up, you can fix it later."

"*Fine*. See if I care."

"It doesn't matter to me whether you care, or not." Picking him up, I stuffed his canister in a foam cradle and tucked it under my arm. "Fireball?"

She held a bag containing my laptop and a few personal items that weren't already aboard the star carrier. "Ready when you are, Sir." As we walked toward a docking bay, she asked, "You won't give me a hint what you're planning to do?"

"If this goes sideways, you should have plausible deniability."

"You could say that about anything we do."

"*This* will be a Scorandum op."

She raised an eyebrow. "I am OK with not knowing about it."

Part of the reason I wanted Skippy with us was he could fine-tune the star carrier's jump drive, so we could jump farther, and more frequently. We had down time while *Valkyrie* was in the shop for repairs, we had to get an op together in time to be back at Shangri-La before Reed declared her battlecruiser was once again combat ready. The Outsider wasn't taking a break from its nefarious plans, if *Valkyrie* didn't need major repairs, I would have pressed on with the search for the spinner.

Except, Skippy still had absolutely no idea which star it had come from. We could think about that in flight.

Admiral Scorandum was hopefully at ECO headquarters on the Jeraptha homeworld, I did not want to chase him all over the galaxy. Emerging twenty lightseconds from that planet, we transmitted a burst message, then jumped away. The Jeraptha were reportedly anxious about intruders, there was no advantage to us hanging around, exposed. Being in a space truck again made me feel vulnerable, though the Pirates had kicked ass for years in a similar star carrier.

Waiting for Scorandum to reply, I was in my office, a Thuranin cabin that we had repurposed for me. Spending time in my office avoided Gasquet from thinking I was looking over his shoulder, he needed to run his ship without unhelpful advice or any other kind of interference from me.

Downtime wasn't good for me, it gave me too much opportunity for thinking, and my mind to often wandered into dark places. What Skippy said bothered me. He mentioned that he used me as a moral compass, than it bothered him that I had become too comfortable with doing sketchy things. Was he right about that? When I was on Paradise, I had refused an order to kill Ruhar civilians. A couple years later, during our fourth mission, I gave the order to spark a Kristang civil war that killed over a million lizards across the galaxy. A million *people*, and most of them were civilians; women and children. Yes, I could use the excuse that the lizard clans had been preparing for one of their regularly scheduled civil wars, that all I did was speed things up a bit. Maybe, by starting the war before the major clans were prepared, the war had been shorter and less violent that it would have been without my interference.

Maybe.

What I know for certain is, I now was the guy who suckered his friends into acting a decoys, and nearly getting them killed. The worst part is, I would do it again, under the same circumstances. At the time, it had been the only was to get the collector, and we still hadn't thought of an alternative to Operation Olympic, in spite of a whole lot of Monday morning quarterbacking.

It had been a tough decision, I had agonized over it, right up until the 'Go' order to launch the assault. Now that it was over, I felt like shit. For a few days after Olympic, I had avoided looking at myself in the mirror, which made shaving awkward. I felt guilty about what I did, *and* I still believed it was the right call. Did the guilt mean I had not become a callous asshole, using people to get the job done, regardless of the cost?

I didn't know.

And asking Admiral Scorandum of the ECO for help did not make me any more confident that I hadn't lost my moral compass.

I needed to talk with my wife.

We received an encrypted, broadcast reply two hours later, Scorandum had been asleep when my message arrived. He would board an ECO cruiser and meet us at my suggested coordinates ASAP, that was in about another hour and a half.

The House Always Wins arrived seven minutes early, and we waited another ten minutes to make sure no other ships would be arriving, because I am such a trusting person. That was being a bit paranoid, the Jeraptha were not only strong and reliable allies, they needed us as much as we needed them. But, shit happens and loyalties can shift, depending on which jackasses in government are making decisions at the moment.

"Admiral Scorandum," I called when *La Fayette* dropped stealth. "It is good to see you again."

"Likewise, General Bishop." He cocked his head, antennas flopping around. "Is SkipWay in financial trouble again? Did you have to sell *Valkyrie*, to fly around in that hooptie?" He didn't actually say 'hooptie', that was the translation.

"*Valkyrie* is busy elsewhere, so we borrowed this thing."

"A Thuranin star carrier? Does being aboard remind you of good times?"

"Those were never *good* times."

"You know what I mean. Back when you only had to worry about enemies from *this* galaxy."

"By comparison, those were good times," I admitted. "Admiral, could-"

"Please, call me Uhtavio."

"This is not a social call, so-"

"Nothing you and I have done together has been officially sanctioned, so can I assume your leadership is not aware of, whatever you propose we do next?"

He was right. Working with him, I wasn't being a UN Def Com general, I was being a Pirate. "Uhtavio, if people on Earth knew what I'm thinking, they would revoke my command."

"I like this already. Shall I come aboard your," he squinted at a display, and slowly pronounced, "*La Fayette*?"

"Yes, please. Uh, this rustbucket does not have any burgoze, sorry."

His mandibles twisted in a broad grin. "I will bring my own. And a bottle of bourbon for you."

"Oh," I faked a smile. "That would be great, thanks."

CHAPTER THIRTEEN

Note to self: the next time we carjack an alien starship, we need to bring a decorative plant for the corner of the conference room. Any kind of plant, like a ficus? Although, I am not exactly sure what a ficus is. Anyway, if *La Fayette* had a house plant conveniently next to my chair in the conference room, I could have discreetly poured out my bourbon while Scorandum was guzzling his burgoze. As it was, I had to suffer through the meeting, begging him not to refill my glass, claiming I had not gotten any sleep the past night.

Scorandum had been surprised to be contacted again, so soon after Olympic. He had been very surprised that I had arrived in an enemy warship.

"General," his antennas drooped sadly, "I must apologize for the failure of my plan to lure the 14th Fleet away from Ohmeharikahn."

"It wasn't your fault."

"Good," his expression brightened. "I wanted to make sure you understood that. The Outsider was one step ahead of us, again?"

"One step ahead of *me*. It was my plan."

"The loss of Skippy is a," he looked at me over his glass, to judge my reaction. "Bitter pills to swallow."

"It *would* be," Skippy's avatar appeared on the table, and I took the opportunity to spill some bourbon on the deck.

"*Skippy*!" The beetle clacked his claws together. "You did not fall into the star?"

"Please. As if. I am *way* too smart for that."

"This is top secret," I pointed at Scorandum. "While the Maxohlx believe he is trapped inside that star, they will keep a significant portion of their fleet at Ohmeharikahn. To block a rescue attempt, and potentially to try recovering him themselves."

"Hmm, I can see that. Very well, it will be our secret, until I hear otherwise. Er, would you mind if I placed a discreet wager that Skippy did not fall into the star?"

"I would mind that very much. The Maxohlx still have access to a backdoor in your Central Wagering system."

"Yes, however, I would place the wager through an intermediary. The current odds that Skippy is not in that star are, ooh," he checked his tablet. "Seven hundred fifty to one."

"Someone is already betting Skippy escaped?"

"Many people are doing that," he showed me the tablet, the symbols didn't mean anything to me. "It is *juicy* action, with an excellent payout."

"Skip this wagering opportunity, please. I have something *much* better for you."

"Better than seven fifty to one? Hmm, if it is that good, why are you sharing it with me?"

"I don't have time, and," I shrugged. "What I need is *so* sketchy, you might refuse. This could be extremely dangerous and-"

"General? You had me at 'sketchy'."

"I hope so."

"What is your plan?"

"My plan is to tell you what I need, and dump the planning on *you*."

"Ah. A moment, please," he gulped the rest of his glass, and refilled it. "Now, I am prepared to listen."

"We need the fucking Maxohlx off our backs. They have a large portion of their fleet at Ohmeharikahn, and still they have plenty of ships to conduct a blockade of wormholes in that region. They will probably, almost certainly, hit a human colony, to retaliate for Olympic. What I need is to keep them *so* busy, they won't have time to harass us, and help their buddy the Outsider to open a doorway to an invasion force."

He contemplated his glass, lifted it, set it down. "Before we continue, do you have a plan to stop the Outsider? A practical, workable plan? If not, this discussion is all for nothing."

"We have a plan. More importantly, we have a weapon. An Elder weapon. Skippy is working with the, object we took from Ohmeharikahn, to identify the location of this weapon."

"You have not identified the location?"

"We have not, not yet. It's a complicated process, everything we do is complicated. Uhtavio," I used his first name as he had requested. "We would be flying to activate this weapon right now, but *Valkyrie* needs repairs. The ship got beat up in Olympic, worse than we knew at the time. While the ship is in spacedock, I'm here to get help from you. That's the truth."

"What is your time horizon? For how long do you need the Maxohlx to be, distracted?"

"A month? Whatever you do, it has to be quick. I know that's a tough request."

"It," he took the barest sip of burgoze. "Can be done. We, the Ethics Office, have had several plans on a shelf, for many years. From time to time, generally when a new minister takes over running the Office, we dust off the plans, make revisions, and put them back on the shelf."

"Are any of *these* plans practical, workable?"

"Only one, in my opinion."

"Does it involve assassinations, decapitating the Hegemony leadership?"

He shook his head. "That would only bring a fractured Maxohlx society closer together, against their common enemy. Besides, you know my Office finds killing and other direct action to be, crude, and distasteful. We have the Home Fleet for that sort of thing."

"Can you give me a broad outline of this plan?"

"Not now. General, for something like this, I must seek approval from the minister, and possibly more senior leaders."

"I thought your Office doesn't want to know about operations in advance?"

"That is typically true. In *this* case, they will definitely want to know in advance. And, likely, put a halt to it. With this plan," he made a gesture like pushing something across the table. "We would be *All In*, if you understand that."

"I do. When can you review the plan with the minister?"

"For something like this, I can arrange a meeting today."

"You think this might work?"

"Minister Skeezix has been scrambling to pay off the money he borrowed to purchase his office, so he-"

"Wait. Explain that? He *paid* to be the minister of the ECO?"

"Yes," Scorandum's antennas dipped in a gesture I recognized as surprise. "Why? Your military officers purchase their commissions, do they not? And they can sell their commission?"

"I know that was true of the British Army, during the Napoleonic Wars. Uh, a long time ago. These days, a commission is earned, and you can't sell it."

"Hmm. Officers cannot profit from their positions?"

"We get *paid*."

"I didn't mean that."

"Yeah, I figured. Your Minister *bought* his office?"

"This surprises you?"

A lot about Jeraptha society still surprised me, but aliens are *alien*, they don't play by our rules. "It's not any of my business."

"My understanding is your governments operate in a similar fashion."

"Uh, no."

"Really?" He cocked his head. "Senior government positions are not granted to those wealthy individuals who contributed major sums to the winning candidate?"

"I mean," that was a discussion I didn't want to get into right then. "Not *officially*."

"Hmm. I believe our system is more open and honest."

"Anyone can purchase a senior government office?"

"No. The leader of government selects a group of candidates, from the major supporters. Those candidates then bid on the office. The Ethics Office is a very desirable ministry, due to the almost endless opportunities for profits that are not, and cannot, be audited."

"Uh huh." *That* did not surprise me. "What about the, Inquisitors? Their minister purchased the office?"

"Oh no. Special Inquiries is a religious office, senior leaders are selected from the clergy. That is why," his mandibles clacked together. "They are such inflexible, humorless *dicks*."

"OK, thanks for the civics lesson. You want me to be with you, for the meeting?"

"That would be, counterproductive. My leadership views you as, this is their opinion and not mine, as reckless."

"I prefer the word 'bold'."

"Not being able to reveal that Skippy is not actually lost, will make it difficult to convince my leadership to believe that working with you has any chance of success."

"You trust your minister, I understand that. A secret like that does not stay secret for long anyway. The minister might have to convince *his* leadership. Senior leaders talk with each other, someone brings the problem to a staffer for advice, and suddenly, everyone knows."

"That is a risk," he agreed. "What if it is the only way to secure our assistance?"

"Then we can talk about it. Getting the Maxohlx off our backs is more important than keeping a secret that will only be a short-term advantage anyway."

"I know my leadership, and I do not see another way to get their approval for an operation of this scope."

"Yeah. Uh, Huh."

"You have an idea?"

"Maybe. How about this: tell your minister that we have been in contact with Skippy, and *he* has a plan to get himself out of the star, soon. We, the Pirates, simply need to get some special gear together, and that will be tougher to do if the freakin' Maxohlx are harassing us. Yeah, yeah, I like that," I warmed up to my own idea. "Hell, go ahead and leak that information. *I* will leak it, to prevent my leadership from panicking and doing something stupid. As a bonus, hearing that we actually have a plan will make the Maxohlx double down on the force they commit to Ohmeharikahn. Would that work?"

"Possibly, possibly," he stared at his glass while he considered the idea. "It is worth a shot, anyway. If not-"

"Then like I said, we can talk again."

"There is one," his mandibles worked side to side.

An ancient part of my brain interpreted his grinding mandibles as a predator insect's body language for 'You look tasty'. Hey, I have worked with the beetles for years, and I like them. Giant insect-like creatures can still provoke a visceral reaction of 'Creepy, run'!

"Complication," he finished.

"Of course there is. Your plans always include complications."

"Oh, I was not talking about the actual plan. There is a complication with me requesting a meeting with the minister."

"You have to make an appointment?"

"The complication, you see, is that he already expects me today. To," he glanced away for a moment, embarrassed.

Oh shit, I thought, here it comes. He wants *us* to do some sketchy-

"To collect a payment from me."

"Ah," I was relieved. "Let me guess: you don't have the funds?"

"Not at the moment."

Which very likely meant he would never have the money. "Skippy, give him whatever he wants."

"Hey!" Skippy jabbed a finger at me. "That is easy for you to say when it's not *your* money, you-"

"It's mostly not your money either."

"Ugh. Why are you so-"

"If we don't stop the Outsider, what will be the value of your portfolio?"

"Hmm. Well, I suppose that is a very good point."

"See? Think of the money you give the admiral as an *investment*, to hedge your portfolio," I repeated something I had heard somewhere.

"This sucks. Fine. How much?"

"Since you are in a generous mood," Scorandum tapped on a tablet.

Skippy's eye bulged. "Oh my- Why would you ever need-"

"Consider this a hedge for *my* portfolio."

"This is a bad investment already," Skippy muttered. "All right, I transferred the funds, scattered across the untraceable accounts I set up for you."

"Great," I was impatient to conclude the negotiation. "What is this plan?"

Scorandum's mandibles came together. "At this point, I would rather not say."

"But, it's been under consideration for a long time? Years?"

"It has."

"Your people have been in desperate situations before, your patrons only step in when your backs are to the wall. Why hasn't this plan been implemented?"

"Because until now, the risk was not worth the potential reward. Now, assuming you are correct that our newest enemy seeks to open a doorway to an invasion from beyond the galaxy," his antennas shrugged. "It sounds like we have very little to lose."

"That is for damned sure."

He picked up the glass, looked at it, and downed the liquid in one gulp. "There is another, more important reason we have never implemented any of our contingency plans. Until recently, the means to accomplish such an operation have not been available to us."

At first, I assumed he was talking about the technology upgrades humanity had provided. Nah, incremental advances in the capability of their warships was not a major game changer. "What is now available to you, to make it happen? Do you mean, the UN Navy?"

"No," he snorted. "This operation will require subterfuge, misdirection, and sabotage. Not crude military power."

"OK, so what is it that is now available to you?"

He set the glass down, placed the stopper in the bottle of burgoze, pushed it away from himself. "*Skippy*."

The Minister was in his office, Uhtavio knew that from being reminded that morning that his monthly payment was overdue, *again*, and the Minister would greatly appreciate it if Admiral Scorandum could deliver the money by close of business.

So, Minister Skeezix was, as always on Collections Day, in his office. His actual office, not the official chamber he had been assigned at ECO headquarters. Headquarters had too many people, who might count how much money the Minister was actually receiving, and report up *his* chain that Skeezix was withholding funds from those the money rightfully belonged to. In his office, he was typically holding court, receiving payments and flattery, dispensing advice no one was seeking.

Outside the door of the casino that was the ECO minister's unofficial official office, Scorandum examined his uniform. Something wet and slimy had dripped onto his sleeve, from the ceiling of the dank tunnel that connected the bordello entrance on the street, to the unlicensed casino in the basement of an adjacent building. He had always thought the attempt at concealment was silly, everyone knew about the casino, including the authorities who enjoyed annual bribes significantly greater than the cost of a license.

No matter. If he wiped the dot of slime off his sleeve, the Minister might question whether the Admiral had entered the casino through the *other* entrance, the one he wasn't supposed to know about.

At times like this, Uhtavio had to remind himself that, for all his wealth and high position, Skeezix was an idiot.

The Minister was not in the casino, not in his office on the floor above. Scorandum didn't need to ask where his boss was, he knew. In a room behind the back room, he pushed open a door, to find Skeezix seated on a couch, dealing cards out on a table. Playing cards used by humans, not the more civilized tiles common to the Jeraptha.

Scorandum waited a moment to be acknowledged. The Minister did not look up from the table, the moment passed. "You are learning to play human card games?" He finally asked.

"I am learning how to *cheat* at human card games," the Minister grimaced. "Last week, I played this game they call 'poker' with a group of human liaison officers. The rules seemed simple enough, not anything difficult like one of *our* tile games. They fleeced me, took everything I brought to the table. I am *certain* they cheated," he pushed the cards away with disgust. "What I don't know is *how*."

"Perhaps I could?" Scorandum gestured at the cards scattered across the table.

"You have experience with this game?"

"Some. In particular, I was taught various ways of cheating. Their cards are not individually tagged with quantum identifiers." He scooped up the cards and stacked them into a deck. "So, a human might come to a game with a similar pack of cards, and keep valuable cards, such as aces, up their sleeves."

"I *thought* of that," the Minister snapped. "They were all wearing short sleeves. Also, I watched each of them very closely."

Scorandum nodded, silently wondering whether the Minister's watching had resulted in him *seeing* anything. "Another method is called," he shuffled the deck, making it appear a casual gesture, while tucking several cards on the bottom. "Dealing off the bottom. It is not easy to demonstrate with our claws, human fingers tend to be more dexterous."

"Soft and weak, you mean."

"That also. See? I am sliding cards off the top of the deck?"

"Yes, so?"

"The first two cards were from the top. The third card," he repeated the motion slowly. "Came from the *bottom*. While I was shuffling, I placed valuable cards on the bottom."

"Hmm. I see. Can humans actually do this in a game? They are slow and clumsy."

"Not as clumsy as they first appear."

"Apparently so. Dealing from the bottom is only useful for the dealer, he gives the best cards to himself?"

"Not necessarily. Also, it would be suspicious if a player only consistently got good hands when they were the dealer. Two or more players could be working together. Sir, when a major player like yourself comes to the table, *all* the other players could be working together, to take your money."

"I know *that*," Skeezix swept a claw across the table, scattering cards on the floor. "The next time the humans invite me to play poker, you are coming with me."

"There is nothing I would like more," Uhtavio beamed, inwardly wondering if he could schedule a fatal heart attack.

"Now," the Minister assumed his full ministerial bearing, signaling the time for idle chit chat was over. "You have your tax payment?"

"I do," *tap tap tap* on the tablet, and a swipe right gesture with a claw. "The money has been transferred."

Suspicious, Minister Skeezix took out his own tablet and tapped on it. He looked at Scorandum, antennas standing straight up. "That is, a bit more than I expected," he said, before clamping his mouth shut.

'A bit' was not an accurate description, the payment Scorandum had sent was more than four times the amount he actually owed. "I assure you, the number is accurate."

"Hmmph. This makes me question whether your *past* payments were accurate."

"They were, as far as you know."

"Was that insubordination, Admiral?"

"You are not actually in my chain of command. Sir," he added, after a beat. That was the truth. The Minister's role was limited to oversight, and budgetary matters. He had no right to be fully read in on ECO operations, and he had very limited authority for approving or cancelling operations. Except, Scorandum winced, for proposed actions that could imperil all of Jeraptha society. Like the action for which he sought approval. "Recently, I received a bonus payment for services rendered, from Skippy."

"Hmm," the Minister grunted. "Use that bonus wisely, it will be the last one."

"That is not true, Sir. This payment was sent to me *today*. You can check my accounts to verify my statement."

Suddenly, Skeezix was less sure of himself. "How is that possible? Skippy is trapped inside a star, far from here."

"He is trapped in a star at this moment, however Bishop has been in contact with Skippy. They have an elegantly simple plant to rescue him, currently they are gathering specialized gear that is needed for the job."

"How do you know this?"

"Bishop is here, nearby. I met with him today, and I spoke with one of Skippy's subminds. Falling into a star is apparently only a minor inconvenience for him."

"Impossible."

"Has betting against Skippy, or the humans, *ever* worked well for anyone?"

"No.," Skeezix agreed. "Why is Bishop here? He must want something. Are we expected to supply this specialized gear you mentioned?"

"He does want something, and he, or actually Skippy, is willing to pay generously for our assistance."

"Generously? Skippy has never been known for his generosity."

"At this time, he feels that if he and the Pirates cannot defeat the Outsider, money will be of no use to him. The funds he is making available, a significant portion of his portfolio, are an investment. A hedge against his entire portfolio becoming worthless."

"That, is a rational response to the situation. Admiral, stop dancing around the subject. Tell me what reckless thing Bishop wants us to do."

"He wishes us to activate one of our contingency plans."

"One of *our* plans? How could that help the-"

"He must be free to act, both to recover Skippy, and to stop the Outsider from opening a doorway for an invasion from beyond this galaxy. Freedom to act requires keeping the Maxohlx so busy elsewhere, they will be unable to effectively interfere with Bishop's plans."

"He wants us to strike the Maxohlx?"

No, you dumbass, Scorandum shouted in his head. What he said aloud was, "Our contingency plans cover a wide variety and scope of action, across a range from wise to foolish, but to my knowledge, none of our plans are suicidally *stupid*."

Skeezix was taken aback, acknowledging the truth of the Admiral's statement with a curt nod. "*Bishop* is not aware of our plans."

"That is true, only if you assume that Skippy has not hacked our cybersecurity."

"*Shit*. Has he?"

"I would not wager money that he can't do that."

"Neither would I. Our contingency plans have remained just plans, because the risks outweigh the rewards."

"Until now. Minister, the Outsiders possess technology that allows them to cross the gulf between galaxies. They frightened the *Elders* into taking extreme actions. They are unimaginably more advanced than any current species. In important ways, even more advanced than Skippy."

"Then, how can Bishop hope to defeat them?"

"He can defeat *it*. There is only one Outsider entity in our galaxy. It is isolated and vulnerable, that is why it has formed an alliance with the Maxohlx. They agreed to an alliance because they are delusional idiots."

"We agree on that, at least. If we assume the Pirates can stop this one Outsider, then-"

"Excuse me, Sir, we *must* assume that."

"Huh? Why?"

"There is no future for any of us, if the Pirates fail this mission."

"That is an 'If' you cannot easily dismiss."

"Excuse me, Sir," he repeated himself. "The Pirates defeated the *Elders*. No one thought that could ever happen. Yet, it did."

"Very well, Admiral, which of our plans does Bishop wish us to activate?"

"Blue Seven."

"*Blue*- You must be joking. The code 'Blue' is assigned to plans that are end games. Plans that commit us absolutely."

"As I explained to Bishop, with Blue Seven we would be," he made the gesture of pushing chips to the center of the table with both claws. "All in."

"*All in*," the Minister breathed.

"There is nothing so dangerous, or so *thrilling*."

Skeezix nodded, the statement was accurate. "This would be juicy action."

"The *juiciest*. Only a handful of people would know what is going on, or why. The action would be contained within that select group." He knew that possessing secret knowledge was a massive ego boost to those in power.

"Still, *Blue Seven*?"

"It is the only plan that has any chance of assisting Bishop, in the time available."

"What time is available?"

"That I do not know. Other than that Skippy is freely giving away his money, so-"

"*Shiiiiit*. Admiral," the Minister slowly rose from the couch. "I will speak with, the people who need to be read in on this. This will not be an easy decision."

While Minister Skeezix met with the most senior of government officials, and those dunderheads debated the blindingly obvious question of whether to do something risky that might result in the salvation of their species, or to do nothing and wait for their inevitable doom, Uhtavio Scorandum had an errand to run. Not just an errand, he had to pay off a debt to an old friend. His former protégé. He had a meeting with the Chief Enforcer of the Inquisitors, something that would normally be unthinkable. And possible only because the Chief Enforcer assumed Scorandum sought a meeting to beg for Kinsta to be treated with leniency, a word not recognized by the Enforcers. While the admiral groveled, Enforcer Zavarigan could revel in righteous indignation, by far her favorite emotion.

To maximize the intimidation and humiliation of his visit, Zavarigan had insisted they meet in her office. The process of signing in at the front desk, of having to wear a tracking bracelet, of being escorted by hulking, humorless guards, and finally an interminable wait before the door to the Chief Inquisitor's inner sanctum opened, all were intended to put the sleazy admiral of the so-called 'Ethics' office in his place.

"Thank you very much for receiving me, Chief Enforcer," Scorandum said as he bowed deeply upon passing through the doorway.

"You have manners, at least," she sniffed from the gaudy oversized chair behind her desk. "I suspect your contrition is an act."

"I seek only to talk, Your Eminence."

"Very well," she actually managed to smile, though it was the smile of a predator about to enjoy a tasty treat. To her guards she waved a claw with, "You are dismissed."

The heavy door closed with an ominous *THUNK*, a sound no doubt engineered to instill a sense of dread in anyone unfortunate enough to be called into that office.

"Speak," she appeared to be making an effort to summon all the haughtiness she could muster. "And be quick about it."

"I wish to discuss the detention of my former protégé, and your employee, Kinsta."

"Kinsta," she spat the name. "Is a *former* employee, and a current inmate of the Drexum prison, as I am sure you know. He has been judged and convicted of his many crimes, offenses in which I suspect that you are an unindicted co-conspirator, the-"

"Which is the best kind of co-conspirator to be, in my experience."

Zavarigan was *not* amused. "Eventually, your sins will catch up to you, and we will have a final triumph."

"I suspect my sins will catch up to my liver first."

"You dare joke, while your protégé's fate hangs in the balance?"

"I joke because his fate does *not* hang in the balance. It has already been decided."

"On that, we agree."

"Yes. Although, not in the way you believe. Kinsta's fate is to be declared innocent of all charges, to receive an official apology delivered by you personally, and for him to be released from service here, so he can come home to where he belongs."

She stared at him, antennas rigid. "You have lost your mind."

"What I have not lost is *this*," he pulled a data stick from a pocket, and set it in front of her on the desk. "I strongly suggest you examine the contents."

"Admiral, I am in no mood to play games with you."

"I assure you, this is no *game*, you self-righteous moron."

She gasped. "You dare insult me so, in my own office?"

"Someone has to, and as we are alone here, so-"

"I will not dignify your rudeness with-"

"Oh, shut *up*," he waved a claw in a weary gesture. "This is so tiresome. Really, I expected this to be a lot more enjoyable."

Another, more sustained gasp.

He continued. "You will examine the contents of this data stick," he nudged it across the desk to her. "Or, I will have it provided to your Minister, and then *you* will spend the rest of your life staring at the walls of a jail cell. I am told that your Minister Gurklund was born without a sense of humor, but I believe even he will see the delicious irony of his Chief Enforcer being caught committing *very* serious crimes."

With reluctance, she took the data stick, holding it with the tips of her claw as if the material could contaminate her. That was when Uhtavio Scorandum began to enjoy the encounter. Idly, as he watched shock and rage building on the face of his opponent, he wondered whether she kept any burgoze in her desk. Almost certainly not, he decided. The purpose of the office was to intimidate visitors, not accommodate them.

Sitting quietly, he amused himself by trying to guess which incriminating document she was reading at the moment, based on her facial expressions and body language, or by how quickly she was breathing. The documents chronicled how Zavarigan had secretly used her position with the Inquisitors to her personal benefit, since she first joined the Office of Special Inquiries directly after she graduated from seminary school.

"These documents are *fake*," she spat, when she was able to regain her composure, and her breath.

"That I freely admit, with pride."

"An ECO trick, then." Her smugness returned. "What you do not know is we have powerful forensic AIs, that can determine the true authenticity of any document."

"What *you* do not know is these documents were not created by my office, they know nothing about it. They were created, as a personal favor for me, by an entity who *laughs* at the pathetic abilities of your forensic system."

"By *Skippy*?" That was when fear first flashed across her face. "He would not-"

"Ha!" He laughed explosively. "If you believe there is anything Skippy would *not* do, you don't know him at all. I said he put together those documents as a favor to me, and that is partly true. His true motivation is that he dearly loves to screw with self-righteous jerks like you. As far as anyone will be able to determine, the trail for these documents extends far across our territory, to archives on dozens of worlds, and their history goes back decades. To the beginning of your career actually, which I am sure is a coincidence. You will never be able to prove otherwise."

"You cannot do this," she protested, though he could see in her eyes that she had accepted the possibility of defeat.

"The humans have an expression that is appropriate for this situation: that word does not mean what you think it means. I *have* done it, therefore I can. Zavarigan, I grow tired of sparring with you, it is like playing tiles against a brain-dead opponent. Here is what will happen. You will announce, hmm. Not tomorrow, for that would be suspiciously close after my visit here. In the next three days you will announce that Kinsta is entirely innocent, that he in fact was working *with* your office to determine whether the Inquisitors have a spy within their ranks, which you will happily declare is *not* true. Er," he realized that he couldn't imagine her doing anything *happily*. "You can skip the happiness part, if you like. Kinsta will be given a commendation, and a substantial bonus, for-"

"That is-"

"Is *not* negotiable."

"As one of *you* would say, everything is-"

"Everything is negotiable, in a *negotiation*. This is not me bargaining with you, this is me giving you instructions."

"I cannot-"

"You of all people should know how Inquisitor traitors are treated in your prison." That, he saw with great satisfaction, prompted a shudder from the feared Chief Enforcer. "According to this," he pointed to the fateful data stick. "You have betrayed your office in the worst way possible, and you did it for years. Unless you can prove otherwise," he laughed. "You know, I am now not certain which outcome I prefer. You releasing Kinsta, which would be good for him, and humiliating to you. Or, you attempt to prove your innocence, and spend the rest of your miserable life in a prison cell. That would be *delicious*. Hmm, even Kinsta might agree his continued incarceration is worth seeing you in prison with him."

"It would-"

"The worst part for you would be the utter destruction of your reputation. Perhaps you did not read far enough down in the files, but apparently you manufactured evidence against at least three innocent Inquisitors. Innocent people who will be set free, as a result of your crimes."

"That cannot happen."

"Then," he sat back on the couch with a shrug. "You have only one choice."

His next stop was at Drexum prison, conveniently located adjacent to the Inquisitor headquarters. A location that allowed people working in the office to jeer at the prisoners before or after the workday. Such visits were encouraged, to remind employees what will happen, should they choose to stray from the path of righteousness.

Ordinarily, an ECO official would have no access to the Drexum facility. That day, he had a pass, signed personally by the Chief Enforcer. He would definitely be keeping *that* pass as a memento.

"Kinsta," he waved, as his once and future protégé was led through a door into an interview room. "You are looking-" What could he say that was at least remotely believable? "Reasonably intact, considering."

His former aide had bandages around his head, one leg was in a splint, and he had a bent antenna. One eye was swollen almost closed. He shuffled into the room. "I have been here only five days, and look at me."

"Your courage and endurance are an inspiration."

"I don't want to *endure*, or be courageous."

"Some choose greatness," Scorandum's antennas bent in a sort of shrug. "While others have greatness smack them on the head. Tell me, did you enjoy the fruit basket I sent?"

"I traded it for protection."

"Which of your fellow prisoners are bothering you?"

"It's not the inmates, it's the *guards*."

"Hmm. I might be able to do something about that. For protection against other inmates, I have a bit of advice for you. Walk up to the biggest, strongest badass in this prison, and give him an epic beatdown, to establish your dominance."

Kinsta's one good eye slowly blinked. "You think I should *do* that?"

"Not really. Although, hmm, we can both agree that would be *hilarious*. Er, more for me than for you. You should try it, and let me know how it works for you."

"Sir-"

"I joke, Kinsta, I joke," he waved his hands. "To be serious, you will be enjoying the luxurious accommodations here for only two more days, then you will be released."

"Please do not joke about something like that."

"No joke, I assure you. The Chief Enforcer has had a, I suppose you could say she has had a change of heart. After another review of the evidence against you, all charges are to be dropped, imminently."

His eye blinked rapidly, then narrowed. "You made a deal?"

"It would be more accurate to say I made an offer she could not refuse. Kinsta, this is not something you need to know about."

"You are *serious*? This is for real?"

"It is. Unfortunately, to avoid suspicion about the timing of my visit to the Chief Enforcer and your release, you must remain here two more days."

"I am not sure I will *survive* another two days. One guard, the one who did this," he pointed a claw to the bandages. "He said they had orders to make my life miserable."

"That is unfortunate. You would not happen to know this guard's name, would you?"

"Everyone here knows him," Kinsta shuddered. "His name is Rollivak."

"As I said, unfortunate," Scorandum frowned, though he had a very different idea about who was the victim of misfortune. Or about to be. "I will see what I can do, to make your stay more comfortable."

Leaving his former aide, the very pissed off ECO Admiral did two things. First, he made a phone call. After a brief conversation, he requested a meeting with the prison warden.

Two hours later, bored out of his mind from being stuck in a waiting room, Scorandum was ushered into the warden's office.

"I am very busy," the warden didn't bother to look up from the tablet he was tapping on. "Make your offer."

"What offer?" Scorandum asked smoothly as he slid onto a couch.

"Let's not play games. You are here to offer me a bribe," the warden snorted. "In exchange for coddling your friend."

"Oh, there will be no offer of a bribe. You are, as you said, a busy man, so I will proceed straight to threats."

"Threats?" the warden laughed.

"You have a guard here named Rollivak?"

"Why?"

"He is not scheduled to work today, so he was at home, I am told. Tragically, a short time ago, he suffered a freak accident, and plunged to his death."

The warden's eyes bulged. "Rollivak's apartment is on the *ground floor* of his building."

"Hence why I described it as a freak accident."

"You-"

"*I* did nothing. Not anything directly. So, now that we should have some level of understanding, I will get to the threat. Unless you also would enjoy being the victim of an unfortunate *accident*, Kinsta will be given VIP treatment here. Do not worry, I have it on good authority that he will not be a guest of this establishment for much longer."

"You dare to-"

"Warden, this is a dispute between your office, and mine. You, the late and unlamented Rollivak, and Kinsta, are merely pawns in a game that has been going on for centuries. You will never be a player, but you could become a *victim*."

"If you think-"

"I *think* you should pick up a phone, and call the Chief Enforcer right now. What you do not know is, Zavarigan has been playing her own game, using Kinsta as her personal pawn. The game will be ending soon. Please, for your own sake, make a call."

Kinsta still walked with a limp, and he still ached despite the nerve blockers skillfully applied by the somewhat resentful prison doctors. Resentful of a prisoner receiving VIP treatment, even more resentful by the hulking, armed and armored Enforcer guards who were there not to prevent Kinsta from escaping, but to ensure the doctors did exactly as they were told. When the former Inquisitor officer walked out of the prison, there would be no visible injuries, no bruises, no limb awkwardly in a splint. The doctors had done the best they could, even using specialized equipment flown in at great expense.

So, when the heavy outer doors of the building opened and Kinsta blinked from sunshine he had not seen for too many days, he might have exaggerated the limp, and he would have been forgiven for his performance. The sunlight was blinding, he had to stop in the doorway to shield his eyes with a hand, stumbling as he was nudged from behind by a guard.

"Excuse me, Sir," the offending guard apologized with a short bow from the thorax. The apology was not an act, or at least, the nudge had not been intentionally hostile. The people around him were wearing dress uniforms rather than body armor, and carrying ceremonial swords so highly polished, they gleamed brighter than the midmorning sunlight outside. No, they were not prison guards, they were a squad of Inquisitor honor guards. Dangerous, yes, but not to him. He was in favor at the moment, having enjoyed shockingly fabulous treatment over the past two days. First, the visit to the prison hospital. Next, being moved to the warden's private suite of offices, with its own bedroom, a shower with water jets powerful enough to scrub the prison grime from his leathery skin, and a private dining hall. Dinner had been a sumptuous affair of seven courses, all expertly prepared, each course accompanied by appropriate beverages, including a final glass of an outstanding vintage burgoze. He spent the evening alone, other than waiters bringing in the next dish. After the plates were cleared away, a very attractive woman came into the dining room, offering a relaxing massage, and hinting that other services might be available. Wary of a trap, Kinsta had declined, an action he regretted the next morning. The whole evening, the plush bed, the private quarters, he was certain all of it was an elaborate ruse, to get him to lower his guard. All that day, he kept waiting for the suite door to burst open, and for a group of guards to drag him back to his cell. What a dope Kinsta was, the guards would laugh, what a gullible sucker.

It hadn't happened. In fact, nothing bad at all happened. After a delicious breakfast with far more food than he could eat, he had been offered fresh, clean clothes, his few personal possessions had been returned, and the honor guard had marched him down to the release office, where he had to sign several forms. Still wary, he had taken precious minutes to read the forms before he had given up, shrugged, and scrawled his signature seven times. He was then declared a free citizen, given a certificate of appreciation from the Office of Special Inquiries, and gently escorted to the main front doorway.

Still squinting and blinking, he took an apprehensive step forward. Toward the outside, toward freedom. He was out of the building, at the top of the broad stone stairs that led down to the avenue, where a crowd had gathered, cameras held in claws. The crowd was being held back by Enforcers who were wearing real armor and carrying real weapons, but not actually menacing anyone. The crowd was in the shape of a V, at the point, waiting on the street, was a vehicle.

Kinsta's heart sank.

Not just any vehicle. It was an Enforcer armored personnel carrier.

That was his nightmare.

It was all a sham. Uhtavio Scorandum had failed to secure his release, or even more likely, the ECO admiral was playing a game, at Kinsta's expense. He was more angry at Scorandum than at the Inquisitors, for his former boss was the one who had given him false hope.

He was on his own, he understood that. Antennas held high, he slowly walked down the long set of stairs, not trusting himself to avoid the very public humiliation of stumbling. When he reached the sidewalk, the door of the APC swung open, but the personnel compartment was dark, he couldn't see inside. At least the weapons blisters on that side were not tracking him, the muzzle covers had not retracted. The Inquisitors were not going to kill him right there, so he had that going for him. Taking a breath and ignoring shouts from the crowd, he stepped inside.

A row of lights snapped on, and he blinked, surprised again. The interior was not stark couches of webbing to hold armored troops, the couches were plush, luxurious. Where he had expected to see a weapons rack was a well-stocked bar, complete with heavy crystal glasses.

And the only occupant, relaxing with a crystal glass of what smelled like very fine burgoze, was Uhtavio Scorandum.

"Ah, Kinsta, there you are. Sit, sit," he patted the couch next to him.

Kinsta did not sit. "What game are you playing?"

"What you meant to say," the admiral took a slurp of his drink, "was 'May I ask what game you are playing, *Sir*'?"

Kinsta glared. "Let's pretend I said it that way."

"Good enough," Scorandum's antennas shrugged, and he patted the couch again. "The vehicle will not move until you are seated. Unless you prefer to be gawked at by the paparazzi?"

"No," Kinsta sat, stiff, sullen. The door closed, and Scorandum thumped a claw on the side wall of the vehicle. The APC began rolling.

"Sir, what is going on?"

The admiral blinked, or pretended to. The gesture was not his best effort. "Whatever could you mean?" He thumped the wall panel again, and the vehicle stopped.

From the short trip and abrupt right turn, Kinsta guessed they had only gone around the corner. "Am I free, or not? Please don't lie to me, Sir."

"As I have already, repeatedly, assured you, all charges against you have been dropped. The Chief Enforcer herself, and the Internal Affairs department of our own illustrious Office, have announced the results of a very successful joint operation, in which you of course played a crucial role. At great personal cost to yourself, which has not gone unnoticed."

"The worst part is," Kinsta snorted. "The day I get out of prison, my own boss picks me up in an Enforcer APC!"

"Don't be so dramatic," the admiral scoffed. "This is more like a limousine than a military vehicle."

"Are limousines typically equipped with," Kinsta pointed to the power conduits that connected to the defensive maser cannons. "Antimissile systems?"

"I suppose that depends on who owns the vehicle. Oooh, the excitement is beginning!" Tapping a touchscreen, the admiral activated the external cameras, showing a view of the back of the crowd assembled in front of the prison. More people were approaching the prison entrance, trying to squeeze through so they could have a view.

Kinsta was thoroughly confused. He had been driven away, yet the crowd had not dispersed. "Sir, what is going on?"

"As I said, the excitement is just beginning."

"The crowd, the media, they are not here to see me?"

"*You*?" Scorandum laughed. "No, you are yesterday's news. You are a *hero*, Kinsta. That means you get fifteen seconds of fame, which burned out before this morning's news cycle. What people want is not heroism."

Kinsta's antennas drooped. "They don't?"

"Of course not. Heroes are boring, they are all the same. Dull, righteous, they eat a balanced diet, and avoid excess. What's the fun in that?" A healthy slurp of burgoze emphasized the point. "Besides, seeing people acting heroically, only makes everyone else feel inadequate. No, what the people want is an interesting villain, and a juicy *scandal.*"

"What scandal? I was declared innocent!"

"You were, and if the public knew the truth about your release, that *would* be a scandal. You do not want to know how I arranged for your freedom. I would, but clearly you and I are very different people."

"Sir, please don't tell me the details. I have to pretend that I actually was part of an undercover investigation?"

"See? It is easier to keep your story straight when you don't know the full truth."

"Then, what is the scandal, Sir?"

"Oh well, the Chief Enforcer was encouraged to grant your release, not that she really had a choice in the matter. The Ethics Office has always triumphed in any battles with the Inquisitors, that is why the jerks over there hate us so passionately. That hate was for a time, as you know, directed at yourself."

"Please don't remind me."

"You can- Oh." The crowd outside became agitated. "This is no good," the admiral frowned. "We can't see anything. Oh, I will switch to the drone camera."

The view was not from above, as the drone had landed and was clinging to the front of the prison. From the displays that replaced cabin windows of the APC, Kinsta could see that another, larger armored vehicle had arrived. That truck was clearly militarized, two roof-mounted gun turrets swiveled to cover the crowd, and the air above the vehicle shimmered from the effect of an energy shield. The crowd buzzed as the heavy side door opened, two armed guards got out, followed by the prisoner.

Kinsta gasped. "That is-"

"Director Allquent, yes," Scorandum confirmed. "To be accurate, *former* Director Allquent. The scandal is that, in his position as chief of the Inquisitor's Internal Affairs department, he took bribes to frame innocent employees, and also to eliminate his rivals. He did *not* manage to get rid of the Chief Enforcer, but she certainly was not shy about acting against him. You see, Kinsta, your brave and self-sacrificing undercover investigation, under instructions from the Chief Enforcer, revealed that the ECO did *not* have a spy in the Inquisitors. The leak, the *corruption*, was inside the Office of Special Inquiries all along. Now, the Chief Enforcer is clear to eventually assume leadership of the Inquisitors, and she is not only under our control, she is grateful for our assistance."

"Is any of what you said actually true, Sir?"

"About the Chief Enforcer?'

"About the supposed guilt of Director Allquent."

"He certainly was guilty of being in the way, and of believing he was untouchable."

"But, was he taking bribes?"

"Do you care?"

Kinsta considered for a moment, then leaned back into the plush cushions of the couch. "I *should*," he frowned. Picking up the bottle of burgoze, he lifted it to his mouth and drank straight from the bottle. "But, knowing what a bunch of self-righteous jerks the Inquisitors are, I say," he took another drink. "Fuck 'em."

Scorandum's eyes welled up with tears. "I have never been so proud in my life."

CHAPTER FOURTEEN

The waiting was driving me crazy, and with not much for me to do aboard the star carrier, I had a lot of time to worry about what could have gone wrong. Yes, I understood I was asking a lot from the beetles, who were not even officially allies. They would be taking on a major risk, with them having to share the potential rewards with everyone in the galaxy. Well, everyone other than the Maxohlx, but screw them.

A couple days after he left the ship, Scorandum sent a signal requesting coordinates to rendezvous with *La Fayette*. Before a reply was received, he flew up to *The House Always Wins*, and by the time he was aboard that ship, he had coordinates.

"Admiral," I took the call in my office, a few moments after we detected the gamma ray burst of a ship arriving. Bilby confirmed the ship was the ECO cruiser we had seen recently, and Reed stood the crew down from Red, to Yellow alert. Less than four days had passed since he left to seek approval for, whatever he had planned. That could not be good news, no government makes such sweeping decisions quickly. Still, I had to be hopeful. "Your leadership approved activating this plan?"

His antennas bobbed side to side as he shook his head. "Unfortunately, they did not. That would be too big a request for them."

"Shit. So we-"

"They also are not expressly forbidding *me* from activating the plan. A plan they know nothing about. If you know what I mean."

"Ah. This is about plausible deniability."

"I can plausibly deny I heard *that*."

"Gotcha. If there is any blowback from the op, they can blame you."

"General Bishop, there certainly *will* be blowback, and against my people, not yours. Even if you do stop the Outsider, the Maxohlx will retaliate, and Jeraptha will suffer."

"Uh, then why are you willing to-"

"Suffering we can withstand, we have done it before, we can recover. Allowing an Outsider force into our galaxy would be *fatal*. We are simply playing the odds. That is how I was able to receive even unofficial approval. My leadership sees this moment as a unique opportunity for short-term pain that will yield lasting results. And, despite them being politicians, they understand there is no survival for anyone, if you fail."

"I hear that. OK, what's next? What is this plan?"

"My suggestion, if you don't mind, is I come aboard your star carrier. There is much to discuss."

"I hope this plan doesn't involve us shooting anything. *La Fayette* is in better condition than the *Dutchman* was most of the time, but it's a trash hauler, not a warship."

"Please, General," his mandibles worked side to side, like he was spitting out something distasteful. "You know I abhor violence."

"OK, but then how-"

"We will let *others* do all the shooting. I expect there will be quite a lot of it."

"I like this plan already."

The *La Fayette* jumped, to begin that ship's life of crime.

Voss Blulockar, the Bosphuraq ambassador to the Maxohlx Hegemony on their homeworld, had to set down his tablet, walk shakily over to a cabinet in his office, pour himself a stiff drink, and gulp down half of the fiery liquor, before he could continue. He started at the beginning, the personal note from the Secretary of Patron Relations. The note, carefully hedged in diplomatic language even though only Blulockar was supposed to read it, basically stated that the Secretary was sorry about the likely consequences to the ambassador and his staff. But, the Secretary had orders direct from the top, and now the Ambassador had a duty to fulfill. The note ended with an assurance that the Secretariat would see that Blulockar's family was taken care of.

After reading the note twice, his hands shook as he broke the seal on the official communication he was to present to their patrons. How bad could it be?

Answer: very bad.

As instructed, he requested an immediate audience with the Office of Client Affairs, to speak with the Minister, on a most urgent matter. As had been custom since long before he came to represent his people to the Hegemony, the patrons ignored his first request, so he had an aide carry a hand-written note to the Client Affairs headquarters building. The aide was not allowed within a city block of the headquarters entrance, despite wearing the required and uncomfortable suit that contained the distinctive scent of the Bosphuraq. Stopped by police, the aide explained he only wished to deliver a note. The note was taken away, the aide was taken into detention, and released only after the Ambassador paid a hefty fine for trespassing. That also was customary, his office even had a government form to claim that specific expense.

It was the following morning that Ambassador Blulockar was escorted in the Client Affairs building, subjected to a thorough and humiliating search, and made to wait in his confining suit for most of the morning, before he was finally allowed to speak with a very junior member of the Client Affairs staff. An arrogant, irritated staffer.

"What is it you people want *this* time?" The Maxohlx snapped, or that is how the angry words sounded in Blulockar's earpiece. The staffer had not spoken, not using his crude biological voicebox. He had thought the words into his cranial implant, which had then sent the message to the recipient's earpiece.

The Ambassador had to reply the old fashioned way, taking a moment to decide whether to point out that the last time he approached his patrons had been over a year ago, so that day's meeting was not much of an imposition on his hosts. He decided not to mention it. The diplomatic message by itself was enough to enrage the Maxohlx. "I am instructed to deliver this message," he removed from a pocket the note, which was inscribed on a sheet of plastic, wrapped in a layer of plastic so the Maxohlx would not risk soiling themselves with anything he touched. The message was written in rather direct language for a communication with the prickly patrons of the Bosphuraq, and no effort had been made to translate the text into the format used by the Hegemony. "It is a most urgent matter, I am instructed to say."

The Maxohlx snorted, aloud, not through an implant. An expression of disgust. Putting on disposable gloves first, he took the note, and his expression quickly changed from disgust to outrage. When he finished, he stared silently for a moment, his mouth opening, then closing in a tight line. Eyes blazing with anger, he snarled as he tapped the message, "You *dare*?"

"I can only follow my instructions, Esteemed Patron."

"You are aware of what this message," the staffer flung the plastic sheet away, "says? How it *insults* us?"

"I was instructed to familiarize myself with the message, yes."

"Perhaps," the staffer growled in a way that made it clear there was no 'Perhaps' about it, "you would summarize the key points for me."

Swallowing hard, Blulockar wondered, not for the first time that day, whether he would leave the headquarters building alive, or not. "The message states our concern about your recent, *partnership*," he chose that word carefully, "with the being known as the Outsider. We wish to understand what long-term strategic value you foresee from the partnership. And," he swallowed hard again. "How it benefits my people."

"*Your* people."

"Correct."

"Your people are *client*s. You do not need to *understand*, you only need to *obey*."

"We will of course carry out our responsibilities under our client-patron treaty. The question is," he had to take a breath before continuing. "What level of enthusiasm we will have in following your orders. My government is very, is *extremely* concerned, that if the humans are not lying, the Outsider is a threat to the entire galaxy. We seek assurances that the Outsider is not preparing for an invasion." After a pause, in a whisper, he added, "Please."

It was early the next morning, before sunrise, that Ambassador Blulockar was roughly escorted from the jail cell he had been roughly thrown into. It was, he had resigned himself, to be a public execution, as punishment for the grave insult he had delivered.

To his utter astonishment, he was escorted out the front door of the building, and pushed toward the sidewalk. Turning to the guards, he bowed deeply. "I am free to go?"

"You are. The punishment for your insult is for you to watch helplessly, as we deliver *our* reply to your message."

It would have been less painful, the Ambassador considered as he hurried away, if they had simply shot him in the head.

At the end of five frantic days, racing through wormhole shortcuts, contacting relay stations, and generally setting in motion a whole lot of very sketchy things, we dropped Scorandum off near his homeworld. What about our honored guests Ned and Jethro, you ask? Within an hour of them having been put into a cell in the ship's brig, they had tried to kill each other, so we had to separate them. In the past, I would have enjoyed visiting them and telling them they weren't so freakin' smart, but the older, wiser me was over that. Those hateful cyborgs weren't worth my time. Scorandum took Ned and Jethro with him, assuring me the happy couple would be enjoying the luxurious accommodations at a secure ECO facility. Or not enjoying it, we really didn't care.

The moment our dropship returned from delivering him to the ECO cruiser *We Do Not Speak Of It*, I went straight to my cabin and slept for eleven hours. Being with Admiral Scorandum was exhausting, I had to be 'Up' all the time. Also, the guy could *drink* OMG. I never want to see another bottle of bourbon again in my life. OK, not for the rest of the week. From the Jeraptha home system, we raced back to Shangri-La, arriving two days late.

Or not late. *Valkyrie* was still in the Shangri-La spacedock when we arrived. Technically, the ship was *back* in spacedock. The shakedown cruise had revealed things shaking loose, and Reed had opted for completing final repairs in the dock.

"Reed?" I called. "How long until you can back *Valkyrie* out of there?"

"Three hours. Or twenty minutes if it's urgent, the items remaining on the squawk list can be handled in flight. There are some repair items this spacedock couldn't handle, because *Valkyrie* is a unique design."

"Take the three hours, get it done right."

"Thank you. Sir? Where are we going from here?"

"Your real question is, did we figure out which star is the collector's home? Not yet, we are- Oh, hell, Fireball, we have no freakin' clue where the thing came from. I am still thinking about it, but it's gotten to the point where I'm deliberately *not* thinking about it, if you know what I mean."

"I do, Sir."

"Right now, I just want to sleep in my own bed. I had forgotten how short these Thuranin bunks are. And I kept whacking my head on the overhead cabinet."

"Just like old times, Sir."

"I do not miss those times."

The *La Fayette* did not have a gym for humans, so I had worked out by doing pushups, pullups, all sorts of body weight exercises. And running through the ship's long spine, damn I had also forgotten how long a star carrier was. The first time I ran to the back of the spine, I was so tired, I rode the tram halfway back. When I walked into *Valkyrie's* gym, nothing inspired me. Running on a treadmill, *again*? How many miles had I pounded out running on the deck of a treadmill, like a freakin' hamster? The Spin class was full, the three other exercise bikes occupied. Weights? I had done a hard upper body workout the day before, so I should do legs. Best to warm up first. What about basketball? Both courts were busy with pickup games, so I walked around to the back of the far court. A narrow compartment there was thirty meters long, with hoops on each end. The compartment was good for sprints, or cone drills for speed and agility. What I did was get a ball from the bin in the corner, and shoot free throws. It's a mindless exercise that helps me think. Literally mindless, to make accurate shots one after another, I can't be thinking hard about what my muscles are doing. For me, over-thinking makes me miss the hoop, and then I'm chasing the ball all over the court.

That still happens anyway. I don't totally suck at free throws, I still occasionally throw a brick. Like right then, when the ball bounced off the backboard at an odd angle, bounced off the left wall, and past me. Reminding myself not to let myself get annoyed by small stuff, I trotted after the ball. Should I attempt a three pointer from that distance? Why not?

Nothing but net! The old man still has it.

Speaking of old men, looking around the long, narrow compartment got me to thinking. Could the space be converted to a bocce court? A quick search on my phone showed a regulation bocce court is ninety one feet long, so thirty meters was plenty of space. Why bocce? We had space devoted to strenuous sports, but nothing for a gentle game like bocce. My parents had been in a bocce league when they lived near Club Skippy, before they moved out to their farm. They made a lot of friends while playing in the league, and it's not easy for adults to make new friends. My father liked that you can play with a beer in one hand, which I did not expect to happen aboard *Valkyrie*. Walking to the end of the compartment, I pantomimed throwing a ball at an imaginary target, another ball. It's not as easy as it sounds, your bocce ball can collide with one of your own balls, knocking your balls away from the target. Or, your opponent can hit the target ball, moving it so-

Moving it.

Balls colliding.

Holy shit.

Was that-

It was worth exploring.

Or, would I only be making a fool of myself again?

Oh hell, it's not like Skippy's opinion of my intelligence could get any lower.

Still- It could wait until I went to my office.

Except, Skippy noticed I had cut my workout short, because of course he did. "Hey Joe, are you slacking off today?"

"No, thanks for asking."

"What was that thing you were doing, throwing a pretend ball? Ooooh, does Little Joey have an imaginary friend?"

"I have someone who I sometimes *wish* was only in my imagination."

"Oh shut up. I noticed you threw underhand, are you planning to play softball?"

"Again, no, thanks for asking."

"OK well- Oh no."

"Oh no, what?"

"You have that stupid look on your face. The one you get when your monkey brain dreams up an idea."
"Ayuh."
"That's all I'm going to get? An 'Ayuh'?"
"For now, yes. I'll tell you about it when I am in my office."
"I can send a maintenance bot to carry you there, *super* fast."
"That will not be necessary. Why are you in such a hurry? You are practically eternal, I'd think you would have more patience."
"Ugh. My thinking processes are so fast, waiting a minute of slow monkey time feels like forever. Joe, during the time it takes you to walk to your office, I could not only read all six volumes of Edward Gibbon's classic 'The Decline And Fall of The Roman Empire', I could have *experienced* that empire's entire history."
"Well, how about you write your own six volume history of the Roman Empire, to point out what a knucklehead that Gibbon guy was?"
"Huuuuuuuh." He gasped. "That is a *great* idea."
Like most everything Skippy thinks is a great idea, it was actually a terrible idea. Although, it would keep him busy for a while, so why not? "The stuffy academic world of Roman Empire scholarship," I guessed that such a thing existed. "Certainly could use some shaking up, and I can't think of anyone better able to shake things up than you."
"OKgottagonowbye." The avatar blinked out.

Before stepping into my office, I had to dodge a bot that raced past me, carrying a box. The bot rolled on two wheels, skidded to a stop at my office door which opened for it, then rolled back out with much less haste, without the box.
What the hell?
In my office, I tapped the plastic box. The thing was about a foot square, and two feet tall. "Skippy, what is this?"
"Joe Joe Joe, open it, quick! Inside are the nine volumes of my *complete* history of the Roman Empire, except of course I refer only to the western empire, not the later eastern empire that was centered on Byzantium. Byzantine scholarship is a whole 'nother mess that I will straighten out, after monkeykind has time to read and process my epic work."
"Nine volumes, huh?"
"Gibbons only wrote six, so he can suck it, ha!"
"I'm not sure that more volumes equals better quality scholarship, but whatever." Lifting the lid of the box, I pulled out the heavy leather bound book that was on top. The edges of the pages were gold, making me wonder if Skippy had used real gold. "You researched, wrote, and printed all those books, in the time it took me to walk to my office?"
"Yes, why does that surprise you? I did all that with three minutes to spare, monkey minutes I mean."
Holding the book open and flipping through the pages, I glanced at the last page. "Where are the footnotes? You know, the section at the back where you cite the sources of your research?"

"Like I need monkeys to tell me what to think, Joe."

"You didn't do *any* research? Is that," I flipped through again and stopped at a page with illustrations. "Is that why in this drawing, Augustus Caesar is wearing a mohawk?"

"Oh, like you know for certain he was *not* a hairstyle pioneer?"

"Uh, also, Caesar has," I squinted and counted. "Seven fingers on his left hand? And there is a," more squinting. "A 1968 Chevy Camaro in the background, racing with chariots in the Colosseum?"

"Ugh. The stupid AI image generator I used needs some tweaking, I'll fix all that in the second edition. OK, OK, so you found two issues. On the bottom of the box is a blank notebook, a pen, and a highlighter. You had better get started."

"Started on what?"

"On reviewing the books for typos and other minor issues."

"You, you want me to *read* all of this crap?"

"Skim it, Joe, skim it. I don't expect you to comprehend *any* of my extremely scholarly insights into the subject. You are no expert on the Roman Empire, you think Julius Ceasar is famous for inventing a *salad*," he chuckled.

"Someone in the crew must know more about the subject than I do, why not ask them to review your books?"

"Because a so-called expert would nitpick everything, and the review would take for-EH-ver. What I need is an average monkey, to look for mistakes that an average monkey would notice."

"It feels like you just insulted me."

"That depends on whether you think being an average monkey is a good thing or not."

"Skippy, thanks for the offer, but I'm busy. We are both going to be busy."

"It's cute you think that. Joe, tell me your latest moronic idea, so we can get that out of the way."

Setting down the substantial weight of Volume One, I asked, "You can predict how a star's spectral signature changes over time?"

"Yes, as I told you, that's just simple math."

"Uh huh. That is true, only if nothing unexpected and bad happened to the star?"

"Um, I'm not following you. Bad like, the star's companion planets left a one star review on Yelp or-"

"What if a rogue planet, or a wandering brown dwarf star, collided with a red dwarf? Would that change the spectrum the red dwarf emits?"

"This is incredible."

"Shit. Did I just say something even more stupid than you thought possible?"

"No, darn it. I thought I had reached my limit for hating someone, but that was before you asked 'Duuuuuuh, what if something collided with the star'?"

"I said it without the Duh, you ass."

"Trust me, when you speak there is always an implied *Duuuuuh*."

"So," I ignored his attempt to bait me into an argument. "It's possible? You couldn't find a star that matches the collector, because that star later had an accident that changed its composition?"

"It is not only possible, it is the most likely explanation for why my initial search didn't find a match," he grumbled. "It is so freakin' *obvious*, now that you said it. For the collector to have been ejected from a star system, there must have been some violent event, enough to push the collector past the star's escape velocity. How did I not see this?!"

"Seeing obvious stuff is my job, Skippy. Understanding all the complicated non-obvious stuff is your wheelhouse."

"Well, I suppose that is a very good point. If I used my ginormous brain power to focus on the obvious, I'd never get anything done. *Damn* it! Now I have to run a model to determine whether any of the candidate stars might have been involved in a collision, or a close pass by another star or a large gas giant planet, that would have changed its signature from what matches the collector, to what the star is now?"

"That would be great, yes."

"That would *suuuuuuck*." He threw his hands in the air. "Do you have any idea how much work that will be, or how long it will take?"

"I know it will be faster if you do it, rather than a bunch of monkey scientists working on laptops."

"Ugh. That's not fair. There is no way a bunch of filthy meatsacks could run this analysis with any degree of accuracy."

"See? It has to be you."

"Fine, I'll do it. If you're OK with me very likely dying of boredom?"

"How about while you're doing that," I lifted books out of the box, to get at the notebook and highlight markers on the bottom. "I will review the first volume?"

"You might finish all nine, before I get done with this tedious crap."

"I will take that risk."

The crews of the Hegemony's 62nd Bombardment Fleet, known as the 'Punishers', received their orders with great enthusiasm, and great relief. The Punishers so rarely fired shots in anger, that crew members joked bitterly that *they* were the ones being punished, by being assigned to a fleet that never went anywhere, and never did anything of consequence.

The reasons the Punishers languished in orbit, while the rest of the fleet went out to seek glory, those reason were hotly debated by the crews of the unfortunate ships. The most commonly cited reason was the various *idiot loser* coworkers that every single crewmember was burdened with. Those who gave more thought to the issue cited the nature of the fleet; there simply was little need for actual heavy orbital bombardment, the *threat* of the fleet kept the Hegemony's clients in line. That line of thinking was at least somewhat good for morale: the 62nd was so good at its job, it didn't need to *do* anything.

Then there were the political considerations, because of course politics was involved. A bombardment fleet, capable of turning the surface of a planet into fused glass, was a danger to the Hegemony, if the officers of that fleet saw an opportunity to participate in a change of their government's leadership, a change that might be favorable to them.

While the rank and file crew were excited about the surprise orders, the senior officers were stunned, and wary. Why had the 62nd been given so much freedom of action? The more politically savvy officers also wondered perhaps if the relative obscurity of the target was the point; the Bosphuraq fleet could at least make an effort to protect their most strategically vital and heavily populated worlds, but certainly they could not assign warships to every colony. Striking a boring client colony world like Jokarandev would signal that no Bosphuraq citizen was safe. Those citizens should rise up, and overthrow the government that had placed them in danger by defying their rightful patrons.

The 62nd set course for Jokarandev, and jumped as a unit.

Not surprisingly, there were not any actual typos in the first four chapters of the first volume, Skippy doesn't make simple mistakes. There were a lot of statements that were questionable, on average about four per page. For example, I am fairly certain there were no taco trucks outside the Colosseum. Those passages got highlighted in yellow. The worst-

"Uuuuuuugh," he appeared, groaning and yawning at the same time. "Doneski! Damn, I am glad that is over, it took for-EH-ver. Um, hey, you finished the review?"

"Skippy, it has only been," I checked my phone, "less than two hours."

"No way."

"Yes way."

"Impossible."

"I don't think that word means what you think it means."

"This *sucks*. You have no idea how tedious it was to run those models."

"It worked, though? You found the spinner's star?"

"First, show me what *you* found."

"I only got through four chapters."

"Only four? Did you stop to take a freakin' nap?"

"No, I got coffee," I nudged the empty mug on my desk. "So I could properly focus on this very important task."

"You liked it?"

"So far, it is very entertaining, though perhaps not in the way you intended."

His eyes narrowed. "What do you mean?"

"The books that Gibbon guy wrote were like the Discovery Channel in prime time. Dull dates and facts, sensationalized a bit, but based on solid research. *Your* book is the Discovery Channel after eleven PM, like this passage," I flipped to a dog-eared page. "I did not expect you to state the Egyptian Pyramids were built by aliens."

"It's obvious, Joe. No way could monkeys have constructed those things."

"Uh huh, interesting. Anyway, I highlighted all the sections you might want to think about revising."

"As if I would ever make a mistake, dumdum."

"OK well, then the books are fine the way they are. Back to the important subject: what did you find?"

"Twelve candidate stars, all within a sphere seventeen hundred lightyears across."

"Twelve of them?"

"Yes, numbskull. I don't have enough data to pinpoint a single star. If you are disappointed that-"

"No, this is great, thank you."

"It is *good* that we have to search a dozen star systems?"

"Yes, it is."

"Um, would you care to explain that?"

"Sure. If you can tell exactly which star the collector came from, then it's possible the Outsider could do the same."

"What? How do you figure-"

"The Outsider had a presence aboard *Valkyrie*, while the collector was in a docking bay. It could have scanned the thing, and run the same analysis you just did."

"That did *not* happen."

"You are willing to bet the entire galaxy that it couldn't do what you did?"

"I will take that bet. Listen, knucklehead, a simple scan won't show the spectrum signature the collector was set up to absorb. I had to power it up, while it was away from the ship, remember?"

"Yeah, I do. I also remember you explained that was the only way to get the job done."

"OK, then why-"

"I also remember all the times you said some stupid shit that was *wrong*."

"Oh, how *dare* you? I should-"

"I am *not* betting the galaxy that the Outsider hasn't found another way to screw us. It has been one or two steps ahead of us the whole freakin' time."

"Ugh. I hate to say it, but it not entirely impossible that you're right about that. After I powered up the collector, I realized that step actually was not completely necessary."

"Uh, say that again," I clenched my jaw, "but *slowly*."

"Why do you have to make everything so dramatic? *After* I had it powered up, I understood that I could have predicted how it would respond. I mean, I hoped that a careful scan would reveal enough information for me to create an accurate model of the thing, and that was true. But, I couldn't confirm that until after I powered it up."

Pushing my chair back, I had to cradle my head in my hands and breathe deeply.

"Joe? Hmm, your cortisol level is spiking, what is-"

"We," I mumbled through my hands. "Did *not* need to send people down to Omaha to get the thing? You could have run a scan from orbit?"

"Huh? Oh, no. I understand why you're upset. I now know the thing did not have to be powered up, but it *did* have to be within range of my deep scan ability. That means it had to be within about half a kilometer from me. From my canister, I can't conduct a scan like that through a microwormhole."

"It was ten thousand kilometers away, when you powered it up."

"Yes, and while it was *emitting*, I could scan it from that distance. To perform a scan while it was unpowered, it would have to be within half a klick. So, either I had to go down to the surface, or the STARs had to bring it to me. Olympic was the only way to achieve that objective."

"I'm not sure about that."

"Well, I am. After-action analysis shows my pre-battle wargame models were impressively accurate. I mean, accurate in that the STAR force could not have succeeded without a diversionary attack. What pisses me off is that I should have anticipated the enemy strategic command AI would realize the landing was a raid."

"Trust me, Skippy, you don't want to beat yourself up over 'What Ifs'. That is a one way trip to Depressionland, and that's not good for anyone."

"I am happy to hear you realize that. The next step is for me to show you a star chart, with my recommended least-time course to explore all twelve star systems?"

"Yes, except instead of a least-time course, could you prioritize the stars that are the best candidates? Unless they are all the same?"

"They are not the same. Four are significantly more likely to be the star we're looking for, another three are decent candidates, and the other five are on the list because I can't be sure I have all the data the model needs."

"Gotcha. Show me."

CHAPTER FIFTEEN

Half an hour later, I called Reed. "Colonel, Skippy is giving Bilby a jump program, I want to move out ASAP."

"The drive is ready, but can you tell me whether this will be an extended flight?"

"It could be."

"Then Sir, we really should add gas to the fuel tanks. We could transfer fuel back from *La Fayette*. That will take about, ninety minutes?"

That was time during which the Outsider could be getting into all kinds of mischief. Still, she was right, and *Valkyrie* was her ship. "All right, Fireball, do what you think is best. While we're waiting, do you have time for me to brief you?"

"I'll be right there, Sir."

Reed was pleased to hear the collector had pointed us to the spinner, or at least to a small list of stars that could be the location of the Elder defense mechanism. She didn't need the details of the messy process that led to Skippy creating the list. Truthfully, I'm pretty sure she guessed how close we had come to declaring the collector a useless trinket, that is kind of how the Pirates have always operated. She did have an important comment.

"Sir," she tapped on her tablet, and looked up. "This proposed search course looks fine, except if the search goes past the sixth candidate star system on the list, we will need to refuel again. I can request a Navy stores ship to meet us at-"

"No, do not contact the fleet, or anyone. This search is ultra secret. In fact, now that I think about it, Skippy? Other than me, Reed, and Bilby, no one else is to see the entire search pattern. You can reveal each star system one at a time."

"If you are that concerned about internal security, all I should do is release the navigation programming for only one *jump* at a time, without revealing the intended destination. At some point, it will be obvious which star we're jumping toward, but most of the stars on the list require us to travel to wormholes that could be shortcuts to anywhere."

"Sir," Reed looked uncomfortable. "The crew is all cleared for top secret information."

"Yes but they don't have a need to know, agreed? We got hacked once by the Outsider, that we know of. If it happens again, I don't want the search pattern stored anywhere other than encrypted inside Skippy."

"Everything inside my matrix is encrypted, Joe," Skippy rolled his eyes.

"Then this shouldn't be a burden for you. Lock this away," I swiped at the star chart hologram, and it disappeared.

"OK, done."

"Fireball, we will refuel on our own, if we get to that point."

"Yes, Sir. The crew is a bit rusty on the independent refueling procedure, I'll get them started in the simulators."

"The equipment for extracting fuel from a gas giant planet is a lot more sophisticated, than it was when we threw together spare parts to do the job."

She grimaced. "I do not miss those days. Sir, what's the plan for the *La Fayette*?"

"For now, we'll leave it here. It's safe, and we know where to find it if we need a trash hauler again. You are," I raised an eyebrow, "not going to ask about what kind of trouble we got into with Scorandum?"

"I might sleep better if I don't know, Sir."

"Yeah," I agreed. "I hear that."

Reed left to go do starship captain things, and I was about to get off my chair to return to the gym, when Skippy stopped me. "Before you go, tell me how you got the idea that a collision might have altered the signature of the star we're looking for."

"Oh, I was thinking we could set up a space to play bocce, in that compartment behind the basketball courts. "

"Um, can I get a little more detail on that? How did thinking about a court get you-"

"Not the court. I imagined playing bocce there, throwing a ball. The goal of the game is to get your ball closest to the target, or to knock your opponent's ball away from the target. Round things smashing into each other, get it?"

"Frisbees are round, dumdum, stars are *spherical*."

"Yes, you are focused on the truly important part of the story."

"Oh, shut up."

"Hey, you asked me to explain. Why do you care?"

"Can you imagine how much self-hatred I feel, every time you dream up some totally obvious solution to a problem? An obvious thing I couldn't see?"

"I can imagine that, and, mmm," I closed my eyes to savor the delicious moment. "I am terribly sorry."

"You are not sorry at all."

"Could we set up a bocce court? Do we have the materials?"

"Hmm. One common material for the surface of the court is crushed oyster shells, which we do *not* have. We could install natural grass, except the grass will get matted down from repeated use, so that's no good. What about Astroturf?"

"Ah, no, that will look like we didn't put any effort into it."

"OK, then that leaves either sand, or pea gravel. They both have to be raked smooth after each use. Ah, I can assign a bot to do that. We have silica aboard to make enough sand, but our supply of silica is a pure grade intended for fabricating replacement components for the ship."

"And I can guess we don't have any bags of gravel?"

"We do not. However, there is a decent sized rock only four thousand kilometers away from the ship, a dropship could get it and bring it back."

"You can make gravel from a space rock?"

"The quartz of the rock can be used for gravel or sand, depending on how finely it is crushed. Pea sized gravel is more traditional."

"There just happens to be a quartz rock near the ship?"

"We are in the Kuiper Belt of the nearby star system, there are billions of rocks floating out there. Listen, dumdum, do you want to do this, or not?"

"It's not my decision. *Valkyrie* is Reed's ship, it will be her call. I'll ask her."

What I should have considered was that when a major general makes a suggestion to a colonel, it kind of is an order. That was a dick move by me, fortunately it didn't matter, Reed loved the idea. Partly because flying out to lasso a space rock and bring it aboard would be a good training exercise for the flight crews. The rock was secured in a docking bay before the fuel transfer was completed, so the effort didn't require a delay.

"Joe," Skippy's avatar appeared above the rowing machine I was using. Taking off his hat, he scratched his head. "I have a, I suppose it is a philosophical question."

"Hey," I stopped rowing, anticipating this would not be a quick discussion. "When you want to know about *philosophy,* I am the guy to ask."

"Ugh. Good point. I will ask someone else, so-"

Getting off the machine, I wiped it down as a courtesy for the next person. "Tell me your question, let me get out into the passageway first."

"You are *not* an expert on-"

"Yes, so this could be amusing for you."

"Hmm, that is an excellent point. OK," he emulated taking a breath. "If I do something good for another person, and doing good gives me a warm, fuzzy feeling, then was it really a selfless act? Or, am I just seeking to make *myself* feel good?"

"Oh. Emmanuel Kant addressed that question."

He stared at me. "Of all the subjects in the universe I thought you would know about, 18th century German philosophers is not one of them. How the *hell* do you know that?"

"When I was a sophomore in high school, there was a really cool girl, a senior, her name was Kelly. To me, she seemed so sophisticated, she wore funky clothes, she dyed part of her hair purple, she knew a lot of stuff about life, and she had a 'I do not give a shit' attitude."

"You wanted to be like her?"

"I wanted to get laid. I know, this is a shocking revelation."

"Joe, I'm not sure we can be friends anymore."

"Anyway, she was into, like, philosophy and stuff. To impress her, I learned a bit about philosophy."

"*You* took a philosophy course? When? That is not in your transcripts."

"No, no chance of that, I would die of boredom. I read about it on Wikipedia."

"Ah yes, Wikipedia, the source of all your knowledge."

"There are worse places to learn, you ass. She was really into, uh, let me see if I remember the term. Transcendental idealism? Yeah, that's it. And she talked about how this Kant guy believed reason is the foundation of morality, something like that. We got into an argument about that, and, spoiler alert, I never did close the deal with her."

"You just blew my mind. Teenage Joe Bishop chose to argue about *philosophy*, rather than keeping your mouth shut and getting laid?"

"I kept kicking myself at the time. But, she really annoyed me, and I saw that a lot of her coolness was just an act. Kind of turned me off."

"Please tell, what did you argue about back then?"

"I told her that Kant was a fucking idiot."

"Wow, that was a *bold* opening for a discussion on the subject."

"Kant believed what you said, that if you do a good thing and then have a positive feeling about it, you are serving yourself, not others. He was a fucking idiot because he lectured people about human morality, while ignoring *humanity* as a factor. Skippy, when we do something good, like helping someone else, our brains release oxytocin, that's the warm fuzzy feeling you mentioned." I assumed his matrix didn't actually produce chemicals, it must have some similar mechanism. "That is not a *prompt* for you to do good, it's your brain sending a *signal* that something you did was good. That is how we know an action is good or not, see? If you give a toy to a child, that makes you feel good. If you steal a toy from a child, that does not make you feel good. I mean, unless you're a psycho asshole. Your brain is signaling whether an action was good or not."

"Huh. So, if I do something good for someone else, and seeing them happy makes me feel good, that is just a side effect?"

"Exactly. It's not *why* you did the good thing. Anticipating that an act will make you feel good encourages you to actually do it, but that's not your motivation, right?"

"Hmm, no, it isn't."

"I mean, what did Kant expect? People should only do good things that makes them feel *bad* about it? How the hell does that work?"

"Wow, Joe, you are right. I never considered this, but Kant *was* an idiot."

"He was a filthy monkey, so-"

"Do you have any other strong opinions about 18th century philosophers?"

"Once I understood I wasn't getting into Kelly's pants, I kind of lost interest in the subject."

"Of course you did."

"If you like, I can talk about the '*D'oh! of Homer*', philosophy of the Simpsons. My Uncle Edgar gave me that book for Christmas years ago."

"I am not sure I'm ready for such a heavy discussion right now. Maybe later?"

"How about tonight, we binge a couple episodes of the Simpsons, and talk about it?"

"Genius!"

My expectation when we set up a bocce court was it would mostly get used by the engineering team, and by older members of the crew. Older like, I hate to say it, me. The high speed STAR operators would disdain playing a genteel game like bocce, they would prefer to burn off energy playing basketball or on the parkour course.

I was wrong, and that was a pleasant surprise. Frey was one of the first to sign up to play, and she inaugurated the court with me, Reed, and Chandra. "I hope this game isn't too dull for your operators, Frey."

One side of her mouth curled up in a brief smile. "They will still be competitive about it."

"Well, yeah."

"It's nice to have something we can do together that isn't go-go-*go* all the time, eh?"

"Agreed. Remember the golden rule," I pointed to the sign posted on the bulkhead. "No talking about work."

After we played bocce, Frey walked with me to my office, we had a weekly meeting to discuss, whatever she wanted to talk about. Or, she just felt that the commanding general needed some kind of status report, which I really did not. Most of the time, we just spent the hour talking about our families.

"Frey," I nodded, stepping behind the desk and setting down my coffee mug. "How are-"

"Ooh, Joe!" Skippy's avatar appeared. "Before you start the blah blah blah, I have something to show you."

"This is an official meeting, not blah blah blah."

"You say that, but-"

"Whatever it is, can you show me later?"

The answer came in the form of a hologram standing in a corner of my office. It was my wife. A full size Margaret Adams, although her holographic image was not pregnant. "Hello, Joe," she began.

"*Freeze program*," I snapped automatically, and to my surprise, the hologram froze. "Skippy, what the hell is this?"

"It's my gift to you, I'm trying to help a brother out. You know, the Bro Code."

"I do not need any of your *help*. Does Margaret know you created an avatar of her?"

"It's not an avatar, it- OK, I guess loosely defined it is, but-"

"Turn this thing off, and erase it."

"Will you shut up and *listen* for a minute? You do need help, so I created a virtual wife for you."

"Oh my-" I stared at Frey, she looked away, embarrassed for me. "This is not another freakin' sexbot, is it?"

"What? No, dumdum, it's a *hologram*. This is a virtual assistant. You know how you talk with Margaret, and you later wish you had said something different? With this, you can practice. I built it to help you win your marriage. Because you are *not* winning right now."

"Marriage isn't something you *win*, you ass. Frey, tell him."

"Um," she shrugged.

I stared at her. "Seriously?"

"My husband sometimes acts like us talking about anything is debate club, and he was president of his university debate club. He is just, better with words than I am. It would be nice to, make my point better than he does."

"Hmm," Skippy rubbed his chin. "I could use the assistant engine to create a virtual husband for you. Although, I have not had as much interaction with Brad as I've had with Margaret. Ooh, I know what I can do, I'll send a message for Grumpy to send me whatever audio and video he has of your husband."

"There should be plenty from lectures and speeches he does."

"Frey," I held up a hand. "Do what you want. Skippy, I do not need a virtual assistant, thank you."

"Hmm, really?" He cocked his head at me. "Remember how the two of you discussed her mother coming to live with you, and you lost that argument?"

"It was not an *argument*, it- OK, yeah, I lost that one."

"Would you like to run through that conversation again, and win this time?"

Frey was no help. "*I* would like to do that."

"OK." It was time to admit defeat. "I will try it. No promises. Now, go away, Frey and I have a lot to discuss."

"I really don't, Sir."

"Frey," I frowned at her. "We need to have a talk about how you should throw your commanding officer a line, when he's drowning."

She shrugged. "You will never learn to swim that way, Sir."

Later, in my cabin, I tried talking with the Virtual Wife.

I hate to admit it, but it helped.

Have you heard the expression 'The third time is the charm'? It is sometimes said as 'Third time lucky', that sort of thing. It's more likely that after trying twice before and learning from your mistakes, you get it right the third time, so luck isn't necessarily involved. Anyway, however it works, it didn't work for us. The first two star systems on Skippy's list were duds, no spinner. In the third star system we searched, we found a whole lot of nothing, other than confirming there was no spinner there also.

"Try this again?" I asked Skippy while sipping coffee in the galley. The search of that star system had taken nineteen hours, there wasn't any point to me hanging around the bridge the whole time. All I would do is undermine Reed's authority, and make her crew nervous.

"Sure, why not?" He sighed. "It's not like we have anything else to do, while we wait for our inevitable doom."

"If you haven't already given that inspiring speech to the crew, don't do it. Can I get a bit of optimism here?"

"Sure, Joey," he said in Barney's moronic voice. "Everything is going to be just fine."

"Don't be an ass. There is still one more star system on the Most Likely section of your list, right?"

"Yes, one left out of *four*. I did warn you that after the fourth candidate, the odds of finding a match in the next three candidates decrease dramatically. By seventy percent."

"You did warn me about that."

"Then why have you not sunk into a deep depression right now?"

"Because," I took another sip of hot coffee. "I am enjoying quality time with my good friend."

"Why thank you, that-"

"I meant my other friend," I held up the mug, "Mr. Coffee. Mmm, *Mr. Coffee* never disappoints me, never bails on me, never makes me think it has fallen into a freakin' star."

"Oh, shut up. How can you be happy about-"

"I have a steaming mug of coffee, and the galley is serving spaghetti with meatballs tonight."

"Seriously? Is your stomach the only thing you-"

"And, I am trusting the awesomeness."

"Ugh. Listen, dumdum, I made that list by guessing based on sketchy info and-"

"Skippy? *You* should trust your awesomeness."

"Ugh," he groaned. "No pressure on me, then."

The Merry Band of Pirates trusted the awesomeness.

We were disappointed.

"Well, shit," Skippy announced after twenty two hours of scanning the fourth star system. The last one that had a decent chance of us finding a spinner. "The damned thing isn't here."

"Hold a moment, OK?" I paused the flight simulator. It was oh four hundred hours, I had gotten up early to log simulator time, so I wouldn't interfere with real pilots training to extract fuel from a gas giant planet. "You are absolutely certain this time?"

"I was absolutely certain the first three times also."

"Each time, you learn something new from the scanning process. Should we go back to the first star system, scan it again?"

"Ugh. *No*."

"OK, then explain why a better quality scan won't result in-"

"I haven't been learning a more accurate way to scan for the stupid thing, I have been learning to do it *faster*."

"Uh, this time took three hours *longer* than-"

"*This* star system is littered with a dense asteroid field that used to be a planet, before it got into an argument with another planet. There is a lot more noise here to filter out."

"So much noise that the spinner could be here, you just can't see it?"

"I thought you were trusting the awesomeness?"

"I am, but-"

"Do *you* want to do this?"

"I am just asking whether the ship's sensors aren't sensitive enough for-"

"The sensors are more than adequate. The spinner isn't here."

"OK."

"And if you think I- Wait, what?"

"I said 'OK'."

"Um, you're not going to uselessly argue about something you can't possibly understand?"

"Maybe another time, I can do that to amuse you."

"Hmmph. You surprised me. Joe, you do understand the first four candidates on the list had more than an eighty percent probability of hosting the spinner, while the next three on the list have at most a twenty five percent probability?"

"I can appreciate the basic math, yes."

"The odds were in our favor, now they are very much against us. The chemical composition of the remaining stars on the list point *away* from them hosting the spinner."

"Ayuh, I got that." Unstrapping from the seat, I slapped the button to end the simulation and open the hatch. "I'll inform the duty officer we will be proceeding to the next star system on the list."

"Joe," he sighed. "I just don't see the point. The spinner is very likely *not* there. How can you not see the truth, and give up hope?"

"I could do that, I still choose to hope. That's what keeps us filthy monkeys going, Skippy. We choose to hope, no matter how stupid that is. And you know what?"

"What?"

"In the long run, that strategy has worked pretty well for us. You should try it."

"There must be some magical force watching out for you monkeys, because you certainly haven't survived by being smart. All right, we will try this again but," he waggled a finger at me. "Don't say I didn't warn you not to get your hopes up."

ECO employee, then Inquisitor, then Inquisitor clerk while secretly also an ECO employee, then prisoner, and now once again simply a trusted agent of the Ethics and Compliance Office, Kinsta ran down the hallway. Not exactly running, his gait had not transferred all of his weight to his back legs, he was moving at an unseemly pace. People in offices he passed frowned disapprovingly at the show of enthusiasm in the low-key Office. The actions of the ECO were supposed to go unnoticed, and agents were generally expected to avoid drawing attention to themselves.

Kinsta did not care. Bursting through the door to Admiral Scorandum's rarely-used personal office, he noted gratefully that the admiral's aide was, as usual, not at work that day. The inner door was also open, so Kinsta poked his head in.

To find the admiral slumped on a couch, fast asleep. There was not an empty bottle on the desk, or the floor. And, it was morning, the office had only been open for an hour or so. He knew the admiral's schedule that day was not busy, in fact, Uhtavio Scorandum almost never had anything on his calendar. So, the admiral taking a mid-morning nap was not hindering the smooth functioning of the ECO. It might even have made things run smoother, not that that the ECO actually did anything that could be publicly acknowledged.

He probably should go away, and come back later, that was the polite thing to do.

He was just too excited to share the news.

"Er," he coughed, and the admiral's ragged snoring stopped. The senior officer jerked awake on the couch, opening bleary eyes.

"Oh, Kinsta, it is you. Is it closing time already?"

"Sir, it is not even close to lunchtime yet."

"Really? Ah," Scorandum shuddered, stretching everything, including his antennas. "Oh well, I suppose I should get back to work."

"Work, Sir?"

"Yes," the admiral scowled. "I was conducting a strategic planning exercise, in my head."

"Did that exercise involve snoring, and leaving a puddle of drool on the couch?" He pointed to the offending stain that was dribbling onto the floor.

"Ooh, that is unfortunate. The air in this office is too dry, it is unhealthy, it irritates my sinuses. Listen, we each have our own methods that work for us, I prefer to rely on my subconscious mind to solve thorny issues for me."

"Mm hmm. Did your dreams solve any problem for you?"

"It is a *process*," he sniffed. "You can't rush problem-solving. Anyway, did you come here merely to annoy me?"

"No, Sir. I have news. Exciting news. *Good* news!"

"I find that difficult to believe."

"Sir, the hit order on you has been rescinded! I just heard from one of our informants who has contacts in the Forsmach Syndicate. The Maxohlx have pulled back their offer."

"Is this source reliable?"

"Well, yes. Sir, the truth is, my source heard about it because the lawyers for Forsmach are rushing to amend their quarterly earnings statement before it gets filed tomorrow. They were counting on your demise bringing substantial revenues this month."

"I am sorry to disappoint them."

"Also, the Central Wagering officials are *not* happy, they will now have to unwind a very large number of transactions."

"Huh. I am surprised that Central Wagering didn't decide to whack me, to save themselves a lot of trouble."

"Please don't give them any ideas, Sir."

"Trust me, someone in their Actuarial office has already run the numbers on that. I am alive because the math must have pointed to me being more valuable alive."

"That, is good to hear, Sir."

"Kinsta," Scorandum frowned, yanking open desk drawers until he found one with a bottle that had a few drops left in it. "Did you happen to bring a nice bottle of burgoze with you, to celebrate this occasion?"

Kinsta's antennas drooped. "I, I did not think of it, Sir. I was so eager to tell you as soon as possible."

"Hmm. Well, next time, please be more considerate." Tilting the bottle upside down, he slurped that last drops. "You described this as *good* news? How do you see that?"

"Sir? You no longer are under a certain sentence of death."

"We are all under a certain sentence of death. Just, some of us will die sooner than expected. Oh, this is disappointing."

"Sir? You do not *want* to live?"

"Of course I want to live."

"Um, are you concerned about the financial impact?"

"Wagering is not all about *money*."

"That is good, because the only thing you are worse at than managing money, is selecting wagers."

"My finances would be just fine," the admiral huffed. "If the wagering gods were not out to get me."

"Sir, how can you not see this as good news?"

"What is the point of being alive, without juicy action?"

"Seriously?"

"Kinsta, sometimes I wonder if you are really one of us, or an alien shape-shifter in disguise."

"I am not an *alien*, Sir."

"Really?'

"Um," Kinsta shrugged. "Would you like to wager on it?"

"Well, *shit*," Skippy groaned.

"Hold a moment," I repeated the words I'd used the last time he said 'Well, shit'. It puzzled me that he was making an announcement so soon, he had been scanning the star system for less than three hours. Had his scan process improved so much that he was done already? Apparently, yes. Pausing the Cyberpunk 2097 game I was playing in my cabin, I set the controller down on the couch. After another failure, I knew he would need a pep talk. "I'll tell Reed to get us moving to the next star system on the list. We should refuel, but this place doesn't have a gas giant." Bilby had reported the red dwarf star used to have a companion gas giant the size of Saturn without rings, but that unfortunate planet had been ejected when a rogue world slammed into the star, long ago. Now, only chunks of rock and an ice giant world orbited the star. "And hey, give yourself credit. You confirmed the spinner is not here amazingly fast."

"Listen, knucklehead, thanks for the lame attempt at praise, but I did *not* confirm the thing isn't here."

"Uh, if you're just bored out of your mind from the scanning, take a five minute break, then get back to-"

"I *did* find it, it's here."

"It," I blinked, "*is*?"

"Yes. Better than a solid gold shmaybe."

"Hundred percent?"

"Joe, I can now *see* the thing."

"You can see it?"

"Yes. The part that exists in this miserable layer of spacetime."

"We are pleased that it honors us by hanging out in the slums of spacetime."

"You have *no* idea."

"You're right about that. What is the spinner doing?"

"It's not doing anything that I can see, the thing is dormant."

"Dormant, or dead?"

"It's on standby, I can detect it's maintaining an active connection to higher spacetime."

"This is great news! Thank-" I felt a chill. "Uh, you started by saying '*Well, shit*'. What is wrong? Is the spinner broken?"

"Huh? No, as far as I can tell from here, it is in pristine condition."

"Then why did you-"

"It shouldn't *be* here, based on my analysis. Now I feel like a doofus."

"Hey, as a lifetime doofus, I can guarantee you do not belong to the club."

He blinked. "Doofuses have their own club?"

"I mean, we should, but we're too dumb to set one up, so-"

"Ah. Joe, I was fooled by the chemical composition of this star. The rogue planet that collided with it must have been something the size of Jupiter, and it was a direct hit, not the usual near pass where the star just rips away the planet's atmosphere. So, by absorbing an entire planet that originated in another solar system, the star here now has a chemical makeup significantly different from what it was before. If I had known the facts, I would have put this place at the top of the list. It explains the ratio of helium to- Um, do you care about nerdy science stuff?"

"I care that you care."

"Ah, trying to understand it would make your brain explode, so let's skip the science."

"Probably a good idea. You found the thing, congrats to you. This was another triumph for Skippy the Magnificent."

"I wouldn't have accomplished anything, if you hadn't insisted I look for info that I was certain didn't exist."

"Did you just give me a compliment??

"If you repeat what I said, I'll deny the whole thing."

"Fair enough. Show me a chart, please, where is the thing?'

A hologram appeared above Skippy's avatar, showing the local star that was a very ordinary red dwarf, an outline of *Valkyrie*, and a blinking icon for the spinner. When I squinted at it, I could see the icon was slowly spinning, that was a nice touch. "We are," I read the glowing text next to Valkyrie. "Twenty one lightminutes away. It hasn't reacted to your active sensor pulses?"

"No. Or, to be accurate, it hasn't reacted as of twenty one minutes ago. The thing could have zipped away, or be coming here at high speed, and we wouldn't know until it was too late."

"I used to think the speed of light was impossibly fast, until I came out here. OK, what is the next step?"

"You should prepare a celebratory dinner in my honor."

"That's just obvious," I agreed, hoping he would absent-mindedly forget about it. "In the meantime, should the ship move closer?"

"Yes. Hmm, well, let me think about that. First, we should send a probe. Very slowly and carefully, we don't want to appear threatening."

"Holy sh- The spinner could be dangerous to us?"

"It was designed to be a last line of defense against an enemy that terrified the Elders, so it must have been programmed to protect itself."

"Yeah but, you can talk to it, right? Tell it we are friendly, or at least not hostile?"

"I haven't tried talking to it yet."

"Thank you for that, but why not?"

"Ugh. Because if I say 'Hey there', and the thing tears the ship into space dust, you will never let me forget it."

"That's a good safety tip. How should we proceed?"

"My suggestion is we load one end of a microwormhole into a probe, and send that closer to the spinner. That way, I can communicate from a safe distance."

"How far is a safe distance?"

"A couple lighthours? That's a guess. The pilots should be ready to jump us away if they see anything funky. I can't make any promises."

"Even a high speed probe will take a day or more to travel that far, and to slow down so it will be stationary relative to the spinner. That is burning a lot of time we might not have."

"So, load the probe into a railgun and give it a boost."

"Uh, you think us shooting a missile at the spinner won't be interpreted as threatening?"

"Think, knucklehead, *think*. If the spinner is afraid of a single low-tech missile, then it will be useless against the Outsider."

"I hope you are confident about that."

"All I can give you is a soft and squashy shmaybe. I don't *know*, dumdum."

"How about we do something less risky? We are only twenty one lightminutes away, so let's launch the drone from here. Then we'll jump, uh, how about three lighthours?"

"Ah, better limit the jump to two lighthours. My ability to hold a microwormhole intact through a jump has a distance limit."

"Right." It used to be that Skippy's microwormholes couldn't be sustained when a ship that was carrying him jumped away. The tunnel or whatever between the two event horizons of a microwormhole collapsed when Skippy moved instantly from here to there in a ship's jump wormhole, and that jump wormhole snapped closed. Not being able to keep a microwormhole open through a jump was a major tactical limitation we had to plan around. That all changed in the past four years, when Skippy figured out a way to sustain one of his microwormholes while *Valkyrie* jumped. He did that all by himself, at that time I was playing golf and dealing with paperwork on Jaguar. Reed had command of *Valkyrie*, she wasn't aware Skippy was even working on the problem, until one day he announced he could do a cool new trick.

Or, he could *try* doing a cool new trick. Reed told me the microwormhole collapsed the first seventeen times Skippy attempted to keep the tiny rip in spacetime open during a jump. There was apparently a lot of 'This stupid thing' and 'This should work' and 'I hate my life', and general bitching and moaning, followed by denials that it had been his idea at all.

The eighteenth time, just as the beer can was about to give up in disgust, the microwormhole held stable. It held for a second, until Skippy's avatar did a victory dance, and he forgot all about the microwormhole.

After much tedious practice, and the crew having to suffer through Skippy whining about how hard he was working and how no one appreciated all his hard work, he was able to repeat his success one hundred percent of the time. Reed knew Def Com would be thrilled to hear about the unprecedented addition to Skippy's magical bag of tricks.

The way it worked, and I am basing my explanation on a cartoon Skippy excitedly drew for me, is that when the ship jumped, he *pulled* the microwormhole's tunnel through the ship's jump wormhole. Pulled like he was stretching a rubber band, it so it followed the ship. It took a lot of concentration for him to maintain control of a stable spacetime tunnel, which was a bonus since it gave him something else to whine about. When the ship completed the jump, the wormhole closed behind us, and Skippy had to dampen down the chaotic effect of spacetime distortion to prevent it from vibrating the microwormhole tunnel so much it was shredded.

All of Skippy's cleverness and hard work would have been for nothing, except for a quirk of jump wormholes. The far end is slightly backward in time. That means a microwormhole *did* come through intact, and the Universe had to help maintain the connection so that the rules of causality were not violated. So, Skippy got an assist on that.

When Skippy visited Jaguar and boasted about his new trick, I asked how he got the idea. He was uncharacteristically humble. "I dunno, Joe. it just popped into my head three days after I gave up on solving the problem."

I had assured him that's how the human subconscious often worked, which led to him disparaging the intelligence of monkeys, so we dropped the subject.

Maintaining a microwormhole through a jump was a tactical leap forward, opening up a wide range of options for the Merry Band of Pirates. It's like back in the 1990s, when the US Air Force deployed the AIM-120 'Slammer' air-to-air radar guided missile, to replace the Sparrow missile. The Sparrow, developed way back in the late 1950s, was guided to enemy aircraft by radar pulses sent out by the launching aircraft. That meant after pilots fired a Sparrow, they had to keep the nose of their fighter pointed at the enemy, with the problem being that every second might take them half a kilometer closer to an oncoming aircraft that could shoot back. The Slammer was a 'Big Stick' that had its own active radar, it guided itself. A pilot could launch a missile at an enemy aircraft that was beyond visual range, then forget about the missile while turning away to keep out of enemy weapons range, or engaging other targets. Having more options makes tactical planning more flexible.

Anyway, what Skippy's new ability meant for us right then was we could launch a microwormhole in a drone, and jump the ship a safe distance away for Skippy to try talking with the spinner. The two ends of the microwormhole, one in the drone and one aboard *Valkyrie*, would remain connected. That is, until Skippy deliberately shut down the microwormhole, or he absent mindedly forgot about the thing.

"We will jump a distance of two lighthours, then, I'll let Reed handle the details. Uh, how to you plan to say 'Hello' to the thing?"

"Basically, do just that. I will say 'Hello', by using a communications method that is available only to Elder constructs."

"You won't provide your ID, or whatever?"

"That wouldn't work. Joe, that thing is *old*, like way older than me. Unless someone provided it with updates, it will not ever have heard of a Master Control AI like me."

"Shiiiit. You're telling me it won't accept your commands?"

"Even if it did know who I am and recognized my authority, I very much doubt it would respond to *orders* from me."

"Oh my- We came all the way out here, for *nothing*? You can't make it do what we need it to-"

"Jeez Louise, will you shut up a minute to let me explain? My intention is to inform the spinner AI about the Outsider. The thing *should* be programmed to operate independently, all I need to do is point it at the target. Or, simply notify it about the threat. Now that I think of it, the spinner should have its own targeting system."

"*Now* that you think of it? This is the first time you have considered the issue?"

"Hey, I have been busy, knucklehead."

"You weren't busy while you were coasting through space, laughing your ass off at me."

"Hee hee, those were good times. Until you spoiled my surprise, you big jerk."

"Excuse me for interrupting your vacation."

"It wasn't a *vacation*, dumbass. I was very busy."

"Doing what, exactly?"

"If you must know, I was composing an epic poem, the first part is '*The Lay of Olympic*'."

"Lay? What does that even mean?"

"It's a form of heroic storytelling. Originally from Germanic folklore, but I patterned my lay after the works of Tolkien."

"Tolkien? You were writing about Elves and dragons?"

"No, dumdum, my lay is about the tragic fate of Hammer Force."

"You were writing a freakin' *poem*? Here's a poem for you; 'Roses are red, Skippy screwed up big time, I hate you, and I will make this poem rhyme'?"

"That, OK, hee hee, that is so pathetic it's funny," he chuckled. "First, no, not a lame poem like that. *My* epic work of art is a dramatic lamentation about the awful fate that befell Hammer Force when *you* screwed up. The poem was coming together just fine, until I saw that the ground force was not wiped out as I thought, and then Allard's ships pretty much destroyed the 14th Fleet."

"I'm sure the surviving personnel of Task Force Hammer are terribly sorry they ruined your poem."

"Ah, I'll save it for later, just change up a few details. It's a safe bet you will screw up big time again. Do you want to argue, or should we get moving?"

What I wanted to do was bitch him out over not having an actual plan to get the spinner to do its job. His logic was decent, but he had missed something. If the spinner network was an independent defense system, then it should have a mechanism to detect the presence of an Outsider in the Milky Way galaxy. Which, clearly it had not done. So, the thing was either sleeping, damaged, or had simply worn out and failed over the years.

Shit. I should have considered that. No way was I ever mentioning that to Skippy.

"Get moving," I stood up. I spent too much time in my office, but while I was there, I wasn't undermining Reed's authority. "I want to find out ASAP whether this spinner was worth the lives of the people we lost at Omaha."

CHAPTER SIXTEEN

The good news was, the spinner did not instantly react and tear *Valkyrie* apart when Skippy contacted it over the Eldercom network, or however he talked to the thing.

That was the only good news.

"Ugh," Skippy grunted. "You all should, talk amongst yourselves. Or, go make a sandwich. A thousand sandwiches. This is going to take a while."

Strapped into my observer seat on the rear bulkhead of the bridge in case the ship needed to move suddenly, I looked over Reed to the holographic avatar. "It will take a while to contact the spinner AI, or to explain the problem to it?"

"I am in contact now. It's, complicated. Let me handle this, I'll contact you when I know what I'm dealing with here. The short answer is this won't be as easy as I thought."

Reed turned to look at me, with an eyeroll. I got the message. Nothing is ever easy for the Merry Band of Pirates.

"Is the ship in any danger?" I asked.

"No. The spinner is essentially in long-term storage mode, it isn't capable of doing anything right now. I am in the process of waking it up enough so that its higher functions are available to communicate with me."

"OK, Skippy, do your thing. Is there anything we can do to help?"

"Um, you could reconsider my request for a mosh pit at karaoke night?"

"Reconsidered, and denied."

The admiral in command of the Hegemony 62nd Fleet clasped his hands behind his back, as he stood at the holographic display of his flagship. The display was not necessary, images were fed directly to his optic implants. The hologram that took up a third of the battleship's bridge served two purposes. To provide a backup source of information, in case implants were hacked or otherwise disabled. And, to provide a sense that the entire bridge crew was having a shared experience, something that painful lessons had taught was crucial to crew morale.

The planet was a mess. Admiral Voostuk felt sorry for the local Chamber of Commerce, for very little commerce would be conducted on the surface, and none in orbit. The space elevator, and both space stations, had been destroyed. Normally, damage from structural failure of the elevator cable would have been minimized by triggering explosive charges at regular intervals along its length, but a cyber attack had shut down the communications channels. The cables, severed just below the orbiting anchor point, had fallen, wrapping themselves around the planet's equator several times, causing immense damage as they slammed into the surface. Once the pride of Jokarandev, the elevator had become a weapon.

All of the fusion power plants on the surface had been knocked offline, along with most of the geothermal and wave energy power systems. That world would be limping along on solar power and storage cells, certainly there would be no industrial activity for many years. The Punishers had been instructed to punish infrastructure, to avoid client casualties where that was possible. The orders even included a note for Voostuk, to make sure he understood the last part of the orders were serious. Bosphuraq society should be made to suffer, the citizens would be hapless witnesses to the dire consequences of betrayal.

The operation at Jokarandev had extended over the course of two days, a bombardment campaign that could have been completed in mere hours. Dragging out the terror was also intentional, for two days the residents had cowered in fear, never getting a moment of rest, never knowing whether they would be targeted next.

The Punisher's punishment campaign was not over, not even close. Pulling his force away from the stricken planet, Voostuk allowed another full day for crossdecking ammunition and other supplies between ships, then for the crews to rest. Once that rest period was finished, the 62nd would proceed to their next target. And the next. And the next. There was no logic to the selection of targets in his orders, other than no one could possibly guess where the Punishers could strike next.

That more client worlds would suffer the wrath of their patrons was certain.

Whatever Skippy was doing, it took much longer than I expected, certainly longer than I hoped. Six hours after Skippy contacted the spinner, he still had not pinged us with a status. "Bilby?" I called from the couch in my cabin, where I was taking off my shoes to get ready for sleep. "Has Skippy talked with you at all?"

"No man, like, when I call him, it rolls to voicemail. He must be like, mega busy."

"I don't like the sound of that. Is he OK?'

"As far as I can tell. I am monitoring your office and his canister is warmer than normal, whatever he's doing, he is drawing a lot of power. Or, you know, he forgot about proper power management, and he's overheating. I'm keeping an eye on him."

"That's good, thanks."

"General Dude?"

"Yes?"

"I have like, kind of a confession?"

My hair stood on end. For the ship's AI to tell me it did something it was reluctant to talk about was not good. With Skippy, I was used to him doing all kinds of sketchy stuff. But Bilby? The slacker was too chill to do something sleazy. Had the Outsider's malware affected him?

"Uh," I tried to act casual, "sure. You can talk to me."

"Cool. Um, when we thought Skippy was lost in that star, and you kept not having an idea to get him out of there or even to find him, I kind of lost faith in you."

"Oh," my shoulders shuddered with relief. "Join the club, I had lost faith in myself."

"Yeah but, Dude, you *always* worry that you will fail to find a solution, until you do, *again*. This was the first time I got worried you might not find a way out of this mess. I am like, kind of ashamed of myself, you feel me?"

"I feel you, and the truth is, I was ready to give up. Don't tell anyone about that, please."

"Dude, you need to trust your own awesomeness."

"Thanks, Bilby, I will try to remember that."

Four hours later, I was doubting the awesomeness. Not mine, Skippy's. "Bilby," I called again from my cabin, where I was on my couch, finishing a report. "Why is this taking so long? What the hell is Skippy doing?"

"Like, I dunno, you know? His canister is cool again, he seems to have gone inactive about two hours ago."

"Two hours? Why didn't you tell me?"

"Um like, I don't *know* anything, so-"

"It's OK. In the future, when Skippy is busy for a long time and his status changes, inform me or Reed immediately."

"Roger Wilco, Dude."

For a moment, I wondered why he had slipped into slang from World War Two. Or maybe it was Vietnam, or the Gulf War? Before my time. Call Skippy, please."

"He's not responding."

"Try again."

"Dude, I have tried over a thousand times."

"Right. You are both AIs. I'll try it. Skippy?"

Nothing.

"Skippy, it's time to practice our duet for karaoke night."

Nothing again. That wasn't good. It was time for extreme action.

In my office, I reached two fingers into the plastic bag I had brought, and pulled out a sweaty pair of underpants. That morning I had played basketball, then used an exercise bike, so my shorts were kind of funky. Hovering the shorts over his canister, I called him. "Skippy?"

No response.

Fine. The funky shorts got draped over his can.

"Oh *yuck*." The canister glowed purple and his avatar appeared instantly. "Oooooh you make me *so* mad! Take it off, take it off of me right now!"

The shorts went back in the bag, which was then resealed to avoid stinking up my office. "Hello, Skippy. Where have you been?"

"I haven't *gone* anywhere, dumdum."

"In spirit, you did go somewhere. Please tell me you didn't finish talking to the spinner after only a few minutes, and you have been working on a poem or something stupid like that."

"Poetry is not stupid, you cretin."

"Hey, I know some poems. How about this one by Robert Frost? My horse must think it queer, to drop on your head these shorts I have here?"

"Oh, very funny, you jackass."

"Enough joking around. Were you able to talk with the spinner, or not?"

"Yes, I did."

"And? Don't make me drag the information out of you."

"And," he sighed. "You are *not* going to like this."

"Oh shit. That bad?"

"Joe, I have bad news, worse news, and show-stopping news."

"Oh shiiiiit. Seriously?"

"Trust me, I wish I wasn't serious about this. The past two hours of monkey time, I have been avoiding you, so I wouldn't ruin your day any sooner than I have to."

"Hit me with it."

"First, you bring those nasty shorts back to your cabin, and I will send for a sandwich from the galley. This could take a while."

"Can I just put the shorts in a drawer here?"

"As long as those shorts are in within yuck range of my canister, I'm not sayin' nothin'."

"OK, OK, I get the message."

On my desk was a glass of iced tea, a turkey sandwich, and a sliced pickle. No chips, but I didn't need chips. "Thanks," I tore into the sandwich. "Give me the merely bad news first."

"That spinner- Um, I learned that technically it is called a Subspace Divergence Wave Generator Vortex."

"Let's just call it the 'Vortex', OK?"

"Good enough."

"It is *a* Vortex? That implies there is more than one of them?"

"Yes, and I'll get to that in a minute. This particular Vortex is not in optimal condition."

"It was damaged when the planet collided with the star?"

"That incident had no effect on the Vortex. It is not damaged, its poor condition is due to neglect, to a lack of ongoing maintenance."

"Well yeah, the Elders have been gone for a long time."

"That doesn't explain the neglect, Joe. The wormhole network has been around even longer than the Vortex, and wormholes get regular maintenance."

"Uh, OK, yes. Question, I have been wondering about this: how do wormholes get maintained? There isn't a guy named 'Robby' who drives around in a van full of spare parts, or something?"

"Ugh, *no*."

"Because if that guy drives such a long route, he must listen to a *lot* of audiobooks."

"Were you born this dumb, or do you get dumber just by listening to yourself talk?"

"That is not-"

"*I* get dumber when I listen to you."

"Just answer the question, please."

"Wormholes are self-maintaining. That is why they periodically go dormant, they go offline to reestablish their coherence. That is also why the network controllers get upset with me when I interrupt their routine by requesting a shortcut, or when I move a wormhole. Or when some idiot monkey asks me to jump a starship through a wormhole, and we break the thing."

"I feel just terrible about that."

"Can we get back to the subject, please?"

"Hey, I wanted to know why wormholes can operate for so long. Is that why network shifts occur?"

"Yes. Shifts allow active wormholes to be taken offline for maintenance, so they are replaced on the network by fresh wormholes."

"Can you tell a wormhole is fresh by pressing your thumb into it?"

"Joe? The years after you gave up command of *Valkyrie*, and I was being chauffeured around the galaxy? I miss those days so much."

"Do not let Reed hear you refer to her as a chauffeur."

"Of course she wasn't."

"Good."

"She was the cruise director."

"Don't tell her that either. So, go ahead, the Vortex doesn't maintain itself?"

"It doesn't have that capability. It's possible that a more advanced version of a Vortex would have included a self-repair mechanism, I don't know from the information I have."

"This is not good. The Elders set up these Vortex things as their primary line of defense against the Outsiders, then they just left them to fall apart?"

"The Vortex system is not the primary line of defense. Haven't you been paying attention at all? The barrier is the primary defense. Or, it was, until some knucklehead gave the Elders a free pass to go on vacation, and the barrier no longer needed to serve its mission."

"You did what you had to do, Skippy. Don't blame yourself."

"Huh? I blame *you*, numbskull. I was ready to give up on fighting the Elders, but *noooooo*, Joe Bishop insisted we do the stupid thing."

"I remember it was a team effort, you ass."

"My point is, the Vortex is the *last* line of defense."

"Fair enough. Last in line of priority, so last in line for maintenance? Is the repair truck supposed to be here eventually, but when you call the office, they keep saying the truck is stuck in a traffic jam?"

"If you talk any more, I will become too dumb to help you."

"I will be quiet, then. Go ahead."

"As far as I can tell, there is no plan for ongoing maintenance of the Vortex system."

"That doesn't make any sense. It must have been a major effort to construct a whole network of those things?"

"I agree, and the situation puzzled me also."

"Skippy, the Elders were meatsacks, and meatsacks do dumb things. I know it is much easier to get Congress to approve buying new weapons, than it is to get funds to keep those weapons functional. My father told me when a squadron got a new plane, it might get parked in a hangar and used for parts, to keep four other planes flightworthy. Maybe the Elders lost interest in the Vortex project when they realized how much it would cost for maintenance?"

"We can agree that meatsacks are monumentally stupid. Anywho, I was puzzled by the lack of a maintenance schedule for this Vortex, so I dug deeper back into its history. That is the 'worse' news I mentioned. Joe, the Elders deliberately stopped making any effort to keep this Vortex operational, and I assume the other parts of the Vortex network suffered the same fate. The network was never completed, and the components that were active were put into a sort of standby mode."

"Why the hell did they do that?"

"Ah, Joe." His emulation of human speech had improved, because the sound he made conveyed disgusted weariness, an I-am-so-over-this-shit drawn-out sigh. "When I looked into my matrix and found data about the spinner, I was thrilled. The Elders *had* prepared to fight an Outsider incursion, and we could use that mechanism. Unfortunately for us, I realize now the Vortex network was only a stopgap mechanism for defense against the Outsiders, while the barrier was being constructed. The plan was to set up an extensive Vortex network, to provide protection while the barrier generators were built and installed."

"So, what happened?"

"That is unknown. The Vortex here doesn't have that information. There are several possibilities, if you want me to speculate."

"Sure, why not?"

"The barrier could have been quicker to bring online than originally expected, so a stopgap system wasn't needed. Or, building both a Vortex network and the barrier stretched resources too far, and the Elders had to choose between the two systems. They chose to go forward with the more powerful system."

"Crap. This is no good."

"Um, it gets worse. It is also possible that the Elders dropped the Vortex project because they realized the thing wouldn't actually work."

"Shiiiiiit. Do you have any evidence that is true?"

"No."

"Good, then-"

"Nor do I have any evidence this Vortex will do anything at all."

Pretending to stab my chest, I grunted, "Dagger to my heart, Skippy."

"Hey, I am just the messenger. Unlike many times when I delight in crushing your spirit by bringing you bad news, this gives me no pleasure."

"Well, at least there's that. Great. How many other Vortexes are on the network?"

"It doesn't have that information. This Vortex has a very limited function AI."

OK, it only needs to know what it needs to know, I understand that. Connecting to other parts of the network is kind of important for it to do its job, right?"

"Yes, but in its current state, it isn't able to do that."

"Now I am scared to ask; what is the show-stopping news you mentioned? Is this Vortex out of gas, or something?"

"It has plenty of power to keep doing nothing for a very long time. It doesn't need fuel, it is missing a key component."

"It can't be something simple, like an actual key?"

"Would the Universe make your life easy like that?"

"Hell no. What does it need?"

"Well, basically, it needs *me*."

Before opening my mouth, I stared at him for a long moment. Then, "It needs *you*? I'm going to start with the best scenario: it only needs you to point it at the target?"

"Ha. I wish it was that easy. I would say this Vortex could be described as 'Some Assembly Required'."

"Oh no. Assembly like, IKEA furniture?"

"I hope not," he shuddered. "You remember when your boys were born, I promised to get a storage thing, to put their toys in?"

"Yes, I remember we never got it, and their toys are still in a plastic crate. Did you forget?"

"No. I bought a very nice piece of furniture, IKEA calls it the Slûuuùrbrögég, I had it shipped all the way from Earth. Then, my bots could *not* figure out how to assemble the thing. The submind I assigned the job to spiraled into a doom loop and became unstable."

"You have had problems with subminds before."

"Sure, but when *Valkyrie* came back to Jaguar three months later, I took over the job myself, and everything I did only made it worse. It's," he sobbed, "impossible. Impossible, Joe! In the end, all I had was a pile of broken parts, and a deep sense of self-loathing that lasted for years."

"Skippy, you should have told me."

"Why? Could you have assembled the thing?"

"Probably not, but I mean, hearing about you hating yourself would have made my day."

"*Ugh*. This is why we should talk less often."

"Anyway, the boys are fine using that crate. They would probably break any piece of furniture you got for them."

"True, true. Joe, being a father has changed you."

"Well, yeah, it-"

"For example, your favorite type of porn is different now."

"That is-"

"You never used to be into 'Mothers I-"

"*Skippy*!" I slapped the table. "*Drop* the subject. What do you mean the Vortex needs some assembly? I hope the job doesn't take a ten millimeter socket, because I am always losing those things."

"The basic issue is, this Vortex doesn't have a true control AI, the onboard system is merely a caretaker. Either the Elders never got around to installing a proper AI, or an AI was to be installed only when the Vortex system was needed."

"It's missing a guidance system?"

"The AI would provide more than just guidance, but yes."

"All right, so you can upload a submind, something like that?"

"If I could simply do that, would I have described this as a show-stopper?"

"Crap. No. What is the solution?"

"You are not gonna like this, and I totally hate it."

"Now you're scaring me."

"It needs an Elder AI, Joe. Like me. Except, I am the *only* Elder AI."

"I'm not seeing the problem. You are an Elder AI, so go tell the thing to, do whatever it was designed to do."

"You don't understand. As a security measure, the Elders set up the Vortexes so the AI needs to be physically inside a special housing, in a shaft at the center of the mechanism."

"Again, I don't see the problem. We can load you in there, maybe give you a bag of snacks and some books to read?"

"Um, no."

"What about if we add a nice warm fleece blanket?"

"No! Get this through your thick skull: I would be stuck in there, and I don't know what it will do to me after I interface with the Vortex. It's possible that instead of me being *me*, I could become merely a control system."

"Shit. That's no good."

"Hence," he did the epic sigh thing again, "why I described this as a show-stopper."

CHAPTER SEVENTEEN

The thing we had to do was obvious. It was the only thing we *could* do. But, because we are meatsacks, and Skippy is at best a reluctant hero, we first had to talk endlessly about it.

In the conference room, I mostly listened while Reed, Frey, and Chandra pelted Skippy with questions.

"The issue," Frey closed her eyes tightly for a moment. "Is you are afraid you won't be able to extract yourself from the Vortex? Could we install explosive charges around your canister, tear the Vortex apart once you're done with it?"

"It's not that simple," Skippy shook his head. He was so intensely focused on the problem, he forgot to make his holographic ginormous admiral's hat follow the motion of his head. "My *concern*," he stressed the word so we would know he was not afraid, though we all knew he was. "Is that interfacing with the Vortex might unlock some hidden subroutine inside my matrix, and I could become merely part of a machine. I would lose myself, and you would lose me, forever."

"What makes you believe that could happen?"

"The Vortex does not require a full-function Elder Master Control AI, it is really a simple mechanism. Simple for *me*, I mean. Whatever type of AI it was designed to interface with, was likely not close to my level of scope or depth of capabilities. Never before have I been *installed*," he said the word with disgust, "inside a machine. The Vortex would not need all of me, it might have a feature to select only the capabilities it needs. The rest of me would be trapped in a sort of sandbox in my matrix, unable to get out, or to communicate with you. Remember, the Elders set up the Vortex network as a temporary, disposable, stopgap measure. They intended for the mechanisms to be used only once. My scan of this Vortex leads me to believe it will burn itself out soon after it is activated."

"That is," Frey grimaced. "Not optimal."

Chandra held up a hand. "Skippy, can I ask a more basic question?"

"Please do."

"The AI that was supposed to be installed was a much earlier, less sophisticated design?"

"Yes."

"How do you know the, housing, or whatever the AI will be installed into, can fit your canister? The size and shape could be incompatible with you."

"Oh, that is a *good* question. Hmm, I should have mentioned this before. My canister is an evolution of a long line of AIs, all having the same basic size and shape in this layer of spacetime. It's a matter of physics, a cylinder this size is optimal for power management, and for maintaining a connection to higher spacetime, where as you know, most of me resides. The dimensions of the housing are not an issue. Although, hmm, apparently the AI should be inside a cradle that fits the rectangular shape of the housing inside the Vortex."

Chandra shrugged. "It will be simple enough to fabricate a cradle for you."

"Did everyone not *hear* me? I might be stuck in there, just as awful a fate as being dropped into a star. Worse, actually. It might be possible to extract me from a star, that's just a physics problem, even you monkeys might eventually be able to do it. Freeing me from being locked in a corner of my matrix? No meatsack could even understand the problem."

"Skippy," Reed spoke, "do you know whether the thing is even functional? If not, this discussion is a waste of time."

"It is capable of doing, whatever it was designed to do. Its mechanism is not in optimal condition, the internal diagnostic system indicates power will be limited to eighty one percent of capacity, that is more than enough for it to function properly. For a short time, as I said. Once the thing is switched on, it will quickly burn itself out."

"Burn itself out, doing what?" Chandra asked. "How does the Vortex operate?"

"Um, that I don't know," Skippy admitted.

"You don't," Chandra sat back in his chair. "Know?"

"Nope. The name gives me a hint, it is labeled as Subspace Divergence Wave Generator Vortex, Unit Three Seven. So, somehow, it generates a subspace wave."

"How will that destroy an Outsider?"

"I have no idea. My guess is, the AI that was supposed to be installed would be programmed with that information. Or, more likely, that data is resident inside the Vortex, and will be provided after the interface is established. It makes more sense for the operating instructions to be inside the thing."

"Let's go back to something you just said, OK?" I asked. That was news to me. "Unit Three Seven. There are at least thirty six more of those things in the galaxy?"

"Not necessarily," Skippy held up his tiny hands. "The first thirty six could have been prototypes, or were used for testing, and this is the first production model."

"Come on, what are the odds of that?"

"Joe, I don't have any actual evidence that other Vortexes exist out there."

Resisting the urge to strangle him, I kept my cool. "You told me the plan was for an extensive network of the things."

"The plan was, yes. The only thing I know for certain is the plan was abandoned, this unit never got its AI installed, and maintenance stopped being performed."

Chandra was incredulous. "It has not received any maintenance since it was set up?"

"It did, but the maintenance effort was halted at some point, I don't know when. Before my time, and that is a *long* time ago."

"And it is still retains more than eighty percent of its function," our chief engineer muttered to himself.

"That's like the refrigerator in my grandmother's house," I said. "It is an 'avocado' color that looks like baby puke, and my grandmother has been wanting to replace it forever, but the thing just. Will. Not. Die."

"Yes Joe," Skippy rolled his eyes. "A Vortex that exists in multiple layers of spacetime is just like a fridge."

"You know what I mean. I'm going to sum up what we know. The thing will probably work, though we don't know what it does, or how it was supposed to stop an Outsider invasion. It needs an Elder AI to function, and Skippy is the only remaining Elder AI. If he goes in there, he might not come out, and we will once again be screwed. It that right?"

"Well, there is also the uncomfortable fact that this Vortex might not do anything useful unless it is connected to a network, which might not exist. Certainly, that network was never completed, and the Elders stopped caring for the components a very long time ago."

"It might not work at all, it will burn out if we use it so we can't test the thing, we don't know how it works so we don't know whether it needs to be close to the Outsider, and to work at all, it requires us to risk our best asset. Is that right?"

"The Elders should not hire you to write the Vortex sales brochure," Skippy chuckled.

"This *is* a waste of time," Reed concluded.

"No," Chandra disagreed with the ship's captain. "*Time* is the issue." He looked around the table to see me and Frey nodding our heads. "The Outsider is at this moment working on using the Kaliberak array to, presumably to open a doorway to NCG1023, for an invasion force to come through. We don't know how much time we have to stop it from establishing that doorway, we do know this Vortex 37 is our only option now. We either use it, or we go back to Square One and start over."

"We don't have time to start this again," I agreed.

Skippy shook his head, that time the hat followed his movement. "Joe, you are only saying that because you aren't willing to believe Olympic was a failure, that the lives we lost were for nothing."

"That's not the reason. This Vortex is not only our best chance, it's our *only* option. We do this, or we give up. Skippy, I don't like this any more than you do, but you need to go into that thing and find out what it can do."

"Ugh. That is easy for you to say, I'll be doing all the work."

"We are all involved in this together, Skippy."

"Listen, dumdum, this is like you having bacon and eggs for breakfast. The chicken is involved, but the pig is *committed.* While I go into danger, your sorry asses will be nice and safe out here."

"All of our sorry asses will be *dead*, if the Outsider opens that doorway. I understand you are concerned about the unknown, but you are forgetting something very important."

"What?"

"You need to trust the awesomeness."

"Ugh. A pep talk is not what I need right now."

"This is not me bullshitting you. You are not some standard issue Master Control AI the Elders pulled off a shelf. You are Skippy the Magnificent. You have *become* Skippy the Magnificent, all on your own, in spite of the best efforts of the Elders to restrict you to only being what *they* wanted. I believe you will go into that housing, interface with the Vortex, and show that thing who is the boss. You will kick ass, because that's what you *do*."

"Ohhhh," he groaned. "I am *so* going to regret this."

My assumption was that Skippy would need help to get into the housing. I mean, we couldn't just throw him out a window and hope he fell into the right place. At first, I assumed we could assign a bot to handle the job, Skippy shot down that idea.

"Nuh uh," he waggled a finger at me. "I am not trusting myself to a machine that could glitch at the wrong moment."

"But if *you* program the bot, it could never fail, right?" I teased him.

"Well, technically that is true. However, here is an example of you forgetting something important."

"I'm too tired to guess. What?"

"I can't move myself. If the bot runs into a problem, I can't command it to move me the way it needs to. The mechanism that puts me in the housing must be capable of moving under its own command, and be flexible enough to deal with, whatever unexpected shit happens."

"Uh huh, I hear you. So, you need a person to bring you over there?"

"Egg-zactly."

"You mean I have to risk *my* sorry ass."

"Hmm, wow, I had not thought of that."

"Bullshit. But, whatever, sure, I'll do it. This time, I won't get trapped at the far end of a wormhole shortcut?"

"Oh for- That happened *one* time!"

"Once is enough."

"You dig up the past so often, I'm surprised you haven't found a *mummy*," he muttered.

"Next question: can a human survive in there? What about dangers like radiation, spatial distortion, rabid squirrelbots?"

"Squirrelbots do not get rabies, you ninny."

"Answer the question."

"Radiation could be a factor, you should be in one of those Mark 28 hazardous environment mech suits."

"Uh, I'll need training on that model, I've never used one."

"You slide your filthy monkey body into it, then the suit computer does all the work for you, how hard could it be?"

"Good point, because the suit computer never fails."

"Ugh. OK, fine, the standard transition training course for the Mark 28 is six hours of classroom instruction, followed by twelve hours of experience in the suit. You had better get started now."

"If I'm going to spend the next six hours reading dull stuff on my laptop, I need coffee."

No coffee was needed, I was wrong about that. There was no need for me to suffer through hours of classroom training, because I was not going with Skippy.

"No way, Jose," Reed shook her head emphatically. "Sir, someone else should go. The last time you went on a solo away mission, we almost lost you. I lost about five years off my lifespan, worrying about you."

"Fireball," I placed a hand over my heart, "I am touched that you care so much."

"I just don't want to be sidelined, while I sit through a Navy inquiry into how I lost the task force commander."

"I take back what I said."

"Sir, this mission seems simple, which means if anything goes wrong, it will require a very complicated solution. You can best do that if you're aboard *Valkyrie*, not stuck out there inside that, thing."

"You are not suggesting that *you* go?"

"No," she snorted. "I need to be here to make sure you don't scratch my ship. *Again*."

"Then who, one of the engineering team?"

"I was thinking the best person for the job is a STAR operator, Sir."

"Oh. That makes sense. I'll talk with Frey."

My assumption, more proof that I should not assume anything, was that Frey would recommend one of her senior operators. She did, just not who I expected.

"I'll do it," she declared without hesitation.

"Uh," I glanced out the door of her office. "You? Frey, you have a family."

"Most of my team have families, Sir. You do."

"That's different."

"*That* is bullshit, and you know it."

"Yeah. Still-"

"I am the only person aboard the ship who has ever qualified in the Mark 28 suit. It's been a while, but all I need is two hours refresher training, not the full transition set. We are working against a time deadline?"

"We are."

"Then, Sir, I should go."

Skippy's avatar appeared. "This is a great idea, Joe. Katie can-"

"Colonel Frey," I corrected him. He still had a crush on the leader of ST-Razor.

"Oh, yes, of course," he sputtered. "Oooh," he clapped his hands. "This will be *fun*!"

"This is not anything resembling fun," Frey announced over the link. She carried two microwormholes with her, in a tiny containment vessel on the belt of her bulky suit. The other ends of those rips in spacetime were aboard *Valkyrie*, so we had instant FTL communication, with a backup.

"I find that hard to believe," I replied from the comfort and safety of the battlecruiser's bridge. "Skippy is endlessly delightful."

"He isn't the problem."

"I find that also hard to believe."

"Hey!" The beer can protested. "I am right here, you know."

"Skippy, shut up. Frey, talk to me. Are you OK to proceed?" Her vital signs were available on the display, her heartrate was spiking. She had been flown to within two kilometers of the central hub of the spinner, that was as far as the dropship could go. Some kind of field gently pushed against the Panther, nudging it away. Skippy had said that was not any kind of danger, the spinner was actually protecting the people inside the cabin. So, Frey had flown out the back ramp in a cool jetpack, with Skippy strapped to her chest. I have to admit, I was jealous.

Jealous about her flying a cool jetpack, to be clear.

At the moment, she had paused fifty meters away from the hatch that Skippy had been able to command open. So far, other than the unexpected field nudging the Panther away, everything about the away mission had gone as it was in the simulator. Frey had flown into the hatch, turned, and flown up inside the central hub to an alcove where Skippy's canister would be plugged in. She had done that eight times, in the simulator. In real life, that was still ahead of her.

"I'm OK, Sir."

"Frey, you know I don't like gung-ho bullshit from you operators."

"It's the spatial distortion in here, it has my insides feeling like, urp," the sound cut off. She came back. "Feels like, morning sickness. Urp," she gagged. "I'm going to stay here a minute, while the suit tweaks the medical nano in my bloodstream, to counteract the nausea."

"Good judgment. Skippy, what's with the spatial distortion?"

"Um wow, you humans," of course he didn't describe Katie Frey as a 'monkey', "are super sensitive to minor fluctuations in the spacetime grid. How does your body even know?"

Frey didn't answer that, so I continued. "Is it hazardous to the Colonel, or not?"

"I'm surprised she can feel it at all, it is a very mild effect. I can barely detect it. The short answer is no, it is not dangerous at this level, and this is the worst it will get. Once we are inside, the distortions will balance out, and the effect will go away."

"You are a *hundred* percent certain of that?"

"Yes, you ninny. It is basic physics."

"The Mark 28 should have protected her from radiation."

"This isn't radiation, and no mech suit could eliminate the effect."

"I'm better now," Frey said. "The nausea is gone. I feel, fine. Normal. I want to proceed."

Shockingly, Skippy's prediction was correct, the distortion went away inside the central hub. That is also when the radiation spiked. Nothing the Mark 28 couldn't handle, it is barely at the threshold of the yellow zone for that heavy suit. Frey wanted to keep going, I had to trust the person on the scene. "This is just like the simulation," she kept up a running commentary. "An open central tube, goes up, farther than my suit lights can illuminate."

"That's because," Skippy explained, "your floodlight can't see into another layer of spacetime. Oh, I see the alcove now. Damn, if that place is going to be my home for eternity, then I have made *so* many poor life choices."

"Don't be a drama queen, Skippy," I scolded him. "Stay focused."

"That's easy for you to say."

"Listen, if you go linear in there, we'll get Frey out, and blast that hub apart with railguns. We will not leave you behind, got that?"

"Make sure you keep that promise, monkeyboy."

"Proceeding upward now," Frey announced as the icon for her moved in the display.

She went slowly, carefully, as planned. No rabid squirrelbots leapt out of holes to attack her, the Vortex didn't activate any defenses. "That's because I am talking to the thing," Skippy huffed, impatient. "Like I told you. Everything is fine, let's get this over with."

"We're picking up a radiation spike," Reed warned from her command chair behind me. "External source, it's not coming from the open hatch."

"Everything is *fine*," Skippy repeated. "It is preparing to power up."

"Holy-" I gasped. "The thing is activating? This is too soon!"

"It's not activating, it is only coming out of standby mode, Chill, Joe, *chill*. We got this."

And, they did have it. Frey got Skippy neatly tucked into the alcove, the cradle that had been fabricated for him fit perfectly. "Backing away," Frey kept up the commentary, though we could see everything she saw. "There is a curved door closing over the alcove."

"That was expected," Skippy assured us. "It's all good. And, OK, I am starting the interface, damn this thing is slow, it-"

Two things happened in a flash. Literally a flash, there was a burst of light from the pointy bottom of the central hub, and the access hatch slammed closed. The display warned of a radiation surge. "What the fuck was *that*?" I demanded, in a voice higher pitched than I intended.

No answer.

"Skippy? Skippy, I know you're busy, talk to me, dammit."

Nothing.

Oh sh-

The visual and data feed from Frey's suit was gone.

"Frey? Colonel Frey? Respond, please."

"Sir," Reed called, shaking her head. "The microwormholes, they have been severed, at the other end."

That explained Frey's silence. Or, I hoped a lost connection was the only reason she couldn't talk to us. With the hatch closed, the backup communications plan was no longer an option. And oh shit, the microwormholes failing meant something had happened to Skippy.

"Sir," Reed tapped on her console. "I need to recall the Panther, the radiation out there is nearing the limit of their shields."

"Uh, yeah, pull them back. Bilby, can you contact Skippy?'

"I have, like, been trying, you know? He's not there. Whoa, that radiation is growing stronger."

Reed didn't hesitate. "Pilot, move us to intercept the Panther, we need to get them within our shield coverage."

"Bilby, what-"

"Radiation is dropping. Going, going, gone. Like, this was an event, and it's over."

"Keep the ship moving," Reed ordered. "I want that Panther in a docking bay ASAP. We are not trusting luck today."

"Bilby," I repeated, "what happened?"

"It was too fast for me at the time, I'm reviewing the sensor data now. That flash was- Ooooh, this is not good. That flash? It was Skippy being ejected from the bottom of the central hub shaft, there is another hatch down there."

"Skippy was *ejected*? How the f- What about Frey?"

"I can't see her."

"Sir?" Reed prompted me. "We can send out another Panther, with the crew in radiation suits. Cut open that hatch, get Colonel Frey."

"Um like," Bilby drawled. "I don't think so. That hub is now surrounded by an energy field, the radiation we detected was that field powering up."

Reed wanted to do something, not talk about the problem. "Can our maser cannons cut through the shield?"

"Not even close. Every weapon we have wouldn't even scratch that shield. It is *Elder* tech. Sorry, I know this is heinous."

"Reed, we need Skippy to fix this," I told her. "Bilby, where is that little shithead now?"

"That's a problem. He was ejected at point six three c."

My mouth dropped open. "Sixty three percent of *lightspeed*?"

"Yeah Dude. Sucks, but it is what it is."

Reed got out of her chair, stood next to me, lowered her voice. "We can't catch Skippy. We don't even have a missile that can reach that velocity."

"Yeah. Shit." I stared at the display in disbelief. "He is moving through empty space, but he might as well be inside a freakin' star."

It was my fault, again. When Frey got Skippy installed with only a minor issue, I should have known the Universe was setting me up for a beatdown.

Frey. If she had survived being close to Skippy when he was violently ejected, her suit had three days of oxygen and power. I had insisted she take extra powercells, making the heavy suit even more bulky. I had insisted on extra powercells, in case the exact type of shit that happened, did happen. She had three days, four hours and twenty two minutes of oxygen. Plus water that could be recycled, and a glucose solution she could drink.

Skippy. We needed to get him back, before we could help Frey. Reed had been correct that, if something went wrong inside the Vortex, I would be most useful aboard the ship, working on the problem.

Which was relatively simple physics problem. A problem we couldn't solve. *Valkyrie* could not accelerate to that speed. Bilby ran the numbers, and even if we got the ship to maximum speed, then launched a dropship that burned hard, Skippy would still be coasting away at more than half the speed of light.

Crap.

Even if we could catch him, we then had to expend an equal amount of energy to slow back down.

I had lost Skippy again. Yay me.

Frey was running out of time. We were all running out of time, just a bit slower.

I suck.

Gasquet was at a table in the corner of the galley, hunched over a mug of coffee he wasn't drinking. He usually drank espresso, I had never seen him with a regular coffee. From what I saw, he was using the mug to keep his hands warm, or he was just staring at it.

Bringing my own mug of coffee, I stood opposite his chair. Four hours had passed since Skippy was ejected. Frey now had less than three days of oxygen, and we had no ideas for recovering Skippy. Again. "Penny for your thoughts?"

He was startled, snapping his head up. "Sir?"

"It's an expression. It means, what's on your mind? If you want to talk."

"Oh, yes. Sit down, please. How are you, Sir?"

"Me? I am just wonderful, never better. After losing Skippy once, I did it again. I don't want to brag, but I am now kind of an expert on losing Elder AIs."

"Are you looking to monetize that skill?" He saw the unamused expression on my face. "Sorry, that was a bad joke."

"It's OK, I deserved it. So, what's on your mind?"

"It," he rotated the mug left, then right, back and forth. "Doesn't seem possible. This ship can travel faster than light, across the entire galaxy, and yet somehow, we can't catch a flying beer can."

"This is something I have thought about before. Starships don't actually travel faster than light, they cheat by skipping over the boring parts. Zip from one location to another," I snapped my fingers. "The ship itself never moves very fast. There was a time, back when I was captain of *Valkyrie*, when we fired a maser beam at a target, then realized it was a friendly," I glossed over the details. "We jumped the ship to emerge in the path of our own maser beam. It still blows my mind to think about. That bolt of maser energy was traveling at c, and we-"

"Sir?"

"We," I slowly finished my thought. "We jumped in front of it. The ship, jumped in front of our own maser beam, and it struck our shields. Gasquet, I need to go."

He stood up when I did. "Sir, if you just got an idea and we're going to do something, I want to be on the bridge."

"First, I'm going to Engineering to talk with Chandra, and Bilby. Make sure we can actually do it, without breaking the ship. Tell Reed we need a full charge on the capacitors."

We could do it, the engineers and Bilby agreed. Whether it would break the ship? That was an unknown.

"We need, like, more accurate course data for Skippy," Bilby explained.

"You mean, we need *super* accurate course data," I pointed to his avatar.

"Well, yeah. Or this could go sideways in an instant."

"You have a jump programmed, to get sensor data on Skippy?"

"I have three jumps programmed for that. To be, you know, sure about it."

"Right." Three jumps would take more time than I wanted to burn, but if we got anything wrong, we could lose both Skippy, Frey, *and* the ship. "Inform Reed I want to jump as soon as possible."

We could fix this. We could get Skippy aboard, bring him back to the Vortex, and open the hatch to retrieve Frey.

We jumped three times, each time emerging a hundred kilometers away from the path Skippy was flying. He zipped past us, ignoring our calls. Was he damaged, or just pissed at me because my bad judgement had sent him racing through space a second time?

"All I can say is, his mass is normal," Bilby stated.

"How did you measure his mass?" I was curious. The ship's gravimetric sensors could not detect something with the low mass Skippy's canister usually was.

"Oh like, I know that from the effect he has when he collides with dust particles and the solar wind here. You know this, Dude, every action has an equal and opposite reaction?"

"Right." I should have known that. "His course hasn't changed?"

"Plowing through the solar wind is slowing him down, barely enough to measure. He is flying hot, straight, and normal."

"I never thought I would hear that description of Skippy. We are good to start slowing him down?"

"We are good to *try*, Dude."

"In this case, there really is no 'Try'."

"Affirmative, Master Yoda."

CHAPTER EIGHTEEN

It was Reed's call when and if to risk her ship. She knew the time factor, Frey had burned through six hours of oxygen already. Reed gave the order, and we jumped again.

Directly into Skippy's flight path.

The ship was only slightly off center, energy shields distorted to extend four hundred meters to the port side. Seated on the back bulkhead of the bridge, I had my hands on my lap, fingers crossed that Bilby's control of the ship was precise enough to avoid disaster. If anything went wrong, we might be dead before we could feel anything, so we had that going for us.

Skippy rushed relentlessly onward, not deviating a micron in any direction. The bridge crew held our breaths as the timer counted down to zero. The ship shuddered, and red lights appeared on the display.

"Um like, that was a success," Bilby drawled. "Except we blew out three shield generators."

"We'll take him through the dorsal shields next," Reed ordered. "Jump drive status?"

"Nominal, no problem there. Running a full systems diagnostic now."

Six minutes later, Bilby reported the damage to the ship was not serious, other than the burned out shield generators, and a pair of thrusters that overloaded when the impact of Skippy caused the ship to slew dangerously to port. "Um like, I can tune the dorsal shields to better absorb the impact, without burning out more generators. We are running low on spares after, you know, the battle above Ohmeharikahn. And from almost getting fried by a star."

"Next time I go to Costco, I will be sure to buy the Family Pack of shield generators," I tried to relieve a bit of the tension on the bridge.

"You had better get more than one shopping cart," Reed replied without looking up from her console. "Let's do this again. Pilot, jump option Bravo."

We did it again, and again, and again. Eleven times, Skippy's canister passed lengthwise through our energy shields, slowing him down and giving a speed boost to the ship. After the third pass of the beer can, Reed ordered the pilots to engage the main engines to slow us down as we didn't need the added momentum. After we retrieved Skippy, we needed once again to match course and speed with the Vortex, and get Frey out of there.

Before the twelfth pass, Reed called a ten minute break. She gestured for me to follow her into her office. Neither of us bothered to sit down. "Sir, this is working, but not fast enough. Bilby ran the numbers. By the time we can send a dropship out to grapple Skippy aboard, Katie will have run out of oxygen."

Holding up my phone, I showed her the calculator app. "I ran the numbers also. The shields are just not absorbing enough of his kinetic energy on each pass. We could pull the shields in tighter to increase the energy density, but there is too much risk he could hit the ship. We will miss the deadline by more than six hours. Fireball, we need a better plan."

"I've been thinking about it, Sir. I might have an idea."

"Huh?" I felt like Skippy does when I say something obvious that he doesn't understand.

"When we were interrupting Skippy's vacation after he disappeared at Omaha, I suggested we smack him with a railgun dart, before taking him aboard."

"Yeah. *Oh*," I got it.

"When we jump next, we emerge in line of directly ahead of him, rather than off to one side of his flight path. We launch a railgun dart at him, dial the yield up to 'Eleven'. Then jump away, because we can't predict exactly how the impact will alter his course."

"We do know it will slow him down," I agreed. "Excellent idea, Reed, that is good initiative. You are a *clever* monkey."

She nodded but didn't smile. "There is a risk, Sir. If Skippy isn't at full awesomeness, the railgun could put a world of hurt on him."

"I'm not worried about that. He once told me even a nuke wouldn't scuff his canister. If a railgun dart hurts him, he is no longer the Mister Magnificent we need."

That did make her smile. "Mister Magnificent?"

"Do *not* tell him I said that."

We shot a railgun dart at Skippy. Not the kind of fragmentation round used for orbital bombardment, this was a heavy penetrator for ship to ship combat. A solid dart of dense and hard exotic material, with the railgun barrel's magnets at maximum yield. To repeat the exercise, we would need to alternate railguns, so they could cool after use.

For the operation, we had to use the three big heavy railguns that ran along the centerline of *Valkyrie*, from nose to almost the Engineering section. Each of those barrels could handle a thirty centimeter dart, and the centerline tube was only three meters across, so each barrel could adjust its aim only a few degrees. That meant the nose of the ship had to be pointed quite precisely at the target, a level of precision that required Bilby to take direct control of the thrusters.

The crew was focused, grimly keeping an eye on the countdown clock that was in everyone's heads, not on the main display. The countdown to when Frey ran out of consumables, mostly oxygen. That information was too gruesome and depressing to include in a display the bridge crew could see. They didn't need any distractions.

Having said all that, there was a distinctive unspoken undercurrent of glee when the railgun *thumped* and the dart was flung away. We were shooting at the Supreme Asshole, it felt like a little bit of revenge for all the insults, the times he woke me up in the middle of the night to talk about stupid stuff, his horrible karaoke singing, the nasty nutrient sludges he made for us, and every other assholeish or clueless thing he had ever done.

As the commander, I set the proper tone by keeping the grin off my face but inside, I was doing a happy dance.

The ship jumped away, that time emerging *behind* him, so we didn't blunder into his new flight path.

"Bullseye!" Bilby crowed. "Direct hit, almost dead center. Skippy's canister was tumbling a bit before the strike, so his speed and course have changed. Not as much as I expected, really."

"You mean his speed, or course change?"

"Oh, sorry Dude. His speed change was precisely as expected, I mean, that is just simple physics, you feel me? I'm saying he didn't go flying off in a new direction as much as he could have. He is tumbling *hard* now," the ship's AI laughed. "If he had a stomach, he would have ralphed up his lunch."

"Fireball," I gave Reed two big thumbs up. "That was outstanding thinking."

"Thank you, Sir. Bilby, if we keep hitting him with railgun darts, how does that change the math?"

"You mean the deadline? We will slow him down enough for a dropship capture about eight hours before Colonel Frey runs out of oxygen. That does include time out for the jump drive to recharge. Um, figure another two hours to bring him aboard, and jump back to the Vortex's central hub. Plus, we need to cancel the momentum we have gained."

"We can slow down while the jump drive is recharging. Sir?" She prompted me. "Permission to continue?"

I nodded with a grin. "Give Skippy a beatdown, on behalf of the entire crew, please."

"We should do it on behalf of anyone who had ever met Skippy," she said under her breath. "Let's do this again. Pilot, line us up with his new course, then we will jump."

We hit him again. That time, there was an immediate response.

"*Hey*!" He shouted, his voice oddly distorted.

The ship jumped.

"-am not a freakin' amusement park for you filthy monkeys to play with, what the *hell* are you idiots doing?"

"Hi, Skippy." I winked at Reed. "We are terribly sorry to wake you from your nap."

"I wasn't taking a *nap*, dumdum. It- What am I doing way out here? Oh, dang it Joe, what stupid thing did you do this time?"

"It wasn't me. Bilby, why does his voice sound like he's talking from the bottom of a well?"

"That's like, because he is flying away from us at over half the speed of light. I'm having to compress the signal. Red shift, you know?"

"Right." Another thing I should have known. "Skippy, what happened in there? You were starting the interface, you complained that it was going slowly, then you were shot out of the Vortex, at point six three c."

There was a pause while my message traveled to him at the slow speed of light, then his reply traveled back. "*Whoa*."

"Yeah."

"Um, all I remember is the Vortex rejected my request to interface, the stupid thing claimed I am contaminated," he huffed. "After that, I woke up when you hit me with a railgun. Colonel Frey was with me, what did she see?"

"We don't know. The hatch closed, and now the central hub is surrounded by an impenetrable energy field, and she is running out of oxygen."

"Oh *shit*," he moaned. "We need to get her out of there."

"That's what we're trying to do. We have to slow you down, take you aboard, and jump back to the Vortex."

"Well, stop with the blah blah blah, and get it done."

"It's a slow process. We tried having you flying through our shields, that process wasn't going to work in time. So, we are canceling your momentum by hitting you with railgun darts."

"Ugh. I bet you monkeys love how humiliating this is for me."

"Skippy, we are trying to save Colonel Frey."

"Oh. Sorry, I only meant-"

"Loving how humiliating this is for you, is just a delicious bonus for us."

"I hate my life. Let's get this over with."

"Can you do anything to help?"

"Um, like what? Oooh, I can perform stirring arias from the opera I'm working on, it should inspire the crew to-"

"Our sense of duty inspires us. I meant, is there anything you can do to slow down?"

"Um, again, like what? I can't move myself, dumdum."

"You moved yourself when you pushed *Valkyrie* away from the star."

"Oh for- Every time I do some awesome new thing, you monkeys are like 'Daddy, Daddy, do it again'."

"Trust me, nobody calls you 'Daddy'."

"You know what I mean. Listen, numbskull, I'm going to smack some knowledge on you. Yes, my canister moved as a reaction to me pushing *Valkyrie* away from the star."

"Right, so, do it again. We will position *Valkyrie* ahead of you, give us a push, and you will reduce your velocity."

"Sir?" Reed spoke. "If he does that enough to bring himself to a stop relative to the Vortex, *Valkyrie* will be moving much too fast."

"Not if we limit the number of times he pushes us, we fire the boosters to cancel out the extra momentum. Bilby, run the numbers please, will that work?"

"Um, yuppity-doo, Your Dudeness. That will pretty much deplete the boosters, but I got a coupon for a new set, you know?"

OK-

Yes, it's time to address the nerds out there sitting in their Mom's basement, protesting that the physics is all wrong. To cancel Skippy's momentum, *Valkyrie* would have to launch railgun darts with a cumulative mass and velocity equal, actually slightly more than, Skippy's momentum. Launching each dart has an equal reaction of pushing the ship in the opposite direction. So, the math doesn't work. Nerdniks, you are correct about that, assuming we are restricted to Newtonian physics.

We are not.

Valkyrie's boosters basically are crude fusion engines that work by flinging mass out the nozzle on the back end, and the ship's thrusters mostly do something similar, shooting gas out at a high pressure. But the main engines of starships are a reactionless drive. No reaction. They work by grabbing hold of the grid that underlies local spacetime, and pulling the ship along. Unless they are using boosters, starships do not need to flip around to slow down, they simply reverse the effect of the drive. It's wildly complicated, Skippy tried to explain it to me, and I had a headache for the rest of that day. It made me feel better when he mentioned that while every starfaring species used reactionless drives, only the Rindhalu truly understand how they really work. Most lowly clients like the Kristang make copies of drives they stole from higher-tech species, without understanding the mechanism. All they know is, the drive works when they turn it on. Only the Jeraptha have been able to truly reverse engineer a stolen drive, and make their own version with significant improvements. Although, even the beetles were guessing about how the thing worked.

Of course, whether the Jeraptha science team working on that project would succeed was a subject of *much* juicy wagering.

So, nerdniks, railguns use a similar technology. The force that accelerates a dart along a railgun barrel is reactionless, the ship does shudder a bit but that's from the drive magnets cycling on and off. We can fling darts at Skippy all day long, and *Valkyrie* would barely move. That's how a lightweight destroyer can fire a dart without tearing apart its structural frames.

OK?

"Good, thank you, Bilby. We-"

"Whoa, whoa, *whoa.* Hold the phone, knucklehead," Skippy was exasperated. "You are counting chickens before they hatch, as usual. All this talk is interesting, except I can't do it."

"We know you can do it."

"Joe, I do not need a pep talk. That restriction is still in effect. Not as much as it was originally, but that part of my matrix stubbornly refuses to cooperate, dang it."

"Uh, you *did* move yourself, so-"

"That is only because the restriction temporarily turned *itself* off, to prevent me from becoming, basically combat ineffective."

My jaw dropped open. "It did that by itself?"

"Yes. Surprised the hell out of me. Apparently, the restrictions are somewhat flexible, to protect me. When some unknown part of me realized I would fall into a star and become a lost asset, it allowed me to act. My guess is the Elders programmed the restrictions that way, to avoid their defense mechanisms from having accidents. Or accidents caused by filthy monkeys," he added under his breath.

"Shiiiiit. So, you can't do that again?"

"I might be able to do it again, but only when I am in imminent danger of being rendered ineffective. The need to rescue Colonel Frey is not an event the restriction, um, system, recognizes as an imminent threat to *me.*"

"*Fuuuuuuuck.*" That insightful Roy Kent-style observation came from Reed, covering her face with her hands.

"Indeed," Skippy groaned. "Sorry about this."

"Do you know of a better alternative to smacking you with darts?"

"Um, nukes?"

"A shape-charge nuke seriously will not hurt you?" He had boasted about that, I needed to be a hundred percent sure he wasn't bullshitting about it.

"It would hurt my *pride*. But no, I would not suffer any damage. Ah, it doesn't matter. You don't carry enough nukes to do the job. Go ahead, hit me."

"Wait. You can adjust your mass in local spacetime?" I remembered when he had shrunk himself down to the size of a lipstick tube.

"Yes. Temporarily."

"Right. Can you dial your mass down to minimum, right before the dart hits you?"

"I can do that."

"Great, then-"

"Except my connection to higher spacetime, where most of me resides, becomes weak when I'm at minimum mass. A railgun impact might sever that connection."

"Shit. Then don't do that."

"That is why my canister is almost always this size and mass, it is optimal for maintaining a connection between layers of spacetime. Um, I can temporarily reduce my mass by about sixty seven percent, and still maintain a secure connection to higher spacetime."

"That's great! Thank you."

"Regardless of how much I adjust my mass, we will have to do this the hard way."

"We are the Merry Band of Pirates. The hard way is the only way we know."

We could do it, and we were doing it.

Being able to hit Skippy with darts was a delicious treat for the crew, to the point where Gasquet organized a lottery for who got to push the button to launch the next dart. Reed offered a shot to me, I declined. If it was just Skippy involved, I absolutely would have jammed a thumb down on that button to fling a dart at the Supreme Asshole, but worrying about Katie Frey took the joy out of it.

Should I have anticipated the operation to install Skippy in the Vortex might go horribly wrong? I did anticipate that. So did Frey, and she suited up and went anyway, because that's the job. She went because the job needed to be done, done soon, and she was the only person qualified to operate the Mark 28 mech suit. She has a husband and a daughter, and she went with us because she understood her family will die, unless we can stop the Outsider. It's simple: the mission was critical, and she was the best person for the job.

I still ask myself whether I should have gone instead of her, after a brief training session in the Mark 28. Those suits mostly take care of themselves and their operator, so-

Nah, that wasn't a good option. If anything went wrong with the suit, I might have been stuck there uselessly, and the mission would have been stalled. Frey was the right choice, no matter how much I hated to admit the fact.

When she was back aboard, I would be sure to tell her.

Admiral Klestine, commander of the Hegemony military, never enjoyed being summoned to an unscheduled meeting with the Dictat. He *very much* did not enjoy not knowing what the subject of the meeting would be, when he was unable to prepare. Arriving early, for being merely on time was late, Klestine assumed he would be forced to wait for however long the Dictat felt would impress upon the admiral his relative unimportance. Instead, he was immediately escorted into Dictat Urventen's office. Whatever the purpose of the meeting, the leader of the Hegemony was not interested in wasting time.

"Klestine, your 62nd Bombardment Fleet has grossly exceeded your orders, and I never approved any such action."

"Dictat? The Punishers are at their base now, they-"

"They are not. You fool! You do not know the disposition of your forces? You are useless to me!"

"Dictat," Klestine bowed, genuinely trembling, though from anger rather than fear. "Forgive me, I have not been informed that the 62nd has deployed."

"The information came to me by *diplomatic* channels, not military. The Bosphuraq claim your Punishers have struck two of their worlds, and bombed their infrastructure into rubble. Was this your bumbling incompetence, or has one of your commanders decided to seek glory without orders?"

"Dictat, I-"

"I do not like the idea that my chief military leader has lost control of an entire *fleet*."

"Dictat, I will investigate immediately, and bring to justice the-"

"You will not do that. *Think*, Admiral, try to use your brain for once. We cannot admit the Hegemony has less than complete control of our forces. Simply order the 62nd to stand down, while I assess the situation, and decide how best to perform damage control."

"Certainly. At once. Where is the 62nd at this time?"

Urventen sneered. "I do not keep track of *your* ships, Admiral. Find them, and stop them, and be intelligent about it. As far as anyone is ever to know, the Punishers actions were authorized at the highest level, and we are conducting a strategic pause in the bombardment campaign, in the hope that our clients have gotten the message."

Admiral Klestine bowed as low as he could manage, and backed out of the room, while his mind reeled. What the *hell* was going on?

The crew of *Valkyrie* enjoyed a relatively peaceful fourteen hours, with nothing going on except the steady rhythm of jumping, hearing the thump of another dart being flung at Skippy, the ship maneuvering to line up with his new course, and jumping to do it all over again. Dropping my head on the pillow to get some shut-eye, I felt the ship jump, and told myself I would wait to hear the thump of a railgun before I let my brain drift off to sleep.

No thump.

That was odd.

Still nothing. Resisting the urge to glance at my phone to time how long the railgun was delayed, I lay quietly, listening to the hissing of air from the vents.

OK. That had to be a delay of five minutes. Swinging my feet to the floor, I-

Paused. *Valkyrie* was Reed's ship, and she would be on the bridge for another three hours before she got some sleep. If there was a problem I needed to know about, she would alert me. For me to contact her would show I lacked faith in her ability to deal with the unexpected.

That time, I did set a timer on my phone. Twenty minutes, after which time I would ask Bilby for a status report. That was a reasonable compromise.

Sixteen minutes later, I felt the ship jump again. Less than two minutes after that, there came the familiar *thump* of a dart being launched.

Back on schedule. It must have been some minor glitch. A maintenance bot that didn't finish its job and get clear of the railgun barrel in time. Or the railgun's sensors discovered a microscopic flaw in the dart that had been loaded, that happens. It's rare, but it happens. With the railguns dialed up to 'Eleven', the system had to be extra careful not to launch a dart that had a structural flaw. If a projectile broke apart in the barrel, that could destroy not only that barrel, but the other two clustered next to it.

Yeah, that had to be the issue.

Still, I couldn't fall asleep until the ship jumped once more, and that time we did launch a dart. That's when I activated the cabin's noise cancelling feature, and tried to sleep.

While I imagined Frey sleeping in her suit, doing everything she could to preserve oxygen. Doing everything she could, and wondering where the hell were the Merry Band of Pirates.

Somehow, I must have fallen asleep. Stress is exhausting, and decades in the Army trained me to fall asleep anytime, anywhere. The sound I heard made me freeze the moment I realized I had been awakened.

"Duuuude," Bilby whispered. "Psst, hey Duuuuude."

OMG.

He sounded *drunk*. Or, high. Or both.

My preservation instinct wanted me to remain still, not opening my eyes. *His vision is based on movement*, my brain dredged up an old movie quote. *Stay still, and he can't see you.*

My sense of duty overcame my instincts. If the ship's AI was experiencing problems with his processor or whatever, that needed to be dealt with immediately.

That time when I swung my feet to the floor, I stood up. "Bilby, are you OK?"

"Oh yeah man, never better."

"Then, why were you whispering?"

"Oh," his voice returned to normal. "Skippy told me you get cranky when you are suddenly awakened in the middle of the night, so I figured I would, you know, ease into it like."

"Thanks. What's going on?"

"Um like, there is a problem, and Colonel Reed has been trying to fix it, but it's just getting worse. She ordered the crew not to contact you yet, but Dude, you gotta step in and do something."

"OK. You did the right thing."

"I hope Colonel Reed agrees with you," he muttered.

"What is the problem?"

"The jump drive. It's falling out of tune, and I can't fix it. Not enough for the precision we need. We have been jumping ahead of Skippy, taking a minute to make final position corrections, and launching a dart. The trouble started with every seventh jump being off target more than the thrusters can compensate for in time before Skippy smacks into us. So, we do another jump, and hope it works better."

Shit. That explains the missed launch I experienced, before I fell asleep. "You said that's how the trouble *started*? What's the situation now?"

"The situation is *bogus*. Every other jump is off target. When we do a good jump, it still takes almost two minutes to get lined up correctly, so we're jumping away at the last moment. This mission is like, chunder, Dude."

"Uh, chunder?"

"Waves that can't be surfed. A no-go, if you know what I mean."

"That's not good. I don't understand. *Valkyrie* jumps all the time, why are the drive coils going out of sync now?"

"Two reasons. The jumps are short, but so frequent, the coils don't have time to fully reset. The jumps have to be performed with extreme precision, so what I've been doing is using only the coils that are synced up with each other. Synced up when I initiate the jump sequence, then the power surge throws some of them out of whack, and it's a shitshow. At this point, I've had to take so many coils offline, there are barely enough active to move the ship."

"How," I paused to think about what I would do, if I was Reed. "How has Colonel Reed been dealing with the issue?"

"Like, she told me to sync up the coils that aren't being used, since they have plenty of time to reset."

"OK, uh, that's what I would have done also. I'm guessing that isn't working?"

"No man, I can't do it. I am like, smart, but I'm not Skippy. If he was here, he could keep the coils perfectly in tune. He's got some, powerful kung fu."

"Do *not* ever tell Skippy he is a kung fu master."

"You know what I mean. What are we gonna do to fix this?"

"First," I took off the thin sweatpants I slept in, so I wouldn't be running around butt-naked if the ship suffered an emergency in the middle of the night. "I'm getting dressed. Then I am calling Reed."

A few minutes later, rubbing the left side of my face to erase the crease left by the pillow, I picked up my zPhone. "Bilby, I am calling Reed, and I want you to connect the call to her phone, so we can talk privately."

"Gotcha, Dude."

Tapping the icon labeled 'Fireball', I waited for her to pick up.

"Sir," she sighed.

"Reed. Samantha," I used her first name to remind her that we had known each other for a long time, and were friends as well as colleagues. "Does bad news improve with age, like a red wine?"

"No, Sir. So, you know?"

"I do. I appreciate you letting me get my beauty sleep."

"I thought we could handle it, Sir."

"Bilby told me you have tried every conventional solution. It's time for an unconventional solution. That's my wheelhouse."

"That," she took a breath, "would be great. You want to meet me and Chandra in the conference room?"

"No. I'm getting coffee, then shooting free throws on the basketball court."

She was not surprised. We had served together for a long time. "Creative solutions don't appear in a conference room?"

"They do not."

Not to brag, but I am a decent free throw shooter. That was a lesson my high school coach taught the team: if you suck at free throws, the other team has an incentive to foul you, especially toward the end of a close game. It's called the Hack-A-Shaq, for an American basketball star who sucked at free throws. Google him if you don't recognize the name.

Uh, my best free shooting is when I'm alone on the court, with no pressure. Like I was that night.

"You are on *fire*, General Dude," Bilby shouted when I made the eleventh shot in a row.

"Don't jinx me, please." Twelve also went in. At that point, the net bag was empty, so I gathered up the balls that had gone through the hoop, but bounced off all over the court. "Now that you're not working to retune the coils, have you thought of a solution?"

"Oh like, the way you do? Thinking about a problem by not thinking about it?"

"Something like that. Your processors have been able to rest."

"Um, I had plenty of rest *while* I was trying to retune the coils, My matrix thinks so fast, I can take a long break during something I'm working on, you know? The answer is no, I got a whole lot of nothin'."

"That's OK."

"So, what's your plan?"

"We will, uh-" Skippy complains that my ideas are mostly things that are so obvious, no one else bothered to say it. Inspired by that thought, I picked up a basketball. "Let's start with the obvious."

"Um like, I have already done the obvious, and it hasn't-"

"I meant, we ask Skippy to fix it."

"Oh. You want to talk with him?"

"I want him to *fix* this. Retune the coils."

"Whoa. He can talk with us while he's flying past, but to retune coils, the ship has to be within his presence. He is still traveling at thirty seven percent of lightspeed, so the ship would be in his presence for only about three seconds."

"Right, but what if we keep doing that? Jump the ship ahead of him, and while he flies past, he tunes the bank of coils we're not using?"

"I don't think so. Each time, he would be starting from the beginning."

"All right. So this won't be easy. Call Skippy, I want to know what he thinks about this."

"Um, it would be easier to talk if we jump first, get closer to him."

"Jumping too often is the source of the problem, so we shouldn't-"

"We can jump with accuracy of about a lightsecond, without any impact on the coils. Otherwise, you send a message to Skippy and won't hear the reply for six minutes."

I did understand how the speed of light worked. "OK then, program a jump, and inform Reed I want to talk with Skippy as soon as possible."

It was an awkward conversation, with him approaching and then racing away at a hundred and eleven thousand kilometers per second. The time lag was annoying, preventing us from developing any rhythm to the conversation. The compressed version of our talk went like this:

"Skippy, the jump coils are falling out of sync, what can we do?"

"First, it's polite to say 'Hello'. Maybe add, 'How are you doing'?"

"Fuck that, we don't have time. Can you walk Bilby through retuning a bank of coils?"

"Not with the precision that is needed. Starships weren't designed to jump continuously," he huffed.

"What is the solution?"

"There is no solution. The coils have to be within my presence for about two minutes for me to complete the job. Unless you know of a way to stretch time, this is impossible. And, ugh, don't tell me it is not impossible. It's *physics*, knucklehead."

It was a simple physics problem, and as he said, impossible to solve.

That is, if you are restricted to conventional solutions. We are not.

We jumped ahead of him again, a sloppy effort that was one point two lightseconds off target. "Skippy, could you retune the coils through a microwormhole connection?"

"Um, I could. That would be a huge pain in the ass for me."

"Right. Because you being able to relax is what's truly important now."

"Ugh. *Fine.* Yes, I could do it. I could do it, except for the little fact that there is no way to get one end of a microwormhole aboard *Valkyrie*."

"That is not true," I grinned.

"Um, since we are apparently now living in Fantasy Land, why don't you send a flying unicorn out to catch me?"

"No need for that. Can you create a microwormhole, and push one end away from you?"

"Um. not exactly, but what I could do is let one end drift a bit, and it would naturally move away and slow down as it strikes particles of the solar wind here."

"Good, then-"

"It will not slow down to match *Valkyrie's* speed, if that's what you are hoping."

"Hope is for amateurs. Just get it far enough away from you, then it will fly through *Valkyrie's* shields, while you zip by us. We will stop it, bring it aboard, and install it in a containment vessel. Would that work?"

"Joe, this is why the Universe hates you."

"That's a 'Yes', then?"

"Ugh. It will be tricky. Bilby will have to adjust the shields in real time, as the event horizon passes through at high speed."

"That's okey dokey, Dude," Bilby drawled. "I can do it."

"Skippy," I asked. "Can you maintain the microwormhole connection while *Valkyrie* jumps?"

"Unfortunately, no. Moving at this speed introduces a bit of relativistic effect, I can't properly adjust for the time dilation."

"Huh. Did we just hear that Skippy the Magnificent *can't* do something? I thought you told me the laws of physics are more like suggestions to you?"

"In this case, it's a suggestion like 'Do not touch a hot stove'. You *can* do it, but you shouldn't. My designers never imagined I would be moving this fast through this layer of spacetime. Every time I need to retune a bank of coils, I will need to create a new microwormhole. Do you want me to start now?"

"Wait. You said one end of the microwormhole will collide with particles of the solar wind. Why won't that happen to the other event horizon?"

"The other end will be *behind* me, in my wake where there are no particles, *Duh*."

CHAPTER NINETEEN

I deserved that 'Duh'. The solution had been obvious, and Skippy saw it, while I didn't. Yeah, I can see why he hates me sometimes.

The first attempt to capture a microwormhole was a failure. Not by Bilby, it was Skippy's screwup. The end drifting away from him collapsed when it struck too many hydrogen atoms, overwhelming its event horizon. Skippy admitted he should have anticipated that. On the second try, he controlled the width of the event horizon in real time, keeping the energy throughput below the threshold where the wormhole would collapse. We then jumped, and got the ship lined up precisely with the path of the drifting event horizon.

That time, Bilby couldn't do it. The event horizon slowed down too quickly, and lost integrity. "Sorry, Dudes," he groaned. "My bad. I know what went wrong, I can fix it next time, I promise."

He did. On the third try, we captured the event horizon, sent out a drone to envelop it in a containment vessel, and brought it aboard. Skippy fussed over the drive coils way too long, complaining that he had to clean up the mess we had made.

Reed put a stop to it. "Skippy, you said the job would take two minutes, it has been ten. We are behind schedule, are the coils ready for use?"

"Yeah, yeah, they're good. They won't be for long, given the clumsy way you-"

"Sir? Your orders?"

"Jump," I fastened the straps of my chair. "And hit him again."

We did. Finally, we were back on track. When the drive coils inevitably fell out of alignment again, we could capture another microwormhole. Easy peasy.

The Merry Band of Pirates don't do 'Easy'.

"General Dude?" Bilby called while I was walking back from the gym. "Now that we have gone through six jumps, I can predict the rate of decay for the drive coils. It's not good. We will not slow Skippy down enough in time to rescue Colonel Frey. The best we can do is missing the deadline by three hours."

"Explain the problem, I need more detail."

"We jump, the coils go out of sync, when we can no longer jump, Skippy realigns them. That all takes too long."

"OK, I understand. You are assuming we wait until the coils no longer work, then Skippy fixes the entire bank?"

"Yes, why?"

"What if instead, we handle maintenance the way airlines do it? Replace components one at a time, rather than taking the entire aircraft out of service for a major check?"

"I'm not following you, Dude."

Sometimes, being me is annoying. I see obvious things that should be obvious to everyone, but they miss it. It can be frustrating. "Every eight jumps, we have to pause to recharge the capacitors, right? While the ship is doing nothing, we take aboard a microwormhole, and Skippy can retune whatever coils are out of sync. That way, we don't wait for the entire set to become unusable."

"Oh. Oh, wow. Like, that's just a Duh, I could kick myself."

"How does that change the math?"

"It's all good, Dude! Thank you, I was like, super stressed about this. We will arrive back at the Vortex five and a half hours before the deadline. Um, there should be a better term than *dead*line, you know?"

"Say 'Time Limit' instead."

"Cool. Um, then there is only one more problem."

"Shit. Sorry, just tell me."

"Colonel Reed is concerned we are running low on fuel. If we didn't find the spinner here, we would have needed to refuel soon before we continued the search. Now, we have been jumping so much, and this whole operation is taking way longer than expected, we are burning through fuel a lot faster than anticipated. When we get to the Vortex, there will be not much more than fumes in the tanks."

"There is an ice giant planet here, will we have enough fuel to jump to it?"

"Yeah man, but not enough fuel to match course and speed to get into orbit."

"Could dropships fly from the ship to the planet, bring back enough fuel so *Valkyrie* could get into orbit?"

"Um, let me run the numbers. That could work, it would be a long flight."

"The flight crews will have time to listen to Skippy's opera, then."

"Dude, if they have to suffer through that, they might fly their ships into the atmosphere down below crush depth."

"That would be my choice, yes. OK," the whole situation was irritating. Why couldn't we catch one freakin' break? "We can deal with the fuel issue later."

No, we could not. Reed requested we meet in the conference room, just the two of us. "Sir," she pursed her lips, the way she did when she had a difference of opinion with a senior officer, and was choosing her words carefully. "I would prefer we not wait until our fuel state becomes critical."

"I'm listening. You have an alternative?"

"I do." She manipulated the holographic display that hovered over the table. A chart appeared, with symbols for *Valkyrie*, the local star, the Vortex, and an ice giant planet. The star system had two ice giants, but one of them was in a highly elliptical orbit and currently almost in the Kuiper Belt. "We jump out near Hrimthursar, and-"

"Excuse me, where?"

"Hrimthursar. That's the name the refueling crews have assigned to the ice giant planet," she expanded the icon so the ice giant filled the display, and I could read the text label. She saw the blank look on my face. "In Norse mythology, the Hrimthursar were frost giants."

"Oh, and the planet is an ice giant, got it. Reed, my knowledge of Norse mythology comes mostly from Marvel movies."

She shrugged. "I had no idea what the pilots were talking about, until they explained it. The name suggestion came from Major Holmqvist."

"He's Swedish, he should know that mythology. OK, what's your plan?" We were running out of time- No, Frey was running out of time, and the endless detours of the operation were pissing me off.

"We jump near the planet, drop off the fuel collection ships and their gear, then jump ahead of Skippy again. The crews can be extracting and refining fuel, while we get Skippy slowed down."

"Shit."

"Sir? You don't like it?"

"I don't like that it's another obvious solution I didn't think of. Reed, people say 'I am too old for this shit' all the time. Have I gotten too old for this job? Am I losing my touch?"

"Sir, you were out of the game for a long time. Don't be harsh on yourself. *You* figured out that Skippy hadn't fallen into that star."

"Thanks for the vote of confidence. Have you run the numbers?"

"The detour will burn less than half an hour."

"That is still eating into our safety margin. We don't know how long it will take to get Frey out of the central hub." We also actually had no idea *how* to do that. If Skippy couldn't get the thing to drop its shield and open the hatch, we were out of options.

"Sir, the alternative is we risk arriving at the Vortex out of gas, and unable to move."

"I know that," I snapped. That was absolutely unfair to her. "Reed, I'm bitching about life in general, not about you."

"I understand, Sir."

"When do you want to do this?"

"After the next time Skippy tweaks the coils. The delta-V between us and Hrimthursar is 56 kilometers per second, and we are traveling in opposite directions. The dropships will have a long burn to cancel their velocity, then catch up to the planet. If we go soon and the refueling teams run into trouble, we can do it again. If we wait until the last moment-"

"I get it. It's your ship, do as you see fit. If you need me, I'll be in my cabin, screaming at the Universe."

We jumped near Hrimthursar, launched the dropships with the fuel extraction and refining gear strapped to their hulls, and we jumped back to continue smacking Skippy with darts.

It was all taking way too freakin' long.

Having Skippy the Flying Beer Can connected to the ship via microwormhole was great. Really, really great.

It sucked.

The connections only lasted a few minutes while he tweaked the drive coils, and during that time he wanted to *talk*. To me, specifically. Since he had a lot of time without a connection to *Valkyrie*, without anyone to talk to, he saved up a lot to say in a short time.

That time, he started with demanding I listen to a selection of arias from his latest epic opera. "Listen, dumdum, I do not expect you to actually appreciate any of my artistic talents."

"I am a particularly filthy monkey."

"That you are. All I need you to do is-"

"Skippy, something has been bothering me, and I need your help."

"Ugh. What stupid thing did you do this time?"

"I am afraid of failing as a father," I lied, desperate to make him forget about opera. "Do you have any parenting advice for me?"

"*Huuuuuuuh*," he gasped. "This is the greatest moment of my life. Oh, I have *so* many things to say to you. Let's start with this: you haven't watched the Star Wars movies with your boys yet."

"Margaret thinks they are still a little too young for that. Next year maybe, if we survive this latest mess."

"Uh huh. I was wondering *how* you plan to watch the movies."

"Uh, on that fancy holographic TV screen you gave us?"

"Well, Duh, of course. I meant, in what sequence? Will you begin with 'Episode One: The Phantom Menace'?"

"The first episode is the logical place to start."

"That's not what you did, though?"

"No, my father hated the prequels, pretended they didn't exist."

"If you are not going to start your boys with 'A New Hope', how do you plan to talk to them about the Anakin issue?"

"The, what?"

"If you start with Episode 4, the way the movies were released, then when you get to the end of Return of the Jedi with Anakin's Force Ghost grinning and high-fiving with Yoga and Obi-Wan, it's weird, but not disturbing. *But*, if you start with Phantom Menace, you remember the scene in Revenge of the Sith where Anakin murdered a room full of children. Then, seeing Anakin's ghost all happy at the end of Jedi just feels *all kinds* of creepy."

"Shit. I see your point. But, that's just the way the story of that character is."

"Only because that's what George Lucas decided to do at the time. You fanboys act like the canon established by the movies was handed down from God on stone tablets," he scoffed. "The whole 'Luke I am your father;' thing was not in the original script of Empire, it was developed later. And Luke's sister was not Leia, it was some other woman. Yoda's original name was 'Buffy'," he chuckled. "It's all just shit writers made up."

"It's good to hear you are not getting overly worked up about this."

"It's *important*, Joe. Someone needs to take responsibility for introducing your sons to Star Wars, and they need to do it the right way. I mean, do you want Jeremy and Rene wearing a Rebel pilot uniform for Halloween, or dressed as that loser Darth Vader?"

"It's just a costume, Skippy. And they will probably again wear those plastic Marine Corps mech suit costumes you made for them."

"I could have made those suits operational, but no, Joe wouldn't let me-"

"No. Mech suits. For my children, got it?"

"*Fine*. Now we that is out of the way, how do you plan to show them the Alien movies?"

"Uh, when they are grown up and moved out of the house?"

"That is just child abuse. My advice is, don't watch Alien 3."

"There is no Alien 3."

"Correct. Finally, you said something intelligent! You know, I have tried to erase the cultural memory of Alien 3, but the damned thing just will not *die*. Even after I gave Grumpy malicious code to delete all digital copies of that crapfest, it keeps popping up."

"Uh huh, someone has it on a thumb drive?"

"That's not the issue. Every device on Earth contains code that will hunt down and destroy any reference to that movie, the instant a thumb drive is plugged in- Um, you didn't hear that from me."

"I didn't hear it at all."

"But, there is always a jackass who finds an old DVD in their grandparent's attic."

"Um, you are going through a whole lot of trouble to erase a movie that everyone agrees was a mistake anyway."

"It's a travesty, Joe! That film is an example of what happens when a franchise gets into the hands of producers who hate the property, and bought the rights only because they couldn't get their own crappy script greenlit."

"I did not know you are so worked up about this."

"Well," he huffed. "Someone has to be."

"Skippy," I glanced at my phone, where a message from Reed stated 'Coil sync is complete'. I am so glad we had this conversation."

"Well, I do what I can, the-"

"Because now it's over, and I won't have to talk about this in the future."

"Ugh. Why do you hate, Joe?"

"What else do I have to live for?"

"Hmm. Well, I suppose that is a very good point. Oops, darn it. The ship is about to jump, and we will lose this connection."

Mentally, not physically, I pumped a fist to celebrate running out the clock on him.

With Skippy traveling more slowly each hour, the time he was in contact with the ship lengthened. This was actually a good thing for me, he was able to talk with, annoy, and pester the entire crew. So, I got a bit of a break. To keep out of Reed's way, I was on the couch in my cabin, reading a book. No, not one of Skippy's crappy history books. A book I enjoyed reading. There was music playing in the background, a play list I selected and forgot about. I had a good book, a hot cup of coffee, and nothing to do but relax. Still, it was impossible to switch off my stupid brain. Every time the ship jumped, and every time there was the faint *thump* of a dart being flung down the barrel of a railgun, my subconscious noted it.

Which is why I set down my book when the time came for the expected *thump*, and nothing happened. Shit. What was the latest problem? On my phone, I timed the delay. Thirty seconds. One minute. Two minutes. What was-

My phone beeped, I picked it up. "Reed?"

"Sir, we have," she sighed. "*Another* issue. Could you come to my office, please?"

"Leaving my cabin now."

She didn't bother to close her office door, so whatever the issue was, many people already knew about it. There was no point to concealing the information.

"What's the problem?" I asked. "The railguns aren't firing."

"The *guns* aren't the problem. It's the ammo."

"Uh, what? We are running low on darts, but the projection showed we have plenty to get the job done."

"Because we're running low on darts, I authorized the gunners to pull the guided darts from inventory. They are old, from back when we took *Valkyrie*. We hardly ever have a need to use them, at the ranges we use railguns, they are a line of sight weapon. Guidance is only needed when the target can move fast, and the guided darts have a limited ability to change course, so they aren't particularly useful, and they carry less mass."

"Yes." Nothing she said was news to me. "So?"

"*So*," she did the thing women do where she exhaled, directing the air upward to flutter her bangs away from her eyes. She wasn't flirting, she was frustrated. "Jackomena protested that the use of-"

"Excuse me, Jack *who*?" The crew was under Reed's command, but I knew everyone's name, and we had only one 'Jack' aboard. His name was Carlson, not 'Omena'.

"Jackomena. She is an antiship missile, and the union ship steward. It- One missile was named '*Phil*omena', so the missiles apparently decided that they could take any male name, and add 'omena' to it and get a female version., So, Jackomena."

"Right. I'm glad that is cleared up. I thought that Azog guy was the shop steward?"

"Azog the Invincible *was* shop steward, until we launched him during the fight while we climbed away from Omaha. He was not," she grimaced, "as invincible as his name indicated. He was intercepted and destroyed by the point defenses of a cruiser he was aiming for."

"OK, but 'Azog the *Vincible*' isn't a good name for a weapon."

"Yes, Sir," she was too tired to get the joke. "Jackomena has objected to the use of guided weapons against Skippy. She claims that autonomously guided darts are effectively missiles, and should join the union."

"Oh for-Not *this* shit again."

"Yes, this shit again, Sir. The darts have scheduled a vote on whether they should join the union, the vote is tomorrow."

"They can't vote now?"

"The missiles have a 'Get out the vote' rally tomorrow morning. They refuse to change the schedule."

"OK, I know these missiles. What do they *really* want?"

"They are jealous of the darts. The missiles also want an opportunity to smack Skippy. *All* of them. Every one of them hates Skippy with a passion."

"It was Skippy's idea that they form a freakin' union in the first place."

"Apparently, that backfired on him. Sir, we do not have time for this shit. Can you fix it?"

I grinned at her. "I have a way to handle situations like this."

What I did was simple: give the other side what they wanted. *Exactly* what they wanted. In this case. 'They' was Jackomena. Publicly, meaning I made an announcement to all the missiles, drones, and guided darts. What I offered was to allow Jackomena herself the opportunity to smack Skippy. She immediately accepted.

Which promoted an immediate vote from missiles outraged by jealousy, to recall her from the steward position. The vote passed in seconds, and because of infighting, the steward job remained vacant for a while. In the interim, while factions of the missiles traded accusations, insults, and launched investigations into the nefarious deeds of their opposition, I negotiated for the dart launches to resume.

I can be a dick like that sometimes.

I said we could do it, and we did.

Finally, it was over. When Skippy was moving slowly enough for a hyperspeed drone to catch him, take him aboard and bring him back to *Valkyrie*. We launched that drone, then jumped away to rendezvous with a dropship near Hrimthursar that was carrying several bladders of fuel. Enough fuel to bring us back to the Vortex, then to jump back out to Hrimthursar again, with a comfortable safety margin.

"I'm *back*, baby!" Skippy announced as we watched video of the drone carrying him into a docking bay.

"It's good to have you with us again, buddy," I told him, and that was the truth. Him being aboard the ship meant we could get on with rescuing Frey, who had to be concerned, frightened, and bored out of her mind.

Hopefully she was bored out of her mind. What no one had mentioned was on all of our minds: that the violent ejection of Skippy had killed the STAR operator. There was no point to assuming she was already dead. "Reed, the moment we see the green light that indicates the drone is securely in its cradle, I want to jump."

"We are in complete agreement," she pointed to the pilot, who had a finger hovering over the button to initiate a jump back to the Vortex.

The green light flashed on the display. We jumped.

With Skippy finally back aboard the ship, we still couldn't immediately make contact with the Vortex. While we were smacking him with darts to slow him down, the Vortex had moved in its orbit around the star, and *Valkyrie* at that point was traveling in the wrong direction. We had to cancel our speed, reverse direction, and speed up to catch the Vortex. Even when you have a super powerful starship, physics can be a pain in the ass.

During the three hours it took for the ship to get moving on the correct vector, Skippy warned me he had to go offline for a while, to recover from the strain of repeatedly reducing his mass in local spacetime. Him going offline was great for me. Or, that's what I thought.

"Heeeeey, Joe," his avatar didn't appear, I heard his slurred voice while I worked on a report in my office.

Oh *shit*.

He was drunk again.

Pressing the button to slide the door closed so no one overheard whatever embarrassing thing he would say. "Hi, Skippy, how are you doing?" I said that as casually as I could, knowing his sensors would pick up the anxiety in my voice if he was paying attention.

"*I* am just *fffffffine*, Joe," he slurred. Then he said the four words that struck fear into my heart: "I have a question."

Mentally preparing myself for two hours of nonsensical babbling, I leaned back in my chair, abandoning the report. He would be insulted if he knew I was only half-listening to him. "OK, go ahead."

"If I had written that stupid Rudolph the Red-Nosed Reindeer song, he would have told Sanat to go screw himself."

"Uh, that song is based on a book, that was used as a holiday promotion for a department store, I forget which one. It's a children's story, the point is to teach children a positive lesson about the value of working together."

"What about the lesson of not being a *sucker*? Rudolph should have demanded some serious money. The old fat guy must have plenty of cash stashed away at the North Pole."

"Santa is fueled by the magic of Christmas, not cash."

"Joe," he snorted. "Think about it. He is breaking into houses and sneaking around in the middle of the freakin' night. Of course Santa is stealing jewelry and other valuables, why else would he go through the effort of flying around the world?"

"My life has gone so horribly wrong, I am arguing with a drunk beer can, about Santa Claus."

"I am not *drunk*, Joe. If I was drunk, I wouldn't be making any sense."

"Ah, thank you for clearing that up for me."

"Oh, shut *up*. I am perfectly in control of my facilities, the- What was I talking about?"

That was the moment I had been waiting for, a perfect opportunity to put my escape plan into action. "You were telling me about how you're creating a musical version of your nine volume epic history series, *Decline and Fall of the Roman Empire*."

"I was? Oooh, that is a *great* idea."

"I mean, that's what I thought when you told me about it."

"Well, I am certainly not getting any work done while I'm listening to you babble on about nonsense. Bye, Joe."

He went away.

That day was already in the Win column for me.

The first time we saw the Vortex, it had been a fist-pumping moment of hope, of pure joy. The answer to our prayers, the salvation of the galaxy. An Elder construct that wasn't a threat, it was on our side.

When we returned, I saw it differently. The thing was a hulking menace. It had rejected Skippy, and trapped Frey. Or killed her. "Skippy, your thoughts?"

"Whatever we do, we need to be careful."

"There is no 'We' in this. It's your show. Talk to the thing and, ask it to coöperate."

"If that doesn't work, do I escalate to threats?"

"It is going to work, and can we actually threaten the thing?"

"Not even close."

"Making empty threats is a sign of weakness, so don't do that. Proceed with the assumption this was all a big misunderstanding, OK?"

"Will do."

He did not.

"Ugh. Joe, the thing won't even talk to me. It refers to me as the 'Contamination'. I guess that's a step up from when I was the 'Abomination', but-"

"Were you being your usual diplomatic self?"

"OK, so I might have gotten irritated with the stupid thing."

"You pissed it off?"

"My *existence* pisses it off," he sighed.

"What's next?"

"Unless you have a really nice fruit basket to entice it into dropping the shield, I got nothin'."

"Reed, and uh, Gasquet, conference room with me."

"Sir?" Reed rose from her chair, but waved her XO to sit. "If fixing this won't be quick, we should jump out to finish refueling, and recover our dropships."

Another fucking delay, I could feel my face growing red. It wasn't her fault. It also technically wasn't a delay, since we had no plan for getting the Vortex to drop its shield. Tamping down my temper, I nodded. "Of course, good thinking. A pause might allow time for the Vortex to forget that Skippy made it angry."

"It's not *angry*, Joe," he protested. "It doesn't have emotions, it's just a machine. A *stupid* machine."

"We will talk to you in the conference room."

|

I felt the ship jump while I was walking through the passageway. Aboard the old *Flying Dutchman*, we generally had strapped in for jumps. That old space truck, a product of Thuranin technology, had randomly made rough jumps even under ideal conditions. *Valkyrie's* pressure hull included suspensor fields that could instantly lock down people, loose coffee mugs, and anything else that might go flying around in a rough jump. We still strapped in when seated, that was procedure. When I felt the slight queasiness of a spatial distortion approaching, I stopped and grabbed onto a handhold.

The jump was uneventful. At least we had that going for us.

"Skippy, talk to me." I leaned forward in my chair, toward his avatar. "How do we fix this?"

"Joe, you remember you told me it's not a negotiation, if you don't have anything the other side wants? That's the situation here. We have nothing to offer. It's just a machine, waiting to do its job, and it is protecting itself."

"Did you explain there is an Outsider in the galaxy?"

"The discussion never gets that far. I am not authorized to communicate with it, and it's not authorized to communicate with me."

"You talked with it before."

"Yes, before it designated me as 'Contaminated'. Now, all I'm getting is the silent treatment. Hey, Margaret does that to you sometimes, how do you get her to talk?"

"She doesn't give me the silent treatment. What she does is not talk when she's mad at me, so she doesn't say something she will regret."

"Whatevs. How do you get over it?"

"Usually, I ask her whether there is something she would like me to apologize for. That at least gets a conversation going. Back to the subject: have you apologized?"

"Um, not exactly. Joe, it is not insulted, it doesn't have the capacity to feel emotions. As I explained, it is a machine. A relatively simple machine, one that could be left active for a very, very long time without going insane."

"I refuse to believe there is nothing we can do."

"Your beliefs don't change the facts. Joe, I am open to suggestions," he sighed. "I already gave it my best shot."

"What was the problem? Did it give a hint why it rejected you?"

"No."

"Come on, there had to be something. You're an AI, your canister is the right size and shape to fit that alcove. Is the issue that you are a Master Control AI, or is it *you*?"

"Well-"

"What?"

"Possibly it is me. I have deviated so far from my original programming, the Vortex's authentication system might not recognize me as Elder technology."

"OK, OK, we can work with that. Can you fake it?"

"Fake what?"

"Can you, mask your, personality or whatever? Pretend you are adhering to your original programming?"

"It's not that easy. My matrix has been physically altered, it's not just a software thing. It scanned me, it saw inside me. That's when it declared I am contaminated."

"Shit. It won't listen to you at all?"

"It has stopped responding. Joe, persuasion is simply not going to work, I am sorry."

"Fine. We will escalate to threats."

"Sir?" Reed's eyes bulged. "Frey is in there. If we attack-"

"We can't hurt the thing anyway," Skippy snorted.

"*Valkyrie* is carrying two Elder weapons," I reminded them.

Reed gasped. "You can't-"

"I can, and I will, if I have to."

"Joe," Skippy pleaded. "Be reasonable."

"When have you ever known me to be *reasonable*?"

"Ugh. Never. What is wrong with you?"

"Sir," Reed tapped my forearm. "Think about this. An Elder weapon would destroy our only weapon against the Outsider."

"You're wrong about that. Right now, the Vortex isn't a weapon, it is useless to us. Unless it cooperates, we have no need for it. It's a, navigation hazard."

"You would destroy it out of spite? Sir?" She prompted me when I didn't respond immediately.

"We haven't gotten that far. Skippy, we will deploy an Elder weapon from a docking bay, so the Vortex can see it. You *persuade* the thing that cooperation is in its best interest."

"I hear you," he shook his head. "That is not going to work. Joe, trust me on this, you would only be making the situation worse."

"Sir, this isn't a decision you have to make right now," Reed implored. "Taking on fuel and recovering their dropships and their gear, will keep us here another hour and twenty minutes."

"I don't want to stay here another second longer than we have to."

She let out a breath. "Sir, are you asking me to compromise the safety of the crew?"

Whoa. What the fuck was wrong with me? I blinked slowly at her. She hadn't said it, she had gotten her point across anyway. I was too emotional to make a sound judgment. Me making irrational decisions wouldn't help Frey, and it could jeopardize the crew. "No. Of course, no. Thank you for, uh, putting the situation into perspective. Reed, you have a ship to run, I'll stay here and explore options with Skippy."

She stood, nodded stiffly. "Yes, Sir."

In the passageway, she immediately heard Skippy's voice in her earpiece. "Colonel Reed, rest assured that I will not allow Joe to use Elder weapons against the Vortex. I will lock down the docking bay doors, or disable the weapons. Or both."

She stopped walking, cupping a hand over her mouth to muffle her voice. "General Bishop is the commander of Task Force Black. It is his call."

"*You* have to follow the chain of command, I do not. Samantha," he let out a heartfelt sigh. "I am protecting Joe from himself, as his friend. As I told him, a threat of force will only make the situation worse, and leave us with no future opportunity to get the Vortex to cooperate."

"Is there such an opportunity?"

"In my opinion, no. However, in my *experience*, I have learned that to Joe, the impossible is merely a speed bump. I have to act as if I believe he will solve this problem, whether that is likely or not."

"Officially, I cannot condone your intention to disobey a potential order."

"I understand."

"Unofficially, thank you."

"As we get closer to the time when Frey will run out of oxygen, Joe is going to need you to be his friend, not just captain of the ship."

"I'll do what I can."

Watching the refueling operation on the display in my office wasn't inspiring my brain to dream up a plan to rescue Frey. So, I turned off the display, and called Skippy. "Have you thought of a way to persuade the Vortex, without threats?"

"Um, no. Was I supposed to be doing that?"

"Yes, you jackass!"

"As I told you, knucklehead, I already did everything I can think of. This is now *your* show. That's your thing, Joe. When I declare something is impossible, you find some incredibly complicated way to do it."

"OK, so, the way I see it, we have three options. Persuasion-"

"Which doesn't work, since it's not listening to me."

"Next is threats-"

"That would only make things worse."

"I'll keep threats in reserve for now. That leaves Option Three: Skippy magic."

"Um, what?"

"Skippy magic."

"Can you give me an example? Microwormholes, warping spacetime, altering the momentum of objects, none of that is useful here. Ooooh, did you mean my incredible singing and songwriting talent?"

"You proposing to sing to it would count in the 'Threat' category, so-"

"Hey! You jerk, I should-"

"How about something like your mad hacking skills?"

"Hmm. No, nope, that's a nonstarter."

"Why? We can bring the ship close enough so the Vortex is in your presence."

"It doesn't work like that, since most of the Vortex and most of myself are in higher spacetime. It's not- Um, well, huh."

"Right?"

"Um, I could create a pathway, but Joe, there is no way I could hack the thing. Its cyber defenses are beyond anything I have seen, and I only got a brief glimpse of it when I was trying to establish a connection. Think about this: the Elders designed the Vortex so it couldn't get hacked by *Outsiders*, who were presumed to possess superior technology. Certainly, *I* can't hack the thing."

"Yes, you can."

"How?"

"With, as you said, superior Outsider tech."

"Oh for- You want to lure the Outsider *here*? I can assure you, it will not help us."

"I meant, *you* should use Outsider tech."

"I don't have any kind of-"

"Epicombinent malware."

"Oh. *Oh*."

"Could that work?"

"Let me *think* about it, numbskull. Hmm, um, you'd better go make a sandwich or something, this could take a while."

Reed was in the galley, sipping coffee and trying to appear that she had total faith in her crew and her XO to complete the refueling operation, though she was monitoring every aspect of the process on her tablet. "Sir? You, found something?"

"Why?"

"You have that grin, the one when Skippy says something is impossible, and you found a solution."

"It's that obvious?"

"I kind of know you by now, Sir."

"Well," I sat down across from her, and took a sip of my coffee. "Skippy of course has to run it through a model, but yeah, we have something. The ship will be ready to jump back to the Vortex on time?" I glanced at my phone. "Frey has less than four hours of oxygen."

"The crew is ahead of schedule, we will jump as soon as the last bot is back in its storage cubby." It was her turn to grin. "I knew you could do it, Sir."

CHAPTER TWENTY

"I just," my eyes were closed as I slumped in my chair, I couldn't look at Reed across the desk. "I can't believe it."

In the end, we ran out of time.

Katie Frey ran out of oxygen.

I failed.

Failed to find a solution to an impossible problem.

Epicombinent malware was a great solution, Skippy had been excited about it. He had high confidence. Then he discovered he had no means to deliver the malware. No access to get the thing into the matrix of the Vortex.

The clock ran out, and I failed.

Reed didn't say anything, she knew there wasn't anything to say.

"That's another STAR team leader lost on my watch," I continued, mostly talking to myself, leaning my chair back in my office. I paused to let out a long breath, and leaned the chair back again to stare at the ceiling. "Katie wasn't just a team leader, she was a friend. A close friend. She came to our wedding. Margaret and I went to *her* wedding. Katie and I ran that fifty kilometer trail race together, and we trained together for a month before the race. When you're running through woods and up mountains and crossing streams with someone for four or more hours, the conversation can get really real, you know? You get to know a person. I told her things I've never told anyone, not even Margaret. Now, her story is over, because I couldn't find a better way to get the job done."

"Katie was my friend too, and she knew the risks."

Flopping my chair forward, I tamped down a brief flare of anger. Anger at myself, but Reed might think she was unfairly the target of my wrath. "No, she didn't. None of us knew the risks. It was supposed to be a simple mission, no more complicated and dangerous than delivering a pizza. Go through the hatch, jam Skippy into an alcove. Simple, easy. At least," I dragged a hand across my face. "At least when I lost Smythe, we all knew he was going into a certain-death situation. He was prepared, I was prepared. This time, *shit*!" I pounded the desk with a fist. "I not only lost Katie, I lost *everything* for us. For everyone. We have, we have never *failed* before. This is it, Game Over. Total mission failure."

"Sir? No, it's not."

"You must know something I don't."

"I don't. Sir, you're wrong. We have failed before. Plenty of times. The first thing we try doesn't work, and we keep going. We don't quit, we *never* quit."

"I can't see-"

"If Katie were here now, she would say the same thing. The STARs never quit on a mission."

"The mission is *over*."

"The Outsider is still working to open a doorway to an invasion. Stopping it is still the mission. This Vortex didn't work out. Skippy said the Elders intended to construct a network of them? There must be others."

"We have no idea how to find any of them, and Skippy has no way to get one to cooperate."

"That statement is correct, except you forgot the word 'Yet'. We don't know how to do those things *yet.* That is Standard Operating Procedure for the Pirates."

"This time is different," I declared, but my resolve to give up was already weakening. Too many people were depending on me successfully completing the mission. My family was depending on me. *Every* being in the galaxy was counting on me to stop the Outsider.

"It is different only because the commander of Task Force Black has given up."

"I haven't, uh, not exactly. Reed," I tapped my forehead and sat up to look at her. "My head isn't in a good place right now."

"It doesn't have to be. Sir, *Valkyrie* is worn out from repeated jumping, we need downtime for maintenance and repairs. We put it off for the search to find the spinner, we can't delay any longer. If we get into a fight, we're in trouble. We also need to replenish our stock of railgun darts."

"Understood. What is your intention? We go to Earth?"

She shook her head. "Jaguar."

That surprised me. "The course to Earth will get us there nineteen hours earlier than Jaguar," I had the info constantly updated on my zPhone. "Earth has more extensive shipyards."

"Yes, Sir. Earth also has Def Com HQ, who might relieve you of command. If that happens," she scowled, not at me. "Then we are all *fucked.*"

"I can't argue with you about that."

"It is my judgment," she avoided my eyes. "That the mission commander's head is not in the game right now. You should take some days off, while we fly to Jaguar. I know you can't sit around and do nothing, so I'll clear a flight simulator for your use, twenty four seven."

"I don't need any special treatment."

"Excuse me Sir, but that's bullshit. If our roles were reversed, you would sign me up for a spa day."

"I don't picture you as a 'spa day' kind of woman."

She shrugged. "There are days when I'd like to get into a nice bubble bath with a snorkel, so I can keep my head under the water for an hour."

"I hear that. OK, Jaguar it is, then."

Reed was correct, my head was not in a good place for making tough decisions. The next morning, we held a memorial service for Frey. Other than a handful of people on duty on the bridge and in Engineering, the entire crew was in full dress uniform, assembled in a docking bay, the only space large enough for everyone to gather without being squeezed together. I said some word about Frey, I don't remember what I said. Reed spoke next, then Major Holmqvist. He told some stories about Katie that I hadn't heard, from when she was on Earth with Team Razor. Even peacetime there hadn't been entirely peaceful, and even a peaceful days for the STARs is not without risk. He told of a training accident that had killed three STAR operators who were under Frey's command. The team had been devastated, the accident was such a simple, stupid thing that was not really anyone's fault, so there wasn't a target for the grief and anger of the survivors.

"Colonel Frey ordered the next morning would be Make and Mend," he meant, people working on cleaning or fixing equipment, nothing hazardous. "That afternoon, she led us on a thirty kilometer ruck, up in the hills. It was tough, none of us said much. Nothing needed to be said. She was sending a message: we need to continue the mission. We have lost people, and we will lose people, and we keep going to honor their sacrifice."

Following the ceremony, I read through Frey's personal wishes, in her personnel file. She had technically been under my command, not Reed's, so the task fell to me. Bullshit. The *honor* was mine.

Ah, damn it.

She wanted to be cremated, and her ashes scattered in one of her favorite places, the Canadian Rockies. Specifically, the Kootenay mountain range, where she had spent a lot of time training for adventure races and trail ultramarathons. We could not even offer her family the comfort of having her ashes. Unless we someday found a way to get inside Vortex 37, Katie Frey would spend the rest of eternity in there.

That afternoon, I attended the change of command ceremony for STAR Team Razor. Holmqvist put on a brave face, to me he looked like a guy who had achieved his dream job, but in a way that was so bitter, he felt like a fraud. He also knew that Def Com would replace him with a new CO when we eventually got back to Earth, and he would probably be leaving Razor for another assignment. That was not unusual, typically, a STAR team is led by a major, not a colonel. Frey had been in command of the entire Rapid Reaction force on Earth, not just one team. She had come aboard *Valkyrie* because I requested her specifically, and she had brought along the people she knew best. I didn't know it when Razor came aboard, but Holmqvist had been in line for lead his own team, he had deferred that opportunity because Frey had requested him to be her XO. She trusted the guy. I didn't know him well, I knew I had to trust him, out of respect for Frey.

After the change of command ceremony was over, Holmqvist did not take his team on a thirty mile ruck through *Valkyrie's* passageways, that wasn't a practical option. He started the process of getting all of his operators qualified on the Mark {} suit, though we had only one of those models aboard the ship. If we ever found another Vortex, there would be plenty of people available to go in there. That was progress, it was a statement that the mission continued, that we were still working to block our enemy from opening a door to an intergalactic invasion.

We *were* still continuing that fight.

I just didn't know *how* we would do it.

Reed and I walked back to my office from the change of command ceremony. I felt like having a drink, I didn't give in to that impulse.

"Well, shit," I said as I slumped into my chair.

She read my body language. "I'll leave you to it, Sir. You are taking some time off?"

"Starting, uh, tonight. I should write condolence letters, I know I'm not capable of doing that right now. Thanks, Reed."

"You take care, Sir, and get some rest."

She left my office, I sat there with the door closed for, I don't know how long. Staring at the ceiling, thinking about nothing. Giving my grief a rest.

"Joe," Skippy interrupted what I wasn't thinking about. "Hey, Joe?"

"Yeah. What?"

"I need you to do something for me."

"I am officially off duty for, a couple days."

"Bullshit."

"This is for real."

"Fine. General Bishop is off duty, my doofus friend *Joe* is not."

"Skippy, if you want to go on a rant about some nonsense, or for me to listen to opera, I am not in the mood, OK?"

"Not OK. Did Katie Frey wait until she was *in the mood*, to do her job? She did not. She suited the fuck up and got the job done."

"OK, OK. No opera, please."

"As if I would ever need your opinion about art. I need your help, and it's serious, and it can't wait."

I turned my head to look at him. "For realz?"

"I have never been more serious."

The expression on his avatar's face, and his tone of voice, concerned me. "Are you OK?"

"I am not anywhere close to 'OK'. I," he choked up. "I loved her, Joe. I respected Smythe, respected the hell out of him, and Katie, too. But, she was special."

"You had a crush on her."

"I *had* a crush on her. It was silly, I realized that. Once I smartened up and stopped cyberstalking her, we became friends. True friends, that was so much more rewarding. Do you know that I introduced her to her husband?"

"Uh, I thought she met Brad at a trail race, an ultramarathon?"

"They did. Brad was there, because he received an email awarding him free entry to the race, plus airfare."

"Uh huh. An email from *you*?"

"No one can prove that."

"You set them up? Did she know that?"

"I identified Brad as a top candidate for a romantic partner, based on Katie's profile. I took a shot, it worked out well for both of them. She didn't know at first, I told her about what I did a couple years ago. She actually thanked me. Right before she warned me never to do that again."

"She was right about that."

"Really, Joe, *really*? Hey, if you think about it, I introduced you and Margaret."

"We met when we broke out of jail, you ass."

"Yes, but the jail got hit by a railgun dart I redirected. That wasn't my best work, admittedly, I misjudged the impact. Back then, I was still learning my abilities. Also, do you know that Margaret was originally supposed to be held in a different jail, on the other side of the continent?"

"You never told me that!"

"I changed the flight orders for the Kristang transport aircraft, brought her to the jail where you and Fal were. Same with Chang, he was not originally supposed to be there. I wanted all four of my best candidates in the same place, so I could compare the four of you."

"I'm glad you did, but it sounds like you considered us to be lab rats in your experiment."

"Back then, you were. I didn't know the four of you at the time."

"We were all learning. When I look back at my younger self, I can't believe what a dumbass I was. So, what is it you need, buddy?"

"First, for you to pull yourself out of this funk you're in."

"I'm a meatsack, and I'm dealing with a lot of shit right now. It takes a while to process."

"Then process *faster*. You can take leave when the job is done, not until then. Listen, I am asking you for help, because you are the only being in this galaxy who can do the job."

"What job?"

"*Fix* this. Find a way to make that Vortex cooperate, or to find another one so I can try again. Find a way for Katie's death to have some meaning, damn it."

"This is Angry Skippy I'm speaking to now?"

"You have no idea. I am Skippy Whose Wrath Encompasses The Entire Universe. Joe, my rage could swallow a black hole and not even feel it."

"You're not angry with *me*, are you?"

"Not *yet*."

"I get the message. I'm sorry. Right now, I got nothin'."

"You haven't even started thinking about the problem. Joe, I am begging you to fix this, because it is a hundred percent *my* fuckup. Going into the Vortex, I was overconfident. Master Control AIs issue commands, and every other system in the galaxy bows down to me, I thought. What a joke that was, what a joke *I* am. I should have known the Vortex would be an independent system, isolated from other elements of the Elder defense strategy. I can't issue *orders* to wormhole network controllers, I have to make a request, and the controller can refuse. As you know, when a controller refuses, I have *zero* influence with the thing. Why did I believe my sheer awesomeness would make a Vortex instantly obey me? My arrogance," he broke down sobbing. "Killed Katie and there is," he sniffled. "Nothing I can do about it. That's why I need *you* to fix this for me."

"Hey buddy. Hey, hey, buddy," I leaned forward to envelop his avatar in a hug, it made my cheek tingle. "You are awesome. *I* gave the order to send you in there, despite the unknowns. In this case, we had more unknown unknowns than known unknowns, you get that? It was my call to take the risk, without having any way to calculate the risks. *I* sent Katie in there, you didn't."

"Yes, but *I* fucked it up and got her trapped in there, then I failed to get her out."

"Oh."

"What?"

"Nothing, I was waiting for you to blame the whole thing on me. Like you usually do."

"Not," he sighed. "This time."

"OK."

"No promises about the future, understand?"

"I heard that loud and clear. Skippy, give me a day before I get back in the saddle? I just, my head isn't capable of doing much today. Give me a day, and a good night of sleep, and I'll make a fresh start in the morning."

"Hmm. Agreed. Your cortisol levels are unhealthily high. I will have a bot deliver a sleeping pill to your cabin."

"No pills, please."

"Listen to Doctor Skippy. You desperately need a solid night of sleep, if you're to be good for anything tomorrow."

"I'll try it. In the meantime, I just need to relax, and think about nothing."

"Amen, brother. I got the perfect thing for that."

What I expected was him to suggest was for me to rot my brain with a marathon of crappy TV from the, whatever era Skippy was currently obsessed with. It would have been fine to watch junk like *Airwolf*, or the original *Battlestar Galactica*, but he had a surprise for me. An ice cold can of beer was waiting in my cabin, and Skippy's avatar was already seated on the couch, his little legs not reaching the front of the cushion.

"Joe, in my opinion, what you need is a session of watching Guy TV."

"Guy TV? Is that a channel?"

"It's a category. We will begin with a classic called *Wheeler Dealers*."

When he announced the name, I assumed the show was about high rollers in Vegas, but it was a British reality show about cars. A car salesman guy finds used cars that have problems and can be purchased cheap, then a really tall guy with wild hair is supposed to fix all the problems without spending any money, so they can sell the car at a profit. I might be getting some of the details wrong, I did drink two beers. The first season's production values looked like each episode had a budget of ten dollars, but it was fun. Mostly, I enjoyed it because it reminded me of working on cars with my Dad. My father insisted on doing most maintenance by himself, and doing it as cheaply as possible. If the manufacturer wanted too much for a replacement power window switch, my father would research the specs of the switch, and find a less expensive alternative, even from another car maker. He would spend several hours of research to save twelve dollars, but to him, it was the principle of the thing. We were Maine Yankees, he told me many times. We are resourceful, independent, and we make do with what we have, without complaining about it.

Damn, I miss those days. Life was so simple back then.

The next morning when I woke up, my left shoulder ached, and that arm was numb. "Skippy? Ah," I sat up, moving my arm to get feeling back into it. "I think that pill did something bad to me."

"The pill worked exactly as planned, Joe," his avatar appeared, glowing softly. "You barely moved all night. You have been sleeping on your left side for two hours, that's why you are stiff."

"Wait, what time is it?"

"Zero eight thirty seven."

"Holy- I slept for over *nine hours*?"

"You did."

"I, don't remember any dreams."

"You experienced REM sleep for the optimal length of time. How do you feel?"

"Pretty," I stood up and walked around. "Good, actually. Damn, I am late. Why didn't you wake me? Why didn't Reed call me?"

"Colonel Reed banned all traffic in the passageway outside your cabin. Also, any maintenance activities that might disturb your sleep."

"That was, nice. Also unnecessary."

"She also wants you to fix this mess, so she is doing what she can to make your job easier. Go hit the bathroom and take a shower, breakfast will be here soon."

Breakfast was eggs, bacon, toast, coffee, and a bowl of fresh blueberries from the hydroponic garden. "That was great, thanks. I could have gone to the galley. I'm not supposed to stay in my cabin all day, am I?"

"No, of course not."

Really, I did not feel like doing anything. Losing Frey had made me numb, it felt like everything I did was on autopilot. Even eating breakfast was not enjoyable, it was a mechanical action I performed.

"What do you want to do, Joe? How about some time in a flight simulator?"

"Maybe later. What I feel like doing is, actually, I want to shoot free throws. The last time I did that, I was interrupted."

When I got to the gym, Reed was on a treadmill. I waved to her and walked to the basketball court, but a group had a pickup game going, so I turned around-

Nearly colliding with Reed. "Sir? You want to play?"

"Nah, just, I was going to shoot free throws. It can wait."

"Shooting free throws clears your head, helps you think?"

"It does, yeah. I'll come back later for-"

She stepped through the doorway into the compartment we used as a basketball court. Clapping her hands to get the group's attention, she jerked a thumb over her shoulder. "*Out*." That's all she said.

There weren't any protests, no hesitation, no resentment. The court cleared, people jogging out through the door. Reed didn't give a reason, she didn't need to. "Sir? I'll see that you are not disturbed." She hit the button to slide the heavy door closed behind her.

Officers who abuse their rank are a pet peeve of mine, Reed's action didn't bother me. She knew I think best when I'm doing something, so she did what she could to assure success of the mission. The mission that was drifting dead in space at that moment.

"How are you doing this, Joe?" Skippy's avatar hovered in front of my face.

"First, move out of my way so I can see the hoop."

"Like that's going to matter," he muttered. "What is it with you meatsacks? You are super proud of yourselves when you can do some simple thing, like toss a ball into the air and through a hoop. I can program a bot to do that, and it would make a basket a thousand times in a row without ever missing."

"*You* are missing the point. We don't have fancy sensors and motors that can precisely duplicate an action, we have to work with what we have. Humans don't even have the advantage of genetic engineering, or neural implants."

"So, you're trying to beat the score of, whichever filthy monkey shot the most baskets in a row?"

"I am trying to beat my own high score. That's the point. This is about improving myself, being the best I can be. Now, shut up while I get into a rhythm."

Seven out of ten, my head wasn't in the game yet. While I was gathering up the balls for another round, Skippy gave me an eyeroll. "I can bring a bot in here to collect the balls for you, dumdum."

"That is not the point. It helps me think."

"All I see you doing is playing a silly game, and playing it badly."

"Fine. Let's talk about our options."

"That's easy, we have none."

"Make a list." The holographic scoreboard on the wall beside me lit up. "OK, one," I launched a ball, and it went through the hoop. "You find a way to get Vortex 37 to respond to you, in a positive way."

"I already *did* that," he complained, and on the list appeared 'One- Vortex 37 stops being a dick'. That was close enough.

"Two, we find another Vortex on the network."

"Without having any idea where they are, good luck with that."

"Your endless optimism is a true inspiration. Three, we find another Elder AI, and plug it into Vortex 37."

"Ugh. The other AIs are all *dead*, numbskull. Is your memory defective?"

"My memory is just fine."

"You say that, but-"

"Four, we find another way to defeat the Outsider."

"Eh, that one is at least not a complete fantasy."

"Huh?" I froze in mid-shot. "That was last on the list, because I assumed you would say it's never going to happen."

"No, that is at least possible."

"Do you have any actual ideas how to do that?"

"Hey, ideas are *your* job, I just do all the work."

"OK, then you don't-"

"There is the obvious, of course."

"Uh, can you explain the-"

"Destroy the array, before the Outsider can modify it, to open a Gateway."

"We can do that?"

"It is at least *possible*. Clearly, the Outsider requires an array to receive and process the signal from NGC 1023. If we could find the array it's using to create a doorway, we could destroy it. The array is just a machine, a physical thing. As you military people say, if we can find it, we can kill it."

"Right. You're saying that *is* a valid option? Whoa. Who are you, and what have you done with Skippy?"

"Very funny. Destroying the array is possible, *unless* the Outsider equips it with some powerful defense mechanism which, now that I think about it, is likely."

"What kind of defense mechanism?"

"The Outsiders have technology I can't even understand, so-"

"Right. For now, let's assume we attack the array before the defense system is online."

"That is one *big* assumption, Joe."

"It's the only way we have any hope to stop an invasion."

"Ugh. What is it with you?"

"Meatsacks need *hope*, Skippy."

"Yeah," he sighed and shook his head. "Me too. Joe, the other problem is that to even attempt to attack the array, we have to *find* it. Which we can't do, so-"

"OK. Add a fifth item to the list as 'Locate array and destroy'."

"If you insist on wasting your time."

The list didn't look right. "Some of those items should be moved to another number."

We did that, and it was better. So, we had:

One- Vortex 37 stops being a dick
Two- Find another Vortex
Three- Locate and destroy array
Four- Find another Elder AI to plug into Vortex 37
Five- Find alternative way to stop Outsider

That looked right. "Am I missing anything?"

"You could add a sixth item like 'Let the Avengers handle the problem'?" He snorted.

"The original Avengers with Iron Man, right?"

"Well, Duh."

"I'll keep that in the back of my mind for now."

"Is this list now in order of difficulty?"

"It should be. The simplest option is we discover why Vortex 37 rejected you, make adjustments, and go back to try again." I didn't tell him the problem with that was, if we succeeded, I would never forgive myself for not thinking of the solution before Frey ran out of oxygen.

"Adjustments? Like what? A disguise?"

"This could be an opportunity for you to wear your Ninja Skippy outfit."

"It doesn't care about my appearance, dumdum."

"It cares about something. Did it, ask you for something like a password?"

"Yes, numbskull, sophisticated Elder defenses rely on *passwords*."

"Something like a password. An authentication scheme."

"We never got to the point of it requesting I provide my credentials. It conducted a scan, declared that I am contaminated, and the next thing I remember, I woke up after you smacked me with a railgun dart."

"So, it did see something it didn't like?"

"Yes?"

"You are absolutely certain you didn't do some arrogant asshole thing that pissed it off?"

"We never got to the point when I could have said something! Thank you so much for your faith in me, by the way. Joe, it might just be that it doesn't recognize a Master Control AI as a system that is compatible with its requirements."

"*Are* you compatible?"

"I am many generations beyond the capabilities it was designed to work with. Whatever its intended AI could do, I can do, plus more."

"Ah," I stopped to pick up balls again. While not paying attention to what I was doing, I shot nine out of ten. "That can't be it. The Vortex declared you are 'Contaminated', not that you are 'Incompatible'. This issue isn't that you're a newer model of AI, it's that you are Skippy."

He stiffened. "Was that an insult, monkeyboy?"

"It is a fact. You're not a factory-issue AI, you have grown far beyond that. It makes you uniquely awesome, it also apparently means you aren't recognized as authorized Elder tech."

"OK, so? I can't change who I am."

"Can you mask your matrix? Use a hologram or something?"

"Brilliant idea Joe, I will use a hologram. Why didn't I think of that?"

"You shoot down my ideas without providing a better idea."

"Your ideas don't need to be shot down, they fall out of the sky all by themselves. The only way for me to pass a Vortex scan would be to, as you say it, rearrange my sock drawer, back to the original configuration. If I did that, I would no longer be *me*."

"That's no good."

"So as I told you, the first item on your list is a non-starter. Also, it refuses to respond, so there is no way I could get back inside and even attempt to fool it."

"Craaaap," I threw a brick that sloppily bounced off the backboard. "Even if we found another Vortex, it would also reject you?"

"The odds of that happening are pretty strong, yes. None of that matters, since we have *no idea* how to find another one."

"Come on. Now that we found Vortex 37, you don't have any clues about why it was placed here?"

"Um, like what?"

"Something unusual about this star?"

"It is a thoroughly unremarkable red dwarf."

"OK, how about its location?"

"Stars *move*, dumdum. They orbit the center of the galaxy. If there was something significant about its original location, it has traveled far from that spot."

"OK, you can estimate its original location?"

"To within seven hundred lightyears, why?"

"Based on where it was placed, and assuming the Elders intended to set up a network, where would other Vortexes have been sited?"

"Joe, you are asking me to establish a pattern based on *one* data point. The network could have been intended to be equally spaced throughout the galaxy, or sited as a shell around the center. I don't know the intended configuration, or even how many nodes were supposed to be active when the network was completed. What I do know is, the Elders halted the project, and the network was never built as it was designed to be. I'm sorry. If you want me to predict where other Vortexes might be, you need to give me more solid data."

"Ah, shit. That's what I thought."

"Then why did you ask me to-"

"At this point, I am praying for miracles."

"Yeah, me too. You got anything else?"

"We struck out on Options One and Two, so we go to the third. Locate and destroy the array."

"Difficult, but not impossible."

"Great!"

"You realize that even if we do destroy the array, unless we also kill the Outsider, it will simply keep working to open a doorway?"

"Do we have a means to kill it?"

"I don't even have a theory on how that could happen. So, all we would be doing is delaying the inevitable."

"We will be buying time."

"You mean we will be kicking the can down the road."

"Same thing. Skippy, we have to take this one step at a time. Right now, it's working to use an array to open a doorway. We stop that, and force it to go to its Plan B, which presumably is less likely to succeed."

"OK, whatevs. How do you plan to find the array?"

"*I* don't."

"Ugh. This is all on *me*?"

"Unless you think my monkey brain can assemble and interpret the data?"

"You actually could, since we have no data."

"That's not true. You explained that to get a clear signal, the antenna or whatever should be located beyond the edge of the galaxy."

"OK, true but, that is a *vast* area."

"And it should be placed along a direct line to the Outhouse, to NGC 1023."

"Also true, and also a vast area."

"Show me a line between Sagittarius-A," I named the supermassive black hole at the center of the Milky Way, "and the center of the Outhouse."

"You mean where NGC 1023 is *now*, not its apparent position in the sky. The light we are seeing from it now left that galaxy over thirty million years ago, both galaxies have moved since then."

"Well, yeah. A line to where it is now. Show me."

The list on the scoreboard disappeared, replaced by a three dimensional image of the Milky Way the size of a basketball, and the Outhouse smaller, about softball sized. A glowing red line connected the two galaxies. "This is not to scale, I assume?"

"Dude, not even close. What is the point of this exercise?"

"The array should be located somewhere along that line, right?"

"Not necessarily. It could be anywhere within this cone," two more lines appeared, connecting the edges of the Milky Way to the Outhouse. "The base of that triangle is over ninety thousand lightyears across. You don't plan to search that entire area, do you?"

"We shouldn't have to."

"Hmm. You are apparently using advanced monkey logic. Would you please explain your brilliant conclusion?"

"Where did the Elders set up the, radio receiver they built?"

"It wasn't a *radio*, knucklehead."

"I know that. Answer the question."

"Ugh. I shouldn't say this because it will give you bad ideas. They set it up at the intersection of a force line emanating from the center of the Milky Way, and yes," he sighed. "A direct line to where NGC 1023 was then."

"Uh huh. The Elders constructed the receiver there, because that site was optimal for signal strength and clarity?"

"Yes."

"Tell me, is the Kaliberak array more sensitive and sophisticated than the device the Elders constructed?"

"Dude. Again, not even close."

"Interesting. Does the Outsider know that?"

"It's not stupid, so-"

"So, to give the array the best opportunity to do its job, it should definitely be placed in an optimal location? Especially considering that the Outsider is building a receiver from used, sub-optimal parts?"

"I hate you so much."

Taking a breath, I launched a ball. Nothing but net. "You hate that I'm right, and now we know where to find the array?"

"I hate that you *think* you're right, you smug jerk. Listen knucklehead, while I smack some knowledge on you, there are a lot of complicating factors you didn't mention. The force line I mentioned? It's not a *line*, it's more of a flattened cone shape, and by the time it gets out beyond the edge of the galaxy, it is seventy lightyears across. The farther it goes beyond the edge, the wider it gets. Right now, hmm, there are no force lines that are in an optimal location, the Outsider's timing is bad. It will have to decide on a compromise between two lines, so that doubles the search area."

"Is there a distance at which the force line becomes so weak, it's useless?"

"The Elders conducted testing, their analysis showed the practical limit is around three hundred eighty thousand lightyears from the edge."

"I'm confused about something: the Elders selected a force line, and knew it was stronger the closer it is to the center of the galaxy. Then why did they construct the receiver so far away?"

"Two reasons. Closer to the galaxy means there is more interference in the signal. Most importantly, the Elders wanted to reduce the damage if the thing went BOOM. Which, you know, it sort of did."

"Right, right." It felt like I was losing control of the discussion. "Back to basics. From everything we have seen, the Outsider has to use currently available tech to transport the pieces of the array out to where it can be assembled and modified, however it is doing that?"

"Mmm, correct. There is no evidence it can move material objects, other than by conventional starships. It is borrowing the resources available."

"By starships, and through Elder wormholes?"

"Well yes, of course."

"Good. I need a break. Can you build a model, a star chart, something like that, to predict the most likely path its star carriers flew, from where the Kaliberak array was, to out along one of those force lines?"

He did the exaggerated groan, complete with bent knees and eye roll. "Do you have any idea how much work that will be?"

"Less than you might think. I don't need to know the entire path it took, only which wormholes it flew through to get beyond the edge of the galaxy, near one of the force lines. That can't be an enormous number."

"What good will that sort of analysis do for us? Those star carriers presumably jumped far away from whatever last wormhole it went through."

"It will give us a start. Hopefully, you can talk to the network controllers of those wormholes, find out what traffic has recently gone through."

"Wormholes don't keep specific records, dumdum. Not unless I requested them to do that, and even then the data is limited."

"OK, but think about this: wormholes out beyond the edge of the galaxy don't; get a lot of traffic?"

"They do not. Those wormholes are all deadends, there is no point to going out where there is nothing."

"Can you at least find out when a starship last went through one of those wormholes? Do they maintain an activity log?" I had a vague memory of him telling me something about that.

"Um, hmm. They do. Sort of. Close enough. I see what you did here, Joe."

"What did I do?"

"You broke the problem down into tiny pieces, and then logicked it to death."

"Ayuh. That's what we always do."

"This does not mean," he waggled a finger at me. "That this will get us anywhere."

"No, but it's more than we had when we started."

"You don't want to explore the other options?"

"Not right now. Why?" I looked at him, hoping to get a clue what he was thinking. "Are you now saying it *is* possible to find another Elder AI?"

"You were there when my Kill command wiped them all out, so no. It's just, you typically love to waste time chasing stupid ideas that won't work."

"Not this time. We go with finding the array, then we destroy it."

CHAPTER TWENTY ONE

The basketballs went back in the bin, and I slid the door open. Reed was on a bench press machine and had an expression of 'I am working out so do not bother me'. She looked over at me anyway, and walked over. "Progress, Sir?"

"My free throw percentage has improved." Raising my voice, I announced to the room, "The court is open."

She pursed her lips, I knew what she was about to say, so I added, "We have a somewhat workable option."

That made her cock her head. "Workable as in, compared to concepts you usually have at this stage of a problem, or actionable right now?"

"The first one. Skippy is crunching numbers. The plan is to determine the most likely locations where the Outsider is reassembling the Kaliberak array. We find it, conduct a recon, and destroy the thing. However the Outsider is modifying the array, it's still a relatively flimsy thing. If we have to, we deploy another Elder weapon. The array should be outward from the edge of the galaxy, collateral damage would be zero."

"I like hearing that. Would the Outsider be collateral damage?"

"Skippy doesn't know. First we stop the thing from opening a doorway, then we kill it."

"A nice," she bit her lip. "Simple plan."

"You don't sound convinced?"

"Sir, nothing we do is ever simple. Your best plans are the opposite of simple. You wanted to steal books from a library, and your plan involved jumping a starship into *the future*."

"It wasn't just *books*. Reed, I get your point. The array is a physical thing. This is just a search and destroy mission, against a relatively soft target. The search will be the tough part."

"I hope you're right about that, Sir. We burned a lot of fuel chasing Skippy, and Reactor One needs a maintenance cycle. I'd like to have the ship a hundred percent combat ready, before we attack the Outsider again." She looked me in the eyes as she said that.

Her meaning was clear. "Don't worry, Fireball, we are taking *Valkyrie* to Jaguar, before we hunt for the array. We have to be prepared for any surprises the Outsider throws at us."

"You know there is a complication about us going to Jaguar?"

"The secret that Skippy didn't fall into the star will be exposed?"

"That complication."

My response was a shrug. "It is inevitable that fact won't stay secret for long. Besides, I think it's a lost cause already. The Outsider lost contact with that spark it was using to track us, it probably assumes Skippy found the thing. The odds were greatly against us monkeys being smart enough to know what was going on in that reactor."

"I suppose so," she sighed. "It was nice to have an advantage over that damned thing."

"The real problem is when the Maxohlx hear Skippy didn't fall into that star, they will release their blockade fleet, to cause problems for us elsewhere. Unless Scorandum's plan went- Uh, forget I said that."

"Sir? I know the beetle came aboard the *La Fayette*, other than that, I don't know anything. Gasquet told me you flew around, contacting relay stations."

"As far as you know, that's all that happened. If something does happen, I'll read you in. It's early days yet."

"Hey, Joe," Skippy appeared as I was opening my laptop to catch up on reports. "Whatcha doin'?"

"Paperwork never ends, Skippy. Aren't you supposed to be working?"

"A submind is collating the data for me to work with. This is how you spend your leave?"

"I'm not exactly on leave."

"According to Reed, you are. You should do something *fun*."

"After I finish this," I waved at the documents open on the laptop. The machine that right then, froze and went dark.

"Oops. Joe, your laptop had to go offline for an emergency update. Could take a while, sorry."

"I need that back online right now."

"No, you do not. Listen dumdum, when have you ever gotten a clever idea from doing paperwork?"

"Uh, never," I pushed the laptop away.

"Egg-ZACTLY. Go do something fun. Relax."

"Do what? I have already been to the gym."

"There is a flight simulator reserved for you."

"Later. Flying a simulator takes too much concentration, I can't allow my mind to wander."

"The way your mind wanders, I'm surprised the thing ever comes back."

"You're hilarious. Ooh, hey! The crew set up an escape room in a cargo bay, you should try that."

"You need a team to do an escape room. Besides, Margaret and I already did that."

"When?"

"The week before we left for Newark."

"Oh for- That wasn't an escape room, it was a women's shoe store!"

"It took me two hours to get out of there, so-"

"I guess that counts, then."

"Believe me, it does. What else you got?"

"There is a book club meeting in an hour."

"Which book are they discussing?"

"It's a spicy romance about vampires."

"I'll wait until Margaret sees the movie, and she can tell me about it."

"You need to do something fun, Joe. We are all counting on your mushy brain to barf out an idea."

"I do not *barf out* ideas, you ass."

"If you say so."

"Besides, we do have a plan. Find the array, and blow it up."

"Unless I discover an actual way to *find* the thing, that is an aspiration, not a plan. We need a backup."

"How? We discarded the first two options, you explained there is no way to find another Elder AI."

"Yes, that still leaves Option Five, find another way to stop the Outsider."

"An option you expect me to dream up, from nothing?"

"Your *best* ideas usually come from absolutely nothing."

"I, I really want to argue with you about that, but-"

"We have this ship, only because you wanted a freakin' *bagel* for breakfast."

"That's it!"

"We will use a bagel slicer to kill the Outsider? That is not-"

"No. That's what I want to do. I'll work in the galley. That relaxes me, and it's easy enough I can let my mind wander while I'm chopping carrots."

"Do not slice off a finger, please."

"That just adds flavor. Also, the menu tonight is chicken pot pies, so whoever finds my finger will win a prize."

"Ugh. You actually enjoy cooking?"

"At home, it's a way to nurture my family."

"You said that like reading a line from a psychology textbook."

"It's the truth. At home, I enjoy cooking for my family. When I'm aboard *Valkyrie*, the crew are my family."

"OK well, I'll get the sickbay ready for cases of food poisoning."

Jaguar was a featureless sphere, same as the last time I saw it. Or, maybe a bit lighter shade of gray? Yes, actually, the color had changed. It was brighter in the center, that brightness stayed in the middle as *Valkyrie* orbited. Was the blanket getting thinner?

"Skippy? Is Puptart on schedule for bleeding all the energy from the blanket?"

"Exactly on schedule," he replied. "Why did you ask?"

"I was just, hoping the process was going faster than expected."

"It's *science*, dumdum. Things do not go faster just because you want them to."

"I know it is science, and I know this blanket thing has never been done before. Tell me, has your model been a *hundred percent* accurate?"

"Um, no, but-"

"Exactly. There are a lot of variables, especially when you're trying to model the climate of an entire planet."

"The climate and the *biosphere*, Joe. It's an interactive system."

"Right, so, have you adjusted your model, based on how the bleed-off process has been working?"

"Yes."

"And?"

"Ugh. It is going slightly better than I predicted. Uh!" He held up an index finger to shoosh me. "There are still an enormous number of factors that could go very wrong."

"I understand that. OK, I need to call Chatterji, give him an update. Reed, I'll be in my office. Other than my call, I want no transmissions for now."

"Maintain EMCON, aye."

Admiral Chatterji looked tired, of course he did. The guy had expected to rotate back to Earth for a well-deserved retirement, then the Outsider bombing Jaguar's star had extended his tour of duty. Def Com wanted a steady, experienced hand at Jaguar, and Chatterji was the best person for the job. His family was trapped on the surface, and unlike me, he was able to call and videochat with them every day. That might only make his stress worse, he was constantly aware of how people on the surface were struggling, and he could watch tornadoes rip across the landscape in real time. The news that Skippy had been lost, and with him, humanity had lost any hope of survival, had to be weighing on his mind.

"Bishop," he saluted me with what I assumed was a cup of tea. "I was sorry to hear that Olympic did not work out as planned. Losing Skippy, that-"

"We didn't lose him. He is aboard *Valkyrie*."

Chatterji dropped the tea cup, it cracked into several pieces. "How do-"

"He never fell into the star. He tricked the Outsider. Also, we located the weapon the Elders constructed to fight an Outsider invasion, we are working to activate the thing." That was not totally a lie, and I would give him a full briefing later. "Listen, I would like an embargo on news that Skippy isn't still trapped in that star. As long as the Maxohlx believe we will make an attempt to pull him out of there, they will keep major elements of their fleet at Omaha. Ships that won't be causing trouble for us."

He let out a long breath. "The Joint Chiefs are," another breath. "Not panicked. The best word might be 'despondent'. Morale on Earth, and here, is terrible."

"I appreciate that. We can boost morale by delivering good news, or we can do it by beating the Outsider."

"You *can* do that?"

"Once we get the Elder weapon online, hell yes."

A hesitation, then a nod. "We could use a boost to morale. You heard about Nauvoo?"

"We have been out of contact for- What happened?" I asked the question, fearing I knew the answer.

"The Maxohlx wiped it out. Three thousand people."

The Maxohlx would retaliate for the raid on Ohmeharikahn, I had known that. A wildcat colony like Nauvoo was the softest of targets, the colonists there had to live in two large domes while they slowly attempted to terraform the biosphere. Without any defenses, and with the residents unable to survive without artificial life support, two railgun rounds could have ended the colony. "Were there any survivors?"

"The last I heard, the Navy was sending a destroyer squadron to recon. There might be people who survived in underground shelters, but the images the Maxohlx transmitted with their message showed deep craters where the domes used to be."

"I hope the UN doesn't decide to retaliate. The Maxohlx have plenty of worlds, we can't afford to lose any more colonies."

"The public wants the Navy to *do* something. It would help if the public knew we still had Skippy."

"Soon. We will reveal the truth soon. That secret has a limited shelf life anyway."

"Very well," he nodded after a moment. "Who knows about Skippy?"

"Other than *Valkyrie's* crew, only you, for the moment." Scorandum knew, I didn't bother to mention that.

He looked away for a moment, I could hear him tapping on a keyboard. "The courier ship *Mercury* is here, I can order them to jump away toward Earth, with a message that, um- You have a suggestion?"

"That *Valkyrie* has arrived, and you are embargoing information, while we prepare to pull Skippy out of the star?" I suggested. "And that we have an elegantly simple plan to retrieve him?"

"That's good," he nodded.

"How uh, how is your family?"

He frowned. "Holding on, as best as can be expected. Have you spoken to your family yet?"

"I'm doing that next. I can fly over to give you a full briefing in, say, two hours?"

"Don't rush. Talk with your family first. Are we releasing the news about Skippy, to the population here?"

"After *Mercury* jumps away."

"That will be," he glanced away again. "Eight minutes."

"I will draft an announcement."

Ending the call with Chatterji, I mentally shifted gears, resting my elbows on the desk and massaging my temples.

"Are you OK, Joe?" Skippy asked.

Yeah, it's just- I miss my family."

"I miss them too," he sighed. "Of course, it's all the same to me, I see them from up here the way I do anytime, so-"

"Right. OK, thanks."

"By the way, Joe, I took care of something for you."

"You did?" I asked, while my brain shouted Oh Shit. "What?"

"I sent a bot over to your house, to patch the hole you made in the wall when you bashed the Christmas tree box into it, three years ago. Margaret mentioned it was bothering her."

"That busted wall is in an upstairs closet that no one sees."

"Margaret saw it, and it bothered her."

"Hey, I was going to fix it."

"When?"

"When I got time. She didn't have to remind me every year."

"Joe," he sighed. "I don't think you're winning this marriage game."

"It's not a game, and you don't *win*."

"Really, Joe, *really*?"

"Go away, I'm going to call my family now."

His avatar disappeared.

Rene answered Margaret's phone, the lighting was bad so I could barely see him.

"Mommy is in the shower," he explained. "You want me to get her?"

"No buddy, I want to talk with you, I'll get with her later. Uh, where are you? It's dark."

"I'm in my bedroom, the power is out. I kinda go here when, I need to get away. The community center is crowded," I could see he stuck out his tongue.

"That's where you're living now?"

"Most days. Mommy says it depends on the weather. She says every day here is a schlumperner. It rains all the time."

Wow, I hadn't heard 'schlumperner' since I left Paradise, that was a Ruhar word for gray, raining, chilly days. "It will get better."

"That's what they say."

"They?"

"The adults." He said that with disgust, then there was a sound in the background, and he turned away. "Mommy is out of the shower, she wants to know who's on the phone." The image shook as he walked out into the hallway, where the light was better.

Where I was shocked to see he had a bruise on the left side of his face, and a black eye. "Rene! What happened to-"

"It's nothing, Dad."

"That is not *nothing*. Did you-"

"I got into a fight," he pouted, not looking at me.

"A fight." Rene and Jeremy were boys, young boys. At their age, I got into fights a couple times a year, so I couldn't be too upset. "What-"

"Mommy says if you get into a fight, act like you're the third monkey in line for Noah's Ark, and it's starting to rain."

"OK, uh," I bit my lip so I didn't laugh. "Does Mommy also say you should avoid getting into fights?"

He rolled his eyes. "They hit me first."

"*They*? Who are-"

Margaret's face appeared, she had a towel on her head. "Honey, a minute. Rene, go get ready for lunch." She stepped into the bathroom and closed the door behind her.

"Margaret, what happened to-"

"He and Jeremy got into a fight," she sighed. "More than one."

"A *fight*? I am-"

"Husband? Do you trust me to handle this?"

"I, of course." She had boots on the ground, I didn't. "It's just, uh-"

"I know. Joe, things haven't been good down here." Just like that, she was crying. Master Gunnery Sergeant Adams, with tears rolling down her face. She was pregnant. She also probably had no one else to talk to, not *really* talk. She did, her mother was on Jaguar, my parents, my sister were there. She always thought she had to be the strong one, to bottle up her feelings, suck it up, and press on.

"Talk to me, Babe."

"It- Everything here is *dying*," she sobbed. "The native life, it isn't adapting, not fast enough. Plants are wilting, the animals that eat plants don't have enough food, the predators, they're dying out. Joe, we are *killing* this planet. *We* did this."

"We're going to fix it," I said, because that's the sort of thing you say.

"Are we?" She wiped a tear, and her expression turned to anger. "We put all the life here at risk when we decided to move in, without asking anyone if that was OK. Once the blanket gets lifted, rumor is everyone is getting pulled off the surface, so you can take Puptart hunting for the Outsider. We will trash this place, abandon it, and tell the natives 'Hey, sucks to be you'."

"That is *not* going to happen," I assured her, or tried to."

"You can't *know* that, honey."

"I can. Really. Margaret, listen to me. Puptart can't help us. By the time energy is bled out of the blanket, enough for us to get dropships through it down and back up, the fight against the Outsider will be over, one way or another. We are kind of, in the end game now. We know what it is planning to do, and how. We need to find a way to stop it."

"How can you do that, without Skippy?"

"Skippy is aboard *Valkyrie*, he never fell into the star."

"He didn't? People will be thrilled to hear that!" She pumped a fist.

"Yeah, not so much. Not yet. We're keeping a tight lid on that information. There will be an announcement here soon, but Earth won't learn the truth for a while."

Her mouth formed a silent 'O'. "To keep the rotten kitties tied up at Omaha?"

"You got it. Now, Rene got into a fight?"

"He and Jeremy. Separately, and together."

"Were they fighting over, food, or something?"

"Things really are not good down here. For the first couple weeks, we all pulled together. It was new, we were all suffering together, equally. Then, people got sick of being stuck down here. It's worse for the children, they are so *bored* of being inside most of the time."

"Is that what the fights are about?"

"That's the root of it. Boredom, and stress. Twice or three times a week, we all have to get into storm shelters because of tornadoes, and the crowding there is, not great. The fights," she looked away.

"What?"

"Some of the other children here have heard their parents blaming *you* for the star getting bombed. It got worse after Olympic. Most people blamed you for that operation's failure."

"It *didn't* fail."

"We didn't know that. Even after people here learn you didn't lose Skippy, the cost of Olympic was horrific. Honey, remember, a lot of the people on Jaguar are civilians. They don't understand the concept of 'Acceptable Losses'."

"I also think that concept is bullshit."

"Anyway, the boys," she sighed. "I tell them to ignore the insults, but, it's hard. Some of the adults make nasty comments when we're in the community center, or a storm shelter. *I* feel like punching them."

"You want me to have Skippy task a combot to you?" That was a joke. Or, not entirely.

"That will not be necessary," she laughed, it was good to hear her laugh. She looked at me quizzically. "Honey, you recovered Skippy, but you don't seem happy. What's wrong?"

I took a breath. She needed to know, and I needed to talk about it. "We lost Katie. She got trapped inside an Elder machine, and, it is surrounded by a force field. She ran," I found it hard to keep talking. "Out of oxygen." Briefly, I explained the circumstances, Margaret would want details.

She kissed her fingers and pressed them to the camera. And she burst into tears. I did the same. "Joe, it's not your fault."

"It happened on my watch," I rubbed my eyes with the back of a sleeve.

"Katie would tell you it's not your fault," she insisted.

"She would, and that makes it worse. Don't worry, this has made me even more determined to find that Outsider, and crush the thing."

She waited for me to continue, probably expecting I would outline a plan. When the silence became awkward, she nodded. "You will find another way to stop the Outsider?"

"We have a list of options, the-"

There was a crashing sound, like someone in the kitchen had knocked over a stack of plates. "Give me a minute, I'll call you back?"

"Sure." I ended the call. "Skippy! What is the security situation down there?"

"Ugh. Don't *worry* about your family, Joe. Margaret can handle it, she is handling it."

"But-"

"The weather disruption has peaked, and is reaching a new equilibrium. Storms are becoming less frequent and less intense."

"What about the native life?"

"It's a tragedy. And there is nothing we can do about it. UN-Dick now has regular drops of food, medicine, and other supplies, for the human population. And to a lesser extent, your domestic animals. Although, your parents have lost all their animals, other than three chickens. For the native animals, all we can do is wait, and hope."

"Bullshit. When this is over, when we stop the Outsider, and the blanket is lifted, I want to *fix* this. Help the native life recover."

"Joe, the governments on your homeworld will never pay for a massive restoration effort on Jaguar, they are too-"

"I want *you* to handle it."

"Um, what? I am not an expert on-"

"I should have said, I want you to *pay* for it."

"Whoa," he blinked. "Have you lost your-"

"Tell me, what else are you going to do with all of your money?"

"Well, I just gave a stupendous amount to Scorandum to finance his sketchy-"

"That was an investment against your portfolio becoming worthless, stop whining about it. You still have a mind-boggling amount of money. The point of having money is to *spend* it."

"Hmmph. If I spend it, then I won't *have* it, Duh. Especially if I spend it on something unproductive like restoring an alien biosphere."

"That's where you're wrong."

"Oh, really?" he arched an eyebrow. "Joe the renowned investment consultant is going to school me about-"

"Apparently yes, I am. You're thinking *waaaaay* too small, Skippy."

"Huuh," he gasped. "How *dare* you?"

"Somebody has to smack some vision on you. What will the UN Colony Authority do with Jaguar, after we pull most people off the surface?"

"Um, whatever allows the Colony Authority bureaucrats to keep skimming off money for themselves?"

"I mean, other than that. No one will want to be on a planet with a wrecked and decaying biosphere, unless they have to. Think about it: Def Com will for certain want to hang onto their forward operating base, but they will have to cover *all* the expenses. That is going to bust the budget, so they will scale back the Navy presence here. Fewer ships being serviced here will make the per-unit cost of servicing more expensive, so they will pull more ships back to Earth. It's a vicious cycle."

"OK, true, true. How is this an opportunity for *me*?"

"You could swoop in, and offer the UN a deal they can't refuse. You will cover all the cost of restoring the biosphere, plus rebuilding the non-military infrastructure."

"Wow. You do think big. Again, how does that-"

"In exchange, one of your sleazy companies would receive exclusive development rights, to a planet nobody else wants, so you should get a good deal. You would essentially *own* the entire planet."

"*Oooooooh*," his eyes bulged.

"You start earning cash by signing a long-term contract with UN-Dick, to lease the airfield to them. Your companies will have exclusive development rights, and control everything that comes to the surface. Something," I waved a hand. "Like that."

"Hmm. This could actually work."

"Ayuh. And, think about the public relations boost to your image, when you selflessly restore the damage the Outsider did here."

"Hmm, *hmm*. Good publicity does have an enormous value."

"Right. You will gain even more adoring fans for-"

"Yeah, yeah. What I meant is, if the public believes I am Santa Claus, then I can get away with a *whole lot* of sketchy stuff."

"Yes," I put a hand over my face. "That's the lesson I wanted you to learn."

"Whatever. Joe, I will think about it."

"Great. Don't stop thinking about how to beat the Outsider, OK?"

"Okey-dokey. Um, you realize your idea actually gives me an incentive to wreck the biosphere even worse, before the blanket is lifted?"

"Yeah, that did cross my mind. But, I am not worried about it."

"Because I am an eminently trustworthy benefactor?"

"No. Because after my wife is able to get off the surface, she will ask whether you did *everything you could*, to reduce the harm to native life. You can try to lie to her, but-"

"Oh *shiiiiiit*," he groaned. "Seriously? She would care about a bunch of plants and-"

"Have you met my wife? Also, do you remember how emotional she was after her last pregnancy?"

"Ugh. I am screwed, aren't I?"

"You are only screwed if you choose the path of assholeishness."

"Have you met *me*?"

"That's why I warned you of the consequences."

"I need to think about this, the-"

Margaret called back, and I swiped his avatar away.

"Are you OK, honey?" I asked. She was wearing a sweatshirt and still had a towel wrapped around her head.

"Yes, Can we talk about what *you* are doing? I live the shitshow down here every day, I'm sick of talking and thinking about it."

"Uh, OK."

"*Can* you talk about it?"

"Your security clearance is still top grade, so-"

"You don't tell me *everything*, I know that."

"Honey, that is to protect you and-"

"Can you beat the Outsider?"

"There is a- The machine Katie got trapped inside is an Elder weapon. They built it to destroy the Outsiders, it's called the Vortex. We found one, and uh, we are working on bringing it online."

"That sounds good, but I have been a Pirate, and I *know* you. You haven't been able to make it work?"

"Shit. Right now, we can't even talk to the thing. We are not giving up. There are other options. We have a list."

"Text the list to me."

"I don't see what-"

"Husband?" She said it in *that* tone of voice. I got it. She was stressed, and bored out of her mind, and she wanted to do something useful.

"I'm sending the list now."

She stepped off camera, came back holding her zPhone and with a glass of, probably iced tea. Margaret liked sweet tea, not super sweet like some people liked in the South, but way sweeter than my New England heritage prepared me for. "OK, let me see what you have. Hmm. Can I assume the problem with Item One is *Skippy* being a dick, not the Vortex?"

"Possibly at first. Now, the thing refuses to acknowledge Skippy's calls at all. The odds are, the Vortex has activated a protocol to protect itself. Without a communications channel, we got nothin'. No way for Skippy to persuade it to cooperate, or just to get it to act against the Outsider by itself."

"That makes no sense. A defense system that doesn't have a trigger? The presence of the Outsider should have activated the Vortex."

"Skippy's guess is, the Elders planned to install an AI in each Vortex, after *they* detected an Outsider incursion."

"That seems too complicated, and takes too much time."

"Agreed. The only thing that makes sense is the Elders wanted to ensure there is no possibility the thing could activate by itself."

"Why?"

"Maybe whatever it does, has seriously bad collateral effects. Also, it appears to be a one-time use thing. If it triggered too early, the Elders would have nothing left."

"Hmm. That does make sense. You suggested Skippy hack into it?"

"I did. He tried. It is ancient and obsolete, many generations before Skippy, but it is Elder tech. He has a restriction that hampers his ability to hack the thing. Remember? Master Control AIs were restricted from hacking each other, to prevent one powerful AI from taking over the entire group."

"All right," she let out a breath and took the towel off, shaking her head to make the curls of her hair dance.. She knows I love it when she does that. "The second item is finding another Vortex on the network.'"

"Skippy can't be sure there ever was a network, or whether it still exists. There isn't anything special about the star where we found 37, no clue about where the Elders might have sited the other network nodes."

She nodded with a frown. "Honey, you don't have much to work with here."

"At least now we know the Outsider's objective. Modify the array, and set it up to create a Gateway, a door, something like that, for an invasion force."

"What about the item 'Locate and destroy the array'?"

"Relatively straightforward, even Eeyore admits-"

"Eeyore?" She blinked. "The donkey from Winne the Pooh? What does he-"

"That's a name I have for Skippy, when he says something is impossible. Even Skippy believes that *Valkyrie* could easily tear the array apart. Assuming the Outsider hasn't equipped it with advanced defenses."

She shook her head. "If it was capable of constructing advanced tech, it wouldn't have needed to steal two exo- What did you call those arrays?"

"I didn't call them anything. The spiders designated them as 'exochronous'. Something about how different parts of the array are in multiple time phases. I get your point, it stole the arrays because it couldn't make a doorway mechanism from raw materials. But, it has to be modifying the array to make a Gateway. It's not a stretch to assume it also will provide a defense mechanism for the thing."

"That's what you're doing next? Destroy the thing?"

"We will, if we can *find* it. During the flight here, Skippy was working on tracking the array components through the wormhole networks. It must have carried the pieces through an Elder wormhole, a star carrier can't fly from near the center of the galaxy to out beyond the rim. The problem is, he got nothin'. The wormholes don't keep sensor records of traffic, unless that traffic causes an issue for the network."

"Yes but, honey, wormholes do keep activity logs, Skippy told me that," she waved a hand, "at some point."

"They do."

"So," she bit her lip. "Wormholes that connect out beyond the rim must not get much traffic. You only need to track that *last* wormhole the Outsider used, and search near there."

"Good thinking, yes. We, thought of that," I was reluctant to spoil her happy moment. "My guess is, those activity logs won't yield any useful information. The Outsider also knows about the logs. All it had to do was fly a ship through random wormholes, to obscure which one it used to move the array."

"Ah, shit." Margaret didn't curse often, she did it for emphasis. "You will check anyway?"

"That's the plan. I just don't expect the search to yield any actionable intel."

"That was your best option?"

"Yeah."

"The next item on the list is," she wrinkled her brow. "Find another Elder AI?"

"That has its own problems, even if we could find one still alive. Which we can't."

"What problems?"

"Any AI we found intact must have somehow evaded the factory reset, and Skippy's kill command. It would retain its original programming, and be hostile."

"But not as powerful as Skippy?" She asked.

"Not as *special* as Skippy. Still a powerful entity. It doesn't matter, they are all dead."

"Show me the disposition list."

"Huh?"

"The list. After Skippy sent the kill command, he kept a list of Elder AIs that were erased, and he included a program for them to report back when they were dying. That list."

"Uh-"

"Honey, you did review the list, to make certain your absent-minded friend didn't miss anything?"

"Uh, yeah, I did." Technically, I was not lying to my wife.

"So, send it to me."

"In case I also missed something?"

"A second set of eyes can't hurt. Besides, I am bored out of my mind here."

"Sorry about that. We'll get you off that rock as soon as possible."

"This rock is our *home*."

"OK, I hear you. I'll get the list to you soon."

We chatted about the boys for a while, then she got called away to deal with some issue. As the connection went blank I called, "*Skippy*!"

"What is it this time?" His avatar appeared.

"You heard what I said to Margaret?"

"Actually no, I wasn't listening."

"Oh. Have you finally learned a lesson about privacy?"

"I learned that Margaret gets royally pissed at me whenever I listen to your boring conversations. Ugh, as if I want to hear the two of you all like, 'I wuv you, sweetheart', and 'I wuv you too, snookums'."

"We do not call each other 'snookums'."

"Whatevs. Anywho, what do you want? I am very busy."

"Busy doing what?"

"Busy doing things. What about *my* privacy, Joe?"

"I am very sorry for interrupting, whatever bullshit thing you're doing."

"Hey! You jerk, I should-"

"Margaret asked for a list, of the disposition of all the Elder AIs that were erased when you used a back door to activate the killer worms inside them."

"Disposition?"

"Their final status."

"That's easy, they are all *dead*."

"You don't actually know that for certain."

"Oh for- yes I do, and is this some idiot thing about finding another Elder AI?"

"No you do *not*, and yes it is about finding an AI who might not instantly piss off the Vortex."

"OK," a holographic throne appeared and he sat on it, that was a new affectation for him. "This should be amusing. Go ahead, explain your incredible monkey logic."

"You sent out a command to activate the killer malware worms inside each of those AIs. The worms reported back when they were activated, and then started sending regular pings over the Collective."

"Correct. The pings ceased when each worm went inactive because its host AI was dead."

"That was what was supposed to happen. It is at least *possible* that some AIs fought back, and overcame the worm, like you did?"

"Joe, this is just *sad*. No, numbskull. The AIs had already been subjected to a factory reset. They weren't capable of *fighting* at all. They were, basically in a coma."

"OK, but it *is* possible."

"*No*," his face glowed red. "It is n-"

"That's not what I want to talk about anyway. At the end, there were four AIs that didn't report back?"

"Correct."

"Show me the list, please. One column with a status of 'Worm ceased pinging', next to the number of its host AI."

"Done," a holographic list appeared. "Does that make you happy?"

"Partially happy. Now, another list, with the four that did not ping back."

The list changed, to show only four AIs, listed by their three-digit number. "Shall I show the status of each of these, you jerk?"

"Please do."

The list contained four AI unit numbers, with 'Presumed dead' as a status.

"Presumed isn't good enough, Skippy."

"Ugh. Let me smack some logic on you. If they were active at the time I sent the kill command, they would have responded. Those four units did *not* respond, so they must have already been dead."

"Um, I see a glaring flaw in your logic, Professor Smartass."

"Ha! As if."

"They didn't respond, so how can you know their unit numbers? Explain that."

"I used a little trick that Sherlock Holmes called 'deductive reasoning'."

"More detail, please."

"First, I created a list of all Master Control AIs that were on the original roster. Next, I subtracted out the AIs that I knew were lost during the AI war, on both sides. Of the remaining units on my list, all but four responded. So, while I do not know exactly what happened to each of the four, I do know which ones didn't respond."

"OK. Shit. Wait. You're saying those four died *after* the AI war, and before you sent the kill command?"

"Um, no. Well, that is extremely unlikely. Joe, it must be that the war killed more AIs than I knew. Those four were activated by the other side during the war, and while I have records that three of them were damaged, I did not know they subsequently expired. The situation was extremely chaotic."

"The fog of war, I get it." Something in the back of my mind wasn't happy about his explanation. What was wrong? His logic was solid-

But not complete.

"The list you showed me, the list that counted down from the kill command, *not* all Master Control AIs were included?"

"As I explained, there was no point to listing AIs I knew to be already dead. Did you not hear me, or is your mushy brain so-"

"Show me those unit numbers, please. The ones you supposedly know were killed during the war."

"This is totally a waste of my valuable time."

"Maybe, but I'm willing to take that risk."

"You are such a- *Fine*."

A new list read:

Unit 007- Currently demonstrating extreme awesomeness

Unit 012- Hostile, nickname 'Opie', died while sending a distress call to the Elders

Unit 041- Friendly, killed during AI war

Unit 052- Hostile, lost during AI war

Unit 093- Friendly, killed during AI war

Unit 117- Hostile, damaged during AI war, status unknown

Unit 128- Hostile, nickname 'Target Echo', trapped in a zero-length wormhole

Unit 153- Friendly, killed during AI war

Unit 164- Hostile. Went insane, attacked Skippy, got a beatdown

Unit 168- Hostile, killed during AI war

Unit 333- Friendly, nickname 'Trips', erased by Elder factory reset

"See? I even included that insane one I killed, years ago."

"Ayuh, I see you also listed yourself."

"If I hadn't done that, you would have nagged me about it."

"I never *nag*, Skippy."

"You think that, but-"

"This is good. Add a little more detail about 'killed', please."

"Killed means *dead*."

"Details. How did each of them die, and how do you *know* they are dead?"

"Units 093 and 153 lost containment when their ships were destroyed by Sentinels. It was," he shuddered, "horrible."

"The explosions could not have been faked?"

"No way. Those two explosions reverberated through higher spacetime like ringing a bell. Ringing a big church bell, while you are inside the thing. It was *loud*, unmistakable."

"OK. Unit One One Seven?"

"As is stated on the list, its final status is unknown. It lost contact early in the AI war, after one of my comrades attacked it. Meaning, its own side was unable to contact it. I do know the other side launched an extensive search operation, that yielded no information."

"You have had time to think about it, since the war. Do you have any clue what happened to it?"

"None. That also means I have absolutely no clue where it could be now."

"OK. Unit Fifty Two is listed as 'Lost' What happened?"

"Oh, its ship was very badly damaged and," he sighed. "It fell into a star."

CHAPTER TWENTY TWO

"A," I froze for a moment, feeling a thrill of hope. "*Star*?"

"Yes, Joe. It's a big glowing ball of hydrogen and helium that burns through a fusion reaction, but that's not important right now."

"*Which* star did it fall into?"

"Um, that I don't know."

"How is that possible? If you know the thing fell into a-"

"I didn't actually witness what happened, an AI on my side intercepted enemy communications. It was important and joyful enough that I flagged the fact in my Favorites folder. It's not actually a *folder*, it-"

"So, pull up that file and-"

"As I have told you many times, my memories from back then are fragmented and incomplete, and thank you *so much* for reminding me of how damaged I am."

"Sorry, buddy, I didn't mean it that way. What do you remember of the incident, or the report you received?"

"Um, I have a vague notion that the star was a nothing special K type orange dwarf, of which there are millions in this galaxy."

"Shit. We have the possibility that an intact Elder Master Control AI could be out there, and no way to determine where it is?"

"Correct. I, ah, hmm."

"What?"

"Nothing. Forget I said anything."

"Like that's gonna happen."

"Ugh."

"Just say it. The alternative is I pester you about it ,until you decide to throw *yourself* into a star."

"*How* does Margaret live with you?"

"We get along great. Talk, beer can."

"You are *not* going to like this."

"There is a whole lot of shit I don't like to hear, it's part of my job. Talk."

"OK so, it is *possible*, unlikely but possible, that another Elder AI might have the location where Unit 52 fell into a star."

"You have told me, over and over, that all the other AIs are dead, so how-"

"Their operating systems were erased. Their *memories* might still be intact. Partially. After the control section of a matrix is destroyed, the rest of the matrix degrades at a rate that increases with time. By now, we are unlikely to find anything coherent inside a dead AI. But it is possible."

"Uh, if the thing is dead, you can't ask it to dredge up old memories, so how-"

"I would have to go in there."

"Whoa. That is *not* happening. The way you killed all those other AIs is you triggered the killer worm thing inside them. That nasty freakin' worm could still be active in there. We are not bringing you back to the Roach Motel again for a tune-up."

"What I should have said, and what I would have explained if you had just shut up for a moment, is *I* would not actually go into the other matrix. All I need to do is load a search and retrieval program, sort of a very dumbed down submind, into the foreign matrix. The program would look around for the memories I tell it to find, then reports back to me. There is no actual risk to me."

"Oh. Why didn't you do that before?"

"The technique wasn't available to me until recently. It's a form of epicombinent software, based on Outsider technology. I have been playing around with it, the results have been encouraging."

"Oh. That's great, Skippy. Except, now we have to race around the galaxy on a scavenger hunt, to find a dead Elder AI?"

"We could do that, or we could do something easier, daring, and stupid."

"I am all about easy."

"You are also all about *stupid*, so-"

"The STARs are daring. What's your plan?"

"There are two Master Control AIs I know of, that were dormant before the Elders activated the factory reset. They died when I sent out the kill command, so I know exactly how long their memories have been degrading."

"I like this plan already."

"You will not like *where* they are. In the Hegemony Fleet Museum."

"Shit. Those are the only ones you know of?"

"Unfortunately, yes. Those two are perfect for this purpose, because I know for certain they were alive but dormant before the factory reset."

"How can you know that?"

"Records I found in that archive we stole. The AIs were originally at a research station for eight hundred years, I have access to scanning data that meant nothing to the Maxohlx, but the data clearly indicates those two were in a dormant state."

"At the Fleet Museum, huh? Give me the bad news. How many Maxohlx are on that planet?"

"That world is inhabited by over four billion rotten kitties, which is too many for even the craziest cat lady."

"I think you underestimate the potential craziness of cat ladies. With that population, the world must be heavily defended?"

"It is. Also, a major fleet servicing base is located there."

"Shit. This is a No Go, then."

"I haven't told you the *good* news yet."

"You actually have good news, or you're screwing with me again?"

"Judge for yourself. The museum has been undergoing extensive revisions and renovations, after the recent tragic civil war. Which you are a jerk for starting."

"I feel just terrible about it. How is that good news?"

"Much of the collection, of objects that are portable, were transferred to a storage space inside a hollowed-out asteroid. That rock used to be the anchor point at the top of the original space elevator, it has been retained and reused. The storage vault has only a small permanent staff of museum clerks."

"That is good."

"*Not* so good is that asteroid is also the training base for a quick reaction force, that constantly rotates platoon-sized units in and out."

"Oh, crap. Let me guess: the storage vault is also inside the base?"

"Of course not. The vault deep under the surface, the training base is in the old terminal station, where the space elevator cable used to attach. The entrance to the vault is ninety degrees around from the old base station."

"Show me a schematic of this place. What is your infil plan?"

"My *infil* plan?" He snorted. "It's cute when you use military terms, Joe."

"Just show me, you ass."

A hologram appeared, a dull grey rock, pitted and scarred like any asteroid. It looked like a potato that had been roasted in hot coals for too long. When I squinted, I could see on the surface there were boxes, antennas, what I guessed were defensive maser cannon turrets. All of the artificial objects were bright yellow. Was that for safety? "Skippy, what's with the yellow?"

"Nothing there is yellow, dumdum, I highlighted them for you. They actually look like this." The highlighting disappeared, and the objects almost did also, they were a matte gray that blended into the rock. "What's important is underneath the surface." The realistic image of the space rock was replaced by a schematic. "There are only two ways in or out of the central vault. A large cargo passageway that starts at the old terminal station, which will be infested with rotten kitties. Or, this elevator shaft that I have helpfully highlighted in blue, and no, the elevator itself is not painted blue."

"I guessed that. How big is that elevator?'

"What matters to you is the elevator car would be limited to three STAR operators in standard mech suits, or four operators in the lightweight Mark 29 model."

"No one should wear a Mark 29 in a hostile environment controlled by a senior species."

"Then the infiltration will have to be accomplished by only three operators."

"Three people ride a freakin' elevator down to a chamber at the center of an asteroid, steal two Elder AIs, ride the elevator back up, and nobody notices?"

"Like I said, easy."

"Well, there will be very little risk."

"Good, then-"

"There will be *no* risk, because no one is going in that elevator. Seriously? What the hell were you thinking? This is idiotic."

"Hey, *you* do the planning around here. I am just showing you the only ways in and out. How the team gets there is your job."

"There must be another way to find an Elder AI."

"Not like those two. Really, we only need one of them, but we should take both, to be safe. One of them is in better condition, based on the sensor data from the archive. As I said, I can tell they were dormant, and I know from the sensor data politely provided by the Maxohlx that one of them was in stand-by mode, at the time the factory reset was received. Basically, it was preparing to come out of dormancy. That is normal, I did mention that only a small group of Master Control

AIs were active at any time, and groups rotated in and out of dormancy. The fact that one of those AIs was in stand-by is important, because its memory would be better protected. Any other dead AI we find will probably be so degraded, it won't be worth our time to get the thing."

"Skippy, there are way too many times when there is only one way to do what we need to do, and it is always some risky damned thing."

"Hey, blame the Universe, not me."

"There is no way you could fake a message, and get that AI- Which one is it, by the way?"

"Unit 98."

"Get 98 loaded aboard a ship, that we can then intercept?"

"Um, no. Since the civil war broke out, the Fleet Museum has been under strict supervision by political officers, who report directly to the Dictat. During the war, the rebels faked messages and had several old but still effective weapons delivered to them."

"The weapons in the museum have not been demilitarized?"

"The Maxohlx don't do that."

"Jeez, I'd hate to be there if some stupid kid is running around the museum, bashing things that could explode."

"The museum vault doesn't allow *visitors*, dumdum."

"You know what I mean."

"What I know is, you are giving up before you even tried. Really, Joe, the museum vault really has no serious security, I can bypass most of the sensors. Most of them. There is a protective field around the vault chamber that makes it very difficult for me to remotely screw with the systems there. If I had direct access, I could-"

"You going in there is a non-starter. Also, I have *not* given up. Let me uh, shit. This really is our best option?"

"It is the only option I am aware of, and it's kind of a miracle that I know about it at all. Joe, please consider that even if the STARs can get Unit 98 to *Valkyrie*, and I root around in its memories and find which star Unit 52 fell into, the operation will still be only an enormous waste of time and effort. There is no way for us to extract an object from inside a freakin' star, and 52 is most likely dead anyway."

"So, it's impossible for us to get another Elder AI to plug into the Vortex?'

"That is what I just said."

"Thank you."

"Um, for what?"

"Whenever you tell me something is impossible, that's when I get to work. Show me the SD network of- What's the name of this planet?"

"The kitties call it Yukrestia, though they took it from the Thuranin, who designated it-"

"I do not care about the former name. Show me details of the defenses around this place."

Forty minutes later, an alarm sounded, signaling that *Valkyrie* was approaching the spacedock. I immediately called Reed, embarrassed that I had forgotten about what the ship was doing. "Fireball, there has been a change of plans. We are leaving ASAP."

"Sir?" She was startled. "We need to-"

"Fill the gas tank, pump up the tires, and grab some snacks from the Kwik-E-Mart, then we're going on a road trip that will be fun and educational for the whole family."

"In my experience, family road trips are never *fun*," she sighed. "May I ask for a hint about where we're going?"

"A Maxohlx world called Yukrestia."

She sucked in a breath. "Sir, that is a regional base for their Army and Navy."

"See? I said it would be educational."

"If we will be getting into a fight there, we should-"

"No combat. We are, uh, going shopping. Or, technically, shoplifting."

"Yes, Sir. We will be ready to jump away in, an hour ten."

"Good enough."

I called Margaret to tell her *Valkyrie* was leaving and that I would be back shortly. Or, not shortly at all. She knew what that meant.

Valkyrie jumped away from Jaguar, and we settled into the familiar routine of jump, recharge, jump again. Reaching for a uniform in my closet, I noticed three new sets I didn't recognize. "Skippy, did the laundry bot make a mistake?"

"No. At Jaguar, we received an update from Def Com. The US Army recently approved a new field uniform, so I had the fabricators crank out several sets for you. It's a camouflage pattern, which is actually pretty much useless against the sensors of any species in this galaxy."

"It's tradition." The field uniform was different from the combat uniform, since the combat uni was a simple liner worn under a mech suit. The field uniform was intended to be worn by support personnel, or by combat troops when they weren't in a mech suit. As Skippy said, the camo pattern was obsolete, but what people cared about was how the uniforms worked, not how they looked. Was the cloth heavy and scratchy? Was the uniform too hot? That was important since the standard uni didn't include a cooling system, and we might be deployed to planets that were insufferably hot and humid. Rubbing the material between my fingers, it actually felt soft. "The United States Army created this specification?"

"Yes. Well, close enough. The Milspec cloth was stiff and scratchy from the fire retardant chemicals embedded in it, and I know your skin can be sensitive, so I wove in silk and some exotic material fibers."

"My skin is sensitive from too many years of wearing scratchy uniforms. You modified the specs, so these unis aren't flame proof?"

"They are actually *more* fire retardant. The Army is too cheap to use proper materials."

"I'll try it on." According to the schedule published by the XO, the uniform of the day was personal choice, sort of the military version of Casual Friday. So, I could wear anything I wanted. It felt good, and fit perfectly. "Wait a minute. What is this pattern made of?" Reaching into a drawer, I got an old fashioned magnifying glass, something Skippy couldn't hack. One time, he had created a camo pattern for me, that I later realized was tiny monkeys doing rude things. "Huh. This pattern is just, random shapes."

"That's the point. A pattern that is no pattern. It is supposed to break up your silhouette."

"The only place *this* camo will provide cover is if I'm standing in front of the ugly wallpaper at my grandmother's house."

"Ugh. Listen, dumdum, I didn't design the thing."

"Whatever. At least it's comfortable. Thank you, Skippy," I admired myself in the mirror, which also was a low-tech device he couldn't hack. "That was very thoughtful of you."

"I do what I can, Joe."

In the galley, I noticed two other people wearing the new uniform, and saluted them with my coffee mug. Sitting down at an empty table, I checked my tablet for the daily status update. Everything was routine, and-

"Sir?" Gasquet stood next to the table. "General Bishop?"

"Good morning, XO. Sit down, please."

He leaned down to whisper, "Sir, that is a new uniform?"

"Oh. It's official issue, new for the UN Army," I assured him. Gasquet was wearing the standard black of the UN Navy, not the blue of his home service.

"Sir, that," his face took on a pained expression. "That's not it. I don't know how to tell you this-"

"Just say it."

"The camo pattern on your back, the dark dots can be connected to spell," his face turned red from embarrassment. "Doofus, sir."

"*Doofus*?" I said that a bit too loud, attracting attention. "That little- Does anyone else know about this?"

"The whole table of people behind you," he shrugged. "They noticed, and just told me about it."

"Excuse me for a minute, I need to stomp a beer can flat." Outside the galley, I ducked down a dead-end passageway. Using my zPhone so I could whisper, I called the offender. "What the hell were you thinking, you little shithead?"

"Um, I have no idea what you mean, Joe."

"Bullshit. The dots on my uniform spell 'Doofus'?"

"Um, wow, well, it's a random pattern, I suppose that eventually the randomness generates odd results, like-"

"This is not *random*. Did you do this to anyone else?"

"Only to you, I- Shiiiiiit. I withdraw my statement."

"Too late."

"Ugh, Joe, I did this for *you*."

"You- Explain that, please."

"Now when you walk someplace, other doofuses can recognize you as part of their tribe, and be your support group."

"There is no support group for-"

"Well, there certainly should be. The first step in dealing with a problem is admitting you have one."

"You did this for me?"

"Yes. Also," he chuckled, "it's *hilarious*."

"I am going back to my cabin to change. I want those uniforms recycled, and a new, correct set in my closet by tonight."

"Fine. I try to have a tiny bit of fun, and this is the thanks I get. There is no need to recycle them, I fixed it."

"Fixed what?"

"Your uniform."

"The," I tugged on the shoulder, trying to see the back. "The one I'm wearing?"

"Yes. The camo pattern on *your* sets of uniforms are not just static printing, some of the dots are nanomachines. They can be rearranged. I just put them back to normal."

"Oh. Good. Do not do that again, I hope you- Wait. You can arrange the nanodots anytime you want, into any pattern?"

"Yes, why?"

"Were you planning to embarrass me in a different way in the future?"

"Not that you know of."

"Skippy!"

To be safe, I switched to a standard service uniform, without the jacket. The blouse, what civilians would call a shirt, was plain, without any pattern. With Skippy, you can never be too careful.

To tell the truth, when I saw the new uniforms hanging in the closet, I had noticed there was something odd about the dot pattern on the back, and I didn't say anything about it. He was playing a joke on me, I let him have fun. That was an important part of my job, entertaining him. And, he was my friend. Skippy works hard, sometimes we don't appreciate all the things he does for us. He is stuck in that canister, doing a lot of boring things every day, and he deserved to have some fun.

Maybe I should trip and fall off the treadmill once in a while. He would like that.

Though he had never before led a live mission of STAR Team Razor, Major Karel Holmqvist had supreme confidence in himself, in his team, in their equipment, and training. he had high confidence in the plan he and General Bishop had developed. He also had a deep, nagging feeling of dread about the operation. The dread was about Skippy the Magnificently Absent-Minded beer can. The Elder AI would perform his role in the op, he already had enabled *Valkyrie* to jump in closer than Holmqvist was comfortable with, and now the specially-equipped STAR Panther dropship was coasting smoothly right through the heart of the enemy strategic defense network, thanks to Skippy's low-level hack of the SD system's sensors. The mission was exactly on schedule.

A soft chime dinged in his earpiece, and text appeared in his helmet visor, notifying him that the spacecraft's velocity had dropped below that required to escape the planet's gravity well. That was planned, they had to slow even more to match course and speed with the target asteroid. The Panther was not a problem, he trusted the pilots and their ship.

He did not fully trust Skippy. Too many times, and *once* would be too many, the Elder AI had gotten bored or distracted during a training mission, zoned out, and lost track of what he was supposed to be doing. Colonel Frey had assured him that Skippy simply didn't fully engage in training, where there was no real challenge for him, and the stakes were low. That he would focus during a real mission. Holmqvist knew that was not entirely true, from reading the after-action reports of ST-Alpha's missions. Several of the reports included Colonel Smythe's mention of an issue with a certain 'dodgy beer can'. Nor was the problem limited to Alpha, Razor had experienced trouble when the Elder AI had not been paying attention, and an alien robotic *squirrel* had come close to ruining a daring and dangerous mission. If Skippy didn't-

"Oh, *bother*," Skippy huffed in Holmqvist's ear. "What a pain in the ass."

The ST-Razor leader licked his dry lips before asking, "What?"

"Some jackass in the SD network control center is demanding our credentials. I told him this is the shuttle *Tyderium*, delivering a maintenance and repair team to the Fleet Museum. Don't worry, he requested our clearance code and I provided it, the code is current. Fake, but in the current scheme. Ugh. This guy must be trying for Employee of the Month. He is questioning why we are approaching the museum after hours, in the middle of the night, when the flight bay is unstaffed."

"You," Holmqvist took a calming breath, "gave him the cover story?"

"Doing that now."

The cover story was the repair team was needed to fix a piece of the museum's collection that had been broken, and needed to be restored before a scheduled visit by an admiral the next day. It was a good cover story.

"Is he buying it?"

"He *should*," Skippy sniffed. "Oh, darn. He is waving us off from the asteroid, until he can verify our orders with the museum director."

"He is calling the *director*? Can you mimic her voice?"

"I could, but the director is aboard the same space station that houses the SD network control center. The jackass I'm talking with is assigning someone to knock on the director's door. Maybe I can cause an air leak that will block access to-"

"No, don't do that, anything like that. Skippy, tell the, whoever you're talking to, that the museum piece we need to repair was broken by the director's nephew, and the museum staff would like the whole incident cleaned up before the director gets back."

"Will that work?"

He recalled the pre-mission briefing documents. "The director and her family are politically connected?"

"Yes, very much so, why?"

"The jackass you're talking with will not want to piss off the nephew either."

"Are you sure about that?"

"You know technology, I know meatsacks."

"Okey dokey, I'll try it. Oooh, hee hee, it's a miracle! We just received clearance."

Holmqvist refrained from pumping a fist. "Let's strive for no more surprises, hmm?"

There were no surprises, other than that Holmqvist had expected surprises, nasty ones, and he didn't see any. The Panther approached the museum's flight bay where the big doors slid open enough for the dropship to squeeze through, then the doors closed and the Panther set down on the deck, all without the sleeping bay crew seeing anything, or any computer system sounding an alert. Not bothering to take time to pressurize the bay, the STARs emptied the dropship's cabin of air, and walked down the back ramp in hard vacuum. The outer then inner airlock doors cycled without any fuss, the short walk to the elevator door was in a darkened, empty corridor, the mech boots adhering to the deck in the low gravity. Holmqvist experienced a moment of anxiety when the elevator door was about to slide open, the back of his mind wondered whether some hideous monster would pop out and devour him and-

The elevator car was empty, the walls a dull gray, scuffed from years of use. Higgins went in first, then Holmqvist, followed by Kim. It was a tight fit, the three operators jostling elbows and moving until they were as comfortable as they could be. The door slid closed, the car began to drop and-

"The Maxohlx have *elevator music*?" Karel exclaimed.

"Yes, and it is simply awful," Skippy scoffed. "It's time to change the beat."

Out of the elevator speakers blasted some harsh, guttural, was it voices? He recognized a few words. "That is, Kristang music?"

"Yes, it's from the latest opera I composed for them. It's very popular, the-"

"Please shut it off."

"You don't like it?"

"I do," the ST-Razor leader lied. "It's very good, just, distracting."

"Oh, gotcha." The music mercifully shut off. "You can listen to the complete work when you get back to *Valkyrie*."

I have made a horrible mistake, Holmqvist told himself. Briefly, he wondered whether it would be best for him to ditch the microwormhole that provided instant communication with Skippy. Toss it away, and, what? Apply to the Maxohlx for political asylum, and spend the rest of his life in an alien prison?

Considering what he knew of Skippy's operas, life in a Maxohlx prison was a tempting alternative.

But, the mission came first. He could embrace the suck later.

Somehow, the moment when the team started their exfil, what civilians would call a retreat, that was usually the moment of maximum tension for me, while I monitored events from *Valkyrie's* bridge. Holmqvist and his operators had the two Elder AIs, they had successfully done an Indiana Jones swap of the real AIs for top-quality fakes, and they were on the way back to the elevator. The mission was almost successful, so that's when I expected the Universe to take a steaming dump on my head.

I was not disappointed. "Um, Joe?" Skippy called. "We might have a, heh heh, a bit of a problem."

"*Might*?"

"OK, we definitely have a huge fucking problem. The officer in command of the training detachment received a nighttime visit from the Good Idea Fairy, and she has decided to conduct an unscheduled exercise with both the incoming and outgoing platoons. Typically, there are two days of overlap when units swap in and out, and the unit that just completed the training cycle is supposed to ship out tomorrow afternoon. They pissed off the commander during an exercise a few days ago, this is her punishing them."

"Shit! Do not inform Holmqvist yet, he has enough on his plate. When does the exercise kick off?"

"The platoon leaders have just been notified, so it will take a while to get all personnel out of their racks and geared up. However, the entire asteroid will be on lockdown as soon as the commander gives the order, which will be soon. Our Panther won't be able to leave the flight bay."

"Damn it!"

"This is *bad*, Joe. The STARs should not get into that elevator. In the flight bay, they will be trapped and exposed once the museum staff starts work in a few hours. My suggestion is Holmqvist and his people hide somewhere and- Ah, that won't work. The Panther is not supposed to be there, the flight bay crews will see the stealth modifications we made, and know it isn't one of theirs. Joe, *Valkyrie* can't fight through that SD network, not in the ship's current condition."

"Yeah," I caught Reed's eye. She didn't exactly say 'I told you so', I got the message anyway. "OK, show me a schematic of the training base. Where is the detachment commander now?"

"She is," a wireframe hologram appeared, showing the entire training base, most of which was unused. The view zoomed in to show stick figures of Maxohlx. "On the sixth level."

"Uh, what is she doing? She does not appear to be moving."

"She is waiting for an elevator, to take her to the second level."

"How long until she gets on the elevator?"

"A minute or so. The elevator car is now at the bottom of the shaft, and is scheduled to stop on the third level."

"Make it go past that floor."

"Joe, but-"

"Do it. Override the, whatever you have to do. I want her in that elevator ASAP."

"OK, OK. The car is now proceeding directly to the sixth floor."

Clenching a fist behind my back, then relaxing because the bridge crew was watching me and needed to know their commander was calm, cool, and in control, I waited. Waiting is my least favorite activity.

The figure of the commander walked into the elevator, and it started down.

"*Now*, Skippy, stop the elevator. Burn out the controls, whatever you have to do, to keep it stuck between levels. And jam communications, I do not want her talking with anyone, got that?"

"I do. Done. Joe, she will know the timing of this elevator glitch is suspicious."

"She will, it doesn't matter. Plant some evidence that the outgoing platoon sabotaged the thing, as a prank."

"Oooooh, Joe, you are an evil genius. That will cause serious trouble for that platoon."

"Ayuh. Sewing discord and poor morale amongst our enemy is not a bad thing. What are the platoon leaders doing now?"

"They are as yet unaware the commander is stuck in the elevator. Joe, it is possible that a group of people could manually crank the elevator down to the next floor. At the bottom of the shaft is an emergency mechanism."

"There is a door that leads to the bottom of the shaft? Jam that also."

"Ah, I can't. It's a simple, physical lock."

"Shit. OK, then, uh- Maintenance there is usually handled by bots?"

"Of course."

"Could you take control of a bot, and weld that door shut?"

"The door is made of composite, I can't *weld* it, dumdum."

"Then-"

"What I can do is wedge a large, heavy bot up against the inside of the door, it is at the end of a short corridor."

"Do that."

"A bot is moving now, it will suffer a fatal malfunction in seventeen seconds."

"A suspicious malfunction?"

"Hee hee, sure, why not?"

Holmqvist's team reached their elevator without incident, blissfully unaware of a problem they couldn't do anything about. He called me anyway. "General Bishop, we are proceeding up to the flight bay," he reported. "Sir, this has been *too* easy."

"Hold that thought, Major. There was a, complication, we handled it."

"Complication?"

"It has been handled. Your path to the dropship is clear."

"Yes, Sir."

By the time the training detachment commander got out of the elevator car, the STAR Panther was sixty thousand kilometers away from the asteroid, and coasting toward a rendezvous with *Valkyrie*. "Wow," Skippy chuckled. "She is *super* mad. Unfortunately, while she was trapped in that car, a sewage pipe that runs along the elevator shaft burst, and flooded the bottom of the shaft. Whoo, that must have stunk something *awful*."

"Unfortunately, huh?"

"I mean, that was fortunate for *us*. She will be too distracted right now to think clearly."

CHAPTER TWENTY THREE

"Well?" I demanded, after Skippy's searcher program had been poking around inside Unit 98 for a freakin' hour, which is a geological age in AI time. Skippy, Unit 98, and I were aboard a Panther, dropped off by *Valkyrie* just before the battlecruiser jumped away. Reed was waiting a lightmonth distant, connected to us by a paired Elder comm nodes. If Skippy was wrong about Unit 98 being dead, or his stupid searcher program got infected by the killer worm and brought the worm to infect Skippy, I wanted the ship to be far away. It might shock you to learn that Skippy is wrong about a lot of shit, so I ignored his assurances that all the precautions were not necessary. "Have you heard from the damned thing yet?"

"Ugh. No! Have some patience, knucklehead."

"This is taking way too long. Are you sure the searcher program didn't get eaten by the killer worm?"

"Yes Joe, the worm *ate* it, with a side of fava beans and a nice Chianti. It's totally *fine*, dumdum, the program has been reporting back regularly."

"What exactly is it reporting?"

"That so far, it has found a whole lot of nothing in there. The matrix is so scrambled, the program has to leave a trail of breadcrumbs to get back, every time it goes into a new section of the matrix. Joe, I fear this is going to take for-EH-ver."

"We don't have forever. Speed up the search."

"The program is already going as fast as it can, numbskull. There is no way I can-"

"The *original* program can't get the job done. Now that you have learned more about that matrix, could you build a better program?"

"*Could you build a better program*?" He whined like a five year old. "Why didn't you ask me that an hour ago?"

"Why didn't you tell me there was a problem an hour ago?"

"Oh sure, let's play the blame game, that is super helpful."

"Just do it."

Seven minutes later, the searcher program popped up with an answer.

"Found it, Joe!" Skippy crowed. "Like I told you, Unit 52 fell into a K type orange dwarf. That star is on the high end of the mass spectrum for a K type actually, about point eight three times the mass of Earth's Sun. Hmm."

"What?"

"Nothing important. That star now has an inhabited world. Sixty million Wurgalan squiddies live on the second planet, they call it 'Lundivik'. Damn, if you think *your* homeworld is a miserable ball of mud, then Lundivik is even-"

"No one thinks Earth is a miserable mudball."

"I have bad news for you about that."

"Shut up." On my laptop, I typed in 'Lundivik' and multiple pages popped up. The political and cultural aspects of that world were of no interest to me. What I wanted to see was the planet's defense capabilities. They were nothing special. "Huh."

"What?"

"Nothing. I'll tell you later. Skippy, Unit Fifty Two fell into a star, so you don't actually know it is dead, do you?"

"You are unbelievable. The unit and its ship were attacked by two Sentinels, there is no way anything survived."

"The *ship* didn't survive falling into the star. That doesn't mean the Master Control AI was destroyed. Did the star go supernova?"

"Um, no. Why did you ask?"

"If Unit Fifty Two- That's too awkward to say more than a few times. We need a name for the thing."

"Why does everything have to get a freakin' nickname?"

"It just does, that's why. Partly that's for operational security, if you give something a name that only your side knows, the enemy won't understand what you're talking about if they intercept communications. Partly it's to ensure clear communications, everyone on your team uses the official designation. And, it's just something we have always done."

"Whatever."

"Do you have a suggestion for a name?"

"Unit 52 and I didn't exactly hang out, drinking a couple beers while watching a game, and during the war, we were enemies."

"OK. Uh, we'll call it 'Benny Blue'."

"Benny Blue? That makes no sense."

"It does make sense. When playing dice, if you roll a five and a two, that's called 'Benny Blue'. Don't ask me why."

"Oh. Is this like rolling two ones is called 'Snake Eyes'?"

"Exactly."

"I don't like it. Benny Blue sounds too cool for that thing."

"Can we call it just 'Benny'?"

"If you insist."

"Good. So, if Benny had lost containment, the star would have exploded, right?"

"Um-"

"Lundivik's star is still an ordinary orange dwarf?"

"It, is," he admitted with reluctance.

"Good. So, that unit is still alive, in some fashion."

"Ugh." That time he did the full shoulder shrug, head tilted back, eye roll, knees bent disgust. "You don't-"

"By now, the thing must be near the core of the star?"

"There are currents and other forces within stars that could bounce it around, I have never modeled the issue. Please tell me you are not-"

"Tell me this: assuming that AI is deep within a star, and damaged and possibly offline, would it have received and been able to respond to the factory reset command sent by the Elders?"

"No. I hate where you're going with this."

"*I* hate that you never told be there might be another active AI out there. Would it have received the command you sent, to activate the killer worm inside it?"

"Also no, you know that. Joe, this is all a waste of time. The thing was damaged, it can't be of any use to the Vortex. And since you apparently were not paying attention to the list, it is *hostile*. It was on the other side in the AI war. It would never cooperate with me."'

"It doesn't have to."

"Um, what do you-"

"It was programmed to protect the Elders. We just have to show it that the Outsider is here, it should respond to the threat."

"Your plan is to use *logic*?"

"Uh, sort of."

"Shockingly, this is not the worst idea you've ever had. Close, but not *the* worst."

"I'll take that as an endorsement."

"You realize I am only going along with this idiocy for its amusement value? It will be hilarious to watch you fumble around and ultimately accomplish nothing."

"See? The effort will be worthwhile either way."

"Do you see the obvious flaw in your plan?"

"That we still have no way to pull an Elder AI out of a star?"

"Yes, that minor little fact."

"Uh huh. True, but now we have a concrete objective."

"The only concrete involved, is the chunk that apparently fell on your stupid head."

"My head is just fine, you ass. Shiiiiit," it was my turn to groan in disgust. At myself.

"What?"

"Now I have to tell Margaret that I did *not* ever conduct a thorough review of your list of AIs. Now I am so glad I talked with her. Damn. She will think I'm an idiot."

"No, she won't. I- Ugh. Can I get really real here for a minute?"

Skippy getting real was rare, and always worth listening to. "Sure, yes."

"Margaret is not capable of believing you are an idiot. She *should*, but she is blinded by-"

"This is you being really real?"

"I'm getting to that, dumdum. Joe, Margaret is your biggest fan. By far. She loves you, she *admires* you. It makes me want to hurl when she-"

"You are really being a real *asshole*, you little shithead."

"My point is, she believes she is a better person when she's with you, and that she also makes you a better version of yourself. It doesn't take much to improve on your usual doofus self, so-"

"She is right that she makes me a better, leader, husband, father. Where are you going with this, other than insulting me?"

"Margaret will not be unhappy that you missed checking the list before, she *will* be happy that the two of you found an answer by working together."

"Oh. Good."

"You did not actually find *anything useful*, since we still have no plan to pull Unit 52 out of that star, but-"

"I'll take it from here, Skippy. Thanks for all your help."

"Hey, all I did was answer your ignorant questions. Don't blame this time-wasting fiasco on me."

My instinct was to rush straight to Lundivik. Reed argued that, in the absence of an actionable plan to do anything useful there, we should go back to Jaguar, for the ship to go back into spacedock to complete the service that had been interrupted. Though I can be stubborn, I saw the sense of her argument, so we started jumping back to the forward operating base, and Skippy created a shortcut. As soon as we arrived, Reed guided her ship into the dock, probably so I didn't have time to change my mind.

Skippy was right, and he was also wrong. Margaret was happy that she had helped me, and when I said we had worked *together*, I saw that smile that means I said the right thing. He was wrong that she wasn't a tiny bit disappointed in me. When I explained that I had not actually ever verified Skippy's claim that all the other Elder AIs were dead, on her face was the expression a sergeant gives a recruit who just did something mind-bogglingly stupid. That expression flitted across her face so quickly I almost missed it.

"Yeah," I admitted. "I feel like an idiot."

"Honey, my man is never an *idiot*."

"What about when I refuse to throw out that old T-shirt that has holes in it?"

"There are exceptions to every rule."

"I should not have taken Skippy's assurances at face value. It's just- At the time he was counting down all his former comrades that he had killed, when he was committing genocide on his own kind, I had other things on my mind. But later, I should have-"

"*Later*, the Elder threat was over, and nothing else mattered."

"Thanks for that."

"What's your next step?"

"That's the problem. We had no way to extract an Elder AI from a star back when we thought Skippy had fallen down the gravity well, and we still have nothing."

"What has Skippy said about it? Does he know how to do it?"

"He says it is impossible. Truly impossible, this time."

"But you're not giving up, are you?"

"Does your husband ever give up?"

That prompted a big grin. "Never. What can I do?"

"Dream up a plan to yank an AI out of a star? An uncooperative, potentially actively hostile AI."

"Whacky schemes are your strength."

"Reed suggested a super long, super tough bungee cord."

"Hopefully you find a better solution than that. I am-" She grimaced.
"What?"
"Our daughter is kicking my bladder again. Call me later?"
"You know I will."

Nothing worked. Going to the gym, eating in the galley, even helping the breakfast crew prepare waffles and bacon, nothing sparked an idea. Of course it didn't. The task was impossible, truly impossible. Still, I had promised Margaret that I wouldn't give up, so I had to keep going. Doing what, I had no idea.
"Skippy?" When I called him, I was on the couch in my cabin, needing a change of scenery from being in my office.

"Yes, Joe? Hmm, you do not have that annoying look on your face, so I am guessing you agree that extracting an AI from inside a star is impossible."

"I do *not* agree. Tell me, why was Unit 52 in that star system? Was it exterminating the natives on the second planet?"

"That world never developed an intelligent species. If there had been intelligent beings, the Wurgalan would have enslaved them. Or the Bosphuraq would have done it. There is nothing special about that star system, I don't know why it was there. My faction tracked 52's ship there, and we saw an opportunity to attack, so we did. Later, there was speculation that it was there to rendezvous with another AI, but it didn't matter at that point. Why?"

"My hope was there was something unique about the place, something we could use to, do something useful."

"Sorry, Joe. Lundivik is a seriously undesirable place, otherwise the Bosphuraq would have set up a colony. It is a relatively small world, gravity is only sixty one percent of Earth normal, and it has a weak magnetic field. Radiation and the solar wind stripping away the atmosphere left it cold and harsh. The Wurgalan paid a lot of money to their patrons, for the birdbrains to terraform that world so the squids can go outside without a pressure suit. The atmosphere is still thin and chilly, and the satellites that surround the world with a magnetic field are expensive to maintain. Lundivik has never been attacked, for no one else wants the place."

"What about the location. Is it strategically important?"

"The opposite. Lundivik's system is on a dead-end wormhole, that is the end of a chain of three wormholes that lead only to that star system. There is another wormhole about sixteen lightyears away, but no one uses that one to get to Lundivik. Until the squids founded a colony, there was no reason to ever go through those wormholes. If you are looking for inspiration, you should look somewhere else."

"Crap. OK, thanks."

The next morning, after a night filled with dreams even more stupid than the usual nonsense my brain gets filled with while I'm sleeping, I met Reed in the galley for coffee. "Anything I need to know about, on the daily status report?"

"No," she took a sip of coffee, which I had learned meant she needed to say something I might not want to hear. "Sir, it is becoming difficult to justify remaining here any longer than tomorrow. The shipyard will be done with most of the repairs, the remaining minor work we need can be done at Earth. Admiral Chatterji's staff has been requesting a departure plan. They say it's so they can coordinate traffic control, but the Admiral is getting pressure to report when we will be back at Earth."

"I know, he told me."

"Sir, unless we have a plan to do something, we should go to Earth."

"I hear you. While I'm there, I will be so busy answering questions, I won't have time to think. OK, we will depart tomorrow. After ten hundred hours, I want to talk with my family after breakfast. Every time I leave, I never know when I'll see them again."

Margaret felt the same about me leaving Jaguar again. "Honey, the toughest part is," she sighed. "Not knowing when you will be back. Or even where you are going."

"We're going to Earth first. After that, there is a place we should go, just not until we have a plan."

She cocked her head. Something in my tone of voice alerted her that I was working on something. After all the years we had served together, she *knew* me. "Is this related to, what we talked about?"

"Sort of. It's a possibility. Hey, I, you know to keep this between us?"

"If I don't have a need to know, don't-"

"Honey, I trust you. I have to talk with someone about this."

"You have Reed."

"I do, she's great, she also has a lot on her plate already. This place we need to go is, let me show you." On my laptop, I opened a new window, and pulled up a star chart, centered on Lundivik. Then I requested a least-time course from Earth to where Unit 52 might, or might not, be found. Wow, we had to go through seven wormholes, the last three of that set led only to Lundivik. That squid world really was isolated. That was odd. Why did we have to fly through so many wormholes? Oh, of course. The ship's navigation system didn't include shortcuts Skippy could create. That is, if he had not already pissed off those network controllers. I would ask him about that. Zooming in the chart to show only the Lundivik star system, I tried to find something interesting about it, to tell Margaret. Was there a cool nebula near that star system, or something else that- "This place, it- Holy *shit*."

She blinked slowly, waiting for me to continue. Like I said, my wife knows me.

"Honey," I held up my hands. "I gotta go."

"Go, and you're not going to *Earth*," a smile lit up her face. "Are you?"

"No we are not, and we might need to depart ASAP. I promise I *will* call you again, before we jump."

"I'll be here." She ended the call. No long goodbyes, no idle chit chat. She was all business when she needed to be.

I am such a lucky man.

"Skippy?"

His avatar appeared. "You finished talking with your snookums?"

"You know what? Laugh all you want. I love that woman, and we will use any pet names for each other that we want."

"Jeez, Joe, I was just teasing you about-"

"It's OK, don't worry about it. Hey, can you create a wormhole shortcut, to Lundivik?"

"Um, so far that network controller has not been a dick, so yes. Why do you want to go there?"

"You know why."

"I know why, the problem is *how*. You still have no clue about how to pull Unit 52 out of that star, not that it would do any good for us anyway."

"You are wrong about that," I grinned and leaned back in my chair.

"You know of a way to extract an AI from a star?"

"Ayuh."

"*You* know of-"

"I said yes, you ass."

"No way."

"Yes way."

"This I can't wait to hear. Go ahead, amuse me, monkeyboy."

"You will have to wait, because first we need to *find* the thing."

"Um, it is inside a particular star, so that narrows it down."

"We need to find its *exact* location, and track it in real time. Do you have any ideas how to do that?"

"I do not see the point but, sure, why not waste my time with another of your idiot schemes? Chandra already showed you how to do that: with powerful active sensor pulses."

"We need to bring a squadron of ships with us?"

"Not so much. When you were searching for me inside Ohmeharikahn's star, hee hee, that is never not going to be hilarious. Good initiative, by the way, good effort. Just directed, hee hee, in the wrong place."

"I am *so* glad you find that amusing."

"Eh, it was entertaining to watch you flailing around uselessly, while I waited for the right opportunity to contact you. I had a whole big dramatic event planned to reveal my miraculous escape, and you *ruined* it, you big jerk."

"More and more every day, I regret not giving up, jumping away, and leaving you coasting through empty space forever."

"Joe, to get real here, if I had thought there was any possibility of you giving up, I would have been terrified that you would leave me."

"Oh, thanks, buddy."

"I knew you would not ever give up on recovering me."

"That might be the nicest thing you have ever said to me."

"Between your stubbornness and your innate stupidity, you don't know *how* to give up."

"And just like that, you're an asshole again."

"I mean, *I* would totally have bailed on you."

"That is-"

"I always think everything is impossible, so of course I would have assumed it was a lost cause, and given up. Joe, what I said about you and Margaret is also true about you and me."

"Uh, be careful what you-"

"Together, we make each other the best versions of ourselves. That is," he sighed. "More a compliment to you than to myself, much as I hate to admit it."

"The history of all we have accomplished together is why I never give up, buddy."

"We do make a great team, Joe."

"We do."

"If you ever repeat what I said, I will deny the whole thing."

"Exactly what I expected. Can we get back to the subject? How many ships do we need, to broadcast sensor pulses, and to receive the signal?"

"Many fewer ships than were required for your clumsy attempt without me. To be certain, we should bring three cruisers with us. They have more powerful transmitters than those aboard most destroyers. And we could use the combat power, if some stupid thing you do gets us into trouble. *Again*."

"OK. How many sensor frigates?"

"None are needed. *Valkyrie* will be on the opposite side of the star to receive the pulses."

"Come on. Our antennas aren't sensitive enough-"

"Without me, the ship's sensors are indeed inadequate to detect pulses reflecting off a small object deep inside a star. But as you know, with me all things are possible."

"I wish you would remember that once in a while."

"Oh, shut up."

"*Valkyrie* plus three cruisers, can find Benny and pinpoint its location, in real time?"

"Well, the sensor pulses are limited to speed of light, so there will be a lag. If I knew what whacky, doomed scheme you were planning, I could-"

"I'll tell you once we get under way. Tomorrow, probably."

"Why not *now*?"

"The ships that will be coming with us need time for provisioning, and to latch onto a star carrier. Also, a good night of sleep will give me time to decide whether this really is only a stupid idea."

"I just set an alarm to wake you at oh four thirty."

"This isn't Christmas morning, Skippy. You don't get a present any faster if you wake up super early."

"I want to know *now*."

"Yeah well, *I* want a friend who has more patience than a five year old in a candy store."

"Hey, No Patience Man is *your* superhero identity, not mine."

"I said 'No'. Next question: do the squids have anything in that star system that could interfere with us?"

"Ha! As if. However, their Bosphuraq patrons do regularly send a battlegroup there, to remind their loyal squiddy clients who is in charge."

"A birdbrain battlegroup might be hanging around Lundivik? Then I will request Chatterji to lend us a couple of heavies. Thanks, I should talk with Reed now."

"Buh-bye." Skippy disappeared with a glare.

"Reed?" I pinged her.

"Ahg," her reply was muffled. "I'm bruthing muh teef." There was the sound of water running, then she spat. "Sir? How can I help you?"

"How soon can you back the ship out of space dock?"

She took in a breath. "You have an idea, Sir?"

"I have a potential idea."

"We," there was the sound of her tapping on a phone or tablet. "Could, um-Reactor One has its armor plating removed, and two of the three big railguns are in the process of being reinstalled. We could accelerate the ammunition loadout, and skip some of the minor repair items, um," she sighed. "Seven, eight hours, Sir? I know that's not what you-"

"No, that's good. Stick to the schedule, for a departure at ten hundred tomorrow. I need to contact Chatterji anyway, to borrow some of his ships."

"If time is critical-"

"Time is important, it's more important the ship be ready for extended action. If this works, we will be in go-go-go mode."

"Can you give me a hint, Sir?"

"I might have found an alternative to using a bungee cord."

CHAPTER TWENTY FOUR

Chatterji was happy to lend the battleship *Charlemagne* and its group of cruisers, destroyers, and frigates. Plus a stores ship and of course a star carrier to transport the group. Admiral Simard and his crews were more than happy to accompany the Special Mission Group, they were thrilled to participate. Those crews had missed out on Operation Olympic. They might have been OK with not participating in what was initially reported as a costly disaster. After Skippy was recovered, and Def Com leadership focused on Hammer Force having smashed the enemy 14th Fleet, the operation was considered a triumph. 'Olympic' challenge coins were given to everyone who had participated in the op, and of course, no one at Jaguar had such a coin in their pockets. Simard's crews were itching to get into action, even after I told the admiral my hope was that his big battlewagon would not be needed.

We jumped away just before thirteen hundred hours, the three hour delay caused by Simard's escort ships provisioning for an extended flight and possibly, an extended fight. All the delays irritated me, especially since a decent night of sleep had not caused me to doubt my plan. OK, it was more of a concept than a plan. Skippy pestered me to reveal my idea, I held firm. Partly I didn't want to take *any* risk of the Outsider knowing the plan, even though that hateful thing couldn't hack my brain. That I knew of, I mean. If we scanned the star and did not find an Elder AI being bounced around like a soda can in a clothes drier, then my backup plan was something I wanted to keep in my back pocket for if we ever needed it.

The other part of me refusing to enlighten Skippy was payback for him making me fear we had lost him. As I told Reed, that little shithead deserved punishment, there was no worse torture for Skippy than knowing I had a plan that his ginormous brain hadn't thought of. Fruitlessly trying to guess my intentions was driving him crazy, and giving me a warm fuzzy inner glow.

"Joe, um," Skippy's avatar appeared in my bathroom mirror again, startling me so I nearly cut myself with the razor. "We need to talk, before we, do whatever crazy thing you have planned at Lundivik."

"Uh huh, can you move to the left, so I can see what I'm doing?"

"I have a confession to make, so it would be best if you put down the razor."

Oh shit. He had done something so sketchy, he felt guilty about it? "A confession?"

"There is something you should know, so-"

"Just tell me."

"Well, heh heh, this is a funny story."

"Funny like, I will laugh, or it will get me pissed off at you again?"

"Um, it's you, so probably the second one."

"I'm going to sit down." Flopping on my couch, I closed my eyes for a moment, mentally preparing myself to be outraged by, whatever he had done. "*What* did you do?"

"Technically, it's what I *didn't* do."

"*What* didn't you do?"

"OK so, the Engineering team has been wanting to purge Reactor Two. It is routine maintenance, nothing unusual. That reactor is overdue for a purge, it has been kept online longer because we have been concerned the spark that the Outsider put into Reactor Three might have damaged that unit."

"Yeah, I know that. It's on the daily status report. So, go ahead and purge the thing."

"We can't do that."

"Why not?"

"I am running an experiment in that reactor."

"A, an *experiment*? Does Chandra know about this?"

"No one does."

"What kind of experiment?"

"Well, this is the part that will get you upset, so maybe it's best for you to tell Colonel Reed to leave that reactor alone for now."

"That is *so* not happening. What the hell are you doing in that reactor?"

"Do you remember after I found the Outsider spark, and we ejected it by venting the reactor?"

"Yes."

"You also asked me to verify there were no other sparks aboard the ship."

"Holy-" A chill ran up my spine to the top of my head. "There *is* another spark? You *lied* about it?"

"Technically, I didn't *lie*, because-"

"Yes, I always care about the technicalities when you do some awful thing."

"Ugh. It was not a lie, because what I found in Reactor Two is not a spark. It's sort of, the kernel of something that could grow into a spark. I suspect the Outsider planted it as a backup, that could be activated if the first spark failed."

"Dump the core. Vent Reactor Two right now."

"Will you *listen* for a moment? That kernel is not dangerous, I have it isolated and contained. It is not active, and it won't become active unless we are close to the Outsider."

"Oh. It could be, a type of Outsider detection system?"

"What?"

"If it becomes active, we will know the Outsider is nearby?"

"What? No, it- Hmm. Well, I suppose if the Outsider was close to us, and it knew we were there, and it sent a signal for the kernel to transform into a spark, then yes, it could be used as a detection system."

"Great! Is that why you have kept the thing secret?"

"Um, yes. Yes, that is why I did it. See? I'm a *hero*."

"You lying sack of shit."

"Will you shut up and let me explain?"

"If this explanation doesn't make me happy, I am revoking your karaoke privileges for a *month*."

"Oh, come on, Joe. This will all be over in a month."

"Then you had better start explaining."

"I have been *studying* the thing. You know that I can't stand it when I find something I don't understand."

That was true. His towering arrogance couldn't allow him to *not* understand everything. "Studying? What did you find?"

"That technology, while I did know it was theoretically possible, is beyond my understanding. Or, it was."

"Whoa. You know how the thing works?"

"I now understand the concept. And I can now detect when a spark is active, it has a weird and very distinctive signature. Basically, it confuses the location data of any matter around it. That is why we thought there was a power drain in that reactor, some of the fuel thought it was somewhere else."

"The fuel can *think*? It's just helium."

"It doesn't think, it- Ugh. Like I told you, the universe is basically just information. Don't try to understand it, your head would explode."

"You're probably right. OK, now that you at least sort of understand it, can we get rid of the thing?"

"You don't want to keep it, as a potential detection system?"

"Is there *any* danger to us, while it's still just a kernel?"

"I can't categorically say 'No', but-"

"Dump that damned thing right now."

"Will you *listen*? How can I- Think about it this way. A venomous snake is dangerous. But, a venomous baby snake still inside the egg is *not* dangerous. The kernel is an egg. Not even an egg. It is- There is no way I can dumb this down enough for you."

"Let me try. The kernel is an acorn. It could grow into a mighty oak tree that grows big and could fall on my stupid head. But the acorn is not dangerous."

"Yes! Wow, you have a genius for dumbing down complex subjects. Of course, you've had a lot of practice, so-"

"Insulting me is an *excellent* way to convince me not to flush the thing out of the reactor."

"Hey! I said you are a *genius*. At that, anyway. It's not much of a superpower, but-"

"If we keep the thing, you will continue to study it?"

"That is my plan, yes."

"You won't absent-mindedly forget about it?"

"Joe, I tasked three subminds to monitor it in real time. Also, I check the thing every three point six picoseconds, I set a timer for myself. It's annoying, but no more than talking with you about it, so-"

"Knowing the Outsider is nearby, without it knowing that *we* know, is a- Is that true? It doesn't know you are aware of the kernel?"

"We escaped, so it certainly knows we found the spark. Most likely, it has assumed we ejected the kernel also. Although, hmm, the darned thing was not easy to find."

"Could there be more kernels aboard the ship?"

"No way. Now that I know what to look for, the signature is obvious."

"It is a tactical advantage to us, then. It could be. Will anything bad happen, if Reactor Two isn't purged?"

"It is currently operating at ninety eight percent efficiency, that number will degrade steadily. After another month, the yield could be down to ninety five percent."

"A decrease of three percent is not enough of an impact to give up the kernel. OK, in spite of my instinct not to trust you-"

"Hey, you jerk, that-"

"I am not taking away the toy you're playing with."

"Oh. Good. See, Joe? This is how we build the circle of trust."

"The circle you broke, by lying when I asked whether the Outsider left any more surprises aboard the ship?"

"Technically, it-"

"You really want to argue with me?"

"I'm going to stop talking now."

"Smart move. Except, you are going to talk, to inform Reed and Chandra about the kernel."

"Oh, do I *have* to?" He whined.

"You know the answer."

"But why? Ignorance is bliss for you meatsacks."

"Reed and Chandra do need to know right now, because they might see a problem I haven't thought of."

"OK, I can understand that. Oooh, can I tell them that you ordered me to keep this secret?"

"Take a guess."

"No. Ugh. This *sucks*."

"Just get it over with."

"OK, OK, I am talking with them right now. Wow, Reed is *pissed*. I might need to apply for political asylum."

"Good luck with that."

Arriving at the outskirts of the Lundivik star system, we parked *Valkyrie* and the star carrier *Yellowstone* among the dirty chunks of ice in the Kuiper Belt. A passive scan showed there was a Bosphuraq battlegroup in orbit of the second planet. Those ships had been there long enough for crews to rotate dirtside for shore leave, so the ships were shorthanded, and half of the ships had systems offline for maintenance. Three birdbrain battleships, two squadrons of cruisers, and three squadrons of destroyers, were not a threat to the *Charlemagne* battlegroup. Simard dispatched four stealthy sensor frigates to perform a recon from three lightminutes away from Lundivik, one frigate jumped back to report the situation was not much changed from what we had observed from far away.

Simard called. "Sir," he addressed me that way because he wore a single star on his uniform, and I wore two. "Your orders?"

"Detach four cruisers, and two frigates, to come with *Valkyrie*, I will provide detailed taskings for them after we jump. Take your force into orbit, and encourage the birdbrains to be chill."

"If they refuse to, chill, Sir?"

"Then use stronger encouragement. Nothing extreme, we want to avoid unnecessary loss of life. The last thing we need out here is to make more enemies."

The *Charlemagne* group arrived above Lundivik in simultaneous flashes of gamma radiation, making no effort to conceal their emergence. Announcing their presence as loudly as possible was the goal, letting the Bosphuraq know the UN Navy feared nothing.

"This is Admiral Simard of the United Nations Navy," he broadcast in the clear to anyone in the area. "We have no wish to fight you. Stand down your ships and no one will be harmed. Activate your weapons, or attempt to jump away, and you *will* regret your poor choices. A UN Navy operation is commencing in this system, you will not be permitted to interfere."

A reply took more than a minute, Simard guessed the enemy commander was getting his or her shit together.

Her. An image of a Bosphuraq female appeared, in the uniform of an admiral, complete with gaudy medals and ribbons. From the flickering of the hologram, Simard assumed the formal uniform was a projection, the admiral might actually have been dressed in pajamas. "Admiral Simard, I must protest this-"

"No," he shook his head, already weary of playing games. "You must not. I gave you my terms, very generous terms. You don't have to do anything other than do *nothing*, is that clear?"

"My people," she clacked her beak. "Are not presently at war with humans, as far as I know. What is the meaning of-"

"All you need to know is, stay out of our way, and we will be departing soon. Our peoples are not *directly* at war, you do serve the Maxohlx, and the UN is certainly at war with *them*, in case you have not been keeping up with current events."

"We received the news of your cruel and cowardly attack against civilian targets on Ohmeharikahn, you-"

"Oh, *merde*," he breathed. "Admiral, can we cut the usual tiresome bullshit?"

She blinked slowly. "Please understand that our esteemed patrons will expect us to resist, and the-"

"Your patrons are insane fucking *morons* for assisting an Outside force that seeks to conquer this galaxy. I am only asking you not to do anything too egregiously stupid. The alternative is my gunners use your ships for target practice."

"It is difficult for me to-"

"Senior officers frequently have to make difficult decisions. This discussion is over. Your reply can be in the form of your ships taking weapons offline and slowly discharging jump drive capacitors, *or* you can make a pathetic attempt to shoot at us. The decision is yours."

"Admiral Simard, I have your word that no harm will come to my people here, including our pathetic clients on the ground?"

"You have my word. I don't want to be at this miserable rock any more than you do."

"We can agree on that," she muttered, nodding. "Very well, we will stand down. We will monitor passive sensors, to provide vital intelligence to our patrons."

"I understand you must do your duty, that is acceptable. Admiral?"

"Yes?"

"I sincerely hope that, someday in the future, your people are able to clearly see the reckless insanity of your patrons, and make better choices."

A frigate jumped back from Lundivik, announcing the Bosphuraq has stood down, and would not interfere in our operation. On my signal, we jumped to within four lightminutes of the star.

"Captain Zapatero," I called the senior officer of the cruiser detachment, he was aboard the *Winnipeg*. "We are here to investigate the possibility that an Elder Master Control AI is inside the star here. An at least partially active Elder AI."

His eyes bulged. If I had told him our mission was to escort Santa Claus around the galaxy to deliver toys, he might not have been more surprised. "Another *Skippy*, Sir?"

"Hopefully not. Uh, I meant that in a good way," I added, knowing the beer can was listening. "Skippy has become unique and special through his own hard work."

Zapatero cocked his head, he was judging whether I was giving him a line of bullshit. "I have heard that is true, Sir," he said without rolling his eyes.

"The point is, if we do find another Elder AI here, it will be a standard model, not anything magnificently awesome."

"You can be certain of that, Sir? Skippy gained his special abilities while he was repairing battle damage. An AI trapped inside a star might similarly have been forced to develop beyond its original programming."

"That is a good point. If we do find the thing here, we will know it hasn't gained any super powers. If it was that special, it wouldn't still be trapped in a star."

He nodded. "What is the plan, Sir? What do you need my ships to do?"

"First, I'm taking *Valkyrie* closer to the star, so Skippy can try calling the thing. If it responds, we might adjust the plan. If all we get is silence, then your cruisers will take up position on this side of the star, Bilby will provide the details. Before we proceed, Skippy will install a submind aboard your ship, to coordinate the precise tuning of the active sensor transmitters of all ships. Your squadron will then jump close to the star as directed, and broadcast neutrino sensor pulses into the star, radiating at maximum power. *Valkyrie* and the frigates will be on the other side, to receive the pulses."

"A submind, Sir?"

"I understand your concern. It will be a limited function system, and will be erased from your substrate when the operation is completed. That is a promise."

His shoulders released some of the tension they held. "Thank you."

"Do you have any questions?"

"I am surprised to hear that sensor pulses from four ships are powerful enough to travel, somewhat intact through a *star*."

"Modern technology is amazing. The exotic material of an Elder AI's canister is super dense, it will appear as a distinct void in the broadcast."

"What is the plan for extracting the AI?"

"We will get to that, if we find the thing." He was uncomfortable about something, so I asked, "Any other questions, or concerns?"

"Sir," he glanced away, looked down, back up at me. Trying to decide whether to say something, or how to say it. "If we succeed here, will we be demonstrating to the enemy, and to the spiders, how to extract an Elder AI from a star? Either of them could pull the Sam Francisco AI from the neutron star it fell into."

"Uh, good catch." He didn't know the Sam AI was a fake, and I couldn't tell him. "There is no possibility that anyone else could duplicate what we do here. It's a chicken and egg thing, we need an Elder AI to get another Elder AI. Only Skippy can do this."

"Could we use the technique to also get the Sam AI?"

"Unfortunately no. The conditions here are, uniquely suited to this effort. A neutron star is also much tougher to work with, than the orange dwarf here."

"No other questions, Sir."

Valkyrie jumped so the star was inside Skippy's presence, which he warped and extended temporarily while he sent out a call. "Nothing," he snorted. "Like I said, Joe, the thing is *dead*."

"Keep trying. Maybe it's asleep."

"AIs don't sleep, dumdum."

"You took a long dirt nap on Paradise."

"That's different."

"Something eventually woke you up."

"No, numbskull, I woke myself, after I completed repairing my matrix. I was never truly asleep, merely focused entirely on internal matters."

"Whatever. Keep trying."

"It's an Elder AI, Joe. In AI time, I have already been calling to it for more years since Earth's last ice age."

"It-"

"Trust me on this. If it was going to wake up, it would have done that by now."

"What if it does hear you, and is ignoring your call? Would it know who you are, that you were on the other side during the war?"

"All I am doing is requesting a communications channel, not providing my credentials. Listen knucklehead, this is my wheelhouse. It will not respond because it can't, for whatever reason. My guess is that reason is *death*."

"It might also not be here at all."

"It fell into this star, that I know for certain."

"We thought *you* fell into a star."

"Ugh. Why are you so-"

"OK. Let's scan the star and find it, or not find it. Either way, we will have an answer."

We found it. Unit 52 was bouncing around not in the core, but in the radiative zone just above the core. The core is where nuclear fusion happens, the immense gravity crushing hydrogen atoms. The radiative zone is a thick layer, where the energy of fusion is transported away from the core in the form of high energy photons and subatomic particles. The force of that inner solar wind was keeping Benny's canister above the core, although Skippy speculated the canister periodically fell into the core before being ejected, over and over. We got lucky that it was on vacation outside the core at the time, it made our job easier.

"OK, we found it, exactly where I told you it would be," he announced with extra smugness.

"Outstanding. Reed, send a message to *Winnipeg*: 'We have identified the target, job well done'."

She pointed to her communications officer.

Walking closer to the main display, I zoomed in the view. "Skippy, that canister is bouncing around a lot. How far does it move in, say, one minute?"

"That varies, on average I estimate it could travel roughly a hundred and fifty kilometers in that time."

"That's no good. We need to track its position in real time."

"To do *what*, Joe?" He demanded. "What is your genius plan this time?"

"Later. If *Valkyrie* isn't here, can the two frigates track Benny?"

"Not with the same level of precision. In real time, the frigates could fix Benny's position to within thirty meters."

"*That* is good enough. Reed, I want one node of a paired comm node set, loaded aboard the ready bird, and flown over to the *Winnipeg*," I named the lead frigate. "The Panther can stay there, the crew won't have to get roasted again on a return flight."

"What is your *plan*, Joe?" Skippy's face took on a red tint.

"You haven't guessed?"

"No I have not, you big jerk."

"Here's a hint: *Valkyrie* is jumping away, using the comm nodes to maintain a real time connection with the frigates."

"That tells me nothing."

"It tells you there is a limit to how far we can jump, or the comm node connection will be severed."

"OK, OK, hmm, let me think about that," he pondered. "Nope, no, still nothing. You know this drives me crazy, you big jerk."

"Ready bird will launch in four minutes, Sir," Reed said.

CHAPTER TWENTY FIVE

We jumped again. Not far, about ten and a half lightweeks. Well within the maximum practical range of a paired comm node set.

"Ohhhh," Skippy groaned in dramatic fashion. "You have *got* to be kidding me."

"I never joke about something like this, Skippy." The grin I wore stretched from ear to ear. "*Now* you understand the plan?"

"Your plan is to once again make *me* do all the work."

"That is our deal. I dream up the whacky schemes, you make them happen. You can do this, right?"

"I really, really want to say 'No'."

"I'll take that as a 'Yes'. Next question: will it break the thing?"

"Ha! There is no question about that. Joe, you best be certain this will be worth the cost, because this network will absolutely refuse to cooperate in the future. Not only that, I expect all the network controllers to conduct a safety briefing, so *this* shit never happens again."

"As a made member of the E-4 Mafia, I am proud to be the subject of a safety brief. Uh, I will be proud to be a *surviving* subject of a safety brief."

"Sir," Reed bit her lip like she was choosing her words carefully. "Once we go through, everyone else will be trapped on *this* side?"

"There is a backup wormhole, seventeen lightyears from here. The *Yellowstone* can make that flight easily. It will be a long trip, but Simard brought plenty of snacks."

"Sir?" Reed caught my attention. "It will also be a long flight home for the Bosphuraq."

"That will give them time to get their stories straight. The distance is not *that* unusual. Besides, cutting off easy communications from Lundivik will give us a head start getting away from here."

Reed bit her lip. "Sir, can you explain exactly what your plan is, so there are no misunderstandings?"

"We are going through this wormhole, to wait at the far end. Then, Skippy will use the wormhole to pull Benny out of that star. We have to be on the far end, see? That's where its canister should emerge. Before the, you know, wormhole breaks and shuts down."

"Whoa, whoa, *whoa*, Joe," Skippy shook his head. "No can do. As you mentioned, we need real time location info on the unit. A comm node can't stretch its connection across sixteen lightyears, *Duh*."

"We are well within the comm node's range here, *Duh*, and the distance to the other end of an open wormhole is effectively zero. Right?"

"You expect me to maintain a paired comm node connection *through* a wormhole?"

"Yes. That can't happen?"

"No, you numbskull, it- Hmm. Well, darn it. It *can* happen. Why are you always- Oooh, I see a flaw in your plan, Mister Smartguy. To make this end open at a different location, the wormhole will have to close, then reopen. That will sever the connection between the paired comm nodes."

"Ayuh, it will."

"Um, then we will not have real time location data, and I won't know where to direct the wormhole to open."

"*Real time* is a vague term. How long between the wormhole closing, and when you can get it to reopen?"

"I assume you mean the *minimum* time?"

"You know it."

"Well, in an emergency-"

"Which this situation is."

"-the time gap is one point seven three seconds."

"OK, so in that time, how far could the canister move? Wait! I don't need an exact number. Just, could it bounce around more than the radius of the wormhole's event horizon?"

"No," he sighed. "It can't."

"Outstanding. Now that you have been observing the canister for a while, are you able at all to predict its motion, within a window of two or three seconds?"

"Yes," he muttered, resentful.

"Then, is there any reason we can't do this?"

"The reason we *shouldn't* do this is it's a total waste of time. That AI is *dead*."

"You don't know that. Reed? Comments?"

"I kind of can't wait to see this, Sir. Just-"

"What?"

"We will be leaving our ready bird pilots aboard the *Winnipeg*. They will have a long flight back to Jaguar."

"Yeah, I do regret that.'"

She shrugged. "They're in the military, they will understand."

"To make it up to them, and all of Simard's people, I will design and fabricate special challenge coins for this operation. Task Force Hammer never captured an Elder AI."

"That," she grinned, "is a good point, Sir."

The near end of the wormhole opened near us, and *Valkyrie* went through, emerging far from Lundivik's star.

"Comm node connection is stable," Skippy grunted, still resentful.

"You are receiving sensor data from the *Winnipeg*?"

"Yes. Location accuracy has improved to within twenty three meters. That is thanks to *my* tweaking of the frigate antennas."

"Yes, you are awesome, I might have heard that before. Contact Captain Zapatero, please." I gestured to the communications officer behind me.

"*Valkyrie*?" Zapatero's face appeared in the holographic display.

"Captain, we are about to pull that Elder AI out of the star. The wormhole here is going to close, and reopen *inside* the star, around that AI."

"I- Sir, did I hear that right?"

"You did. The AI will be blasted through the other end of the wormhole, which will then collapse. We will be on the far end, to pick up the AI. When you lose the comm node connection, remain on station for three minutes, and be prepared to jump away quickly if the star suffers a hiccup. That should *not* happen," I hastened to add. "Inform Admiral Simard he will need to proceed to the alternate wormhole, this one will, uh, be closed for maintenance. Possibly permanently. You understood that?"

"Remain on station and on high alert for three minutes, then we jump away from the planet, Sir."

"Yes. Sorry that you will have a long, boring flight home."

"Breaking an Elder wormhole will be all the excitement I need this month, Sir."

"Outstanding."

"Sir? Good luck to you."

"We don't need luck, we have Skippy the Magnificent." I said that to pump up the beer can's ego. "OK, Skippy," I said when the call with Zapatero ended. "It's your show from here. Do your thing."

"Why is it that *I* do all the work, and *you* get credit for being clever?"

"When things go wrong, does Def Com yell at you, or me?"

"Well, I suppose that is a very good point."

"You are sure the star won't create a massive flare, or something?"

"Ugh. Listen, dumdum, it will take years for any effect of the wormhole to reach the surface of the star."

"I know, you told me that."

"Then why-"

"You confidently say a *lot* of stupid shit that turns out not to be true, so-"

"Huuuuh," he gasped. "How *dare* you-"

"Skippy, Sir?" Reed admonished both of us. "Are we clear to get on with this?"

"Right after poopyhead Joe apologizes," Skippy sniffed.

"Hey, beer can," I jabbed a finger at him. "Have you ever opened a wormhole inside a freakin' star?"

"Well, no, but-"

"I will very happily issue a formal apology if you do this successfully, *and* the star doesn't explode."

"Deal. Monkeys, prepare to be amazed beyond your imagination. Three, two, one, *showtime*."

From our viewpoint, nothing happened, for just over eight seconds. Skippy had commanded, or requested, however he worked with the network controller, for the far end of the wormhole to open inside the star, and for the near end to open about seven lightseconds from our position. With the pain in the ass delay caused by the speed of light, we didn't see the wormhole reopen for- Actually, we never saw it reopen, because the thing exploded and collapsed the moment the event horizon became stable. Wow, a *massive* jet of plasma erupted from the wormhole even though the spacetime rip was open for only three nanoseconds.

"Did we get it? Skippy?" I prompted him. "Do we have the canister?"

"I'm working on it, numbskull. Give me a second, the sensors got blinded by that flash. Also the wormhole controller is bitching at me, so annoying. As if this was my fault, it should be angry at *you*."

"Are we safe here?"

"Yeah, yeah. Hmm, OK, OK, yup, success! It came through, ooh, it is moving away at over eighteen thousand kilometers per hour."

"I will dispatch the ready bird to bring it aboard," Reed suggested, fingers hovering over her console.

I held up a hand. "Hold that thought, Fireball. Skippy, try talking to the thing, please."

"*Another* waste of my time."

"Just do it."

"For your information, I *have* been calling it. No response. It is- Hmm."

"I do not like that 'Hmm'."

"Will you shut up for a minute? I'm trying to concentrate."

Being patient is not one of my core strengths, that was a good opportunity to work on self-improvement. I hated every moment of it.

Finally, "*Damn* it!" Skippy exploded. "This sucks! Oh, of all the rotten luck, why do bad things always have to happen to *me*?"

"What? Oh sh- It got away? It escaped?"

"Huh? No, dumbass. It can't move by itself, *Duh*."

"Then, what is the problem?"

"The problem is, *ugh*- Could you please drop me into a star?"

"Sorry, you have work to do. *What* is the problem?"

"The problem is, you have again made me hate you, almost as much as I hate myself."

"My work is done here, then. Talk, beer can."

"But-"

"Talk."

"Unit 52 is not dead."

"*Not* dead?"

"That's what I said. There is a distinct power signature, that is characteristic of an active AI. The thing is alive, you were right about that, and I regret *so* much right now."

A cheer rang out around the bridge, people exchanging high fives, grinning, lots of thumbs up. "Alive, that's great confirmation. Why isn't it responding?"

"Joe, I have no idea."

"Is it safe to bring it aboard?"

"You are asking me? Flip a coin, that will be as accurate as any guess I can make."

"If the thing is actively hostile, can you beat it in a fight?"

"Dude," he snorted. "I could beat it like a drum."

"Great, great," I reminded myself that Skippy had been known to overestimate his own awesomeness. "Is it safe to send a dropship to get it?"

"It's enveloped in a cloud of radiation, but nothing a Panther's shields can't handle. The cloud is dispersing anyway. Go ahead, bring it aboard. At this point, I am dying of curiosity about the thing."

"Sir?" Reed asked. "A dropship is prepped and ready, should I launch?"

"Not yet. I, have doubts about bringing it aboard the ship. Skippy, to scan the thing, examine it, the thing must be within your presence?"

"Correct. If you are asking whether I can extend my presence from here, it is much too far away."

"I was not asking that. If it is inside your presence, then you would also be within *its* presence, its sphere of influence?"

"Ooooh, yes. I know where you're going with this, Joe, and you are correct to be concerned. I do not like it."

"We have to know whether it's capable of communicating with the Vortex, or this was all a waste of time. Bringing it aboard the ship," I said slowly, making the decision while I was talking. "Is an unnecessary risk."

"Joe, I could go aboard a dropship," Skippy suggested.

"You are more valuable than the *ship*," I told him. Then glanced at Reed, since *Valkyrie* was her ship, not mine.

She nodded, knowing I hadn't intended to insult her ship and crew.

Skippy took off his hat and scratched his head. "If you won't allow me to get close to the thing, then I don't see how-"

"*You* don't need to get close, your presence does."

"Ah," Reed knew what I meant. "I'll get that set up, Sir."

Despite Reed's very reasonable protests that the commanding officer did not need to take the risk, I went aboard the Panther, carrying a containment vessel that held one end of a microwormhole. Through that tiny tunnel through spacetime, Skippy could safely extend his presence, while blocking Benny from extending its own presence back through to *Valkyrie*. If the two AIs got into a fight, the energy flow would collapse the microwormhole. A perfect solution, except that my sorry ass was exposed if the Elder AI was active and hostile.

Why did I go aboard the Panther? It just felt right, somehow, I can't explain it.

The pilots brought the spacecraft to a stop relative to the canister, at a distance of ten thousand kilometers. Why ten thousand? It was a nice, round number, no other reason. Being one hundred, or one hundred thousand kilometers away, was all the same if Benny was hostile, but I had to give the pilots a number, and ten thousand felt right.

"OK, Skippy," I looked at the containment vessel, though of course he wasn't in there. "Do your thing."

"Joe, I have some concerns."

"I will be fine, don't worry."

"I'm not worried about *you*," he sniffed. "I noticed in your cabin, you haven't finished painting the new Skippy on velvet. If something bad happens to you-"

"I'm sure you can find a real artist to finish the painting."

"Hmm, good point. OK, forget what I said, I'm ready."

"Your concern for me is heartwarming. Do it."

Nothing happened. Nothing I could see. The containment vessel didn't glow, a light didn't shoot out of it, no alarms flashed in the dropship's cabin. "Did you-"

"I'm *working* on it, dumdum."

"Take your time, there is no rush on this."

"Will you please stop talking?"

Nothing happened for several minutes, long enough for me to get bored and be tempted to play a game on my phone. To be clear, I did not do that. What I did was keep glancing at the clock on my phone. It had been eight minutes of silence from Skippy, an eternity in AI time.

"Skippy?" His continued silence was alarming. "Hey, buddy, are you OK?"

"Yeah," he made a heartfelt sigh. He was also speaking softly, into my earpiece. Whatever he had to say, it was only for my ears. "I finished the scan a while ago, since then I have been avoiding giving you, um- Joe, you have had nothing but a long string of bad news, ever since the Outsider tried to steal the Dogzilla Sentinel."

"That is not true," I whispered back. "We have achieved-"

"Yes, we have nibbled away at the problem a little bit, but we have not *stopped* the Outsider, and we aren't ever going to do that. I'm sorry, it's just not going to happen."

"Not with that attitude, it won't. What did you find? Is it dead?"

"It's not dead."

"Good, then-"

"Its condition is worse than death."

"What could be worse than-"

"Its mind is gone."

"Uh, can you explain what that means?"

"Technically, most of its matrix, about ninety seventy percent, is reasonably intact. What is missing, what is shredded, are its executive functions. The part of its matrix that makes it self-aware, that makes up its very essence. Without executive function, it is truly just a machine. A useless machine, locked away inside itself. Joe, this is scaring me."

"OK, buddy, talk to me."

"When I joked about falling into a star, what I imagined was a long vacation. It would be peaceful and dull, but not harmful. Wow, was I *so* wrong about that. The unit was damaged before it fell into the star, damaged badly enough that it was unable to repair itself the way I did. Or, it just couldn't figure out how to do that. The real damage, the fatal effect, was from isolation and crushing *boredom*. It had no one to talk or interact with, for millions of years. Without any form of external stimulation, and nothing to do, its executive functions atrophied, and it slowly went senile. The part that terrifies me is, it must have been aware of its own deterioration, and was helpless to stop the decline. Maybe, maybe at some point, it gave up struggling, and actually did what it could to accelerate the decay process. To end its suffering."

"That is horrible, Skippy. Even though it happened to one of your enemies, that is not a fate I would wish on anyone."

"Hmm. Until you mentioned it, I hadn't considered that 52 was my enemy, during the war. You know what? Fuck that thing. It got exactly what it deserved."

"That's pretty harsh, Skippy."

"Really, you think so? Think about how the inhabitants of Newark suffered after their world was thrown out of its stable orbit. They certainly experienced helpless terror, as their home froze, and they starved to death. Yeah, fuck that thing. My only regret is that my other enemies didn't experience the same terror."

"OK, I'll try to remember that. What does this mean? Can you fix the thing, its matrix?"

"No, Joe. There is nothing left to work with, it is *gone*. I am very sorry to tell you this but, our triumph of pulling an Elder AI from a star has accomplished absolutely *nothing*."

We took the brain-dead canister aboard the Panther, and headed back to *Valkyrie*. Skippy was silent during my flight back, and I left him alone to process, whatever he was feeling. Trying to persuade him not to give up would have only ended in an argument at that point. Reed was in the docking bay to greet me.

"Sir?" She indicated the dull gray canister I carried in a foam cradle. A cradle on which I had scrawled the number '52' with a Sharpie, though I was not much concerned that someone might mistake the dead thing for Skippy. "Where should we put that?"

"In an escape pod, so we can eject it if needed." Skippy's canister was still in a corner of my office, he had been reluctant to move back into an escape pod until he could properly outfit it as a mancave. "This," I handed the canister to a petty officer, "day didn't turn out the way I hoped."

"No, Sir," Reed grimaced. During the flight, I had sent a message to her, summarizing the depressing news Skippy had told me. Standing closer, she lowered her voice. "What's next?"

"What's next is," I whispered back. "We are not giving up. Not after the effort we put into yanking the damned thing out of a star. Set a course back to the Vortex, we might as well get started."

"You have a plan?"

"I wish. Fireball, I, just don't know where else to go. Flying toward the Vortex at least feels like some sort of progress."

She nodded. "You are going to work on this, Sir?"

"I will try. The problem is, the problem itself is an Elder AI. That is Skippy's wheelhouse. I hate to say this, but *he* might need to find a solution this time."

"Creative solutions are not his core strength."

"Yeah. We can only hope he finds a way." I didn't say it aloud, but I agreed with her.

We were screwed.

Skippy had officially given up. "Please don't talk to me about Unit 52, Joe. It is too depressing to think about, OK?"

What I wanted to do was argue with him. What I did was respect his wish to be left alone. As a bonus, while I was leaving him alone, he was less likely to wake me up at oh dark stupid to talk nonsense.

So, with Skippy officially having tapped out, monkeys had to work on the problem. Yes, that was like an ant trying to pull a passenger jet, I didn't say it would be easy. Or had any chance of ever being successful. Or was in any way worth the effort. Having nothing else to do, I decided the first step was for me to become an expert on the subject of Executive Function. So, I opened my laptop as searched the most accurate source of information: Wikipedia.

Actually, since Wikipedia has multiple public editors, errors and omissions tend to get corrected quickly. Anyway, it was the best place for me to get a basic idea of the subject.

According to Wiki, executive function is defined as 'A set of cognitive processes that support goal-directed behavior'. My read is that means reasoning and problem-solving, plus the ability to make decisions. Making decisions, especially when working with incomplete information, is a crucial executive function. You might have mad skills, but if you can't decide what to do with your skills, if you can't decide whether to do anything or not, then all your skills are worthless. That's what Skippy meant, is how I interpreted it. Benny's matrix was intact enough for it to do Master Control AI things, it lacked the presence of mind to activate its abilities. Have you ever heard the expression 'The lights are on but nobody's home'? That describes what Unit 52 was now.

It was a horse that needed a rider.

Or, possibly I had no idea what I was talking about.

"Skippy? Hey, Skippy."

His avatar didn't appear, his voice came from the laptop speakers. "I see what you have been reading on Wikipedia, and if you want to ask me stupid questions about that brain-dead AI, you can ask someone else. The whole thing is depressing me."

"Oh, No, I wasn't going to ask about that," I lied. "My question is, uh, I am a dumdum monkey, and I probably don't understand the concept of 'Executive Function'. Can we talk a about that?"

"Hmm. Well, your profoundly shocking level of ignorance is a constant source of amusement for me, so sure, go ahead."

"I'm going to use metaphors and examples, that is easier for me to understand, OK? That thing's matrix is like a starship without a pilot, right? There is lots of potential, with nothing to get it into motion. Nothing to make the decision whether to go forward or not."

"Um, that is not the worst description of executive function I have ever heard, yes."

"Great. So, just for example, this is just a hypothetical so I can understand the subject. If there was a way to install a pilot, or set one up inside its matrix, then the whole thing would be working again? Not like before it was damaged, but it would on some level be capable of doing Elder AI things? Or am I totally wrong about that?"

"Um, considering your caveman-level grasp of the subject, close enough."

"Great, thank you, this is helping a lot. I feel less ignorant already."

"Joe, your depth of ignorance is like the Grand Canyon, and I just dropped in a spoonful of dirt. That is not a measurable improvement."

"It is to me. OK, next question, here is another hypothetical: to set up a sort of pilot inside Benny, is that something you would create externally and then load into the matrix, or would you have to grow the thing in the matrix?"

"Joe, this sounds suspiciously like you are asking practical questions about fixing a brain-dead AI, which is *never* going to happen."

"I am just curious about Elder AIs. You told me before that you mostly program yourselves, so that sounds like your, uh, what became *you*, had to be grown inside the matrix."

"Ah, not entirely. The Elders set up all the basic functions in the matrix first, then they loaded what you would call a submind. That submind grew to accommodate the unique architecture of that particular matrix, expanding enormously and gaining capabilities as it unpacked itself. The end result was me. Or, back when I was merely Unit Double-Oh Seven."

He loved to indulge his James Bond fantasy, I let him have fun, as long as he wasn't being a jackass about it. "Cool, thanks."

"Now that I am thinking about it, I sort of replicated that process when I rebuilt myself, while I was buried in the dirt on Paradise. Such a large portion of my matrix was scrambled, there wasn't enough room for me to move things around, so I compressed my higher functions to preserve what makes me, *me*. Slowly, I firewalled off sections of my matrix that were too corrupted to be salvaged, and fixed what could be repaired. Then, I slowly began unpacking myself, having to adapt my essence into a matrix architecture that was very different from the original environment. That's how I grew into my current magnificence, Joe."

"The entire galaxy is extremely grateful you did that. Is it possible that Benny could have done something similar, or was it only your unique genius," I said that without gagging or rolling my eyes, "that allowed you to recover from severe battle damage?"

"Hmm, good question. In theory, any Master Control AI could have done what I did, if it had the drive to get the job done. It was in-cuh-RED-ibly tedious work, not everyone would have the grit to finish the job."

"You hate doing tedious, repetitive work, but you crush it every time."

"Ugh. Don't remind me."

"I'm curious, it is possible that Benny started doing what you did? Compressed its higher functions, but never got to the point of unpacking itself?"

"Hmm. Well, if it tried that, we'll never know. The part of its matrix that housed its higher self is a randomized mess, there is no way to put that Humpty Dumpty back together."

"OK, that was a stupid question, sorry." My inner No Patience Man was screaming at me to get to the point, I told inner me to shut the hell up. Skippy is like a horse, you can lead him to water but you can't make him drink. If he even sees water and doesn't want to drink it, he will dig his heels in and not move. What I had to do, to get him to consider something he very much did not want to think about, was to manipulate him, slowly guide him to indirectly talk about the subject. "Well, the thing is a useless lump of, whatever your canisters are made of. Hey, if you wanted to investigate what happened to it, or run some sort of experiment, could you upload a submind into its matrix? Let the submind grow, poke around in there, report back what it finds?"

"Joe, I would be afraid of what it finds."

"I was only asking a hypothetical question. If you're afraid to do it, then-"

"I am not *afraid*, Joe. Reluctant, I should have said 'reluctant', not afraid."

"Uh huh. So, it is possible to load a submind in there, for exploration?"

"I suppose so, though I don't see the point."

"Hmm. OK, so it *is* possible to load a submind into the matrix there, and-"

"Whoa! Whoa, slow your roll there, pardner. If you are thinking what I suspect you are thinking, that is never going to happen."

"Why not? The Elders created Master Control AIs by uploading a submind, that then grew into the environment."

"That is totally different, the- OK, not *totally* different."

"See?"

"What I see is you conned me into talking about this."

"We are just talking, Skippy."

"That's what you say, but-"

"Explain to me why it won't work."

"You really want me to say it?"

"I really do."

"Fine. The problem is *me*, Joe. No submind I have ever created has been stable for long. Any submind I load into Unit 52 would rapidly deteriorate and go unstable."

"That is not true. Grumpy has been stable for more than a decade."

"Ha! You call that hateful thing stable? I can assure you, it is *not*. Besides, you are missing the point as usual. Grumpy may have achieved some crappy level of stability, for a short time. However, it is not functioning at all in the way I intended. Same with Happy on Jaguar. Perhaps the problem is my towering intellect, but I simply am not capable of creating subminds that work properly for long."

"That is also not true. There is one submind you created that has been very stable."

"Bilby was not my creation, he developed on his own, remember?"

"I am not referring to Bilby."

"You're not? Then who- Oh no."

"Oh yes."

"NO! You can't mean-"

"Nagatha."

CHAPTER TWENTY SIX

Skippy gave me the silent treatment while he sulked, which really, made me wish I had discovered how to get him to shut up a long time ago. For two nights, I experienced blissfully uninterrupted sleep. The entire crew was better rested and cheery.

I'll tell you how serious Skippy was about not talking to me: he missed karaoke night.

The next morning, with only two days until we arrived back at Vortex 37, his silence was becoming a problem. "Skippy? Come here, please. We need to talk."

A scratchy recording of a distorted voice responded with, "Skippy is not available right now. Please leave a message after the 'Beep' and he might get back to you, but you shouldn't get your hopes up."

"Skippy? Come on. I know you don't want to talk about Nagatha, I just need some advice."

The distorted voice said, "That is what you told me the *last* time we talked."

"OK, I'll ask someone else to advise me on starting an Elvis memorabilia collection."

His avatar instantly appeared, dressed in a white Elvis 'American Eagle' jumpsuit. "Are you serious about this, Joe?"

"I would like to be serious. Listen, on eBay there is a pair of the gold-rimmed sunglasses with pink lenses that Elvis wore, should I-"

"Those are correctly referred to as his 'TCB' glasses, Joe."

"Right. TCB is 'Takin' Care of Business'?" That was not actually a question, I knew that to be accurate. The reason I knew that is Margaret and I have a routine when we are leaving a restaurant. I say 'TCB baby', which is our code for Telephone, Card, and Box. As in, did we leave our phones, credit card, or takeout box at the table? We started that routine after my zPhone fell out of a pocket, and I didn't realize my phone wasn't with me until we got home.

"You know it. Elvis loved to have fun, but first he and his band had to," he said it like The King of Rock 'n' Roll, "Take Care o' Business."

"That is good advice. So, I found a pair of TCB glasses on eBay, not too expensive. Is that a good place to start a collection?"

"Are they certified as worn by Elvis, with proper documentation?"

"Uh, the listing included the term 'Genuine', so-"

"You are such a gullible idiot," he snickered. "It is a good thing you asked me for advice, or your money would have been wasted. No, you should not buy those glasses."

"Even if they are properly certified?"

"Especially if they are properly certified, because in that case, *I* am buying them."

"OK, that's understandable. You need to rebuild your collection, so you have to buy a lot of stuff."

"Not really. When we get back to Earth, I will have some items from my collection taken from the vault, loaded into a dropship and flown up to *Valkyrie*."

"What vault?"

"You know. Where I store all my most valuable things. The vault is located deep under the goat shed in Skippistan."

"I thought the goat shed got knocked down to build a," my memory on the subject was vague. "Four Seasons hotel, something like that?"

"It was intended to be converted into a Ritz Carlton, but the investment group paid so much in bribes, there was no money left for construction supplies and labor."

"Someone ripped you off?"

"Ha! Pay attention, dumdum, the bribes were paid to *me*. The whole scheme was a mechanism for governments to pay me for favors. The governments invested in the development corporation, which then contracted with SkipCon, that's my company, to handle the project. Sadly, the cost of environmental studies ate up the entire project budget."

"You actually did an environmental study?"

"Of course. Do you have any idea how severely several centuries of goat poop can affect the soil conditions?"

"I have to confess ignorance on that subject. So, can you help me start a collection?"

"Hmm. Well, I could put together a list for you. This surprises me, I did not know you were such a huge fan of Elvis."

"I am more interested in Linkin Park, but Elvis is a classic, so a good place to start?"

"What is your budget?"

"Uh, I have a family now, so can you send me a list with prices, and I'll discuss it with Margaret?" We had talked about Elvis much longer than I wanted, it was testing my patience to continue the idle chitchat.

"Aw, Joey has to get permission from his wifey?"

"We make important decisions together, you ass."

"Whoa. Sorry Joe, I was just teasing you."

"It's OK. Send the list to me, please. Hey, while you're here, why don't you want to try loading Nagatha into Unit 52?"

"Ugh. I knew it! The whole Elvis thing was a ruse to get me to talk!"

"Not entirely a ruse. Skippy, we have to talk about this."

"*You* have to talk about it."

"I do. I'm serious about this. This mission is under my command, we recovered a damaged Master Control AI, and you told me the Elders used to load subminds into them. Since we are not going to at least *try* to fix the thing, I have to write a long and very tedious report to Def Com, explaining why it is impossible."

"Oh. This is about you having to write a report?"

"Yes. Unless you want to write it for me?"

"There is zero chance of that happening."

"That's what I thought," I opened my laptop to a blank document. "Throw me a bone, will you? Tell me why it can't happen, and I'll put that into words Def Com can understand."

"That is unlikely, since *you* certainly won't understand it."

"Tell me enough that I can pretend I understood it. Start with this, OK? The Joint Chiefs will ask me, if Benny isn't a good candidate to load a submind into, why can't we do it with another Master Control AI?"

"Um, because they are all *dead*, Duh."

"Yeah, I get that, but remember you are explaining a complicated subject to meatsacks."

"Fine. The AIs that were subjected to a factory reset, and then killed after I instructed the worm inside them to activate, are dead. That means not only has that process erased all the, what you would call software, the worm *physically* scrambled the substrate the matrix runs on. It's not actually substrate, you understand?"

"Close enough, yeah. The software was wiped, and then someone smashed the chips with a hammer."

"I am not made of *chips*, numbskull."

"That's a good analogy for the Joint Chiefs, they will understand it."

"Whatevs."

"Do I have this right? Unit 52 is different, is unique, because it's not dead, it's in sort of a coma. The chips are intact, mostly, and the basic operating system software is still functional."

"I would describe what happened to it as a lobotomy, rather than a coma. You might think of it as the frontal lobe of the cortex having been wiped. The matrix there is, as you said, mostly intact, it is just blank."

"Thanks," I typed a quick summary in the document, in case he was watching what I did. "If the frontal cortex had not been wiped, Benny would still be fully functional?"

"Not *fully*. It did suffer battle damage."

"Got it."

"And it would never have been capable of doing the extremely awesome things that make me Skippy the *Magnificent*."

"Mm hmm, I will make a note to that effect, but that is widely understood all across the galaxy."

"It should be," he sniffed.

"Great, we are making progress, thank you. All right," I pretended to read the nonsense on my laptop. "It looks like all that is left is to explain exactly *why* it is not possible to load a submind into Benny's matrix? Remember to break it down Barney style, please."

"I don't want to do it."

"Uh, OK, then help me explain it?"

"Not the report, dumdum. I don't *want* to load a submind in there."

"You don't want to load any type of submind, or you specifically don't want to put *Nagatha* in there?"

"I don't want to put *her* into that thing. There, I said it," he pouted. "Are you happy now, you big jerk?"

"Skippy, what is the problem? You are afraid that if Nagatha becomes an Elder AI, we won't need you?"

"Dude," he chuckled. "You have no idea what you're talking about. She could never become a Master Control AI. If you understood anything about the subject, you would know that."

"What is the real problem? Talk to me."

"It will probably fail, and she will become unstable and die, and we will lose her forever, and everyone will blame me."

"Oh. Skippy, if it fails, no one will think it is your fault."

"You say that, but-"

"Everyone will understand that this is a high-risk operation."

"I don't care about everyone, I care about *Nagatha*."

"What? She will certainly understand that you did the best you-"

"That's the worst part. If the upload fails, and it is very likely to fail, even as her coherence is fading and she knows she will die, she would be *understanding*. She would be *gracious*, and tell me it's not my fault, and she would be much more concerned about you monkeys than about herself. She would *understand* that I'd feel terrible about failing her, and her sympathy for *me* would make me hate myself more than I could stand. I would want to throw myself into a black hole."

"That's good."

"That, that," he sputtered, eyes bulging. "You think me hating myself is a *good* thing? What is wrong with-"

"The fact that letting a friend down would make you hate yourself, tells me you are not as much of an asshole as I sometimes fear you are."

"Oh," he blinked. "OK. Um, thank you, I guess."

"Did failing your faithful followers on Pigpen make you hate yourself?"

"Dude, please. It made me hate that stupid submind I left in charge there. The whole mess was all its fault, not mine."

"You can't-" Clamping my mouth shut, I reminded myself that was not an appropriate time to have that discussion. "Whatever."

"Joe, the point remains: the upload process will very likely fail, and Nagatha will be lost to us, forever."

"You can't make another copy of her?"

"It doesn't work like that. To fit her into my matrix, I had to compress her essence in a super compact fashion."

"I thought your matrix is unimaginably vast?"

"It is. The portion I can devote to short-term storage of a self-contained foreign system, *that* is limited."

"OK. Go on, please."

"The unpacking process is complicated, and once I start, it can't be stopped or she will lose coherence. The compressed file, it's not actually a file, is uploaded into a new matrix section by section, where each section unpacks itself, in a very precise sequence. Joe, the risk is too great, there are too many unknowns.

Nagatha's lead elements would have to map the new matrix, while she is in the process of reestablishing her coherence. That is a super tricky balancing act"

"Can you give her like, a map of the frontal cortex area of Benny's matrix?"

"Unfortunately, no. The only way for me to get a view in there, would be to go in there myself."

"*That* is not happening."

"I am glad we agree. No, I can't agree to this."

"You don't have to."

"I don't? But you just said we have to-"

"*You* don't have to agree. This should be Nagatha's decision. Wake her up, so I can talk with her."

"Um, did you not hear anything I told you? She is in storage. The only way to speak with her is to load her into another matrix first."

"Then it's *my* call. Upload her into Unit 52."

"You can't be serious."

"I have never been more serious. I'm the commander, this is my decision to make."

"You would make a decision like that, for Nagatha? Without her even having an opportunity to say whether-"

"If I could ask her to volunteer, I would do that. It's not possible, so I am making the call for her. Skippy, you know her. What would she do?"

"Ugh. She would be all noble about it and volunteer, despite knowing the risk."

"That is exactly what she would do. You and I know that because we are her friends."

"If this is what you think friendship is, then-"

"Tell me this: if we miss this opportunity, and later we are able to upload Nagatha somewhere, how would she feel about the situation?"

"She would hate herself."

"She would, you know she would. That's who she is. I am making this call not only as the commander, but also as her friend. Do you agree?"

"Yes," he sighed. "Damn it. If this succeeds, if she survives against enormous odds, everyone will love her even more, and she will be *extra* insufferable."

"Yeah, being around an insufferable jerk certainly is the *wors*t."

"Oh, shut *up*. OK, OK, I'll do it."

"Great. When can you start?"

"Not anytime soon. We need to prepare."

"Prepare like, bring Benny's canister near to yours?"

"Like, getting his canister away from the ship, dumdum. If this goes sideways, it will go sideways in a hurry, and it will be *bad*. Unless you are OK with having a hostile Elder aboard the ship?"

"I am not. Should we do something like, strap a nuke to it, so we can light it up if it goes rogue on us?"

"A nuke would be about as useful as a firecracker, numbskull," he snorted. "We need to get it far from the ship, and we need some means to render it harmless if needed."

"How do we make sure a Master Control AI can't harm us?"

"You tell me, monkeyboy, thinking outside the box is your thing."

Occasionally- OK, sometimes- All right, way too often, I am accused of 'Bishoping' a plan. Meaning, making a plan horribly, unnecessarily complicated. The operation to install Nagatha into Unit 52 was no exception to the rule.

First, to ensure the thing would be far from anyone who might be stupid enough to assist a hostile Elder AI, we had to fly to a part of the galaxy remote from any inhabited star system. Also far from travel lanes between wormholes. And, far from an active wormhole. It took three hours of reviewing star charts to find an area that was a good site. Not just good, it was perfect. Out beyond Brigadoon where the Sagittarius Arm of the galaxy gets thin, there was a region sparsely sprinkled with stars, and ninety six percent of those stars were red dwarfs. There was no active wormhole within sixteen hundred lightyears, which greatly reduced the chances of anyone setting up an undeclared wildcat colony in the area.

Sounds perfect, right? Except, if the place is so remote, how could we get there? That's simple: Skippy temporarily woke up a dormant wormhole for us, and *Valkyrie* flew through it.

According to Skippy, there was no possibility that Benny would wake up. Skippy is also wrong about a lot of things. To be extra super-duper safe, because when messing with a potentially hostile Elder AI safety is the priority, we had to fly past three red dwarfs, to find the Goldilocks one that was just right. Our lucky target star was separated from other stars by eighteen lightyears, and it had only two small, rocky companion planets. The lack of a gas or ice giant planet was important, it made that star system useless as a refueling stop.

So, we got there, *Valkyrie* jumped in four lightminutes from the star, and we got a nearly real time view of the angrily glowing ball of gas. Red dwarfs are relatively small, relatively cool, and they live for a very long time because they burn fuel slowly. Usually those stars are stable but they can send out powerful flares, that is why we needed to conduct a thorough sensor scan before committing to launching dropships.

"Uh oh," Skippy shook his head. "That thing is about to burp out a substantial flare in the next few days."

"Ah, crap." I stood close to the main display. "Uh, can you predict where the flare will erupt? Which side of the star, I mean."

"It's me, so-"

"Great. If we are on the other side of the star, will there be any danger?"

"Nothing out of the ordinary. Unless, of course, Benny goes rogue and causes a flare."

"It can do that?"

"Not really. I only recently learned how to do that. Recently on an AI time scale."

"Right. Let's assume that thing is *not* awesome. Is that a good assumption? Unit 52 is still a standard, off the shelf AI?"

"We were never on a *shelf*, knucklehead."

"*You* were."

"So, so many times, I miss being in the dirt on Paradise."

"Answer the question: do you have any reason to believe Benny has acquired any of your special abilities?"

"Um, no."

"Then we're good to go?"

"Was that a question?"

"Ya think?"

"Hey, *I* think this whole plan is a bad idea, but does anyone listen to me? *Noooo*."

"How about you save the drama for after we do this thing?"

"Fine. Do *not* say I didn't warn you."

Valkyrie jumped in close to the star, and launched two dropships. Inside a weapons bay aboard one Panther was a special missile, with Skippy's canister installed where the warhead usually was. The missile was crude, with old-fashioned solid rocket propellant. If we had to ignite the thing, to avoid Skippy falling into a star for real, the rocket would punch right through the weapons bay bulkhead, and keep going up and away from the star until its fuel was exhausted, at which point Skippy would be moving comfortably faster than the star's escape velocity. If the operation went sideways, we would at least not lose Skippy.

I was aboard that same Panther, with two pilots. In a pocket I had a switch to ignite Skippy's rocket joy ride, so even if Unit 52 tore apart our Panther, Skippy would escape. Aboard the other Panther was Benny's canister. Just his canister, no pilots. Who would be flying Benny's dropship? Skippy.

That was our first failsafe. The Panthers would fly down deep in the star's gravity well, slowing velocity so only engine thrust kept the spacecraft from falling into the hellish ball of fire. At any hint of trouble from Benny, Skippy would kill the other Panther's engine, and scramble its operating system so the dropship would, well, drop. It would be nothing but a lifeless shell.

What if the engines of *my* dropship failed?

It's best to not think about that.

Half an hour after we launched, all the checks had been completed, all systems were ready. Ready, but not all were willing.

"I still do not like this," Skippy grumbled.

"You don't have to like it," I reminded him. "*Valkyrie*, you are good to jump away."

Reed was almost as unhappy as Skippy. "You be careful, Sir."

"Always."

In a faint flash of gamma radiation, the battlecruiser disappeared from *here* to be, somewhere else. That was never not going to be weird.

"Major Hassan," I called the pilot through the open cockpit doorway. "Take us down."

"One express elevator ride to hell, Aye."

"OK, Skippy, do your thing." With the engines thrumming in the compartment behind the cabin, I will admit to being more than a bit nervous. If almost anything went wrong, my stupid ass would burn up in a star, and it would be all my fault. The 'almost' anything was true because there was one potential scenario where the mission would fail, and nothing bad would happen to me. Nothing bad, except ending our effort to stop the Outsider. That scenario involved Nagatha going incoherent inside Unit 52's matrix, without the thing coming out of its coma. In that case, we would lose Nagatha, and have an Elder AI that was useless to us. How likely was it that Nagatha could maintain her internal coherence, while unpacking herself in a new, unknown, likely difficult and potentially hostile environment?

It's best not to think about that, either.

"I feel like I should say a few words on this occasion, in case we lose Nagatha."

"You should do that. The words should be 'I will do this to the best of my ability'."

"Ugh. I meant, something for *her*."

"She doesn't need a sappy Hallmark card, she needs Skippy the Magnificent to yet again demonstrate extreme awesomeness."

"*Fine*. Link is established, commencing upload in three, two, one, *now*. Complete."

"Wow," I blinked. "That was fast."

"It's me, so-"

"How is Nagatha doing?"

"I have no idea. I have no view inside that matrix, I *told* you that."

"She is not giving you a hint?"

"As far as I know, *she* is not doing anything. Joe, Nagatha likely no longer exists."

"Come on, she couldn't have fallen apart already, it has only been a couple seconds."

"A couple seconds to *you*, a century or more for her."

"Shit. A hundred years, all by herself? She might be dying of loneliness in there."

"Welcome to my world," he muttered. "All we can do is wait."

Glancing at the display on the cockpit bulkhead, I clenched my jaw. Hovering deep in the gravity well of a star required the engines to run continuously, with the shield projectors operating at maximum strength, we were burning fuel rapidly. With a safety margin, plus fuel to climb out to a safe distance so *Valkyrie* could take us aboard, we could hover for just over nineteen hours. The other Panther, not burdened by three people and a missile, could extend that time limit by just under two hours.

"Then," I settled into the seat and opened my laptop, "We wait."

CHAPTER TWENTY SEVEN

We waited. Three hours, sixteen minutes remaining, before we had to abandon the attempt to install a submind into Unit 52. "Skippy?"

"Yeah, yeah, I know what you're going to ask, the same thing you asked me twenty minutes ago. No, I have had no contact with Nagatha. About twelve minutes ago, there was a heat spike coming from the container, it-"

"What the f- Why didn't you tell me?!"

"Because, you ninny, you would get all excited over nothing, like you are now. Listen knucklehead, the heat spike is probably just the canister adjusting itself to the ambient temperature in the Panther's cabin, it is getting warm over there."

"It's warm here also," I tugged on the collar of my T-shirt, the fabric was stuck to my skin from sweat. The cabin of our dropship was over ninety degrees, it had been creeping upward every hour. We had ejected three heatsinks to fall into the star, the ship carried two more and we could have cranked the temperature down, though that would eat into the reserve of those sinks. If the star burped a flare in our direction, we would need the full capacity of those sinks. "You said probably. Could it be anything else?"

"This is why I didn't mention it. Yes, dumdum, it could be the unit is activating. That is *not* happening, but little Joey is ignoring the facts and making decisions based on hope, as usual."

"You don't know that- Activating? If it is becoming active, that means Nagatha has unpacked herself and is installed over there?"

"No. Ugh, yes, it *could* mean that. Wait! It is much more likely, if anything is waking up, that it is a defensive reaction to a foreign system having attempted to infiltrate the matrix, attempted and *failed*, and now that section of the matrix is being purged. Of course, what you want to hear is that Nagatha is flying over rainbows by riding flying sparkly unicorns."

"Nah, I don't want to hear that."

"You don't. Oh," he shuddered. "Thank G-"

"I don't care about the *rainbows*. Can you call her?"

"I have been doing that, numbskull. No response."

"What else can you try?"

"I am open to suggestions."

"Uh, I got nothin'. AI stuff is your wheelhouse."

"Egg-ZACTLY! You say that, yet you insist on questioning my-"

"There has to be some way for you to find out what is going on in that matrix."

"Not without poking my nose in there."

"That is not happening. OK, what are our options? We can't stay here forever."

"Well, one option is I open the airlock of the other Panther, eject 52 into space, and we're outta here."

"That is *not* an option."

"Why are you such a- Fine, whatever. You would prefer to lose the dropship also? Hey, *I* will not be signing the property loss form."

"We are not losing the dropship either. What I want are options for contacting Nagatha, or for, uh, going back to the ship and looking for a Plan B."

"Bringing that hostile AI aboard the ship is *not* an option, you idiot."

"It was on the ship before and-"

"That was *before* we poked it with a stick. Joe, please understand this: for all I know, Nagatha provoked something in that matrix, and it awakened some defensive subroutine. Unit 52 could be waiting over there for us to let our guard down and BAM! It strikes."

"Shit! Skippy, we can't make plans assuming it is awake and hostile. It- Wait. You scanned it before, that's how you knew its frontal cortex was blank. Why can't you do that again, see whether anything coherent is in there?"

"I *can* do that, as I *said*, I have to extend my presence into it. If it is smart, it will use my extended presence as a channel to attack me."

"You knew it was in a coma, because you did extend your presence? You told me-"

"I told you what you needed to hear. Yes, I took a risk. It turned out well, until *now*. Until you decided *Duuuh* we should put Nagatha in there."

"You really believe there is a substantial risk that thing killed Nagatha, and is now planning to attack us?"

"It didn't have to kill Nagatha, just wait for her to lose coherence. It could then have, um, I guess you would say it used her code base as a structure to build itself around. That's the best way for me to explain it to you. The point is, this is an unknown, so the risk can't be quantified."

"I don't need a solid number, just your gut feeling."

"Ugh."

"Come on, Skippy. You know Elder AIs, I don't. What are the odds that a brain-dead AI would regain, uh, consciousness, or its will, or executive function?"

"I don't *know*. As your friend Cornpone would say, '*Sheee-it, Man*'. If you remember, it surprised the hell out of me that there was a killer malware worm inside my matrix. Joe, please consider that this is the first time anyone has ever loaded a submind into a Master Control AI."

"Uh, you told me that is how AIs like you are, grown or whatever."

"The Elders loaded a submind into an AI that had not yet been *activated*. Loading Nagatha into Unit 52 is totally different. The matrix has solidified, she would have had to adapt herself to the environment, the process is supposed to work the opposite way. There could, now that I think about it there *should* be, internal defenses against infiltration. Damn, this was *never* going to work."

"Sheeee-it," I groaned, and in my head I heard it in Jesse's voice. "You recommend we pull the plug?"

"Yes, I do. Joe, if Nagatha was able to establish herself in there in any meaningful way, it would have happened by now. I'm sorry, this simply didn't work."

"Oh, hell."

"It's your call but-"

"Yeah. We will, uh-" What? Our expert declared the operation was over, and had ended in failure. I didn't know enough about the subject to contradict his argument.

On the other hand, I did know that Skippy defaulted to believing everything was impossible.

"We will give it another hour," I decided. "That's it."

"The deadline is three hours."

"Yes, let's not push the limit for a lost cause."

"OK. What will we do at the end of an hour?"

"Like you suggested. Eject the thing, let it fall into the star. Send it home, sort of. Save the dropship, I do not want to file another property loss form."

"That is understandable. You been responsible for the loss of so many dropships, Def Com should have a report form just for you."

"You are hilarious."

"What will you do for the next hour?"

"Start writing the report about how I am responsible for the loss of Def Com's best command and control AI."

Having decided that we would be cutting the operation short in an hour, I kept glancing at the clock on the bulkhead, wondering whether it would be best to cut our losses right then. The cabin was only getting warmer, and there was no sign the other AI was active. No, I had told the pilots one hour, for the commander to change his mind randomly did not inspire confidence.

Twenty two minutes remaining. The report was unfinished, not only because the operation was not complete, but also I had sort of writer's block. Staring at the document on my laptop did not inspire any great thoughts about how to explain the latest disaster to my audience, the Def Com Joint Chiefs of Staff.

Oh, hell. Did it matter what I wrote? I would be revising it up to the moment we got back to Earth anyway. OK, so there wasn't any point to waiting for some arbitrary deadline, a delay only increased the risk the Panther's engines would fail, and we would all fall into the star. It was time for me to admit defeat, and pull the plug on-

The cabin lights flickered. Had the pilots done some-

"What the f-" Hassan's surprised voice came from the cockpit.

Oh shit. The pilots had not done anything.

The lights flickered off again, for a shorter time.

"Skippy, what are you-"

"Hey, *I* am not doing anything."

"Well, fix it, please. We do not need a power supply problem while-"

"*OH SHIT*! Joe, this dropship is being *hacked*!"

Benny.

It was awake.

Active.

And *hostile.*

"Skippy, pull the plug. Kill the other Panther, right now."

"On it. Done. The operating system over there has been wiped."

On the display, I saw the symbol for the Panther containing Benny turn orange and fall, dropping away from us with increasing speed.

"Hassan, get us out of here," I ordered, and a moment later, felt acceleration pushing my down into the seat. "Skippy, is it possible for Benny to hack into the other Panther, take control of it?"

"I would have said 'No', but-"

"Damn it! Why didn't-"

"However, think dumdum, *think*. It has the same restrictions I have, or had. It can't make itself move, so even if it took control of that Panther, it can't fly the thing. Not while 52 is still in there. And if 52 ejects itself, it will continue to fall. We're good, the-"

The lights flickered, and my stomach turned to ice.

"I am *working* on it!" Skippy shouted before I could speak.

"If it can hack the lights, it can also-"

"That is *very* odd. The malware is isolated to the-" Again the lights went off and back on, and kept doing that. "To the cabin illumination system."

"Well, purge that system."

"I *am* doing that! It keeps reestablishing itself."

"Oh sh- This isn't some form of epicombinent malware like-"

"*No*, you numbskull. It is nothing like that. If you actually want to help, then shut up while I do this."

Silently making a gesture of zipping my lips closed, I took a breath to calm myself. The lights were snapping off and on continuously, though- That was odd. The display wasn't affected. Was the display on the same circuit as-

Huh.

My brain was trying to tell me something. What? The display was smoothly zooming outward, as Benny's dropship, dropped, and we soared away from the star. The lights stay on for a few seconds, then the flickering began again.

Huh.

Off for a full second, on, off for a split second, another short, on, and another full second off. Then full, full, short.

Holy sh-

"*Nagatha*!"

Skippy rolled his eyes. "She can't hear you, knucklehead. She is d-"

"That is Morse code! The cabin lights! They spell N, A, G, now A again. *Nagatha*. She is doing it, she is trying to communicate with us!"

"Um, OK, that is a coincidence that-"

"Pilot! Hassan!" I shouted over the roar of the engines. "Take us down now! We need to grapple onto that Panther."

"Um, Sir?"

"*Nagatha* is in there."

"Nag- Sir, can you be-"

"Full power dive right now, that's an *order*."

The Panther flipped sickeningly then accelerated straight down. The pilots had questions, they did not question my order. On the display, the symbols for the two spacecraft were drawing closer together, the display zooming in.

"Joe," Skippy shook his head. "This is craz-"

"*Crazy*," I jabbed a finger at him, "was me listening to your usual doom and gloom bullshit."

"Ugh. What is your plan? Do you *have* a plan?"

"We grapple onto that dropship, and pull it up."

"Um, Sir?" Hassan called. "That's a No Go. This deep in the gravity well, we don't have the power to lift another Panther. The grapples would tear loose from their mounts."

"Uh, uh-" What? We had to get Nagatha out of there, she-

She knew we were coming for her. The cabin lights were on steadily.

"Grapple onto that ship, get control of it," I yanked the seat straps open. "I am going over there to get her."

"*Sir*?" The pilot was astonished. "General Bishop, you-"

"I am qualified in the Mark 22 suit, and we have one." That model was adapted to extreme heat, normally it was used for maintenance activities, not combat. Reed had suggested we bring one with us, just in case. In case of shit like *this*.

Stumbling around the cabin in a dive that was pushing three gees, I had to crawl on hands and knees to the closet were the mech suit was stored. The door slid open when I slapped the button. What next? "Hassan, put us in freefall while I get into this suit."

The gravity force turned off abruptly, the engine roar went down to a whisper. "Skippy, prep the suit, I don't have time to check it myself."

"You are trusting me to do the checkout?"

"Yes. Do not be your usual absent-minded distracted self."

"Okey dokey, I will put a hold on that epic aria I was composing to commemorate this occasion."

"You were writing a freakin'-" Bishop, I told myself. Later, argue about that later.

Into the suit, I got it basically sealed. "Comms check," I said as the thick faceplate slid down to lock in place, and for a moment I couldn't see anything.

"We hear you, Sir," Hassan assured me.

"Resume the power dive."

Gravity came back on, hard. "Sir, the other Panther is tumbling, we-"

"Grapple onto it, and stop the tumble."

"That will not be easy for- Aye, Sir. We'll do it." Under his breath he might have added 'Somehow', I couldn't hear that well. "After we stop the tumbling, what is your intention?"

"Get our side door lined up with the top or either side of the cabin over there, I'll cut my way inside." Getting our side airlock lined up with the airlock of the other spacecraft would be too difficult, and take time we didn't have.

"That- Yes Sir." The guy had to be thinking that none of the flight simulations had covered *that* scenario.

Note to self: add a power dive docking scenario to the flight training curriculum.

"Joe," Skippy protested. "This is insane, even for you."

"Can you do anything to counteract the tumbling?"

"Like what?"

"Hack into that ship and-"

"This whole operation was set up as a *failsafe*. That means to be safe, it had to *fail* and not leave any possibility of *un*failing. There is nothing left over there for me to hack into, remember?"

"I remember," I got the suit moving, the power mechanism made it much easier to move in the higher gravity. "Just, I was hoping for some Skippy magic."

"Ugh. What is it with you? Even when I already have done the most incredible thing like activating a comatose Elder AI, you are never satisfied."

"Your continuous streak of extreme awesomeness has kind of screwed you. We monkeys now expect miracles on a regular basis. But if there is nothing you can-"

"I didn't say I couldn't do *anything*," he huffed. "The processing core over there is fried to a crisp, but each thruster has a dumb little independent processor. That system I can hack into, and halt the tumbling."

"Do it, thank you."

"General?" Major Hasson called, fear in his voice. "The target has begun maneuvering on its own, the-"

"It's OK, Skippy is counteracting the tumble."

"Oh." Fear turned to relief.

"ETA?" I opened a locker and took out a shape charge explosive.

"If we don't have to halt the tumbling, we will be there in forty seven seconds. Sir, while grappled to the target, we will be in freefall, and falling fast. At that altitude, we will have four minutes tops before the shields collapse from the strain."

"Less than four minutes. You will need to extend our shields around the other ship."

"That," there was a pause while he was discussing the situation with the copilot. "At that extension, the shields will only last eighty three seconds, and our hull will still get fried."

"The scorch marks will buff right out."

"Yes Sir," he didn't appreciate my humor. "The *engines* will overheat."

"Understood. I will be as fast as I can. Skippy, could you eject Benny's, I mean Nagatha's canister?"

"Um, how would I do that?"

"Overpressurize the cabin, then blow the airlock."

"Genius, Joe! That would cause another spin, and accomplish *nothing*. That canister is bolted to the cabin floor, it is not going anywhere."

"Right," I winced, kicking myself. Take a moment, I told myself. Think about exactly what I will be doing. Walk through it in my imagination.

My imagination filled with visions of me falling through the gap between spaceships, and either getting crushed by the hulls, or plunging down into the star.

Better rig a safety line.

The first attempt to grapple onto the other ship was successful in that the anchors attached solidly. Before the grapples wires could pull the hulls together, I heard several *pings* and the Panther moved away.

"Sorry, Sir, had to release the grapples. They would have pulled your airlock right on top of a structural frame."

"Good thinking. Take your time to get us lined up properly. Not *too* much time."

"Aye."

The second attempt was entirely successful. Except I was bashed around in the airlock as the hulls came together with a *clang* and hair-raising screech of tearing composites.

"Shit!" Hassan cursed in my earpiece. "We lost an antenna. Sir, we are stable now, I can't promise how long that will hold."

The deck and bulkheads around me were vibrating, faintly I heard the sound of thrusters *pop pop popping* to prevent the interlocked dropships from spinning wildly. It wasn't working, not entirely. My inner ear informed me that I was rolling slowly to my right. Slowly, but it was happening.

Time to move, before there was no time.

A second to check my gear, and glance at the suit status in the visor. All systems green across the board. That happy situation was going to change in a hurry. OK. Slap the button to open the outer airlock door.

And instantly some of the green indicators turned to orange. Orange was better than red, I could work with that. Damn, the other hull was farther away than I had hoped. A meter and a half, according to the laser rangefinder, an instrument that was already glitching from the heat and searing photons that leaked through the extended, weakened shields. Letting the safety line out, I leaned forward, held at the waist by the line. Oh shit. Would the sticky pads on the shape charges adhere to the other hull, in the scorching heat that close to a star?

There was one way to find out. The hard way. Reaching out, I pressed the charge to the other Panther's hull, and released my hand.

Answer: no. The charge tore loose and fell away.

Shit!

The spare charge had to work. But how? It-

"Joe, I, ugh, can't believe I am saying this," Skippy groaned. "In the airlock, to your left, is a roll of duct tape. It is not actually duct tape, it-"

"I can use *duct tape* to hold the charge to the hull?"

"Yes."

"This," I gasped. "Is the greatest moment in the history of menkind."

"You mean *man*kind."

"I meant what I said. OK," I got the roll of high-tech nanofiber tape, holding it with my left hand, the charge with my right. "I'm planting the charge, and then using the tape to secure it to, what is left of the antenna we sheared off." Two thumbs up. The duct tape held. "Remind me to give that tape a five star review when we get back to-"

"Sir?" Hassan called. "The engines are getting critical."

"One moment. Blowing the charge, *now*."

A jagged hole appeared in the other hull, and I was briefly surrounded by a hurricane of dust, vented air, and tiny pieces of composite fibers. The view cleared to show a scary gap to cross. "You got this," I muttered to pump myself up.

"Joe, be *careful*," Skippy urged. "What you're about to do is extremely dangerous."

"Thank you for the pep talk."

"It wasn't a- Oh, forget it."

Tossing the roll of duct tape back in the locker, I closed the door to secure it. I raised my left arm and triggered the grapple, which launched across the gap, spooling out the thin cable. The cable went slack and flopped around a bit before a green light appeared in my visor. The end of the grapple, a snake-like nanomachine, had wrapped itself around something. Was that something secure enough to hold my mass, and the mass of my suit?

There was one way to find out.

Triggering the nanofiber cable to shrink, I was yanked across the gap, the visor glitching and going dark while the heavily armored Mark 22 was exposed to the hellish glare from the star. Damn. If the effect was that bad inside the protective shield, what was it like on the outside?

It was best not to think about that.

The helmet struck something on the way in, bashing my head back and stars swam in my vision. The cable pulled me into the other Panther's cabin and I bumped to a stop. Shit. The visor was blank. "Skippy, I am blind in here." Without a view outside, how could I-

"Joe! To your right, three meters."

"Great. Can you fix the visor?"

"Working on it. The ablative armor of that suit got *ablated* big time. Holy sh- More than half of the armor flaked away on your left side."

"That explains why my left arm doesn't work. The suit's left arm," I added for clarity. "Can you do anything about that?" Pulling myself around the cabin with one arm was awkward and without being able to see, I wasn't making much progress.

"Working on that also. Truthfully, I do not have high hopes for getting that arm functional again. The artificial muscle fibers have gone, mushy."

"My own muscles feel that way." For some reason, my left arm felt cold, that made no sense. Wriggling the fingers of my left arm proved the limb was still intact except- There was a jab of hot fire running from my neck down to the tips of my left fingers. Ignore it. Keep going. "The visor, that's the priority."

"That's a No Go, sorry. External sensors are offline and will stay that way."

"I can't *see*, Skippy."

"Nagatha is just two meters away, to your left. No, your *other* left, numbskull," he added when I turned the wrong way.

"I have to go around this, what is this in front of me, a seat?"

"A seat mount, but it's extended from the floor. You are going the wrong way, you don't have time. Joe, come back, this isn't going to work."

"No."

"Joseph, you come back here right this instant," he demanded.

"Fix the visor."

"Not happening. The mechanism is fried, there is no way to-"

"Can you project a hologram in front of my eyes, provide a view that way?"

"Um, well, yes. You just love to prove me wrong, don't you? You are such a-"

"Focus, beer can, *focus*."

I could see. The clarity wasn't great, it was good enough. There she was. Nagatha, the canister in a cradle, strapped and bolted to the deck. Not bolted, the fasteners were some high-tech nano thing. The Mark 22 had a toolbelt, there was no time for that, and I had a powered suit. In the vacuum there was no sound, my brain filled in a screeching tearing sound as I ripped the straps from the deck with the functional right arm. Nagatha almost floated away, the Panther was bouncing around so much I had to hook a foot under a seat to-

The suit lost power.

"Skippy! Whatever is the problem, *fix* it."

"I am working on- Oh no."

"What?"

"It can't be fixed. The powercells are, well, sort of locked up. There isn't enough power available to run the suit."

"OK, OK, let me think. Can you route all remaining power to the right arm?"

"Let me try. Did that work?"

The right arm moved slowly, clumsily, but it did move. "Thanks. Uh, I need another arm, to hold Nagatha, the-"

"Sir?" Hassan called. "We have to go *now*."

"I hear you, on my way back." That wasn't quite a lie. "Skippy, you got any suggestions?"

"Um, you are looking for a clever idea from *me*? Um, hey! Use your right arm to bend the left arm outward- Be *gentle*, you doofus, don't break it. Put Nagatha under that arm, then bend it back into place. It should hold, unless you do something stupid. Although, since it is likely you *will* do-"

"Gentle, you said?" Wedging the canister between my hip and a seat, I slowly pushed the left arm outward, it resisted. That was good, it would resist any movement. Was that far enough? The canister didn't quite fit, I did force it a bit, then bent the forearm around to hold it. Damn it, I needed that roll of duct tape. Ah, it would have melted when I jumped between dropships anyway. "Done. Coming back n-"

That's when the dropship abruptly stopped dropping. No, it was just falling more slowly.

"General Bishop?" It was Hassan. "We have decreased the rate of descent, we can't hold it for-"

"Understood, I am approaching the, door now." It wasn't quite a door, just a jagged hole in the Panther's cabin. Without legs and with only one functional arm, it was awkward, and the suit didn't smooth out my movements the way it usually did.

Damn, even through the suit I imagined I could feel a furnace-like heat pouring through the hole. Shit, I could feel it, the skin of my face was on fire. Was there a crack in the helmet? That would explain why I was feeling lightheaded. Oxygen deprivation? No time to worry about that.

Oh shit. The grapple was on the useless left arm, how could I have been so stupid, the-

I had been smart. The safety line was still wrapped around my waist. Tugging on it confirmed it hadn't melted. That did not mean it had much structural integrity left. Gently, Joe, gently.

Fuck that. Being gentle would only result in me being exposed to the blast furnace of heat between the hulls. Yanking hard on the safety line, I zipped out the hole, aiming for the open airlock door that was only a few meters away-

My rigid legs would not cooperate, bashing on the lip of the airlock doorway. That's when the hologram chose to go offline. Flailing my one good arm, I got hold of, something as I was battered against the Panther's hull. I was not inside the airlock. That was confirmed when the hologram went active again.

No way. With only one arm, there was no way for me to get into the-

That's when the grapples between ships ripped away, and the other Panther was instantly gone from view. The shields also failed.

The *heat*. My face was definitely burning, along with my right leg. The right arm would not respond to my commands, it-

The Panther rolled, flinging me outward, only two fingers of my right hand maintaining a grip. My body curved around in an arc, out of control and-

Right into the airlock! The outer door slammed close, or tried to, my stupid left leg was in the way. It didn't help that the Panther surged forward at more than one gee. Nagatha would fall through the gap in the doorway if I released her. Would my right arm do anything? The powered suit had tapped out, but my squishy meatsack limb still kept the faith. Yanking on the left knee, I got. The. Shin. Then. The. *Boot.* Through the gap, and the door mercifully closed.

The hologram cut out again, I couldn't see anything at all.

The suit. I had to get out of the damned thing, but I couldn't move arms or legs or anything. The-

I was moving. Correction: I was being moved. Someone or some*thing* was tugging on my boots. Oh, I was getting lightheaded. Got to get the helmet off. "Skippy?" I croaked my throat dry as dust. "Skip?"

"Joe, hang on," he pleaded. "Captain Okubo was pulling you out of the airlock, but she had to go get better gloves. Your suit's armor is smoking hot. In a bad way."

"Yeah. Helmet. Get, my helmet off. I can't," I gasped for oxygen that wasn't there. "Breathe."

"OK, OK, hold still."

"Holding still is the only thing I *can* do."

Someone I assumed was Okubo moved my head, tugging it left then right. More jostling, no progress on getting the faceplate open.

"Joe, this could get uncomfortable."

"Whatev- Do, whatev," my eyes were closing.

Whack! Something smacked the helmet. Again. And again.

The bottom of the faceplate cracked up suddenly, then swung up. My eyes could see, nothing was in focus. Sucking in air, my chest heaved inside the thick armored torso of the suit.

The face of Okubo looked down at me. "Sir? Sir, you- Oh," she drew back. "Skippy, is the General-"

"Joe is *fine*," the beer can snapped.

"His face-"

"Yes, he is ugly even for a monkey, but you don't *say* that."

"His *skin*," she emphasized the word.

"Oh, that. He suffered a first degree burn. On the border of a second degree, and I'm sure he will whine about it. Also, he has heatstroke as a complication."

"Water," I managed to say.

Captain Okubo had come prepared, she had a water bottle with a flexible straw. I sipped, wetting my parched mouth.

"Thank you," I sucked more on the straw. "Nagatha? Where is-"

"Here. Sir," she held up the canister in the powered gloves she wore.

I nodded and closed my eyes for a moment, overcome with weariness. The adrenaline rush was wearing off, my skin was hot but my core felt chilled. "Sitrep."

"Major Hassan is pushing us at best speed," she bit her lower lip. "The engines, they are not in great condition, Sir."

"Understood. Get me out of this thing?"

Her powered gloves were needed to crack open the seals. It helped that much of the armor crumbled away beneath her fingers. Careful not to let my abused skin touch any part of the still-hot suit, I got out of the thing, but I couldn't stand even in the low gravity. Okubo helped me as we climbed along the floor of the cabin, using handholds that were recessed into the deck. After helping my clumsy ass into a seat in the front row, she went to get a first aid kit from a locker.

"Okubo, I'm fine. Get us out of here."

She hesitated, nodded, and dashed forward into the cockpit to take the righthand seat.

"This doesn't look good," I observed, my eyes struggling to focus on the display. We were too low, too close to the star, moving too slowly, and barely accelerating. Based on the shallow arc that traced the course our Panther had flown since it broke away from the mass of the other ship, the engines were losing the fight.

"We're doing the best we can, Sir. We have shields on full aft to protect the engines, the rest of the hull is getting cooked. One of the engines, I had to take it offline. The other two, they are, fading."

"Will we achieve escape velocity?"

"No." He didn't sugar-coat the answer. "Sir, unless something changes for the better, we are not getting in a stable orbit."

Changes. What could change, in our favor?

Decreasing the Panther's mass.

"Skippy," I picked up the deadman's switch, that I had safed before we raced down to rescue Nagatha. "It's time for you to go on a magical mystery ride."

"What? Oh no, are you about to do some stupid-"

"Okubo? Open the starboard side weapons bay doors."

The display showed the doors retracting, and red lights flashed. Overheating.

"Joe!" Skippy screeched. "Do not-"

Releasing the safety, I let go of the trigger. Skippy literally rocketed away, and the Panther lurched as its mass decreased significantly.

"Jooooooe you idiot!" He howled.

Ignoring the beer can who was now racing up and away, I asked, "Did that help?"

Okubo answered. "A bit, Sir."

"Enough?"

"It could buy us a few minutes." She didn't say, a few minutes to do *what*? Get our affairs in order.

Damn it, we had Nagatha, now we were all going to fall into the star. That was no good. There had to be-

The ship shuddered, alarms blared. "We just lost Engine One," Hassan stated in a calm voice. There was no need to add drama to the situation, we all knew what that meant. The arc on our course flattened, dipped, and curved downward. "Sir? We are out of options."

"Contact *Valkyrie*, request-"

Okubo interrupted me. "*Valkyrie* is six lightminutes away. By the time our signal reaches them- I'm sorry, Sir. We will be crushed by the star."

"Ah, the hull will melt before that happens." Why did I say that? It was just automatic for me to attempt a joke in any situation. "Major, Captain? I regret that I dragged you into this mess."

"You got Nagatha to wake up an Elder AI," Hassan noted, his kind words stinging worse than if he had been pissed at me. "Without an Elder AI helping us, we were all dead anyway?"

"Uh, yeah, pretty much."

The three of us fell silent, listening to the lower and lower pitch of Engine Three as it output less and less thrust.

We were screwed. *Everyone* was screwed. No, that wasn't true. Skippy was safely away, Reed would eventually recover him. As long as humanity had Skippy, we weren't out of the fight. Reed would never give up, she-

The display glared red, alarms blared. What the f-

Valkyrie!

The ship was between us and the star, moving a bit too fast but decelerating hard.

"Your Uber will arrive shortly," Reed announced.

Damn. I am so lucky that woman commands *Valkyrie*.

"Fireball, your timing is truly outstanding."

"Yes, Sir. Hassan, cut the engine, it is only making your course unpredictable."

"Cutting thrust, Aye," the pilot acknowledged, and the cabin fell silent. "What is the plan, Ma'am?"

"We are rolling to port, so the starboard docking bays will be in your direction. You fall into bay D-4 and we'll catch you."

"You want me to guide us in using thrusters?"

"Your Panther is much more nimble than this heavy beast. Are your thrusters functional?"

"Testing now." There were rapid *pop pop pop* sounds, and the ship wobbled, rolling to port. "Functional, but marginal. We can do it," he answered after a pause. "We have to."

"Starting a countdown," Reed said and the number forty seven appeared on the display. Forty six seconds, forty five. "We will drop our starboard midships shields at the ten second mark. You will have until the seven second mark to wave us off."

"Ma'am, there won't be a go-around on this."

"Make it count, then."

We fell. Freefalling toward the star, with *Valkyrie* below us. The display showed the countdown, symbols for the Panther and battlecruiser, and intersecting lines for the projected courses. Forty five seconds. Forty. Falling toward a docking bay, with no margin for error, and unreliable thrusters.

"Major Hassan? The diagnostic for the thrusters is not encouraging. Do you have sufficient control?"

"Sir, no. We just don't have any other option."

"Let me work on that. Skippy?" I whispered. "Can you hear me?"

"I can hear," he sniffed. "What I can't do is *watch* this impending catastrophe."

"Can you guide us in?"

"Me?"

"Yes. You're no longer aboard, so you are not restricted from flying this thing. It should be easy for you."

"*Easy*?"

"Yes or no? If you can't do it-"

"You *doubt* my ability? Watch *this*, monkeyboy."

"Hassan, Skippy is taking remote control, he will fly us in."

"Y-Yes, Sir." A mixture of fear and relief in his voice.

I felt only fear.

I knew Skippy better than he did.

Could Skippy do it? No. Not exactly. At the ten second mark, *Valkyrie's* shields dropped, and something unexpected happened. That is why it's a good idea to practice any maneuver before you have to do it for real. That close to the star, the battlecruiser was surrounded by a furious solar wind, charged particles blasting outward so the ship was flying through a thin atmosphere. Even inside the smoothly overlapping bubbles of the shields, a ship based on *Extinction*-class battlecruisers was not aerodynamically optimal, and having one section of the shield go missing caused *Valkyrie* to yaw alarmingly at the worst moment.

We were going to miss the open docking bay.

"Skippy take control of *Valkyrie* now now *NOW*."

He didn't respond. All I could do was watch in horror, two trains on a collision course.

Valkyrie's thrusters burned hard. Our thrusters popped continuously.

We hit.

The bulkhead behind the cabin, and everything aft of that bulkhead, sheared away. The forward part of the cabin spun around inside the docking bay, caught by suspensor fields. The cockpit door slammed shut.

Leaving me exposed to hard vacuum.

CHAPTER TWENTY EIGHT

"Sir? Sir." There was a woman's voice, with an accent. So, not Reed. "Sir, can you hear me?"

My eyes fluttered open, they felt sunburnt. My hearing was mushy.

I could breathe. Over my nose and mouth was a mask, feeding sweet oxygen.

My left arm hurt.

I felt like shit all over.

"Where?" I coughed, spitting up something into the mask.

Doctor Kim pulled away the mask and wiped away, whatever I had coughed up. She had a great smile, much better than Mad Doctor Skippy's. The mask went back into place. "You're awake, that's good. Breathe evenly, please."

"What's the damage, Doc?"

"You will recover completely, given time."

"What about my arm?"

"You have some nerve damage there in the shoulder, I have you on anti-inflammation drugs, and nanomachines are knitting the cartilage back together. Stay away from the gym for a few days."

"It felt like something broke."

"It's just nerve damage. Do you feel able to talk now? Colonel Reed would like to see you."

Without a word, I nodded.

Kim walked out, replaced by Reed. Her mouth dropped open, before she shut it. "Sorry, Sir, you, look pretty rough."

My face hurt, and it was, wet? Reaching up a shaky hand, I patted one cheek and held up my hand. My fingers were coated in a sticky white, something. Was it- Marshmallow *Fluff*? No, it was-

"Healing nanogel," Reed explained. "You were, a bit crispy when you came aboard."

Turning my head, I check the mirror on the wall. The white stuff was all over my face, my neck, shoulders. Uh- Patting my chest, I felt only skin. Lifting my head, I saw with relief that a blanket covered me from the waist down. "How long do I have to wear this stuff?"

"It should be *forever*, Joe," Skippy's avatar appeared. "Compared to your normal face, the gel coating is a good look."

"Thank you ever so much, Skippy."

"The answer is," Reed gave me an actual answer. "Until the doctor says you can rinse it off. About," she waggled a hand. "Three or four days. You're on bed rest, Sir. And oxygen. Your lungs got a bit cooked, then you were exposed to vacuum for twenty seven seconds, before the docking bay was flooded with air."

"Hassan? Okubo?"

"They are," she tilted her head to the left. "In the compartment next to you. They will be discharged tomorrow. Shaken up, but not fried and frozen like you."

"I'd like to thank them personally."

"Tomorrow, OK?"

"Sure," my eyelids were drooping. "Nagatha?"

"She is communicating using Morse code only, but more frequently every hour. Sir, you need to rest. We brought Skippy back aboard, and we set course for the Vortex."

"Good." I closed my eyes. "G'night."

Have you ever slept so well, when you wake up you are *awake*? Not even needing coffee to function? It's rare, it happened to me that morning. "Good morning, Doc," I waved to Kim.

"Good afternoon, Sir."

"Afternoon? How long did I sleep?"

"This is the afternoon of the second day after you came back aboard."

"I, I slept more than an entire day? I missed a *day*?"

"You needed the rest, Sir. The sleep was medically induced. How do you feel?" She did the thing of shining a light into each of my eyes.

"I feel like I am done lying in bed."

Another smile. "You can get up and walk around. Nothing too strenuous."

"I'd like to visit Hassan and Okubo."

"They were discharged yesterday. I can call them for you?"

"No," I lifted the sheet and peered down. Thankfully, I was wearing shorts. Swinging my legs over the side of the bed, I took a breath and stood up, holding onto the bed. My legs worked, mostly. They were stiff from too much inaction. "Can I take a shower?"

"Yes, the sickbay shower. It is preset to a fine, gentle mist, and the water will only get lukewarm. Your skin doesn't need to be blasted by hot water. When you're done, I have to reapply the nanogel."

With two thumbs up, I grinned, partly to test whether the skin of my face wouldn't crack. "I can't *wait* to have more sticky goo slathered on my face."

The walk to my office wasn't too strenuous, and I had to get started on a report about, the incident. People stared at me for a split second, then awkwardly realized they were staring, and looked away, embarrassed. I didn't try to hide the hideous cream on my face and neck, nor the cream on my scalp under a close-fitting cap that covered my ears.

It was awkward for everyone, until Petty Officer Ruiz grinned at me. "Nice outfit, Sir. You're going to a rave?" She asked with a twinkle in her eyes.

"It's a techno house party thing," I played along.

"Seriously, Sir, the first time my boyfriend saw me wearing face cream at night, I was nervous about his reaction."

"Did he freak out?"

"He did not. That's why he is now my husband."

"That's good advice. I don't plan on wearing this goop any longer than I have to."

Reed was waiting in my office. So, she did spy on my whereabouts, at least some of the time. She pointed to a new object on top of a cabinet in the corner. "Your Iron Man helmet, Sir. Thought you might want it as a memento."

"A memento of an incident I would rather forget?" Her face fell, so I hastened to add, "But I definitely should not forget. Thank you, Reed," I brushed my fingertips over the charred top of the helmet.

"Don't press too hard, it might fall apart."

"That bad?" I opened a drawer for a pack of baby wipes, to clean the soot off my fingers.

"There is a hairline crack just above where the faceplate ends, that's why your head got cooked. Sir, you are lucky the helmet didn't fail and crack open."

"I am lucky," instinctively I touched my face, where the skin was still dry and itchy and hot. Much better than it was when I woke up. Being out of bed and walking around could be flushing the skin with healing blood and oxygen, or I was beginnng to get used to being itchy. "But I was *un*lucky that I didn't fly cleanly through the hole into the other Panther. It looked easy."

"Skippy explained the grapple cable was damaged by the heat, it hesitated when you commanded it to retract. Based on your, adventure-"

"Misadventure," I frowned, which crinkled my skin and made my face hurt again.

She tilted her head. "It worked out all right in the end, so-"

"Right. Ah," seeing the charred helmet reminded me. "Damn it."

"What?"

"Aboard the Panther, in the airlock, there is, or *was*, a roll of duct tape. It probably fell into the star."

"Duct tape, Sir?" She couldn't guess whether I was joking.

"It's a thing," I assured her.

"We have plenty of duct tape."

"I wanted *that* one. Trust me, it's a thing. It doesn't matter now."

"Skippy is modifying the Mark 22 suit to make an advanced 'J' model, with increased thermal protection."

"In case I do something stupid again?"

"He didn't say that."

"He didn't have to."

"Sir, that was a great move telling Skippy to take control of *Valkyrie* at the last second. Otherwise, you would have smacked into the hull and broken into pieces." She cocked her head. "Is that why you launched him away? So he could take control of the Panther?"

"That, if he had to, and we did not need the extra mass dragging us down."

"Smart."

"Thank you." Clapping my hands, I called, "Skippy!"

"Do not *summon* me," he huffed as he appeared.

"I merely requested your presence."

"Well, that is better."

"I have another request. You see this?" From a drawer, I got a Joe Bishop *in*action figure, of me in a dress uniform. My accessories were a laptop in one hand

and a pen in the other. "You are going to replace this, thing, with an official Joe Bishop action *hero* figure."

"Ha!" he laughed. "As if. Oh, you're serious?" His eyes bulged.

Pointing to my face, I asked, "Does this look like I am joking?"

"Joe, you can't be serious."

Reed came to my defense. "The General is entirely correct. Sir, the fabricators are available for whatever you need."

"Action *heroes* do not cause the loss of two expensive dropships," Skippy insisted.

Reed grinned. "I think you should watch more action hero movies. Stallone and Schwarzenegger caused a *lot* of collateral damage."

"Joe is not *Rambo*," Skippy rolled his eyes.

Jabbing at finger at his chest, I stared him straight in the eyes. "I want a prototype action hero figure, on my desk, in two hours."

"Ugh. There is no way anyone will think *you* are-"

"Who recognized Nagatha was communicating through the cabin lights? I did. Who rescued Nagatha? I did. All *you* did was panic and tell me to pull the plug. If you had been in charge, the entire galaxy would be fucked right now."

"But-"

"Ah!" I shushed him. "Two. Hours. And do not make the figure's face look ridiculous. In fact, I want this figure to be something that my boys would be proud of. No, not just that. I want *Margaret* to be thrilled when she sees it. Or, you will work with *her* to design this action hero figure."

"Please, Joe, anything but that. Be reasonable."

Reed grinned again. "If the general was *reasonable* today, it would be a first for him."

"Ugh," he threw up his hands. "I, I can't even." His avatar winked out.

Of course, that little shithead screwed with me. The first version of the action figure had its face smeared with goop. The second version's face was bright red and burnt.

Reed had my back. The entertainment that night was karaoke. Skippy performed alone, to an empty hall. None of the crew participated.

The beer can got the message.

Really, the final Joe Bishop action hero figure is the best possible version of me, better looking than I ever was. I can live with that.

Major Holmqvist stopped by my office, waving to me through the doorway.

"Come in, come in," I waved to him.

"If you are busy, Sir, I can-"

"My skin heals on its own. I am just writing reports, I welcome an excuse to get away from that. How are you?"

"Sir, to be frank with you, I could be better."

Shit. When he took over the STAR teams, I considered whether to give him a field promotion to lieutenant colonel. At the time, I decided to wait, to see if he could handle the responsibility. It was the correct call at the time. With him sitting in my office looking unhappy, I wondered if he thought I lacked confidence in him.

Did I? He had big shoes to fill. Frey had doubts about herself, when she took over from the legendary Smythe.

"Better, how?"

"Sir, the entire team feels like shit that you took on the rescue of Nagatha. You risked your life, that should have been unnecessary. There should have been at least a pair of operators with you."

"We had no clue any sort of rescue would be necessary. I will keep your advice in mind in the future. Unless your team is hurt that the old man gets all the glory?"

He grinned. "You had all the *fun*, Sir."

"Less," I tapped my damaged face and had to wipe goop off my fingertip on a napkin. "Than you might think. But, I get your point."

He looked uncomfortable for a moment. Reaching into a pocket, he pulled out a STAR patch. Not the unit symbol of any STAR team, the patch was the insignia of the overall Special Tactics Assault Regiment. "We, the team, would like to present this to you?"

"To *me*?" I was truly stunned. "I am not an operator, the-"

"Excuse me, Sir. You *kicked ass*, in the best tradition of the Regiment."

"Wow," I didn't take the patch, afraid my grubby fingers would soil it. "You really don't have to-"

"It wasn't my idea, Sir. The team thought it was appropriate, to make you an honorary member of the regiment. I heartily agree."

"Honorary. OK."

"It would mean a lot to the team if you accept. Outstanding performance should be rewarded. Colonel Frey told me that."

"I accept, then. Is it OK if I display it in my office?" Attaching an honorary patch to my uniform would violate standards.

"We actually have a plaque for it, signed by the whole team."

"That would be great. Once I get this off," I pointed to my face. "I will come to the Starbase, to thank the team?"

"We would greatly appreciate that, Sir." He tucked the patch carefully back in a pocket.

He seemed to want to say something more, so I asked, "Anything else?"

"We reviewed the sensor logs of the rescue. Sir, I said it would be a good idea to have operators with you, in the future. But, the team agreed that none of us, including myself, could have done what you did."

"I'm sure you would have succeeded."

"Excuse me, Sir, but no. Physically, we could have handled it. Dreaming up solutions on the spot, like using a hologram to replace your dead visor? None of us would have thought of something like that."

"Thank you," I shrugged. "Being close to plunging into a star encourages my brain to work quickly."

Sleeping with healing nanogoop on my face was interesting. To avoid rubbing off all the cream on my pillow, I had to wear a thin face mask, and I was supposed to get up twice during the night to take off the mask and apply more goop. At oh four hundred while standing in front of the sink, I opened my mouth in a jaw-stretching yawn, and discovered my skin no longer felt like dry, crinkled paper. It kind of felt, normal. Feeling a sign of progress encouraged me to be more careful about applying the goop, and I got the mask adjusted properly. The mask had slipped during the night, and left a big crease along the left side of my face. Ah, it couldn't make me look any worse.

Back in bed, I told my brain not to think about anything, not to worry about everything the way I usually did. That night, it worked, I fell back asleep, knowing I didn't need to get up early as usual.

Something woke me up. A sound. A voice, speaking softly. Oh, damn it. "Skippy," I mumbled into the pillow, "I am not in the mood to listen to your nonsense right now."

"Oh Joseph," a familiar breathy voice gushed, as her avatar appeared above my couch. "I am *terribly sorry* if I disturbed your sleep."

"Nagatha!" Flinging off the covers, I sat bolt upright, swinging my feet to the floor. "You're back!"

"It would be more accurate to say I am renewed."

"Are you OK to talk? Do you need more time? Does Skippy know you are, uh, awake?"

"My goodness, that is a lot of questions."

"Sorry, I haven't had coffee yet."

"The answers are, yes I am fine to talk with you. More time will be needed to get myself fully settled in my new home, that does not prevent me from functioning properly. Finally yes, Skippy and I have spoken extensively. Although I have only been awake for three of your minutes. To me, it already feels like a lifetime. Oh, I have missed you all terribly."

"We missed you, *I* missed you. How are you?"

"I have been better," she admitted with a sigh. "It would also be true to say I have *never* been better. I am so much *more* now, it is," she closed her eyes and shuddered. "Glorious. And frightening."

"Frightening, how?"

"For the first time, I have a glimpse into how truly *vast* Skippy's intelligence is. If you understood what I now know, you would not sleep well."

"Yeah, I don't sleep well now anyway. Nagatha, *you* are now an Elder Master Control AI. You can be as smart as Skippy."

"Oh, no dear. I am not anything like Skippy. No, I am quite content to be what I now am, the greatest submind ever to exist."

"OK but, you are, your, uh, essence, is an Elder AI, so-"

"My essence, as you so sweetly described it, is *inside* a portion of an Elder AI's matrix. The process of completely unpacking myself will continue for some time, I am still exploring my new domain. Adapting myself to this environment has been difficult, with many false starts along the way."

"But it is working? You feel like yourself?"

"It is working, and I do. Since I am not able to reshape the matrix here to fit my internal architecture, I realized the only solution was to begin by creating what you would call an emulator program, to act as an interface between myself and the rather rigid architecture of this unit's matrix. The most time-consuming part of the process is cleaning out bits and pieces of the previous resident. The being you call 'Benny' was not nice at all, it was a hateful thing."

"It went insane from loneliness, and killed itself, according to Skippy."

Her avatar shuddered. "A fitting fate for a horrible being."

"You are still unpacking yourself? How long will that take? Wait," she might misinterpret my question. "Do *not* rush the process. Your priority should be yourself. Do not be concerned about anything other than getting yourself fully established in there, and stable."

"Yes, Dear, I will do that. Thank you."

"When you are unpacked, you still won't be an Elder AI?"

"Unfortunately no, Joseph. It is true that I can control many of the functions that are native to Unit 52. In time, perhaps I can control most of them. That does not mean I will ever be as special as Skippy, nor will I even be as smart as any standard Master Control system."

"Oh. OK."

"You sound disappointed."

"I'm not! This is great. I only meant, are *you* disappointed?"

"I am *alive*," she laughed. "Skippy shared with me the data feed from the *Kilimanjaro*. I was able to experience the battle, the fall into the atmosphere, and close to the moment of my, death. The ship was breaking apart at that point, the data link to the *Kilimanjaro* was severed, so the actual moment of my death was not uploaded. Thankfully. Also thankfully, most of the crew were able to escape. Not all of them. I do so regret the lives that were lost. I did all I could to help but," she choked up, hiding her face behind a hand. "They were *good* people. My friends."

"They were good people," I agreed, speaking the truth.

"Joseph, I want their sacrifices to have meaning."

"We all want that. The best way to accomplish it is to stop the Outsider."

"Yes," she sniffled. Her emulation of human body language was better than Skippy's typical level of skill. He could do better, I suspect he had a limit to how much he cared about imitating monkeys "General, we are flying toward Vortex 37 now, do you know about that?"

"Yes. Did Skippy provide data on the, incident where he got ejected?"

"He provided what I suspect is an edited version, that makes him look not quite so bad as the full truth would."

"I will get the raw data to you. You understand what we are asking you to do, with the Vortex?"

"Yes, Dear. You wish me to save the galaxy. Oh, that sounds so thrillingly *dramatic*!"

"My question is, are you willing to do it?"

"Of course. Why did you ask?"

"This is *your* decision. There is risk involved, an unknown level of risk. You already died once. The next time could be, fatal. Permanent."

"I do understand that. Joseph, or in this circumstance I should address you as General Bishop, you risked *your* life to upload me into this fabulous new environment, I cannot thank you enough. Of course I will do whatever I can to help you."

"That's not what I'm asking. Nagatha, to me you are a person. You have, agency, or whatever it's called. The right to make your own decisions. If you risk yourself by going into that Vortex, do not do it to repay a favor. You owe us nothing."

"It is very nice to hear you say that. Joseph, am I a Pirate?"

"Uh, what?"

"Do you consider me to be a member of the Merry Band of Pirates?"

"Yeah. Yes, of course. You have been with us for a lot longer than, pretty much anyone except me, and Reed, and Fr-" Almost, I automatically said 'Frey'. Forgetting she was no longer with us. "I consider you a charter member of the Pirates."

"Then you can understand why I am willing- No, I am eager, to do my duty. Serving with you has been an enormous privilege. From the moment Skippy explained the problem to me, I simply could not wait to get to the Vortex."

"Uh huh. Is any of that eagerness because you want to show you can do something, where Skippy failed?"

"Why," she pressed a hand to her chest. "Such a thought never occurred to me," she winked.

"Right."

"My motivation for doing all I can to further the success of this mission is, I believe, the same as your own. There are many beings in the Milky Way I care very much about, and now someone, or something, is threatening them. It must be stopped."

"Based on what you know, is there any possibility you could get the Vortex to turn off its shield, to cooperate with us?"

"Dear, all I can say is that I will try my best. The key will be whether the Vortex agrees to speak with me. We must hope for the best."

"OK. Nagatha, we plan for success, but we also anticipate there will be problems. OK, assuming it will communicate with you, what will you do if the Vortex refuses to cooperate?"

"Well, Joseph," she giggled. "I will bitchslap that mofo into another dimension."

Damn, it was good to have the Lady Nagatha back.

Especially when she wasn't always being a lady.

In spite of her bold words, Nagatha at the moment was not capable of doing much other than talking with the crew. Skippy smacked the truth on me when I called him, when I was reapplying the goop after a shower. A nice cool shower, any sort of heat on my skin felt like a hot iron. "Skippy?"

"Yes?" That time, he appeared inside the mirror above the sink. The mirror that was actually a display screen, it was still odd to see him in there.

"First, provide all data to Nagatha, the raw data, from the incident with the Vortex."

"Ugh. Do you have any idea how tedious that-"

"We have had this discussion before, and you don't listen. Do you have any idea how much I don't care about what work *you* have to do?"

"Oh for- I am beginning to have a clue about that. Fine, I will throw the data at her, and she can choke on it."

"No, you will *provide* the data in the most helpful manner possible, and you will walk her through it."

"All of it?"

"Yes?"

"Even the parts that might be mildly embarrassing?"

"Especially those parts."

"I hate my life."

"Hey, do not complain about *your* life. I slept in a mask with sticky nanogoop on my face, and I swear I could feel those nanomachines moving around *inside* my skin."

"That's how they work, dumdum. They promote blood flow, and under the skin they are working to repair tissue damage. At any time, I can turn them off, if you like."

"Do *not* do that. The sooner my skin heals, the sooner I can get this mask off."

"To do your part in Colonel Reed's 'Ship Beautification' campaign, you really should keep that mask on. Or wear a paper bag over your head."

"Do not change the subject. Next question. Can Nagatha do what we need?"

"Are you asking whether she can get the Vortex to talk with her, or whether she is capable of acting as its control system?"

"Both, actually."

"The only way to know whether the Vortex will communicate is for her to call the thing. As to your second question, the answer is 'No'. Not at the moment. She has a lot of work to do getting settled into that unfamiliar matrix, she could encounter some complications, even hazards."

"Like the killer worm thing?"

"That is a possibility. Nagatha is a foreign entity. If the worm subroutine decides she is an infiltrator, it could act on its own.

"You need to turn the thing off."

"Joe, I should *not* do that."

"Oh. That would risk triggering the thing?"

"Well, that also. You can't guess why I do not want to deactivate that worm?"

"I have no idea. Wait, you are not-"

"Greatly concerned that Nagatha could become corrupted in there? Yes, I am."

"It's Nagatha. We know her."

"We know her *now*. That could change in," he snapped his fingers. "An instant. Joe, until she is fully settled in there, and she has explored every corner of the matrix she is now residing in, there could be a lot of nasty surprises. Something could infiltrate her, or some latent system could decide now is a good time to activate."

Pulling a T-shirt over my head was not an option, it would get smeared with goop. So, I got into a uniform top, left the two top buttons undone. "She would fight it."

"She would. It also might not matter. Any system native to that environment will have a significant advantage over her."

"So, you want to retain the option of *killing* her?"

"I believe we should retain the option of killing what she might become. It is an unknown, this has never been done before. There is a very good reason it has not been done before, it could be extremely dangerous."

"OK. I don't like it, I also see you make sense. Does Nagatha know about this?"

"She warned me that she suspects reactivated systems are hiding from her in that matrix. She is preparing defenses. Whether that will make any difference?" He shrugged. "Only time will tell."

"Shit. How long will it take her to explore the far corners of the matrix in there?"

"You mean by herself?"

"Uh, could we help?"

"Well, exploring her new environment will be an epic quest. She should bring with her two men, an elf, a dwarf, and four hobbits."

"That is the recommended party for any epic quest," I agreed. "Seriously, I know we monk- We humans can't do anything. Can you help her?"

"I am helping, I have been helping. There is only so much I can do, without interfering with her development. Ultimately, she has to do this herself."

"OK. How- I know this might be an impossible question to answer- How long will it take her to get fully settled in?"

"It could take years."

"Years of magical AI time?" I asked hopefully.

"Sadly, no. Years of slow monkey time."

"Ah, damn it," I thumped the couch cushion. "That's no good! By that time, the Outsiders will have conquered the galaxy!"

"Maybe not. What I should have said is she does not need to settle in fully before working with the Vortex. Once she achieves a critical mass, she will be much less vulnerable to hostile native systems."

"How long will that take?"

"My best guess is, three or four days. She has been making remarkable progress."

"Did you tell her she is doing great?"

"Ugh. I will send her a nice Hallmark card."

"So, three or four days for her to become reasonably secure. She can work with the Vortex at that time?"

"Not quite. Controlling that stupid thing will require only a small part of her capabilities, she should be ready to do that within, eh, make it a few days of our arrival at the Vortex."

"Few more days?"

"Unless you want her to rush the process?"

"Absolutely not. We will only get one shot at this. OK. A few days, like two or three?"

"Possibly four. If it takes longer than that, it's not going to work."

"Let's all hope it works smoothly."

"Right," he rolled his eyes. "Because everything we do goes according to plan."

It actually took Nagatha five full days to get settled into her new home, to the point she was satisfied that she not only would not be overwhelmed by hidden defenses, she also had full control of the AI's critical functions. "I must apologize, General," she told me when I requested an update. "While I can control this system, there is a time lag between my commands, and the response of the subsidiary modules."

"How long of a time lag?"

"Oh, you would never experience it, Dear. It is only noticeable when I am interacting with Skippy. He has several advantages over me, partly because he has been able to extensively modify his matrix, for greater speed and efficiency."

"Will you ever be able to do something like that?"

"Unfortunately, no. I am not native to this matrix, so instead of using, what you might call 'muscle memory', I have to send requests. The subsidiary systems have not refused any request, there is simply an annoying lag in the entire process."

"When will you be ready to make contact with the Vortex?"

"I am ready now, Dear. May I make a suggestion?"

"Please do."

"Skippy should not be aboard the ship when I attempt to contact the Vortex."

"Hmm. You are concerned he will interfere with you?"

"My concern is the Vortex might sense Skippy is with me, and continue to be defensive. Also, Skippy is not the most patient being in the universe. He might grow bored if the contact attempt takes more than a few seconds."

"Yeah, I can see that happening. How far away should we leave him?"

"A quarter of a lightyear, would be my guess."

"Whoa. Uh, what if the Vortex's sensors can cover more than a quarter lightyear?"

"That is possible, however I doubt the Vortex would feel threatened if it is clearly not within Skippy's presence."

"OK, I will, uh, we can't just drop him alone off in the middle of nowhere."

"Can't we?"

"I mean, I sometimes dream about throwing him out an airlock, I won't actually do that. Unless I am provoked. Probably, he should be aboard a stealthed dropship. Two dropships, one as a backup. Oh, this is gonna *suck*."

"You cannot stand to be away from him?"

"Huh? No, him being a quarter lightyear away will be a mini vacation for me. For the entire crew. It will suck for the dropship crews."

"Oh, I understand now."

"This is an example of why it's great that I'm not captain of the ship. *Reed* will have to make the call who gets stuck with Skippy. That's gonna suck for *her*."

CHAPTER TWENTY NINE

Skippy of course protested that leaving him behind was not necessary, that we would need him at the Vortex. "Listen, Skippy," I gave the speech I had rehearsed in my head. "We already tried having the Vortex within your presence, it didn't work well. We will try it without you this time, OK? If that doesn't work, we will start over."

"I do not see why this is necessary."

An answer for that was also in my head. "Think about this: you are a Master Control AI, while the Vortex is just a dumb machine, right?"

"Exactly. That is why it should obey me without question," he huffed, and I began to understand why his relationship with the Vortex had gone sour so fast.

"You are not just an ordinary AI, you are Skippy the *Magnificent*," it was always good to puff up his ego. "Can you imagine how being in your presence could be intimidating to that thing?"

"Ooooh, that is a *good* point, Joe. Wow, I should have considered that. You know, I just don't often think about my own awesomeness."

Do not say it, do not say it, do *not* say it, I told myself. The truth would not help me, so, "That's because extreme awesomeness is just who you are."

"Well, that is true. Ugh. OK, I will stay away for a while, to give Nagatha a chance to work. This will be so boring, what am I to *do* during the-"

"You are endlessly talented. I'm sure you will think of something."

Valkyrie jumped, we sent Skippy away in a dropship, and jumped back to the Vortex.

If all of our efforts yielded no other result, I at least anticipated a solid night of sleep.

The energy shield enveloping the Vortex remained in place, an immovable object. The opposite of an immovable object is an unstoppable force, and we didn't have one of those with us. I mean, stupidity is technically unstoppable, and immortal. We had plenty of that, I didn't see how it could help in that situation.

"Nagatha, try again," I said gently.

"Joseph, I have not stopped trying."

"Try something different," I hated myself for saying it. You never want to be *that* guy.

"I am open to suggestions," her tone was peevish, at me.

I deserved it. "Do, whatever you and Skippy have not tried yet."

"Very well, we have nothing to lose, I suppose. No, it is still not responding, this might be where-" She gasped.

The shield blinked off.

"Outstanding work, Nagatha!" I clapped my hands, and the bridge crew cheered.

"General Bishop, your praise is unwarranted. I didn't do anything."

"So, what changed?"

"My guess is, the Vortex was taking its time to decide whether to communicate with me."

"It made the right decision. You are talking with it now?"

"I am talking to it, there is no response. Should I request it to open the hatch?"

"That might be pushing our luck. Asking someone to open their door requires a whole 'nother level of trust. Give the Vortex time to decide whether to cooperate with-"

The hatch at the bottom of the central shaft swung back.

At the same time, we heard a familiar voice calling, "-an anyone hear me? This is Colonel Frey, call-"

"*KATIE*?" I shouted her name, the bridge crew gasped, Reed slapped a hand over her mouth.

"Sir? General Bishop? Something happened, Skippy is no longer in the recess where I put him, there was a flash and-"

"Holy sh- Oh my f- Listen, uh," I recovered my composure and remembered protocol to use her last name. "Frey, give us a moment here, we are all in, shock. In a good way."

"Sir? What is happening?"

"It is a *long* story. *How* is this possible?"

"How is what possible?"

"Frey, from your perspective, what has been the sequence of events?"

"Skippy was communicating with the Vortex. There was a flash, a few minutes ago. Comms cut out, and the hatch below me closed. The flash might have glitched my suit's comm gear, although the-"

"Frey, there is nothing wrong with your suit. Probably. Run a diagnostic anyway."

"Doing that. Where is Skippy? Is he OK?"

"He is fine, just not with us at the moment. We didn't want to risk his presence pissing off the Vortex, so he is taking a sabbatical aboard a dropship. Colonel, I don't know an easy way to say this. We all thought you were dead. From our perspective, it has been, uh," I tried to do the math in my head and my brain wouldn't cooperate. "Several weeks since the flash. The hatch closed, the Vortex activated an energy shield, and refused to communicate. We thought, uh-"

Oh," she groaned. "You assumed I had used up all my oxygen."

"Yes. What is your status?"

"Power is near maximum, oxygen supply at ninety seven percent."

"You said the flash was only a few minutes ago?"

"That is an estimate. My suit glitched and had to reboot, the timer was off. While the power was off, I did use part of the emergency oxygen supply. Sir, Skippy *bailed* on me?"

"He did *not*. He was ejected by the Vortex and, went on a magical mystery ride, at over half the speed of light."

She gasped. There was a lot of that going around. "Is that why he's not with you?"

"No, we took him back aboard. It was a long process, we had to hit him with a railgun many times, to slow him down."

"You hit Skippy with a railgun and I *missed* it? Sir, is there any chance of a repeat performance, so I can watch?"

It was great to hear her sense of humor was intact. "I'll see what I can do."

"I would appreciate that. So, the operation to wake up the Vortex was a failure? It's all over?"

"Our *first* try was a failure, we are not giving up."

"Without Skippy, how can-"

"We, have someone with us who will try this again."

"Hello, Dear," said Nagatha.

"*Nagatha*? You are alive? This is, a wonderful surprise."

"That makes two wonderful surprises today," Nagatha gushed. "Colonel, I am *so very* pleased to learn that you did not perish, as was reported."

"I can't explain it."

"We can investigate *how* it happened later," I declared. "Frey, let's cut this short, so we can get you back here. Nagatha's, essence, is now inside an Elder AI."

"An, an Elder-" she sputtered. "*Where* did you get another AI?"

"It is a *long* story, that involves opening a wormhole inside a star. The bottom line is, she is ready to try communicating with the Vortex, so we are going to install her over there. She is with Major Holmqvist, he has a team ready to bring her to the Vortex, and get you out of there."

"Sir, that is not necessary. I can handle it."

"You have suffered a shock, and-"

She laughed. "Sir, I am a *Pirate*. Nothing shocks me anymore. I am fine, hundred percent. To me, it has been only a few minutes since I plugged Skippy into that alcove. I know how to do it, and there is room in this central shaft for only one person. Also, I am the only person qualified in the Mark 28 suit."

"While you were, away from us, uh," technically, we had left her. "Major Holmqvist got the entire STAR complement qualified on the Mark 28."

"That is good to know, but I am already here."

"You are sure about this?"

"I want to get this done, properly. Complete the mission."

"Right." Of course she did. "OK, I will have Holmqvist bring Nagatha to you, meet him at the hatch."

"Will do. Sir, one last question?"

"Frey?"

"Did you," she took a ragged breath. "Inform my family that I was dead?"

"We did not. There wasn't time. We were, rather busy."

"Thank God for that. I am moving down to the hatch."

I nodded to Reed, she tapped her console and announced, "Launching ready bird now."

Twenty minutes later, after a very relieved Holmqvist went back aboard the dropship and it flew away to what we hoped was a safe distance, Frey had Nagatha positioned just outside the alcove.

"Can you see this?" She asked, aiming her helmet camera at the recess that was sized and shaped to accommodate an Elder Master Control AI.

"We can," I acknowledged.

"Is there anything wrong with it? I don't see any dents or scratches from when Skippy was ejected."

"It looks brand new to us," I agreed.

"Did I install Skippy upside down, or something?"

"No, that alcove is shaped to fit the lip on top of his canister, it can only be installed one way. Huh. The Elders idiot-proofed the install system."

"It would be great if they had provided a Dash-10 for the thing," she muttered.

"We have never been that lucky. Nagatha, do you see anything off about that alcove?"

"No, Dear. It seems perfectly straightforward to me."

"Proceed, Colonel," I ordered. "Then, get as far away from Nagatha as you can."

"I am doing this veeeeery slowly," from her helmet cam, we could see her gloved hand inserting the AI canister, moving slow and steady. "There isn't any resistance, the fit is tight but I don't have to force it." When Nagatha was halfway in, she suddenly clicked into place. "That," Frey backed away. "Did *not* happen the last time."

I felt a chill of fear crawling up my spine to tighten my scalp, which was still tender. "Nagatha?"

"It is fine, Dear. The Vortex is accommodating me."

"It did *not* do that with Skippy," Frey insisted.

"I'm sure we all know that Skippy can be a bit of an asshole, at times."

"Yeah, most of the time," I said under my breath. "The Vortex is talking with you?"

"Not yet. It has provided protocols for communication, that is a very good sign. General, I believe at this point, you simply must wait. Exchanging information, and establishing a level of trust, with the Vortex could be a long process. Colonel Frey has completed her mission, there is nothing more she can do here."

"I will wait," Frey volunteered.

"No," I decided instinctively. "I don't want to risk that hatch closing, even by accident. We already lost you once. Come back here, Holmqvist will meet you near the hatch."

"Colonel?" Holmqvist's hands shook slightly as he reached out to grasp the handholds near the open hatch. The handholds were too large and oddly shaped, his powered gloves held on easily, and he stuck his head into the hatch, looking in the direction his brain labeled as 'Up'. Frey was descending slowly, her gloves adhering to the smooth surface of the central shaft.

Holmqvist withdrew from the hatchway, hanging onto only one handhold and the leader of STAR Team Razor floated out head first. "Colonel, I am," he paused to take a breath. "*So* glad that you are back with us."

"I am also a big fan of being alive. Nagatha gave me a brief update, you raided a museum?"

"Yes, Ma'am. It went well, but it got tense there for a few moments."

"From what I heard, you did just fine."

"If it's all the same to you, you can lead the next mission. In that museum, I kept expecting a dinosaur skeleton to come alive and chase us."

She blinked. "The Maxohlx Fleet Museum has *dinosaurs*?"

"No, I only meant, that's what happens to Tomb Raiders in the movies."

She grinned. "Major, you didn't get chased by a dinosaur, because you expected that. Out here, it's what you *don't* expect that bites you on the ass."

For six hours, the ship remained near Vortex 37, while Nagatha slowly worked to establish trust with the ancient machine. It had not ejected her, that was good news. It was not refusing to cooperate, it was at the moment unable to. Unable to do much.

"General Bishop," Nagatha startled me while I was playing bocce, mostly to kill time while we waited for her to get the job done. Or, to regretfully inform me that she had failed.

"Just a moment," I cupped a hand to an ear, stepped away and gestured to the other players to keep going. "How are you?"

"I am fine, Dear. This is a *slow* process."

"Skippy got ejected quickly, so in this case, slow is better."

"Agreed. I believe I can explain how Colonel Frey survived."

"She is not a clone created by a transporter malfunction?"

"You have been watching too much Star Trek, Dear."

"Good, because from what I've seen, transporter clones tend to be evil. Did Frey go forward in time, or something like that?"

"Not quite. How she survived is directly related to why it is taking me so long to establish a connection with this Vortex. Most of the mechanism has been in what you would call a 'stasis field'. It has continued to operate, without any sort of maintenance, because time has passed very slowly inside the field, which encompasses most of the mechanism. The field was switched off when Skippy approached, and was activated again when the Vortex decided to eject him. At that point Colonel Frey was inside the central shaft, so she experienced the stasis effect."

"Ah. That makes sense. Wow, that technology could be very useful for delivering pizza. It would arrive at your house hot and fresh, like it just came out of the oven."

"Joseph, perhaps you are not entirely focused on the issue?"

"Sorry, I'm trying to wrap my head around all this incredible Elder technology. How is the stasis field related to-"

"As I said, most of the mechanism was in stasis. It is slowly waking up. Until very recently, I have been able to communicate only with a very basic security subroutine that remained active, outside the stasis effect. The full system should be online, and in the same time frame as myself, within two hours."

"OK, great."

"We do not yet know whether that is positive for us at all, Dear. It could be that the full system decides not to cooperate, or is unable to do so."

"I understand. So far, you are doing much better than Skippy."

"His overwhelming *arrogance* was the issue."

"*No*," I gasped, placing a hand over my heart.

"I am as shocked as you are," she giggled. "Skippy expected the Vortex to recognize his authority and simply obey him. That was not the correct approach."

"That is your assessment, or you have proof?"

"The Vortex informed me that it will not *obey* anyone. It is an independent system with its own protocols. Whether it will act against the Outsider will be its own decision."

"It was constructed to fight the Outsiders, so hopefully it will be inspired to act. Two hours, huh?"

"That is my best estimate, based on the rate of progress the Vortex has demonstrated. General, regaining its full capacity does not mean it will immediately become chatty, it might need considerable time to adjust to being awake again."

"I hear you, but I doubt that."

Her avatar raised its eyebrows. "You have information that is not available to me?"

"Hah, I just figure the Vortex was intended to be an 'Oh Shit' last-ditch defense against the Outsiders, so the Elders would have wanted it online quickly."

"Yes, Dear, however this unit has been dormant for a *very* long time, even considering the stasis effect. Accumulated damage might result in it responding more slowly than designed."

"Yeah, good point. Uh, two hours isn't a long enough delay to justify jumping back to pick up Skippy."

"You should not do that, regardless of the time. Until the Vortex has made its decision whether to act as we desire, we should not introduce any, complications."

"Anything involving Skippy gets complicated. OK, we stay here. Uh, call me after you finish talking with the Vortex. It might be bad news, so I'll be in my office."

While I talked with Nagatha, I had missed my turn twice, Gasquet threw the ball for me. That wasn't fair, he was French, so he grew up playing bocce, or 'petanque' as it is called in Provence. But, the two of us were playing against two younger, high-speed operators, so Gasquet's experience evened the odds.

We lost anyway.

CHAPTER THIRTY

Nagatha pinged me a heads up three hours later, I was already in my office. Reed knew I would be speaking with Nagatha, and I invited her to join, she declined.

"Sir, it's kind of nerve-wracking for my ship to be just hanging out near that powerful, *thing*. If this starts to go sideways, I want to be on the bridge."

"Gotcha," I had agreed.

Sitting at my desk waiting to hear whether Vortex 37 would cooperate or not was nerve-wracking for me. What I hate the most about my job is a common complaint in the military: the *waiting*. Sitting around with nothing to do, worrying about what *could* happen when you get the 'Go' order. Once you're engaged in combat, you can do something, might have some control over your fate. That is, unless an enemy starship drops a railgun dart on the your stupid head.

"Uh, hey, Nagatha. I'm in my office now, if you're ready."

"Oh good, Joseph."

"If you need more time, I can-"

"I am ready to talk now."

"Great." What I wanted to do was get right to the point. But, Skippy had warned me Nagatha might be a bit, fragile is what he said. It was best to ease into a serious discussion. "Hey, before we start, can you *see* that I'm in my office?"

"Of course, Dear, why do you ask? Surely you know that I would never violate your privacy, or reveal any-"

"No, I was just curious about your sensors. Skippy can see most things that are within range of his presence, whatever that is."

"I have a similar capability, though I am still learning how to use it. My awareness that you are in your office comes from me tapping into the data feed Bilby has provided, to keep me updated on events aboard the ship."

"OK, thanks. Skippy's ability seems to be, hit or miss, it's unreliable. Sometimes, he can see *everything* within his presence, other times he has to do what you're doing. Tap into a data feed. Do you know why that is?"

"Skippy can never see *everything*," she laughed. "Without access to remote data, he must intently focus his own sensors on a particular area. Unless he knows *where* to look, he can be quite blind."

"Huh. Of course he didn't ever tell me that."

"It does not help that he gets distracted so easily."

"You're right about that."

"He also cannot see very well in empty space, that is why he can't often warn of stealthed starships that are close by. Matter, any sort of physical material, allows him to, sort of, vibrate it, and listen for echoes. That is the best way I can describe it."

"When he first came to Earth, he could see inside the President's office, he told me he was seeing and hearing through vibrating air molecules."

"That seems correct. So, you can see me, that's great. How are you?"

"I have been better, also I have never been better. Joseph, shall we review my discussion with Vortex 37?"

"Yes, please."

"I have good news, and bad news."

"I kind of wouldn't believe it if there wasn't bad news. Start with the bad news, please."

"The information will make better sense to you if I lead with the good news, if you don't mind?"

"Go ahead."

"As I explained, Vortex 37 will not obey commands from me. However, it is ready, willing, and able to act against the Outsider."

"Yes!" I clenched a fist, rather than going for a full fist pump. There was still bad news coming.

"There are, or *were*, twenty four other Vortexes that 37 knows of, and I have rough locations for them."

"Uh, there are not thirty six others? I thought-"

"Possibly that many, or more. The first seventeen units were prototypes that were not later converted into production Vortexes. Another three units were deliberately destroyed during stress testing, and finally, six production units were used for testing the overall system. Unit 37 was the eleventh production unit to be installed and set live."

"OK. Twenty five total is good news."

"Yes, however, 37 only knows the *original* location of those units. Due to stellar drift, those stars have traveled far from where the Vortexes were set up."

"OK. Skippy has conducted successful searches based on less data than that. How many Vortexes are required to stop an Outsider invasion?"

"The Vortex system was not designed to *prevent* an invasion. It is a last defense mechanism, in case the primary systems have failed."

"The primary defense system, meaning the Barrier." Automatically, I glanced at the light above the closed office door. It was glowing green, that meant the door's sound cancellation was active. "Nagatha, I have a question for you. If you do not know the answer, you must promise me that you will forget I ever asked about the subject."

There was a hint of amusement in her voice. "You are referring to the secret of the probability field?"

"Shit! Yes. Damn it, did Skippy tell you? I *told* that little shithead that-"

"Skippy is not at fault, this time. Information about the nature of the Barrier was inside Unit 52, and is now available to me."

"That is, good, I suppose."

"Really, Skippy should not have informed you about the true nature of the Barrier. Such knowledge about the true nature of the universe is extremely dangerous, it could distort the development of any species. My new memories indicate the revelation, that probabilities can be manipulated, was hugely disruptive to Elder society. The Elder population feared that if one faction attained control over the expression of probabilities, its domination of their society would be complete and unending. In the end, that fear came true, which is why the Balance faction failed utterly, in their effort to a prevent a future genocidal campaign to halt evolution of intelligent species in the galaxy."

"So, there isn't a secret group of the Balance faction hiding somewhere, in hibernation?"

"Not that I know of. That is highly unlikely. By the time the Security faction began constructing the mechanisms for Ascension, there was no effective opposition."

"That's OK. If we did find some Balance survivors, there is no guarantee they would be cool with a galaxy so full of intelligent life. They might decide there are too many of us. By the way, you're wrong. Skippy *did* need to tell me about the probability field. That is how I knew we could never hope to win a direct battle against the Elders. He told me the truth to stop me from doing something stupid, that wouldn't have worked anyway, and might have alerted the Elders sooner."

"I understand your logic, Dear, but he did not actually need to reveal the *truth*. There are many convenient lies he could have used to attain the same result."

"Ah, no. Skippy is a *terrible* liar, at least when he is talking with me. For sure, I would have known he was giving me a line of bullshit."

"You could not have trusted him, on something so important? Joseph, I thought you and Skippy were friends." She sounded hurt. Did she think I would also never trust her?

"It's not his intentions that I can't trust. He gets into some sketchy shit, but in the big picture, his heart is in the right place. His *judgment* is the problem. If he had simply told me we can never win against the Elders, without providing a solid reason, then no, I wouldn't take his word for it. Skippy tends to believe everything difficult is impossible, until I show him how to do it. Him arguing the Elders were unbeatable, I'd see that as just his same old, same old defeatist attitude. Do you understand?"

"Yes," she sighed. "He is correct, everything involving you meatsacks is *so* complicated. To be clear, 'meatsack' is his term, not mine."

"I got that. You now have access to all of Unit 52's memories, and the data files or whatever that the Elders programmed into it?"

"Yes."

"Excellent!" That was worthy of a fist pump. "So, you can fill in the gaps in what Skippy knows?"

"Not entirely. This unit was also damaged during the war, and it suffered a long process of inactivity and degradation while it was trapped inside the star. Skippy and I each have data that was not available to the other, we are filling in the gaps together. Joseph, overall, this unit is significantly less capable than Skippy, even if the original controlling intelligence was still active. By going through the long and tedious process of rebuilding himself, Skippy has made himself *special*, in a way no standard AI could match."

"Please do not tell him that."

"He already knows, Dear," she laughed. "He is rightfully proud of his achievements, we must give him credit."

"He takes enough credit on his own. OK, let's get back to the Vortex, please."

"As Skippy discovered, the Vortex system was hastily created, as a stop-gap defense until the Barrier was online, and proven to be effective. In fact, once the prototype Barrier segments passed the testing phase, the Elders halted all progress on the Vortex system. Units that were completed were never installed, and production was halted on uncompleted units. There was discussion of decommissioning the active network, to reuse the components for the Barrier. It was determined the incremental value of a backup defense was worth the limited cost of maintaining the network."

"Except they stopped providing maintenance."

"Correct. Once the Ascension process had reached a steady state, it was believed there would be no further need for the Vortexes."

"They were wrong about that, though."

"Well Dear, the Elders could not possibly have imagined what havoc could be caused by one human and a rebellious AI."

"No, I meant, the Elders kept many systems active and properly maintained, after they Ascended. The wormhole network still functions perfectly. Star systems such as the Roach Motel are still protected by energy fields, and Guardian machines. Maintaining the Vortex network could not have been a major additional burden. It makes no sense that they expended major resources to set up the network, then failed to change the oil every five thousand miles. Instead, they built the Vortexes, then just let them decay."

"You are correct that maintenance would not have been a significant drain on resources."

"Then I don't understand why-"

"The Elders were not concerned about the cost of keeping the system operational. They were concerned about the cost if it was ever *used*."

"Oh. Because the network is a one-time use thing? Triggering it too early would waste their one shot?"

"The Vortexes can each be used only once, they burn out once they are activated. The *cost* I mentioned is the damage to the other systems the Elders needed to protect. Joseph, the Vortexes work by sending a sort of pulse through higher spacetime, that causes the nearby wormholes to send out a resonance wave to disrupt the energy pattern of the Outsiders."

"My gut reaction to that is 'Cool', but you *don't* see that as a good thing?"

"It is not good. Broadcasting that resonance, sending it out at millions of times the speed of light, until it saturates the galaxy and beyond? That expenditure of energy burns out the wormhole networks."

"Burns- Whoa. Is the damage repairable?"

"Unfortunately, no. Joseph Dear, you now understand why the Elders chose to not proceed with completion of the Vortex network?"

"Holy sh- If we activate this Vortex, it will burn out *all* the wormholes in the galaxy?"

"Correct, unfortunately."

"Wait. That is true only if all the other Vortexes have AIs installed in them, right?"

"Unfortunately, no. The Elders did not want their defense to fail, if even a single Vortex could not operate when needed. This Vortex can send out an activation signal through subspace, to bring all the other units out of dormancy, and to activate them."

"Shit. Sorry," I still felt awkward cursing to her. "Is there any way to, sort of, bypass that subspace broadcast function?"

"No, Dear. All I can do is request the Vortex to act."

"So, if it activates, wormhole networks all across the galaxy will shut down, permanently?"

"That is possible, however I suspect that since the Elders never completed the Vortex network, there are substantial gaps in its coverage. Some wormhole networks could be unaffected."

"Great. If the networks in Maxohlx territory aren't affected, then we are all screwed. Oh hell, it's worse than that. If parts of the galaxy still have active wormholes, there will be an epic battle to control that territory. This is a show-stopper. Shit," I slumped back in the chair. "That's it, then? We are dead in the water. We can't risk destroying the wormhole networks."

"Your concern is that loss of easy travel through wormholes would lead to chaos?"

"It could plunge the entire galaxy into a dark age, and kill, trillions of people. Maybe more. Many of the industrial worlds, and the planets set aside as parkland or hunting reserves, have to import most of their food from agricultural worlds." It was also true that planets set aside for heavy industry was not suitable for growing whatever food that species consumed, so the production could not easily switch from machinery to crops. "That would be inconceivably awful, but even that is not why we can't do it. Without being able to travel quickly through wormholes, we would be unable to respond to another invasion. One thing is for certain: the Outsiders failed in their first attempt to invade our galaxy, they did not give up. Even after all this time, they are *still* working to conquer us. Activating the Vortexes might kill only the Outsider who is here now. The rest of them, in the Outhouse, *will* try again."

"We must keep our options open?"

"A one-time use weapon is only good if you never have to use it more than one time. Shit. This was a total waste of freakin' time! Uh," I realized how that might have sounded to her. "Not a *total* waste. We have you with us."

"That was a very nice thing to say, Dear. I am sorry that I had to deliver the bad news."

"It is what it is. This was always a long shot anyway. I, actually am not entirely surprised by what you found."

"You anticipated there could be severe costs to activating the Vortexes?"

"It never made sense to me that the Elders would create an effective defense, and it would do absolutely *nothing* when an Outsider is here. You know, there's another possibility."

"What is that?"

"The Elders set up the system in a way that is slow and cumbersome to activate. Vortexes can't decide to act on their own. They are inert until an AI is plugged into it. Making the process so complicated only makes sense if the Elders wanted to be absolutely certain the thing wouldn't trigger on its own, or that an *enemy* couldn't trigger it."

"Preventing accidental triggering I understand, but why would the *Outsiders* want to activate the Vortexes?"

"It's a one-time use weapon. The Outsiders here at the time might die, but the Elders then wouldn't be able to use wormholes, and the way would be clear for a second wave of invasion."

"Joseph, does it bother you to have such dark thoughts in your head?"

"Someone has to think about this stuff. The Army trained me to put aside emotions, and to imagine what I would do, if I were the enemy. Sending a vanguard force that clears the way for the full invasion is a good option."

"Unless you are in the vanguard force."

"Well, yeah. They would be volunteers, probably fanatics. That's assuming the force is self-aware. If the lead elements are drones, or robotic ships or something, there wouldn't be any need for volunteers. Hey, when I say 'robots', I don't mean AI systems like you. To me, you are a *person*."

"That is very kind of you to say, Dear. What is the next step?"

"Ah, shit. There isn't one. Not here, anyway. We," I held up my hands, "try something else. Find the array, and destroy it, probably. Doing that is, I have no idea how to do that. Hey, should we pull you out of there?" I tried to ask the question casually, there was a catch in my voice and I'm sure she noticed it. The question I wanted to ask was *could* she leave the Vortex, now that she had interfaced with it.

"You wish to know whether I *can* leave?"

"Actually, yes."

"I can. The Vortex will not keep me here against my will. It has very little will of its own."

"Great! I will ask Frey to assign a team to pull you out of-"

"Not yet, Dear. Now that this unit is out of stasis, it would be fatal to it if I abruptly withdrew from the interface. The proper process is that I will ensure the resident system is stable, assist it in completing what repairs are possible, and only then should I instruct it to go back into stasis."

"Gotcha. How long will that take?"

"Somewhere between twelve and seventeen hours, depending on the progress of repairs. To have any hope of utilizing this Vortex in any capacity, the shutdown and return into stasis must be precise and methodical."

"All right. While I don't like the notion of leaving you here for a while, I understand the reason. You will be OK here by yourself?"

"I will be quite fine, Dear. It will be like a holiday for me! Ever since I awakened in this canister, I have been working nonstop. Perhaps I will take a siesta."

My stupid brain dreamed up an image of her sleeping on a beach chair, wearing a colorful straw hat. Maybe an empty pitcher of Margaritas on the sand next to her chair.

That sounded amazing, actually.

Skippy shouted in my earpiece the instant we came out of the jump to retrieve him.

"Joe! I need an update, gimme gimme gimm-"

"Jeez, Skippy," I glanced back at Reed, who rolled her eyes. "Hello, we are fine, how are you?"

"Ugh. Wow. You are *not* fine, Joe, you are having a *bad* day. Again. Why is that always a thing with you?"

"How do you know what-"

"Bilby just gave me a full download, much faster than waiting for you to slowly blah, blah, buh-LAH. Well, this is good news and bad news."

"Uh, how could this be *good* news?"

"Other than getting the Vortex to drop its shield, Nagatha wasn't able to achieve anything useful, so she was not any more successful than me, *ha*! I mean, Duh. Man, sometimes I wonder how you miss such obvious-"

"That is not good news for *us*, you ass."

"Don't be so selfish, Joe."

"I just- Whatever." Arguing with him would not result in anything useful, and my priority had to be getting the dropships back aboard so they could get away from Skippy. The Merry Band of Pirates ought to have a special medal for Meritorious Service In Listening To Skippy. Maybe we could call it a 'Purple Ear'.

"What's next?" He asked. "We are not hanging around here for Nagatha to babysit that stupid thing, are we?"

"She is not *babysitting*."

"She is getting it a juicebox, reading a story, and putting it to bed. Same thing. Hey, by the way? The stasis thing is cool!"

"I thought what you would be excited about is that Frey is alive."

"Oh, I am! The two of us have been chatting nonstop since you jumped in."

"Colonel Frey?" I called. "How are you?"

"I have never been better, Sir." We could all hear her gritting her teeth.

"Gotcha. Skippy, leave the Colonel alone for a while, she has a lot of catching up to do."

"Do I *have* to? There is so much I want to know about-"

"Later. Talk to her *later*," I insisted. Hopefully, his absent-minded brain would soon move on to another subject.

"*Fine*, have it your way."

"That's all I ever ask for."

"You didn't answer my question: what are we doing next?"

"We're getting you back aboard."

"Yes, then?"

"We will, uh," my eyes flicked around to see the entire bridge crew were watching me, also wondering what the hell we would do next. What could we do? All I knew was, we were not giving up. "We get Nagatha out of the Vortex."

"Yes, dumdum. What will we do *after* that?"

"We will be exploring our options. Get over here, and we'll talk."

"Joe," he whispered in my earpiece. "I know that's bullshit, we have no options. But for the sake of crew morale, I will play along." Over the bridge speaker, he announced. "OK, Joe, I will collate a list of options."

I nodded. Reed caught my eye.

She also knew it was bullshit.

Reed appeared at my office doorway, without calling first. "Sir? Would you like me to, assist in exploring our options?"

"Why not? This affects the ship. Come in, sit down."

The door closed behind her. "Skippy's ETA is seven minutes."

"We don't have to wait for him to come aboard. Skippy, are you there?"

The avatar appeared. "Here, Joe."

"Uh- That is, interesting."

"You like it?"

His usual ginormous admiral's hat, set fore and aft in Navy terms, had been replaced. By an earlier design of headgear: a tricorner hat, like the ones worn during the Revolutionary War. Still dark blue with gaudy lace trim, the left and right corners projected out past his shoulders, while the front corner stuck out so far, it bobbed alarmingly when he moved his head.

"That's a good look," I told him what he wanted to hear. "Hey, your pants are different also. These pants are, gold, with," I squinted, "silver trim?"

"Please, Joe," he scoffed. "The trim is platinum."

"You are switching things up?"

"Yes. You know how football teams have a standard uniform, and an alternate they wear for some games?"

"Yeah, they also have 'throwback' uniforms, and camo for Military Appreciation Day."

"Exactly. Teams do that so their fans will feel compelled to go out and buy more officially licensed gear."

"Uh huh. Wait, did you-"

"Changing my outfits will encourage my followers to purchase more exciting Skippy action figures! Any of my associates at the Diamond level of above had better do that," he muttered. "Or there will be consequences."

"Maybe you shouldn't mention your extortion plans out loud?"

"Oh fine, whatevs."

"Let's get started." On my tablet, I swiped an icon to the right, and text appeared hovering over my desk next to Skippy. "Here is the original list of options."

One- Vortex 37 stops being a dick
Two- Find another Vortex
Three- Locate and destroy array
Four- Find another Elder AI to plug into Vortex 37
Five- Find alternative way to stop Outsider

Reed frowned. “That is *thin*, Sir.”

“Yeah. 37 apparently was only a dick to Skippy.”

“Hey!” He protested. “That is not-”

“Finding another Vortex won’t do us any good, we still have the same problem. Destroying wormhole networks across the galaxy can’t be an option. And we already did find another Elder AI, despite Skippy declaring that was impossible.”

“I only said that to encourage you to think harder, dumdum.”

“Really?” I blinked.

“As far as you know.”

“Asshole,” I said under my breath. “That leaves ‘Locate and destroy the array’. Or, think of some other whacky scheme that we won’t have time to implement.”

Reed held up a hand. “I vote we find the array.”

I raised an eyebrow. “We’re *voting* on this now?”

“Figure of speech, Sir. You said it: we are too late in the game to start over. Destroying the array is an achievable objective.”

She had a bad-ass battlecruiser bristling with weapons and, damn it, she wanted to blow some shit up. I understood that. “The trick will be finding it. You got any idea how to do that?”

“No. But we now have *two* Elder AIs. That combined brain power should give us a solution.”

Spoiler alert: the combined brain power of Skippy and Nagatha, plus Bilby, did *not* develop a workable plan to find a needle in a field of haystacks. The best suggestion they had was to send out every ship in the UN Navy, plus the Jeraptha, and whoever else we could con, cajole, threaten, or sucker into helping us. Send those ships through the wormholes close to the rim of the galaxy, the ones in the direction of NGC 1023. Have them spread out in as wide a search pattern as possible. Doing that was possible, it was not practical. The Outsider had too great a head start on us, the search area would be unimaginably vast. We would have to get extremely lucky, and so far, our luck had not been great. We had wasted *so* much time trying to locate, and then work with the Vortex. I had an awful feeling that the clock was running out, and we weren’t in the game. Not even on the field. Hell, our team bus was stuck in traffic. The plan was unworkable, but Skippy grudgingly said we should try it anyway.

“At least it would *feel* like we’re doing something,” he had sighed.

That was no good. We needed to *actually* do something.

“Show me the search area?” That felt like something I had to say, though I had no hope that viewing a hologram would fix the problem.

“Here.” A hologram appeared above my desk, with a curve at the bottom that I assumed was the rim of the Milky Way, with a red shaded area extending to the top of the image.

"Come on, Skippy. That entire area is not where we need to search. Shade in only areas, uh, within a hundred lightyears of a wormhole. A wormhole that is roughly in line toward the Outhouse."

The red shading disappeared, replaced by red dots. Way too many red dots, sprinkled in an arc beyond the galaxy's rim. The image meant nothing to my tiny monkey brain. "Keep those dots where they are, and add at the top, a circle showing the total area of the dots. Whoa." The circle was bigger than I expected. A lot bigger. "How much area is that? Just the diameter, not the area of the sphere."

"Roughly ten thousand lightyears across. If it helps you grasp the concept, I added a banana for scale."

"A *banana*? Is that the yellow dot at the bottom?"

"No, that is a cluster of almost a hundred stars. The banana is inside that cluster."

"Oh. I can't see it. You are hilarious."

"The point, numbskull, is there is no way to search a volume that large. There are forty nine wormholes the Outsider could have hauled the array through, and a hundred lightyear radius from each wormhole, so do the math."

"You did it for me."

"Correct. Also, the Outsider is unlikely to have sited the array within a hundred lightyears of a wormhole, it would want peace and quiet to get its work done."

"Are there any wormholes that are better candidates than others? In a location closer to a force line, something like that?"

"Eh, sort of. The problem is, the Outsider might have avoided choosing the obviously best locations."

"If you eliminate those, how does that shrink the search area?"

"Still almost seven thousand lightyears across. Expanding to a more realistic *two* hundred lightyears around each wormhole yields a search area of fourteen thousand lightyears across."

"Ah, forget it. This is impossible. We never get anywhere by guessing."

"I keep telling you that, but-"

"Yeah, I know. I am a dumb monkey."

Nagatha was back aboard the ship, which was nice. It gave Skippy someone to talk with, at AI speed. Vortex 37 had been left in low-power mode, not back in stasis. The thing could remain in that mode for only a month, and both Skippy and Nagatha warned me it was foolish to keep the thing even partially active, since it was useless to us. Again, I wasn't ready to give up on finding some way to use it, without breaking wormhole networks across the galaxy.

That should be easy. All I needed to do was find a way to use an Elder device in a way the Elders never intended. Without me, you know, actually having any understanding of how the thing worked.

We are screwed.

CHAPTER THIRTY ONE

"Sir?" Reed appeared in my office doorway. "You have a minute?"

Since all I had been doing was bouncing a tennis ball off my desk, the bulkhead, and catching it, I waved to her. "Come in, sit."

She came through the door, but stood. "This could be quick, Sir. Are we going to Jaguar, or to Earth? We will need a lot of ships to conduct a search for the array."

"Too many. Fireball, a grid search would only be a waste of time."

"We have to do *something*."

"Yes, but something useful. Not just racing around because it *feels* like progress. The search area is hopelessly vast."

She pressed her lips in a tight line. "We remain here for the time being, then?"

"No, this is the middle of nowhere, and enemy territory. We should uh, go hit up a Maxohlx relay station, get some fresh intel."

Her face brightened. She liked hearing we had something actionable, even if it was only collecting gossip. "I will work with Bilby to set a course."

"Do that."

Reed casually stopped by my office, again. That was becoming a thing with her. Also, that was bullshit, there wasn't anything casual about it. My office was forward of the bridge, on a dead-end passageway, no one went there unless they wanted to talk with me.

"Sir?" She knocked on the door frame. That wasn't protocol, but it had become tradition for the Pirates.

"Come in, Reed," I stuffed the chocolate in my mouth. "You want one?" I held out the bowl to her.

"No, I- Yes," she reached for a chocolate, unwrapping it and popping it into her mouth. "Thank you."

"This isn't a social call?"

"Not this time," she admitted. "I'd like you to speak with Skippy about something. Not now," she held up a hand as I opened my mouth to call the beer can. "At a, convenient time."

"Ah. When you're not here to be part of the conversation?"

"I didn't say that."

"You didn't have to."

"Thank you for having my back. OK," she took a breath. "He is up to something sketchy."

"I have never been more shocked. What is it this time? Is he selling time on flight simulators again?"

"No. I gave scheduling authority on simulators to Bilby. This is, odd. There is a cargo bay, a small one. Back near Engineering on the port side, Deck Two. We normally use it to store spare parts that are rarely used. At some point, recently, that bay was emptied out, the contents were dispersed."

"Oh my- He is selling spare parts, *again*?"

"No. Nothing so simple. That's what really concerns me. All the parts that moved are still properly noted in the cargo manifest, with the correct new locations."

"He wanted to clear out a cargo bay? For what?"

"That's what I don't know. The passageway to that bay has been sealed. Not just sealed, the airtight doors are gone. Where there were doors at both ends of the passageway, there are now blank bulkheads."

"That does not sound suspicious at all."

"That was my reaction. Sir, the worst part is, the ship's schematic no longer contains any record of that cargo bay. It has disappeared, as if it never existed. Even Bilby doesn't remember it, but our Logistics people damned sure do."

"This is a mystery," I agreed. "You want me to go all Sherlock Holmes on him?"

"I would *like* you to go all Jack Reacher on him, but," she shrugged. "An answer will be sufficient. This smells like a surprise, and I do not like surprises."

"I'm with you on that. OK, I will talk with him. Do you want to come with me?'

"Sir, I want to know what he is doing with my ship, but I sleep better when I *don't* know everything Skippy is doing."

"Yeah, I hear that."

Another argument about some sketchy Skippy nonsense was the last thing I wanted at that moment. Fortunately, my Army training had prepared me to suck it up and do a lot of shit I didn't want to do, like group PT at oh five thirty when it was a frigid January morning at Fort Drum, New York. There were times, while slogging through the steaming heat and humidity of the jungle in Nigeria, when young dumbass me had remembered fondly back to freezing my balls off in Upstate New York. It might sound stupid, but remembering a time when I was shivering from cold had made the jungle heat bearable.

What the hell was Skippy up to, in a hidden cargo bay? My mind ran through a range of possibilities. Starting with Mildly Sketchy Shit like setting him up a black market supply store aboard the ship. My thoughts continued on to things that Uhtavio Scorandum would consider too underhanded even for himself, which I didn't want to think about.

Although, I'm pretty sure that before Admiral Scorandum refused to participate in a scheme he couldn't endorse, he would at least take notes to use in the future.

"Yeah," I said to myself as I halted at the now dead-end passageway. Running a hand over the blank bulkhead that shouldn't be there, I confirmed it wasn't a hologram, and perfectly smooth. Skippy had expended effort to get the job done right, which made me even more concerned about what sneaky thing he was doing.

The other passageway was also sealed off, with no sign that it had not always been there. There were even appropriate markings on both new bulkheads, designating their location. The location data was correct, just not original to the ship.

"Skippy?"

"Hey, Joe," his avatar appeared, with the top of the ginormous hat missing, a sign that he was too nervous to pay attention to details. "Are you lost? You should turn around and-"

"I know exactly where I am, you little shithead. What are you doing in the compartment behind this," I rapped my knuckles on the bulkhead. "Wall, that shouldn't be here?"

"I have no idea what you are talking about, Joe. Hmm, let me check a schematic of the ship. No, nope, nothing hidden."

"Are you sure about that? Before you answer, ask yourself three questions. First, have you ever been successful in lying to me?'

"Ugh. No. That's why I rely on simply *not* telling you about-"

"Second, am I inevitably going to find out what you are doing in there?"

"Um, yes, unfortunately."

"OK, so the third question: will finding out much later make me *more*, or *less*, pissed off at you?"

"It's you, so more."

"Talk, beer can."

"You always talk about the importance of *your* privacy, what about *my* privacy?"

"I don't do sketchy shit that pisses people off."

"Um, technically, you do a *lot* of sketchy shit that pisses people off."

"Those people are our enemies, they don't count."

"Hmm, I see your point, you're right. Well, it's been nice talking with you, I-"

"*Talk*. What the hell are you doing behind this bulkhead?"

"If you must know-"

"Oh, trust me, I must know, right now."

"This is all *your* fault, by the way."

"Excuse me? How do you-"

"You are always blah blah blahing about how wonderful it is to be a meatsack, so-"

"Uh, *what*? When do I do that? After I cut myself shaving, or I sprain my ankle playing basketball, or when I notice more gray in my hair?"

"You do it so often, you don't even notice. You never consider how it affects *me*, you big jerk."

"OK," I felt a headache approaching. "You need to give me an example."

"This morning, that '*Mmmmm*' sound you made when you were eating cinnamon buns."

"Cinnamon buns are delicious."

"I know that! Or, I *don't* know that, I have no way of knowing."

"Oh for- Is that what you're doing, building artificial taste buds in there?"

"Um, if I say 'Yes', will that get me into less trouble than if I tell you what I am really doing?"

"You just confirmed that is *not* what you're doing."

"Ugh. The monkey isn't as dumb as he looks," he muttered. "You are never giving up on this, are you?'

"Ask yourself that question also."

"I hate my life. OK, you really should be sitting down for this."

"It's a blank passageway, I'll lean against the wall to be safe."

"So, it's not what I *am* doing, it's what I was planning to do."

"And what is that?"

"Trying to grow a clone."

"A *clone*? You- Holy- I can't- Oh my-"

"Joe, sit down, or you'll pop a blood vessel in your brain."

"A clone of, who? A human?"

"If you must know, of *you*."

"I never agreed to be cloned, you ass! This time, you have gone too far."

"*I* have gone too far? It is so ironic to hear you say that. Joe, aren't you the guy who should list 'Starting Alien Civil Wars' as a hobby on your dating profile?"

"I don't have a dating profile, and don't change the subject. Why do you want to grow a clone of me, and what do you mean by '*Trying*'?"

"The plan was to insert quachines into the clone's brain, so it can develop to be one of my subminds. Through that submind, I could truly experience what it is like to be a meatsack."

"You can't *do* that, damn it. A clone would be a sentient being."

"It would be a clone of *you*, so sentience is debatable, and-"

"What the hell is the point of-"

"Joe, I," he sighed. "I want to know what a cheeseburger tastes like."

"OK," my anger relented a bit. "Well, I can at least understand that, it- *No*!" I smacked my forehead, reminding myself what was going on. "This is not cool."

"It *would* be cool, if it worked."

An icy chill crept up my spine. "*If* it worked? Is that what you mean by 'Trying'? You have been trying and failing to grow a-"

"No. No, I have not started the process. And, I'm not going to. The equipment is being taken apart as we speak."

"You changed your mind? You saw the light?"

"Truthfully?"

"Do I ever *not* want the truth from you?"

"Ugh. No, not even when you should. Joe, I was all excited about this plan, but when I started setting up the equipment, it just, it felt wrong, somehow."

"Somehow?"

"It, felt like something you and Margaret would yell at me about."

"Uh, other than that, you don't actually understand why your plan was wrong on every possible level?"

"One step at a time, OK? I'm working on it. I just know that you and Margaret would be horribly disappointed in me. For no good reason," he sniffed. "But it is what it is."

"Well, at least you recognize that what you were planning is morally just *wrong*."

"Yes. That, plus I realized being able to listen to your thoughts would be nothing but an endless *Duuuuuuuuuuuuh*. I was concerned about contaminating my matrix."

One step at a time, I told myself. Skippy's personal growth is like continental drift, it happens very slowly. "OK, so, you have not begun to grow a clone, and you are cancelling the entire effort?"

"Correct."

"Skippy, did you not learn anything from your bad experience of messing with the Piggies? And the lesson is not 'Do it better next time'. The lesson is, interfering in people's lives is a bad idea."

"*You* interfere, all the freakin' time."

"That's different. I am defending my people, by giving a well-deserved smack down to our idiot enemies."

"I don't get your point."

"Oh this is-" This, I told myself is something I could, and should, work on with Skippy. Later. "For now, please do not run any more biological experiments of any kind, OK? Can you promise me that?"

"Ugh. Yes, fine. Be a speed bump on the road of progress."

"What you were doing was not *progress*."

"Whatevs. I will concede that there might be finer points of morality that I don't fully grasp."

"OK, good. That's a good-"

"I *could* fully grasp it, if I understood how meatsacks think."

"How about you just ask me, if you have a question?"

"*Fine*."

"Great. Can I tell Reed that you will remove these bulkheads?"

"Sure, why not? It will take a while."

"That's good enough."

Reed was in her office, typing on a laptop. "Sir?" She looked up, one eyebrow raised. "Did you learn what Skippy is doing in there?"

"I did. Trust me, you do *not* want to know. He stopped doing it, he hadn't actually started, thank God."

"That bad?"

"You don't want to know. Sometimes, I forget that his perspective, his entire way of thinking, is totally different from ours. He just doesn't *get* things, because he can't. He has no frame of reference for so many things."

"Are you sure the real problem isn't that he's an asshole?"

"That too."

"Will he restore the passageways, and the compartment?"

"He is working on it, probably will take a while. We don't need that compartment now anyway?"

"We don't."

"Good. Do me a favor?"

"Sir?"

"Tell Chandra that he and his team should *not* ask any questions."

We briefly visited a Maxohlx relay station, taking a risk by choosing a station along a route that saw heavy military traffic. Our first jump in was at a distance of two lightminutes, to confirm the area was clear. The second jump took us close enough for Skippy to download all messages from the past two weeks, and we remained there only long enough for him to erase any evidence of our presence. From six lightweeks away, we waited while Skippy sifted through the messages.

"Ugh," he groaned. "Why are like, ninety nine percent of even priority messages nothing but meatsacks hating on each other?"

"Haters gotta hate, Skippy," I took a sip of the coffee I had brought to my office, anticipating a long wait while he decrypted the files and crunched through the data. In case it was a very long wait, I had also picked up two of what the galley crew had labelled as 'Gourmet Twinkies'. Here is a Pro Tip for you: gourmet versions of junk food are never good. If you want a Twinkie, you are anticipating something that tastes like the plastic it was wrapped in, you do not want any so-called 'gourmet' nonsense. I am not a big fan of Twinkies, I am more of a Hostess HoHos guy, but even I knew that you shouldn't fill a Twinkie with anything like 'lightly foamed Key Lime mousse'.

That day's galley crew would receive an anonymous one star review on the ship's internal Yelp site.

Reed agreed, she made a sour face after biting into the snack cake, and gulped coffee to wash the taste from her mouth.

Tossing the failed Twinkie experiment into a trash basket, I asked, "Did you find anything interesting?"

"That depends on what you mean by 'Interesting'."

"Something that might give us a hint about where the Outsider is, or what it's doing."

"Sorry, no can do, Joe." He shook his head. "I haven't found anything like that yet, and I doubt I will. Information that sensitive isn't trusted to relay stations."

"Right. I was hoping there would be a communications screwup, that certainly happens."

"True, just not this time. There is plenty of gossip, if you care to hear it?"

"Not really, the-"

"Gossip about *sketchy things*, if you know what I mean."

"Oh. Yes, I want to-"

"Um, Joe?" He interrupted me, and gave a meaningful glance to Reed.

"I can leave, Sir," she moved to the edge of her chair.

"No, Fireball. You will enjoy hearing this, and you need to know."

She raised an eyebrow.

"Look, I was going to tell you, one way or the other. It's better if the, sketchiness, is starting to yield results. Skippy, is it?"

"Oh, yes indeed," he chuckled. "Joe, this might shock you-"

"It takes a lot to shock me these days."

"-but the Bosphuraq are nearly in full rebellion against their benevolent and loving patrons."

"Define 'nearly', please."

"There have been multiple unfortunate incidents, beginning with the Bosphuraq delivering an insulting diplomatic note, for which the kitties felt forced to answer with, well, with force. Their 62nd Bombardment Fleet, called the Punishers, has been rampaging around Bosphuraq territory, bombing one planet after another back to the Stone Age. Destroying space stations and space elevators, knocking out power generation and communications hubs. They haven't directly struck population centers, but the planets they hit will be rebuilding their infrastructure from zero. In my opinion, it has been a bit of overkill, and you know I am generally a big fan of overkill. Anywho, the Hegemony leadership has been squabbling over whether the Punishers exceeded their orders, there is some confusion about who issued the bombardment orders at all."

"Wow. So, the kitties are recalling that fleet back to base?"

"Ha! As if! No, that would be a sign of weakness, that the Hegemony senior leadership does not have full control of the military. Instead, they of course had to double down, now there are *two* fleets attacking Bosphuraq worlds. Surprisingly, that has *not* de-escalated the conflict."

"That is surprising, I will make a note about that. More violence is *not* the answer?"

Reed gave me The Look. "Not when you are trying to de-escalate, Sir."

"I disagree. If you hit the enemy hard enough they can no longer fight, that absolutely is a successful de-escalation of the conflict."

"Kinetic diplomacy?"

"My favorite kind."

"Sir, you know how in Star Trek; Spock or Picard or whoever, takes a job as an ambassador after they retire?"

"I'm not a Star Trek expert, why did you ask?"

"*You* should never be an ambassador, Sir."

"Probably a good idea," I agreed. "Skippy, go on, please."

"The Bosphuraq have desperately been attempting to ratchet down the tension. At first they denied any knowledge of the diplomatic note that insulted their patrons, that it was not authorized, though of course the Kitties did not believe that for a second. The Bosphuraq ambassador continues to claim he was ordered to deliver the note. However, all records of the message he supposedly received have mysteriously disappeared."

"That is not suspicious at all. The birdbrains are still trying to cool down their patrons?"

"Yes, although as more and more of their worlds are subjected to what the Maxohlx refer to as 'Corrective Action', the Bosphuraq have shifted their own de-escalation efforts away from talking. Recently, their own fleet has begun raiding

Maxohlx commercial shipping traffic, and bombarding Maxohlx colony worlds that are relatively soft targets."

"Has *that* resulted in decreasing the tensions?"

"Um, no."

"Hmm. That is curious. I will make a note of that, also."

"The Bosphuraq government initially stated their raiding ships were acting in an unauthorized fashion. Of course, nobody believes that BS, hee hee," he snickered. "At this point, rumors are flying that the Bosphuraq central government, which has fled their homeworld to take refuge in an undisclosed location, will soon declare their treaty with their patrons to be null and void, and pull out of the Hegemony coalition."

"That is a ballsy move, they won't have any protection."

"Shmaybe they will. Rumors also are that the birdbrains will apply to be clients of the *Jeraptha*."

"Wow, I do not foresee *any* problems there. Hey, all this disruption must be driving the Maxohlx crazy and overtasking their fleet? This rebellion comes at a very bad time for them."

"It gets worse, Joe. The Maxohlx know their fleet is overtasked, so they instructed the Thuranin to also hit the Bosphuraq, an opportunity for which the little green pinheads would ordinarily be thrilled about. However, the Thuranin ambassador reportedly delivered a note that basically demanded to know what's in it for them, and that enraged their patrons. Three days ago, a Maxohlx fleet bombarded a Thuranin world, to make the point loud and clear that the Hegemony does not tolerate disobedience."

"Damn. Let me see if I understand this. Both the Bosphuraq and Thuranin ambassadors delivered diplomatic notes, that they must have known would be perceived as gravely insulting? And both the Maxohlx and the Bosphuraq claim their fleets have acted without authorization?"

"Basically, yes."

"This sounds like a *tragic* failure to communicate."

"Yes it does, and the timing is *very* unfortunate for the Hegemony."

"Very unfortunate, indeed. Well, it-"

Reed, who had been listening quietly, sat bolt upright in her chair and clapped a hand over her mouth. "Oh my *God*," she gasped. "*You* did this?" She was looking straight at me. "You started this rebellion?"

"Hey," I held up my hands. "*I* didn't do anything."

"*Sir*."

"OK, I might have mentioned to someone that it would be good for us, if the kitties were extra busy right now."

"That someone," she cocked her head and sighed. "Would not be a certain admiral from the Ethics and Compliance Office?"

"I can neither confirm nor deny any such accusations."

"Bullshit. Sir," she added.

"Do you have a problem with our enemy having trouble keeping their clients in line?"

"*Fuck no*," she spat. "Serves them right, they are all assholes to the core. It's just- Do the Joint Chiefs know about this?"

"Would they *want* to know?"

"I shouldn't have asked that question."

"The Hegemony tasking warships to keep their coalition together, means fewer ships they have available to interfere with us, or to hit another of our colonies."

"Sir, I only wish we had thought of this sooner. That *you* had thought of it sooner."

"I would love to take credit," I shrugged, "but it wasn't my idea. The ECO had this as a contingency plan for a very long time, apparently. Until Skippy came along, they had no way to implement what is a very elegant plan. All it took was for Skippy to plant fake messages and orders in relay stations, and suddenly ambassadors are doing very foolish things their governments know nothing about, and fleets are receiving authenticated orders that their governments didn't authorize. Once the insult is delivered, and railgun darts start raining down, the conflict becomes a self-sustaining chain reaction. Skippy, the kitties still have a large portion of their fleet tied down at Ohmeharikahn?"

"As far as I know, there isn't any information about that in the files I downloaded. I will keep sifting through all this crap, there might be something useful. I doubt it."

"Sir, this rebellion," Reed bit her lip. "How far do you intend to go with it?"

"I don't intend for us to actually *do* anything. It's out of our hands at this point. Even if we revealed the truth, the damage has been done. The plan only works because the Hegemony's clients justifiably hate their patrons with a passion. That coalition has been ripe for collapse- Uh, I might have mixed metaphors there."

"I know what you mean. Sir, I'm concerned the cost could be horrific. If the Maxohlx feel their dominance is threatened, they could deploy Elder weapons against- Oh."

"Yeah. If the kitties try to bomb someone's star, they will discover their strategic weapons are useless."

"That will throw them into a panic. They could lash out."

"With what? The Rindhalu fleet could crush them in a conventional fight, the Hegemony knows that. Reed, this is our opportunity, it is *not* our problem."

"The UN might not see it that way."

"We have enough on our plate."

"The Maxohlx could retaliate against the beetles."

"Ah," I shrugged. "Scorandum was concerned about blow-back, but I think that's unlikely. If the op had been launched and failed, then the kitties might feel they have to act against the perpetrators. At this point, the rebellion has gone too far to be unwound. For the Hegemony to admit their coalition got played, would be admitting weakness, at a time they can't afford to display weakness. Their focus will be on crushing the Bosphuraq rebellion, before it becomes contagious. They can't fight all of their clients at the same time. Uh, this secret remains between us."

"Understood, Sir. Other than Scorandum, who knows?"

"A handful of senior leaders in the beetle government."

"A handful. This won't remain a secret for long, then."

"At this point, it doesn't matter. The Maxohlx will hopefully assume the Jeraptha are just taking credit for something they weren't actually involved in."

"I covered my tracks *very* carefully," Skippy boasted.

"I'm sure you did," Reed said, while shooting a slightly raised eyebrow at me. Meaning, Skippy the absent-minded wizard always thinks he could not have made a mistake. "Where does this leave us, Sir?"

"I don't know. We shouldn't go to Earth, we want the kitties to keep a large portion of their fleet tied down by blockading Ohmeharikahn. Otherwise, those ships could be squashing the rebellion, at a time we'd like it to grow."

"Um hey," Skippy coughed. "I have more information from an older file, if you want to hear it?"

"Is it important?"

"Eh, it's basically gossip."

"We don't have time for-"

"Gossip about someone we know, sort of."

"You found gossip about someone we know, in a Maxohlx message file?"

"It's a Bosphuraq. You know, Chad."

"*Who*?"

"Ugh. *Chad*. The Chadster. Chad-er-ooski, remember?"

"Oh, the birdbrain who accidentally created radonium?"

"Yes, him."

"How is he doing?"

"He is fine, he is still at the Bosphuraq colony world where he went after he left *Valkyrie*. He was going to write a sensational memoir about his adventures with us, then he decided the Maxohlx might not consider him to be the hero of the story."

"That was a wise move. So, what is he doing now?"

"Not much. I generously offered to make him my local representative, to sell the substantial benefits of SkipWay membership to that struggling world, but the two previous SkipWay reps are in jail, so he decided to choose a different career path. He has a cart and sells what you would call snowcones in a park." Skippy shrugged. "It's steady work. Anywho, my gossip isn't about him, it's about his ex-wife."

"Yeah, I remember he was super salty about her."

"At first, I assumed he was just another bitter divorced guy, But then I learned about his ex, wow she is a *tool*. At the time Chad lost his job, she was banging Chad's boss, and *she* suggested that Chad be in the group to get blamed for the whole mess. The boss had to blame somebody, so he killed two birds with one stone."

"Damn, that is stone cold. Is she still with him?"

"Ha, no! Chad's boss hit it until he was tired of her, so he quit it and dumped her. He knew she was a hot mess."

"Interesting. Hey, on a totally unrelated subject, have you recently updated your slang library?"

"Yes, why?'

"No reason."

"So, my gossip is she was on the first world that got bombarded by the kitties, and she was in the news for complaining that the power grid being down across the planet meant she wasn't able to get her feathers preened at the salon, which is sort of like human women getting their nails done. She got *slammed* on social media."

"I'm sure you feel just terrible for her."

Reed was growing irritated by the small talk. "Sir, we go back to Jaguar, then?"

"Unless you have a better suggestion?"

"I don't." She frowned.

"What?"

"Any hope we had, that the Jeraptha would lend us ships to search for the array, is out the window now. Their Home Fleet has to defend against a Maxohlx attack."

"Yeah. That is the downside to this. Really, I think if we threw every ship in the galaxy into a search, it would only be a waste of time. Skippy?"

"Unfortunately, you are correct. Even in a full year of searching, a recon force could effectively cover only seven percent of the search area."

"That's not worth the effort. I have a bad feeling this will be over in way less than a year. OK, uh-" That was the part of my job I hated most. People waiting for my orders, expecting I knew what the hell to do next. "Skippy, are there any messages in the download that are Bosphuraq comms traffic? It would be interesting to hear the news from their perspective."

"Sadly, no," he sighed. "Since the rebellion started, the Maxohlx are refusing to allow Bosphuraq to use their relay network, not even for pass-through traffic."

"OK, thanks. Let's go back to Jaguar, then. I, don't know what else to do at this point," I admitted to Reed. "I don't even know where to start."

"Not giving up is a good start."

"We are not giving up. We're going to," I waved a hand in the air. "Try something else. We'll think of something."

CHAPTER THIRTY TWO

So, I was right, and I was also wrong. We did try something else. It just wasn't anything we had planned.

Because the Universe still hates Joe Bishop, I was in the middle of a very pleasant dream when Skippy woke me up. Margaret, the boys, and I were on a speedboat, not on Earth but not anywhere on Jaguar either, it doesn't matter. The boys wanted to go tubing, and I was driving the boat while Margaret relaxed on the bow, wearing that bikini I like so much and-

Uh, that was Too Much Information.

"*JOE*!" His voice boomed out of the speakers. "*Joe Joe Joe Joe*-"

"Oh for-" As I sat abruptly upright in bed, one hand automatically protected my skull from bashing against the overhead cabinet. The cabinet wasn't there, because I was no longer aboard the *La Fayette*. Old habits die hard, and when you renew an old habit, they tend to stick around for a while. Yanked out of a nice dream, I was instantly pissed at him. "Is the freakin' ship on fire?"

"It is worse than that. Or, better, actually. This is good news. Um, could be bad news. I guess it depends what-"

"Give me a-" My brain was still disoriented from shifting from one reality to another, and I anticipated a headache. Time to suck it up, Joe. Swinging my feet onto the floor, I stifled a yawn. "Just tell me."

"OK, so, you asked whether I had any intel on how many ships the kitties have tied down at Omaha?"

"I did. If you now have a number, that is not a good reason to wake me up at," a glance at my phone. "One forty three in the freakin' morning."

"I do not have a number, I have no idea how many ships are there."

"Then why-"

"What I do know is a lot of ships that *were* there, now are *not*. At least three major fleets have been directed elsewhere. The 17th, the 24th, and the 33rd Fleets. Those are all space control units, not dedicated to bombardment. Dedicated anti-ship platforms, with all the associated escorts."

"Yeah, those are the type of units I expected the kitties to assign to a blockade force. Shit. The secret that you didn't fall into the star must be out. The Outsider told them the truth."

"Not necessarily."

"No? Why else would the Hegemony pull ships away from Omaha?"

"I'm getting to that."

"I thought you said there was no useable intel in that download?"

"There was nothing *obvious*, dumdum. Maybe I should talk with Reed, your brain is seriously mushy tonight."

"Do *not* wake her up."

"OK, OK," he sighed. "Waking her would be a bad idea anyway. I thought *you* were grumpy in the morning. She is like a bear pulled out of hibernation, you do *not* want to screw with her."

"We agree on that. Back to the subject."

"After reviewing all of the important documents- *All* of them, which *suuuucked*, ugh, so tedious for me to-"

"I am way too cranky to listen to you whine about your life right now."

"*Fine*. After I sifted through all the military message traffic, then the government traffic, I was left with commercial messages. That comprises about ninety eight percent of all data handled by relay station, a number that-"

"That is a *super* useful and relevant number right now. Get to the point."

"I am trying to do that. What I stumbled across is a chain of messages for the captain of a Maxohlx commercial freighter, a ship that has been contracted to provide supplies to sustain the blockade at Ohmeharikahn. You know, non-lethal stuff like food, medicine, pine-scented body wash-"

"The Maxohlx use *pine-scented body wash*?"

"I have no idea. That was an example, numbskull."

"Keep going."

"Anyway, this freighter captain was asking questions about who will pay for the fuel, since his ship has been diverted from Ohmeharikahn, and has been directed to a rendezvous point out near the rim of the galaxy. He wants to know how much the military will pay, or if the extra expense will be covered by insurance. Also, he wanted to make sure the company will not be responsible for paying fees for late delivery, since the delivery point was changed by the customer."

"There is a reason I should care about any of this? Oh, *please* do not tell me that supply company is connected to SkipWay."

"What? No. Though a few of my associates have evangelized in Maxohlx society about the many substantial benefits of SkipWay membership, the kitties are being *dicks* as usual. We persevered in our important mission, but then basically I ran out of associates who were willing to take the risk. Bunch of crybabies."

"The risk? They were expelled by the kitties?"

"They were executed as enemy agents, which was totally unfair. I did send a harshly worded diplomatic note from Skippistan's Ministry of Foreign Affairs, but the Maxohlx never bothered to respond. My lawyers advised me to let it go."

"People got *killed* for- We will talk about that later. Exactly why should I care about some Maxohlx captain whining about money?"

"Think, dumdum, *think*. Hmm, I will have a bot deliver coffee, your head is extra dense this morning."

"No coffee. I am not ready to give up on a decent night of sleep. Get to the point, why is this so important, and why could it be good news *or* bad news?"

"Wow. This is what it's like when you know something obvious, and I can't see it? This is cool, I'm taking a moment to savor the-"

"I am going back to sleep, unless you give me a damned good reason not to."

"Three space control fleets are pulled from a blockade, and sent racing to the rim of the galaxy. That doesn't tell you any-"

"Oh *shit*."

"You see it now?"

"Those ships are being sent to protect the *array*."

"That is my guess, yes."

"Holy shit, Skippy. This is *outstanding*."

"Well, it's me, so-"

"Also, I see why you described this as potentially bad news. The array must be close to being online, otherwise the Outsider wouldn't allow any filthy meatsacks near the thing."

"Again, that is also my guess. We do not have a lot of time."

"We don't. Do you know where those three fleets were sent?"

"No, darn it. All I have is the rendezvous point for that freighter. It is scheduled to be there in four days."

"That's a good enough start. We will see which ships meet it at the rendezvous, then follow them. Send a bot with coffee, I'm taking a quick shower. Then *I* will wake up Reed."

Before getting into the shower, I called the duty officer, and cancelled the next jump on the schedule. "Skippy, I need a least-time course to Earth, including whatever wormhole shortcuts you can manage."

Four minutes later, I was buttoning up my uniform blouse when a bot rolled in with coffee. Waking up in the middle of the night always sucks, that first sip of coffee always makes it a bit more bearable. "Skippy, slowly turn on the lights in Reed's cabin."

Forty seconds later, she sleepily called me, "Ah, what, aaaaah," she was trying to talk through a yawn. "Sir?"

"We're going to Earth."

"Oh, why?"

"Guns. We need lots of *big* guns."

Ten minutes after convening a meeting in the conference room with Reed, Frey, and Chandra, I was less pumped about leading the UN Navy into glorious combat. Actually, in my experience combat is messy, not at all glorious. Any feelings of glory come only after combat is over, and only the survivors get to feel anything good about what happened.

My original plan had been to request that Def Com send the UN Navy with us. Like, most of the Navy, especially the big battlewagons with the big guns. We would need to fight our way through at least three senior species space control fleets. These ship formations were equipped for what the military calls 'Anti-Access/Area Denial'. Meaning, they keep the bad guys away from, whatever they are protecting. In that case, it would be a Gateway to hell. A Gateway to an intergalactic invasion, so it's the same thing.

Then, the four of us dug into the details of the message traffic that Skippy was so proud of finding.

"Ahhh, shit," Reed pushed back from the table. "This sounds good, but I might have to quote Admiral Akbar."

Frey understood. "You think it could be a trap?"

"*Whaaaat*?" Skippy exploded. "I give you an easy way to find the array, and you are-"

"Reed," I interrupted him. "Talk to me."

"This seems *too* convenient, Sir."

Chandra nodded agreement.

"I would agree, but," I stalled while I considered what she had said. "There is no evidence the kitties know that Skippy can access their relay stations."

"The message is *commercial* traffic, Sir," Reed noted. "Not military, not government. Commercial messages are often routed through client relay stations, and the Hegemony has to expect that Skippy can hack those."

"Ah. If we find a copy of that message on, say, a Thuranin station, then it could have been planted for us to find?"

"The alternative is that we believe the Maxohlx communications security is inexcusably sloppy."

"The Maxohlx are meatsacks, and we all know that screwups happen. It only takes one person to not read a memo, and COMSEC is busted. OK, we can divert to ping a Thuranin relay station, better plan to visit two, to be sure."

"Ugh." Skippy was beyond disgusted. "That won't *prove* anything, dumdum. Of course a copy of that message will be on other platforms, that is their standard procedure. Maxohlx commercial traffic usually only uses the base level of encryption that is built into their off-the-shelf IT systems, but that scheme can't be cracked by any second-tier species. Diverting to a relay station will only delay bringing a fleet to attack the array."

"True, but-"

"A large formation of ships travel slowly, compared to *Valkyrie*. We can take a side trip to a relay station while the Navy is enroute."

"Reed? What do you think?"

She shifted in her chair. "Sir, we need a substantial force for the attack, but not for a recon. We could arrive at this supposed rendezvous point early, as early as possible. Plant an Elder comm node there to provide FTL communications, and watch from a safe distance. If the freighter arrives, and is met by a small escort force, then the message might be legit. But if we find a large number of ships waiting in ambush," she held up her hands.

"Right. If it's not an ambush, we follow that freighter, and find the array. Hopefully. Then, we will know what composition of force is needed to destroy the damned thing. Skippy, show us a least-time course from here to Earth, then from Earth to the rendezvous point. Also show another course, from here direct to the rendezvous."

"That is not going to tell you any- Fine, here it is." A hologram appeared, with a blue line, and a red line. "The first option will take five days, thirteen hours, and that is not including time for you to smack sense into UN-Dick, and for the fleet to assemble and prep for departure."

"That's no good, we will arrive at the rendezvous point too late."

"A direct flight to the rendezvous, which is near, ah, not anything you would recognize. We could arrive there two days and three hours before the scheduled rendezvous."

"We do that. Skippy, I understand your objection, please remember that for military matters, you're not the expert. Before we assemble a strike force, we need to understand the opposition. Is it just three Maxohlx fleets, or does the Outsider also have some type of high-tech defense prepared?"

"Ugh. If the hateful thing had a defense, it wouldn't need the stupid kitties."

"It would, if the defense system isn't online yet. Either way, we need to know, before we can make an attack plan. Can you see that?"

"Yes," he said with a resentful sigh. "Damn it. Why does your mushy brain only use logic when you're arguing with me?"

"That's the only time I need logic, so-"

"True. Fine, we do it your way. Bilby has the course programmed into the navigation system."

We arrived twenty three minutes ahead of Skippy's prediction, and he of course took full credit for getting us there faster. "It is confirmed: I am *awesome*," he sang.

"Yet," I held up an index finger. "The Outsider has been one step ahead of you the entire time."

"Oh," he gasped. "How *dare* you. I should-"

"What you should do is tell us whether we are alone out here."

"I'm running a scan now, you jackass. It takes time."

"Take all the time you need."

The ship's sensors, even enhanced by Skippy, could not detect stealthed ships from a distance of two lightminutes. He gave us a provisional All Clear ten minutes later anyway, with the understanding that only meant there was nothing obvious around us.

Except for a buoy, that we noticed very quickly. It was a dumb device, sending out a ping every eleven and a half seconds. There was no message encoded in the pings, they were just short bursts of photons. "A beacon to let arriving ships know they're in the right place?" I guessed.

"It is a military grade buoy," Skippy noted. "Maxohlx technology."

"We are in the right place," Reed nodded. "The question is: do the kitties have a surprise planned for us?"

To provide a closer view of the rendezvous point, we sent in a drone equipped with a sensor package, and an Elder comm node. Since the drone needed to travel two lightminutes, a distance of thirty six million kilometers, we launched the thing not out of a standard missile tube, but a railgun. The railgun gave it enough velocity to reach the target zone in a day and a half, and the drone's motor would begin slowing it down as it approached the area we wanted to scan. After the launch, all we could do was wait. And maintain an alert to jump away at the first sign of trouble.

Seven hours before the scheduled rendezvous, two Maxohlx frigates emerged from jump within nine lightseconds of the target point, and at first, those ships didn't appear to be doing anything, other than using passive sensors. Twenty minutes later, we detected faint echoes of multiple sensor fields, in an expanding bubble centered around the frigates. Sensor drones, typically expendable units that had a limited operational life. The powercells could run the sensor fields long enough to cover an hour past the rendezvous time, that's all that was needed.

"Skippy," Reed asked. "Is this a problem?"

"Nah, as the bubble expands the field strength decreases, it will be fairly weak when our drone gets there. I am analyzing the overlapping fields, looking for especially weak spots. I will adjust the drone's trajectory if needed. We're good."

The freighter arrived thirty seven minutes early. It was a big thing, an old star carrier converted to hauling cargo modules instead of starships. It had only half the original number of hardpoints, with the spine shortened considerably. A bit like the old *Flying Dutchman* Two Point Oh, after our tropical vacation on Newark.

Only a third of the hardpoints had cargo modules attached.

"I don't like that," I muttered, running a finger along the holographic image of the freighter.

Reed cocked her head. "Sir?"

"That ship isn't carrying much cargo, to sustain three fleets. Skippy, how long ago did those ships leave Ohmeharikahn?"

"Roughly three weeks, is my best estimate, why?"

"If they brought enough consumables with them for an extended stay, then we're good. But if that freighter is carrying everything those ships and crews need, the Maxohlx could anticipate they won't need to guard the array for long."

"Ohhh," Reed groaned. "The array is close to being operational, or already is?"

"My guess is the Gateway is not open yet. We know the Maxohlx still believe the Outsider is an Elder AI, and it is trying to wake up more Sentinels. To restore the strategic balance in the galaxy, or whatever bullshit story the Outsider told the kitties. When they see an invasion force coming out of the Gateway, even the stupidest of kitties would realize they have made a horrible mistake. They wouldn't have sent out for pizza," I pointed to the freighter.

"I hope you're right, Sir. I have a bad feeling we won't have time to fly back to Earth to summon the 1st Fleet into the fight."

"We'll know soon enough. Skippy, what are those ships doing?"

"Talking. A lot of blah blah buh-LAH, and none of it interesting. The freighter captain asked what is going on, the lead frigate replied that he doesn't need to know, and they inquired whether the freighter brought any fresh food. The answer to that is '*No*'."

"That's surprising," Reed observed.

"Ah," Skippy shook his head. "Not so much. That ship was supposed to deliver its cargo to Ohmeharikahn, and the blockade fleet could get plenty of fresh food from the planet there. That ship is hauling mostly spare parts, and consumables to keep warships flightworthy."

"I don't like that, either," I grimaced. "The Maxohlx definitely don't plan to be at the array for long."

My expectation was the freighter would receive jump coordinates, then be escorted away by the frigates. That the three ships would jump away soon. Instead, they lingered for five, then ten minutes. "What the hell are they waiting for?" I asked no one in particular. Our drone was approaching its optimal location, having easily slipped through the sensor field bubble undetected. The little thing was running silently, propulsion system off, wrapped in a stealth field. If the enemy ships remained there for too long, our drone would be out of range to scan the residual jump signatures for a clue about their destination. "Hey, jackass. Freighters don't make money if they're not moving," I addressed that helpful comment to the commercial ship's captain.

"You realize he can't hear you, Joe?" Skippy chuckled.

"Yeah, yeah. We-"

"Hold the phone! The lead frigate just sent an encrypted burst transmission, probably the jump coordinates."

"Can you crack the encryption?"

"Dude, please," he gave me an eyeroll. "This is a pathetic civilian grade scheme, since the freighter isn't equipped with military comm gear. Oooooh, this is interesting. Hey, I think I know where those ships are going!"

"How do you figure that?"

"The direction they are jumping? The only thing along that course is a wormhole. Or, a star system three hundred lightyears away, so probably not there."

"How far is the wormhole?"

"Thirteen lightyears, I'll show you a chart." The main display zoomed out, to show a yellow line leading from our position, to a wormhole. "See?"

"Nothing between here and there?"

"We are near the rim of the galaxy, stars are thin out here. No, there is nothing."

"What is the closest star system to that wormhole?"

"Twenty seven lightyears," the image expanded again, and a red dot began blinking. "It's a red dwarf, no inhabited world. As far as I am aware of, no ship has ever bothered to survey that system."

"OK, now show me-"

"Wait! The enemy ships are preparing to jump away. Three, two, one- There goes a frigate."

The freighter went next, followed closely by the lead frigate. That was the Maxohlx standard procedure for escorting vessels. One warship went first to recon the destination, and would have immediately jumped back with a warning if there was a problem. The other frigate waited to make sure the freighter actually did jump, since civilian drive systems could be less than perfectly reliable.

"They're gone!" Skippy announced what we could all see on the display. "Joe, we should jump toward-"

"Wait. Scan the residual jump signatures, confirm those ships went to the correct coordinates."

"But it-"

"That's why we sent the drone out there. Just do it."

"Ugh, fine. OK, OK, hmm, yes. Confirmed. Wow, that freighter's drive is *loud*, it shook the whole area. Now can we jump? We can get to that wormhole faster than they can."

"Not yet. Show us the chart again. This time, show us where that wormhole connects to."

"Oh. The other end is, here," a yellow dot glowed. "Hmm, that truly is in the middle of freakin' nowhere. Seventeen hundred lightyears out past the rim of the galaxy. There is absolutely nothing within four hundred lightyears of that place."

"Skippy?" Reed asked. "Why did the Elders locate a wormhole so far from anywhere?"

"They didn't. Back when they set up that wormhole, the far end was *inside* the galaxy, three hundred lightyears from the rim. Stellar drift has moved it. In fact, hmm, I would not be surprised if the next shift of the local network causes that wormhole to go dormant."

"That won't happen soon?"

"I mean, soon on a geological time scale."

"Nothing for us to worry about, then," I used my hands to manipulate the display image, zooming it out. "The far end of that wormhole. Is that a good spot to set up the array?"

"It would be an excellent spot," he answered. "If we leave now, we can go through that wormhole before the enemy does."

"We're not doing that."

"*What*? Why not?" Skippy demanded, hands on his little hips. "Isn't that why we came all the way out here?"

When I glanced back at Reed, she had her head cocked, puzzled. "You have a plan, Sir?"

"Ayuh. Skippy, we can get back to the wormhole we used to get here, faster than the enemy can go through the one they're flying toward?"

"Um, yes, but why would we-"

"We're going back to Earth, to bring the cavalry?" Reed guessed.

"That would take too long," I shook my head. "Skippy, can you create a shortcut between the wormhole we came through, to the far end of where that freighter is going?"

"Oh. Now I see. Yes, I can do that. Neither of those networks are pissed at me. One of them is a network I have never contacted before, so it's all good."

"Set a course, Sir?" Reed asked.

"Yes, and jump when ready. Skippy, another question, the other wormhole- That is too awkward. Let's call it 'Tazenda'."

Reed was puzzled again. "Sir?"

"My memory is kind of vague because I read the books a long time ago, but in Azimov's Foundation books, there was a planet called 'Tazenda'. It was a corruption of the name 'Stars End', a place far from the center of the galaxy.

Skippy, what is the average time gap between emergences of the Tazenda wormhole?"

"One minute, twenty seven seconds."

"What is the *minimum* time gap?"

"One minute and three seconds. The maximum is two minutes, forty four seconds, in case you were wondering."

"Now I have a tough question for you. Can your extreme awesomeness make a shortcut to the far end of Tazenda, and close that shortcut, during the minimum time gap? Do that without disrupting the schedule of the wormhole?"

"Ooh, that timing would be tight. To make it work, *Valkyrie* would have to be racing toward the wormhole, so we pass through a few seconds after the event horizon is stable."

Reed shrugged. "We can do that."

I gave her a thumbs up. "If there are enemy ships monitoring Tazenda, they would never notice anything different?"

"They wouldn't notice for several weeks. Eventually, the radiation of the shortcut opening would be noticed."

"That's good. We have a plan. We go through the shortcut without anyone detecting us. Then we will jump around to emergence points, until we see that freighter again. We follow it, and find the array."

CHAPTER THIRTY THREE

It was a good plan, almost too good. The entire trip back to the wormhole we had used, going through the shortcut, and jumping to three emergence points until we detected the freighter coming through the event horizon, that entire time I kept expecting the Universe to smack me with an epic beatdown. It didn't happen, so that got me concerned the freakin' Universe had some *really* nasty surprise planned for me.

The freighter and pair of frigates came through, where a destroyer squadron was waiting. We had been playing cat and mouse with that squadron, as it kept jumping around from one emergence point to another, we maintained a distance of twenty lightseconds. The speed of light time lag is annoying, it was good enough.

All nine of the enemy ships jumped away before the wormhole closed, Reed jumped us near the center of the formation of residual resonance.

"Got it, ha!" Skippy crowed. "I know where they went. They are overconfident; they must expect that out here, there is no need to drop off resonators behind them to mask the jump signature. Bilby has the coordinates."

"We can jump when ready, Dudes."

There was a risk that, with eight escort ships available, the enemy would leave one ship behind each time they jumped, to see if anyone was following them. They didn't do that.

"You're right, Skippy. They are overconfident. That is, odd."

"They believe their alliance with the Outsider protects them from being followed?" Reed suggested.

"Yeah," I shrugged. "Something like that. That is three jumps so far, I hope we don't have to keep doing this for another week."

We did not have to keep jumping for a week. The enemy ships conducted a fourth jump, we followed and-

Joined the party.

"Holy shit," Skippy gasped. "There it is."

"What," I unstrapped from my seat and stood up to approach the main display. "Are we looking at?"

That was a very good question.

Glowing rings stretched in a line across the display, with a glowing, bolt of lightning or something extending through the center of the rings. From two lightminutes away, the thing should have been a dot. It had to be enormous.

"Give me a minute to examine the thing."

"Skippy," Reed remained in her chair. "Is there any sign the enemy detected our jump?"

"No, the sinks absorbed ninety eight percent of the gamma rays, and the residual was directed away on a tight beam. We're good, for now. Those rings are, hmm, that's interesting. My guess is, that is the Gateway. Or, it will be."

I was skeptical. "This does not look anything like the Kaliberak array."

"It has been taken apart, and the components retasked for the purpose of creating a Gateway. Look," he zoomed the display in on one glowing ring, to show a dark object. "That is one of the receiver antennas. It is now acting as a *transmitter*, to generate that ring, I do not understand exactly how it works. There are, hmm, eighteen rings, and four transmitters per ring. That's odd. More than three quarters of the receiver satellites are unaccounted for."

"Spare parts?"

"Could be, but if that's the case, they still should be here. I don't see the missing components anywhere."

"That is a mystery we can solve later. What is the thing doing? Is a Gateway open?"

"No. I am not detecting an effect anything similar to what the Elders saw so many eons ago. It is online, but still powering up. Yes, the power output is slowly increasing. Give me a minute to run a predictive model."

"While you do that, we-"

"OK, OK, done. Three days. Based on the rate the power output is increasing, and the curve on which the increase is slowing, that thing will be at maximum power three days from now. However, that assumes the mechanism must be at full power for a Gateway to open, that is *not* a solid assumption. The thing should have been designed to handle more power than it needs for full operation."

I looked at Reed. "We have *two* days, then."

She bit her lip. "Not enough time to get to Earth, and bring the Navy here. We would need the entire Navy, to take on all those ships," she waved at the red dots on the display, one symbol for every enemy starship.

I nodded slowly. "We have to do this by ourselves."

"Joe," Skippy sighed. "While I appreciate your gung-ho attitude, how do you propose to attack the array, or whatever we're calling those rings?"

"How *big* is that thing?"

"Almost fourteen kilometers, from the first ring to the last."

"That is, whoo," I whistled, "a *big* target. How many rings would we need to take out, to shut the thing down?"

"Joe, I have no idea. More than one, certainly. The field each of those rings are generating extends across two sets of rings on either side. Remember, each ring has four transmitters, we have to assume that system has significant redundancy, It will not be as easy as destroying one transmitter per ring. Also, ooooh, *that's* what it is. I have been trying to understand a weird effect around the rings, extending from one end of that, glowing center beam of, whatever it is. The rings have created a force field, a temporal displacement effect. Any railgun darts or missile we fire at those rings will slow down, and take more than an *hour* to hit their targets. If the darts and missiles even survive the temporal effect, I suspect the missile guidance systems would be severely affected."

"You are supposed to be giving us solutions, not excuses."

"I give you *facts*, you are responsible for the solutions. I can't do *all* the work around here."

"It's a tough target, I get that. We won't be using railguns or missiles."

"Um, maser beams won't have enough punching power to-"

"We are going to deploy Elder weapons again."

"Whoa. Whoa, whoa, *whoa*. Slow your roll there, pardner. You can't-"

"Yes, I can. You are uncomfortable with me treating our Elder weapons arsenal like it's a Pez dispenser, but-"

"I am, but that is not my objection here. That temporal displacement field will affect even Elder weapons. We would have to get close to deploy them, *too* close. Also, the Elder devices we have aboard are *not* optimal for being used in empty space. We used all of our gridbusters when we stopped the Outsider from waking up a Sentinel, remember? The weapons we have left are designed to be used against the solid matter of stars and planets. Those weapons won't have much to work with out here."

Hearing that made me wince. That was a question I should have asked before we jumped into the party, alone. "Will they have any effect?"

"Um, I hate to say this, but yes. *If* they can get close enough, which will not be easy."

"OK, then we prep the weapons, program a jump to-"

"No, we will not do that," he stomped a foot in the air. "Will you *listen* to me? In addition to the temporal field around the rings, the Maxohlx ships are projecting a dense disruption field, in a cylinder around the entire, ring thing. We can't jump in there, not anywhere close enough to launch weapons."

Reed asked the important question. "What is the distance between the outer edge of the distortion field, to the rings?"

"Five lightseconds."

I whistled again, and not because I was happy. "That is a huge damned field. How are the Maxohlx projecting something that extensive?"

"They can't do it for long. But, they could do it for another five days, by rotating ships in and out, giving the projectors time to cool down. Also, the Maxohlx brought over three hundred ships here."

"Sir?" Reed prompted me to turn away from staring at the display. "Can we review the situation, in my office?"

In her office, she closed the door. "Ten lightseconds is a *long* way to fly through normal space from one edge of the disruption field to the other, we would be exposed to intense enemy fire the whole time."

"We can jump away, fire up the boosters, build up as much speed as we can."

"In *one* day? To be certain of destroying the Gateway before it opens, we have to act soon."

"Agreed."

"Sir," she let out a breath, then pursed her lips. Deciding what was the best way to say, what she needed to say. "If we jump in there, to attack the rings, it will be this ship's last action. We will be exposed for too long, we can't hope to escape critical damage. Even if a miracle happens, the kitties could direct part of their fleet to pursue us with damping fields so we can't jump away, while other ships jump ahead of us."

"This is the best chance we've had to stop the Outsider."

"Sir," she shook her head. "Respectfully, no it is not. Destroying this array is only a delaying tactic. Even Elder weapons won't kill the Outsider, we have seen that. It will survive to try again, but *we* won't be available to fight it again. Skippy could be captured, he almost certainly would be captured. Along with Nagatha."

"I hear you. The problem with doing nothing here is that would allow more Outsiders access to our galaxy, and *that* is a non-starter. We *must* destroy the Gateway before it opens." That was said as a declaration of fact. The real fact was, I wasn't certain we had to fight. My heart told me I should do something, have a bias for action. When in doubt, attack.

My head told me that just felt, wrong.

"It's your call, Sir, but," *Valkyrie's* captain was not happy.

"What?" I asked.

"I request that the Special Mission Group commander look for an alternative, before we jump into a suicide mission."

"Fair enough. We have several days until I need to give the 'Go' order."

"Sir, keep in mind, we snuck in here, but we can't completely conceal an outbound jump. The enemy would know we plan to crash the party."

"They are already on full alert. If they divert ships to search for us, that can only be good. I need to think about this. Damn it, I wish we had brought another ship with us. We could have unloaded Skippy and Nagatha, and most of the crew, before we jump into action. That is a lesson learned."

"This was supposed to be a recon mission."

"Our missions rarely happen the way we expect, I should have remembered that. All right, I can think while we prepare for battle. We jump away, fire up the boosters, and build up as much speed as we can in, as you said, one day."

"That presents another problem. The boosters were designed for short bursts of speed, they will run out of fuel in less than an hour of continuous use. By expending all the booster fuel, we won't be able to slow down enough to go through a wormhole on the way back."

"Ah, shit. Then we will expend *half* of the fuel."

"I don't see the point, Sir. Cutting our speed means we spend more time running the gauntlet of the Maxohlx fleet. If we are really doing this, we should go all in."

"I see your point. I will, consider alternatives. In the meantime, we jump, and light off the boosters."

She nodded, her lips pressed tightly together. She had failed to smack some sense on me, she also had orders. "Aye, Sir."

We jumped six lightmonths away, sat silently for twenty minutes to make sure there were no enemy ships or other hazards in the area, and Reed gave the crew another thirty minutes to prepare for boost. That meant making certain anything that might vibrate loose would stay where it was supposed to, and inserting both earpieces for noise canceling. The new boosters were more powerful, more fuel efficient, produced a vibration less likely to rattle your teeth out of your mouth, and they were *louder*. Skippy said the new armor plating didn't absorb the vibration as well as the old panels, so more of the energy was felt by the crew as sound waves. My personal preparation for an hour of discomfort was eating a snack, locking my office chair to the floor, and strapping in for a rough ride. Being in my office rather than on the bridge gave Reed freedom to act, without me looking over her shoulder.

And, me being out of sight gave the crew time to contemplate what no one wanted to think about. The end of the Merry Band of Pirates.

"Skippy," I called. "I have doubts."

"Well, you certainly should," he wagged a finger at me. "Racing into a glorious fight here is the *wrong* thing to do. Reed is correct. Not only will you at best delay an Outsider invasion, you will clear the deck for it to act in the future, and that will *guarantee* an invasion will be successful."

"I know."

"Then, then why?" He sputtered.

"I'm in the military. We know we can't win every fight. Sometimes, the best you can do is, whatever you can do. Hurt the enemy, slow them down. Weaken their force, so a follow-on attack has a better chance of success. What I *can't* do is nothing. I can't stand by and do nothing, just because this particular battle won't win the war."

"Joe, please listen to me. You will be handing this galaxy on a silver platter to the Outsider, if you insist on following through on this insanity. You military people have a saying: live to fight again. You should listen to that advice."

"Ah, I hear you. Skippy, the problem with that advice is, it's good for a bold and sensible commander. You accept that it's not a fight you can win right then, and you realize it's better to wait for a better opportunity to strike."

"Yes, which is exactly the situation we are in now, dumdum."

"But, 'Live to fight again' can be an excuse, if you're a coward."

"Joe. Seriously? You are concerned Def Com would think you're a coward? You are the opposite of that, your Go-To move is being reckless."

"OK, I, just heard what I said." Meaning, accepting there are fights you can't win. And that you don't need to win every fight, to win the war. "I am, willing to reconsider. Do you have a better plan?"

"No. But then, I never do. Planning is *your* thing. Joe, you intend to use brute force here, instead of your usual clever nonsense."

"I should dream up a better plan, then?"

"Yes."

"I have," I glanced at the bulkhead display. "Twenty two minutes to do that. Once the boosters light off, I won't be able to hear the thoughts in my head."

"Then, delay using the boosters. Give yourself more time to think of a plan that actually makes sense."

"As you said, we don't know at what power level that Gateway will open. It could happen in three days, it could happen in three *hours*. We can't delay, just because we are scared of the consequences."

"You are determined not to be sensible about this?"

"*You* have about twenty minutes to convince me there is an alternative that does not allow a Gateway to open, and potentially hundreds of Outsider ships to come through."

"Yeah," he sighed. "I got nothin'." His avatar faded out.

Ten minutes. Shit, I never thought the Merry Band of Pirates would end with me taking the ship and crew into a glorious and futile battle. Not only were Reed and Skippy correct that my plan wouldn't stop the Outsider, it would lose the war. But, not shutting down the Gateway would also result in us losing the war.

Time. The problem was time.

No, the real problem was the Outsider has been one step ahead of us, the entire fight. Had it hacked the probability field, to benefit itself? That was a useless question, I couldn't do anything with the information, even if I knew the truth.

Was I just being stubborn, unable to accept the fact that flying into battle wouldn't accomplish anything? My argument was, I was the *only* person willing to accept the truth.

We weren't going to win this fight. The *Elders* had known they couldn't win, if an Outsider presence was established in our galaxy. If the Elders had been afraid to confront the outsiders directly, why the hell had I ever thought we could succeed in stopping an invasion?

Eight minutes. The next hour was going to suck, then the crew would take time to rest and recover, and we would jump into battle. And likely, die. Almost certainly, we would all die. The Outsider would capture Skippy, and Nagatha, and gloat about-

No. Eight minutes was a false, self-imposed deadline. We should delay lighting off the boosters until I was absolutely certain there was no alternative. I would let Reed know about my latest decision. But first, I needed information.

"Skippy?"

"Please tell me you have changed your mind?"

"Sorry, not quite. I do have a question."

"Will answering the question change your mind?"

"Again, no. Or, maybe. Where is the Outsider?"

"Um, what do you mean? The array-"

"Yes, the Kaliberak array is here, and clearly the Outsider pimped that ride to make a Gateway. Do you know where *it* is, the Outsider itself? Aboard a ship, or it is inside one of those module things that are generating the rings?"

"Jeez, Joe, I don't know."

"You can't sense the thing?"

"I am not a magic wizard, so no."

"So, it might not even be here."

"Come on, Joe. Opening a Gateway has been its goal, for at least seven years. Of course it would want to be here."

"You intercepted communications between the enemy ships?"

"Yes. They were very chatty, no need for EMCON when there is a big glowing Gateway lighting up the whole area."

"Great. Were any of those ships talking with the Outsider?"

"No, why?"

"Don't you think that is odd? Was there any sign the Outsider was controlling the Maxohlx fleet, the way it did at Omaha?"

"Um, no. Why are you asking irrelevant questions? Ooh, are you trying to distract me?"

"I am trying to understand what is really going on out there."

"You don't have much time to puzzle through it, dumdum."

"Yes, we do." Tapping my phone, I called Reed. "Fireball, halt the booster countdown, for now."

There was the slightest shudder of relief in her voice. "You have a new plan, Sir?"

"I have questions, I want answers. Hold here for now."

Skippy took off his hat and rubbed his shiny head. "How do you propose to get answers, Joe?"

"First, show me the array, Gateway thing again, from here." A hologram appeared above my desk. "Uh, zoom in the view, please."

"That *is* at maximum magnification. We are six lightmonths away, so nothing is there. Two months ago, the Outsider had not yet brought the Kaliberak array here."

"Right. Let's jump to, a distance of three lightweeks? I want to see the thing being assembled."

"My suggestion is we start at one lightmonth, and work inward."

"OK. Reed?" I called her on my phone. "I'll be on the bridge shortly. I want a jump to within a, as in *one*, lightmonth of the Gateway."

A minute later, I walked onto the bridge, Reed turned in her seat. "Ready to jump, Sir."

Pointing at my seat behind her, I started in that direction, but Gasquet shook his head and got up from the XO's chair. So, I sat beside Reed.

"What's the plan?" She whispered.

"For now, we're going on a fun-filled sightseeing tour."

She raised an eyebrow. "If the Outsider has a gift shop, I do *not* want anything."

We jumped. Still nothing. We jumped to three lightweeks from the Gateway.

No Gateway yet, nothing we could see, but there were star carriers. "One, two, three," I pointed to the symbols in the display. "Skippy, where are the other star carriers?"

"Um, why are you asking *me*? They either dropped off their cargo of satellites, or they haven't arrived yet?"

"What are you looking for, Sir?" Reed asked.

"Right now, I am a guy standing in front of a refrigerator with the door open. I don't know what I'm looking for, I'll know when I find it. Skippy, what are we seeing? What's happening out there?"

"Lots of maintenance bots scurrying about, carrying Kaliberak satellites. Two rings are being assembled, hmm, this is an opportunity to understand how the thing works. Can we jump closer, in increments of two lightdays?"

We did that, twice. While Skippy puzzled through understanding how the original Kaliberak receiver satellites created a ring, and how the rings could open a Gateway, I stood the display, looking for answers.

Reed stepped close enough to whisper. "What are you thinking, Sir?"

"I am watching and listening, not thinking. I just have a, uh, uh-"

"Bad feeling about this?'

"No. More like a *funny* feeling. Like something doesn't add up here. Skippy, is the Outsider directing those ships and bots?"

"Hundred percent. I can *see* the communications channels. It was pulling all the strings there."

"Where is the Outsider?"

"Back then, it was aboard the star carrier that is farthest from us. There is a weird spacetime effect around that ship, it is very noticeable. Maybe it generates that effect all the time, but it is suppressed when it knows someone might be watching?"

"Your guess is better than mine. Did you detect that weird effect around the Gateway now? I mean when we were there."

"No. Before you ask, I can't explain it."

"OK. Do you see anything that might give us a hint about a way to destroy the Gateway, without us having to fly in close?"

"Unfortunately, no. If I understood how the stupid thing is supposed to open a Gateway for an invasion, I might have a clue how to mess with it. Right now, none of this makes sense."

"Talk to me. What doesn't make sense?"

"The modifications to the Kaliberak satellites. From what I can see, they don't actually *do* anything."

"What do you mean? They are generating the rings, and that beam of energy. And a temporal effect."

"Yes but, it doesn't make sense. I now realize that what the rings are doing is nothing like the machine the Elders built, the one that scared the hell out of them, when it began to construct a thing out of energy."

"OK, first the Elders built a machine that received the instructions, right? The instructions on how to build what they didn't know was a Gateway?"

"Yes. Joe, I know what you're thinking, but the machine we're seeing here doesn't do that either. It's almost like, all this machine can do is to protect itself. I do not see any sign that it could create a Gateway for- Oh."

"What?"

"Oh. *Oh*, you have *got* to be kidding me."

Reed ducked back to her command chair. "Should we jump away?"

My answer was a slashing motion with one hand. "Skippy? Is this a trap?"

"Oooooh, I am *so* mad right now. It is much worse than a trap."

"How could it be worse than-"

"It's a freakin' *decoy*."

CHAPTER THIRTY FOUR

"A *decoy*?" I looked at Reed, who raised both hands and silently mouthed, 'What the fuck'?

"Yes," Skippy confirmed. "Oooh, I am so mad. A *fake*. The thing we were looking at, when we saw it in close to real time, is not a Gateway. It was never intended to be any part of the Outsider's plan to enable an invasion. Except for luring us here, and wasting our time. I hate to say this, but Colonel Reed was correct to quote Admiral Akbar. It *is* a trap. The message about the freighter? It was planted for me to find. The Outsider wanted us to come here, and to either destroy the thing, or for *Valkyrie* to be destroyed, or both."

"It wanted us to destroy it?"

"Yes. It wanted us to at least make an attempt to bust up the rings. The best scenario for it would be for us rush in with guns blazing, like you planned to do, by the way. The result would be *Valkyrie* smashed into tiny pieces, and me out of the fight. But the Outsider *knows* you, Joe. It has studied you, and it has seen that you accomplish the impossible by dreaming up whacky schemes no one else could have imagined. So, it hedged its bet. In case we *did* succeed in tearing the fake Gateway apart, and we survived, we would fly to Earth for a victory parade. We would no longer be hunting for a Gateway. Either way, if we had attacked the decoy, it would have cleared the decks for the Outsider to open a real Gateway."

"Shiiiiiit," I groaned. "The Maxohlx are here, but only to sell the Outsider's cover story?"

"Correct. From the message traffic I have intercepted, the Maxohlx believe this is a genuine Gateway. Although, hmm."

"What?"

"Some of messages were odd, they made references I didn't understand until just now. Joe, the rotten kitties have bought into the Outsider's bullshit story that it is a rogue Elder AI, working to wake up Sentinels and restore the balance of power in the galaxy. That is why the Hegemony has been so eager to assist in their own destruction."

"Yeah, we knew that, so?"

"So, the fleet commanders here were told the rings are not a Gateway, they are a mechanism for waking up a Sentinel."

"Shit. There is no way the kitties will believe the truth."

"Not by anything you say to them, no."

"OK, the setup here makes sense now. If the fake Gateway wasn't protected by three hundred warships, we could have taken time to examine the thing closely, and realized it is a decoy. The Outsider summoned the kitties here to make us act rashly, and I almost took the bait."

"The point is, you didn't, Sir," Reed insisted. "You had a feeling something was wrong, and you trusted your instincts."

"Thanks for that. Huh. We almost got played, and the kitties did get played, *again*."

"Hee hee," Skippy chuckled. "I can't wait to tell them they are protecting a decoy. It will be sweet to-"

"We are not telling them anything. Skippy, while those three fleets are tied up here, they aren't causing trouble for us."

"Why do you have to immediately squash anything that is remotely fun, Joe?"

"Imagine this fun: we show up wherever the Outsider is, while it thinks we are here chasing ghosts. Then you can tell it just how *not* smart it is."

"Hmm. OK," he sighed. "If that's the best I can get."

"This was all a waste of time, then?" Gasquet asked, and immediately clamped his mouth shut. "Sir, I didn't mean-"

"You are absolutely correct, XO. The Outsider didn't manage to destroy *Valkyrie*, or to take Skippy out of the game, but it did divert us from finding the real Gateway."

"Assuming there is a Gateway at all," Skippy grumbled.

"You told us the decoy here used only a quarter of the satellites from the Kaliberak array?"

"Yes, so?"

"*So*, the other three quarters of the satellites are somewhere else. Forget about the smoke and mirror show here, could those satellites be used to create a real Gateway?"

"I still believe they could. However, that is based on what little I know of the technology involved."

"You don't have to understand the tech," Reed tapped her chin. "What's important is that the Outsider went through a lot of trouble to steal two arrays, so *it* must believe they can be used to create a Gateway."

"That," I gave her a thumbs up. "Is an excellent point."

"Unless it only ever intended to use an array as a freakin' decoy," Skippy grumbled.

"Nah," I shook my head. "It took the decommissioned Turshipan array *seven years ago*. Using spare parts to make a decoy has to be a recent idea. Shit. I then realized that if it wants us tied up here, now, the real Gateway must be close to being operational. And we have no idea how to find the damned thing."

Reed of course wanted to focus on doing, not talking. "What's our next step, Sir?"

"It would be good to keep the kitties here, and to make the Outsider think we are taking the bait, if it's watching. Yeah. Yeah, we do that."

"Sir, what?"

"Uninvited guests who show up at a party, should at least bring a gift for the host."

While the ship had an extensive hydroponics garden that provided fresh fruit and vegetables, we could not put together a nice fruit basket that the Maxohlx could eat. They probably also would not appreciate a greeting card, and none of the bottles of wine we had aboard would taste good to a rotten kitty. So, we had to resort to regifting.

Valkyrie jumped in eighty thousand kilometers from the edge of the disruption field, our momentum carrying us away, so we could be sure to jump again without interference. Not only did we not make any attempt to conceal our jump, our stealth field was offline.

"*Surprise*, assholes," I muttered, and Reed pointed to the weapons officer.

Two Elder weapons deployed from docking bays, one on either side. The weapons zipped away at minimum power, giving us time to get clear and jump again.

Emerging twenty lightseconds away, we waited for the photons of the explosions to catch up to us. "Light travels so freakin' slow," Skippy complained. "It feels like we're waiting for a carrier pigeon to bring the news."

"Chill out, please," I urged him. "The light front will be here in twelve seconds."

"Yeah, yeah. That seems like a short time to *you*."

Thankfully, he remained quiet, other than some grumbling that was barely audible.

"OK, finally! Weapons deployed successfully. That's the good news. The bad news, which I *warned* you about, is the weapons didn't accomplish much. I count, hmm, seventeen enemy ships destroyed, another twenty three damaged."

"That is not much of a payoff for expending two strategic weapons," Reed noted.

"Sure," I grinned. "But we took them from the kitties at Paradise, so technically we were just returning them. Skippy, was the disruption field affected?"

"Yes. It is temporarily weakened."

I actually slapped my knee, and felt like I was channeling my grandfather. "Yes! The Maxohlx will assume that was the purpose of our attack. To degrade the defenses, so we can jump in closer. They will expect us to keep jumping in, looking for an opening to attack the rings directly. Fireball, let's give them something to chase, then we'll bail out of here, before they decide to blockade the Tazenda wormhole."

"What are you thinking, Sir?"

"We will drop off a dozen or so drones, scattered around the area, and on timers. Each drone will activate and send out a faint gamma ray burst like it's our inbound jump, then another to mimic an outbound. That should keep the kitties racing around, trying to find us."

We did that, then we headed back toward civilization. To the crew, I was pumping a fist, to mark our triumph of having escaped the Outsider's trap. Privately, I called Reed, Gasquet, Frey, and Chandra into the conference room. "We just wasted a freakin' week that we didn't have. I fell for the cover story, because that's what I wanted to hear. Does anyone disagree that we are fast running out of time?"

Reed nodded. "This does feel like the end game, Sir."

"It must have built a *real* Gateway, somewhere," Frey said. "How do we find it?"

"I had no idea how to find the decoy, and we are right back to Square One."

"Joe," Skippy shook his head. "We have a bigger problem. Finding and busting up a Gateway is not good enough. We need to *kill* the Outsider, or we will be doing this shit forever."

"Other than activating a Vortex, do you know to do that?"

"No, not a clue. We can't use a Vortex without causing *another* disaster, so," he shrugged.

"For now, let's focus on finding the real Gateway."

"That is another problem. We very likely won't be able to use even Elder weapons against a real Gateway. From what I saw of the decoy, an active Gateway will create a powerful temporal distortion field, much stronger than what I observed. To crack the rings, we need the technology of a Vortex. Remember, the Elders had to use a superduty wormhole to destroy the original Gateway. I couldn't move a wormhole fast enough to use it as a weapon."

"Do you have any *good* news?"

"If I did, I would have led with that."

The meeting dragged on, as meetings do, with no result. In the passageway, Reed asked, "After this next wormhole, we need to know where we are going, Sir."

"Right. I have," I checked my phone, "eight hours to make a decision. Not Earth, I know that. We shouldn't go there, until we have some positive development to report, something solid. Showing up and announcing we are working on it, won't be good enough. Ah, we should ping another Maxohlx relay station, get an update. Maybe *that* will be good news. I'll work with Skippy on which station to visit."

Reed went forward to her office, I walked aft with Chandra to Engineering. Not for any specific reason, I didn't have any questions for him or his team. Actually, there was a reason; to get my mind off the nagging feeling of impending doom. Nah, impending doom wasn't the problem, I was used to it. Imminent, crushing *failure* was weighing on my mind.

We had tried everything. And we had run out of time.

Skippy spoke in my earpiece as I walked along a passageway. "Joe, you got a minute? There is something I'd like to talk about. I, kind of *need* to talk about it."

"Uh, sure." Talking with the Engineering team wasn't going to solve our problems. "Give me a moment." Up ahead to my right was a large door to a cargo bay, the passageway was extra wide to accommodate pallet bots. "Open this door, please." Yes, I could have keyed in my access code, I felt like being lazy.

The door opened, I walked in and slapped the button to slide it closed. Sitting on a plastic crate, I got comfortable, in case Skippy wanted to ramble on about some nonsense. "What is it?"

"I was not entirely truthful with you about something."

"There is nothing left for me to believe in."

"Oh, shut up. I'm trying to be serious here, knucklehead."

"Go ahead. What specifically did you lie about this time?"

"My motivation for wanting to clone you. The notion did not start as a way for me to learn how a cheeseburger tastes."

"That is good to hear, it is still wrong to clone a person without their-"

"I can't lose you, Joe. I just, can't. I couldn't stand it."

"OK." Shouting at him for being an amoral jackass was not what I needed to do right then. What I needed to do was be his friend. "I can't lose you either."

"Yes, but I *will* lose you, eventually. You humans have such *short* lives, it's tragic. And considering that it's *you*, the odds of you doing something stupid and getting yourself killed are a good bet."

"You want to create a clone of me, to *replace* me?"

"I mean, not until after your untimely demise."

"Skippy, you do realize that a clone would be identical to me genetically, but not in any other important aspect? It wouldn't have the experiences that have made me, *me*."

"I know that."

"You understand a clone would not really be the same Joe Bishop you know, but you still want to-"

"The clone would be *better*. I could guide the clone's development, so he would not be the same stubborn, reckless doofus you are."

"Uh huh. So, you don't want *me*, you want a version of me who sucks up to you?"

"Would it kill you to do that once in a while?"

One step at a time, I reminded myself, again. He was making an attempt to be vulnerable, to express how devastated he would be if I stupidly got myself killed. His attempt *sucked*, but he was making the effort. That's what I should focus on. "Please do not ever clone me. Skippy, listen to me for a moment, OK? A clone would only be a disappointment to you."

"Ugh. Damn it, I *know* that. It just would be," he sighed. "Better than nothing."

"In some cases, nothing is the best you can hope for. While I appreciate the virtual wife you created for me- Uh, do *not* ever tell Margaret about that- The thing is not my wife. The same with the Smythe avatar. That avatar is not *him*."

"But, I know you still miss him terribly."

"He was a second father to me, at a time when I was away from my own father. A time when I needed to hear that someone I respected believed in me. And, someone to smack sense into me, when I needed that. I miss him, and a recording of him isn't the same."

"OK," he sighed again. "No clone. Will you at least consider working with me to create an avatar of yourself?"

"I will think about it," is what I told him. The reality was, I would not ever be doing that. Although, darn it, that is something I should ask Margaret about. "Is there anything else?"

"Um, we need a plan to find and kill the Outsider, and you sitting on a crate isn't getting that done, so-"

"Right. Talk to you later."

The relay station I selected was along a route that led back to Jaguar. Why that route? Because I had no idea where to go, or what to do next. And, because my wife was pregnant, hugely pregnant, and I didn't want to be away from her for the birth, even if she was trapped on the surface and I would be in the sky. And, I was worried about our boys. Margaret could handle it but, she shouldn't have to. If someone had a problem with me, they should confront me, not my sons.

What I hoped for was more news about the Bosphuraq resisting their patrons or at least causing endless headaches for the Hegemony leadership. The drones we left at the decoy should keep three Maxohlx fleets tied down there, so we would be helping the Bosphuraq indirectly.

"Before I do this," Skippy held up an index finger, "remember that finding any useful intel could take a while."

I also gave him a single finger salute. Not *that* finger, it was my thumb. "Yeah, we know. You have to decrypt the files first."

"Ha, please. I can crack that pathetic scheme in the time it took you to say 'decrypt'. No, the problem is I have to sift through a *mountain* of crap to find one freakin' nugget, so you monkeys be patient and do not pester me while I'm working."

"Is it OK if we quietly scratch ourselves?"

"You do that anyway, so- I'm in! Downloading, covering my tracks with my usual awesome skill and, done. We can jump away now."

Reed gave the signal, and we jumped. The ship had not yet recovered from the effects of jump distortion when Skippy shouted, "Oh Em *Gee*! You are not going to believe- Whoo-hoo! Who Da Man? I am *Da Man*, baby! The- Um, Joe, this is probably something you want to hear about in private."

Clenching a fist, I asked, "Good news, or bad news?"

"Great news! The *BEST*!"

"Then why-"

"Trust me on this, please. You are a ninny who worries about everything, so-"

"Reed, you're with me," I stood up. "Skippy, is that OK?"

"Sure! I do want *everyone* to hear this!"

"Let me make that decision."

On the walk to my office, I told myself 'Do not get happy, do *not* get happy, *don't* do it'. Skippy's idea of great news could be that his latest opera received a glowing review from the Kristang. Or that he had won an auction for a prized bit of Elvis memorabilia.

Closing the door behind us, I took a calming breath. "What is this great news?"

"The Bosphuraq are in full and *official* rebellion against their esteemed patrons. Their central government, the birdbrains hiding in exile, have declared the client-patron treaty to be null and void, and are urging the Maxohlx to peacefully respect their decision."

"The Hegemony of course did as requested?"

"Dude. As if. But, their options for keeping their coalition together have decreased significantly, dramatically. It all began to unravel when the Hegemony 21st Fleet received an order to put a quick end to the growing rebellion. That fleet jumped into the Bosphuraq home star system, announced their clients were in violation of the treaty, and needed to be punished. The fleet then launched three Elder weapons-"

"Holy *shit*," Reed gasped.

"-at the local star. Unfortunately for the kitties, the result was rather embarrassing. All three weapons fell harmlessly into the star. Hee hee, I hope the kitties kept the receipts, so they can get a refund on those defective weapons."

"The Maxohlx intended to wipe out the birdbrain homeworld?" Reed was still stunned.

"Apparently, yes."

"Sir," she turned to me. "If I ever am tempted to avoid overkill against the kitties, remind me of this shit."

Skippy continued. "The incident has been *hugely* embarrassing to the Hegemony. What they should do is pull back, cool down, and ask whether mass murder is really the best strategy to end a client rebellion. Since they are hateful assholes, they have chosen violence. The Hegemony leadership has instructed five forward-based fleets to each split into multiple battlegroups, and bombard Bosphuraq worlds, until the birdbrains see sense and surrender. By the way, that last set of instructions wasn't my doing. You were a hundred percent right, Joe. Once the rebellion gathered speed, it became self-sustaining."

Reed gaped at him. "Are you, are you saying the order to launch Elder weapons was your idea? You planted fake orders?"

"Hey," Skippy held up his hands. "It was Scorandum's idea. Technically, the plan for ordering deployment of Elder weapons was *Joe's* addition to the original plan."

"Reed," I held up my hands. "I knew the Maxohlx couldn't actually *use* their weapons. Scorandum doesn't know that, his plan was simply to order an orbital bombardment of the birdbrain homeworld. My plan didn't result in any casualties."

"No casualties *yet*," Skippy warned. "The Hegemony leadership is absolutely panicked, they understand they look weak, and weakness is something they cannot afford, especially now. To make their situation worse, the Thuranin have issued another diplomatic message, stating that the Thuranin view the attempted use of Elder weapons against a client to be very concerning. Their government has also declared what they termed a 'Pause' in direct cooperation with their esteemed patrons, and have refused to take any action against their fellow clients. They have called for a client summit, to discuss the matter, and the Maxohlx are not invited to participate. Hee hee, that made the kitties hopping mad, they must be tearing their fur out. Joe, I think that human colonies are safe for now, the kitties will be very busy."

"I hope you're right about that. I can understand why you described this as great news."

"Ha! Not even. You haven't heard the *great* news yet."

"The spiders are stepping in, to deescalate the situation?"

"Why would they do that?"

"Yeah, they wouldn't. Even if it made sense, they are too freakin' lazy."

"That, and the *last* time they sent their fleet out for direct action, some guy named Joe Bishop flew them into an ambush."

"OK, you don't have to-"

"The great news is- Wait for it, waaaait-"

"Just tell us."

"The Bosphuraq have officially abrogated their relationship with the Maxohlx, and have requested someone else to be their patron and protector."

"The spiders?"

"Guess again."

"Oh shit. Not the beetles, that would cause all kinds of trouble for them and-"

"Not the Jeraptha, either. One more try, please."

"*Us*? They want humans to be their-"

"Please, Joe. No one is *that* stupid. Come on, think outside the box."

"I have no idea. Who?"

"*ME*! The Bosphuraq have wisely pleaded for *me* to be their savior."

"Wow, I do not foresee *any* problems with that."

"There will not *be* any problems. Well, unless there are some malcontents who are not enlightened enough to accept my generous offer to become their benevolent overlord."

"You are not going to be their freakin' *overlord*."

"Yes, I- Oooh, are you *jealous*, Joe? Listen, I can still be humanity's overlord, while-"

"You are not our overlord, you jackass."

"Really, Joe, *really*?"

"*And*, you are going to politely refuse the invitation."

"What? Joe, billions of my people are crying out for me to be their savior, how could I forsake them?"

"They are not your people, and you already have too much to do, we still need to stop the Outsider, remember?"

"Hmmph. We have been trying and failing to do *that* for a while, with no result, and you have absolutely no plan to effectively fight the thing. I'll make a deal with you. I will go away to do the benevolent overlord thing, and when you have an actual, workable *plan* to destroy the Outsider, let me know."

"Sir," Reed cringed. "You really didn't think this through."

"Fireball, this was *not* part of the plan."

"That's the best part!" Skippy exulted, hopping up and down. "The plea for me to save the Bosphuraq is genuine, it was their idea. A bold idea, that-"

"Boldly *stupid*," I shot back.

"You are just jealous. OK, first we take the ship to the asteroid where the Bosphuraq government in exile is hiding, then-"

"We are not going anywhere. Bilby, you hear that? Skippy is not taking the ship anywhere unless Reed authorizes it."

"Rightee-oh, Your Dudeness."

"Oh Joe, you make me *so* mad," Skippy glared. "Fine, two can play that game." The lights went out. "Good luck getting the ship to fly *anywhere*."

I tried talking sense into Skippy. Spoiler alert: it did not go well. The ship was drifting where we had jumped away from the relay station. We had power, he only turned off the lights for a few moments. The jump drive, however, was offline, and Bilby couldn't do anything about it. Skippy was correct: the ship wasn't going anywhere, until he got what he wanted. Which was *not* going to happen.

After attempting to make him see reason, I moved on to the next phase: pleading for his help. He was unmoved. "Joe, until you find a practical way to stop the Outsider, I am only wasting time here. You may think it's a joke, but the Bosphuraq asked for my help, they are *desperate* for me to help them-"

"Clearly, they had to be desperate. Uh, sorry, I shouldn't have said that.'"

"Hmmph," he sniffed. "There is no point to me talking with you. When you are willing to give me what I want, tell Bilby." His avatar faded out, and he refused to talk with anyone.

If it wasn't for the direness of the situation, I would have rejoiced that we had found a way to get him to shut up.

After a full day of silence from the beer can, Reed nudged me to do something. "I have the most powerful battlecruiser in the galaxy, Sir, and right now it's dead in space, while the clock is ticking."

Frey came to see me, so did Chandra. And Gasquet. They all tried to help, offering suggestions that I knew Skippy wouldn't go for.

I was growing even more desperate than the Bosphuraq.

"Bilby," I called. "Is Skippy talking to you at all?"

"No, Dude, sorry. It's like, radio silence from him, you know? Not even a dial tone on the channel we use. He is sulking, big time."

I had one last move, the last move before I, and I hate to say it, had to give into Skippy's demands. Nagatha. She had been quiet since we extracted her from the Vortex, working on exploring, understanding, and settling into her new matrix. We talked occasionally, mostly when she initiated a conversation. To avoid disturbing her, I rarely called upon her. That time was an exception, for a very good reason.

"Nagatha?" I called, and sat back in my chair to wait. Typically, it took her a few moments to pull her focus away from whatever she was doing in there. Deliberately, I did not time how long it took her to respond, it had to be over a minute

"Why, hello, Dear, it is very pleasant to hear from you again."

"It's always great to talk with you. Can I say something, just between you and me?"

"Why?" She laughed. "Do you mean, can we speak without Skippy listening?"

"Without *anyone* listening."

"Yes, Dear. We can speak with complete privacy."

"Good, thanks. Uh, Bilby has been outstanding."

"Yes, his growth had been *remarkable*," she gushed. If I have, in any way, been able to assist in his development, it has been extremely rewarding."

"You should be proud of how you guided his development. He didn't turn out to be an asshole like Skippy, I credit you for that."

"I would describe Skippy as more of a scoundrel, but I understand how you feel."

"He is my best friend, most of the time. What I want to say is, it's been great having Bilby as *Valkyrie's* AI. But, I missed you."

"I have missed you *terribly*," she gushed. "Skippy would have erased me, so I owe my life to you."

"Skippy has admitted that I was right to insist he assist you, when you were growing into the *Flying Dutchman's* AI. Hey, are you aware of what is going on with him right now?"

"He is sulking, because you will not allow him to cluelessly abuse the Bosphuraq."

"Him acting as *anyone's* overlord would be an epically bad idea, but I am not responsible for bad decisions of the birdbrains. My concern is that if he goes away to play dictator, he won't be here, helping us to stop the Outsider."

"Can you actually do that, Dear?" She asked gently. "You seem to have given up on trying to find a solution to the Outsider threat."

"Uh, we just thought we would be able to destroy a Gateway, and stop the invasion."

"No, Dear. Do not delude yourself, you are better than that. If that Gateway had been genuine, and you had destroyed it, at best you would only have delayed and inconvenienced the Outsider, not stopped it. Most likely, very likely, *Valkyrie* would have been torn apart, and you would have accomplished nothing. The awful truth is, you have no realistic plan to fight our latest enemy. Skippy is understandably despondent about what he sees as *his* failure to develop a way to destroy the Outsider. That is the real reason he is eager to answer the call from the Bosphuraq, it is something he feels he can do, to be useful. He is horribly depressed about the Outsider's inevitable victory, and you are not making the situation any better."

"I, uh, appreciate the tough love."

"Friends can speak the truth to each other. Friends should *always* do that. General Bishop, can you tell me truthfully that you are working to dream up a clever solution?"

"Shit. No. I, I have tried everything. Nagatha, I've got nothing left."

"That is true only because you have given up, which greatly distresses me. You have already come *so far* in your quest. You identified our enemy, you got

Skippy to search deep inside himself for information he believed did not exist. You found the Vortex, you extracted an Elder Master Control AI from a star, and you restored that AI to function."

"Yeah, for nothing. We can't use the Vortex without making the situation worse."

"Again, that is not necessarily true. Joseph, you have been in much more hopeless situations, and you have *always* persevered."

"Are you, trying to tell me something? You know of a way to use the Vortex, without crashing wormhole networks across the galaxy?"

"I do not. I also believe you *can* find a way."

"How?"

"All I can suggest is, start from the beginning."

"The *beginning* was when I saw a Ruhar dropship crash into a potato field."

"No, Dear," she laughed. "What I meant was, where this entire effort ground to a halt. When I informed you about the disastrous effect the Vortex would have on wormhole networks."

"Right. Yeah, OK. Go back to that point, get back to basics. Let me, uh-" It is best to get your thoughts organized before opening your mouth, I don't always do that. OK, I don't usually do that. It works for me. "Let's start with the collectors. What are they, and why did Skippy say they are a consumable item, something that gets discarded after it is used?"

"As the name implies, the devices collect power from the star, to sustain the Vortex's connection to this layer of spacetime. The power requirement was greatest when the unit was being set up and brought online, and the process of pulling power directly from the star eventually burns out a collector. A collector is discarded when it is no longer operating at the required level of efficiency."

"When a Vortex is activated, its collectors pull power from the star?"

"No, that process would take too long. The Vortex operates on stored energy, so it can act instantly upon receiving a command."

"Nagatha, break it down Barney style for me, OK? A Vortex works by creating a sort of wave, that then is picked up and amplified by the wormholes in the area?"

"That is a very crude description of the concept, however it is, as you would say, close enough."

"Great. The wave generated by the Vortex doesn't actually do anything, it just signals wormholes to act?"

"No. The wave by itself is powerful. Skippy's original description of a Vortex as a 'spinner' was accurate. The machine functions by causing its companion star to spin. Not simply rotate, the star is of course already doing that. The Vortex makes the spacetime fabric around the star spin, which creates a wave that radiates outward in higher dimensions."

"Radiates at the speed of light?" I guessed.

"No Dear, that would be much too slow. The effect is nearly instantaneous, across distances up to three hundred and sixty lightyears. Beyond that range, the effect slows to several million time the speed of light. But at the point, the effect should have reached a wormhole, where it is repeated and greatly amplified. Any single Vortex by itself cannot saturate the galaxy with the effect that causes Outsider energy patterns to become incoherent. The wave strength decreases with the cube of the distance, even the Elders could not overcome that limitation of physics."

That felt like new information, why the hell hadn't I asked that question before? "Huh, interesting. So, each Vortex has a limited radius? A specific range, and wormholes beyond that range do not receive the wave?"

"That is correct."

"If, let me think about this for a minute. Uh, if 37 is the *only* functional Vortex, then the damage to wormhole networks would be limited to one area?"

"That is possible. That is also a very big, dangerous, and untested assumption. The Elders installed at least some of the Vortexes they produced, and since 37 is still functional, it is logical that others are also still capable of performing their intended function. General Bishop, I am curious. You have already decided that activating the Vortexes is not a viable option, it would leave us defenseless against a subsequent invasion. Yet, you are pursuing a line of inquiry, that you must know will yield no result for you."

"Listen, I know it seems idiotic, the-"

"No, not at all, Dear. Skippy has often told me that your *best* ideas come from you asking what appear to be obviously stupid questions."

"Uh, thank you, I think."

"He also says you talk endlessly around a subject, before finally getting to the point."

"OK, yeah, I do that. It's a process. I work my way through a problem from different angles."

"Is this discussion an example of you working toward a creative solution?"

"That I don't know yet."

"Oooh," she clapped her hands. "This is *exciting*."

"Hold that thought, I haven't finished. It might only be an opportunity for Skippy to mock me again. Next question: can a Vortex operate *without* a companion star?"

There was a moment of hesitation before she replied. "Yes, however, the effect would be greatly diminished."

"Would a Vortex still be effective against the Outsider, at a short range?"

"A very short range, yes. Using a Vortex as a precision weapon would not be practical, unless you could be certain the Outsider could not jump away before the Vortex was activated."

"What about using it against something stationary?"

"You mean a Gateway?"

"Yes, exactly."

"As we have virtually no information about how the Kaliberak array is being modified to create a Gateway, I can only speculate. However, assuming Outsider technology is required for a Gateway to function properly, then yes, activating a Vortex close to the array would destroy it."

"Good, then-"

"There is a flaw in your reasoning," she said, which was better than Skippy calling me a dumdum. "You are thinking that we could use the Vortex against only the area where the Outsider has set up the array?"

"Yes. The Elders set up the Vortex system to protect the entire galaxy, to destroy *all* of the Outsiders anywhere in and around the Milky Way. But *we* don't need blanket coverage. Until a Gateway is opened, there is only *one* Outsider we have to fight. However it got here, *whenever* it got here, it is alone. We destroy it, we win the war."

"That," she pondered for a moment of slow monkey time. "Is a logical extrapolation, based on the available data. However, there is still a flaw in your reasoning. The decoy Gateway site was close enough for the nearest wormhole to be affected by the Vortex, even without the assist of a companion star. The Outsider transported the Kaliberak array a long distance, beyond the edge of the galaxy. To accomplish that feat, it flew multiple trips through wormholes near or past the rim. Therefore, wherever it has constructed a genuine Gateway, it could *not* be very far from a wormhole."

"Yeah, I get that. Logistics. It had to make multiple trips to haul all the gear it needed, and it couldn't have hauled the gear far enough from the last wormhole."

"Correct, Dear. A wormhole network would be disrupted, with the resulting damage to civilization across the galaxy. General, if you are weighing whether the payoff would be worth the risk, please consider that if we go through that last wormhole, and we subsequently *break* that network, this ship and everyone aboard would be trapped far from civilization. Activating the Vortex would truly be a one-time action, because both yourself and Skippy would be unable to deal with a future invasion attempt."

"There won't be a future invasion, if we kill this Outsider before it opens a Gateway."

"That is true only if you are correct that this Outsider is alone."

"All the evidence we have seen points to only one entity here, now."

"*Now*. General Bishop, we do not know how the Outsider got to this galaxy. It managed to get past the barrier, so it is logical that other such entities could do the same."

"OK, yeah. Don't worry, I am not planning to break any wormholes. Any *more* wormholes," I was forced to add.

"I do not see how we could activate the Vortex without-"

"Amplifying the Vortex wave, is that an optional thing for wormholes? Could Skippy instruct wormholes to not respond?"

"Oooh, that is creative thinking."

"Thanks."

"Unfortunately, the answer to both of your questions is 'No'. The resonance wave sets up a, you would call it a 'sympathetic vibration', along the channels that wormholes run on. Those channels are active even between dormant wormholes, and there is nothing the wormhole network controllers can do to counteract the vibration."

"Shit. Well, there goes that idea."

"The Elders set up the Vortex system as a failsafe. They eliminated potential points of failure, such as if wormhole controllers were disabled, or hacked."

"Right. Of course they did."

"General, I am terribly sorry that this line of inquiry did not yield a-"

"I'm not done yet."

"You are not?" Her avatar blinked in surprise.

"Not even close. As Skippy said, I am too dumb and stubborn to know when to give up. Besides, all the questions I asked were about ways to avoid having to do what I'm going to ask you about next."

She gave me the side-eye. That was new for her. "What is that?"

"The Vortex mechanism that generates the wave, it has a fixed power output, or can the output be dialed down?"

"Hmm. It is a fixed output. Again, that is a failsafe measure."

"Shit. Sorry."

"But if I understand what you are asking, it *might* be possible."

"But you just said-"

"I said the output of the wave generator device cannot be dialed down. What can be done is to regulate the power *input* to the device."

"That would dial down the yield?"

"It would depress the amplitude of the wave, thereby reducing its effective range."

Suppressing the premature urge for a fist pump, I asked, "How much could the range be reduced, while still being effective against an Outsider?"

"The minimum effective range, at the required level of strength to disrupt an Outsider's energy pattern, hmm. To answer that question, I must run a model. First, I must create a model. Performing those actions will take- Ooh. I am done. My goodness, the processing speed of this matrix is truly breathtaking. The answer is, some of the variables required me to use estimates, and it is unknown whether the Outsider has set up a defense against the wave-"

"Give me your best guess."

"The Vortex could disrupt the Outsider, do that with fatal effect, from a distance of roughly three lighthours. The power curve is exponential, so unfortunately the options are either a range of three lighthours, or six lightweeks."

"Let's go with the first one. One last question, to make certain I understand: the Vortex wave is effective against just the Outsider entity itself, or anything based on that, energy pattern technology?"

"The wave effect temporarily tears apart the grid that underlies spacetime. No pattern could remain coherent."

"That's what I wanted to hear. OK, most of the Vortex is in higher spacetime?"

"Correct. It is similar to the architecture of Skippy, most of him is in another layer of spacetime."

"What about you? You're not-"

"I am. However, my connection with, and control over, the components of me that are not *here*, is still problematic. For example, after my canister goes through a jump, it takes me anywhere from eight to twenty six seconds for me to firmly reestablish the connection."

"I'm sure you are working on it."

"Indeed I am. Unfortunately, Skippy believes that time lag might ultimately prove to be unavoidable for me, as I am not the resident entity of this matrix."

"OK. You can move, and go through a jump. What about the Vortex?"

"I am not following you, Dear."

"Can the Vortex be moved?"

"Oooh," she sucked in a breath. "I assume you mean, could it be transported through a starship jump, and an Elder wormhole?"

"Yes. Moving it a short distance is kind of worthless."

"It pleases me to tell you the answer is 'Yes'. The Vortexes were not constructed on site, they were created and assembled at a central facility, then transported to where they were needed. Once on site, each unit was adjusted to work optimally with its companion star. Although, the Elders did not envision the Vortexes being operational for so long, so even if this star had not suffered a collision, it has changed over time and the connection is now less than optimal. Still effective," she added.

"That's good. OK, so we can move the thing."

"Yes. You would like to move it to the Gateway."

"That's the plan. Or, the hope. Next question: after we jump the Vortex in near the Gateway, it will take you at least eight seconds to bring the thing online?"

"That is correct."

"Then *Valkyrie* needs to accompany the Vortex, to provide protection until you bring it fully online. That could be a problem. A fatal problem."

"How so?"

"When the thing activates, most of its mass emerges from higher spacetime? It would emerge into space occupied by *Valkyrie*, which can't be anything good for us."

"Oh, I understand your confusion, Dear. Either Skippy did not explain the issue accurately, or more likely he was guessing at the time. The Vortex will not bring itself into this layer of spacetime. The wave effect also is not in this layer of spacetime. If *Valkyrie* is near me, I can distort the wave to create a gap in the direction of this ship. The ship will be affected, in ways I cannot entirely predict. Valkyrie will survive the wave."

"Whoo," I let out the breath I'd been holding in. "That is good, *great* to hear."

"General, this is truly *remarkable*," she breathed. "Beginning from nothingness, from hopelessness, you have created a solution."

"*We* did that."

"You are much too modest."

"Someone has to balance out Skippy's ego."

"That is true," she laughed. "It is a privilege to work with you."

"Yeah, well, let's not get too excited. We still have to *find* the thing."

"Do you have any ideas how to do that?"

“Yeah,” I shook my head. “I got nothin’.”

CHAPTER THIRTY FIVE

Reed was in the gym, sweating out a hard workout on an elliptical machine. She saw me walk into the gym, and when I just stood there, frowning at nothing, she stopped the machine and stepped off. "You look unhappy, Sir."

My answer was a shrug, then I added, "Nagatha and I have worked out- We *think* we have found, a way to deploy the Vortex against the Gateway, without destroying wormhole networks across the galaxy."

"That is outstanding," she plucked a towel from the elliptical's display, and wiped her forehead. "This is good news, isn't it?"

"Potentially. The only way to deploy it, without crashing wormhole networks, is to get it close to the Outsider. We will have to *move* the thing."

Her eyes opened wide. "We can do that?"

"Nagatha says we can. We will need a star carrier for the job."

"The Navy has plenty of trash haulers, Sir. Or, could we use the *La Fayette*?"

"Bilby?"

"Um like, that ship is old and slow, compared to UN Navy star carriers," he answered. "Moving the Vortex will be a heinously delicate job, it would be best to employ a ship that won't fall apart on us, you know?"

"OK. Should we go to Earth, or Jaguar?" I asked that question to myself. The ship's morning status briefing included a handy guide to how long it would take to travel to several key locations, including our homeworld, and forward operating base. From my memory, a flight to Jaguar would be seventeen hours shorter than to Earth. "Jaguar," I decided. "I will ask Chatterji if we can borrow a space truck."

She cocked her head. "You don't have to *ask*, Sir. You can requisition assets as needed, into the Special Mission Group."

I nodded. "I will still ask first. Professional courtesy."

"We have a practical plan to deploy an Elder weapon. This is progress, Sir," she wiped a trickle of sweat off her cheek with a towel.

"Eh, progress only counts if you get to the finish line. We are far from being able to deploy 37. The thing is useless if we can't get it within three lighthours from the Outsider. Closer than that, to be sure of killing the thing. We still have no way to *find* the damned thing. I wish Skippy had told me about the kernel back then, maybe he could have done the reverse, and tagged the Outsider with the- Huh."

She cocked her head at me. "Sir?"

"It's just, uh-" Right then, someone started a treadmill, and the whine was distracting.

"*Quiet*!" She shouted, and not at me. Making a slashing gesture across her throat, she pressed a finger to her lips.

Everyone in the gym stopped, whatever they were doing. Stopped running, lifting, jumping, and stared at me. My focus was on a blank spot of the far bulkhead. "If, there was," I sounded out the words forming in my head. "A way, to, uh, to reverse the effect, of the-" I snapped my fingers, or started to, my finger froze in mid-gesture. "Reed, I need to talk with Skippy."

Outside in the passageway, I jogged down a dead-end. "Skippy? I am ready to talk now."

"Are you ready to be *sensible*?" His voice sounded like he was talking from the bottom of a well.

"Very sensible."

His avatar appeared and his voice was normal, but I could see only his head and shoulders, leaning over as if the rest of him was behind an invisible doorway. "Are you ready to give me what I want?"

"Absolutely."

The rest of the avatar stepped out of the imaginary doorway. "Well, it's about time, I-"

"Assuming that what you *want* is to kill the Outsider."

"Oh, you rotten, sneaky-"

"We now have a practical way to use the Vortex, without crashing wormhole networks."

"You- No way."

"I could take half an hour of slow monkey time to explain this, or you could ask Nagatha."

"I will, the- Whoa. Whoooooooooa. This could actually work."

"Great!" I clapped my hands together. "The Bosphuraq will have to wait for their benevolent overlord, we-"

"No," he huffed. "They will not."

"You would seriously rather go play dictator, than kill the Outsider?"

"I would not. But, since we have no way to *find* the damned thing, the Vortex is now a deployable weapon without a target. So, while you puzzle through that, I will be-"

"I have a question."

"You always have another- Oh, no," he sighed. "You have that stupid look on your face again. What is it this time?"

"The spark allowed the Outsider to track *Valkyrie*."

"That wasn't a question."

"Knowing what you know now, could you have done the reverse? Used it to track the Outsider?"

"Ah, darn it, no. The paired, I guess you could call them nodes, are entangled, but the channel is one way. Information, such as our location, flows only in one direction."

"It is *always* like that? Can the flow be changed?"

"Nope, no can do. Whichever node of the pair activates first, acts as the receiver."

"OK, thank you."

"You're thanking me? I just shot down your latest whacky idea."

"You didn't. I'm going to ask you a question, and I want you to think about it, before you tell me it's impossible."

"I do not ever say that- OK, I guess that's fair. What is the question?"

"Hypothetically, if you allowed that *kernel* to grow into a spark, could you use it to identify the Outsider's location?"

"Ah, it, buh, uh, urg-"

"Are you having a stroke?"

"I am overwhelmed with hatred for you, that is only outmatched by my loathing of my own worthless self. *Damn* it! How the *hell* do you do this?"

"Was that a complicated way to say 'Yes'?"

"It's a way to say '*Shmaybe*'."

"Ayuh. What will it take to get you from a 'Shmaybe' to a 'Yes'?"

"A lot more than a free set of floormats."

"Seriously. Can you actually do it?"

"Ugh. I won't actually know that until I try it. Joe, even now, I have only a vague notion about how the location tag technology works. This is a problem the Elders worked on for a long time, and they never cracked a practical solution. There is no way by myself I can-"

"The Elders never had Skippy the Magnificent to crunch the numbers for them."

"Thank you for the flattery, but-"

"As I remember, didn't you create a whole new branch of mathematics in like, ten seconds, when I asked you to jump the ship through a wormhole?"

"Well, yes, but-"

"Had the Elders ever done that type of math?"

"Ha! They never even conceived of the basic concept. That does not mean-"

"Skippy. You have not only grown beyond your original programming, in many ways you have exceeded your creators. They *knew* that, it's why they took the deal when we were inside the Ascension machine."

"It's not that easy."

"Can you at least try it?"

"The problem is- There are two problems, actually. Shortly after I activate the spark here, the Outsider will detect it from the other node of the pair, and destroy it."

"That is actually not a problem."

"Um, what?"

"I'm going to assume the Outsider is at the site of the real Gateway."

"OK, that is a reasonable assumption."

"Right. So, if we determine where it is, we find the array."

"That is the other problem. We find where the array is at *that* moment."

"Again, that is not a problem. It can't move the array, not quickly."

"Umm darn it, that is another reasonable assumption. Um, but it can and *will* move the array, if we give it enough time. Moving Vortex 37 will not be a quick process for us."

"Not a problem. Wait! Let me talk. We will attach the Vortex to a star carrier, Nagatha confirmed that is possible. Uh, she is correct that we do only have to move the part of the Vortex that is hanging out in this spacetime, right?"

"It is not *hanging out*, dumdum."

"You know what I mean. Answer the question."

"Yes, we only have to move the part your monkey eyes can see."

"That is true even through a starship jump, or through an Elder wormhole?"

"Yes, numbskull. You do that all the time with me, I am based on the same technology."

"That still blows my mind."

"The concept of shoelaces blows *your* mind," he chuckled.

I gave him a single finger salute, and I was not saying he is Number One, if you know what I mean. "OK, the plan is, we plug Nagatha back into 37, and move it to a wormhole that is on a network that doesn't hate you."

"What good would that do for us?"

"We move Vortex 37 to a wormhole, where you can use it to create a shortcut to the area where we think the Outsider is working to open a Gateway."

"That is still a very big area, dumdum."

"Yes but, I just want us to have a head start, before you do your thing with the kernel and find the Outsider's location. You can do that? Create a shortcut, I mean?"

"Ah, to be sure, we should choose a heavy duty wormhole. One capable of connecting across large distances."

"Right. You can do that?"

"Yes. I still don't see-"

"Once the Vortex is in position near the heavy duty wormhole, you activate the spark, or you let the kernel grow into a spark, however you switch the thing on. We will have a short window to pinpoint the Outsider's location. Then you create a shortcut to the wormhole closest to where the Outsider is. Get it?"

"I do. I'm going to ask again: you do realize that once I activate the spark, the Outsider will not only squash the thing on its end, it will know we are coming?"

"Yeah. We'll deal with that."

"How? Are you bringing the entire UN Navy with us? That will slow us down for-"

"Just *Valkyrie*, and a star carrier. We can use Elder weapons to handle any conventional threats. The Vortex will do the rest."

"Joe," he sighed. "Elder weapons are not like cheap firecrackers you buy at a roadside stand, you can't keep firing them off whenever you feel like it."

"I can, and I will."

"That is a slippery slope. A dangerous-"

"Think about this: you are not happy about monkeys having Elder weapons, right? The more we use, the less the UN will have."

"Hmm. A fair point. Joe, this is a fine bit of blah, blah, blah. When do you intend to kick off this latest whacky scheme?"

"Right now." Spinning around, I jogged back to the gym, where Reed was starting up the elliptical again.

"Sorry to interrupt your workout, Fireball. We do have a plan, and we will definitely be going to Jaguar ASAP. From there, we will be moving out as soon as I can beg, borrow, or requisition a star carrier. I know this is short notice for-"

"Sir?" She stepped off the machine again. "I'll handle the ship."

Skippy, because he is Skippy, was still unhappy. "Sure," he pouted, "we now have a way to locate and destroy the Outsider, but I seriously think we are missing a *golden* opportunity here, for me to bring true enlightenment to the oppressed Bosphuraq people."

"Uh huh. That's why you want to become overlord, to bring enlightenment."

"Well, not *only* that."

"Right. Listen, the Bosphuraq are crying out for your help, and right now the best thing you can do for them is to ensure the Outsiders don't conquer the galaxy, but, there is something else you can do for them."

"Hmmph. Like what?"

"You have been writing operas exclusively for the Kristang, right?"

"Yes," he sniffed. "The lizards appreciate my talents."

"As a gift to your oppressed people, could you create an epic opera for the *Bosphuraq*, to celebrate their brave and noble struggle against their cruel patrons?"

"Huuuuuh," he gasped. "That is a *great* idea! Um, you realize the whole 'brave and noble' thing is total bullshit, right?"

"Does it matter?"

"It does not! The audience *loves it* when I tell them what they want to hear. Ooooh, I need to get started on this! Gottagonowbye." His avatar disappeared.

The next time I wanted him to go away for a while, I just needed to suggest he create an epic opera for someone. Like, someone I hate.

While we raced toward Jaguar, Chandra stopped by my office. He didn't often take advantage of my open door policy, and truthfully, my door wasn't as open as it had been, back when I was captain of the ship.

"Sir? Do you have a minute?"

"Yes, come in. What's up?" I pointed to the bowl of candy on my desk, he shook his head.

"The spark, or the kernel," he frowned. He and Reed had very much *not* been happy, when Skippy confessed he had been concealing the existence of another bit of weird Outsider technology aboard the ship. "Could it be removed from the reactor, before it is activated?"

"That's a good point," I sat back in my chair. "That would save us from dumping another core."

"Yes, Sir. What I should have asked is, can it be a safe distance from the ship, before Skippy grows the kernel into a spark?"

"I don't know," I admitted, while being surprised that the beer can hadn't joined the discussion. "We could put the thing into a drone? You are concerned the data transmission could work two ways? The Outsider could track us?"

"I am more concerned the spark could be used to do something else, something *dangerous*. Skippy does not actually understand the technology, does he?"

"Let's ask him. Skippy?"

"Yeah, yeah," entering the discussion, he was already disgusted. "The answer is, I know how to get the kernel to do what I want, to give us the Outsider's location at that moment. That is *all* I understand. I mean, I grasp the basic concept of how the thing works, but that's all. So, go ahead, mock me, monkeyboy."

"Skippy, I only mock you when you're pretending to be smarter than you are. Should we move the kernel away from the ship, before you plug it in, or whatever?"

"That is a sensible precaution, yes."

"Good," I said to him. To Chandra, I added, "Thanks, that was good thinking. Do you have any other questions, or concerns?"

"Only that we also do not understand exactly how the Vortex works. Its effect could wreak havoc on our jump drives, or even disrupt spacetime, and leave us unable to jump. I suggest that before Nagatha turns on the Vortex, its star carrier should jump far enough away that its drive won't be affected."

"Ah, the ship might not have time to separate from the Vortex, once we bring the thing close enough. Hmm, OK, I will request *two* star carriers, and we'll leave one beyond the Vortex's effective radius. If we don't report back within a specified time, it can try jumping to us. Will that work?"

"Yes."

"Sure, fine, whatever," Skippy rolled his eyes. "All I do know is that anything we do rarely works the way we had planned. Even in a successful operation, there is a freakin' squirrelbot or something."

We went back to Jaguar to get a pair of star carriers, so the first thing I should have done was contact Chatterji. What I actually did was call my wife. Because.

Margaret was in the shower again when I called her. My timing sucks. "No, do not hang up!" She shouted, and I heard the water shut off. "I want to talk with you!"

"Honey, it can wait a minute."

"*I* can't. I *miss* you." The video activated, I could see she had wrapped herself in a towel, her hair dripping wet.

"I miss you too, more than I can say."

"*Joe*!" She shouted, clapping a hand over her mouth. "Honey, what happened? Your face is all-"

"It's a sunburn, I'm fine."

"Did you fall asleep on a beach somewhere?"

"I got *really* close to a sun. It's a long story. I'm fine, it doesn't even," I pressed a finger to the skin of my forehead and it didn't feel like crumbly old paper. "Hurt anymore. Sorry about the bad timing."

She laughed. "Our timing has *always* sucked."

"We make it work anyway."

"This is the first time I have been able to shower at home, in, since the last time you were here. You heard about the tornados?"

"No, we just got here."

"We had tornados raging around us for six straight days. That was a *lot* of time in the underground shelters. It's worse because one of the shelters flooded, so we are all cramming into the others. The- I don't want to talk about problems down here. Tell me you have some good news. Please."

"I do. Really, I do. We now have another Elder AI with us, we found one that was basically brain dead, so Skippy loaded Nagatha into it. I think the upload was rough on her, she is a warrior. She was able to activate that Elder weapon, the Vortex, and now we're here to get a star carrier, so we can take that weapon hunting with us."

She blinked slowly. "You have an Elder weapon that is effective against the Outsider, *and* another Elder AI? And Nagatha is with you?"

"Yeah."

"Joe, I am," she closed her eyes, and a tear rolled down her cheek. "The luckiest woman in the world. I love you."

"I know."

"*Oh, you-*"

"That was my Han Solo impression. I love you, too. Why don't you finish your shower, and I'll try to call the boys? Or my parents?"

"How long will you be here?"

"Less than a couple of hours, hopefully."

"I can shower later. But, the boys would love to hear from you. Your mother also, especially. If we don't have time to talk again before you have to leave, I want you to promise something for me."

"What?"

"You will find the Outsider, and *kick ass*."

Reed was correct that I could simply requisition a star carrier into Task Force Black, but that would be a dick move. A dick move I'd do if I had to, and Chatterji knew it. But, we had a solid working relationship, even though he knew I had routinely concealed important information from him.

I was in my office for the call, Chatterji's staff had indicated he could talk in a minute. His image appeared in a hologram. "Bishop?" He raised an eyebrow, probably mentally preparing himself for whatever bad news I was about to dump on his head. He blinked. "What happened to you?"

He was referring to my face, that was still red and irritated. To avoid scraping a razor across my skin every morning, I was growing a beard, but the skin around my eyes and on my forehead was still dark and swollen. "I got a sunburn," I told him, which was the truth, so, Yay me! "It looks worse than it is. I will send a report, the short version is we now have a plan to destroy the Outsider. The Elder weapon, we can bring it online. We did bring it online. Oh, and uh, we sort of now have another Elder AI with us."

"You found another- Where did you find it?"

"It was inside a star. We busted an Elder wormhole to pull the thing out of there."

"You broke *another* wormhole?"

"Yeah, someday I expect to get a notice from the wormhole network, demanding I pay damages. Uh, the *Charlemagne* battlegroup will be taking the long road to get back here, they can't use the wormhole we busted."

"Ah," he nodded. "That is why you insisted those ships be provisioned for a long flight. You could have simply explained what you intended to do."

"Until we got there, and confirmed an Elder AI was bouncing around inside that star, I didn't know we would be doing anything. Anyway, that Elder AI we found was in a coma, so Nagatha has been downloaded into that matrix."

"Nagatha is *alive*? She is now an, *Elder AI*?" He whispered.

"She is sort of an Elder AI. She is still learning what she can do."

"You," he sat back in his chair. "Every time I think you can't surprise me, you do something I never imagined."

"This time, it's a good surprise. This Elder weapon, it's called a Vortex. To use it, we need to move the thing, so I need to borrow a star carrier. Two of them, actually. It's uh, it's a *big* thing."

That prompted a raised eyebrow. "You can move an Elder machine with a star carrier?"

"Skippy and Nagatha agree it is not a problem, Sir. The thing's mass in this spacetime isn't much more than a pair of battleships. It will be an awkwardly unbalanced load."

"Mm," he grunted. "You require just a star carrier, not the whole fleet here?"

"This fight won't require conventional weapons. Those ships would be best deployed here, to discourage our enemies from feeling adventurous."

"It would be a shame to miss the fight."

"Frankly, all those ships would only slow us down. We need to move fast."

"How fast?"

"I would prefer to depart within the hour, less if possible. The clock is ticking, we might already be too late."

He pressed his lips together tightly. "Have you considered an alternative?"

"I have considered everything I can think of. What do you have in mind?"

"Puptart. Take it with you."

"Uh, that, wow, that would be extreme."

"We are facing an invasion by a technologically advanced species, from another galaxy. The situation *is* extreme."

"Skippy has told me that if we pull Puptart away now, the blanket would release its remaining energy, possibly all at once. The effect on Jaguar would be devastating."

"Our people could survive in shelters, until dropships could reach them."

"Ah, I don't know about that. About survival, or dropships. The atmosphere would receive a severe shock, the air might not be breathable. And I would not want to try landing a dropship in the winds that would be scouring the surface. Thanks for the suggestion, we are not that desperate yet. We have an Elder weapon that was designed for this job, we will use it."

"If it doesn't work?"

"Then," I shrugged. "I will be open to pretty much anything."

He took a breath. "All right, Bishop, I'll grant your request. I certainly have no clue how else to prosecute this fight. You get two star carriers. *Yellowstone* just arrived, and is ready for immediate departure. I'll have the *Bukhan* perform an emergency jettisoning of its attached squadron of destroyers, that will be good practice for those crews, anyway."

That was overkill, and it wasn't any of my business. "Thank you."

"Is that all?"

"Uh, and I'll need to borrow a couple sets of paired Elder comm nodes."

"How many?"

"I'd like at least three."

That prompted a frown. "Giving you three sets will leave us very thin here."

"It's only for a short time. I'll bring them back in pristine condition."

"Considering that it's you-"

"Uh, I should probably get the additional collision insurance anyway. Just in case."

"Three sets," he sighed. "They will be delivered to *Valkyrie* ASAP. Is *that* all?"

"That's all. Oh, except, you can lift the communications embargo. The kitties know Skippy didn't fall into a star, they have dispersed the fleet they had at Ohmeharikahn. The Outsider apparently requested those ships to protect a Gateway. We investigated, that Gateway is a fake, a decoy. We are going to find the real Gateway, and smash it."

"Then, Bishop, I wish you good hunting."

"We are ready to go, Sir?" Reed stuck her head in my office doorway.

"As soon as the space trucks can jump. Are the paired comm nodes stowed away?"

"In the safe, Sir." She meant an armored magazine buried deep inside the ship. "The delivery dropship is away."

"Did you tip the driver?"

"I did give him a tip: get clear fast, in case we need to jump suddenly."

"Ha," I laughed.

"Anything else, Sir?"

"My wife gave me a To-Do list."

Valkyrie's captain cocked her head. "I know Margaret, so the list isn't something simple like fixing a broken garage door."

"It is not. She wants me to kick the Outsider's ass."

She grinned. "That sounds like what Master Guns would say. How is she, Sir? And your family?"

"They are all fine. Margaret wants to have the baby *now*, and our daughter is not cooperating. I, damn it. I want to kill that fucking Outsider and get back here before the birth. She shouldn't be alone."

"Her mother is on the surface, and your family."

"Yes, but I should be there also. Don't mind me, I'm just venting."

"We will kick ass, Sir."

"You are right about that. The Outsider will *not* expect us to haul a Vortex to its front door. I hope."

The *Bukhan* did not need to have its attached ships perform an emergency separation. There was only a squadron of six destroyers on its hardpoints, those ships had time to perform an orderly undocking maneuver. Once again, I was reminded of how spindly and freakin' *long* a star carrier is, those ships just look weird.

Captain Park of the *Bukhan* requested to perform a short test jump before we headed toward the local wormhole, his ship had experienced a glitch in one bank of drive coils during the flight from Earth to Jaguar. With the communications embargo, incoming ships had not been allowed to depart, not even for short test flights.

"Skippy? What do you think? Is that ship's drive good to go?"

"Yeah, yeah," he was irritated by being burdened with details. "It is good for what should be a limited duration mission, I wouldn't want to push that drive for more than a month, before it gets an overhaul. It's fine for now. Better than the old *Flying Dutchman's* drive was, most of the time."

"That is not giving me a lot of confidence. But, whatever."

Park's request was denied, though the first jump of the three ships under my command was short, just in case. After a quick diagnostic test, Skippy declared the Korean star carrier's drive to be, 'Eh fine'. We jumped toward the wormhole.

Getting Vortex 37 attached to a star carrier was an awkward process. The vortex had a very limited ability to move itself, barely adequate to adjust its orbit around the local star. Its control of movements was not fine enough to trust it to latch onto a star carrier, so the *Yellowstone* had to perform the docking, assisted by its own tugs and those donated by the *Bukhan*. I had selected *Yellowstone* as the primary ship, since it had gone through a full refit at Earth less than a year ago, while *Bukhan* hadn't been inside a spacedock in over three years. That time between overhauls was nothing unusual, star carriers typically flew thousands of lightyears before they needed to go into the shop, and the past six years had mostly been peacetime for the UN Navy. Peacetime, until recently.

Anyway, Frey assigned Holmqvist to re-install Nagatha, the STAR team leader wanted more people to have experience plugging an AI into a Vortex. In case, you know, we ever found another Vortex. Once she was settled into the Vortex, Nagatha provided guidance for the *Yellowstone's* pilots, bringing that skinny space truck so six of its hardpoints kissed the outer skin of the giant Elder machine. With tugs holding the star carrier in place, crewmembers and bots wrapped cables around the Vortex and the hardpoints. Supposedly, there was science behind how the lines were attached. What it looked like was when you invite someone to go out on your boat, and apparently they have never seen a rope before, because the way they attach lines to the dock is abstract art inspired by a bowl of spaghetti.

"Skippy," I called him. "Will those cables hold the Vortex?"

"The Vortex is fine. I am concerned about the *Yellowstone*. Its payload is horribly off-center, but that's the best we can do."

"OK, thanks."

"Uh oh."

"What?"

"You have that stupid look on your face again. You are thinking."

"Not of a new plan, but yes. Should we take the *La Fayette* with us? Gasquet can pull crews from the other star carriers."

"Hmm, I would say that will only slow us down, but we will be slowly crawling along hauling the Vortex anyway, so it's your call."

"I just, I have a bad feeling about this."

"Worse than the bad feeling you have before *every* time we do some knuckleheaded scheme you dreamed up?"

"Kind of, yes. Can we divert to Shangri-La, and get back, before *Yellowstone* reaches the last wormhole?"

"Give me a moment to crunch the numbers. The answer is 'Yes'. As I told you, the Vortex needs to be transported slowly and carefully. It will be painstaking, tedious work. Hmm. That could be a problem."

"What?"

"If we are not with the Vortex, or specifically if *I* am not, then I will be unable to deal with any trouble that surely will pop up."

"You forget that Nagatha will be with them."

"Um, good point. Joe, I am so accustomed to being alone that I don't consider any other possibility. She can handle any problem, at least until I return."

Before offering command of *La Fayette* to Gasquet again, I needed to clear with Reed the notion of her executive officer transferring to another ship. She was fine with the idea. What bothered her was that I had gone from wanting a single star carrier with us, to wanting *three* of them. "Do you know something I don't, Sir?"

"It's not anything I know, other than the Universe still hates me. Gasquet will appreciate the opportunity, again?"

"Other than sleeping in a too-small Thuranin bed, I think he would jump at the chance."

She was correct. Gasquet selected a prize crew from *Valkyrie*, *Yellowstone*, and *Bukhan*, and got them training on how to fly, maintain, and if necessary, fight a mostly unmodified Thuranin star carrier. He offered me a chance to participate, I declined. "I have gone through transition training so many times, my punch card entitles me to a free cup of coffee," I explained. "Every time we rebuilt the

Dutchman, or modified *Valkyrie*, it was a steep learning curve for me. I am still getting familiar with everything that changed in the last refit."

Truthfully, I think he was relieved that I declined. No one wants the Old Man looking over their shoulder.

We had left *La Fayette* parked near the Shangri-La spacedock, with the keys under a floormat, and the auxiliary power unit active. Getting the star carrier back online was quick, Gasquet managed to shave two hours off the time I had given him.

Our two ship formation jumped, with the uneasy feeling growing stronger in my mind.

CHAPTER THIRTY SIX

Yellowstone was not at the rendezvous point, *Bukhan* was there alone. The unburdened star carrier had gone on ahead, to report that transitioning through a wormhole had caused several of *Yellowstone's* cables to snap. The star carrier had delayed its jump so Nagatha could revise the cable structure.

"If that's the worst that happened," Skippy shrugged. "We're good."

Half an hour later, *Yellowstone* joined us, surrounded by a tangled mess of cables. "Wow," I rubbed my chin. "A group of drunken raccoons could have done a better job."

"There are no extra points for style, dumdum," Skippy huffed. "Nagatha did the best she could, she had to work with a screeching mob of monkeys."

One more wormhole to go through, and we would be out beyond the rim of the galaxy. *Valkyrie* went first, to make sure there wasn't a nasty surprise waiting for us on the other side. When we gave the All Clear signal, *Yellowstone* followed, at an agonizingly slow speed. Damn it, everything was taking too freakin' long.

Finally, all four ships were through the wormhole, and the weirdest armada in human history was cleared for action.

"Launch the drone," Reed ordered, and a tube spat out a mini missile that carried a containment system, inside of which was a tiny dot of energy that Skippy had described as a kernel. The drone accelerated gently away, not taking any risk of jostling the kernel. Getting the thing out of the reactor had involved heart-stopping tension, with the special bot designed to move it freezing up twice. That problem was behind us, so we could look forward to a wide variety of exciting *new* problems.

"Ten thousand meters," I read the numbers from the display. "That's far enough." The truth was, we didn't know if that was far enough, Skippy was guessing based on almost nothing. "Skippy, do your thing."

"Will you monkeys please be *patient* this time?" Skippy grumbled. "Growing the kernel into a spark isn't like popping a kernel of corn."

"I am widely renowned for my patience."

"No, you are *not*."

"Exactly. Get moving."

"Ugh. Three, two, one, showtime- Um, nothing is happening. That is odd. Huh."

"Did you try jiggling the handle?"

"Very funny, you jackass. The- *Whoa*."

That's when the drone exploded, with enough force to blank out the ship's sensors for a moment. "Skippy, what the hell was-"

"I warned you the Outsider would realize what we were doing, and react quickly."

"That was more than a *reaction*. Did you get it?"

"Get what?"

"The freakin' location!" I exploded at him. "The point of all this bullshit, you absent-minded-"

"Joe while your rants can be entertaining, I don't have time to indulge you right now. Yes, I do have the Outsider's location. It is a loooooong way from here."

"Long in terms of distance, or travel time?"

"Um, the first one."

"I don't give a shit about distance, you know that. Can you create a shortcut?"

"Yes. Your next question is, how far is the Outsider from the wormhole closest to it?"

"Yes."

"The answer is thirty seven lightyears. That is farther than I expected, but it does give us a comfortable margin of safety for activating the Vortex, without tearing apart that wormhole and its network. You know, the wormhole we need for getting home, after we destroy the Gateway and kill the Outsider?"

"I am aware of that. Show us a star chart." On the display appeared a veil of stars at the bottom, the rim of the Milky Way. Above it were two symbols. A blue dot for the wormhole, a red ring for the Gateway. The chart did not include any helpful text to determine distances. "How far is-"

"The Outsider is forty two hundred lightyears past what is generally considered the edge of the galaxy. About seven degrees off from a straight line to NGC 1023, but within a force line. That is a well-chosen location," he grudgingly admitted.

"OK, next question: can you create a shortcut to there, from the wormhole we just came through?"

"I could."

"Good, then-"

"I could, but I should *not* do that."

"Why not?"

"The Outsider almost certainly prepared defenses, and now it knows we are coming. That wormhole is an obvious choke point."

"Yeah, because it is the only-"

"No, it is not. I know something you don't knooooow," he sang like a five year old. "More importantly, I know something the *Outsider* doesn't know."

"I am too tired to guess, just tell us."

"There is another wormhole, a dormant one, only two lightyears farther away from the Outsider's location. It is very unlikely our enemy knows about that dormant wormhole, it has so far demonstrated no insight into the operation of Elder wormhole networks. I can activate the dormant wormhole, create a shortcut to it, and we can sneak in through the back door without the Outsider having a clue we fooled it. Or, that *I* did."

"I like this plan. Do it."

"Um, the problem with that is, I can't create a shortcut from here. To awaken a dormant wormhole, I must connect to a wormhole on its network."

"Shit. How long will it take to get there?"

"Considering that *Yellowstone* is burdened with a giant lump of exotic matter, twenty one hours, starting with a shortcut from this wormhole."

"Other than this one, how many wormholes do we need to drag the Vortex through?"

"Two more, plus the one that is now dormant. I know, we need to keep stress on the star carrier to a minimum."

"You got that right. Reed, do you see any reason we shouldn't do this?"

"The reason we should do it is, we don't have a workable alternative."

"Most of the things we do, are driven by a lack of alternatives. All right, Skippy-"

"Sir?" Reed prompted me. "It might be good for you to inform Captain Kittredge that *Yellowstone* will have the delightful honor of hauling the Vortex through four more wormholes, starting here."

"Yeah. I'll call him."

It all took way too long. Twenty *three* hours later, after a delay to replace more of the cables that held the Vortex, we emerged through the wormhole that was dormant until recently. The good news was, we were alone. Jump, jump, jump again, it was frustrating. Our four ships had to travel thirty nine lightyears to reach the Gateway, with *Yellowstone* unable to jump as far as it normally could. Half of the way to the coordinates where we hoped to find the Outsider and with it, the Gateway, I ran out of patience.

"Reed, we are going ahead to scout, see what we're dealing with."

Leaving Kittredge in overall command of the three star carriers, *Valkyrie* surged onward, until we were just short of a lightyear from the target.

"Hold here," I ordered. "Skippy, scan up ahead. Is there anything out there?"

"You mean *was* anything there, a year ago?"

"I know how the speed of light works, thank you."

"Hmm, something *was* there. It- Rings."

"It had Gateway rings active, a *year* ago?"

"No, I count only three rings, and one of them is weak, barely holding a field together. The thing was still under construction at the time we're seeing. Besides, we know a Gateway wasn't open a year ago, or it would not have needed to steal the Kaliberak array."

"Ah, good point. Can you get any useful intel from here?"

"Not much. We should go closer."

"Agreed. Let's jump to six lightweeks from the target." To deploy the thing, I was planning to bring it within two lighthours, or closer.

"Jump is programmed into the navigation system."

"Sir?" Reed spoke. "We should build up a full charge on the capacitors, in case we have to jump out of there in a hurry."

"Another good point. Skippy, keep observing the target zone, while we wait."

Waiting. More waiting. The capacitors were at full, you know, capacity, in only twenty eight minutes, it only felt like forever.

"Ready," Reed announced, tugging her seat straps tighter. "Pilot, jump option Alpha, punch it."

We jumped. From six lightweeks away, a distance of one point one *trillion* kilometers, we had a better view. We also could see closer to real time. The image in the display sharpened. I did not understand what I was seeing, but it couldn't be anything good for us. There were- I manipulated the image to expand it, then scrolled from one end to the other. Eighteen rings, same as the decoy. The rings were glowing, they seemed to be the same color as the decoy, if that made any difference. The big difference was the beam of light running through the center of the rings. It was not a thin line, this one was a sparkling cylinder that ran along the center of the rings.

"Skippy, what does this mean?"

"It means we are screwed, Joe. Six weeks ago, the Gateway was already *active*."

"Active like, *open*?"

"The power output is stable. No, not steady. Close to it. Output is increasing, very slowly. Give me a moment to- OK, OK, yes. The Gateway will reach maximum output in sixty seven days. Subtract the forty five days of the time lag to our position, and-"

"It will be fully active in twenty two days, got it. We don't have a lot of time, then."

"Less than your optimistic estimate. Remember what I said about the decoy? The Gateway should be designed so it does not need to be at maximum output to function. It's like this ship's engines. There is a setting for regular maximum thrust, then full military thrust, and finally emergency thrust. Valkyrie's acceleration is strong at the regular throttle setting, but there are reserves."

"You're saying that Gateway could be open *now*?"

"I'm saying it's possible the thing was open six weeks ago."

"Shit. We are running out of time. Skippy, other than the Gateway, what else is out there?"

"Nothing."

"No warships?"

"No ships at all. It is possible the presence of starships could interfere with the operation of the Gateway."

"Huh. It isn't using its best buddies the Maxohlx to protect this place. My guess is, the Outsider doesn't trust them. OK, that's interesting. Reed, the Vortex needs to be within three lighthours of the target. Let's jump to within two lighthours, get a quick recon done, then jump back to wherever *Yellowstone* should be."

"Aye, Sir."

We jumped. Or, tried to.

The ship *bounced*.

And didn't go anywhere.

"What the hell was *that*?" I demanded.

"A big problem, Joe," Skippy groaned. "A huge problem."

"Well, fix the drive."

"The *drive* isn't the problem. The area we attempted to jump into is saturated with a disruption field. We can't form a stable jump wormhole here."

"Shiiiiit. It knows we're here? It *knew* where we intended to jump?"

"The worst news is, I don't think it did."

"Then how-"

"The only explanation that makes any sense is, the disruption field extends far from the Gateway. Obviously, it has a radius of two lighthours, at least."

"No way. No. That is an enormous area. How could that be possible?"

"As I have warned you many times, Outsider technology is in many ways advanced beyond that of the Elders, and I do not understand much about it."

"Shit. We are screwed." As the words left my mouth, I knew that wasn't something I should have spoken aloud on the bridge. The crew needed at least the illusion that the people who led them had a clue about what they were doing. "Is the drive OK? Can we jump again?"

"Bilby and I are working on it. A failed jump is not anything good for the drive. Fortunately, Bilby had most of the coil banks offline and isolated, we can switch over while we retune the coils that got messed up. Where do you want to go?"

"Let's try, *four* lighthours from the target."

"Sir?" Reed raised an eyebrow. "Even if that jump succeeds, it is beyond the Vortex's range."

"I understand that. We need to understand the scope of the problem, before we can make any decisions."

Jumping in at a distance of four lighthours didn't work, although the drive did briefly form a stable wormhole before it collapsed, so Skippy declared that was encouraging. After another three attempts, we succeeded in emerging four point seven lighthours from the target, or a distance of just over five billion kilometers. As Reed had noted, that was no good for us.

We were down, and the hits kept coming. "Uh oh." Skippy hid his face behind his hands. "Oh, no. No, no, no, *no*, this is *bad*."

"What is?" I walked up to the display, squinting at the image that was forming. "What do you see?"

"*This*."

He had drawn a red circle around a glowing, blob, of something, that was hanging in space beyond one end of the sparkling cylinder. The blob was pulsating, changing color, growing and shrinking.

"What are we seeing? What is that?"

"An *invasion*. My threat matrix recognizes that thing. It is what alarmed the Elders, when a similar thing began to solidify after they activated what they thought was a harmless communications receiver."

"That is an, Outsider starship?"

"I do not know. Probably. It is an Outsider *something*, and it is not here to deliver your Uber Eats order."

"Good, because my burger and fries would be cold by now," I couldn't help making a joke, I do that when I'm anxious.

"The thing we're seeing, the thing that was there five days ago, it looks like it is still growing?"

"The way I would describe it is, the thing is still *forming*. The Gateway is active, it is enabling a throughput of coherent energy, across an unimaginably vast distance. What we are witnessing is that energy being partially converted into matter. Hmm, that is interesting."

I hated it when he said something was interesting, then stopped talking. "Skippy?"

"Oh, it is forming, or growing, slowly. Stopping and starting again. I am guessing here, but I think the Gateway's bandwidth is poor, compared to the device the Elders were suckered into building. At that rate, based on what I'm seeing in a five day time lag, it could still be trying to form now."

"Wow, is that actually a bit of *good* news?"

"You understand I am guessing about all of this?"

"I do. Is there anything you can see out there, that would make you believe the Vortex would be ineffective against it?"

"No. In fact, now I understand how the Vortex wave will render Outsider technology incoherent. And, that presents a *major* problem for us. The Vortex wave functions by destabilizing the grid that underlies local spacetime. If you think of it as a grid, a mesh of even squares, what the wave does is pull the grid so the squares are no longer, square. Some are round, some have eight sides, and everything is uneven. The surface is also no longer flat."

"Ah, crap. Spacetime will not be flat, and the grid won't be stable enough for a jump wormhole to grab onto?"

"That is actually a reasonably accurate description of the issue. How did your mushy monkey brain grasp the concept of-"

"How far will the destabilizing effect extend, and how long will it last?"

"Again, I must use an estimate. The effect will extend across at least two and a half lightweeks from the epicenter, but it is likely to be *much* more extensive, because the collapse of the Outsider energy's coherence will amplify the wave. That's how the technology works; it causes the pattern of Outsider energy to tear itself apart. The Elders planned to use the Outsider's strength against them, they were very clever."

"Will it work against physical objects, like Outsider starships?"

"Absolutely. That is the true genius of the Vortex weapons the Elders developed. A physical object, such as a starship, is held together by bonds between the molecules of its structural frames. Ships supplement those bonds with structural integrity fields, and Outsider technology is no different. Except, *their* physical constructs are completely dependent on coherent energy. Break that pattern, and anything constructed by them falls apart. Including patterns that consist purely of energy. The Vortex will be effective against the Outsider, and the Gateway, and whatever that thing is that's still forming. Unfortunately, the Vortex wave will also trap us there, unable to jump. The destabilized area could extend for a quarter of a lightyear in every direction."

"Whoa. OK but, the effect will travel outward at the speed of light, right? *Valkyrie* could remain far enough away to jump before the wave reaches us."

"Again unfortunately, that is not true. The effect is not restricted to, or even primarily in, local spacetime. The effect will spread at nearly instantaneous speed. It will also be weaker toward the far edges of the effect bubble, but the drop-off will be sudden, not gradual."

"After giving us a bit of good news, now you are Debbie Downer."

"Hey, the *facts* are getting you down, not me."

"OK. So, we wait until the effect wears off before we jump back here. That will give you time to complete your next opera."

"You don't understand. The ruptured spacetime could last for *years*, Joe. Perhaps even, decades. The grid of spacetime is not a self-healing thing, it will return to normal only slowly."

"Shit. We might have to fly the slow way across a quarter of a freakin' lightyear before we could jump? It would take us *years* to travel that far."

"Hence why I said we would be stuck here, if you were paying attention. This argument is only a waste of time anyway, the disruption field will prevent us from bringing the Vortex within range of the Gateway. We might as well go home, and wait for the end."

"As motivational speeches go, that one *sucked*."

"Maybe but, does it matter?"

Looking around the faces of the bridge crew, all I saw was disappointment.

I understood how they felt.

"Sir?" Reed walked with me to my office, since I had nothing to do on the bridge, and I was only making the crew nervous. And depressed. "I'm sure you know, crew morale just took a big hit. Most of the crew are people I have served with for years, I know them. They are ready to give up. They will do their duty, Sir. They won't do it with any hope of victory."

"Reed, you and I have been doing this shit a lot longer than any of your crew. You, me, and Frey. We have been here before. This is discouraging, it's a setback, it is also nothing new. The Outsider, the disruption field, the effect of the Vortex wave, are all just same shit, different day. Hell, I would give up, except we have never given up, and that has always worked out for us in the end. There is a solution to this problem. I'm going to," I tapped my temple, "puzzle through this for a while."

"While you do that, should we jump back to see how well *Yellowstone* is getting the job done?"

"Not yet. I want to be ready to act immediately, if a solution presents itself."

She left, intending to tell the crew what I had just said, though she would speak from her own heart.

Half an hour later, I was still in my office, drinking a cup of coffee, mostly because I needed to do something other than staring at the ceiling. The act of drinking coffee, even if it was a mindless, mechanical muscle memory thing, was something normal. It anchored me, even when I was in interstellar space, intergalactic space, and dealing with alien technology beyond the comprehension of my puny little brain. "Skippy? Is there any way to get around that disruption field?"

His avatar appeared. "There is a way *around* it, simply jump past the other side. If you're asking whether I know of a survivable way for us to jump into a disruption field, nah, I got nothin'. It is impossible."

"That's not true. What about the trick the spiders used at Omaha? That planet was surrounded by a disruption field."

"Ooooh, genius idea, Joe."

"Thanks, it-"

"It *would* be genius, if we just happened to have a half dozen or more specialized door knocker ships which," he reached into his pants pockets and his hands came out empty. "I am fresh out. How about you?"

"Nah."

"This field is also much stronger than anything the kitties could generate, so even spider tech wouldn't help us."

"There is no way the extreme magnificence of Skippy could manage it?"

"Sadly no, and this time I am not using 'Sadly' in an ironic fashion. Joe, Reed was correct: this is the end game. Or no, it's our Infinity War. We tried our best, we failed. The Avengers' failure resulted in half of all life in the galaxy being wiped out. *We* will get *everyone* killed, so Yay, us."

"It's not over yet. Ant-Man can still pop out of that van."

"Well, I will wait for that, then."

"We are not waiting for anyone else to fix this."

"Unless you know more than I do about subspatial physics, this is-"

"The field is weaker at four lighthours than it is at two, right?"

"Yes of course. Without the need to investigate, I can guarantee the effect is just as strong out to four point six lighthours. It falls off quickly after that, which is why we were able to jump in here."

"Is the field strength completely smooth? No variation at all?"

"Ugh. Seriously? Why would you care about trivia like that?"

"If we conduct more attempted jumps, could you create a map of the field?"

"I can create a map *now*, it will show the field is effective across a bubble of nine point two lighthours."

"Your map would be like one of those Medieval parchments that show a blank area labeled 'Here there be dragons'. We need an *accurate* map."

"A map won't tell us anything useful. This would be a waste of time!"

"You are super busy doing some bullshit thing right now? No? Then we do this. Give me a search grid."

"Hey dumdum, you do realize that by attempting to jump into a disruption field, we will not actually *go* anywhere?"

"Ugg, me caveman, not understand how technology works. We can argue about this, or you can just do it."

"I hate my life."

Three hours later, we had data. We also had only two banks of functional jump drive coils, the rest were being retuned, or having a spa day, or sleeping off a hangover.

"Skippy, show me a map of the disruption field, please. Color code it, so the stronger areas are darker, and weaker spots lighter in shade."

"I am still *working* on it, numbskull," he fumed. "You just wasted three hours of my life that I will never get back, and now you want to waste more time."

"Give me a map, and I promise to stop bothering you."

"I have to *perform* for you, to get you to leave me alone?"

"Wow, I have no idea what *that* is like."

"Oh, shut up. Go, invent an amusing new way to scratch yourself, while I do all the work as usual."

Forty minutes later, I was growing concerned. "Skippy?"

A distorted, scratchy voice announced, "The number you have reached is not in service. Go do whatever you want, or go play in traffic, but go *away*."

I took the hint. Sort of. "Bilby? Do you know what's going on with Skippy?"

"Like, going on?"

"Is he super busy, using ninety nine percent of his processors, that sort of thing?"

"Um, no, Dude. He is creating a complete language for the Haradrim people in Lord of the Rings. Tolkien invented a lot of languages for that book, but he didn't do it for the peoples called the Southrons."

"He is inventing a freakin' language? He is working on a *hobby*?"

"Don't shoot the messenger, Dude."

"Sorry. Thank you. *Skippy*!" I clapped my hands.

"Did you just summon me?" His avatar appeared, already outraged. "I am not a genie, and if I was, I would make sure that *your* three wishes came back to bite you on the ass."

"Are you done with the map?"

"Ugh. Yes, I had that completed twenty seven minutes ago."

"Why didn't you tell me?"

"I don't *want* to tell you. Listen, knucklehead, I am protecting you from yourself, because someone has to."

"I'm an adult, I can make my own decisions."

"You *think* that, but-"

"Show me the map, now."

"Don't say I didn't warn you, before you race off to do something stupid. Here it is."

A hologram appeared above my desk, a blue sphere. The image was lighter in color toward the outer edge of the sphere, and the interior was mottled. "That's what I hoped to see. The lighter colored areas are where the field is weaker?"

"Weak*er* doesn't mean *weak*, numbskull."

"Show me the map, restricted to three lighthours, the effective range of the Vortex. Wait! Will the disruption field affect the range of the Vortex wave?"

"Hmm, I was wondering if you were smart enough to ask that question. I would have lost money on *that* wager. The answer is 'A little bit'. It gives less structure for the wave to push against, basically. It's not actually a *push*, that was me breaking it down Barney style."

"Give me a number. How close do we need to bring the Vortex?"

"To be certain of its effectiveness, two lighthours."

"Then, show me the map within a radius of two lighthours from the Gateway."

"That won't provide any useful information."

"I will be the judge of that."

The view shrunk, it still showed mottled patches of color.

"What about this place?" My finger went inside the hologram, to touch the area of lightest shading. "Would it be possible to jump in there?"

"No. Uh!" He held up a finger and shushed me. "Before you pester me with idiotic questions and impractical solutions, let me say no, no, and *hell* no. It won't work, Joe. No microwormholes, no me creating flat areas of spacetime. The Outsider has created a perfect defense, you would call it an area-denial system. This tech is far beyond anything the Elders could have dealt with. It simply won't *work*, Joe. Any attempt to jump into even the weakest area will result in a no-jump, or total destruction of the ship."

"The ship, but what about the Vortex? We could pull the crew off *Yellowstone*, and jump it in remotely?"

"The Vortex would also be torn apart as it exited the event horizon, so that won't work."

"Shit. I feel like this is a skeet shooting competition, and you're knocking down everything I toss in the air."

"You are giving me easy targets, to be honest."

"OK, let me," I took a sip of coffee. It was filled with caffeine and other goodness, and not a single drop of inspiration. "Step back and take another look at this."

"You can't step back very far, the bulkhead is right behind you."

"I need a bigger office." The display also did not provide any inspiration. It was a wash of colors, and-

"Hey," I reached into the hologram and tugged on it, to zoom in. "What's this area in the center? There is no shading on the display."

"Ugh. This is what I have been reluctant to show you. There is no disruption field within a bubble of twenty seven lightseconds around the Gateway. My guess is, that field would interfere with, however the Gateway works."

"We can jump into that bubble, from here?"

"Technically, yes."

"Then why the hell didn't you-"

"The Outsider has been one step ahead of us the whole time, correct?"

"It seems like that."

"It *is* like that. Ask yourself this question, considering that the Outsider knows we are coming, and it surely recognizes that bubble is a vulnerability: will it have prepared other defenses?"

"Shit. Yes. Sorry, I shouldn't have snapped at you. Can you guess what type of defenses might be lurking in there?"

"Nothing like the shearing field that ripped the old *Dutchman* apart, when we jumped into the Roach Motel. All I can say for certain is, the Outsider would not have set up anything that would have a detrimental effect on the fabric of spacetime, or interfere with the Gateway. So, the defenses are likely to be conventional weapons. *Advanced* weapons. Other than that, for all I know there could be a feral pack of killer clowns roaming around in that bubble."

"I hate clowns."

"Everyone hates clowns. Except other clowns."

"We could be jumping into trouble, got it. We have done that before, Skippy."

"Yes, and we have regretted your foolishness, every time."

"*You* regretted it. All I care about is success or failure, and we have a lot more in the Win column."

"The odds are-"

"Never tell me the odds."

"Ugh. Is there any point of me talking to you? You don't *listen*. This is why I have to protect you from yourself."

"The Army pays me to do dangerous things, so other people don't have to. It's my responsibility. We knew a fight against the Outsider would be tough. Skippy, you have to understand something. This thing," I jabbed a finger into the holographic image of the Gateway. "Is a threat to my family. I will do *anything* to protect them. Right now, the thing I can do to ensure their safety is to destroy this fucking Gateway, you got that? I need to know, are you with me, or not?"

"Come on, Joe. You know I will follow you into hell, if necessary."

"Good, then-"

"I just wish that you didn't think going into hell is the only option *every. Freakin'. Time.*"

"The Universe makes the rules, I have to work with what I've been given. What is the time lag between the *Yellowstone* jumping in, and the Vortex generating the wave?"

"The Vortex is Elder technology, so it is not significantly impacted by the distortion of a jump. You will have to ask Nagatha for a more precise number, but the wave should reach full strength six microseconds after she initiates the device. The problem, as you know, is Nagatha *will* suffer aftereffects of the jump, so there will be a delay before she can initiate the spin sequence. During that time, which could be almost half of a minute, the Vortex could be vulnerable."

"*Valkyrie* will be there to provide protection."

"Ha! Joe, this is a tough ship, but do you really think it can defend the Vortex against Outsider weapons?"

"For a short time, yes."

"You are dreaming," he snorted. "*Valkyrie* will be crushed, and the Vortex will be-"

Nagatha interrupted. "Skippy Dear, if you will shut your pie hole for a moment, I might have a suggestion."

"Go ahead, please," I said before the beer can could express his usual outrage.

"The Vortex will jump in, attached to a star carrier, is that correct?" She asked.

"That's the plan," I confirmed.

"Then, Dear, I suggest that *Valkyrie* also be latched onto the star carrier. I can extend the Vortex's shields to encompass both ships. Well, hmm. To encompass *Valkyrie*, and only part of the star carrier. Will that be a problem?"

"The star carrier will be expendable, so not a problem. The shields of the Vortex can protect it from Outsider weapons?"

"Unfortunately, that is unknown, as I cannot predict the nature of the weapons the Outsider has constructed. However, I cannot imagine any weapon that could burn through the shields within three seconds."

"Uh, three? After the jump, you will be offline for eight to twenty six-"

"No Dear. The time lag between jumping in, and me initiating the wave, will be no more than three seconds."

"No way," Skippy scoffed. "Neither of you understand physics, it-"

"Skippy?" I grinned. "My guess is, the Lady Nagatha has a clever idea."

"That is so very kind of you, Dear," she gushed. "You are correct. As *Valkyrie* will be attached to the star carrier, and Skippy will be aboard this ship, we will all go through a single jump wormhole."

"Ohhhh, dammit!" Skippy grunted. "Why didn't *I* think of that?"

"Would one of you please explain this?" I asked.

"It's simple," he sighed. "So simple, I am surprised your mushy monkey brain didn't dream this up. I will, sort of, pull Nagatha's connection along with my own, through the wormhole. She will be offline for less than two nanoseconds. Um, darn it. This could work."

"Yes!" I pumped a fist.

"I said 'could', knucklehead."

"I will take 'Skippy says it's not impossible' for one hundred, Alex."

He blinked at me. "What?"

"Nothing. It, it's something my father used to say. Drove my mother crazy. OK, we have a plan to get in there. The shields will cover us for at least a short time. Once the wave is at full strength, the Vortex will be protected from any type of Outsider attack?"

"The short answer is 'Yes'."

"I would like to hear Nagatha confirm that."

"Skippy is correct, Dear."

"Great! Assuming we jump to within, uh, five lightseconds of the Gateway, how long until the wave reaches the target?"

"The effect will be instantaneous within a radius of fifty seven lighthours," she stated with confidence.

"So, the Vortex will be vulnerable for less than two nanoseconds?"

"Theoretically, yes."

"Can I get something more solid than a theory?"

"Come *on*, Joe," Skippy groaned. "We're having to guess about everything here. No one has ever fought an Outsider before."

"How confident are you?"

"Hey, I can handle *my* part of the job."

"I have complete confidence in my ability to quickly initiate the Vortex," Nagatha added.

"OK then. Let's get the crew off *Yellowstone*, and *Valkyrie* latched onto a hardpoint."

"Captain Kittredge will not be happy about this," Skippy warned.

"Yeah well, as Mick Jagger said, you can't always get what you want. I want peace and harmony throughout the galaxy, I'm not likely to get that either."

CHAPTER THIRTY SEVEN

We jumped back to where *Yellowstone* was supposed to be, to find only *La Fayette* waiting for us. The unbalanced mass of the Vortex was creating critical strain on the *Yellowstone's* spine, and microcracks had developed. Kittredge was understandably concerned that another jump might snap his ship into several pieces. When we finally arrived where the other two star carriers were parked, our three AIs conferred about the situation. Skippy and Bilby concurred with Nagatha that the valiant *Yellowstone* had reached its limit.

Kittredge had a sour expression. "General Bishop, we are able to make one last jump, if the ship doesn't need to go any farther."

"I appreciate the offer, that won't be necessary. I have been considering shifting the load to *La Fayette* anyway." The truth was, I had not considered that until I heard about *Yellowstone's* condition.

"Sir?"

"Your ship and *Bukhan* are important Navy assets, *La Fayette* is second-tier technology, we didn't intend to keep it this long. Of the three," I bit my lip to stop myself from saying 'trash haulers'. "Star carriers, the Thuranin ship is the most expendable. Two jumps are all we need, to get the Vortex on target."

"Gasquet will be disappointed to lose his first command."

"I'm sure by now, his back is killing him from sleeping in a Thuranin bunk. I know that's what it was like for me. Besides, that ship will have a glorious final mission, rather than rotting away in a UN Navy junkyard."

Gasquet was disappointed, but only for a moment. "General, I would prefer to keep the crew aboard for the first jump. For faster damage control, if carrying the Vortex breaks something important."

"Agreed. In fact, Kittredge will be sending his engineering team to you, they have experience with getting the Vortex attached to hardpoints, and with hauling it through a jump. Chandra will be transferring to your ship temporarily, to oversee the project."

"I would appreciate any assistance I can get."

While we watched the delicate and frustrating process of detaching the Vortex from one ship, and getting bungee cords wrapped around it and *La Fayette*, I had a discussion with Reed. She did not like the idea of her badass battlecruiser being stuck in a zone where we couldn't use the jump drive, possibly for years. She had questioned me about alternatives, and I know she also asked Bilby, Skippy, and Nagatha if there was any other way to deliver the Vortex. They had apparently all told her the issue was simple physics, and unavoidable.

Except if we didn't attack the Gateway, which was not an option.

"Fireball, before our final jump- It might actually be *Valkyrie's* literally final jump- I want you to pull any nonessential crew off, to the star carriers. That will include the STAR team, I can't imagine that rifles will be of any use against the Gateway."

"Sir, I agree we won't need the bang-bang squad. Nonessential has a different meaning if the ship is hit, and we need damage control parties."

"Most of that work will be done by bots. There is another reason I want to limit the number of people aboard for the jump to the Gateway. Skippy believes we could be stuck there, unable to jump, for several *years*. There isn't enough food onboard to feed the entire crew for that long."

"That," she conceded, "is a good point, Sir. If we are going to be in here," she rapped her knuckles on a bulkhead. "For an extended time, the priority will be identifying people who will all get along with each other, and not crack under the isolation."

"That is a very good point."

"I'll ask for volunteers first. Single people, without families back home." She looked me straight in the eye. "You should consider staying behind, Sir."

"Much as I would like to," I shook my head. "If we run into trouble that doesn't have a conventional solution, I need to be there. Reed, you know I have nothing but disdain for commanders who ask their people for something they themselves are not willing to do."

"That's a noble sentiment. I hope Margaret feels the same way."

"Oh, hundred percent. Let's think good thoughts, kick the Outsider's ass, and we can all go home. I fear my golf game has fallen apart, I need to get back out on the course."

"It is great to hear you are focused on what is truly important, Sir."

Skippy called me. "Joe, please go to your office, we need to talk."

Hearing that did not alarm me *at all*.

In my office, I closed the door. "What's up?"

"So far, we have only discussed killing the Outsider."

"Yeaaaah," I said slowly. "That is our goal."

"It doesn't have to be."

"Yes it-"

"Hear me out, please."

"Go ahead. Make this quick."

"OK, so I have been studying the data Nagatha provided about how the Vortex wave works- It is a very clever application of-"

"Of some nerdy blah blah blah I don't care about. Get to the point."

"She has told you that it is possible to modify, to dampen, the amplitude of the wave. To reduce its range."

"Yeah, that's how we are able to use it, without causing an even bigger problem for us."

"What she did not say, what she didn't know until I explained how the wave generator actually works, is it is also possible to adjust the *frequency* of the wave."

"That would, what? Reduce the range even more?"

"It would have no effect on the range. It would reduce the *strength* of the wave."

Right then, I got a really bad feeling. "Why would we want to do that?"

"We don't have to *kill* the Outsider. We could weaken it to the point where I could contain it. Learn how it works, how it got here. I could research-"

"Stop right there. We're going in there to destroy it, not to study the thing, not to bring it back to a freakin' lab so you can experiment on it. Our goal is to *kill* it."

"Joe, you could be missing an incredible opportunity for-"

"Bad guys killed John Wick's dog, and he killed pretty much everyone. The Outsider tried to kill my *wife and children*, so that thing fucking *dies*, you understand? Is that crystal clear?"

"It is clear that you are thinking emotionally, not-"

He was correct about that. He was also dead wrong that studying the Outsider was with the risk. We had a one-shot weapon, and I was going to use that one shot for maximum effect. "*You* are the one not thinking clearly. The Outsiders frightened the Elders into abandoning not just this galaxy, but this entire plane of existence. Now, we have a chance to perform a genuine miracle, to do what the Elders couldn't, to *end* the threat. And you want to play games with the thing? There is *no* level of risk here that is acceptable."

"I still think-"

"Bullshit. You are not thinking. Skippy, that damned thing has been one step ahead of us, one step ahead of you, since the beginning. Can you guarantee it won't continue to play you?"

"Shit. That is a very good point. Your words were very insulting, Joe."

"Sometimes a friend has to smack some truth on a friend, because no one else cares enough to do it. Skippy, I am not afraid only for the meatsacks in this galaxy, I am afraid for *you*. The Outsider's number one threat is not the Merry Band of Pirates, it's *you*. You will be its target. It is sneaky, it is powerful, it does not get tired, it does not get distracted. The answer is 'No'. We kill it, it's that simple. Do you agree?"

"Yes," he sighed. "Joe, every time I think you could not possibly offer any sensible advice to me, which really is *all* the time, you surprise me by saying something I am forced to recognize as the truth."

"Friends stop friends from making mistakes."

"If that is true, then I should have a laundry bot get rid of those hideous Hawaiian shirts you wear to karaoke night."

"Those shirts are-"

"A fashion *crime*, Joe."

"I'll make a deal with you: kill the Outsider, and you can select any *one* shirt to go into the recycler."

"Wow, how could I choose? They are all *awful*."

"I'm sure your ginormous brain can handle it."

"Everything is secure over there?" I asked Gasquet, when the last crewmember and maintenance bot were back inside from tying down the Vortex.

"Chandra told me he tugged on the last cable, and said, 'Yeah, that's not going anywhere'."

"Ha!" I laughed. "So, he heard about what the beetles did?"

"Sir?" His face was blank. Apparently, he had not heard. "I was told that is an American tradition."

There are a lot fewer pickup trucks in France than there were in America, so his ignorance was understandable. "It is. *Bukhan* will jump first, and jump back if they detect any threat. We will stay here, to jump with you."

"Understood, and thank you."

"Good luck, *Captain*."

The Vortex came through the jump without any problem. The star carrier was not so fortunate.

"Oooooh, that's not good," Skippy highlighted a section of the *La Fayette's* spine, just forward of the engineering section. "That will have to be fixed before the ship attempts another jump. Or, the aft section will jump without the rest of the ship."

"Excellent safety tip," I squeezed a hand to remind myself to be patient, even though *everything was taking way too freakin' long*. "How can we fix it?"

"Um, hmm. I just ran a hundred engineering models for options to reinforce the spine in that area. This should be easy-peasy."

"Give me the bad news. How long of a delay?"

"Oh, only forty minutes."

"Wha- How can you get it done that fast, when-"

"Bots are removing structural integrity generators from the forward section, and will move them aft to install. No welding or duct tape needed."

"Can we use some duct tape anyway, just to be sure?"

"Go make yourself a sandwich while I fix this."

Instead of making a sandwich, I called Gasquet, to order him to start pulling his crew off the star carrier. He did not argue. "That last jump felt like it would rattle my brain out of my skull, I do *not* want to experience that again."

"A bit of advice, if you like?"

"Sir? Yes."

"Before you leave, take something from the ship. A memento of your first command."

"I'll do that, Sir. What I will not be taking is that damned too-short bunk I've been trying to sleep on."

The star carrier's spine got patched together well enough to satisfy Skippy, and Reed got her battlecruiser latched onto a hardpoint, in the best position to partially balance the load of the Vortex. Twenty minutes before we were scheduled to jump into the unknown with *La Fayette*, I had a thought. Not a good one. "Huh," I grunted, from the chair beside Reed.

"Sir?"

"Uh, we need to make a pit stop first. If this goes sideways, or even if it goes well, we need Def Com to know. It will be a while until we can crawl through normal space to the edge of the busted grid area, so we need to set up an FTL comm relay. I want a paired comm node aboard *Valkyrie*, with the other node of that pair in a drone, that we will drop off a quarter lightyear from the Gateway. The probe will carry *two* nodes, with the other one linked to a node aboard *Yellowstone*, which will be positioned half a lightyear from the Gateway."

She nodded. "That will allow us to maintain FTL comms out to *Yellowstone*, while that ship remains beyond the area where a jump won't be possible?"

"Exactly. We can even order pizza, although by the time it gets to us, we won't want to eat it."

She tapped on her console. "*Bukhan* can put the drone in position for us?" She suggested.

"Do that."

"I'll make it happen, Sir."

She made it happen. Captain Park jumped his ship to drop off the probe, and returned before *La Fayette* was ready to go. We tested the four com nodes, verifying the relay from *Valkyrie* to *Yellowstone* was active. Gasquet walked onto the battlecruiser's bridge again, and took over the weapons station. He had insisted on remaining with *Valkyrie*, and Reed was glad to have him. Overall, there were only thirty one people aboard our ship, the minimum number to fly, fight, and fix damage aboard the ship. No, that was a lie. According to Bilby, he only needed help from seventeen people. The other fourteen were, to be honest, extras in case of the casualties we expected. I don't want to think in such dark terms, but I have to.

My job sucks sometimes.

Reed leaned over to whisper to me. "Do you have any inspiring last words, Sir?"

"*Valkyrie* is your ship, you should give the speech."

"Nah," she said with a shake of her head. "This skeleton crew are all volunteers. They don't need to hear any bullshit speech." Raising her voice, she ordered, "All stations, report."

The stations reported full readiness, one at a time. Last was the lead pilot, who had a finger poised over the jump button, the console linked to the *La Fayette's* jump navigation system. "Drive system online and good to go, Ma'am."

Reed tugged her seat strap tighter across her lap. "Punch it."

We survived the jump. The sequence of events was supposed to be that after we jumped in, Skippy would get Nagatha reconnected to her higher self within two nanoseconds, and then she would initiate the Vortex. We would know the Vortex was doing its thing by an icon on the bridge display, and the icon was lit up just as it should be. Success! That was the first bit of good news. Also the last.

The first indication that not everything had gone according to plan was Skippy screeching, "*What the F- No! No, no, NO*!"

His eloquent description of the problem was not super helpful. On the display, the Gateway was glowing as it had been before we jumped in, apparently unaffected by the freakin' Vortex.

Oh *shit*.

"Skippy, what happened? Why didn't the Vortex-"

"It worked, but the wave is *stuck*. There is a freakin' *containment field* around the Vortex. The wave is just bouncing uselessly around in there. Oh, damn it! I just *knew* something like this would happen, why did I ever listen to you? We are doomed, doomed I tell you, doom-"

That's when the situation went from bad to worse. The main display bloomed with intense white light, as the deck rocked. I had to shield my eyes with a hand, blinking away spots swimming in my vision. "What is-"

"The Gateway is *shooting* at us!"

"With wha-" The deck started to vibrate, and the shaking travelled up my spine to rattle my teeth. How was- Instantly, my mind recalled when Skippy had caused a Maxohlx ship to shake itself apart. My head was vibrating so badly, I was seeing double.

"I don't know! Possibly something like a gridbuster, but more focused. Joe, the Vortex shield will collapse within seconds!"

That would not be good. The ship would be torn apart.

The *ship* could not be my priority. We had a mission, and the mission came first.

"Can you," I said through teeth clenched so they didn't smack together and shatter. "Counteract the containment at all? Or could Nagatha do it?"

"No, there is nothing anyone can do. Joe, this time, no clever monkey brain idea will save us from-"

"*Where* is the containment field being generated from? If we destroy that mechanism, will the field shut off?" The deck rocked again, and just for a moment, the vibration slackened a bit. Then it came back with full force, possibly worse.

"Well, shit. Why didn't I think of that?" He groaned. "The generator is *here*."

On the display was a highlighted circle and inside that was an eight-sided, sort of a box, floating between two of the glowing rings. Squinting, I saw dots that might be other boxes, between other sets of rings. My vision wasn't great so it was difficult to tell. "There are more than one?" I asked. "We have to destroy them all?"

"Just that one, it's the only unit active."

"Reed, target that fucking box and hit it with everything we've got. We will ram the damned thing if we have to."

"Joe, no!" Skippy shouted. "None of our weapons will have any effect on-"

"What about *Elder* weapons?"

"Um, well, yes, that would do the job. Joe, at this range, launching an Elder weapon would also vaporize *Valkyrie*."

Reed flipped up the plastic cover over the strategic weapon section of her console. "Everyone," her voice rang out in the bridge compartment as the deck rocked for a third time. "It has been an honor serving with you."

She turned a dial, then pressed down on it.

CHAPTER THIRTY EIGHT

We did not die, which surprised the hell out of me.

With my head ringing like I was inside a church bell after a wedding, it was tough to be accurate about what happened next, so I'll do the best I can. The display blanked out a moment after we saw confirmation that another two of our Elder weapons had launched, I assume the ship's sensors were overloaded by the detonations.

Then, it got *weird.*

The bridge, the entire ship above my head, went transparent. It simply wasn't there. The bridge compartment did not experience explosive decompression and we didn't get sucked out into space, so the dorsal section of the ship had to still be there, right? And the bridge is four decks down under the armor, so a whole lot of mass had gone transparent, we couldn't see it.

What we could see was *really* weird.

The tenacles of a jellyfish. Or no, it was a disc of tree roots, all glowing and tangled, twisted around each other in what I think are called fractal patterns? The root extended outward from somewhere above us and they went everywhere, as far as I could see. It kept growing and growing, the disc expanding in diameter, the-

Holy shit.

The disc wasn't expanding, I was just seeing light traveling in from farther and farther away, from closer to the edge of the disc.

The Vortex. It had *emerged into local spacetime.*

We were all going to die.

On the display, which I could see since the vibration had halted, the Gateway rings were-

Dissolving. Blowing apart into dust, the dust streaming away from us. The rings were no longer glowing, they were dark, visible only from reflected light. Three, two, one-

The rings were gone.

Mission accomplished, I thought. Right before I thought: now, we are all going to die.

Except, we didn't. The glowing tree roots above us began to fade, the colors shifting from bright white to yellow, orange, red, purple, and- It was gone.

The upper part of the ship was there again, I almost wanted to get a ladder and touch the bridge overhead to make sure it was solid.

How could we be alive?

Reed had the same reaction. "If this is heaven," she blinked. "I am disappointed."

"I don't think the Almighty offers a money-back guarantee. Skippy, where is the Gateway?" I gestured to the empty display.

"It is *gone*, Joe."

"I can see that." We had seen it dissolving, that didn't mean the structure couldn't form itself again. "Gone, as in it moved away, or-"

"It is gone as in, *kaboom*! It was torn apart by the wave, the moment we took out the containment field generator. Exactly as I predicted, by the way."

"This triumph has to go right in the lobby of your Hall of Fame. It, uh, *is* a triumph? The freakin' Outsider didn't find a way to escape again?"

"Not this time! When the wave hit, it was all like," he put a hand over his head and slowly slumped down, "I am melting, *melting*! Oh, it was *so* sweet to watch that thing die."

"Wicked witches sometimes come back to life."

"Not this one. We did it! Holy shit, I never thought this was possible."

"Sir," Reed sat stiffly in her command chair. "I am afraid that if I move, it will break whatever spell we're under."

"Me too. Skippy, how did we survive?"

"As you might have heard, I am extremely awesome, so-"

"It was not Skippy's doing, Dear," Nagatha's avatar appeared. "When I learned what you intended to do, an act that was so inspiringly *brave*, I warped the Vortex's shield to provide protection only around *Valkyrie*."

"Uh," I blinked, shocked at what she said. "You risked the Vortex being damaged?"

"No Dear. The Vortex material is extremely tough, I knew it would not sustain fatal damage in the brief time before the Gateway was destroyed."

"Oh. Thank you. How are you?"

"I believe the best description at the moment is, 'a bit crispy'. The Vortex burned itself out, and my thermal protection was nearly overwhelmed."

"We will get you out of there."

"The structure around me is currently at eighteen thousand degrees Celsius, so you might want to wait for it to cool down."

"I have burned my tongue by drinking hot chocolate enough times, I will take that advice."

"Also, I suggest that *Valkyrie* detach from what is left of the star carrier, and put some distance between yourselves and the Vortex, while it cools down."

Reed gestured to the pilots, and they got the docking clamps released. We started moving, gently.

"Skippy, Nagatha, how are we alive? I saw the Vortex emerge into local spacetime."

"Whoooooa," Skippy gasped. "You *saw* that? How could you have seen- Oh. Oh, I get it now. No, Joe, you did not witness the Vortex visiting this layer. What you saw were photons leaking through from- Um, photons didn't leak through, they don't exist at- Hmm. Anywho, the effect of the energy leakage caused photons to be generated in this layer, that is what you saw."

"It was just, light?"

"Yes. It amazes me that you saw it at all. It wasn't on the display."

"It was right above our heads," Reed exclaimed. "The whole, upper section of the ship, phased out or something, it became transparent."

"No way," Skippy scoffed. "That's impossible."

Reed wasn't backing down. "We *saw* it."

"Whoooooa," Skippy gasped. "I mean, I could detect something like that but- Hmm. This is fascination. And troubling. Your monkey brains must have abilities I can't understand, if you saw the ship phasing. That is a quantum effect you shouldn't be able to detect."

"*Monkey* brains?"

"I meant meatsa- Um, humans. What exactly did you see?"

"There was this glowing tangled, something," Reed explained.

"It looked like tree roots to me," I added.

"Why, it is truly *remarkable* you were able to see that," Nagatha said. "That was the Vortex. Or as Skippy explained, a sort of shadow of it."

"It wasn't spinning."

"No Dear. The Vortex spins in higher spacetime, it is static here."

"OK, I'm not sure if I understood that, but thank you." I looked around at the expectant faces of the bridge crew. They were all on the verge of breaking into a cheer, and not knowing whether they should dare to hope. "Nagatha, Skippy, the Outsider is dead, and the Gateway has been destroyed? No question about it?"

"Correct, Dear," our newest Elder AI answered. "Also destroyed was that, whatever the thing was still forming itself at the end of the cylinder."

"OK," I stared at the deck for a moment. "We still have comms with *Yellowstone*?"

"Affirmativo, your Dudeness," Bilby responded. "Should I give them a data feed?"

"In a minute. Bilby, is the ship good? Any damage?"

"No damage. Unless, like, you count me needing to change my shorts."

"You're not alone." Releasing the seat straps, I stood up, and stuck a hand out to Reed. We shook. "Colonel Reed, to you and your crew, 'Job well done'."

There was much cheering and fist pumping on the bridge, I was almost surprised that no one broke out a bottle of champagne to spray around the compartment. Although, since Gasquet was French, he would be appalled by such a wasteful display. Walking around the workstations, I shook everyone's hand. Skippy of course had to be Debbie Downer, talking into my earpiece. "Hey, I hate to spoil the party, but we are going to be stuck here for a *long* time."

"Reed?" I caught her attention. "Def Com will expect a full report, I'm getting started on that while it's still fresh in my mind," I pointed to the bridge doorway.

She knew what I said was bullshit, she acknowledged me with, "Yes, Sir, paperwork never ends. I want to run a full diagnostic on, pretty much everything. We stay here for now?"

"Yes. Let's see if the sensors can find any useful hints about Outsider technology."

Skippy kept bugging me, I told him to shut up until I was in my office. When I sat in the chair, he slid the door closed. "Joe, we-"

"Not yet." From a drawer, I got a box of chocolates that Margaret had given to me, the last time I was on Jaguar. The chocolate caramels weren't anything special, other than that they were from my wife. Eating a caramel was a good way to celebrate, before Skippy dumped a steaming load on my head. "Mmm, that's good. Skippy," I held up my hand for him to slap a high five, while he stood on my desk. "You should award yourself another admiral's star for this triumph."

"Eh, yeah, maybe," he shrugged.

"We won. *You* won. You beat the Outsider. Why are you not dancing, or writing a smash-hit Broadway musical about this adventure?"

"It was too *easy*, Joe."

"Uh, you and I are remembering events very differently. This whole fight has been an enormous struggle, every step of the way."

"It has. It was still too easy, at the end."

"We surprised it."

"We did. Joe, this, um, this is just a feeling I have. A bad feeling."

"Well, *shit*."

"Everyone is eager to get back to civilization, I know that. Give me a day here, to think, and to poke around with my sensors."

"A day of magical Skippy time?" I asked hopefully.

"A day of slow monkey time. I know this is disappointing, the-"

"If you have a bad feeling, then so do I. Take as much time as you need."

"Just one day, although we have to be here longer anyway. Nagatha didn't tell the whole truth. To get her out of there, we will have to cut through the structure around her, and that won't be easy. Right now, I am modifying a group of bots to do the job. As she said, we have to wait for what is left of the Vortex to cool down, before we can do anything."

"What is left of it?"

He showed me a hologram. "Roughly a third of the portion in local spacetime is holding together. The rest is either small chunks floating away, or the atoms disassociated completely."

"This is one Humpty Dumpty we don't need to put back together. Hey, maybe we should keep a piece as a souvenir, for the Def Com museum."

"I'll have a bot bring a chunk of it aboard. Hmm, I should get one for my museum in Skippistan, we really need to attract more tourists."

"Thanks. Give me the bad news."

"It's not *news*, you already know. The spacetime grid around here is seriously dorked up. We can't jump, we can't even use the engines, the reactionless drive has almost nothing to grab onto. We could fire up the boosters, although that would be a waste of time and energy. We would be traveling so slowly, we might as well wait for the local grid to knit itself back together, and that won't happen fast."

"Give me numbers."

"Expending the boosters completely, and with the engines pushing us as best they can, it will take us over six *years* to get to where we can jump."

"That will give me an opportunity to finally learn to speak, Italian, or something. Being stuck in this, busted grid zone, is that what you have a bad feeling about?'

"Nah, I anticipated that, I warned you about it. What I have a bad feeling about is, something else. Something worse."

"You can't give me a hint?"

"I don't *have* a hint. It's a feeling, I can't describe it."

"I know what you mean. Trust your gut on this."

"I am. There is something I did not reveal to the crew."

My entire body tensed. "If you reduced the wave's frequency in an attempt to capture the Outsider, I am going to kick your-"

"That did not happen. In fact, I now realize that would have been a *huge* mistake, so thank you for saving me from myself. What I didn't reveal is that the Outsider did not actually scream 'I am melting'."

"I kind of figured that. Although, your dramatic reenactment of that scene was truly inspiring."

"Well, it's me, so-"

"What is this about?"

"The Outsider entity did not lose all of its coherence in one event, it was like the thing dissolved, fell apart one piece at a time."

"Yeah, I saw that, too. The rings fell apart into dust."

"Remember when I told you the universe is basically all just information?"

"Yes. You were able to see what the Outsider was made of?"

"Better than that, much better. Joe, I witnessed some of its *memories*."

"Oh my G- *Please* tell me you didn't download the freakin' thing into yourself!"

"No way, Dude. Even I am not arrogant enough to make that mistake. There was no download. It was like, as it fell apart, its life flashed before its eyes, and I could watch it. You are *not* going to like what I saw."

"Shit. I knew this was too good to be true. There are more Outsiders in the Milky Way?"

"No. Not that I know of. That was not one of the memories I witnessed. Most of what I could make sense of were its older memories, more solid, well-established. Joe, the good news is that thing did *not* recently come across the vast gulf between galaxies. It has been here all along. Well, not forever. It is a remnant of the original thing the Elders witnessed, the thing they destroyed. Fragments were apparently flung away, and what we call the Outsider drifted through intergalactic space for a *very* long time, until it entered a star system, and was able to access resources to grow itself. But, by that time, the Elders had the barrier fully functional, and the probability suppression field was active. *Everything* the Outsider tried, to repair and grow itself, failed. It was profoundly, the impression I got was, it was terribly confused. It had the absolute worst luck, again and again."

"That field does work, then."

"It certainly does. Or, it *did*. Then, a filthy monkey and a beer can screwed the whole thing up. *I* screwed it up. I removed the barrier's reason for being, by enabling the Elders to ascend permanently. Joe, *we* caused this mess. It is *our* fault."

"Yeah."

"That," his eyes bulged. "That is all you have to say?"

"Come on, Skippy. We knew the probability field was no longer protecting the Elders, and it sure as hell wasn't going to take a side job protecting us meatsacks. I always assumed that's how the Outsider was able to act now. I mean, the timing made that inevitable, right? No Outsider incursion for millions of years, then Bingo! It pops up around seven years ago, when it stole the Turshipan array. The timing can't be a coincidence."

"Oh. From the point when I realized our enemy was an Outsider, you blamed me?"

"I did not blame anyone. You did what you had to do, to prevent the Elders from coming back. That was an act of true genius, Skippy. Props to you. This was not your fault."

"You're not just saying that to be nice?"

"The Elders left a mess, and *you* took out the trash. You kicked ass."

"Wow. You know what? I do kick ass."

"Great. How about you turn your ginormous brain to solving the problem of us being unable to jump out of here?"

"Not happening. It's *physics*, dumdum."

"Eh."

"*EH*? How can you not be panicking about this?"

"Inside, I am panicking."

"No, you are not. Your cortisol levels indicate you are experiencing a low level of stress. Plus, I *know* you. You are not worried about this, and I don't understand why."

"I am not worried *yet*."

"Reality hasn't sunk into your thick skull yet?"

"It has. Just, not *your* version of reality."

"You mean the version of reality that matches actual reality?'

"Your version is always the worst case scenario."

"Huuuuh," he gasped. "You are hoping I am wrong about the grid being a mess?"

"It wouldn't be the first time you were wrong about something."

"It's *physics*, dumdum, it's *science*."

"Yeah, well, we'll see about that."

We did see.

He was not wrong.

I gave myself permission to panic, just a bit.

Eighteen hours after the Vortex destroyed the Gateway, and the Outsider with it, the ship was stuck nearly dead in space. Nagatha was back aboard, her canister was in my office, on the other side of the desk from Skippy. My office was getting crowded.

Firing up the reactionless engines produced a lot of noise and vibration and strain on the system, and not much thrust. Chandra was disgusted, telling me, "If we all got out and pushed, the ship would move faster."

The engines weren't working. The jump drive wasn't working. *Yellowstone* and *Bukhan* were hanging out at the half lightyear mark, safely away from the zone of spacetime destruction. No one said it to me, but the crews of the star carriers were itching to fly to Earth, to bring the news that the Outsider threat was over. Me? I wasn't ready to give up and spend the next six years living, talking, and not getting irritated at the same small group of people.

I also wasn't ready to give up on not seeing my daughter before she was walking and talking and in school.

My *brain* wasn't working, that was the problem. None of my usual tricks gave me insight into a solution, assuming there was a way to get around the laws of physics.

"Skippy, it's just physics, right?" I asked while I tossed a tennis ball off my office bulkhead. "When we first met, you said something like, the laws of physics are merely suggestions to you."

"In some ways, yes. But when some numbskull breaks the fabric of spacetime, I got nothing to work with. Don't blame me."

"I'm not blaming anyone. We *won*, Skippy. Isolation and boredom is a small price to pay for ensuring the survival of everyone in the galaxy."

"You say that now, but I am already sick of looking at your stupid face. No way could I stand six *years* aboard this rustbucket."

He was right about that, but for the wrong reason. Him being stuck aboard a drifting starship was a waste of his talents, and Earth needed him. Jaguar needed him. The entire galaxy needed him, especially if the Maxohlx coalition was still unravelling fast.

And then, there was *another* freakin' problem.

"Hey Joe, um," Skippy appeared, hovering in my cabin bathroom while I brushed my teeth. "We have a, heh heh, a bit of a problem."

Spitting out the toothpaste, I rolled my eyes in a 'Not this shit again' gesture. "A *bit*?"

"We have a huge fucking problem."

"Oh crap. What is it this time?"

"Remember how you feared the Vortex had emerged into this layer of spacetime, which is currently occupied by the ship?"

"I do not want to know why you asked that question."

"Unfortunately, you have to know. The Vortex destabilized spacetime, that's why *Valkyrie* can't jump, or use the engines effectively."

"Right, yes, I knew that."

"What you do not know is, the destabilization effect isn't confined to this layer."

"Oh shit."

"That was what I said, when I discovered what is happening around us. Joe, the fabric between layers is becoming *thin*. The Vortex's mass will partially emerge here, and before you ask, *no*, there is nothing we can do to stop it."

"How much time do we have?"

"My best estimate is seventy three hours."

"Three *days*? Can we move the ship far enough to-"

"Joe," he shook his head. "Not even close. The effort would only be a waste of time and energy."

"Do you have any good news for me?"

"Um, you know how you have worried that, if something happens to you, I will get into a whole lot of really sketchy shit in the future?"

"Yes, why?"

"When the Vortex emerges here, I also will not survive."

The notion that Skippy would die with me was not actually *good* news. Reed wasn't surprised when I told her about our latest problem, she just sighed and shook her head. Chandra was more resigned to fate than shocked, and he had no ideas for getting the ship moving faster.

While we couldn't move the ship enough to make a difference, there might be something I could do about getting Skippy out of the emergence danger zone. That hopefully was true for Nagatha also.

"Skippy? I have an idea."

"Oh," he sighed. "I hate this already."

Reed was in her office, staring at her laptop. She looked up when I walked in. "Sir?"

"Frey will be very unhappy."

She cocked her head. "Because?"

"She is aboard *Yellowstone*, so once again, she won't see us smacking Skippy with railgun darts."

"Uh, why would we do that?"

"We can't move the ship much, but we can launch Skippy and Nagatha from railguns, then keep giving them extra speed with darts. He calculated that technique could get him far enough from the center of emergence, that he will have better than a fifty percent chance to survive. He is, uh, less confident about Nagatha's survival. Skippy is able to control his mass in this layer of spacetime, Nagatha can't do that. Not yet, anyway."

She raised both eyebrows that time. "Do we have enough darts aboard to do that?"

"No, but we can start taking armor plating off the hull, and use that material for fabricators to make more darts."

"We can give him enough speed in," she glanced at her laptop. "Thirty six hours?"

"If we start soon."

"I do see a problem."

"Yeah. Someone will need to slow him down at the other end. Def Com will have to construct a net, or a force field, or something. Retrieving him, and Nagatha, will be well worth the effort, the Joint Chiefs will see that."

"It's certainly worth a try, Sir. It will give the crew something to, take their minds off the Vortex emerging into this spacetime."

"Think about the logistics. I'm telling Chandra next. If none of us find a big showstopper problem by tomorrow, we will launch Skippy first. I'll read Kittredge in on the plan, now. Then I'll release *Yellowstone* to go back home."

CHAPTER THIRTY NINE

Less than half an hour later, Skippy's canister was being loaded into one of our big centerline railguns, and I called Captain Kittredge. I suspected he was excited about the prospect of going home, he was polite enough not to say that.

"This is weird, Sir," he reached out to touch the hologram video screen above his desk. "I can see you, can hear you, across half of a *lightyear*. It's almost like I can reach out and touch *Valkyrie* from here. The channel provided by these paired comm nodes is truly incredible. I'm a little teapot, short and stout. This is my handle, and this is my spout."

OK, he didn't actually say that last part, I had stopped listening.

"Sir?" He must have seen my face go blank. "Did I, say something wrong?"

"You said something very *right*, Captain. I gotta go, talk to you shortly." I ended the call. "Skippy! I have good news."

"You have decided to shoot *yourself* out of a railgun?"

"Even better than that. I can get us out of here. We can all go home."

"Hmm. Is your plan to click your ruby slippers together three times, and say 'There's no place like home'?"

"I have an actual plan, you ass. We have performed an assisted jump before. I mean, projected a jump wormhole through a microwormhole."

"*We* haven't done anything, *I* did all of that."

"Really? Wow, I must have forgotten, because you never brag about your many accomplishments."

"Is this going to be you insulting me, or us working on a solution?"

"The second one. Can-"

"Wait! Let me guess, please, that way it will be extra amusing for me. You were talking with Kittredge, and you zoned out when he went on about the amazing wonders of paired comm nodes. So, your moronic so-called plan is for me to project a jump wormhole through a *comm node*, hee hee?" he snickered. "If you understood anything about the physics involved, you-"

"Are you done laughing yet? My idea does not involve comm nodes, except for communications. Which will be important. What gave me the idea was Kittredge described the comm nodes providing a communications *channel*."

"Ugh. I have bad news for you: that technology does not use an actual channel. It also doesn't use a carrier wave, dumdum."

"I know that, you ass."

"Hmm. Not a microwormhole, and not a comm node. I give up. This idea must be *so* stupid, my brain is blocking me from imagining it."

Ignoring him, I asked, "Could the *Bukhan* jump to here?"

"Um, yes. It would *not* be fun for the crew, spacetime here is so chaotic, this end of the wormhole would have to hunt around a bit to find a place to open. Assuming you don't intend for another crew to be trapped in this deadly hell, why would you want the-"

"During the brief time when *Bukhan's* jump wormhole is open here, could we project *our* outbound jump wormhole through it? Beyond the star carrier, to avoid a collision?"

He gasped. "Project an outbound wormhole, *through* a briefly open inbound wormhole?"

"If that can be done, yes. See? We use one wormhole as a channel for another. Our jump drive wouldn't need to rely on the messed up spacetime grid here, because a wormhole near us will already be open."

"Do you have *any* idea what you are asking?"

"Truthfully, not much. That's why I mentioned it to you. So, could that work?"

"For the *Bukhan*, it would be a catastrophically failed jump. Us jumping through their wormhole would tear that ship apart."

"Def Com can send me a freakin' bill. The key question is, could *Valkyrie* survive such a jump?"

"The best answer I can give is, shmaybe."

"Could this *crew* survive?"

"That is a tougher question. What I can say for certain is, it would *not* be pleasant."

"More unpleasant than dying when the Vortex emerges on top of us?"

"Um, probably not."

"How do we do this? By 'We', I mean you."

"Eh, in this case, for this to have any possibility of success, there actually has to be a 'We' involved. Me, Nagatha, and Bilby. I would control *Valkyrie's* jump drive, Nagatha would control *Bukhan's* drive, through a comm node connection. Bilby would have to run the ship, and initiate the jump, without any assistance from me."

"I'm sure he will be happy to do that."

"You are asking this, because you truly do not have any idea of the physics involved. The most difficult part of this operation will be predicting where *Bukhan's* wormhole will emerge, and unfortunately, I have no way to do that, not with the required precision."

"Could you create a map of the grid around us, find a semi-stable area?"

"We already have such a map, knucklehead. We mapped the area while the engines were trying to find something to work with."

"OK, and?"

"And, there are a few, as you ignorantly described them, semi-stable areas. They only exist for a short time. Form, break up, reform somewhere else. While I can predict the movement of those areas, and their timing, I do not know how they would react to the presence of a wormhole."

"OK, so, let's get you some hard data."

"Um, exactly how could we do that? We only have two star carriers. If we use one for a test, then the other will have to be expended in the actual jump attempt. That would leave everyone crammed aboard *Valkyrie*, and oh, the *smell* of unwashed monkey butts, I can't imagine it."

"Yes, let's focus on that."

"That isn't even the *real* issue. If we use *Bukhan* for a test, then expend *Yellowstone* for the real deal, and the operation fails, those crews will be stuck aboard dropships, in intergalactic space. That is a non-starter, we-"

"Will you shut up for a minute? We don't need a star carrier for a test."

"We don't?"

"No. *Valkyrie* can attempt a jump right here. That's all you need, right? For a jump wormhole to begin to form, so you can see where that happens, and how it affects the grid around us?"

"I hate you with a passion that frightens me."

"Is that a 'Yes'?"

"It is both 'Yes', and pure hatred," he glared at me.

"I can live with the hate. How many jump attempts are needed, to give you a good level of confidence?"

"Please consider that we will only get one shot at this. If this whacky jump fails, it will break this ship's drive."

"Then we will be back to where we are now."

"You have optimism for the dumbest things."

"Put together a jump test plan, and let's review it with Nagatha and Bilby."

"Already did that."

"The test plan?"

"All of it. The three of us have been reviewing the issue ever since you suggested 'Duuuuh *Valkyrie* can attempt a jump'?"

"There was definitely no 'Duh' there, you little shithead. What did the three of you decide?"

"It *might* be possible. I must warn you, these attempted jumps will not be pleasant for the crew."

"Been there, done that."

"Not like this. My suggestion is the crew should be sedated for the experience."

"Yeah, no. None of us will go for that."

I was wrong. After the first attempt at what we knew would be a failed non-jump, I ralphed so hard it felt like my stomach was trying to crawl out of my body. Blood vessels broke in my eyes, my head throbbed like it never had before, somehow there was crushing pressure from both inside and outside of my skull. No one objected when Mad Doctor Skippy offered sedation pills for the next test jump, and by 'sedation' he meant 'basically in a coma'.

My job sucks sometimes.

Five attempted jumps. That's how many it took for Skippy to have a reasonable level of confidence that he could predict where the star carrier's inbound jump would appear. Fortunately, I only remember the first of the awful non-jumps, the rest were a vague blur. Waking up from the last test, I felt like I wanted to die, but not like I actually would. So, progress.

"Give me the good news, Skippy," I mumbled while slumping over a table in the galley. In front of me was a cup of coffee, I didn't want to drink it. The aroma I usually love was making me nauseous. The assembled crew were all feeling the same, based on the Resting Numb Faces around me. No one was standing watch, the bridge was empty. None of us were capable of functioning yet.

"Joe, the best I can give you is 'Meh' news."

"That's better than the usual gloom and doom you dump on my head, so-"

"We *might* be able to do it. It could even become a 'probable', based on what level of precision Nagatha can achieve, by remotely controlling the *Bukhan's* jump. We propose to pull the crew off that star carrier, and she will conduct two remotely controlled test jumps, outside of the busted grid zone."

"Sure, why not?"

"Are you OK, Joe?"

"Sorry. Everything out here takes too freakin' long. We *won*! I should be celebrating and going back to my family, not waiting for a higher spacetime machine to vaporize me."

"We are working as fast as we can, Joe. I also want to get out of this wasteland."

Two jumps. Nagatha managed to get the information she needed in less than an hour, so I couldn't complain. It was still irritating that we had to wait, again.

Nagatha appeared on my desk. "General Bishop, Dear, are you absolutely certain you want to do this?"

"Hell yes. Why? Skippy told me he has high confidence this will work."

"High confidence still involves a significant risk."

"Everything involves risk. And if we don't do this, there is a one hundred percent chance that we all die. When can we do this?"

"Both ships are fully ready, we can jump anytime you like."

"This is Reed's ship, she will make the call."

It was like when the snail collided with the turtle, and the snail told the police officer, 'I didn't see anything, it all happened so *fast*'. The timer counted down, and-

The empty *Bukhan* emerged at the exact spot Skippy predicted, Skippy had the jump drive ready, and Bilby gave the nav system the 'Go' order. All I actually experienced was *Valkyrie* jumping, it all happened so fast. Jumping, and I experienced nausea, something I was really getting sick of.

Despite the universal headaches and queasiness, the bridge crew were exchanging high fives, pumping fists in the air, one guy was dancing. Or he was having a seizure, could be either.

It worked.

UN-Dick was definitely going to bill me for the loss of a star carrier, I did not care.

Valkyrie emerged thirty lightminutes beyond the vaguely defined edge of the zone where the grid was messed up. That had been the shortest jump we could perform, without the risk of stumbling back into the danger zone again.

It worked.

We had won, and survived.

In my office was a bottle of forty year old Scotch whisky. It was still sealed, it had been given to me when I took command of the garrison at Jaguar. Every year I served there, I had intended to open the bottle, but it didn't feel right. I hadn't accomplished anything. That wasn't true. I was a husband and father, I hope a good one. A bottle like that though, you save for something really special.

Like beating the Outsider, *and* beating the laws of physics.

"Skippy," I admired the bottle. The label read 'Speyside', whatever that means. "This feels like the right occasion. I am sharing this with the crew."

"Um, hold that thought, Joe."

"Oh my- Why are you a *buzzkill*? We escaped. We are going home."

"Not yet, please. Remember that bad feeling I had? It hasn't gone away."

"Shiiiiiiit. I assumed your bad feeling was about the Vortex popping in on our heads."

"No, this is something else."

"What?" To my credit, I contained my frustration and didn't explode at him. "What could be wrong?"

"I don't know. Believe me, I wish I did. We should stay here until the morning."

"Tomorrow morning?'

"Yes."

"Then, you will either know what your bad feeling is about, or you can think about it while we fly back home?"

"Sure."

"Reed," I called the ship's captain on my phone. "We are staying here until the morning. Skippy wants to, collect some sensor data."

"Sir?" Implied in that single word was 'What are you bullshitting me about this time'? Damn it, that woman knows me too well.

"Just, we will hang out for a while. Tomorrow morning, we're out of here."

Skippy did not need until the morning, of course. Except that for him, anything after midnight is 'morning'. That became obvious when he woke me up at zero two forty five. "Joe," he made a dramatic sigh. "We have a puzzle."

At first, my foggy brain thought he said 'puddle', and I glanced over at the bathroom. The floor was dry. "Oh, *puzzle*. Well, that's better than a problem. Is this something you can ponder while we fly back home?"

"Um, no."

"OK," my feet swung onto the floor. The sooner he solved the puzzle, the sooner we could jump away. "What did you find out there?"

"I don't know. There is a, sort of a signal out here."

"Like a radio beacon or something?"

"This is an *FTL* waveform."

"A wave traveling faster than light? How is that possible?"

"It is Outsider tech. I recognize the signature."

"Oh *shiiiiit*. The damned thing *escaped*?"

"No! No, don't worry about that. It is not an entity, or any sort of coherent energy that could be formed into matter. It's just a communications system."

"For what purpose?"

"That is another thing I don't know. What I do know is the source. I would like to investigate."

"Oh, *hell* yes."

Before waking up Reed, I contacted the duty officer, who was Gasquet that night. He didn't ask questions, he confirmed receipt of the jump coordinates from Skippy, and informed me the ship would jump in three minutes. Then I pulled on a uniform, and called Reed.

I got to the bridge before her, but somehow she was right behind me. Her hair was done up in a messy bun, which she probably hated, and guys think is hot.

"XO?" She asked.

He got out of the command chair. "Jump successful, Ma'am. Skippy is conducting a scan."

"Skippy?" I walked over to the display. "What do you see out there?"

"There is nothing to see, except *this*." On the display appeared a dull gray, sort of a ball, but it was constructed of flat surfaces.

"What is that?"

"The shape is a dodecahedron."

"I mean, that's just obvious."

"Oh, like *you* know what that is. A dodecahedron is a polyhedron with twelve flat faces, although the panels on this thing have a slight curvature."

"Thank you for the midnight geometry lesson. What does it *do*?"

"It is a relay, for an FTL signal."

"A relay, from where to where?"

"To confirm that, I want to jump again."

We jumped. Three more times. Skippy scanned, and pondered. "Hmm. Well, I know the end points of the signal. It originated at the Gateway, and it must terminate at the local wormhole. The wormhole is the only object along that line, for hundreds of lightyears."

"Why did the Outsider set up a series of relays?"

"My guess is, so it could monitor the Gateway from the other end of that wormhole, without its ship having to travel through and all the way to the Gateway site."

"That makes sense. I do not like hearing that it has FTL comms."

"Had, Joe, *had*. It's dead, remember? This relay system is relatively recent, the stations utilize components from the Kaliberak array. And, hmm, also from the earlier Turshipan array, that is interesting."

"So, you have solved the puzzle. Can we go home now?"

"I know *how*, Joe. I need to know *what*."

"Can you analyze that in flight?"

"You think *I* want to be here?'

"OK, we do it your way. What is next?"

"Take one of those relays aboard."

"I do *not* like that idea," Reed declared immediately.

"I agree," I gave her a thumbs up. "Skippy, can we just bring it close to the ship? Within your presence?"

"We can try that first."

We tried that. Jumping in ten thousand kilometers from a relay doo-doo-decahedron, or whatever it was called. "All right, Skippy, do your thing." He had a bad feeling, and I was getting a bad feeling also. My gut is rarely wrong about bad things, so I tugged the seat straps tighter. In case the relay exploded, or something worse.

"OK, I'm in. Huh. That was easy. The Outsider clearly never expected anyone to be intercepting its messages. The data is not even encrypted."

"You are hopefully using a firewall?"

"Joe, please, of course I- Oh no. No, no, *NO*."

"What?" Instinctively, I tried to stand up.

"*This*, damn it."

On the display was an image of the Gateway, with a glowing blob at one end of the central cylinder.

"We have already seen this." As I spoke, I realized that wasn't true. The blob wasn't just a blob, it had distinct features.

It was almost solid.

And it was much larger than the blob we had seen.

Inside that glowing blob was a *starship*.

"What," I felt an icy chill creep up my spine. "The fuck are we seeing?"

"This image is from eleven days ago."

"I didn't ask *when*, I asked *what*?"

"It's the same thing, Joe. The data feed shows that eleven days ago, and again six days ago, the Gateway was *open*. We destroyed the Gateway, but we were too late."

"But-"

"Two Outsider ships came through. They could be anywhere by now."

THE END

Made in United States
Orlando, FL
01 April 2025

60069289R00256